T. Csernis & Julia Bland

DEMON'S FATE
NUMEN CHRONICLES VOLUME TWO

NO ACCENT EDITION

NUMENVERSE

For more information on the world, this series, other books, or to contact the author, head to:
https://www.numenverse.com/

Cover designed by Tate Csernis
Cover drawn by Simon Zhong
Cover edited by Julia Bland

ISBN – Paperback: 978-1-7384052-9-9
ISBN – Hardcover: 978-1-7385210-0-5
ISBN – E-Book: 978-1-7385210-1-2

THE NUMEN CHRONICLES is a collaborative work written by

Tate Csernis (T. Csernis) and Julia Bland (Julia B.)

Each Party retains ownership over their respected Intellectual Property created outside of this collaboration, including but not limited to names, characters, stories, etc. All Collaborative Intellectual Property shall be jointly owned by the Parties, and each Party shall have the right freely to use all Collaborative Intellectual Property for all purposes and uses.

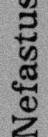

Nefastus

Dawnwood

Dorr

Osasmore

Ultimus

Pristend

Qosa

Yrunlens
Blockade

Idrock

East
Coast

Morrombold

Morroa
Mountains

The
Redwoods

Mor

Yrunlens

Cypress
Forests

Hale

Wru
Plains

Citadel

Chollk

Southern
Badlands

South
Coast

Brabus

Nophia

Roepver

West
Coast

GLOSSARY

Ethos [ee-thos] - The energy within someone that can be used to create or manipulate other energies

✝

Aditus-Insula [adee-tus-in-soo-la] - Translates roughly to Island of Doorways *[Latin]*

✝

Dor-Sanguis [door-san-goo-wis] - Translates roughly to Pain *[Portuguese]* and blood *[Latin]* (aka, Romania)

✝

Nefastus [neh-fas-tus] – Translates to Unlawful *[Latin]* (aka, the Americas)

✝

Numen [noo-men] - God-like beings that chose to show themselves to the world rather than remain anonymous

✝

Aegis [ee-gis] - The Dragon Gods, children of Letholdus

✝

DeiganLupus [day-gan-loo-pus] - Translates roughly to 'refused to turn to the wolf' *[Icelantic, Latin]* (aka, UK)

✝

The Void - The space between the Realms (aka, space)

✝

Proselytus [pros-elly-tus] – A heart-like organ which creates ethos inside a body

✝

Scion [skee-on]

✝

The Seven Realms:
Aegisguard [ee-gis-guard] - The world
(aka, Earth)
Mareaeternum [Mar-ay-ter-num] Translates to eternal tide *[Latin]*
Glaciaqua [Glass-ee-aqua]
Letholdus [Lee-fold-us]
Tengetso [Ten-get-so]
Celitrianas [Sel-it-ree-a-nas]
Yilmana [Yeel-mana]

The Months and Currency

Months

January – Primis
February – Cordus
March – Tertium
April – Aprilis
May – Quintus
June – Iunius
July – Quintilis
August – Tria
September – Novem
October – Decem
November – Undecim
December – Clausula

Currency

Copper – Equivalent of $0.01
Bronze – Equivalent of $0.20
Silver – Equivalent of $2
Gold – Equivalent of $10
Coronam – Equivalent of $100
Cidaris – Equivalent of $1 million

CONTENTS

ARC ONE | | WIZARDS AND WOLVES

ARC TWO | | THE HUNT FOR LUCIOUS

ARC THREE || LOVE AND HATE

ARC FOUR || LILITH

ARC FIVE || HOME

Arc One

✝

Wizards and Wolves

DEMON'S FATE
Numen Chronicles | Volume Two

Chapter One

— ⟨ ✝ ⟩ —

Angels of Tengetso

| **Alucard** |

A flurry of vermillion flames spewed through the rain-soaked streets in pursuit of a speeding black carriage. The stallion pulling its weight whinnied and panted, the crack of the coachman's whip echoing through the sleeping city. But not even a horse could outrun a demon.

The entangling flames raced at the carriage's right side. With the sound of a cocking gun, the carriage's red curtains parted, the window fell, and the arm of a white-robed man reached out with a pistol in his grip. He fired at the flames, but they dispersed before his shot could land and swiftly curved over the carriage's roof to the left side. A pale, clawed hand holding a shimmering golden colt extended out from the fire, and when the trigger was pulled, a whirring bullet fired and embedded into the carriage's front wheel. Before the white-robed man could attempt to fire another shot, the embedded bullet exploded in a flash of blinding light.

As the carriage wheel blew off, the coachman tried to steady the panicking horse, and the white-robed man inside tried to dive out, but the carriage swerved under the weight of its missing wheel and rolled over onto its side, tumbling down the soggy cobblestone street.

The carriage came to a shattering halt. At the end of the road, the mass of vermillion flames landed and twisted together to form the shape of a man. And from the smoke, a pale, crimson-haired vampire emerged.

Alucard.

The faded flames rematerialized the ankle-length fur-trimmed cape he wore over his shoulders, and in the lamplight of the street he stood on, his eyes shimmered like hellfire. He fixed them on the broken, crashed carriage ahead and scowled cautiously, waiting for his enemy to face him.

The carriage roof cracked as a force from within crashed against it. Several thumps came from inside, and after one more, the roof shattered outwards, sending a flurry of splintered wood towards Alucard. The vampire held up his cape, keeping any loose splinters from scathing him, and when the white-robed man climbed out, Alucard holstered his golden colt and stood ready for whatever his opponent was about to throw at him.

With an irritated growl, the blonde-haired man shook the dust and wood from his robes as he stood up straight and glared down the street at him.

Neither of them waited for the other to speak.

The white-robed man immediately held out his hand and fired a beam of blinding white light toward the vampire. Alucard dodged as he summoned a shard of shimmering luciferium from the ground; he launched in towards the man, who dived to his left to evade it. The crystal hit what remained of the carriage, sending it up in flames with a ground-shaking explosion.

Before the man could comprehend, though, Alucard disappeared into vermillion smoke and reappeared in front of him in the blink of an eye. The vampire snatched the man's throat, but when he swung his other hand towards the guy's face, he grunted and grabbed the vampire's wrist. They both growled and snarled, struggling against one another's force.

"*He* sent you, didn't he?" the man uttered through gritted teeth. "You've gathered up my brothers and sisters like cattle—where are they, demon filth?"

Alucard tightened his grip on the man's throat, focusing his ethos into the incantation he uttered under his breath. And as the man scowled in dread, the vampire told him, "They are where you are going."

The man tried to spread his clenched fist to summon another ball of light, but the ground beneath his feet cracked and split, crimson light oozing onto the cobblestone street. His silvery eyes widened, and he opened his mouth to beg, but the cracking ground gaped and pulled him down to whatever hellish fate awaited him in Damien's world below.

Alucard stepped back, watching as the crimson gateway sealed itself, repairing the cracked cobblestone road it had parted to form. It left the faint smell of sulphur in the air and twisting, vine-like scorch marks on the brick.

Silence.

The vampire sighed quietly, and as rain started falling over his face, he tilted his head back, embracing the bitter wet. It was over. That man was the last he'd come to hunt…and now he could go home.

But the pained whine of the horse which had been pulling the carriage snatched his attention. He hurried over to where the beast lay, discovering it had become enthralled within its straps and bands. The dead coachman lay not too far away, but Alucard didn't care about him. He rushed to the horse's side and snapped each strap with his hands; he tugged on the backband, pulling it apart with ease, and when he pulled the coachman's seat and remaining front wheel from the horse's back legs, the beast shrieked and scrambled to its hooves.

Alucard backed off and watched the horse race down the road. The doors of houses and shops lined up the street started opening, lights began flicking on, and the sound of loading weapons stole the serenity of the falling rain. Alucard wasn't going to stick around. He dematerialized into vermillion smoke and raced up into the sky, disappearing above the clouds.

He sped over the city and through a vast, foggy valley, and he didn't stop until he reached a small mining town on the other side of a towering black mountain.

The vampire rematerialized once he touched the ground and followed the dirt path towards the tavern ahead. He wiped the ash from his shoulders and tidied his hair, and once he stepped into the bustling pub, he made his way through the crowd and up the stairs.

A happy bark greeted him when he got into his room. Sabazios, the pony-sized wolfish hellhound raced over and jumped up at him, oblivious to his immense size. But he wasn't strong enough to knock Alucard off his feet.

"Yes, Sabazios, I'm fine," Alucard mumbled as he patted the dog's head and locked his door with his other hand.

Sabazios barked again and followed him to his desk, where a pile of black-enveloped letters lay. The vampire slumped down in his seat and looked over each of them, but there wasn't any new mail among them. He glanced at the standing mirror by his miserable single bed, but a deep, empty darkness swirled around inside. He wouldn't hear from Zalith until much later tonight.

With a quiet whine, Sabazios curled up at Alucard's feet.

"We will head home soon," he said, scratching Sabazios' ears. "I just need to rest for a moment."

His mission to find angels for Damien was finally over—at least in this world. It took him much longer than he would have liked, but time was different in Tengetso. It had been *years* for him, and back home in Aegisguard, he calculated that just over eight months passed. He stared at the math scribbled on a crumpled piece of parchment in front of him, and when he glanced at the clock, he sighed quietly.

"All right," he said, standing up. He hastily gathered all of his papers, envelopes, and trinkets, which he packed into a leather shoulder bag. He then moved towards the mirror and reached behind it. Once he deactivated the linking spell that let him see through other mirrors as if they were windows, the blackness inside faded, and the mirror returned to normal.

He stared at his reflection. In his effort to get the job over with as soon as possible, he'd let his hair grow uncomfortably long. He'd ensure to fix that when he got home.

"Let's go," he mumbled, glancing back at Sabazios.

With a bark of acknowledgement, the hound followed Alucard to the door.

The vampire pulled it open and stepped outside, and once he closed it behind him, he headed down the hall and back downstairs to the bar. He handed his room key to the barmaid, and as she called her goodbyes, he led Sabazios outside and up the path towards the town's exit. It was going to be a tiresome journey home, but the thought of his own bed and clean clothes helped him get over the fatigue weighing down on him. Not only that, but he'd finally be able to talk to Zalith while they were both in the same world. *That* thought had kept him going much longer; all he had to do now was get back to Aegisguard.

Chapter Two

— ⧼ ✝ ⧽ —

After All This Time

| Alucard |

In the kaleidoscopic light of the six Aegisguardian moons, Alucard walked across Dor-Sanguis' vast green fields. Every other time he made this journey home, he thought about how much he craved the feeling of his own bed or the warmth of his castle, but *this* time, he longed for only one thing.

Zalith.

Although they'd communicated through letters and mirrors, he was nervous...and a little cautious. There was so much that he wanted to say—to *ask*; things he felt were better left until they could see each other, better left until a time when Alucard wasn't stressed out by Damien's mission. But through all the angel-hunting, the only thing he could think about was *that demon*. The need he felt for him hadn't faded—none of his feelings had—and now that he was almost home, he might finally get the answers he'd spent so long hoping for.

He set his eyes on the towering castle in the distance, and a smile flickered upon his lips. Zalith would be waiting for him. But with his longing came worry. He wasn't sure whether the demon still felt the same; their frequent communication might mean something entirely different to Zalith, but Alucard tried his best to silence his anxiety and focus on mustering the courage to *ask* him how he felt.

Once he reached his castle, the vampire fiddled nervously with the crucifix which hung around his neck—the same crucifix Zalith gave him the night of their farewell. He hadn't once taken it off; it was all he had of Zalith and having it with him to remind him of that demon helped him through the years.

He made his way into the castle, slipping his hands into his pockets as he set his eyes on the two butlers, who were cleaning the large table in the centre of the room.

Alucard pointed at one of them. "*Pār,*" he instructed. "Ten minutes."

The butler nodded and hurried into the kitchen while Alucard made his way to the far-left door.

With Sabazios following, Alucard made his way through the door to his half of the castle. He headed up to his study, and when he pushed the door open, the hellhound scurried inside and started sniffing around, making sure the room was safe. *Of course* it was safe. No one ever set foot in there, and nothing dared to come near the building.

As he closed the door behind him, Alucard set his eyes on the tall, black mirror standing beside his desk. He knew Zalith was on the other side, waiting, working. Angst instantly consumed him. He hadn't seen the demon in a long time, and as much as he wished to see Zalith, he couldn't help but feel nervous.

However, just as he was about to head to his desk, where his hellhound was waiting for him, a loud crash of thunder echoed from outside. He knew what that sound meant; he knew what that flash of crimson light brought. With a look of dread on his pale face, he pulled off his cape and threw it over the mirror, catching half a glimpse of Zalith, who appeared to be sitting at his own desk, pen-in-hand. He didn't have time to explain.

Moments later, the door to his study balcony swung open, and the Daegelus arrived with an irritated scowl on his face—as usual.

Alucard backed as far away from the mirror as possible in hopes Zalith wouldn't be able to hear. Then, he set his hell-fiery eyes on Damien as he strolled into the study.

The Daegelus focused his cruel sights on the vampire and smiled with such condescendence that it made Alucard frown sullenly. "You look like shit," he said with a smirk, moving closer to Alucard.

He didn't answer. He was sure that he did look terrible; he hadn't yet gotten a chance to tidy himself up since his arrival back home. He hadn't even thought about it. All he wanted to do was see and speak to Zalith. He'd waited so long to talk to him, to ask him about the last night they saw each other, and to be sure of what they were.

When he reached the vampire, Damien placed his hand on his left shoulder—

The moment Damien touched him, Sabazios prepared to attack, but Alucard glared over at the hellhound and subtly shook his head in disapproval. The beast stood down, a worrisome look on its face as it carefully watched Damien.

Damien smiled as he stared at Alucard. "Dare I say you did a good job, Aleksei? For once, have you actually managed to do something of use? And in such acceptable timing."

Looking up at him, Alucard waited. For the first time in what might be forever, he found himself without any care concerning what Damien thought of his performance. He hadn't seen the Daegelus in many years and seeing him again after such a long time didn't make him feel as afraid as it usually would. But as each second in his presence passed, he was beginning to remember how horrified Damien made him feel—how small, how invalid.

But he didn't care. Despite Damien's threatening appearance, Alucard continued to focus all his thoughts and feelings on the demon he so sorely wished to see. However, as a look of disappointment then smothered Damien's face, Alucard felt his calmness fade into dread and angst.

Damien sighed shamefully and slowly dug his claws into the vampire's shoulder. "You did your job well in Tengetso; those creatures you brought me served me well. You also managed to bring me *some* exceptional angels—they will do nicely. However, you failed to bring me the one I wanted," he snarled. Before Alucard could try to speak, the Daegelus struck the wall beside him with his fist. "Are you so stupid as to forget?! Is that what happened?!"

"No," Alucard answered with a cautious frown. "You asked me to find those angels before meeting with—"

"Did I say speak?!" he yelled.

The vampire went silent and waited.

With a deep sigh, Damien pulled his fist from the wall and gripped Alucard's throat. "I asked you to find me *every* angel I need to create this child; you failed to bring me *Lucious*, the one angel I *actually* need! *He* is the most important of them all…and where is he? Where is he, Aleksei?"

Alucard stared vacantly. He'd only just come back from Tengetso and hadn't yet had the chance to search for Lucious. But he dared not argue with the Daegelus.

"You *did* do good, though," Damien uttered, nodding as he slowly pulled his claws from Alucard's shoulders. "Lucious is here in Aegisguard. Find him—and don't falter. I have to speak with my new angels, so I'll come and find you within the next few months," he said, letting go of Alucard.

The vampire watched as Damien turned around and made his way back over to the balcony doors.

"Be a good little brat for me and find Lucifer's ugly, ethos-crafted son for me, too," he instructed, looking back over his shoulder at him. "Detlaff was his name, right?"

"Yes," Alucard confirmed.

"Find him. He might just be more useful to me than you are—and you're not exactly…hmm…special, are you? Just about anyone could do better than you. Yet, I'm stuck with you, aren't I?" he snarled frustratedly. He then spread his wings and disappeared into the night sky, leaving Alucard alone.

Alucard stood where he was for a few moments and dragged his hand over his neck, trying to keep himself from sinking into the despair that had slowly begun to swallow him. His hellhound made its way over and looked up at him, whining quietly as it nuzzled his other hand with its snout. The vampire looked down at the hound and sighed softly, patting its head. He couldn't allow Damien to get to him—not now. He planned for the past few months to use this time to find out how Zalith felt and whether he and the demon might move on to share something more than friendship. That night on the balcony, he felt that he and Zalith *were* more, but he needed confirmation. He always required validation when it came to that demon. Nothing was ever clear enough.

He looked over at the mirror he'd thrown his cape over; he wasn't sure if Zalith heard Damien, but he was glad that he hadn't *seen* it. He wasn't sure what Zalith might think of him if he saw how weak Damien made him feel.

With an irritated scowl, he walked to his desk and pulled his cape from over the mirror. At the same time, the hellhound curled up on the floor beside the mirror and watched Alucard as he pulled out his chair and slumped down into it.

As soon as he came into view, a smile crept across Zalith's face. "Hello, ponytail," he greeted, smirking.

"Fuck off," Alucard snarled as he aggressively snatched a piece of parchment from a pile on his desk. Now he was too irritated to even try asking Zalith what he felt.

Zalith laughed quietly in amusement but then smiled and rested his arms on his desk, staring at the vampire. "Are you okay? Why did you cover the mirror?"

"Yes, and no reason," Alucard grumbled, trying to resist the urge to anxiously fiddle with his ponytail now that Zalith pointed it out—he hadn't had a chance to cut his hair in a long time.

He took a quill from the right top drawer of his desk. Then, he glanced at the demon. The sight of Zalith reminded Alucard just how much he missed him, just how much he longed to feel his embrace once again. He wouldn't admit it, though; not until he didn't feel so pissed off at him.

The same multi-coloured moonlight shone in through the curtains behind Zalith; it radiated into his room, bouncing off every smooth and reflective surface. It felt strange to Alucard, Zalith being in Aegisguard and not Eltaria, but it was also something of a relief. At least he wouldn't have to travel through a nauseating portal to see him.

"What are you writing?" Zalith asked curiously.

"My report," Alucard mumbled.

"And the dog?" he asked, glancing down at the hound lying at Alucard's feet.

"I got lonely," the vampire responded.

Zalith eyed the silent, sleeping hound with a disapproving look on his face. But when he looked at the vampire again, he frowned sadly. "You're not alone anymore; I would've been there with you if I could have," he said as Alucard looked at him. "I have missed you, Alucard—more than I might be able to explain. I want to—"

Before Zalith could finish, a loud knock came at Alucard's door. The vampire huffed irritably and took his eyes off the demon. He looked back at his door and watched as it opened, and one of the butlers stepped into the room.

"We're ready for you, sir," the man said in Dor-Sanguian.

Alucard sighed and glanced at Zalith. "I'll be back in ten minutes or so. Don't leave."

The demon smiled. "Okay."

Then, Alucard got up and left his office, following the butler. He hoped this would be over quickly; he had a lot to get done before he inevitably fell asleep, and he wanted to make sure that he got to tell Zalith *everything* he'd been waiting to say. But at least he had a little more time to prepare himself for that conversation.

| **Zalith** |

Zalith leaned back in his seat and gazed into Alucard's study. He missed the vampire so much; the final month of his absence was a long wait, more so since they hadn't spoken in weeks, but Alucard's mission was over, and Zalith was sure that the vampire would now be free to see him—all he had to do was ask. Of course, the demon had his own business to tend to; things in the Citadel were far from a standard he considered acceptable, and although there was a lot to do, he could afford to take a little time off. They'd manage without him for a day or two.

He didn't want to think about work, though. Alucard was the only thing he wanted on his mind right now. He *adored* that vampire, and seeing him again after what felt like an eternity would be a heart-wrenching relief. It was all he wanted—*Alucard* was all he wanted. He didn't exactly know how to tell him that, but he'd do his best.

The demon glanced around his office, waiting as patiently as he could for Alucard to get back. His thoughts reverted to the night of Alucard's party, the night they had to say farewell. It was a painful goodbye, one of the most disheartening goodbyes he'd ever experienced. But since becoming attached to Alucard, he *always* felt sad whenever they weren't together. That made him surer that he still wanted more with this vampire, so certain that he wanted to ask Alucard *right now* if he still had the same feelings that he expressed the night they danced. But he'd rather meet with Alucard and ask him in person.

As the hellhound whined and lifted its head to stare at him, Zalith glanced back at it. For a few moments, they glared at one another in silence, waiting for Alucard to return. But the seconds were beginning to feel like *hours*. Where was he?

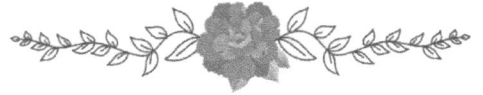

| **Alucard** |

As he made his way back towards his study, Alucard glanced at the tall clock to his right. He'd been gone for *twenty minutes*. Hopefully, Zalith wouldn't be annoyed with him. He exhaled and dragged his hand through his freshly cut hair; he was relieved to be rid of the ponytail once again.

With a quiet sigh, he stepped back into his study.

The demon laughed amusedly, watching through the mirror as Alucard approached his desk and sat down. "What happened to the ponytail?"

Alucard rolled his eyes as he picked up his quill to resume writing. "I had it cut, obviously."

"Well," he said, resting his chin in his hand as he leaned forward, "the ponytail isn't my personal preference, but I think you look adorable either way."

Alucard pouted and turned his head so Zalith couldn't see the embarrassed look on his face. "Whatever," he grumbled, writing his report for Damien.

Amused, Zalith smiled and leaned back in his seat, resting his left leg over his right. "How did the mission go? Did you complete everything Damien asked of you?"

"I did," he mumbled. "I still have to find Lucious, though. He's in Helvetes. Damien didn't tell me to leave right away, though, so I will take some time to rest; these past years have been exhausting," he explained with a sullen sigh.

Zalith then frowned. "*Years*? As far as I'm aware, it's been eight months since we last saw each other."

Realizing that he unintentionally shared the fact that the wait had been longer for him than it had been for Zalith, Alucard stopped writing and glanced at him. He wasn't sure what Zalith might think if he knew it had been a decade for him, but Alucard felt no need to lie. He looked back down at his paper and sighed quietly. "Where I went, time is different—it's... slower. Eight months here amounts to roughly ten years in Tengetso."

Zalith went quiet.

Alucard looked at him and saw a sullen frown on his face. "But it's fine. I was so busy all the time that I barely noticed how long it was taking. I had our talks to look forward to, too... so, it wasn't all that bad. What about you? What have you been up to?" he asked. He didn't want to let the mood become depressing. He'd felt enough of that particular emotion since the night he'd had to say goodbye.

The demon sighed and sat up straight. "Nothing exciting, nothing worth mentioning," he answered. "Just the usual business. Of course, I mentioned in one of my letters that I moved to Nefastus a while ago. I've been taking care of things here."

Alucard nodded as he finished his report. There was so much on his mind; there was so much confusion and angst warring inside him, and there were so many things he needed to ask, but he didn't know how. He intended to ask Zalith straight away if he still felt the same... if he might want something more than friendship, but Damien's appearance left him feeling irritated; he was aware that he snapped at Zalith, and he wasn't sure whether touching on such a subject was currently a good idea.

How could he ignore it, though? Despite Damien's scolding, Alucard couldn't disregard his feelings. He still wanted to be with Zalith; he still wanted to tell him how he felt—to tell him the things he couldn't tell him at his party. Now that Zalith was just an ocean away, Alucard felt so very anxious. His confidence had waned, and as hard as he tried to speak the words which needed speaking, he just couldn't find his voice.

Zalith frowned in concern. "Is something bothering you?"

He had to answer; if for a moment he could forget his nervousness, it had to be now. He glanced at Zalith and frowned in confliction. "I want..." he paused and looked down at his paper; hesitation swiftly warped his tiny moment of confidence. "I want... to sleep," he said defeatedly.

The demon rested his left arm on his desk and smiled. "*I* want to see you—tomorrow, tonight, whichever you'd prefer. But the sooner, the better."

"Why?" Alucard asked, frowning at him. "Why do you want to see me? I'm right here; you can see me."

"You know full well what I mean by see, Alucard. It's been far too long, and I can't bear another moment in your absence."

Alucard took his eyes off the demon and looked back down at his paper. Zalith *had* missed him—he knew that for sure. He also wanted to see him, but he wanted to be sure whether Zalith felt the same as he did. So as he fiddled with the crucifix around his neck, he sighed sullenly and quietly asked him, "Are we... anything?"

"Anything?" Zalith asked with a smirk on his face.

The vampire snarled and attempted to hide his face from Zalith by looking down at his coat belt. "Be straight with me," he implored, trying to unbuckle the belt, but it wouldn't shift. "Have you just been playing with me all this time or is there something more than whatever we are right now?" he asked as his anxiety drastically increased. His heart was now racing, and his hands were trembling.

Before Zalith could say whatever he was about to say with that smirk on his face, Alucard turned to face him and scowled.

The vampire continued, "You confuse me too much. Most of the time, I don't know whether you're serious or just looking for a laugh or reaction. You don't just get to come here and make me feel these things; you don't get to kiss me and dance with me and make me feel like you might just feel the same and then act like this is funny. *Is* this funny?" he asked with distress in his voice. He stopped trying to unbuckle the belt, sighed frustratedly, and glared at Zalith, waiting for him to answer while disguising his fear with anger.

Zalith's smirk faded into an austere frown. "Of course this isn't funny, Alucard. If this were just a game, I would've given up a year ago—sooner, in fact. I'm not wasting your time if that's what you think, and I don't plan to. You've never been any kind of joke to me; there's never been a time I've used you to amuse myself. I take you and what you say very seriously, and although I may appear to smile at what you might consider inappropriate times, it's not because I'm laughing at you. I find you amusing in an endearing, attractive way, not in a condescending manner."

Alucard listened but looked away as a pout appeared on his face.

Zalith smiled and continued, "You make me smile because you make me happy, something I haven't felt so intensely in a long time. I kissed you and danced with you because I want to be as close to you as I possibly can, always. So, please come and see me," he pleaded.

For a few moments, Alucard stared at his desk. Everything Zalith said somewhat silenced the majority of his worry. At least he knew he wasn't a source of entertainment for the demon. Now, his confounding thoughts shifted to whether he was ready to see him or not. *Did* he want to go and see Zalith? Of course he did. Was he ready for what might happen when they saw each other? He wasn't sure; he didn't even know what that would be.

He felt nervous, but he needed to know how Zalith felt; he needed to see if they could share more, so he *had* to go. He was certain he wouldn't find out unless he did; Zalith's failure to answer that part of his question told him that, and he *did* want to see the demon. Being with him always made him feel so wanted, needed, and seen. He craved to feel the contentedness and serenity that he felt when he was with Zalith.

The vampire sighed away his hesitation and looked at the demon. "Okay," he agreed.

Zalith smiled in what looked like relief and happiness. "I'll wait for you in the Citadel. I trust you'll be able to find me."

Alucard rolled his eyes. "You *would* pick the biggest city to live near, wouldn't you?"

"If the crowds bother you, we can meet somewhere more secluded."

"No," Alucard mumbled. "I'll find you."

"How does late afternoon sound?"

The vampire thought to himself for a moment. He'd have to leave early to get to the other side of Aegisguard by late afternoon, but he didn't care. "Fine," he agreed.

"You don't sound as if that's fine," he said with a frown.

He sighed and rested his arms on his desk. "No, it *is* fine. I'll just have to leave around noon to get there. I need to make sure I don't need to do anything here before I leave."

"That's rather early. You're a demon, can't you use the Underworld? Phase?" Zalith asked with concern in his voice.

Alucard frowned despondently. He couldn't phase like other demons, but he didn't want Zalith to know that. "No," he muttered. "I'll be there. It doesn't matter how I get there."

Zalith frowned for a moment... but to Alucard's relief, instead of questioning him, he smiled and nodded. "Okay. Do you plan on heading to bed soon, or do I get to see you for a while longer?" he asked as a smirk crept across his lips.

Struggling to keep a pout off his face, Alucard returned to trying to unbuckle his coat belt; it felt restricting around his waist while he sat there. He could feel Zalith's amused eyes on him as he snarled irritably, trying to pull it off, and once the buckle finally gave way, he yanked it from his waist and chucked it on the floor. The hellhound raised its head in startle, watching Alucard as he pulled his coat off and threw it to the floor with an annoyed grumble.

Alucard then took off his blazer and rested his arms on his desk again. "I have many things to do now that I'm home, but I have time. I should sleep."

Zalith sighed quietly—Alucard knew he was disappointed. But the demon smiled and nodded. "Then I'll see you tomorrow afternoon."

Looking down at his desk, Alucard smiled slightly and said, "Yes."

Zalith then stood up and straightened his blazer. "Goodnight, vampire," he said, smirking.

"Goodnight," Alucard mumbled shyly.

As Zalith left his office, Alucard leaned back in his seat and stared into the mirror for a few moments. He'd see the demon soon; he felt overwhelmed with worry and anxiety, but he wouldn't allow it to keep him from going. He'd waited so long to see him again, to be in his presence, and the time had finally come.

Tomorrow, he was sure he'd find out how Zalith felt and whether they were more than friends. But there was still much to be done before he could sleep. He lied to Zalith, and it made him feel awful, but if he allowed the demon to stay, he was sure that he wouldn't get much else done. He thoroughly enjoyed speaking to him, and it was so very easy to become lost in their conversations. He couldn't let that happen—not tonight.

He took his eyes off the mirror and looked down at the hellhound. "Go and get Ben for me."

The beast stood up and left the room.

Alucard waited, tapping his claws on his desk, and when he heard his hound's claws clipping closer down the hall, he stood up and leaned against his desk, glaring at the door. The beast returned to the room with Ben, the overly muscular, scruffy-faced vampire Alucard had left in charge while he was absent.

Ben immediately smiled as he set his eyes on The Vampire Lord and bowed respectfully before saying, "I thought I heard you get back." He made his way towards Alucard. "How did it go?"

"How have things been here?" he asked, disregarding Ben's question.

Stopping a few feet from Alucard, Ben donned a stern expression. "Quiet," he answered. "Nothing of the wolves, the humans. Dirk's kept the city in order, and I the vampires. Things are pretty much the same."

"Good," Alucard mumbled, "and our guest?"

Ben scoffed. "Making a racket, cries daily."

Amused, Alucard smirked. "I will be away again tomorrow from noon. I need you to keep an eye on the castle for one more day."

"Of course," Ben said with a nod as the hellhound walked past him and sat in front of the mirror. Glancing at the beast, Ben frowned curiously. "Where did you happen across that thing?"

"That thing has a name."

"Sorry—what's his name?"

"Sabazios," Alucard answered.

The beast raised its head and looked up at him with an expectant look on its face.

Intrigued, Ben nodded. "Interesting name."

Uninterested in the small talk, Alucard sighed and crossed his arms. "Attila," he said. "Anything?"

"He *did* send correspondence over the last few months, nothing that might require your immediate attention," he started. "He has made his way into the king's counsel; he's now his advisor. As far as he is concerned, DeiganLupus is, I quote, 'once again yours to do with what you please.'"

"Good. Go now."

With a single nod, Ben turned around and left the room.

Alucard then sighed and returned to his desk; he slumped down in his seat. He had a mound of reports to read, write, and respond to. He'd much rather head to sleep, but he knew he should get some of his work done before tomorrow. So, that's what he would do.

As the night crept onward, he remained at his desk, unaware of how late it might have become and how late it was when he finally chose to take a moment to close his eyes and rest. What harm could a moment's rest do? He leaned his arms on his desk and laid his head on them. He'd get back to work soon. Just a moment. A *few* moments.

Chapter Three

— ⊰ ✟ ⊱ —

Thoughts and Questions

| **Zalith** |

The early morning sunlight shone through the windows of Zalith's office, and a chorus of birds filled the once-silent world outside. Zalith made his way to his desk and set his eyes on the mirror beside it when he sat down. A smile of adoration found its way to his face as he gazed at Alucard, who had fallen asleep at his desk; the vampire told him he was heading to bed last night, but he'd obviously lied. It didn't bother Zalith. He knew too well how hard the vampire worked and how he preferred to do so on his own.

A knock then came at his door; he deadpanned and took his eyes off the sleeping vampire to look over at one of his butlers, who stood in the doorway with a white cup of coffee in his right hand. The demon gestured to his table, instructing the man to place the coffee on it. As the man did so, Zalith glanced back at the mirror, unable to keep himself from admiring Alucard. Despite the fact that he couldn't see his face, he still found it endearingly amusing to see he had allowed himself to pass out mid-work.

Zalith didn't, however, want to make Alucard feel uncomfortable. Once his butler left the room, the sound of his closing door woke the vampire. As much as he wanted to speak with him, Zalith knew that he'd be seeing him in a few hours. Alucard told him he had things to do before leaving for Nefastus, and Zalith didn't want to distract him. So, before Alucard lifted his head and saw him, Zalith stood up and moved out of sight.

| **Alucard** |

Alucard flinched and woke from his sleep. He slowly opened his eyes and glanced around, taking a moment to work out where he was; he'd been away from home for so long that he didn't immediately recognize his own study.

He sighed, sat up, and looked down at his papers. Had he fallen asleep? He glared over at the windows; the sunlight was so bright that he felt as if it might blind him, so he turned his head away and grimaced when his head ached as a result of the rays. Noon wasn't far away, and it made him panic. How could he have allowed himself to fall asleep—and for so long? He didn't want to be late meeting Zalith.

With an irritated scowl, he looked down at Sabazios. The beast was sleeping at the foot of the mirror—

Alucard quickly shifted his eyes to the office inside the mirror. It mortified him to think that Zalith might have caught him napping, but the demon was nowhere to be seen.

The vampire relaxed for a moment and attempted to find the strength to get up and get ready to leave, but when he noticed the steaming cup of what he suspected was coffee on Zalith's desk, he assumed Zalith would soon turn up. So, he stood up and hastily left his study, and the hellhound followed.

He made his way down the empty halls of his castle and to his bedroom. As much as he'd like to get more rest, he had no time, and if he were to meet with Zalith at the decided time, he'd have to leave as soon as he was ready.

He'd be heading to Nefastus…a place he thought he'd never visit again—not willingly. But it was to see Zalith; for that demon, he'd even head back to Tengetso. He took off his shirt and pulled a new black one from the dresser beside his bed as a stubborn pout appeared on his face. Nefastus was a lawless land full of petty criminals, wannabe bandits, irritating pirates, and all manner of things he hated. Of course, it *had* to be Nefastus where Zalith chose to reside. He just hoped the demon's home wasn't in the Citadel; otherwise, he was sure that this meeting wouldn't be very pleasant.

Once he was dressed, he looked down at Sabazios. "Go and get my cape," he grumbled, remembering he'd left it in his study.

The hound barked in response and hurried out of Alucard's room.

Alucard was sure he had more work to do before heading out, but it could wait. He hadn't been in Zalith's presence physically for what felt like an eternity, and he wasn't going to wait a moment longer. Ben would take care of things in his absence.

When Sabazios returned with his fur-collared cape, he took it from the hound and pulled it on. "You can stay here," he told the creature. "I'll be back later."

Sabazios frowned and whined sadly, but he laid down and remained where he was, watching Alucard as he made his way over to the window.

As he stood in front of the open window, Alucard stared at the cloudless blue sky. Hesitation gripped him once again. He wasn't quite sure what he was doing; he wanted to know how Zalith felt, he wanted to understand just how it was that *he* felt—to understand why he missed Zalith so much, why he was always on his mind, and why he desired to be close to him. The thought of seeing Zalith again got him through those years of stressful, endless work. Thinking back to their moments of embrace calmed him, and his hopes of a relationship kept him from sinking into the sadness that gripped him so tightly. The only way to get the answers he needed was to head to Nefastus and meet him, so that was what he would do.

A little over an Aegisguard year ago, they completed their mission to transport vampires from Eltaria to Aegisguard; between their business meetings, they met outside of their work; they'd done so to simply be in one another's company, to do something other than transport vampires. Zalith accompanied him on many of his personal tasks; the demon helped him with the problems Ada caused him, he helped capture and imprison Detlaff, and when Alucard found himself feeling so very lost and alone, Zalith was there to keep him from slipping into the depravity of his life.

Ever since he left for Tengetso, he and Zalith remained in contact through letters and their mirror links. They spoke for what was every week for Zalith. Why would they talk so often if there wasn't more to their friendship? No one had ever managed to make him feel the way Zalith did. Alucard knew that he was a cold, isolated man; he didn't want to spend his time with anyone, and he didn't want to do anything for anyone other than himself. However, when it came to Zalith, he found himself wanting to differ from those facts... to do whatever he could for Zalith. They were friends, business partners, allies... all of that was certain. But what Alucard felt for him was stronger than that. What he felt wasn't friendship, was it?

He felt a *desire* to be around this demon as often as he could. It was unlike anything he felt—unlike anything he would have ever thought he'd feel. That night on the balcony of his castle, he hadn't wanted their embrace to end. But of course, Damien ruined it. Now, he stood there with so many questions, so much confusion, and so much worry. Today, he hoped he'd find out what Zalith thought, and what *he* might want them to be. He was convinced Zalith wanted more; he just needed confirmation. He found Zalith so confusing that he wasn't sure when he might be serious or just pulling his leg in search of amusement.

Did Zalith feel the same? Had Zalith invited him to meet him to tell him that they should remain professional? Had their time apart perhaps changed the way Zalith felt? Alucard dreaded that—it hurt to think about it. Or had Zalith invited him to tell him that he felt the same? To tell him that they could and should share something more than friendship? Why couldn't Zalith just tell him through the mirror? Why did he have to go and physically see him? He knew it was most likely because Zalith would much rather see his reactions in person... but he was going to go despite his suspicions. He had to. It was the only way he'd get answers.

As anxious as he felt, he wouldn't change his mind. He had to know if his feelings were worth paying attention to, and if Zalith was worth it, too. He didn't want to spend another moment away from him, and he needed to know whether this attachment to Zalith would cause him misery. Although he disregarded the things people said about Zalith, the thought of this demon using him still lingered in his head.

He sighed and let go of his worry. Without one more moment of hesitation, he morphed into vermillion smoke and raced into the sky, beginning his journey to Nefastus. Soon, he'd know what Zalith wanted, and he'd be able to decide whether his need for this demon's company was something to explore or something to bury and abandon.

Chapter Four

Nefastus

| **Alucard** |

The Citadel was just as busy as Alucard remembered. Darkly coloured blimps soared through the smoke-filled sky, and not a single bird was in sight other than the owl he appeared as.

Alucard slowly descended and landed on a signpost with over thirty destinations pinned to it. The vampire visited this place many times before and managed to make quite a name for himself. However, that was over a hundred years ago, and he was sure that the people he upset had grown old and died. He still proceeded cautiously, though. The last thing he wanted was people hunting him down like an animal while he tried to spend time with Zalith. As fun as the demon might find such a situation, Alucard wasn't at all in the mood for anything so exhausting.

He glowered at the city's circular centre, watching as hundreds of people shuffled around. The large opening was surrounded by towering, shimmering glass and metal buildings reflecting the sun's light in every direction. Everything was some shade of gold, brown, or silver; the few bronze-stained roads that led deeper into the city were jammed with yelling, arguing people and their horse-drawn carriages. There were taverns on every street and corner, and the streets smelt of alcohol, blood, and smoke. He hated it here.

As several yells echoed from behind him, Alucard sharply turned his feathered head and glared at a group of strangely dressed pirates. They brawled loudly close to the corroded, battered statue of what was once a dragon, which stood not too far from the vast fire tower in the very centre of the city. He watched as they fumbled around, throwing whatever their hands could find on the muddy, littered streets. Shots were fired from their flintlocks, and blood splattered to the ground as fists and maces were thrown.

He recognized their markings and signature weapons. The pirates were the Meshuga, a group of noisy, irritating plunderers he had to deal with so very long ago, and Alucard was bewildered by the fact that they were still around; they shared a single brain cell between them.

Alucard felt utter revolt when looking over this city. It was the living, festering example of pure disorder and disgust, and he had no idea why it was the place Zalith had chosen to not only meet but to live, too. He turned his head once again, setting his hell-fiery eyes on a group of mobsters. They were all dressed in grey-striped, black suits; they had rifles on their backs and black fedoras on their heads. Alucard knew who they were: the Imperito. It seemed as though *they* hadn't died out in the past hundred years, either, and he suspected they probably still thought of themselves as the government in this lawless land. *Morons.*

He watched as the Imperito goons made their way over to the Meshuga pirates and attempted to break up their fight, but they were pulled into it.

Alucard rolled his eyes, shook his head, and scoured the area, searching for Zalith, hoping he had chosen a less chaotic corner of the Citadel to meet. But no. There he was in the far-right corner, watching with a condescending look on his face as the Imperito and Meshuga fought loudly. This time, he'd come dressed in a light tan suit, a white shirt, and a pinstripe-patterned, warm-grey tie. Alucard glared at him, waiting for him to notice so he could fly somewhere less crowded and morph back to his usual form. If someone saw him rematerialize, everyone in earshot would pull out their pitchforks and chase him through the streets.

| **Zalith** |

Standing beside one of the city centre's smaller exits, Zalith had his dark eyes fixed on the fighting people in the distance. He felt no care for them whatsoever; their noise was irritating him—enough for him to get someone to shut them up for him. However, he was far too preoccupied with his thoughts to spare a moment of his time to deal with pointless humans. He'd been in the Citadel for just over a year, and he'd already made immense progress in becoming a governing figure. The occasional fight would still break out, but it wouldn't take long to be dealt with; his people would be along shortly.

He took his sights off the brawl and looked around slowly, hoping to set his gaze on Alucard sometime soon. It was late afternoon, and he was sure that the vampire would be arriving any time now. His excitement to see Alucard was unbearable; it'd been such a long time since he'd seen him, since he'd been in his company. He was but moments away from seeing him again, and his impatience grew as each second passed.

Where was he, though? Dread then struck him. Could Alucard have felt too nervous about coming? He frowned in confliction, but when he set his eyes on a horned eagle owl perched on the tallest signpost on the other side of the centre, a smirk stretched across his face. He'd recognize those eyes anywhere—those eyes which looked as though fire raged inside them. The owl stared back for a few moments, and as it spread its wings, Zalith's worry faded into relief. However, as he held out his arm for the owl to land on, the bird swooped past him. He lowered his arm and turned to face the direction it flew and watched it curve into a deserted alley.

Zalith was aware that Alucard could transform into a fox, but now he knew that he could also become an owl, and it made him wonder what else the vampire could transform into. He smiled curiously and made his way into the alley; he found it adorable that the vampire could shape-shift into animals, but Alucard was here now... and that was what he was going to focus on. He'd sate his curiosity later.

| **Alucard** |

Alucard reached the end of the alley and rematerialized into his normal self. He took a moment to relax, but when he heard Zalith approaching from behind, he turned around. Before Alucard could say anything, Zalith hastily wrapped his arms around him and pulled him into a tight embrace. Alucard felt no desire to struggle or complain; he missed the demon's embrace so sorely that the sudden hug relieved him of his confliction. He slowly moved his arms around Zalith and held him just as tightly, resting the side of his head on the demon's shoulder.

"I've missed you," Zalith said quietly.

The vampire wanted to tell him he missed him as well, but he couldn't find his voice. Not only was he overwhelmed with anxiety, but his hunger abruptly increased, too. Being so close to Zalith was enticing him—he could hear the demon's heart beating; he could smell the blood in his veins. And for a moment, he felt as if he might lose himself. He lifted his head from the demon's shoulder, rested the side of his face on Zalith's cheek, and eyed his neck. He salivated, and his fangs longed to sink into flesh and reward him with sanguine pleasure. It would take no more than half a moment to bite into his skin, to taste him. How he wanted to—how he *needed* to. But he couldn't. He *wouldn't*.

Zalith let go of Alucard and placed his hands on his shoulders, looking at him as he backed off. "Are you okay?" he asked worriedly.

Alucard shifted his gaze to the ground and tried to silence his hunger. It had never been so intense before—such a *struggle*. Ever since killing Ada, ever since he lost himself to that darkness which Damien pulled him from, he found that many of his previous struggles had become so much more overbearing. His anger, his hunger—but he was confident that he could control himself. He had to. The last thing he was going to do was let himself hurt Zalith.

He took his eyes off the ground and slowly set them on Zalith's concerned face. "Yes," he answered.

The demon smiled and moved his hands from Alucard's shoulders to his arms. "Are you going to tell me why you're avoiding crowds?" he asked with a smirk. "And how many different animals can you transform into? It's adorable."

Alucard rolled his eyes, looked over at the wall, and pouted. "I pissed the Imperito off a hundred years or so ago; I don't know if they still remember me," he revealed, trying to hide his embarrassment—Zalith's compliments always flustered him.

"I wouldn't be surprised if they had forgotten you; everyone here is profoundly stupid. If you'd rather not be here, though, we can—"

"I'm fine," Alucard mumbled, pulling free from Zalith's grip. "Where are we going? Or are we going to hang out here for the remainder of the evening?"

Amused, Zalith smiled and held out his arm.

The vampire stared at Zalith for a few moments. Did he want him to take hold of his arm? He felt far too nervous about doing it, but he didn't want to make Zalith think that he didn't want to. *Of course* he wanted to; he enjoyed any contact with him, and he wasn't going to ignore Zalith's evident mutual feeling. So, he dismissed his hesitation and took hold of his arm, and he walked beside him as he led the way out of the alley.

"I thought we could have a drink before we head to my home for dinner—as long as that's okay with you," Zalith said with a smile, glancing at him. "Don't feel compelled to accept. I understand if you'd rather talk here in the city. I would, however, like for you to come back with me. I know there's a lot for us to talk about, and I'd prefer to discuss things over dinner."

Looking down at the ground as they made their way out onto the busy street, Alucard thought about it. He knew how careful of a person Zalith was; he knew he wouldn't just invite him to his home if there wasn't something more to their relationship...would he? And for dinner, too. Alucard wasn't the social type; he wasn't sure whether dinner was something all friends did or if it was reserved for those with closer relationships. Either way, he wanted to say yes. Spending more time with Zalith sounded very appealing.

He took his eyes off the ground and glanced at Zalith. "By dinner, I assume you mean...eat human food?" he asked unsurely; he felt reluctant to say yes right away in case it made him look far too eager.

Zalith looked at him and smiled. "Of course. Unless you can't eat it, then I'm sure I can find an alternative for you."

Alucard looked away again and glared at the passers-by. "I can eat whatever I want, it's just been a while."

"Well, what better place to revitalise than here? And in what better company?" he asked with a pleasant smile as he led the way down a street. "We'll head to a little place not too far away and have a drink, and then we'll head back to my house."

Following, Alucard stared ahead. He felt *so* anxious, but his desire to be in Zalith's company was far more significant. He didn't know what Zalith might have planned for dinner, but he was content with what he already knew. Zalith might not have answered his questions yet, but this invitation to his home assured him that maybe... Zalith felt something similar to what he felt.

He looked at him and said, "We can do that."

Zalith smiled. "Wonderful."

Then, they continued down the street, heading to the place Zalith mentioned. And as he walked beside the demon, Alucard did his best to keep his nervousness hidden.

Chapter Five

— ⊰ ✝ ⊱ —

Of Coffee and Cocoa

| **Alucard** |

Alucard followed Zalith towards a small, secluded café in the very far reaches of the Citadel. The building was made of carob-brown oak, its frames were gold, and it had several shimmering glass windows. The place was all but deserted save for the elf couple sitting inside and the waitress behind the bar cleaning the white mugs. A tempting, chocolatey smell clung to the air, accompanied by the scent of fresh bread and coffee.

Zalith seemed to be directing them inside; however, Alucard didn't *want* to go in, so he pulled his arm free from Zalith's and made his way over to one of the tables lined along the café's front. He pulled out a chair, sat down, and watched Zalith sit opposite him. The demon smiled at him, and Alucard looked away in an attempt to hide his conflicted expression. He wanted to ask Zalith about his feelings; he wanted all of his questions answered *now*. But he knew he had to wait. He knew that Zalith wasn't likely to tell him right away—that just wasn't how this demon worked—and he had already said they wouldn't discuss personal matters until they went to his house. While he *was* eager to ask, he was also curious to know what Zalith had been up to in his absence, so he'd put up with the small talk for now.

The waitress came outside and asked Zalith what he wanted, and as he responded, Alucard turned his attention to the noise in the distance. The Citadel was a lot louder and busier than Dargamoore, and right now, he found himself missing the city where he grew up. There were so many people here, so much commotion, so many humans…and the sounds of their weak little hearts beating around him aroused his hunger. He could kill anyone in this place and no one would raise an eyebrow in concern. Murder was as common as rats on these streets.

Should he? Feeding would make him feel a whole lot less sluggish, and it would sate his growing desire to hunt and sink his teeth into someone. But the more he thought about it, the more uncomfortable he started feeling. A lot of the Citadel people were filthy; he didn't want his lips to meet the skin of someone who hadn't bathed in a week. He *could* use his senses to tell which of his prey was the cleanest, both body and blood, but that could take hours.

"What exactly did Damien have you doing?" Zalith asked curiously.

The vampire snapped out of his trance and set his eyes on him. "Vhat?"

"In Tengetso," Zalith said, smiling. "What were you doing for Damien?"

"Finding angels," he answered with a shrug and rested his arms on the table. "It's...not a very nice place."

"Oh?"

Alucard shrugged again and leaned back in his seat. "It's a wasteland. The Numen throw their unwanted creatures down there; I came across so many different things, all mutations of whatever lives here in Aegisguard. Humans, werewolves, vampires, demons—it was...hmm...there isn't really a word for it—not that I know of, anyway. It's probably worse than Hell. I just did what I had to and left."

"So, that world is a living, breeding cesspool for Damien and the other Numen, I assume."

"Yes. I hope I never have to go back there, and I don't really want to talk about it," he dismissed.

Zalith smiled understandingly but then frowned in concern. "I can't help but notice your irritancy. Why are you so grouchy, Alucard?" he asked with a smirk. "Is something wrong?"

The vampire pouted. "No. I'm just tired," he muttered, looking down at the table. "But I'll be fine," he snapped, glaring at Zalith before he could suggest anything that might shorten their afternoon. He wasn't going to leave the demon's company until he had answers. He didn't care about his weariness or his dangerously increasing hunger. All he cared about was Zalith and his feelings. At least he was able to enjoy the demon's company while he waited to ask, though. There was nothing he wanted more than to be with Zalith, and he wasn't afraid to admit that to himself, but he did wonder whether Zalith felt the same.

"Are you sure?" Zalith persisted.

He nodded and turned his head to stare down the street opposite them. "What have you been doing while I was gone?"

Before Zalith could answer, though, the waitress walked over to their table. They both watched her hand them their drinks, but Alucard eyed her as if *she* was what was being served to him. He could hear her beating heart and smell her coursing blood. He knew that he was hungry, but he hadn't thought he was *this* hungry. He couldn't take his eyes off her throbbing jugular, and he tensed up when his instincts began encouraging him to pounce.

But when the woman walked off, he managed to take his eyes off her and tried to calm down. He could see Zalith smirking at him, though, and embarrassment quickly outweighed any other feeling, and it forced him to look away again.

"Are you hungry?" Zalith asked quietly as he rested his arms on the table and leaned closer with an intrigued look on his face. "Is that why you're grumpy?"

Alucard glared down into his drink. "No," he lied. He then glanced at Zalith. "What is this?" he asked, nodding at the cup that had been placed in front of him. It wasn't coffee; it smelled chocolatey and sweet, not bitter and sharp.

"Hot chocolate," he answered. "I thought you'd prefer something sweeter than coffee, judging by the amount of sugar you tend to use."

The vampire looked back down at his drink and pouted. He wasn't sure about trying something new, but if Zalith thought he'd like it, then he was curious to find out. However, he couldn't focus on his drink. Zalith was right. He *was* hungry, and that was why he felt so irritable. But he still didn't want to drink the blood of anyone in this part of the city. He should, though, shouldn't he? If he didn't—if he remained hungry—he'd be aggravated for the rest of the evening, and Zalith didn't deserve his attitude. Today was supposed to be relaxing for them both, and he didn't want to ruin that because he neglected to feed before he left Dor-Sanguis.

He took his sights off Zalith for a few moments and eyed the people passing by. They all had revolting stenches clinging to them; most of them smelled sick, and one man had recently been infected by a werewolf. But then he spotted an aristocrat dressed in an expensive suit with colours only the wealthiest of people could afford; the man didn't smell sick, and he looked like he took a lot of care in his appearance. Alucard's instinct to attack drastically increased. He was the best option.

Alucard glanced at Zalith and frowned uncomfortably. "I'll... be one moment," he said as he stood up.

Zalith smiled and nodded.

Then, without a moment of hesitation, Alucard trailed the aristocrat, desperate to sate his hunger.

| **Zalith** |

Zalith watched Alucard as he swiftly made his way towards the aristocrat. While he found some amusement in seeing Alucard stalk his food, he wasn't quite sure that he liked the idea of the vampire sinking his teeth into other people—other *men*. In fact, he didn't like the idea of Alucard even *touching* anyone else or someone touching him, whether it be so that the vampire could feed or if it were unwanted contact from another person. Although he felt like it might not yet be his place to feel so possessive, he'd felt this way for a long time, and as he watched the vampire pull the unsuspecting man into the closest alley, Zalith felt almost frustrated.

He looked down at his coffee, trying to keep himself from being irrational. He wouldn't deny that he wished that it was him whom Alucard had chosen to sink his fangs into, but he hadn't, and that made him feel sad. Once again, though, it wasn't his place to make a fuss of such a thing. He and Alucard weren't together—*not yet.*

A smirk made its way onto his face when he started thinking about all the things he wanted to do and say, but he heard Alucard making his way back to the table, so he lost his smirk and looked up from his drink. He followed Alucard with his eyes as he walked back to the table with a much more relaxed expression.

Once the vampire sat back down, Zalith smiled and asked him, "Do you feel better?"

Alucard pulled off his cape, folded it over the back of his seat, and rested his arms on the table. "Yes," he mumbled, looking down at his drink once again.

"Is my jealousy nonsensical?" he questioned, smirking.

He frowned confusedly. "What?"

The demon leaned closer as he gazed at Alucard's face. "I haven't failed to notice that you have preferences when it comes to the people you choose to drink from, Alucard."

"Preferences?"

He smirked again and started slowly moving his hand over Alucard's.

As he looked down at his hand, Alucard shrugged. "I just kill whoever I want. I don't wait for a specific person to come along," he lied, trying to disguise his nervousness with irritancy.

"No?" he asked suggestively.

"I don't know what you're trying to say, so either say it or be quiet," Alucard snarled, looking away from him as he pulled his hand from beneath Zalith's.

Zalith sat up straight, keeping his thoughts to himself. He wanted to tell Alucard how he felt about his feeding habits, but he didn't want to make him uncomfortable. He didn't want to reveal his possessiveness; the last thing he wanted to do was scare Alucard off. There'd be plenty of opportunities to tell him once they'd taken the time to decide where the evening would take them.

Instead of expressing his concerns, he leaned back in his seat and smiled. "Regarding your earlier question: while you were gone, I was working on this city. I've been working towards becoming something of a governing figure here, towards creating some sort of order. The process has been long and not without peril, but I've reached a comfortable point in my feat. The Meshuga and the Imperito still cause annoyances here and there, but they're always dealt with. I've also been keeping up with things back home in Eltaria, waiting for the day I might be able to go back. It might be some time before that happens, but the day will come eventually, nonetheless."

"This city does seem a lot less…revolting than I remember," Alucard agreed.

"I'll take that as a compliment," Zalith said with a smile before sipping his coffee.

Alucard then glanced down at his drink with a hesitant look on his face.

"How are things in Dor-Sanguis?" the demon asked.

He looked at him and shrugged. "Fine. I left Ben in charge again; he's the only person I really trust with the responsibility of the Nosferatu in my absence."

"Naturally," the demon said as Alucard finally sipped his drink. When an almost surprised look appeared on his face, Zalith smiled amusedly. "Better than coffee?"

Alucard placed his cup back down and looked away. "Maybe."

Zalith smirked. "I'll be sure to remember."

"Why? Will we be meeting here often?" he asked skeptically.

"If you'd like," he replied. "It's one of my favourite places to come for coffee."

The vampire looked down at his drink as a conflicted look warped his nervous face.

Zalith was sure that he was thinking…but as he watched Alucard's expression become something of distress, he frowned in concern. He was certain that it was because Alucard wanted answers, and Zalith felt no need to keep them from him. He knew too well how irritable the vampire would become if he took too long to tell him something; the last thing he wanted to do was piss him off or upset him. He wanted to make this man happy however he could, and he felt as though there might not be a thing he wouldn't do for him.

He wanted to head home and immediately tell Alucard how he felt, but he didn't want to overwhelm him. Perhaps that was what Alucard needed, though—to be overwhelmed. He clearly wanted to know how Zalith felt, and he must be aware that it would be a lot to process—but yet, the vampire had still come and seemed adamant to know. Zalith wouldn't make him wait too much longer.

"Do you want to head back *now*?" he suggested. "My groundskeeper isn't too far away with a carriage."

The vampire looked anxious. He seemed to ponder for a moment…but eventually, he nodded and said, "If you want," and then sipped from his hot chocolate.

With a smile, Zalith stood up. "Then let's go."

Alucard stood up and grabbed his cape, but as he pulled it on, he glanced down at his drink. "I want to take this with me," he said, pointing to the cup as he looked at Zalith.

"I can get the staff back home to make you some."

"Fine," he grumbled, turning away from him. "Let's go."

Zalith smirked amusedly as he watched Alucard walk in the wrong direction. "It's this way, Alucard," he called, laughing quietly.

With an embarrassed scowl, Alucard turned around. "Whatever," he muttered, followed by many Dor-Sanguian words that Zalith couldn't understand.

Then, as the vampire passed him, Zalith took hold of his arm with his and began leading the way to where his carriage was waiting.

Chapter Six

— ⋜ ✝ ⋝ —

Words of Eternity

| **Alucard** |

Alucard followed Zalith onto a deserted street where several horse-drawn carriages waited along the road. The demon took him to a black carriage close to the city exit, and once he pulled the door open, he invited Alucard to get in first. With a quiet, "Thank you," Alucard climbed inside, sat down, and watched as Zalith got in and pulled the door shut.

Zalith smiled as he sat beside Alucard. "My home isn't too far away," he said as the carriage began moving along the cobblestone road.

"It's not...loud?" the vampire asked, glancing at him. "To live so close to the Citadel."

"No. The forest surrounding my house tends to keep the noise away."

With a single nod, Alucard turned his head and stared out of the window, watching as the cobblestone trailed off into a dirt road, and the seemingly endless streets of towering stone and metal buildings became redwood and cedar trees.

The vampire rested his chin in his hand, still anxious about his assumption that maybe Zalith felt the same—or something similar, at least. As the demon shuffled beside him, making himself more comfortable in the small carriage, Alucard glanced at him. He wasn't saying or doing anything; it didn't even look like he was thinking. While Alucard was deep in thought, trying to keep himself calm, it seemed as though Zalith was as calm as ever—that was no surprise.

Sometimes—well, most of the time—Alucard found it hard to read Zalith. He wasn't sure whether it was because the demon was just generally hard to read or because he had spent so long away from civilisation and socialising that he'd forgotten what it was like to be in the presence of someone else. Either way, he wanted to know what Zalith was thinking right now. Was he going to ask? Of course he was. He hated when he couldn't assume what the demon might be pondering about.

He looked at the demon, but Zalith was already smirking at him. Flustered, Alucard looked away, and any desire he had to ask questions faded like dust in the wind. It wasn't often that he found himself hesitating or holding back, and this demon was the only person who had *ever* made him do such a thing. Instead of speaking, Alucard looked out the window and focused on the redwood and cedar trees, which were now accompanied by cypress trees. He tried to hide the fact that he was embarrassed, but he was sure that Zalith had seen his nervous expression.

Zalith laughed amusedly and placed his hand on Alucard's shoulder. "Why do you keep looking over here? I know I'm rather desirable to look at, but is there something else—the window, perhaps? Does the forest look different on this side than yours?" he teased.

Shrugging Zalith's hand off, not at all amused, Alucard frowned irritably, still staring out of the window. He watched as the sun slowly set in the distance, filling the sky with an array of oranges and purples.

The demon slowly moved his hand away from Alucard and frowned worriedly. "Is something bothering you?"

Alucard glared at him from the corner of his eye. "How long until we get there?" he mumbled and noticed that the forest tree line was starting to curve outwards; the carriage wheels began scraping against gravel, and the sound of flowing water grew louder. He watched as they passed an open, black metal gate connected to a white stone wall; he assumed they were arriving, so he looked at Zalith, waiting for him to answer.

The carriage then came to a halt; the demon straightened his light tan blazer and smiled. "We're here," he said before unlocking his door.

As Zalith climbed out of the carriage, Alucard exhaled deeply, trying to disguise his anxious feelings with irritancy. He wasn't sure what to expect and being in this new environment wasn't helping. He still didn't know what Zalith was thinking or feeling; he seemed to be so relaxed, and Alucard was feeling unusually on edge. He'd never felt anything like this before, but just as Zalith made him want to do things he hadn't before, he also made the vampire feel things he never thought he would. Alucard always wanted to be alone; he always wanted to be back in his empty castle—but right now, the idea of being just about anywhere with Zalith felt more inviting.

He unlocked his door and climbed out; he stepped onto the white gravel-covered ground and took a few steps forward so that he could see past the black shire carriage horse. Zalith's house wasn't what he'd been expecting; the large, dark-bricked manor adorned a dark grey tiled roof and similarly-coloured wooden panelling around the arched windows. He followed Zalith up the marble stairs from the road and into the courtyard garden, which was decorated with flowerbeds and small orange trees. A water fountain sat in the centre surrounded by a small, white wall, and a gravel path circled it. Another set of stairs led up to the terrace, and as Alucard walked up, he saw that most of the windows had their curtains drawn, but one window on the left side of the house was glowing, candlelight coming from within. Was someone else inside? Did Zalith have a family?

Zalith placed his hand on the vampire's shoulder and leaned into his ear. "My dear friend is staying with me. There's no need to concern yourself with her. She won't bother us, and we won't bother her," he explained before letting go and making his way towards the house.

Watching Zalith as he headed for the front door, Alucard frowned. *She*? His confidence withered a little. A woman? Living in his house? Zalith did mention that he had a friend a while ago when they once went for coffee, and he assumed that this woman must be *that* friend. He also knew that Zalith was gay and had no romantic interest in women, but he couldn't help but feel skeptical.

Zalith looked back over his shoulder at him and waited, so the vampire dismissed his suspicious expression and followed him to the front door.

"I've already had the help prepare us dinner, so it'll be ready whenever we are," the demon said as he unlocked his door and stepped inside.

But Alucard didn't follow him in. Instead, he stood at the threshold and glanced down at the doormat before looking at Zalith expectantly.

Staring back at him, Zalith gestured his arms forward, inviting Alucard to come in.

Unimpressed, Alucard scowled. "Is zhis entertaining to you?"

"A little," he said, smirking. "You may enter."

"*Prost,*" Alucard grumbled, trying to hide the fact that he actually enjoyed Zalith's jest. He stepped into the entrance hall, and when he saw Zalith slip his shoes off, he did the same. The demon then took his cape off for him and hung it from the coat rack.

He followed Zalith through the large hall, and before they turned into the left corridor, he caught a glance of Zalith's office not far from the grand staircase.

The hallway's wood-panelled walls were lined with paintings of people Alucard was sure he'd ask Zalith about later; there were many closed doors and shelves lined with books, as well as plenty of antique furniture and murals covering the walls and ceiling. The *interior* was everything he'd expected Zalith's home to look like.

They reached a closed door with light glowing from behind it. Zalith pushed it open and led the way into a rather cosy-looking living room. A fireplace sat against the back wall, the flames dancing brightly over a bed of wood, and in front of it was a leather couch with a small wooden side table at each end. Six tall arched windows took up most of the left wall, and the gloomy curtains were pulled shut to cover most of them. The walls were black, panelled with dark grey wood; paintings of what looked like angels were dotted here and there, too.

A large painting that hung over the top of the fireplace caught Alucard's eye. It was a portrait of two angelic-looking men, but unlike all the others, these two didn't have white feathered wings—they had no wings at all. While one was standing with his foot on the neck of a dead deer, the other was crouched beside it. They each had rifles in their hands, dressed in hunting gear, and a few dogs were standing in the background in front of a fir-tree forest.

"Do you like it?" Zalith asked.

Taking his eyes off the painting, Alucard glanced at Zalith, who was standing by an oak dining table with two glasses in his hand and a bottle of red wine in his other. The vampire frowned and looked back at the painting. "Is unusual."

"It was in the library—in the castle I worked at before the war. I liked it, so I took it," he explained with a smile.

Alucard looked back at Zalith, watching as he poured the wine.

"Why are you still standing over there?" Zalith asked, placing the bottle on the table. "Sit," he invited, holding his hand out towards the chair beside him.

Keeping his vacant glare, Alucard made his way to the table and sat in the seat Zalith had pulled out for him.

Zalith then sat down. "I should've asked before, but do you need human blood or will what I've had prepared for us sustain you until you return home?" he asked, sipping from his glass. "Unless your rich townsman snack was enough."

Alucard picked up his glass of wine and stared into it for a moment. "Are you preparing to kick me out already, huh?" he asked as bravely as he could, glancing at him, but Zalith didn't seem amused, so he looked back down at his glass. "No, I don't need blood. I've learned to live for months without it; one day won't hurt," he lied. He didn't want to worry Zalith with his feeding habits; when he got back to Dor-Sanguis, he'd find himself more blood.

"And you assume you'll only be here *one* day?" Zalith replied with a suggestive smirk.

Alucard then frowned at him. "You need to do something about your face. It's impossible to tell whether you're offended or not."

"Take your own advice," he said, still smirking.

"At least I don't feel the need to prolong an answer to someone's question," he snarled. "Why do you have to stall? You asked me to come here and said you would answer my questions. I want to know—"

"All in good time, vampire," Zalith said, smiling. "Let's wait for dinner first."

Aggravated, Alucard placed his glass back on the table and glared into it. Why *was* he stalling? Why couldn't they just discuss what they'd come to discuss and move on? Why did he have to sit there and drink wine? Wait for dinner? What was the point in all of this? He didn't see any. He just wanted an answer so he could silence his conflicting thoughts—so he could understand if what he felt wasn't pointless.

Right now, however, he felt as though it was a mistake to have come. Zalith wasn't showing any sign of telling him how he felt or what he thought their relationship was. He seemed to be playing some kind of game for his amusement, and Alucard wouldn't put that past him. This man seemed to find other people's confusion... funny. Zalith said they'd talk once they got back to his house, and now that they were there, it seemed as though Zalith wanted to make him wait even longer. Alucard felt like he might be being a little impatient, but how could he *not*? This was the first time he'd felt so attached to someone, the first time he so sorely desired to be in someone's company, and he didn't want to continue to allow himself to feel this way if it wasn't mutual.

He set his sights on Zalith and frowned in confusion. "I feel as though you're just playing with me. I want to know if that's the case or if you feel something more—you have yet to tell me. You act like this is no big deal, but it's a big deal to *me*. I want to know—I *need* to know that I'm not wasting my time thinking about this all the time. I need to know that what *I* feel isn't a waste of time, that what I think I feel for you is real."

"I can't tell you if what *you* feel is real, Alucard. Only you can know that. But I know that what *I* feel is real, and I *have* tried to tell you; it's just... not so simple."

Still looking at him, Alucard lost his confused frown and sat up straight. "Tell me what you feel," he demanded, "what you *want*."

Zalith exhaled and rested his left leg over his right. "I feel... as though you talk about time like yours is limited," he said, smirking.

Annoyed, Alucard turned away and gritted his teeth—

"Do you think I'd invite you here if I didn't feel anything?" Zalith questioned as he quickly moved his hand over Alucard's. He sighed and placed his glass down in front of him. "Would I spend so much of my time with you if I was playing games?"

"You could, for all I know," he said, his uncertainty outweighing his confidence. Zalith was still avoiding the question, dancing around it, and the vampire could feel his angst building into something suffocating.

He couldn't deal with the anxiety anymore. He hadn't done this before; he would never go out of his way to admit what he felt, especially when, in Aegisguard, such feelings were frowned upon. What he felt was something he thought he'd never feel, and now that he *did* feel it, he owed it to himself to take it seriously, but Zalith didn't seem to be doing the same. He felt embarrassed and nervous, and his mind was shutting down. He just wanted a straight answer, but he still hadn't got one, even after asking Zalith a second time.

Maybe all of this was Zalith's answer. He didn't *want* to answer, did he?

Alucard pulled his hand from beneath Zalith's and stood up. "I shouldn't have come here," he mumbled, looking at the door. "I don't... know why I came. This is all just... fun, no?"

Zalith stared up at him but didn't say anything, and that was all the confirmation Alucard needed.

The vampire scowled and turned around.

"This isn't a joke, nor is it fun in the way you may be implying," Zalith said as Alucard headed for the door.

Alucard didn't want to hear it. All he wanted was an answer to his question. How did Zalith feel? What did he want? But he hadn't got an answer to either and he was just about through with trying to get him to understand how heavy it weighed on his mind. He couldn't face the angst anymore, the fear that his feelings were meaningless. So he'd leave; he'd remove himself from the situation and silence these ridiculous feelings of longing for a man who didn't seem to feel the same.

"So, you're running again?" Zalith called as Alucard reached for the door.

The vampire stopped and scowled over his shoulder at him. "Yes, and this time, I won't look back," he snarled, trying to hide the soul-crushing heartbreak currently taking place inside his chest.

Zalith stood up and smirked. "You just looked back."

Gritting his teeth in anger, Alucard turned to face the door, grabbed the handle, and pulled it open—

Zalith—who shot out of his seat and reached Alucard in the blink of an eye—slammed the door shut as he grabbed the vampire's arm and hastily turned him to face him. Alucard wasn't sure what Zalith was doing; his first instinct was to defend himself, so he grabbed Zalith's wrist, but before he could speak or fight back, Zalith leaned his face into his and kissed his lips.

Alucard scowled as both anger and confusion overwhelmed him. But the feeling of Zalith's soft lips against his own took away the majority of the doubt he felt. It made him consider that perhaps Zalith *might* feel the same; maybe Zalith had longed for this moment as sorely as he had. He kissed Zalith back, and he let the demon's tongue grace his. Zalith's natural bergamot, white sage, and sandalwood scent ensnared him in a state of bewilderment; his heart beat a little faster, and his body shivered in anticipation as Zalith's fingertips caressed the side of his face and slowly stroked down to his neck.

The demon leaned his head back so that it was a mere inch from Alucard's. They stared into one another's eyes, and right now, Alucard wasn't sure if he still felt conflicted. Zalith was always so confusing; although he was annoyed at the demon, he couldn't deny the desire he felt for him. Now that they were this close, he wouldn't waste another moment to get Zalith to see just how much he needed him—how much he *wanted* him.

Alucard lifted his right hand from the door he was pinned against and moved it to the back of Zalith's head. He was confident in what he felt and wanted, and he could see in Zalith's once-empty eyes that he, too, felt something similar. He didn't hesitate. He pulled the demon's face back into his, initiating a long moment of slow, intense kisses. He hadn't known it at first, but this was what he needed—it was what he'd hoped for. He urged Zalith closer, embracing him so tightly that he felt he might hurt the demon. But as Zalith's hand started to wander down past his waist, Alucard frowned and stopped kissing him. He glared disapprovingly at him, hoping Zalith would understand that he wasn't ready for this to go any further.

Zalith smirked and rested his forehead against Alucard's. "Does that answer your questions?"

The strange nervousness that this demon made him feel suddenly returned, forcing him to look away, unable to reply. It *did* answer his questions. He was sure they wouldn't have just kissed like that if this were a game. All he felt now was flustered.

With a smile on his face, Zalith exhaled deeply and placed his hand on the vampire's shoulder as he dragged his thumb over his throat. "The fact of the matter is, Alucard, I enjoy being with you, whether it be communication through a mirror or like this. I don't give my time to just anyone, yet I would give any moment up for you—to be with you. No one has made me feel the things I feel for you; each waking moment, I want to see you, I want to talk to you, and whatever I find myself doing, I am always thinking of you. Something about you captivates me, and I'm not afraid to admit it, and I'm equally unafraid to show it," he explained quietly.

And *that* was the answer Alucard had been waiting for. He got more than what he thought he'd get, but Zalith had a habit of exceeding expectations, and he loved that about him. Alucard was content, he was sure that his feelings weren't meaningless, and he was convinced that he and Zalith might just become something more. That was what he wanted; he'd been sure about that for a while and was confident Zalith wanted more, too. Should he ask? Would the demon ask?

"Now, should we have dinner, or do you still want to leave?" Zalith asked him.

Alucard slowly turned his head to look at him. "Dinner."

With a smile, Zalith took hold of Alucard's hand and led him to the table. They returned to their seats, and the demon topped up their wine glasses.

Zalith then leaned forward and rested his arms on the table. "You mention time a lot for someone who can't die. Why?"

Alucard sighed quietly at his sudden question and glanced down at the table. "I'm not immortal—not entirely. I still treat my time as though it's limited."

The demon smirked. "It's only forever, not long at all."

"Your humour, once again, does not amuse me," Alucard grumbled.

"Time is precious, you're right," he agreed and sipped from his glass. "What do you see yourself doing with your time after this?"

The vampire glanced at him again. "I would…like to think of it as…our time," he said shyly, trying to hide his nervousness with a vacant stare. He hoped *that* would prompt Zalith to ask him if they'd become something more than whatever it was they were right now.

Smiling, Zalith nodded and asked, "What do you see *us* doing with our time?"

However, before he could answer, the door behind Zalith opened. Two butlers walked in, each with a covered plate in their hands. They made their way to the table, placed the plates down simultaneously, waited a moment, and then lifted the lids. They bowed respectfully before leaving just as silently as they had entered.

Alucard looked down at the plate that had been placed in front of him. On the platter lay a large steak and several different vegetables, but the only ones he could name were the carrots and potatoes. There was also a dab of dark sauce. He hadn't seen actual food in such a long time that he wasn't even sure if he was going to be able to eat it. He'd try, though.

Zalith picked up his knife and fork. "You don't have to eat it. I *can* give you something more appetizing," he offered with a suggestive smile.

The vampire wasn't in the mood to deal with drawing blood from some helpless victim. Instead, he took a sip of wine and picked up his knife and fork. As he started to cut his steak, so did Zalith.

As he stared down at the food, Alucard thought to himself for a few moments. It seemed like *he* would have to ask if they were more than friends; Zalith probably knew that he was trying to get *him* to ask and thought it was amusing to wait. Of course he did. But Alucard's eagerness outweighed his shyness, so he stopped cutting and looked at the demon. "I want…. Do you want to…." He frowned, struggling. "Are we…well…what are we?" he asked quietly, unsure of how to word what he was trying to say.

"I, myself, am content with…" he hesitated in his jest and stopped cutting his food. "You and I?" he asked with a sterner tone.

Alucard nodded and rested his arms on the table. "I've never seen myself being with someone…well…romantically," he drawled nervously. "Least of all…a man—*and* a demon."

Zalith frowned slightly. "And that's because?"

"Relationships like these are frowned upon in Aegisguard; people are killed for being gay. Not that I give a shit; I can do whatever I want, I just…never thought I'd feel this way about someone—or that someone would feel this way about me." He could already tell that Zalith was about to ask for more information, so he added, "I also never thought I'd stray away from what people consider normal."

"Do you want to be normal?"

Alucard pouted. "No."

"Then why does it matter? You care about who you care about, and you're attracted to what you're attracted to; society shouldn't influence your wants or needs. If you're worried about it, though, don't be. Here in Nefastus, people don't care the way the rest of Aegisguard might. There's no law here, after all—not yet," he said with a quiet laugh.

"Wouldn't the people you work with think of you differently?"

"Would yours?"

"No. They respect me."

"And I am also respected. Even if they did think of me differently, I wouldn't care."

Looking at him, Alucard half-nodded to acknowledge his words before looking back down at his plate.

"So, am I right in assuming that I'll be the first person you've ever had a romantic relationship with?"

"You say that like you know I'll agree to commit to one."

"Would you?"

The vampire stared into his glass. *Did* he want to commit to a relationship? He was sure that he did. It would be his first, and he couldn't feel any more content about the fact that it would be with Zalith. He didn't want to overthink it, so he shifted his gaze to Zalith and said, "Yes."

Zalith leaned forward and lightly gripped Alucard's jaw in his hand. "Good. Then you are mine, and I am yours," he stated possessively.

Alucard tried to turn his head to hide his nervous frown, but Zalith wouldn't let him. He stared at the demon for a moment, unsure of what he might be thinking, but then Zalith softly kissed his lips, and Alucard couldn't help but smile.

It had been something of a struggle to get the answers he wanted from Zalith, but he finally had them, and he felt as if he couldn't be happier. He was Zalith's, and Zalith was his.

Chapter Seven

— ⊰ ✝ ⊱ —

Dear Friend

| **Zalith** |

An hour after finishing their dinner, Zalith remained at the table with Alucard. He'd gotten exactly what he wanted from this evening, and he was sure Alucard felt just as satisfied. Now, they were in a committed relationship—Alucard was his, just as he had longed for. He was going to do all that he could to make sure things remained that way; he'd do everything in his power to show Alucard just how much he meant to him, and he'd do whatever it would take to make him happy because that was what Alucard deserved.

Zalith felt irrefutably pleased with himself; he managed to answer Alucard's questions and got him to understand that he wanted them to be together. Seeing Alucard in front of him in his own house also blessed him with contentedness. He couldn't want anything more—not yet, anyway. He'd be sure to take their new relationship as slowly as Alucard wanted; he did, after all, take Alucard's wants and needs very seriously and held them above his own. He'd do his best not to make the vampire uncomfortable. He also found himself hoping that it would last—he knew how overbearing he could be, how intrusive, and he hoped such things wouldn't come to frighten Alucard away.

As he gazed at Alucard, he smiled, unable to hide his happiness. He didn't want to spend another moment away from him; he never wanted him to leave, and whatever it may take, Zalith knew he would do whatever he could to ensure this vampire remained in his life.

When Alucard glanced at him, Zalith finished his glass of wine and moved his hand over Alucard's. "Do you have plans for tomorrow?" he asked him.

Alucard slowly took his eyes off his glass and looked at the demon. "Nothing important."

"Then, might I suggest we spend the day together?" he requested hopefully.

"We can," the vampire agreed with *no* hesitation in his voice, "but—"

"But?"

"What will we do?"

Zalith smiled as he took hold of Alucard's hand. "There are a lot of things to do here, or we could head elsewhere if you don't feel comfortable near the Citadel."

Alucard seemed to sink into his thoughts.

The demon frowned curiously. "Why do the Imperito concern you?" he asked as a smirk crept across his face. "What did you do, Alucard?"

He glanced down at his hand and shrugged. "They obviously had a different boss back when I came here. I may have… been the cause of many explosions, many deaths. I wasn't the same back then—I looked for trouble. What better place to find it than here?"

Amused, Zalith grinned and leaned closer to him. "Did they chase you out of town?"

"No." Alucard pouted, looking away. "I got bored, so I left."

"And they remember you after all this time?"

"Maybe," the vampire mumbled.

"What does it mean for you if they *do* remember you?"

"They'll want to kill me," he said with a shrug. "It will be annoying. I don't have the time or patience to deal with humans right now."

Zalith smiled and said, "If it would help you feel more comfortable, I can have every single one of them killed. You'll be visiting often, so I'll do whatever I can to make sure you feel relaxed."

"You'd kill an entire organization just so that I'll walk into the city with you?" Alucard asked with a doubtful expression.

"If that's what it'll take, yes," Zalith said, smirking. "One of my goals has been to exterminate the Imperito and Meshuga gangs, whether through lawful channels or otherwise. And no one would bat an eye, either. The city council have come to appreciate my methods."

The vampire looked back down at his drink and frowned. He was clearly considering it, but ultimately, he said, "No. You don't have to kill anyone. If I need someone dead, I'll do it myself." He then took his eyes off his almost empty glass and looked at Zalith. "Can I have… the thing you got for me at the café?"

He smiled endearingly at him. "I'll have it made for you before we part ways… unless you don't want to."

"What?"

"It's late, and I imagine you'll have to fly home," he said, using his right index finger to move a strand of Alucard's hair out of his face. "There's a guest room if you want to rest, and once morning comes, we can start the day together," he suggested. Of course, he'd much rather them share a room, but he didn't want to be too direct and make the vampire uncomfortable.

Alucard looked back down at his hand with a conflicted frown. "I don't want to impose," he mumbled.

"You could never impose. Just let me know when you're ready, and I'll show you to the room."

"And tomorrow?"

Zalith thought to himself for a moment but then smiled as he gazed at Alucard's curious face. "A walk could be nice, and if it suits you, we can stop somewhere for breakfast."

Alucard nodded. "Okay."

"I think we should also discuss how often we'll be meeting," Zalith said, trying to hide just how eager he was to spend as much time as he could with Alucard. "I understand you have your work to get on with, as I have mine. Currently, mine is less demanding, so *you* tell *me* how often you'd like to meet."

The vampire looked away as that same look of deep thought returned to his face, a look which Zalith found adorable. Alucard seemed to ponder for a moment…and then set his eyes back on the demon. "Sometimes…I can meet once a week, and sometimes…more often. Depends on what I'm doing. If I go home tomorrow afternoon, it will take me the rest of the day and most of the day after to meet with my subordinates and catch up with what I've missed. After that, I'll be free again."

Zalith smirked. "Tomorrow is Sunday, so that means I get to see you again on Tuesday."

"If you want," Alucard mumbled, turning his head once again to hide his nervous expression.

Of course Zalith wanted to see him again so soon. He'd spend every day with him if he could. He smiled and took a moment to admire Alucard's nervous face. "I most certainly do," he agreed.

Just then, he heard the clicking of high heels echoing down the hall. He knew *exactly* who and what was coming, and he didn't want to subject Alucard to that just yet.

He let go of Alucard's hand and stood up. "I'll go and make that drink for you." He then smiled before making his way over to the door.

Alucard frowned strangely and drawled, "Okay…."

Then, Zalith hastily pulled the door open and left the room.

When he stepped out into the candlelit hallway, he immediately set his eyes on Varana, his best friend, as she made her way up the hall. She approached with a curious look on her face, wearing her white satin nightgown, and her bone-straight black hair floated gracefully behind her. The woman's intrigued look, however, faded into one of suspicion as she watched Zalith make his way towards her with a vacant stare on his face, an expression he pulled in an attempt to try and avoid her asking him why he looked so happy.

She stopped a few feet in front of him. "What are you doing?" she questioned skeptically.

"What are *you* doing?" he asked in response.

"I heard voices and thought I'd come to see what was going on," she said, leaning her head to the side to see past him, and as she set her eyes on the door, she scowled suspiciously. "Are you meeting with someone?"

"I am," he confirmed, but he had no interest in telling her who that someone was.

"Who?"

"Does it matter?" he asked, keeping a somewhat amused, calm tone to his voice— he was sure she'd start to make a scene if he let on that he was trying to prevent that from happening.

Varana frowned irritably. "Yes, it does. If there are visitors in my home, I'd like to *at least* know their names."

Zalith smiled. "*My* home," he corrected.

She then scowled impatiently. "Why won't you just tell me?!" she snapped.

With his impatience increasing, Zalith placed his hands on the woman's shoulders, turned her around, and started escorting her away. "I don't make a habit of asking who you're meeting with late at night; can't you grant me the same courtesy?" he stated, leading her through the hall towards the door that would take her back to where she had just come from.

"Can you at least *tell* me who it is?" she muttered with an irritated pout.

He smiled. "No, I don't think I will."

She frowned in frustration, rolled her eyes, and groaned irritably. She leaned back on him to try and make it a struggle for him to continue leading her down the hallway. "Ugh," she complained, "you're so horrible to me."

"I'm the absolute worst," he concurred with a smile.

"I'll just go and see for myself," she said, pulling free from him, but before she could make her way towards the door, Zalith snatched her wrist. She sharply turned her head and glared at him.

With a look of what might be considered hostility on his face, he scowled down at her. "Varana…" he warned.

She snatched her wrist from his grip. "Then just tell me who you're meeting with!" she insisted. "Why do you have to be so secretive?!"

Zalith then sighed tiredly. "My vampire," he answered.

Varana groaned in detest. "*Him*? Still?!" she exclaimed.

He then laughed ever so slightly. "This is why I didn't want to tell you."

With her own scowl of hostility, she glared up at him. "I better not see your little vampire friend around the house, Z; you know how I get," she threatened him.

"I do," he answered, disregarding her threat. "And again, this is *my* house."

"Whatever!" she snarled as she crossed her arms.

Zalith frowned impatiently; he felt reluctant to leave his vampire for much longer. "Would you be so kind as to leave us be, now?" he requested.

She scowled a little harder but rolled her eyes and lowered her arms. "Fine," she mumbled. "Goodnight."

He sighed in relief. "Thank you. Goodnight."

With a sour glow lingering on her face, Varana turned around, made her way back down the hall, and disappeared into a corridor on the right.

As the clicking of her heels faded away, Zalith huffed irritably and headed back down the hall. Before he could return to Alucard, though, he had to head to the kitchen and make the hot chocolate he said he'd make for him, so he turned around and walked towards the kitchen. Alucard would be fine for a few more minutes, wouldn't he?

| **Alucard** |

Alucard waited at the dinner table. A smile clung to his face despite Zalith's abrupt departure; he couldn't be more content with everything he learned tonight. He felt as if he finally understood that Zalith *did* feel the same, and at last, he knew his own feelings weren't meaningless. When he was with Zalith, he didn't have to worry about his problems or his stress…or that drowning sadness. This demon made him feel so happy that he felt like nothing could drag him down into the depravity that was his life before he met Zalith—that loneliness…that hole in his life that he never knew how to fill until he'd experienced the company of someone he adored.

He was nervous about spending the night in a home he'd never been to before, but staying meant he got to spend more time with Zalith, which was all the convincing he needed. Work might be a little hectic to catch up on once he got home, but he didn't want to think about that right now.

With a quiet sigh, he leaned back in his seat. But the echo of Zalith's voice and that of a woman had him feeling someone skeptical. Zalith said his friend was staying with him, and Alucard could only assume that *she* was the woman that he just heard Zalith talking to. Why did Zalith seem to hesitate about having her meet him? Alucard wasn't sure how to feel about being hidden from someone Zalith lived with—someone he clearly cared for. He did, on the other hand, find delight in being called *Zalith's* vampire. If there was something he felt he enjoyed most about Zalith, it was his penchant to claim him.

He might not have seen much of it yet, but it was rather easy to assume that Zalith was possessive, and Alucard found that very attractive.

The door then reopened; Alucard watched Zalith walk in with a white coffee mug in his right hand.

Once he placed the mug in front of Alucard, Zalith returned to his seat and sighed quietly. "My apologies."

Alucard shrugged slightly. "It's fine," he mumbled, trying to keep his skeptical thoughts from outweighing his happiness.

Zalith smiled and placed his hand over Alucard's. "Where were we?"

The vampire frowned and pulled his hand from beneath Zalith's; he grabbed his wine glass and finished the last of his wine. "Tuesday," he answered.

"Yes, Tuesday," Zalith said, resting his arms in front of him. "Should I come to you?"

"If you want," Alucard said as he put his empty glass down.

"Will you have something planned for us, or shall we decide once we meet?"

"I don't know," he mumbled, placing both his hands around the coffee mug as he stared into the hot chocolate inside.

Zalith then frowned. "Are you okay?"

"Why would I not be?"

"You're being grumpy again," he said, smirking.

Alucard took his eyes off his drink and glanced at him. "Why did you not want your friend to see me?"

Zalith sighed and leaned back in his seat. "She can be…overbearing sometimes. I wouldn't wish that upon you. You're most likely to meet her at some point, but not yet."

The vampire rolled his eyes and glared down at his drink. "There is an opera house in Dargamoore," he said, changing the subject. "We can go there on Tuesday. Unless opera isn't something that interests you."

"It sounds delightful," Zalith said with a smile, pulling Alucard's right hand from around his mug and holding it lightly.

Alucard frowned slightly. He wasn't sure why Zalith insisted on holding his hand so much, but he wasn't going to stop him. He enjoyed his touch. The vampire took his eyes off his drink and looked at him. "I can tell you what time the show starts when I get home tomorrow—I'll get someone to find out for me."

Zalith leaned closer to Alucard. "And after that?" he asked suggestively.

Alucard shrugged and shifted his stare to his drink. "I don't know. We'll find something to do if it's not too late. Speaking of, I think I want to lay down now," he mumbled. Now that his confusion and worry were gone, all he felt was fatigue.

"Of course."

He stood up when Zalith did and said, "And I'm taking this with me," as he picked up the mug of hot chocolate.

Zalith smiled and nodded. He then led the way to the door.

Alucard didn't falter. He followed Zalith out of the lounge and through to the main hall. The demon led the way up the grand staircase; when they reached the top, they emerged into a large candlelit hall. Another staircase leading up to the next floor sat on the other side, but Zalith headed to the door to the left of them.

Once he opened the door, Zalith invited Alucard inside. When he walked in, the vampire slowly looked around as the kaleidoscopic moonlight shined in through the arched windows. There were two doors inside the room—one which led to a balcony and one which Alucard assumed led to a bathroom. Draping, black silk curtains had been pulled to conceal most of the windows, and the walls were dark and panelled with darker grey wood; a black, woollen rug stretched across the majority of the floor, and the ceiling was also black with a small unlit chandelier hanging from its centre.

A double bed sat against the left wall with several layers of darkly coloured blankets spread atop it and its two pillows leaning neatly against the headboard. Oakwood dressers stood on either side of the bed, one with a glass lamp atop it. The black walls were bare with nothing but a single mirror on the same wall as the door they'd come through, and two antique-like wardrobes stood to the door's left with a small table between them. It looked as though the room had never been slept in—or stepped in for quite a while, if at all.

"Make yourself at home," Zalith invited as he watched Alucard look around. "Unless... you need a coffin. Do you sleep—"

Alucard sharply turned his head and pointed at him, silencing him. "Don't," he warned with a scowl.

Smirking, Zalith shrugged.

The vampire sighed and sat on the end of the bed. "What time are we going tomorrow?" he asked and then sipped from his mug of hot chocolate.

"I usually wake up just after dawn. If you'd rather wake up later, or sooner, let me know," he said with a smile, still standing in the doorway. "The bathroom is just down the hall, on the right—if you use—"

"Stop," Alucard interjected.

"I'll see you in the morning, Alucard," the demon said amusedly.

Nodding, Alucard looked over at the windows. "*Noapte bună*," he mumbled.

Zalith smiled. "Goodnight."

Alucard listened as Zalith shut the door and walked across the hall, leaving him alone. That didn't go exactly as Alucard thought it would, but thinking about it, he wasn't sure if he would have even had the strength to continue conversing with the demon. His journey to Nefastus had left him feeling exhausted, confused, and irritable. The blood he consumed earlier may have helped for a while, but it was beginning to wear off. The best thing he could do, other than pray on another random human in a country that wasn't his, was sleep and hope he'd feel better in the morning. He may not get to spend the rest of the night with Zalith, but he *would* get to see him again in the morning.

He unbuttoned and pulled off his blazer; he threw it atop one of the dressers before shuffling into the bed. He sat there for a short while, enjoying his drink until nothing was left in the cup, and once he placed the empty mug on the nightstand, he lay on his back and stared up at the ceiling.

The evening couldn't have gone any better. He got his answers—and more. Alucard felt confident with himself and his feelings, and he felt sure of Zalith. He felt closer to him now than ever before, and that gave him a kind of happiness that he thought he'd never experience in his cold, empty life. But it wasn't so empty now. He had Zalith, someone he cared about, and someone he knew cared about him. That was something he hadn't had in many centuries.

Content, he turned onto his side and gazed out at the moons as they slowly drifted across the night sky. It felt strange to think that he'd come to be so close to someone else; he would have never thought he'd be able to have such a thing. He still resented his past; he resented what had been forced on him. But if it weren't for Janus… for Damien, the Numen, and the Diabolus, then he wouldn't have met Zalith. He wouldn't be in Nefastus in Zalith's house; he'd be alone, sinking into his sadness—he couldn't imagine being anywhere else. That was all that mattered.

Zalith filled a hole in his heart—a hole in his *soul*. He just hoped that it would last; he didn't want to think about the what-ifs and the maybes, though. What mattered was that he and Zalith were now together, and he'd do whatever he could to make sure it remained that way. He was already convinced that he wanted to spend every day and night with that demon; Zalith took away his sadness, his emptiness. He made Alucard feel alive, wanted, *and* needed. He made him feel things he'd never felt so intensely before. He even managed to make Alucard forget the dreaded Daegelus, even if it was just for a while.

But he then sighed irritably; his thoughts were always loudest when he was alone. The thought of Damien began sapping away his happiness. He started wondering… what would happen if Damien found out? He scowled and glared back up at the ceiling. He wouldn't find out; Damien was too busy to care what he was doing with his life. No matter what his inner, anxious self thought, he was confident. Zalith wasn't afraid of Damien; he had been sure to show Alucard that fact long ago. He thought that maybe, *just maybe* he could allow himself to be happy with this man, the person who pulled him from the depravity which was his life. He didn't want to be without Zalith—*ever*.

This feeling of contentedness was new—he might even call it joy. He'd never felt so happy, and he was sure from this point onward, he would only feel happier. With a smile on his face, he pulled the blankets over himself and got comfortable. The night would probably drag on if he didn't sleep; there'd be plenty of time tomorrow to bask in his thoughts. So, he closed his eyes and focused on the delightful things that Zalith made him feel. For what seemed like the first time, he was genuinely happy, not a single worry or fear weighing on his mind. And that was because of Zalith, someone he'd hold onto forever.

Chapter Eight

Belong

| Alucard |

The night's silence was interjected by a deafening crash, and a blinding flash of crimson light filled the sky.

Alucard instantly woke and sat up; he stared out of the window as dread filled his eyes and his once-healed heart. He knew what was about to happen—he was sure his serenity was going to be stolen. But there was no sign of the Daegelus. The lightning had struck the gardens out back, but Damien was nowhere to be seen—

"I have certainly underestimated you, Aleksei," came the Daegelus' cold, haunting voice.

The vampire took his eyes off the window and turned his head to stare over at Damien. He stood with his back to the wall across from where Alucard sat. There was a condescending smile on his strangely pale face, and his red and blue eyes glimmered in the dark, their thin-slit pupils glaring right into Alucard's soul. The look of malice on Damien's face kept Alucard both frozen and silent; he couldn't move or speak. All he could do was sit there and wait.

Damien lifted his hand and started to admire his black claws. "I thought you'd be searching for Lucious," he began, glancing at the vampire. "Is that why you're here? In this residence? The same residence that belongs to Eladarin?"

"No," Alucard answered. "I was... I am catching up with Zalith."

"Oh, right." Damien nodded, crossing his arms in front of him. "Is that what this is?"

"Yes," he confirmed.

"I thought you understood how I feel about you and your sad need for friends," he snarled.

Alucard was sure that he knew what was about to happen. He slowly stood up, keeping his stare on the infuriated Daegelus. "'E' is not my vriend," he insisted.

"Oh, so I hear." Damien abruptly sprung forward and snatched Alucard's throat. He pinned him against the wall and glared into his panicked eyes. "This is the last time I will warn you, you pathetic, miserable little shit!" he yelled. "If I have to kill one more person because you can't understand a simple fucking rule, I'll kill you—"

The door opened, and as Zalith entered and before he could say a word, Damien snatched his throat, letting go of Alucard and kicking him to the floor. He pinned the demon against the wall and glared into his confused eyes.

"Perfect timing," Damien said with a grin. He scowled and tightened his grip on the demon's throat. "Did I not warn you about getting close to him?" he questioned. "Did I not tell you what would happen?"

Struggling in his grip, Zalith frowned. "We were simply discussing business," he insisted calmly.

Damien took his eyes off Zalith and looked back over his shoulder at Alucard, who moved to get up, but Damien pointed at him. "Stay where you are," he warned.

Alucard did as he was told and remained on his knees, staring over at Damien in horror. He had no idea what might happen; he knew that Zalith was Damien's favourite subordinate, maybe even his friend. He wouldn't hurt him, would he? Alucard couldn't sit there and think that he wouldn't. There was no telling what Damien might do, but Alucard was sure whatever was about to happen was going to destroy the small amount of happiness he found. And he prepared for it. He let the dread consume him. He let the sorrow wither his joy. Because as such confrontations always did, he knew this would end in someone's death.

The Daegelus took his eyes off Alucard and glared at Zalith. "You should have taken my advice all that time ago, Eladarin," he said as a twisted smile warped his face. "Now, it looks like my boy wants your heart—let's give it to him, shall we?"

Zalith had no time to say or do anything. He took his eyes off Damien to stare down at Alucard—

Damien forced his hand into Zalith's chest and grinned evilly when he glanced back at Alucard; as the vampire stared in terror, too afraid to beg, the Daegelus ripped the demon's heart out and let his lifeless body drop to the floor. Damien then clasped his fist shut and squashed it into a bloody mess. He made his way over to Alucard, who stared at Zalith's face, hoping to see a glimmer of life. But he knew that he was gone. He felt as if Damien had just destroyed his heart, too; he could feel tears trying to escape his eyes, his entire body hurt as if it was being crushed, and as the Daegelus prowled towards him, he trembled and winced in dismay.

"Here you go," Damien said with a smile, letting the bloody mess that was once Zalith's heart trickle through his fingers and down into Alucard's lap. He crouched in front of the vampire and placed his hand on his shoulder. "It could always suffice as a nice snack if you feel hungry," he said, grinning. Then, he stood up and made his way *over to the balcony doors. "I've warned you enough times, Aleksei; don't get close to anyone. They'll always leave you."*

As the Daegelus left the building, Alucard let his tears fall. His breaths became stifled as the pain of knowing that Zalith was gone ensnared him, and it was all his fault. He should have listened—he should have just stayed away. If he didn't let his feelings consume him, if he didn't let himself fall in love, then Zalith would still be alive. But of course... he always fucked up, didn't he? The people he cared about always got hurt because he couldn't listen. First Vanessa and her sons, then Elvin... and now Zalith.

He'd lost the only person he could have ever shared a life with, and never felt so lost.

A crash of thunder woke Alucard.

He opened his eyes with a pained gasp and sat up as fear gripped him fiercely. As he breathed unsteadily, he looked around so frantically that he couldn't even see what he was looking at. Where was he? *When* was he? He gasped for air, his stifled breaths tightening his throat. He gripped the sheets beneath him, trying to focus. The room was still, dark, and silent; the walls were black, the moonlight shined in through the squared windows, and it smelt so overpoweringly of bergamot, white sage, sandalwood, and oak. It took him a moment, but he soon came to realize that he was still in Zalith's house... and there was no sign of Damien or Zalith's lifeless body.

But his heart was still racing. His fear hadn't waned; his dread hadn't yielded. How could it? It may have only been a dream, but Damien was still very real, and so was the situation Alucard found himself in. The Daegelus would never allow him to have a friend, let alone whatever he and Zalith had become. Partners? Companions? Damien would kill Zalith, he'd punish Alucard, and the vampire was sure his rage wouldn't end there.

What had he done? He allowed himself to become too close to Zalith, and now, they were both in horrifying danger. The last thing he wanted was for Zalith to be hurt or killed because of him. He didn't want to lose him. As he sat there staring down at his lap, he tried to understand why this was happening. Why did he think he could have a relationship with anyone? Why did he think he could be happy? He shouldn't. He couldn't. Zalith could be taken away from him in the blink of an eye, and his happiness would go with him. He couldn't let that happen and he shouldn't have let things get this far. He couldn't defy Damien, and he didn't understand why for even a moment he had thought he could.

Just then, a quiet knock came at the door. He didn't lift his head to see who opened it and walked in. He knew.

"Alucard?" Zalith asked. "Are you okay?"

Alucard didn't answer. He couldn't find his voice. All he could do was sit there.

In only a pair of black trousers, Zalith stepped into the room and closed the door behind him. He waled over and sat beside the vampire, placing his hand on his shoulder. "Is everything all right?" he repeated, sounding concerned.

Alucard had no idea what to say. He didn't want Damien to take Zalith away from him, and the only way he could prevent that was to leave—to distance himself from this demon. But how could he? How could he run away from this? He wasn't sure why he was questioning his thoughts—he *should* run, he should leave Zalith behind to protect him. But he didn't want to. The idea of never seeing him again hurt so much that he felt he might allow his pain to escape through tears. Everything Zalith made him feel—it was so intense—and he didn't have the words to explain how sorely he needed it…how desperately he *wanted* it. He'd never felt such happiness and he didn't want to have to throw that away. But if he didn't, Damien would take it.

Staring down at his lap, Alucard frowned sullenly. "I…can't."

"Can't sleep?" he asked, confused.

The vampire shook his head and glanced at Zalith's face. "This," he said quietly. "I…." He frowned sadly and looked back down at his lap. He couldn't say it. He didn't *want* to say it. He'd longed for this for far too long and far too sorely to let his fear rip it away.

As a flash of lightning lit up the room, Alucard flinched in startle and snatched Zalith's wrist. His heart started racing as he waited for Damien to appear, but as another flash of lightning lit up the dark room, his fear slowly faded. It wasn't *him*. But one day, it could be. If the Daegelus caught them together like this, if he caught them together in any situation at all, Alucard was sure he'd take Zalith from him. Alucard wanted nothing more than to be with this demon, to see him, hear him, and feel him. He had become so attached that he couldn't find the strength to let go, not after waiting so long to be with him.

With his fear of losing Zalith increasing, he moved his arms around the demon and held him as tightly as his terror-stricken body would allow him to.

As the vampire rested his head on his shoulder, Zalith smiled and wrapped his arms around him. "It's okay," he said softly.

After a few silent moments in Zalith's arms, Alucard could feel his dread fading. His fear became so irrelevant that he thought he could forget what he dreamt. Zalith already made him feel safe. He knew this demon wasn't afraid of Damien; perhaps that was why Alucard was fighting with himself, keeping himself from running. He didn't want to be alone; he didn't want to be without Zalith. He knew this demon would and could take care of himself, maybe even against someone as powerful as Damien. *Maybe*.

Alucard held him tighter, listening to his calming heartbeat.

So simply…so easily, his fear was gone. Not only did Zalith make him happier than he had ever been, but he also seemed to take away the fear that had haunted him his entire life. No one and nothing had ever done that for Alucard—but Zalith had. Of course he had. How could he not? That was why Alucard had fallen for him. The moment Zalith told Damien to stand down, the moment he had shown Alucard that he wasn't afraid of that man—*that* was when he knew he could allow himself to fall in love. And he had. He couldn't deny it; he *wouldn't* deny it. If he didn't love Zalith, he wouldn't have thought about him every day for the decade he spent away. He wouldn't have been so desperate to see him or be with him. Alucard was sure of how he felt. But could he ever tell him?

Alucard slowly sat up and stared at Zalith's face. He felt as if he could stare at it for the rest of his life—he wanted to. *That* was how sure he was of his feelings. But he then took his eyes off the demon and looked down at his lap. "Did I wake you up?" he asked quietly.

Zalith smiled. "No." He placed his hand on Alucard's shoulder. "Are you going to tell me what happened?"

"Just…a bad dream," he mumbled tiredly. "I get them a lot."

"Is there anything I can do?"

"No."

"Do you want to talk about it?"

"No."

Zalith frowned in worry as he placed both his hands on Alucard's shoulders, and as the vampire looked at him, he stared back with a look of sincerity in his dark eyes. "Tell me. Whatever it is, let me try to help."

Did he want to tell Zalith just how afraid he was of losing him? Did he want to warn him that Damien would kill him if he found out about them? He should, but what would Zalith think of him if he knew the truth? He didn't want to tell him the things Damien had said or the things he had done. He couldn't. But he also couldn't leave Zalith with nothing. He deserved something, and he didn't want the demon to go back to his room and leave him alone in the dark. He was sure that if he sent Zalith away now, his dread would return and result in a sleepless night.

He looked down at his lap. "I just…don't want to lose you," he said sullenly. "I've been alone all my life, and I just feel like I can't…I fear you might leave. The fear…lingers; it makes me feel so…I don't know. I hate it. You could leave at any moment, and I won't be able to do anything about it. This is why I don't let people in, why I live alone, why I have *always* been alone. I thought I could be happy or something. But I'm just afraid."

"You're not going to lose me, Alucard," Zalith said sternly, but sorrow lingered in his voice. He moved his right hand and used it to lift Alucard's head so that he could stare into the vampire's tired eyes. "You don't have to be afraid. I'm here now, and I'll be here for as long as you'll let me. I'm sorry you had to spend such a long time away; if I had known, I would have tried to make things easier. But you're here now, and so am I. I want to spend every moment with you, I want to make you happy, and I want to show you that you don't have to be sad or alone. If there's ever anything you need, just tell me. There isn't a thing I wouldn't do for you," he explained quietly.

Alucard didn't respond. All he could do was stare. The demon's words relieved his sorrow, his pain, and his fear. But he didn't know how to tell him that.

The vampire let Zalith pull his face closer and watched as the demon smiled at him. Zalith then placed a soft, passionate kiss on lips, and it banished what remained of Alucard's dismay. He did his best to fight the nervousness that was now enthralling him and moved his hand to the back of Zalith's head, allowing the demon's kiss to be the first of many. When their tongues met, Alucard felt Zalith tense up; they kissed a little harder, and as Zalith gently pushed Alucard down onto his back, the vampire pulled him closer and rested his head on his pillow.

They kept kissing, but when Zalith's hand began wandering down over his chest, Alucard felt hesitant. He was tired and confused, and he wasn't yet ready for where he suspected this was leading, so he placed his hand on Zalith's shoulder and lightly pushed him away. He then stared up at the demon as an anxious frown possessed his face. Now that his fear had withered, he wanted to go back to sleep, but he didn't want Zalith to go.

"Will you...stay?" he asked nervously. "With me? Here?"

Zalith smiled. "Of course."

The demon laid down beside Alucard as he tried to make himself comfortable. When Alucard stopped shuffling around, Zalith rolled onto his side and gazed at him.

"What are your nightmares about, Alucard?" he asked quietly. "Is it always the same thing?"

Staring up at the ceiling, Alucard sighed. "Mostly."

"What happens?"

The vampire frowned uncomfortably and turned his head to glare at the windows. "Nothing," he grumbled. But Zalith had to know that was a lie—he always knew when he wasn't being honest— and Alucard still felt like the demon deserved to know, but he couldn't bring himself to tell him. As he lay there, his sadness and loneliness slowly returned. He couldn't speak of it. He just wanted to enjoy the happiness that Zalith gave him.

As a hesitant frown made its way to his face, he glanced at the demon, who was still staring and smiling at him. He pouted stubbornly but didn't let the demon's expression stop him. He shuffled closer to him, and Zalith seemed to know what he needed. He moved his arm and allowed Alucard to rest his head on his chest and then eased his arm around him, holding him tightly.

"Don't say anything," Alucard warned.

Zalith remained silent.

"Don't make any stupid comments or whatever."

Still, Zalith said nothing but kept smiling.

Alucard relaxed and slowly closed his eyes. He was convinced that Zalith was moments away from making a snide comment, but he quickly let his guard down. For what felt like the first time ever, he found comfort in rest. Not a single negative thought gripped his mind, no sullen memories drowned him. While Zalith appeared to banish his loneliness during his hours of consciousness, it seemed as though the demon's company did the same for him while he slept. He couldn't wish for anything more.

He allowed himself to gradually drift off to sleep. This time, he was confident he wouldn't be burdened with nightmares—with horror and dread and sadness. Zalith took all of that away.

Chapter Nine

— ⊰ ✝ ⊱ —

In the Sunlight

| **Zalith** |

hen Zalith woke the next morning to Alucard still sleeping beside him, he smiled contently and gazed at his peaceful face. They both had an arm around each other, and Alucard was holding Zalith tightly, even in his sleep.

As he inhaled Alucard's natural scent of cedar wood, cinnamon, warm amber, and roses, an enthralling sense of relief and enticement consumed Zalith. He slowly moved his arm from around him and gently dragged his fingers through his crimson hair. After what had felt like such a long time, Alucard was finally his, and he couldn't be any more satisfied. He would do whatever he could to keep Alucard happy and at his side; he'd never felt this way about anyone before, and he was sure this vampire was the first person that he wanted to keep in his life forever.

But as he lay there, he thought about last night. Something had scared Alucard; he'd never seen the vampire so shaken. But what could have done that to him? Could a simple nightmare scare him as much as he appeared to be? Zalith couldn't help but wonder what it might have been that Alucard saw, and he was pretty sure that the vampire wasn't going to tell him any time soon. He'd not pressure him into telling him, though. He was sure Alucard would tell him in his own time.

And then he thought about the fact that he'd almost lost control. Their kisses had excited him, and he'd fought so fiercely with himself to resist, but he'd pushed Alucard down... and if the vampire hadn't told him to stop, he was certain that things would have escalated quickly. But they hadn't, and as much as he craved every inch of Alucard, he felt glad that things had ended where they had. Not only did he want to take things at Alucard's pace, but he also didn't want to rush; he wanted to savour every single moment with him.

Zalith's eyes wandered down to what he could see of Alucard's back. Ever since he'd known Alucard, there hadn't been a single time where he'd seen him without a shirt—without a *long-sleeved* shirt. He'd never seen any amount of this vampire's skin other than his face, hands, and glimpses of his stomach when he'd examined his wounds. But he'd seen *and* felt enough to know Alucard possessed an appealingly toned body, a body that Zalith wished to see more of. Of course, he wanted to see *everything* he could of Alucard, but it had taken the vampire quite some time to accept physical contact from him, so he was sure it would take an equal amount of time for him to feel comfortable enough to show Zalith more of himself.

The demon pondered; was there more to it? Alucard seemed almost *afraid* to let him see more. Why? He was curious to know, but he believed that Alucard would eventually tell him if that were the case, so he'd wait. He cared so profoundly for the vampire that he'd do his best not to invade his privacy; he'd wait until *Alucard* was ready to tell him the things he kept to himself. The last thing he wanted to do was upset the vampire; he didn't want to hurt him or make him think he was so spiteful as to invade his life and his thoughts. He may be a part of Alucard's life, but he knew he had to be patient.

Alucard then stirred. Zalith smiled, still caressing the vampire's hair, but Alucard didn't lift his head or say anything. The demon's smile became a smirk; he knew Alucard was staring at his body. He didn't feel the need to tell the vampire, though. He continued dragging his fingers through his hair, leaving Alucard to eye him for a few more moments. He knew too well that Alucard wouldn't keep doing it if he knew that Zalith was aware.

Alucard started moving his head, edging his face closer to Zalith's neck, and Zalith's instincts started conflicting with his desires. He knew that he should nudge him away or snap him out of whatever trance he was in—clearly one that had him infatuated with his neck—but his craving to feel Alucard's bite made him hesitate. He let Alucard reach and nuzzle his neck, and the vampire's breath against his skin sent a shiver of anticipation through Zalith's tensing body. He closed his eyes, eagerly awaiting the delight of Alucard's piercing fangs.

However, the vampire didn't bite. He exhaled quietly onto Zalith's neck but then backed away and rested his forehead on the demon's chest.

Zalith held back a whine of disappointment and dragged his fingers through Alucard's hair. "Good morning, darling," he said quietly.

Alucard moved his arm from around him and placed his hand over Zalith's abs. The demon smirked, convinced that Alucard was going to start stroking his body, but to his disappointment, the vampire pushed himself away from him. Alucard rolled over onto his back and rested his hands on his stomach, glaring up at the ceiling.

"*Dimineață*," he muttered.

"Did you sleep well?" Zalith asked, fiddling with Alucard's hair.

The vampire turned his head and set his eyes on the demon's face. For a moment, he just stared at him. His eyes seemed to wander up to Zalith's hair, which was wavy and unkempt from his night of sleep, its longer parts, which were usually combed back over his head, were now free of their usual place and hung roughly three or so inches over his forehead. He wasn't sure if Alucard was staring because he found it funny, or because he liked it.

But when Zalith smiled, Alucard looked back up at the ceiling and answered, "I slept well."

"Good."

As the sunlight flickered through the cracks in the curtains, Zalith noticed the vampire's hell-fiery eyes shimmer an icy blue. He frowned curiously and lifted his head, resting it on the side of his hand so he could look down at the vampire's face. Alucard looked at him and frowned strangely as Zalith waited to see the blue he could have sworn he just noticed, but they looked just as hellish as ever.

"What?" Alucard asked, glaring at him. "Stop staring at me."

"No," Zalith said with a smirk, and as Alucard turned his head to try and hide his face from him, he shuffled closer and moved his body over Alucard's. He placed his arms on either side of the vampire's shoulders and stared down at his nervous face. The sunlight crept in over Alucard's pale skin, and as it did, his fiery eyes faded to an almost white, icy blue. His slit pupils also dilated and became rounded, almost like those of a human. Alucard was obviously aware of it—his attempt to turn away from the sunlight told Zalith that. With a curious smile, Zalith used his thumb to move a strand of Alucard's hair from his face. "Your eyes," he said, waiting for Alucard to look back at him, "why are they different?"

Alucard shrugged and glanced up at him. "They change in the sunlight."

"Why?" he asked, gazing into his eyes as they slowly faded back to their usual hell-fiery pattern when the sun disappeared behind the clouds.

"Because…I'm a vampire."

Zalith smiled doubtfully. "Vampires' eyes are red and don't change."

Alucard rolled his eyes. "I don't know, they just change. I'm not meant to walk in sunlight; I'm supposed to be down in hell with the rest of Lucifer's demons, so they react to the natural light, I guess."

Convinced that he was aggravating Alucard already, Zalith exhaled quietly and smiled. "Well, I find them rather captivating."

The vampire pouted and looked away from him. "Whatever," he grumbled.

He thought he better stop asking him questions, but he couldn't help himself. Alucard made him curious. "Do you feel anything when they change?" he asked, but he was sure that the vampire wasn't going to answer, so as the sunlight crept in once again, he moved his hand to block the light from Alucard's face, making his eyes fade back to their usual hell-fiery appearance.

Scowling, the vampire looked up at him. "Don't do that," he warned.

Zalith didn't heed his warning. With a quiet, amused laugh, he moved his hand so the light hit Alucard's face once more, brightening his eyes to blue. As the vampire snarled irritably, Zalith used his hand to block the sunlight again, watching as Alucard's eyes reverted to their usual colour.

The vampire smacked his hand away. "Stop," he snarled.

Smirking, he moved his hand back, keeping the sunlight out of his face once more.

Alucard gritted his teeth and snatched the demon's wrist. "Are you trying to piss me off?" he growled.

"Maybe," Zalith said, smirking.

Unamused, Alucard let go of Zalith's wrist and turned his head to glare at the wall so the demon couldn't see his eyes. But Zalith ever so slowly moved his hand in the way of the light, blocking it from Alucard's face once again. The vampire snarled loudly and sharply turned his head to glare up at Zalith, but the demon laughed amusedly and gripped Alucard's shoulders; he pulled him with him as he rolled back onto his side. Alucard tried to protest and escape, but Zalith held and embraced him tightly. He grunted in disapproval and tried to pull away but swiftly gave in and calmed down.

As Alucard relaxed, Zalith smiled and rested his head on Alucard's. "All jests aside, Alucard, I'm glad that we're together and that we found each other. I missed you so much—every moment away from you felt like a struggle. Now that you're here, I'll do whatever I can to make you happy. You already make me feel such happiness, even when you're grumpy," he said, smirking.

Laying there, Alucard sighed quietly and moved his arms around Zalith, embracing him in return. Zalith couldn't see his face, but he was confident that he was smiling.

"Do you still want to go for a walk?" Zalith asked quietly.

Alucard seemed to ponder for a moment. Then, he pulled away from Zalith and looked at him. "We can still walk."

Zalith smiled. "I'll go and get dressed."

He got out of bed and headed for the door. When he reached it, he glanced back at Alucard and smirked at him. He watched a flustered frown steal Alucard's pout, and with a quiet, amused laugh, he left the bedroom.

Zalith made his way into the hall, but the moment he left the guest room, he saw Varana making her way up the stairs in an emerald green off-shoulder dress. She set her deep, blood-red eyes on him, and a sour look clung to her face. He headed for his bedroom, which sat across the hall from the guest room, but Varana hurried towards him before he could reach for the door's handle and stopped in front of him.

"There you are," she said with a scowl, glaring up at him as he smiled down at her. "Where have you been?"

She'd obviously just spent the last while looking for him, probably intending to dive into his bed with him as she always would when she wanted attention this early. That didn't irritate him, though. "I was in one of the guest rooms."

A look of revolt and confusion smothered her face. "Why?"

"Because I was checking in on my vampire," he said with a content smile.

"In a guest room? Why isn't he staying with you?" she asked, but then a bitter, snide smile stretched across her face. "Did you get into a fight?"

He deadpanned. "No. I'm just trying to be a gentleman this time around."

Varana snickered amusedly. "Pshh, a gentleman? I didn't realize you were capable of such a thing."

Zalith rolled his eyes. "I'm full of surprises, Varana; you should know that by now."

"And just how long do you think this is going to last?" she questioned, crossing her arms.

He smiled. "The chivalry? For as long as I can bear it."

She scowled in annoyance. "Okay…but seriously, Z…how long do you intend on keeping *this* one around? It's been two years now; based on my lifetime of experience with you, I'm fairly certain that this little relationship of yours has greatly exceeded its expiration date," she said harshly—but an almost desperate stare clung to her face as though she was dreading to hear what he might say in response.

Zalith frowned irritably. "Don't you have something else you could be doing right now?" he mumbled, trying to reach for the door handle behind her.

Blocking the handle with her body, she shrugged. "I'm just saying that your reputation precedes you—"

"Things are different this time," he stated sternly.

"Then explain to me what's so different about this one," she demanded.

Beyond aggravated, he lightly pushed her aside and gripped the door handle. "I don't want to do this with you right now, Varana," he dismissed.

She grabbed his wrist, keeping him from pushing the door open as a stubborn, confounded look warped her face. "At least let me see him then!" she insisted.

"No."

Varana smiled cruelly. "Why not? Is he ugly?"

He tried his best to keep his calm composure. "Of course not. But I'm sure you'd love that, wouldn't you?"

"What are you hiding!?" she yelled frustratedly.

"Nothing, Varana," he answered, trying to push his door open, but she kept him from doing so. "I just don't want the two of you to meet right now. He's important to me, and I'd rather not subject him to your petulant behaviour."

With a sour, hostile scowl, Varana opened her mouth to speak—

"I am done with this conversation," Zalith interjected. This time, he didn't hold back, and pushed his door open, freeing his wrist from her grip. As she stumbled aside, he stepped into his bedroom and turned to face her. "I don't intend on keeping my guest cooped up in his room all day, so I suggest you make yourself scarce," he requested.

Varana clenched her fists in anger, each of them visibly aching to collide with his face. She scowled, gritted her teeth in rage, and turned around, her lengthy, black hair whipping the wall beside her. With a frustrated shriek, she stormed off down the hall as loudly as she could, heading towards her bedroom.

With a quiet, relieved sigh, Zalith pushed his door shut behind him. He wasn't at all interested in giving in to Varana's persistence. She'd see Alucard when *he* wanted her to; no sooner, no later. Ignoring the wall-shaking bang from the slamming of what could only be Varana's bedroom door, he rolled his eyes and disappeared into his walk-in closet. Once he was dressed, he could finally enjoy an entire day with Alucard.

Chapter Ten

Horses

| **Alucard** |

A lucard sat on the end of his bed and glared down at the floor. He listened to the entire conversation between Zalith and that woman, and he didn't like what he heard.

He still didn't understand why Zalith persisted in keeping him hidden from her or why she was so desperate to meet him. That wasn't what had him most perturbed, though. What did she mean by expiration date? *'How long do you intend on keeping this one around?'*—it repeated in his mind over and over. Was he just some sort of temporary fix? Would Zalith eventually get tired of him? Was that what was going to happen? That woman seemed to be convinced of it and she had obviously known Zalith long enough to say so. A lifetime of experience? Chivalry? Alucard couldn't get his head around any of it.

The vampire tried to choose which part of Zalith and Varana's conversation to focus on, but he couldn't. As much as he might want to examine everything he'd just heard, he didn't want to start anxiously overthinking. He wanted to enjoy whatever time he had left with Zalith before heading home to get back to work.

Work... what a tiresome commitment. But he had to do it. If he wanted to rebuild the Nosferatu, if he wanted to keep his people safe, then he had to put in his time and effort.

With a quiet sigh, he dragged his fingers through his hair. He didn't want to think about work. Instead, he thought about what he saw of Zalith's body. He wasn't going to deny the fact that he was *very* attracted to him; it was something he'd felt growing from the moment he'd seen Zalith in his bathroom after crashing that werewolf wedding. But in the moment he'd been fixated on Zalith's abs, he'd let his senses focus on the demon's beating heart... and his blood. He wanted to bite down on Zalith's neck—he wanted to *so desperately* taste Zalith, but he'd resisted. The last thing he wanted to do was hurt the demon and make him hesitant to get so close again.

The door suddenly opened, snatching Alucard's attention, and he watched Zalith walk back in. He was dressed in a light grey shirt with the sleeves rolled up and black trousers. He'd combed his hair back, and he seemed just about ready to head out. In his right hand, he had a white shirt and another pair of black trousers, and once he closed the door behind him, he smiled, made his way over to Alucard, and held the clothes out to him.

"You can borrow these," the demon said. "I imagine you don't want to walk around in the same clothes you slept in."

Alucard glanced up at him and took the clothes. "*Multemesc.* You can…go. You're not watching me get dressed," he grumbled with a scowl, trying to hide his embarrassment.

With a disappointed but devious smile, Zalith reached into his pocket and handed Alucard a comb. "You can borrow this, too." Then, he turned around and headed for the door. "I'll meet you outside in ten minutes," he said as he pulled the door open.

Before Zalith could leave, however, Alucard realized that the shirt had short sleeves. He didn't like that. He looked at Zalith and asked, "Can…I borrow one with long sleeves, please?"

Zalith frowned and made his way back over to Alucard. "Why?" he asked curiously, taking the shirt from him.

"Because short sleeves are uncomfortable," he lied with a hostile tone, hoping to discourage Zalith from asking more questions.

Zalith nodded and said, "Okay, I'll go and find one for you." He made his way back over to the door and left the room.

The vampire waited, listening as Zalith walked across the hall, went into a room, and came back out again. When he came back into the guest room, Alucard glanced at him.

Zalith handed him a white shirt with longer sleeves. "Here."

"*Multemesc,*" Alucard said, taking it from him.

"I'll see you shortly." Zalith smirked at him before leaving him to change alone.

Alucard sighed and unbuttoned his shirt. He took it off and hastily pulled on the white, long-sleeved one Zalith had given him, and then he stood up, changed into the new trousers, and grabbed his blazer from the cabinet he'd left it on last night. He wasn't sure what to do with his old clothes, though. Should he just leave them there? He knew that Zalith had staff, so he left them on the end of the bed and made his way over to the mirror. Once he tidied his hair using the comb Zalith had lent him, he pulled on his blazer and left the room.

As he made his way down the stairs and towards the front door, he slipped the comb into his pocket; he'd return it to Zalith once they met outside. He grabbed his cape from the coat rack and pulled the front door open.

However, when Alucard stepped outside, he couldn't see Zalith. The vampire shut the front door behind him, pulled his cape on over his shoulders, and took a few steps forward. He looked around slowly, searching the porch and courtyard area for the demon. To his right, the groundskeeper was cleaning the carriage with a dripping wet rag and a discontent look on his face, and not too far from the man was a stable with three horses inside. Alucard immediately recognized each breed; he knew more than most about horses, and he'd also often choose the company of an animal over that of another person—except Zalith. But then he rolled his eyes; Zalith never failed to be on his mind. He hadn't forgotten the conversation he heard between him and Varana, either, and he felt increasingly annoyed each time he thought about what that woman said.

With an irritated sigh, he tried to put it out of his mind and made his way towards the stables.

Noticing him as he passed the carriage, the groundskeeper stopped cleaning and stumbled forward. "E-excuse me, sir, you're not permitted to—"

Alucard sharply turned his head and hissed, baring his fangs and sending the groundskeeper cowering behind the carriage. He didn't care what a human might have to say right now.

When he reached the stables, Alucard stopped in front of the black shire mare, the same mare which pulled the carriage last night. She took her copper-brown eyes off the straw was chewing and set her sights on Alucard, staring at him as he placed his hand on her face. The vampire couldn't help but smile; horses were and always had been his favourite animal, and he'd take any chance to greet one.

He stroked the mare's mane. "Did they give you a name?" he asked.

The horse grunted and swayed her head.

"Adalina, huh? That's surprising."

As Adalina returned to chewing straw, Alucard looked at the two horses in a paddock on either side of her. They were Drydenan Warmbloods; the first was an ivory-white-coated mare with a silvery-white mane and striking blue eyes almost the same as his when sunlight hit them. The second was a black stallion, but its face was white. Its eyes, too, were a striking ice blue. He could only assume the stallion was Zalith's and the mare was that woman's. He was curious to know what Zalith named his steed, so he made his way over to it and watched as it finished chewing a carrot.

"What did Zalith call you?" he asked, stroking its black mane.

It snorted quietly and stared at him.

Alucard nodded. "Dimitri? *Ciudat.*"

As Dimitri went back to eating, Alucard glanced at the ivory-white mare and frowned. That was *her* horse—Varana's. He wasn't exactly sure whether he wanted to know what that woman had named her horse, but it wasn't the horse's fault that she had such a petulant owner.

The vampire moved closer and stroked the mare's mane. "And you?" he asked her.

She shook her head and nuzzled his hand.

"Santana," he mumbled. "Okay."

Alucard left Santana and made his way back to Adalina, who grunted in contentedness as the vampire stroked her mane while Dimitri and Santana jealously watched from their paddocks.

"Is that all you have in there?" he asked quietly, seeing that the mare had only straw to chew.

The mare whinnied.

Alucard looked at Dimitri's paddock. "Give me one of them," he requested, looking at the stallion as he stared back, chewing on a carrot.

The stallion reached down and picked up another whole carrot with his teeth and held it out to Alucard, who took it and then handed it to Adalina. The mare snatched it and chewed it ravenously, but after a few seconds, she ten snorted and grunted quietly.

"That's what you get when you eat too quickly," Alucard scolded. "Why the haste? No one's going to take it from you."

Dimitri then snorted irritably and stomped his front left hoof on the ground.

Alucard placed his free hand on the stallion's face. "*Da,* how could I forget about you?" he muttered, stroking the horse's face as it grunted happily.

Adalina snorted quietly and looked in the direction of the door.

Alucard glanced over there, too, and when he saw Zalith leaning against the stable doorframe, smirking at him, the vampire frowned in embarrassment. He took his hands off each horse's face and turned his back on Zalith, trying to hide his face. "Don't say anything," he grumbled.

Zalith stood up straight and made his way over. "Are you having a nice time with your new friends?"

"I am, as a matter of fact," he sneered, glaring at him. "They are far more interesting than people."

Reaching him, Zalith smiled and placed his hand on Alucard's shoulder. "How so?"

"All people do is whine and complain," he mumbled, placing his hand back on Adalina's face. "Unlike people, horses don't irritate you to the point you want to kill them. They are your companion, you trust one another with your life, and your horse will never leave you when you need them." He glanced at Zalith, who was smiling curiously, waiting for him to continue. "People are all the same; they lie, they conspire—they are stupid. Animals are not. If they trust you, they will be your friend for their entire life. They won't run off when a better-looking companion comes along; they won't get tired or bored after a year…maybe two."

Zalith frowned for a moment; he obviously knew that Alucard had heard his conversation with Varana. But instead of bringing it up, he smiled and looked at the horse Alucard was standing beside. "Would you like to take the horses out instead of walking?"

Alucard was admittedly glad that Zalith had chosen to avoid talking about his and Varana's conversation; he wasn't yet ready to listen to what Zalith might have to say. He took his eyes off the horse and looked at Zalith. "I would like that."

As he took his hand off Alucard's shoulder, Zalith smiled and said, "I can use Varana's horse; you can use mine."

"No," Alucard denied, unlocking the gate to Adalina's paddock. "I will take Adalina."

Watching as Alucard made his way into the mare's paddock and began fastening her saddle to her back, Zalith smiled. "Okay," he said, heading to Dimitri's paddock.

Once he mounted the mare, Alucard made himself comfortable and watched Zalith get up on his horse. "Are we going anywhere in particular?"

"Just for a walk," Zalith said with a smile and tapped his horse's side with his foot, making it walk forward.

Alucard made Adalina follow beside Zalith. They headed into the grounds, followed the path to the gates, and navigated the forest path they'd travelled along last night in the carriage.

The vampire then remembered that he still had Zalith's comb, so he took it out of his pocket and held it out to him. "I forgot I had this."

Zalith smiled as he gripped the vampire's hand and pulled him closer, and when he kissed Alucard's lips, the vampire frowned in both startlement and fluster. The demon then took the comb from him and smirked at Alucard, who sat up straight and tried to hide his face by glaring over at the trees on his right.

"You know, even though you're as pale as ice, vampire, I can see when you blush."

Pouting, Alucard turned his head and scowled at Zalith.

The demon slipped his comb into his pocket and said, "Thank you." He tapped his horse's side with his foot. "Come on, this way," he said, steering his horse off the main path and into the forest.

With a curious frown, Alucard made his horse follow Zalith's into the trees. He wasn't sure where the demon was taking him, but he was excited to find out.

Chapter Eleven

Love Letter

| **Alucard** |

For a short while, Alucard and Zalith travelled in serene silence. Every time Alucard glanced at the demon, he caught his gaze, and it made the vampire feel anxious. Why did Zalith stare at him so much?

He frowned and looked ahead; sunlight crept through the rigid leaves of the towering redwood and cypress trees, lighting the leaf-littered ground. Birdsong and the rustling of critters echoed through the quiet, and Alucard felt more relaxed than he had in a long time, even with the demon staring at him.

However, the silence was abruptly interrupted by the loud screech of an owl. They both looked up and set their eyes on a snowy-white barn owl as it descended and made its way towards them. Alucard recognized the bird as one of his messengers; he held out his arm, and the bird perched on his wrist. Between its beak, it held a small, wrapped piece of parchment. The vampire took it from the chirping bird, and then it flew off.

"Business?" Zalith asked curiously as Alucard started unfolding the parchment.

The vampire opened the parchment, revealing a Deiganish-written note. The only words he could read were Ben's name and a few others, but not enough to piece a sentence together, and that made him feel rather stupid, especially next to Zalith. He slowly folded the parchment back up and tucked it into his blazer pocket. "Maybe," he mumbled.

Zalith nodded and stared ahead.

Alucard, on the other hand, couldn't focus on their walk or the calming silence. Ben would have only sent a message if it was important—if it needed his immediate attention. He needed to know what Ben said, but he couldn't read Deiganish. Usually, he'd get Elvin to read his Deiganish mail, but the bard was gone. He *could* ask Zalith, but he felt far too embarrassed to do so. What would the demon think if he found out that he couldn't read the same language that he'd sent him many letters in?

Zalith then glanced at him and asked with a smirk, "What are you hiding? Is that a love letter, Alucard?"

The vampire rolled his eyes. He'd rather tell Zalith he couldn't read than let him think he was receiving love letters. He reached into his pocket and pulled the note out. "Can you... read this for me?" he asked stubbornly, holding it towards him.

Taking the folded parchment from him, Zalith smiled curiously and looked down at it. "Why? Is it from your manstress?" he teased, unfolding the paper.

The vampire snarled and looked away from him. "No. If you must know, I can't read Deiganish."

Zalith glanced at Alucard and smiled, but he didn't have his usual amused or unseemly expression.

Alucard frowned. "What?"

"Nothing. I was just thinking about the invitation you sent me to your party."

Embarrassed, Alucard pouted and looked away.

"No, I loved it," Zalith insisted. "All of your little spelling errors and the way you spelt my name—"

"I spelt that wrong?" he asked, confused.

Zalith smiled. "It's spelt with a Z, but like I said, I loved the way you wrote it. And I was thinking that if it hadn't been for that letter, then... maybe we wouldn't be here right now."

Alucard shrugged. "I was worried you'd ignore it."

The demon smiled and said, "*I* was worried you would've forgotten about me by then."

"I could never forget about you," he mumbled shyly.

Zalith smiled again. "Nor I you." Then, he looked down at the letter. "Aleksei, the packs have been seen congregating in the ruins of Ada's old manor. They've caught word of your return and have begun preparing an assault. Your informant tells me they plan to attack tonight, so I've already gathered the majority of the day and night guards. We're prepared to deal with them in your absence, but their numbers seem to exceed those I had come to know of. Other people not of lycan blood have been seen with the wolves, too, so it would appear that the wolves have allies. Regardless, we will kill whoever attacks with them. But if there is a specific way you want me to approach this dilemma, do let me know. Love from Ben, kiss-kiss-hug-hug."

Alucard scowled at Zalith, watching as a smirk crept across his face. "You're not funny," he snarled, taking the letter back from him. He stuffed the parchment into his pocket and thought to himself for a few moments. He was sure that Ben could handle the werewolves, but this was the first time he'd heard of the wolves having allies. Who were they?

"I assume you have to leave me now?" Zalith asked.

"No," Alucard answered. "Ben can handle it."

The demon smiled contently. "In that case, I feel compelled to ask: if you can't read Deiganish, how were you able to read the letters I sent you while you were away?"

Alucard shrugged. "I had people read them for me and then I killed them."

With an amused smile, Zalith offered, "Well, don't feel as though you have to accept, but I can help you learn to both read and write Deiganish if you want."

As he looked down at his hands and gripped his horse's reins a little tighter, Alucard pouted. It would be useful if he could read and write Deiganish, and he felt as if he could trust Zalith not to belittle him; after all, he hadn't reacted negatively to his admittance just now. "Maybe," he answered quietly.

"I'm also curious to know: why do you have so many names? I've heard many a title used to reference you. Is there a reason you insist particular people use particular names to address you?"

Once again, Zalith was requesting his personal information—this time, however, Alucard felt no need to act hostile. They were partners now, and he felt no reason to keep it from him. "Well, there is," he confirmed, looking at him. "Aleksei is the name the people who raised me gave me, so every other standard person in my life will refer to me as Aleksei. Alucard was the name my mother gave me; I only know it because I could hear her thoughts and often the things she was saying while she was pregnant. I only let people I care about call me that. Aleksei is the name Damien calls me, too— it's... derogatory; he started calling me that like everyone else when—" he caught himself about to reveal something he didn't yet want to tell Zalith. He hesitated and continued, "When...I went to work for him. Emeritus is just my surname—I got that from my mother. And as you know, Caedis is my demon name."

"Why is Aleksei derogatory?"

This time, Alucard couldn't manifest a fast answer. He had no idea what to say. Did he want to tell Zalith *this* truth? No. He couldn't. He took his eyes off the demon and looked down at his hands again. With a quiet sigh, he shrugged and said, "It's just a human name. He thinks it's funny to ignore my demon name."

Zalith frowned but didn't persist. "Who gave you your demon name? Only a demon can name another demon, and from what I've come to know, I think it's safe for me to assume that Lucifer didn't name you Caedis."

"No, he didn't," Alucard confirmed. "It was Lilith. I met her once when I was a child. She was the one who came to help me out of the catacombs when the Diabolus found us."

Zalith frowned. "I thought Lilith did well to keep out of her siblings' squabbles."

"As did I. But she came, got me out of the fight, and left."

"You never searched for an answer?"

"I didn't care and still don't."

Zalith smiled. "Understandable."

Although he was enjoying his time with Zalith, Alucard couldn't help but think about Ben's letter. He'd only been back a single day and the werewolves were already planning moves. Leaving Ben to deal with that by himself might not be the best idea, especially if the wolves had new, unknown allies. No, he had to head back to Dor-Sanguis and get back to work.

The vampire took his eyes off the forest and looked at Zalith. "We should head back now…and then I should head home. I don't want to leave Ben to deal with the wolves just in case their new allies are dangerous."

A saddened frown appeared on Zalith's face. "Of course," he said and made his horse turn around. "Does this mean we have to cancel our date?"

"I don't know," he answered regretfully. "I hope not."

"Well, if it does, I'm sure we can make a new plan," Zalith said, smiling.

The vampire nodded, and then, they headed back towards the house.

| **Zalith** |

As they emerged from the forest onto the road which led to the house, Zalith glanced at Alucard. For a moment, he worried that his questions had upset Alucard and *that* was why he was so hasty to leave. But he was overthinking, wasn't he? Alucard had to get back because of what Ben said in his letter.

He didn't want Alucard to leave; he wanted to spend the rest of the day with him. But he couldn't keep the vampire from returning to deal with his business. He could, however, try to convince Alucard to let him go with him, and that was precisely what he was going to do—and in a way that would give him an amusing but endearing reaction from the vampire.

When they reached the manor, they both dismounted their horses and handed the reins to the groundskeeper, who led them to their paddocks.

"I'll talk to you when I get back," Alucard said as they turned to face each other. "I'll most likely have to talk to Ben and some of my other subordinates, but after that, I'll come and update you."

With a smirk, Zalith wrapped his arms around Alucard and embraced him tightly. "Must you leave, darling?" he asked quietly and sullenly. "I will miss you so sorely."

Alucard slowly moved his arms around Zalith and said, "I have to."

The demon started kissing the side of Alucard's face. "Don't go," he pleaded sadly, hugging him as tightly as he could. "I already miss you."

In response to his clinginess, Alucard frowned and tried to pull away, but Zalith kept hold of him and pecked at his cheek with his lips.

"Stop," Alucard mumbled as he pushed him away, but Zalith could see the smile on his face.

"Can't I come with you?" the demon asked with a forced, saddened frown.

"And do what? Sit around and watch me talk to people?"

"I wouldn't miss such enjoyment for the world."

Rolling his eyes, Alucard sighed. "Fine, fine," he agreed, waving his hand in dismissal, still trying to hide his smile.

Zalith smirked victoriously; there was nothing he enjoyed more than watching Alucard try to hide his smile or his embarrassment. His small act of desperation had clearly amused Alucard, and that was exactly what he had been hoping for. The vampire also agreed to let him go with him, so he had totalled two victories in the same moment.

The demon took hold of Alucard's arm with his. "Will you fly me to your castle, Alucard?" he asked, curious to see how much longer he could keep Alucard from hiding his smile. "Will you carry me in your arms?"

Alucard pouted. "No."

"Then how do we get there?"

"You tell me since you so desperately want to come with me," he sneered.

Smiling, Zalith led the way over to the closest brick wall. "We can phase—*I* can phase and take you with me," he suggested. He was curious to know why Alucard wouldn't phase, but that was a question he'd ask when the time was right. He didn't want to risk ruining this amusing moment. "Where should we go? To the castle or your house?"

"Castle," Alucard said. "You know my house was burned to the ground."

"Do you have plans to build another?" Zalith asked curiously.

"Maybe," Alucard mumbled. "Let's go."

The demon smiled, and without further delay, he created a rift in the wall and led the way forward, leaving Nefastus behind.

Chapter Twelve

— ⨯ ✝ ⨯ —

Unusual Alliances

| Alucard |

Alucard and Zalith emerged from the wall surrounding the vampire's castle. The first thing Alucard set his eyes on was the forest at the foot of the hill. He frowned sadly while he eyed the trees; it was the same area of the forest that Tobias once lived in, and as he stared, both guilt and sorrow enthralled him. Knowing that Tobias was no longer out there hurt; no death had gripped him as tightly as Tobias' had, and he couldn't understand why. Perhaps it was because that man had been his *favourite* friend…or because he died saving Alucard. The vampire wasn't sure, and he didn't want to dwell on it. He had work to do.

The vampire took his eyes off the forest and turned to face Zalith, who finished closing the rift. The demon smiled at him, but he frowned in concern when he clearly noticed Alucard's sadness. Alucard didn't plan to give him a chance to ask if he was okay or not, though. He walked past Zalith, and as the demon followed, he made his way into the castle courtyard.

"I'll have to find Ben and tell him to get messages to everyone I need here. Today was the day I planned to catch up with everything I missed while I was away, so I may as well do that while I'm here."

Zalith smiled and asked, "Is that all you have planned for today?"

Glancing at him as they reached the door, Alucard shrugged. "I still need to look for Lucious; I will begin that job after we've gone to the opera," he said, pushing the door to his castle open. He invited Zalith in first and followed him in. "What will you do while I'm searching for him?"

"Nothing exciting," Zalith said with a sigh but smiled curiously. "Where do you have to look for Lucious?"

"Avalmoor," he answered resentfully. He didn't want to travel to the one place where most of Letholdus' Dragon Gods resided, but what choice did he have? He glanced at Zalith, and he noticed a sullen frown on his face.

Before Alucard could ask what was wrong, the demon smiled at him and asked, "What's it like in Avalmoor?"

As he led the way through the hall and towards the door to his part of the castle, Alucard shrugged and said, "Cold. Always winter. The dragons like the cold and the snow; Letholdus made Avalmoor specifically to accommodate his children. I heard humans have found a way to live there—they find a way to live anywhere…like vermin."

The demon smiled amusedly as they headed through the door. "They *are* very much like vermin. I've heard these dragons are dangerous, though. Is it really a good idea to go alone?"

Alucard headed for his study. "You want to come, don't you?" he asked suspiciously.

Zalith smirked. "Perhaps, but I won't intrude if you don't want me to come."

Alucard felt no need to deny him. In fact, he admittedly hoped that Zalith would ask to come. He didn't want to go alone, and he didn't want to say goodbye to Zalith again for what might be months after only just getting back. The vampire looked away, trying to hide his smile as they turned into another corridor. "You can come."

The sound of rapidly approaching paws snatched Alucard's attention. He stopped walking, looked back over his shoulder, and watched as his hellhound, Sabazios, raced down the hallway towards him. He turned to face the beast, and as it reached him, it jumped up at him, panting excitedly.

Alucard smiled as he patted the hound's head and allowed him to rest his front paws on his shoulders so he could stand on his hind legs and enjoy the attention. But after a few moments, Alucard gently pushed the hound away and looked down at him. "Go and tell Ben I need him," he ordered.

Sabazios barked happily and turned around; he hurried back down the hall and out of sight, the clipping of his claws on the marble flooring fading away.

As they continued walking, Zalith asked Alucard, "Where did you find a docile hellhound?"

"Tengetso," he replied. "I think his pack left him behind because he was hurt. I helped him, and he hasn't stopped following me around since."

"I see," Zalith said and followed the vampire into his study. "Do you know exactly where in Avalmoor to look?"

Alucard walked over to his desk and sighed quietly. "No. I haven't been to Avalmoor in a long time—not since killing Janus. I have people out there, though. I can contact them before I head there," he explained as he turned around and leaned back against the table. "Is Nefastus the only place you've visited since being here?" he asked curiously, but as Zalith moved closer to him, he frowned nervously.

Zalith rested his hands on the table on either side of the vampire and leaned his face into Alucard's. "Currently, yes," he answered with a smirk, his lips a mere inch from Alucard's.

The fact that they were now together made Alucard feel a whole lot more nervous than he had done before; he took his eyes off Zalith and looked down at the floor as he answered, "We'll have to stop in Boszorkány on the way."

"And what's it like *there*?"

He shrugged. "Not too different than here. Boszorkány is one of a few places very similar to Dor-Sanguis."

With an amused *and* intrigued look on his face, Zalith smiled. "Oh?"

Alucard glanced at him. "Well... our languages are similar. Dor-Sanguian's closest relative language is Lupanese; Lupa is just off the coast of Drydenheim—small place, but beautiful. Other similar languages are Aguilian, and then Boszorkian, as I said. People call them romance languages; they are all very similar, yet different."

Still smiling, Zalith moved his right hand from the table and slowly dragged it up Alucard's arm and to the back of his neck. "Are you as familiar with romance as you are with such languages?"

The vampire pouted and looked away from him. "No."

With a quiet, amused laugh, Zalith guided his hand around from the back of Alucard's neck, lightly gripped his jaw, and turned the vampire's head to face him. He then gently pressed his lips against Alucard's.

Although Alucard knew when Zalith was about to kiss him, he still felt surprised each time he did it. It didn't discomfort him, though. He liked it when Zalith randomly kissed him.

The demon kissed Alucard's lips once more and then he smiled and rested his forehead against Alucard's. He stared into his nervous eyes and gently stroked the side of his face with the tips of his fingers. "I'm sure I can show you," he said quietly.

Alucard took his eyes off Zalith again, unsure of what to say in response. He frowned, waiting, and as Zalith smiled, he pouted stubbornly. But his pout soon became a nervous frown when the demon kissed the left side of his neck; a shiver of anticipation spiralled through him as Zalith's lips graced his skin, and he closed his eyes as he gave in to the strange, delightful sensation.

A quiet knock came at the door, startling Alucard. He sharply turned his head and stared at Ben, who was standing in the doorway with a conflicted look on his face. Zalith didn't move, so Alucard placed his hands on the demon's shoulders and gently pushed him away, but Zalith didn't back off without a quiet, reluctant growl.

The demon's aggression intensified the feeling of anticipation, but Alucard did his best to ignore it and turned to face Ben. "What?" he grumbled.

Ben lost his conflicted frown. "Uh... you asked for me, sir."

With a quiet sigh, Alucard nodded and gestured his hand to invite Ben into the room. "Tell me more about what you were telling me in the letter you sent," he said as he walked past Zalith and headed to one of his other cluttered desks. He leaned against the desk and glared at Ben.

Ben cleared his throat and said, "Freja noticed the packs congregating last night. She watched them and informed me this morning of their meetings. She didn't recognize the people seen with the wolves, but she did mention one of them was carrying a staff. I admittedly have no idea what to make of it, but a few of the Adherents said he could be a wizard."

"Wizard?" Alucard questioned and glanced at Zalith, who walked over and stood beside him.

"Yes," Ben confirmed.

Alucard looked down at his cluttered desk and frowned skeptically. Why would a wizard ally with werewolves? Wizards had no business in Dor-Sanguis; wizards had no business with *him*. Either the night guards were idiots, or something new was afoot…something he wasn't yet aware of. Ada wasn't around anymore, so if a wizard had allied with the wolves, someone else must have stepped up and taken Ada's place. But who? He wasn't aware of any other wolves nearly as strong or highly respected enough as her to be able to get *all* the packs to work together to prepare an assault.

He looked back at Ben. "Is Freja still watching them?"

"She has two of her Betas out there right now," he answered.

"Did she say what this staff-wielding man looked like? Specific robe colour, maybe?"

Ben nodded. "White robes."

Alucard snarled irritably. *Of course* he was wearing white; the Selarom Clan wielded ice-white colours, and he knew they were a rather formidable clan. But why were *they* getting involved? Wizard clans hardly ever got involved in business outside of their own country, Divinos. He also knew that some rogue wizards who belonged to no clan wore whites and blacks… so he wondered, could this wizard be a rogue? He glared down at his hands as he placed them on the desk in front of him. "Was there just one?"

"As far as we've been able to tell, yes," Ben said.

The vampire stood up straight with a deep sigh. "I need you to get everyone here for a meeting—now."

Ben nodded and hastily left the room.

"You're concerned," Zalith said, placing his hand on Alucard's shoulder and turning him to face him.

Looking at Zalith's worried face, Alucard huffed quietly. "Annoyed," he corrected.

"Why?"

"I'll tell you when I tell everyone else," he grumbled. "My number of problems is only increasing; I get rid of Ada, and now I have to deal with that aftermath, and wizards along with it."

"I assume it's unusual for a wizard to have allied with werewolves," Zalith said, watching Alucard as he paced impatiently in front of him.

He stopped pacing, placed his hands on the table, and frowned frustratedly. "None of this makes sense. Ada's dead, so the wolves have no reason to unite; they should be scattered and scared, not meeting in the ruins of her house planning to kill me. And a wizard? They keep out of the affairs of other species *and* don't really care what happens outside of Divinos, so why would one come all the way out here to ally with werewolves?"

"Could Ada have forged a relationship with a wizard before her death?"

"I don't know." Alucard sighed, turning to face him. "That woman did all kinds of abnormal things in her life. I don't know why she would need a wizard, but I can ask Dirk. He worked with a dragon, and wizards are close to dragons. Perhaps he'll have something useful to say to me for once."

Amused, Zalith smiled. "I find that quite hard to believe."

Alucard looked away. "People will arrive soon, so we should go to the hall. You don't have to sit through it if you don't want to. I'm sure it's not going to be an interesting conversation."

"On the contrary, anything you say is interesting to me, and I love listening to you speak," he said with a smirk.

With a conflicted pout on his face, Alucard turned around and led the way over to the door. "I have new allies now, too," he mumbled as Zalith followed him. "I don't know how they work or speak; I don't know how stupid they are, either. Dirk found them for me."

As he followed the vampire through the hallways, Zalith asked, "You trust him to find suitable replacements?"

"He's an idiot but he knows how to do his job."

"I wasn't trying to patronize you; I'm just curious. Dirk doesn't look like the smartest of people."

Alucard stepped into the hall and looked around. Not one of the castle's butlers was in sight, and that irritated him more than he already was. The vampire rolled his eyes and made his way over to the kitchen door. When he went inside, he set his eyes on all three butlers, who each had a cigarette in their hand, sitting on the work surfaces while muttering quietly to one another.

An angered scowl possessed Alucard's face as he gritted his teeth. "What the fuck are you all doing out here?!" he yelled in Dor-Sanguian.

As they all flinched in shock, they spun around and set their horrified eyes on him.

One of them stuttered, "S-sorry, My Lord, we were... cleaning... the—"

"The what?"

"The... uh... floor, My Lord," one of them called, pointing to the floor. "It was wet, so we didn't wanna stand on it."

Alucard looked down at the floor, which *wasn't* wet, and there weren't any mops or buckets sitting around, either. He scowled at the three men as they put their cigarettes out and hastily picked up the closest item to each of them.

"W-we'll get back to it, My Lord," another of them said.

The vampire snarled irritably. "I have guests coming. Clean the fucking hall."

They all nodded and simultaneously said, "Yes, My Lord." Then, they scrambled around for their cleaning supplies.

With a roll of his eyes, Alucard turned around and headed back into the hall.

The demon smiled curiously. "Why so angry, vampire?" he asked, following him over to the table.

Alucard pulled off his cape and sat at the head of the table. "They slack off during the day because they're not used to me being here," he muttered as he placed his cape over the arm of his seat. He then slouched back and sighed quietly. "My house burned down, so I live here now."

"I see," Zalith said as he sat in the seat closest to Alucard and rested his arms on the table.

The vampire set his eyes on the incoming butler and watched as the man silently made his way over and handed him a small glass of blood. The butler then bowed humbly and walked off, disappearing back into the kitchen as the other two hurried out with their mops and began cleaning the floor.

As he took a sip from his glass, Alucard glanced at the windows to his left, and when the sunlight hit his face, his eyes faded to ice blue, sending a shiver of pain through his head. He sighed, placed his glass down, and looked at Zalith, who was staring at him. "Why do you stare at me?" he grumbled.

Zalith smirked and moved his hand over Alucard's. He then took hold of it and leaned closer. "Because you're very handsome, Alucard, and I love to look at what I find attractive," he answered.

Taking his eyes off Zalith, Alucard looked down at their hands and frowned. Zalith was leaning as close as he could get with the table in the way, and Alucard wasn't sure whether Zalith was waiting for him to lean closer, too, so that he could kiss him. Either way, Alucard felt far too shy to lean forward. He pulled his hand from Zalith's, picked up his glass, and sipped from it again. He wanted to change the subject before Zalith could say anything else to make him feel even more nervous than he already did, but he couldn't think of anything.

However, he *did* remember that Zalith asked about his eyes this morning. He leaned back in his seat and out of the sunlight, and as his eyes faded back to hell-fiery red, he set them on Zalith. "You asked about my eyes this morning; I *do* feel something when they change."

Zalith laughed slightly. "What an abrupt subject change, and without so much as a smooth transition, too. You're lacking today, Alucard. Should I assume it's because you're tired, or will you tell me what's bothering you?"

"Why are you so sure something is bothering me?"

Zalith smirked. "You make a face, Alucard. We've had this conversation before."

The vampire pouted and looked down at the table. "Nothing is bothering me," he mumbled. "I just thought killing Ada would end the werewolves' desire to kill me."

For a moment, Zalith seemed to ponder…but then he quietly sighed and smiled curiously. "Okay, tell me what you feel when your eyes change."

Alucard looked at him and shrugged slightly. "Pain," he answered.

Guilt smothered Zalith's face. "I'm sorry. If I'd known, I wouldn't have—"

"I don't really notice it anymore," Alucard interjected. "It's more irritating now than painful—it's only painful if I remain in the sunlight for a while."

"In direct light? What if your back's to the sun?" he asked curiously.

"Then I'll be fine," he answered.

Zalith smiled. "I'll remember that."

Ben then walked into the hall, returning from his task of summoning Alucard's subordinates. Zalith and Alucard eyed him closely as he sat in the seat across from the demon and made himself comfortable, and then Alucard glared at him with an expectant look on his face.

"I contacted everyone," Ben said. "They'll be here shortly."

"Right," Alucard mumbled, turning his attention back to Zalith. "If you're coming with me to Avalmoor, we will travel after dusk—I prefer to travel at night," he said to the demon.

With a quiet laugh, Zalith leaned his arms on the table and smiled at Alucard. "How are we going to get there?"

"We could sail…or I can get us there. Either way, we have to stop in Boszorkány."

"How long is the boat trip?"

Alucard thought to himself for a moment. "With Drac pulling the ship, I imagine it being a day to Boszorkány and a day from there to Avalmoor. We'll stop for a day in Boszorkány—Drac will need to rest. While he does, I'm sure we can find something to do there."

Zalith smiled and placed his hand over Alucard's. "That sounds delightful."

As he glanced down at their hands again, Alucard frowned ever so slightly. He wasn't sure how he felt about Ben seeing them talk, let alone seeing Zalith touching him.

At the moment, he didn't want to be so public with their relationship; so he pulled his hand from under Zalith's and picked up his glass. However, he wouldn't let his nervousness devour the excitement that he felt about their trip to Avalmoor; not only would he be travelling to a new country, but he'd also have Zalith at his side while doing so. He couldn't imagine anything more thrilling. He loved travelling and the thought of doing it with someone he enjoyed being with as much as he enjoyed being with Zalith filled him with joy.

He smiled as he set his eyes back on the demon. "We still have the opera to go to. After that, we'll head to Avalmoor. Will you need to go home first?"

Zalith rested his arms in front of him and seemed to ponder for a moment. "I will," he answered. "I'll need to tell Varana that I'm going on a trip. I'll also need to pack clothes. I can do that and meet you back here."

"Okay," Alucard replied and sipped from his glass. "It always snows there and is cold as fuck. You should bring something warm," he advised.

Zalith smiled curiously. "Do *you* feel the cold, Alucard?"

Alucard shrugged as he finished the last of his drink. "I do."

"Then I'll be sure to keep *you* warm," he said with a suggestive grin, and as the vampire looked away in embarrassment, the demon laughed quietly.

Just then, Dirk stepped into the castle, making his arrival known with a loud, "Ahem".

Alucard, Zalith, and Ben watched as the snobby-faced man made his way through the hall. He pulled out a seat several chairs down the table on the same side Zalith was sitting; he took off his coat, placed it over the back of his seat, and then eyed the three of them as he sat down.

The vampire felt immediate displeasure. He didn't like Dirk's strutty attitude *at all*. He glared at the man, who soon lost his stubborn stare and frowned nervously, and then he asked him, "Did you so happen to see anyone else on your way up here?"

"Yes," Dirk replied, resting his arms on the table. "I saw Freja coming up from the forest, and your newest subordinates are currently outside arguing with your groundskeeper. They didn't want to hand their horses over."

Alucard rolled his eyes. He wasn't going to go out there and deal with it. If they didn't come inside within the next few minutes, he'd send Ben out there to get them— but that wouldn't be necessary. Just a few moments later, the last of his subordinates entered the hall. He waited, watching as Freja led the way in and sat beside Ben. Alucard's new scribe stopped beside him, obviously having been expecting to sit in the seat Zalith was occupying, but the vampire knew that Zalith wasn't going to move—the demon's evil glance made that evident—so the scribe walked away and sat beside Zalith instead.

Several other people Alucard hadn't yet met made their way along the table and sat down one after the other. The first was a small, dark-skinned human man; he had not a single hair on his head and wore a cheap shirt and jeans. He didn't look very wealthy at all, and Alucard had no idea who he was or why he was there. But he seemed to know Dirk, who shook his hand as he sat between him and the scribe.

The second was a rather lanky woman with her black hair tied into a ponytail. She had so many earrings in her ears that it looked as though they would soon pull her ears from her head. She sat beside Freja and rested her arms on the table, waiting as the third man sat beside her. He looked as dull as every other human—brown hair, blue eyes, and a face with nothing interesting about it. The last man sat on Dirk's right and was as pale as ice—he was obviously a vampire, but not one Alucard had met before. Alucard made a point of knowing *every* vampire in Dor-Sanguis, and not recognizing him meant he must be from elsewhere.

As boring as all these new people looked, Alucard *was* curious to know who they were and why Dirk had brought them to his meeting. He set his eyes on Freja and asked, "The werewolves: what is happening?"

"Nothing more yet. I assume Ben has informed you?" she asked, glancing at Ben, who nodded. She then looked at Alucard again. "They started congregating in the ruins of Ada's home the night you arrived back from your mission. They've continued to gather; every pack but mine is there—even the smaller, less important packs have joined. There is also a man there we suspect to be a wizard. I gather Ben also told you—"

"Yes," Alucard dismissed and set his sights on Dirk. "The Selarom clan: why would one of them be here in Dor-Sanguis?"

Dirk frowned slightly. "The Selarom clan?"

"Hypothetically," Alucard said.

"They deal in dragon-related issues. Perhaps…they have chosen to concern themselves with the fact that you killed Janus so many years ago?"

"Perhaps. Do they only send one operative at a time?"

"I believe so, yes," Dirk confirmed.

So, there *was* a possibility that this wizard wasn't a rogue and was a member of the Selarom clan. He said to Freja, "Keep watching them." He then looked at Ben. "You said they are planning an attack tonight."

"Yes," Ben said with a nod. "I've prepared both the day and night guards, as mentioned in my correspondence."

"Tell them to stand down. Find the vampires I turned directly; only they will be able to defend against an attack such as this. All of your friends from Eltaria can fight, too."

Ben frowned slightly; clearly, he didn't understand Alucard's reasons.

"The Selarom clan are among the most powerful wizards in the world. They draw their ethos directly from Ephriel. If one is here, and if one is allying with the wolves, we can't treat it lightly. They possess the power of light and will destroy any vampire who cannot walk in the sunlight before they even know what hit them. Do what I said," he instructed, looking back at Ben as the rest of the present people glanced at one another in confliction.

"Why ally with the wolves?" the new vampire called. "Forgive my speaking out, My Lord, but aren't the wolves powerless now that you've killed Ada?"

"Powerless, no. Leaderless? I thought so. Either this wizard is now leading them, or they have a new leader working with this wizard."

The new vampire nodded. "Do you have enough day-walkers to win this fight?"

"I will have," Alucard confirmed. He took his eyes off the vampire and looked at Ben. "After this, go and get Felix's ashes and bring them to me in my study. He's the only vampire trained well enough to take care of fledgling vampires. I'll have to make many new ones if we will be dealing with the Selarom clan. If I kill this one wizard, they will most likely send more, and I have to be prepared."

Ben nodded.

Alucard then set his eyes on the new vampire. "Who are you?" he asked skeptically.

"Remont," he said with a smile. "My friends call me Remy."

"I don't care what your friends call you. In this room, you're my subordinates," he said irritably. "Where are you from?"

Remont frowned slightly "Solitudinem, My Lord."

"And you are here…because?"

"I told you at the party," Dirk announced before Remont could speak. "I formed relations for you with the Solitudinem governments, and Remont is a messenger."

"Right," Alucard mumbled. He'd been away for so long, and he was sure that there was a lot for him to catch up on. He then looked over at the small, dark man. "And you?" he questioned.

He smiled brightly. "Oh, hi," he said. "I'm Dorion. I'm the new prison guard. Dirk put me in charge not too long ago."

As Dorion shared his accolades, Alucard tried to listen, but his attention was stolen by Zalith, who was dragging his foot up the inside of his right leg. He scowled and glanced at the demon, who was staring at him with a suggestive smirk. Alucard rested his chin in his hands to try and hide his pout, and he set his eyes back on Dorion. When Dirk joined in with the conversation, telling everyone how Dorion's last prison functioned, Alucard rolled his eyes and glanced around the table; everyone else was paying attention to Dirk and Dorion.

Alucard didn't care; the prison didn't matter right now because his vampires could feed on the humans in Dargamoor. He set his eyes on the black-haired woman. "You," he called, silencing Dorion and Dirk. "What are you here for?"

She set her dark eyes on him, but she didn't speak a word.

Alucard scowled impatiently—

"She doesn't speak," Dirk announced before Alucard could say anything. "She is Esta from Boszorkány. I also mentioned that I befriended one of the witch covens for you. She is the Boszorkian coven's leader and has been living here in Dor-Sanguis while waiting for a chance to meet you herself."

A witch? Alucard felt undeniably intrigued. He took his eyes off Dirk, moved his hands from his face, and looked at her. "Are you part of a main coven or a smaller one?" he asked in Boszorkian, causing everyone around the table but Esta to frown in confusion.

She smiled and responded in Boszorkian, "The largest in the country."

Dirk scoffed and said to her, "I thought you didn't talk."

The witch ignored him and said to Alucard, "I have many things to discuss with you."

"Later," Alucard said in Deiganish so that everyone could understand.

The vampire leaned back in his seat and caught a glimpse of Zalith's irritated face; he was glowering at Esta. It almost looked as though he was jealous…. *Was* he? The vampire frowned, but as Zalith turned his head to look at him, he set his eyes on Dirk.

"I want you to send me any and all information you have regarding the Selarom clan," he instructed, but as Zalith started dragging his foot up his leg again, he glanced at the demon and frowned. But when Dirk nodded in response, the vampire looked back at Dorion, the new prison guard. "You are familiar with the arrangement; I will be sending a new vampire to collect every Friday," he said, and as Dorion nodded, the vampire went to look at Freja, but scowled and sharply turned his head to glare at Zalith, who was *still* dragging his foot up and down his leg. They stared at one another for a moment, and as the room's silence quickly grew awkward, Alucard set his eyes back on Freja. "Get a few of your wolves to infiltrate whatever congregation is going on in the ruins of Ada's house; I want more information."

Freja nodded.

Zalith kept stroking Alucard's shin with his foot.

Alucard scowled and discreetly kicked the demon's foot away beneath the table. He then set his eyes on Remont. "Find me people to turn—at least ten," he instructed, "and if they can give me more than just their lives, that would be even better."

Remont nodded.

Ignoring Zalith's returning foot against his leg, Alucard set his eyes on the other human sitting between Dirk and the scribe. "What are you here for?" he asked irritably.

The small man looked at Alucard and said, "Pyris. I recently joined the city council, and Dirk is showing me the ropes."

As Pyris went on to explain how he'd met Dirk, Alucard stopped listening, uninterested in what more he had to say. Zalith's constant touching was irritating him more and more until he could no longer ignore it. He sharply turned his head and glared at him. "Stop!" he snapped.

Pyris fell silent and looked around in confusion. Everyone else stared at Alucard, who kept his hostile glare on Zalith, but the demon did nothing but smile at him as if he, too, was waiting for an explanation for his outburst.

Alucard snarled, took his eyes off Zalith, and glared around at everyone. "We are done here," he announced. "If I need to see any of you, I will send someone to find you."

No one questioned the abrupt ending of the meeting. Everyone but he and Zalith stood up and began to make their way towards the castle's exit.

As they left, Alucard glared at Zalith. "Do you find enjoyment in annoying me?" he snarled quietly.

"Yes," Zalith said with a smirk.

Alucard rolled his eyes and stood up. "Whatever," he grumbled. "I have to prepare to wake Felix up," he muttered and left the table.

With a curious smile, Zalith followed beside him, and without another word, Alucard led the way deeper into his castle.

Chapter Thirteen

— ⊰ ✝ ⊱ —

Touch

| **Zalith** |

When they reached Alucard's study, Zalith leaned against one of the desks and watched as the vampire looked through the sheets of paper on his cluttered work surface.

He felt a lot of things right now: guilty about the fact that he'd messed around with Alucard and the sunlight this morning—he had no idea it was hurting him—and he felt like shit about it. He'd also noticed that Alucard wasn't comfortable with him touching him or being affectionate in front of his subordinates, and as much as Zalith didn't want to, he'd stop doing that. The last thing he wanted to do was upset Alucard or make him uncomfortable. Other than that, though, he'd enjoyed getting to watch Alucard order people around again. He loved listening to Alucard's voice, and he adored his accent, too. He'd never pass up a chance to get to listen to him being a boss, either.

As Alucard stacked together some sheet music and put it into one of his desk drawers, Zalith smiled. He observed the pondering expressions on the vampire's adorable face as he cleaned up his desks.

But then the vampire stopped and glared at him. "What?"

Zalith smirk. "What?"

The vampire frowned down at his desk. "We didn't go anywhere for breakfast this morning," he muttered as he took an old quill from the table and chucked it into a nearby trashcan. "I gather you need to eat, so if you want to, I can get someone to go to the city and get whatever you want—unless you would rather we go to the city ourselves."

"Do you have a preference?"

"No," Alucard said with a shrug.

He smiled. "Then we can go to the city ourselves."

But Alucard then frowned in confliction, looked down at the table, and pouted. "I'd rather stay here, actually."

With an amused smile and a slight roll of his eyes, Zalith sighed quietly and said, "Then here we shall stay."

"Think of what you want and I'll send someone to get it after I've woken Felix up."

"Will you be eating with me?" the demon asked.

"Maybe," he muttered, glancing at him. "I'll see how I feel after this," he said as he turned to face the door to his study.

Zalith looked over there too, and watched Ben walk in with a small black urn in his hands.

Ben made his way towards them as Zalith and Alucard eyed him closely. "Here you go," he said, handing the urn to Alucard.

"Go and find Remont; help him find people for me," Alucard then instructed.

Ben nodded, turned around, and left as swiftly as he arrived.

"What do you have to do?" Zalith asked curiously, watching him as he pulled the lid off the urn and placed it on the table.

Alucard slowly tipped the contents of the urn onto the floor; as the black ash began to pile on the ground in front of him, he shrugged and answered, "Simple reawakening ritual. I restore his body with my blood—that's about it," he explained, placing the empty urn on the table next to the lid.

"And what do you need this Felix for?" Zalith asked, watching Alucard pull a small dagger from the bottom drawer of the desk they were standing in front of.

The vampire stretched out his arm so his hand was above the pile of ash, gripped the dagger's sharp edge in his palm, and slowly cut his skin, allowing his blood to drip down onto the ash. "I need more vampires able to walk in the sunlight; in the event that the Selarom clan send more wizards, these new vampires will be useful in the battle they will bring with them. Felix is a brood nurse, a particular type of vampire which specializes in taking care of new vampires; he feeds them, teaches them to hunt and not to kill their victims, etcetera," he explained and placed the knife on the table. He looked down at his palm and watched it heal as the ash below began to sizzle quietly.

With an intrigued look on his face, Zalith nodded. "And vampires turned directly by you gain the ability to walk in the sunlight?"

"Yes," he confirmed.

The sizzling ash started moving around, slithering and writhing like a serpent. It swiftly rose and formed the shape of a man, and Felix's features soon grew. The grey-haired vampire materializd from the bloody ashes, and as his body reformed, he gasped for air as if he'd been starved of it for hours. He sat there on his knees, huddled over in a foetal position with a horrified look on his face. But as he slowly lifted his head and set his eyes on both Alucard and Zalith, he gasped in shock.

Bawling like a child, the naked man abruptly threw himself at Alucard's left leg and wrapped his arms around it. He cried in Dor-Sanguian, so Zalith had no idea what he was saying. He didn't care what he was saying. He *did* care that this man was touching Alucard, who didn't seem at all happy.

Alucard harshly kicked Felix off his leg and scowled down at him in revolt. "Stop crying like a child and get the fuck up," he snarled.

As he was told, Felix stumbled to his feet and stood before his master.

"Go and get some clothes on and then get your ass back here, I have work for you. And be quick; the resistance you currently have against the sunlight will soon wane."

Nodding frantically as tears trickled down his face, Felix scurried out of the room and disappeared, leaving Zalith and Alucard alone.

As he left, Zalith calmed and turned to face Alucard. "What an ugly little man," he mumbled.

Alucard rolled his eyes and turned to face the table. "Ugly is an understatement," he said as he picked up the blade he used to cut his hand. He snatched a glass from the shelf to his right and positioned his wrist over it.

"What are you doing now?" Zalith asked, but this time, in concern.

"They will need my blood to turn people, and I'm not exactly comfortable with a dozen people chewing on my arms."

With a smile, Zalith leaned back against the table and observed as the vampire cut his wrist. "Would you be comfortable with perhaps *one* person in particular… chewing?" he asked, grinning.

The vampire slowly turned his head to glare at him and scowled. Then, without a word, he concentrated on his blood as it slowly filled the glass.

Sure that he might have irritated Alucard with his flirtatious comment, Zalith smiled and sighed quietly. "Does it only require your blood to turn someone into a vampire?" he asked. He already knew that it took both vampire blood *and* venom to turn a human into a vampire, but he just wanted to change the subject.

"Yes," Alucard mumbled. "I told you before that I'm not really a vampire. My blood is what created vampires; I'm simply their creator. I still like to call myself a vampire, though—I feel more like one than I do a demon."

Curious and somewhat eager to listen to Alucard talk more, Zalith smiled. "How is it that you're not really a vampire?"

"Janus made me believe that he turned me into a vampire when all he did was grant me the ability to make a sub-race by removing a curse that had been placed on me when I was born. Lucifer didn't want his son making armies or cults or whatever, so he negated that ability within me. Janus removed that block, and once he was sure I could create the sub-race now called vampires, he took my blood and did with it as he pleased. It didn't take me long to realize he had lied to me—I met a soothsayer a long time ago; he studied my blood after I was cursed with vampirism—apparently, anyway—and told me what I just told you. You know the rest—I killed Janus, blah… blah… whatever."

Zalith smirked deviously as the sweet scent of Alucard's blood became harder to ignore. It might not be the thing he craved most from Alucard, but its scent still aroused him. The demon carefully gripped Alucard's arm as he moved it away from the blood-filled glass, and when the vampire stared at him in confusion, Zalith edged his face closer to the vampire's bleeding wrist, which he pulled closer to his face. He then slowly dragged his tongue over the wound, and as the blood touched his tongue, a shiver of delight electrified through his body. It wasn't *at all* what he had been expecting.

He'd drunk vampire blood before—*and* demon blood—but Alucard's blood tasted nothing like either. It was sweet—*so sweet*—and so unique, unlike anything Zalith had tasted, unlike anything he might have been able to imagine. He didn't have the words to explain it; all he knew was that it made him crave Alucard a whole lot more desperately than he already did, and as he swallowed the blood, he couldn't help but wonder... if Alucard's *blood* tasted this delectable, then his cum probably tasted *exquisite*. And just the thought of it aroused him *intensely*.

The demon lowered Alucard's wrist and pressed him back against the table with a devious gleam in his eyes. As the vampire frowned nervously, Zalith seized his face and kissed his lips. The unexpected aggression only fuelled the intensity, and Alucard's hesitation seemed to melt away.

Their kisses deepened, each moment escalating the desire between them. Zalith's heart raced, and he trembled with anticipation at the thought of Alucard's bare skin against his own. Without breaking the kiss, he pressed his body against the vampire's, a daring move that sent both excitement and angst spiralling through the demon. Encouraged by the lack of resistance, Zalith's primal urges encouraged him to push the boundaries further.

Zalith, hungry for more, trailed hot kisses down Alucard's neck. The vampire tensed but willingly tilted his head, inviting further exploration. Soft kisses peppered Alucard's sensitive skin, the demon's hands gliding down his body to his waist. Sensing Alucard's nervousness, Zalith felt a rush of excitement as the vampire's hand timidly found its way to the back of his head.

As the demon continued his assault on Alucard's neck, the vampire surrendered to the building desire. Alucard's blazer became a casualty of their heated encounter, discarded onto the table with a hungry eagerness. Zalith, unable to contain his fervour, reengaged in a fevered kiss, his right hand venturing under the vampire's shirt. The contact with Alucard's sculpted abs sent shivers down Zalith's spine, the anticipation now reaching an almost unbearable peak.

In response, Alucard reciprocated, his hand tracing over Zalith's shirt, conveying a desire mirroring the demon's own, but he was evidently too nervous, and guided his hand to Zalith's shoulder instead.

Zalith nuzzled into the crook of Alucard's neck, his own breath quickening with the intoxicating mix of desire and excitement. Alucard's quiet sigh of contentment sent a thrill through the demon, a signal that his desires might find the response he craved. Emboldened, he slipped his other hand under the vampire's shirt, his lips claiming Alucard's neck in a fervent exploration.

Gripping Alucard's waist, Zalith pulled him closer; he was sure that the vampire could feel the hard bulge in his trousers. With a tantalizing hope, he waited for Alucard's hand to wander down, anticipating the touch that would push them further towards what Zalith had desired since he first laid eyes on him. Yet, Alucard's hand remained on Zalith's shoulder, a subtle resistance that did little to dampen the demon's longing.

His heart pounded with anticipation, the craving for Alucard consuming him. Moving his hands down Alucard's waist, Zalith's fingers traced a path past the vampire's belt, an invitation for what lay beyond. His senses heightened, Zalith felt the charged air between them, thick with the promise of unrestrained desire. The room seemed to pulse with unspoken tension, the longing for more driving the demon's every move.

Just as Zalith's anticipation reached its peak, Alucard's sudden, nervous murmur shattered the spell. "Stop," he uttered, his hand snatching Zalith's wrist. In that instant, the room echoed with the palpable tension of unfulfilled longing, a delicate balance between restraint and surrender hanging in the air.

Despite his intense desperation for more, Zalith did as Alucard asked. He stopped kissing the vampire's neck and frowned in concern. For a moment, he felt guilt and confliction grip hold of him. While he may feel like he and Alucard had been together for a long time, the reality was that they hadn't been together very long at all. He knew he was very far ahead of where he was meant to be concerning their relationship, and he needed to slow down and remember that he wasn't the only person he had to consider. Alucard was more important than his own needs, and he needed to make sure they both understood where they stood with one another. The last thing he wanted to do was rush into something that the vampire wasn't ready for.

Looking at what he could see of Alucard's nervous face, Zalith frowned in worry. "Does this bother you?" he asked quietly, his wrist still in the vampire's grip.

With a conflicted pout, Alucard seemed to ponder for a few moments. "No," he mumbled, still hiding his face from Zalith.

The demon wasn't convinced. If Alucard wasn't bothered, he wouldn't have just snatched his wrist like that. He knew Alucard was shy, and Zalith felt as though now was a better time than any to ask him how he felt about intimacy and sex. He carefully pulled his wrist from Alucard's grip and placed his hand on the side of the vampire's neck. "Perhaps we should talk," he suggested.

Alucard frowned and slowly lifted his head to look at him. "About what?"

"The touching," he answered.

The vampire looked down, hiding his face again. "What about it?"

Zalith sighed quietly. "I don't want to make you feel uncomfortable at all," he started. "I don't want to make you feel as though you have to rush into anything you might not yet be ready for, and I think it's important for you to know where I currently stand. When it comes to you, I find that I have little to no self-control, and more often than not, I want nothing more than to have sex with you. However, it's very important to me that you're ready, and if you're not, then that's perfectly okay. I just think we need to be on the same page and understand what we both feel. If you wish to take things at a slower pace, I'm more than happy to do so for you," he explained.

Alucard stared down at the floor. He went quiet for a few moments—he was probably thinking about what Zalith had just said. But then he sighed quietly and shrugged. "It doesn't bother me," he said shyly. "I just...I've never... well, before now, I've never been with someone like this—I've never...done this. I have no idea what I'm supposed to do, and I'm afraid that my lack of knowledge will cause me to do something wrong or something to irritate you. I don't want to irritate you," he explained, trying to hide his nervous face from Zalith.

Zalith smiled and rested his forehead on the side of Alucard's head. "You don't have to do anything, Alucard," he replied. "I don't have any expectations. And you haven't done anything wrong, either. I'm simply worried that I might be moving too fast for you and want to know if what I'm doing is okay or not."

The vampire stood there, clearly unsure of what to say. Zalith understood just how nervous he must be feeling, and he wanted to do whatever he could to make the conversation easier for him.

"Have you been and are you comfortable with what's happened so far?" the demon asked.

After a short moment of silence, Alucard glanced at him. "Yes," he answered before looking back down at the floor.

Zalith smiled and continued, "Do you feel comfortable for things to go further, or would you prefer we leave things as they are for now?"

Alucard adorned his adorable look of pondering again. And then, he scowled and pouted. "Yes," he mumbled.

"To leave things as they are?"

"No...to continue."

The demon smiled again. "And would you like me to ask before I try anything new for you?"

Still pouting, he nodded.

"Now, can I have a kiss?" Zalith requested, smirking.

Frowning, the vampire slowly lifted his head and stared at Zalith for a few moments. He looked just as nervous as ever but managed to move his face ever so slightly closer to Zalith's. However, he soon stopped when his nervous expression worsened.

Zalith laughed quietly; this vampire was so cute, especially when he was nervous. The demon smiled and pulled Alucard the rest of the way until his face was in his. Then, he kissed his lips and rested his forehead against Alucard's. "Please don't feel as though your inexperience is a problem—it's not," he said sternly. "We'll take this as slow as you need."

Alucard took his eyes off Zalith and looked down at the floor again. "Okay," he said quietly.

As he then hugged Alucard tightly, Zalith exhaled contently. He was glad they were now on the same page, and although he wasn't sure how slowly or quickly things would progress from here, he was happy knowing that Alucard was comfortable.

Chapter Fourteen

— ≺ ✝ ≻ —

Another Werewolf Conundrum

| Alucard |

Alucard looked through the papers on his desk. Twenty minutes had passed since he sent Felix away; despite the conversation that they just had to ensure that they were both on the same page, the vampire was beginning to feel a little awkward. He was relieved to know that Zalith wasn't expecting him to know what to do and that he was fine with his inexperience, but he still felt nervous.

While they were kissing and touching, he'd become very excited, but his nervousness had quickly consumed him and forced him to push Zalith away. He didn't want that to happen every time they came close, but no matter how hard he tried, he always got so flustered and anxious when Zalith was right in front of him.

He glanced at the demon, who was reading one of the very few Deiganish books that Alucard had in his study. When the demon had kissed his neck, Alucard desperately wanted him to bite him, but he hadn't, and even now, he was feeling agitated by that fact. But he tried not to let it get to him. There were more important things going on right now.

With a quiet sigh, he finished tidying the papers in front of him and leaned back against the desk. He set his eyes on Zalith, who lowered his book and smiled at him, but before either of them could say a word, Felix scurried back into the room fully clothed.

Alucard shifted his attention to the grey-haired man and took the glass of his blood from the table. He made his way to Felix and instructed him, "Go and wait for Ben and Remont; they will come to you with the people you need to turn."

As Alucard handed him the glass, Felix nodded. "You want…me to care for them?"

"Why else would I wake you up? On your way back, tell one of the butlers to come here."

Without a word, Felix turned around and left the room.

Alucard then sighed tiredly and glanced at Zalith. "We can go somewhere else once we send the butler to get what you want to eat."

Zalith smiled as he moved closer to Alucard. When he reached him, he placed his hands on the vampire's waist and pulled him into a light embrace.

While he stood there, Alucard let himself relax and rested his head on the demon's shoulder. Neither of them said anything for a short while, and as Alucard sunk into the demon's warm embrace, he turned his head so that he could bury his face in Zalith's blazer. He quietly inhaled the demon's alluring scent of bergamot, sandalwood, and white sage; it made him smile contently, and as he moved his hand over Zalith's other shoulder, the demon nuzzled the side of Alucard's face.

But when one of his butlers knocked on the door and entered the room, Alucard sighed irritably and took his head off Zalith's shoulder. He looked over at the butler, who nervously waited for his orders with a pen and notepad in his trembling hands.

Alucard stepped back and looked at Zalith. "You can tell the butler what you want for lunch; I have to go and get something," he muttered.

Then, as Zalith nodded and let go of him, Alucard disappeared and reappeared on the tallest floor of his study. He didn't need to get anything at all, he just needed a moment to himself. Although he was content with everything Zalith had asked and discussed with him, he couldn't help but feel worried. He wasn't sure what to expect, he didn't know what to do, and as much as he tried to calm down, he couldn't seem to ignore the constant paranoia that he might do something that irritated Zalith.

He stood in front of the desk beside a bookshelf, staring down at its cluttered surface as he listened to Zalith's mumbled voice coming from the ground floor. He couldn't let his anxiety keep him from enjoying his time with Zalith; as overwhelming as it might be, he'd do his best to ignore it now that he knew Zalith wasn't expecting him to know what to do when they became intimate.

With a quiet sigh, he made his way to the edge of the floor and stared down at Zalith and the butler, who was scribbling the demon's requests into his notepad.

The vampire disappeared and reappeared beside Zalith, startling the butler. "Bring it to the lounge," he instructed.

Nodding, the butler closed his notepad and hurried out of the room to fetch what he had been told.

Zalith smirked as he turned to face him. "What did you have to get?"

"Something," he said with a pout, looking away.

The demon smiled amusedly and glanced around the study. "Well, what do you plan to do after we eat?"

Alucard shrugged and led the way over to the door. "I don't know," he mumbled as he looked at Zalith, who followed beside him. "I'm not going to lie and say I'm not concerned about the wizard. I trust my subordinates' intel, but I'd rather head there and see for myself."

"You're going out there alone?" Zalith asked worriedly.

"To observe," he assured him, but he was convinced that Zalith was going to ask to accompany him. While he enjoyed the demon's company—and as much as he liked working with him—he felt he'd rather deal with this alone. He'd killed Ada, and he wanted to make sure that he *personally* ended any wolf's attempt at reviving that insane woman's mission.

Zalith frowned in concern. "Do you want me to come with you?"

A conflicted expression possessed Alucard's pale face. He'd already decided he wanted to do this alone, but he didn't want to upset Zalith by telling him he couldn't come. "I want to do this alone," he said quietly.

The demon looked away from him as they headed up a staircase. He didn't say anything to Alucard, and the longer the silence dragged on, the more anxious Alucard began to feel. Had he upset Zalith? He had, hadn't he? He knew that Zalith just wanted to spend time with him... but the werewolf situation was *his* business. He didn't want to get Zalith all wrapped up in that, especially after what happened last year with Damien and Ada. He wanted to deal with it quietly, quickly, and alone.

When they reached the top of the stairs, they walked through a deserted, sunlit hallway. He glanced at Zalith again, and when he saw a look of pondering on the demon's face, the vampire frowned. What was he thinking about? Was he mad? Was he considering how angry he was and how he was going to express it? Alucard's anxiety skyrocketed, and as they continued forward, he tried to keep a vacant stare.

"Alucard," Zalith suddenly said.

As his angst spiked and sent a wave of dread through his body, Alucard turned his head and gawped at him.

"Have we spent too much time together?" the demon asked in concern. "Are you trying to tell me you need some time alone... away from me?"

"No," he instantly answered.

"Then why are you going to willfully walk into a trap by yourself?"

Alucard stopped walking and glared at him. "What?"

With an aggravated scowl etched on his face, Zalith turned to face him. "You've already worked out that this gathering of wolves isn't a coincidence—it's a little *too* convenient, isn't it? I *know* how smart you are, and I've known you long enough to know how you prefer to approach this sort of thing. You've obviously worked out that this is a trap, and you're going to waltz right into it, aren't you?"

Alucard frowned irritably and scoffed as he continued walking down the hallway. "Don't antagonize me," he warned.

"Have you forgotten what happened the last time you walked into a trap?" Zalith asked, following him down the hall and ignoring his warning. "When Ada drugged you, and—"

"We're not talking about that," Alucard grumbled as an embarrassed pout struck his face.

Zalith lightly grabbed his arm before he could reach for the door and turned him to face him. "Wasn't it just yesterday that you were telling me you're *not* immortal, Alucard?" he questioned, a stern but worried tone in his voice. "You know that their wizard ally is dangerous, and yet you still want to walk into their trap alone. Do you have any idea how reckless that is? You could be hurt—or worse—and I'm not going to let that happen. If you want to investigate these wolves yourself, I'm coming with you whether you invite me or not," he stated.

As his pout contorted into a vexed glower, Alucard yanked his arm from Zalith's grip and snarled at him. "Do you think I'm so stupid that I'd risk my life?" he snapped. Did Zalith *really* think that he was that brainless? Did he think he was incompetent? He wasn't wrong about it being a reckless move, but it wasn't something Alucard felt he couldn't handle. He had purposely walked into traps so many times before, and he was still standing, still alive. Why would this time be any different?

Zalith sighed quietly and adorned a concerned frown as he lowered his hand. "I do *not* think you're stupid, Alucard," he said sternly. "I care about you so much, and even if you're the smartest person in the world, things can still happen—things you aren't prepared for. I want to come with you so that I can be there to help if anything bad *does* happen. I know you're capable of handling it yourself, but that doesn't keep me from worrying."

Alucard looked down at his hand as he gripped the door handle. He felt as if he may have overreacted. Zalith just cared about him and didn't want him to get hurt—he knew that... and he hadn't meant to snap at him. A guilty, sullen expression stole his scowl, and as he glanced at Zalith, he pushed the door open. "I didn't mean to snap," he muttered, stepping into the room as Zalith followed. "I'm not... used to somebody caring," he admitted.

Following him into the lounge, Zalith gently placed his hand on Alucard's arm, and as the vampire turned to face him, he smiled and said, "It's okay. I'm sorry if it sounded like I was demeaning you—that wasn't my intention at all. I just... you mean so much to me."

With a subtle smile of understanding, Alucard gently shut the door. Zalith trailed behind him as he walked towards the oak table positioned beneath one of the towering arched windows. The walls, adorned in black with opulent gold trim, shimmered in the influx of light cascading through the glass. A plush white rug, reminiscent of the one in his own manor, graced the floor, while an expansive fireplace adorned the back wall.

Alucard pulled one of the chairs out from under the oak table. "We can eat here, and then we can... go and find the wolves," he said as he sat down and rested his arms in front of him.

Zalith smiled in response as he sat across from him.

"What do you want to do about tonight, then?" the vampire asked. "I have no idea how long we'll be out there with the wolves, and I know phasing takes a considerable amount of ethos," he said, watching as a smirk slowly crept across the demon's face. Alucard rolled his eyes and glared out of the window. "You can stay if you want… and go home in the morning to get whatever you'll need for the next few days. I'll need to have people prepare my ship anyway, and I'm sure you won't want to stick around for something so boring. I will also have someone purchase our tickets for the opera."

Smiling, Zalith also rested his arms on the table and gazed at Alucard. "I'd like to spend the night with you, yes," he confirmed. "And that also sounds like a reasonable plan. Do tell me, though… your ship: will we be travelling to Helvetes aboard the same ship you used to transport the vampires?"

"No," Alucard answered, glancing at him. "I have *that* ship—which is used for things such as transportation and is also used to send vampires to other countries whenever they are needed. I have another ship docked behind the castle for matters of a more personal nature. She is… expensive, so I refrain from using that ship unless need be. We will be at sea for a few days—overnight—and this ship is meant for such journeys," he explained.

Zalith's face gleamed with curiosity. "And do I have to wait until the day of our journey to see this other ship of yours?"

"Yes," he said, looking back out the window. "I haven't sailed it for a while, so it might not look its very best."

"Well, either way, I look forward to seeing this other ship of yours and to our journey together," the demon said.

"Make sure you bring clothes suitable for a lot of snow. The last I heard, the snow falls so heavily there that it's sometimes impossible to see where you are going."

"I'll keep that in mind."

"And wear something made of gold," he added. "The Dragon Gods can't sense you if you wear gold."

"Interesting… I'll remember that. Is there anything else I should know?"

Alucard thought to himself for a few moments but there wasn't anything he felt he hadn't already addressed. "No," he answered, and as the sound of approaching footsteps came from outside the door, he turned his attention to it. "*Vino*," he called when a quiet knock disturbed the quiet.

The door opened, and the butler Alucard sent to get Zalith's lunch walked in and made his way over to the table with two covered plates in his hands. He placed one in front of Zalith and the other in front of Alucard; he removed the lids to reveal the food beneath them and then swiftly left the room.

Alucard stared down at what had been presented to him; he didn't recognize any of the food on his plate *at all*. It looked like some kind of red meat—perhaps similar to the steak he had last night—and several different vegetables. He frowned and glanced at Zalith, who had the same thing on his plate. The vampire felt no need to ask what it was, though; he trusted Zalith's food knowledge, especially since he'd enjoyed dinner yesterday. So, as Zalith picked up his knife and fork, so did Alucard.

"Do you have a specific plan in mind for this investigation?" Zalith asked, looking over at him as he ate.

Once he finished the green vegetable he'd chosen to try first, Alucard glanced at him. "Nothing that requires revision," he answered. "We go to where they are, see what they're doing, and kill them if I feel like it," he said with a shrug and shifted his interest back to his food.

Nodding as he ate, Zalith took his eyes off the vampire. "Do you know how many wolves there might be?"

"Most of the larger packs are at least fifty-strong," he answered. "There are three packs, excluding Freja's. So, at least a hundred and fifty of them."

With a concerned look on his face, Zalith stopped cutting his food, rested his arms on the table, and looked at him. "That's a lot of werewolves, Alucard, not forgetting their ally."

"I know," he mumbled, glancing at him. "We'll be fine. We were fine every other time we fought werewolves, no?"

The demon smiled slightly. "Indeed, we were," he concurred.

"We'll go after we've eaten," he said and continued enjoying his food.

With a content nod, Zalith went back to his food, too.

Chapter Fifteen

— ⸢ ✝ ⸥ —

Silver Bite

| **Alucard** |

A s the afternoon crept into dusk, Alucard and Zalith made their way to the castle's main hall, where they prepared to leave and begin their investigation of the congregating werewolves and their apparent wizard ally.

The vampire pulled on his blazer and made sure that both of his colts were firmly within the holsters inside. Sabazios watched him from beside the door as he attached his rapier to his side; the hound then whined quietly, waiting to be told whether he could accompany them on their journey or not.

Alucard sighed and walked over to the hellhound as Zalith followed. He placed his hand on the hound's head and said, "You should stay here in case wolves attack—as Freja said."

"Do we have a plan?" Zalith asked, handing Alucard his cape.

Turning to face him, Alucard took his cape from the demon and then hung it up on the coat rack. "I don't wear it when I know it might get damaged."

Zalith smiled. "Understandable."

"And we can discuss a plan as we walk," he said as he led the way towards the castle door. When they stepped into the courtyard, Alucard glanced at the demon and asked him, "Have you ever fought a wizard before?"

"I've fought many. They sided with the humans during the war in Eltaria. But there are a lot of things here that are different to those back in my world, so I suspect the wizards are no exception."

Alucard stared ahead as they walked down the grass hill and towards the path which lay at its foot. "Their ethos comes from Ephriel—the Angel God—so that makes them susceptible to demon ethos. If you have a true form, using that against him would be the best option. If you only possess a demon form, then any sort of demon ethos will counter him. The Selarom clan specialize in light ethos; neither of us is vulnerable to light, so we'll be fine," he added, looking over at him as they followed the path which used to take them to Alucard's manor.

"Do *you* have a true form," Zalith asked with a smile, gazing at him.

With a slight shrug, Alucard looked away and mumbled, "I can become many things depending on the situation. Fox, owl, pure ethos. My *true* form is what I look like without this manifested body," he explained, gesturing to himself with his hands. "Beneath this, I am... I look much different. You saw some of it while you were taking care of me."

Zalith smirked. "And will I get to see this true form of yours in its entirety?"

"No."

The demon laughed slightly. "I'll show you mine if you show me yours," he said suggestively, his smirk growing more flirtatious by the second.

Alucard frowned at him from the corner of his eye; his confliction fought with his curiosity. Did he want to see Zalith's demon form? Yes, he did. He couldn't deny that he felt curious, not only about what Zalith truly looked like but about what his body looked like under that shirt. But he didn't want to share *his*. He wasn't ready to show Zalith what was hidden beneath his clothes, beneath his *skin*. So he swiftly dismissed any consideration of Zalith's suggestion and glared ahead as he led the way towards the distant forest.

"I don't know how many wolves will be there," he said, changing the subject. "But we've dealt with werewolves together before, so we know what to do. Most Selarom wizards have to remain still to charge attacks, so if we do decide to kill them all, keep moving," he advised, glancing at Zalith. "Light ethos travels in a straight line, so you should make sure to make yourself hard to hit."

Zalith nodded as he stared ahead. "Noted."

"As for the plan, we observe before we attack. I want to see what these wolves are doing and find out why a wizard is with them. Freja and Ben have told me they were planning to attack, so I want to find out if that is true. Either way, tonight ends with them understanding that Ada is dead and so is any hope of them reviving her insane ideas. They may want to start a war, but I want to end it here and now. I have not the strength to deal with werewolves any longer," he muttered.

Zalith then frowned in concern. "Are you okay?" he asked, obviously noticing the tire in his voice.

The vampire looked at him as they entered the forest. "I'm fine," he confirmed as sternly as he could. But as he glared ahead, he sighed quietly to himself. "Ada made my life difficult for four hundred years and I just want it to be over," he admitted. His reluctance to keep his feelings to himself had withered—in fact, he found himself less hesitant to tell Zalith the truth now that they were closer. He thought Zalith deserved to know how he felt and he'd do his best to tell the demon when necessary. After all, Zalith hadn't kept his feelings from him, so he ought to give him the same courtesy.

"Well, Ada's dead, and all we need to do now is make sure the rest of werewolf-kind know that her death ended any chance they may have felt they had at overthrowing you," Zalith said with a smile. "I believe tonight will be the night you get that point across."

Alucard nodded slightly. "I hope so."

"Now, tell me about what you did in Nefastus," Zalith requested, shifting the subject. "You told me that the Imperito are after you because you may have been the cause of many explosions," he said, smirking.

With an amused smile, and glad of the beginning of a new conversation, Alucard started, "Just over a hundred years ago, I was in Nefastus with Attila. A client hired several of my vampires to help him clear up gang drama, but my vampires never came home. So, we went to investigate. The client was a member of the Imperito; they had this no-witnesses policy, so they killed my vampires after they'd done what they had hired them for. You don't just kill my vampires, so I set up explosives in every one of their compounds and watched from the Citadel Tower as they all blew up at the same time. They lost everything they had spent two decades building. I then went to see their leader and made sure he knew it was I who had done it. I've never seen a man cry so much," he said, smirking. "Perhaps… it was a little too much, though, now that I think about it. Back then, I was a little less mature—I liked to cause trouble since I didn't really have much else to do with my time. They deserved it, though."

Zalith laughed and slowly linked his arm with Alucard's. "I see you had very different ways of doing things a hundred years ago. Sometimes, though, a louder approach is the better option."

Alucard frowned nervously when Zalith held his arm and looked away to hide his anxious expression. "Sometimes," he agreed. But then his eyes fixed on something in the darkness. He stopped walking, as did Zalith; he stared into the trees, keeping his eyes focused on what he could now see was the dead body of a werewolf. From where he was standing, it looked as though it had been there for quite some time, but its head was still attached. Why hadn't it been possessed? Why hadn't it become a hellhound?

Also noticing the corpse, Zalith frowned and looked at Alucard.

Wordlessly, Alucard led the way over to the wolf and pulled his arm free of Zalith's once they reached the corpse. The wolf's dirty-gold coat was stained red with its own blood and most of its upper body was twisted, mangled, and enthralled in what looked to be a bear trap—but the teeth of the trap were silver.

"This was left here specifically to trap a werewolf," the vampire said with a frown.

"Perhaps the packs are still fighting amongst one another. Or perhaps… it was left from the times they were enemies," Zalith suggested.

Alucard shook his head. "I've walked through these forests every night continuously for years and I've never seen these traps. This corpse is at least two days old, too. No one has come to see if they have trapped anything, so I can assume that these traps were laid out to keep threats away."

Zalith frowned warily. "To keep *you* away."

"And my allies," Alucard confirmed. "This was one of Tobias' wolves," he said, noticing not only the small tear in the wolf's right ear but its particular coat colour, too. However, he didn't want to think about Tobias—not now. He looked away from the wolf, scoured the surrounding ground with his eyes, and scowled skeptically. "There could be more; we should be careful."

The demon nodded slightly while he glanced at the ground around them. "This must also mean that we're close to where they're gathering."

"*Da.* Ada's old house isn't far from here. We should scour the area alone; you can investigate the north and east of the area, and I the south and west. We need to find out what they're doing and what the wizard's intentions are."

A reluctant look appeared on Zalith's face. "And will we be meeting back up soon?"

Alucard nodded. "Then, we'll decide what to do with them."

Zalith sighed quietly but nodded in agreement. "Okay—be careful," he warned with worry in his voice.

"I will," he said.

As Zalith disappeared into the murky woods, Alucard exhaled deeply and looked down at the dead werewolf. Why hadn't anyone come for him? Why hadn't Freja mentioned this wolf was missing? She *had* said she sent some of *her* Betas out to watch the congregating wolves, but this was one of Tobias' Betas—it was Farley, the same Beta Alucard had gone out of his way to rescue. Now, there he lay, dead on the ground, his life just as pointlessly ended as his Alpha's.

Alucard stood there, staring at the body. His hands started to shake, and both dread and guilt consumed him, gnawing at him with its sharp, jagged teeth, inflicting him with its dismay-inducing venom. Until now, he'd done his best to ignore what happened before Ada's death; he tried to forget what he did, he tried to forget the people he had killed and the people who died because of him. But seeing someone who had been close to Tobias forced him to sink into his postponed guilt—and reality slapped him *hard*. Tobias was dead, and he'd never see him again; Tobias' friends were also still suffering because he hadn't made sure to tie up every loose end he had left after disappearing. He was sure that Farley wasn't the first to die because of his incompetence, and he might not be the last if he failed to end the werewolf dispute tonight.

Now was far from the best time, but he had to let himself grieve, even if it was just the slightest bit, even if it was just for a few seconds. He'd held onto it for so long; he felt as if he couldn't continue ignoring it. If anything, he'd use it to fuel the raging fire that was his anger. Whatever the werewolves were up to, he'd be sure to end it once and for all. It wouldn't bring Tobias back—it wouldn't bring anyone back—but it *would* give

Alucard the relief he needed, the relief of knowing that his vampires would no longer have to watch their backs for traitorous, foul beasts in the place that was supposed to be their sanctuary.

He took his eyes off Farley and morphed into his melanistic fox form. He scurried along the leaf-covered ground, keeping his eyes pierced for traps as he moved deeper into the forest. He wouldn't fall prey to silver teeth.

After a while, Alucard found the clearing where Ada's burned husk of a house stood. The moonlit opening was full of werewolves, some in their human forms, and others in their wolf forms. Alucard used the advantages of his small fox body to prowl closer, and when he found and lay between two small rose bushes, he scanned the area with his hell-fiery eyes. Wolves…wolves…more wolves…but no sign of the white-robed wizard Freja and Ben had mentioned. Where was he?

With a skeptical frown, he examined each wolf, man, and woman he could see from his hiding place. He didn't recognize any of them; some were Deiganish, and others were speaking in Dor-Sanguian about how cold the night was, how they wished they were in some tavern, or what they had for breakfast—nothing useful. They didn't seem to be gathering for an attack. Had Ben and Freja misunderstood their gathering? Alucard didn't know Freja well enough to say, but Ben? Ben wasn't stupid—he wouldn't mistake a social gathering for a call to arms, would he?

Alucard took his eyes off the crowd, wriggled his way back out from under the bush, and silently scurried a small distance forward before settling beside a tree. From where he now lay, he could see more of the opening and a small group inside the ruins of Ada's house. Three wolves were lying at the feet of a white-robed man, who was sitting on a pile of rubble. Several people also lingered against the two standing walls behind him and to his left, keeping watch.

Obviously, the white-robed man was the wizard, but why was he sitting among wolves? Why were the wolves standing around him as if he was their Alpha? Alucard frowned, eying each of the wolves closely. The four grey beasts at his feet were Betas, and the men standing around him might also be Betas. With a confused scowl, Alucard eyed each and every wolf he could currently see in the opening, but there were no Alphas at all. Why?

Setting his eyes back on the wizard, Alucard thought to himself for a few moments. Zalith had probably also located the wizard and had also most likely peered into the minds of several wolves already to find the answers he needed. Alucard sometimes wished he could read minds as easily as Zalith could, but he had to make do with what methods he did have.

He frowned and eyed the wizard; the man looked no older than forty, but his aura told Alucard that he'd been alive for over a hundred years. If they were going to kill this wizard, it wasn't going to be as simple as he might like; the wizard wasn't powerful, but Alucard just wanted to avoid using his true form. However, it was beginning to look as though he might have to use it after all.

Alucard shuffled back and turned around; he might as well find Zalith now. There was no point in him hanging around—he wasn't going to get any answers doing that. However, as he started to scurry forward, the ever-so-quiet rustle of the bushes unsettled him. He stopped moving and scanned the darkness with his eyes, but he couldn't locate the ominous aura he was sensing around him. It had come so suddenly—that minacious chill. He had no idea what to make of it—it felt as though a thousand eyes were on him... as though the gripping, snatching claws of a hundred beasts were reaching to grab his small, furred body. What made it even stranger was the fact that, for a moment, it felt as though that feeling came from inside himself rather than the darkness around him.

He had to find Zalith.

The vampire cautiously continued forward, searching for Zalith's aura. But the twigs snapped behind him, and as he looked over his shoulder, the eager eyes of a prowling werewolf met his. The beast immediately sprung at Alucard before he had a chance to figure out whether to morph out of his fox form and attack or not. There was only one option. He darted forward like a bat out of hell, racing away from the beast as it gave chase, salivating and panting.

As he ran, Alucard considered morphing back to his usual self to fight the beast, but if he did that and killed it, the gathering of wolves would smell its blood and come running. He couldn't run forever, either. The beast had his scent and it would chase him until either he or it could no longer breathe.

Alucard continued sprinting through the forest, avoiding every shimmering silver bear trap he spotted, hoping that the werewolf would be careless enough to step into one, but it seemed to know where they had all been placed. He could feel himself weakening; he'd need to stop soon or he was sure he'd stumble. But then he scowled—*why* was he running? It was just a werewolf. He was going to kill every single one of them anyway, so why postpone its inevitable death? The gathering of wolves wouldn't be able to smell its blood if he didn't spill any—he could simply break its neck... but then it would turn into a hellhound, and he'd rather not deal with that on top of everything else. The fact that he couldn't keep running forever still remained, though.

With a roll of his eyes, he came to his decision. After a few more seconds of running from his pursuer, he leapt forward, morphed out of his fox form, and swiftly swung around and grabbed the wolf as it pounced after him. The beast obviously had no idea who it was chasing—the look of utter horror and confusion smothering its face made that evident. Alucard snatched the beast's neck, but it didn't let its shock become its downfall. The beast swung both its back legs forward and kicked the vampire so harshly that he stumbled back, and the wolf escaped his grip.

The werewolf landed on its back legs, and without taking a moment to recompose itself, it flung forward. Alucard snatched the wolf's arms, but it forced him to the ground with its sheer weight. It almost amused Alucard that the beast was trying so hard, and his laugh only angered the wolf more. It snapped its jaws as the vampire gripped its neck, and it dug its claws into Alucard's shoulders as he snarled angrily. The vampire glanced to his left, a flicker of silver in the moonlight catching his attention, and as he set his eyes on the conveniently placed beartrap, a look of relief found its way to his face. He wouldn't have to put much effort into killing this werewolf.

With a frustrated growl, Alucard forced the beast aside; it struggled, making Alucard's task a whole lot more complicated than it had to be, but once the vampire forced the side of its head down onto the trap's trigger, the wolf yelped and went silent as the trap's teeth clamped shut around its head. But Alucard failed to move his arm in time, and he yelled painfully as the spikes impaled his flesh. He gritted his teeth and gripped his right forearm as it bled profusely, trapped between the wolf's head and silver jaw. He tried to pull the trap apart, but it was silver—even *he* couldn't do anything against that.

It wouldn't take long for the other werewolves to smell the blood of their fallen packmate, and they'd most likely come to investigate. If they found Alucard like this, he wouldn't be able to escape or defend himself. He wasn't going to lay there and wait to be found, but the only way out was waiting and hoping that Zalith would find him first… or tear off his arm like some desperate animal. He shuddered at the thought of severing a limb, but he might not have a choice.

Chapter Sixteen

— ⟨ ✝ ⟩ —

Wizard's Light

| **Zalith** |

From the tree branch he was perched on, Zalith watched the gathering of wolves. He observed each of them carefully, concentrating; it wasn't as easy to look into people's minds from so far away, but he managed. The fact that they were unaware of his presence made it a whole lot easier. If they knew that their thoughts were being listened to, he'd have to physically touch their faces just to stand a chance at getting in.

While he worked, he let his own mind wander a little. As well as feeling concerned about this wizard, he was also worried he might be annoying Alucard with his insistence to follow him everywhere. He wasn't trying to be clingy; he just wanted to protect him and make sure that he was safe. But he feared that if he kept insisting—if he kept spending so much time with Alucard—the vampire might grow tired of him.

He didn't want to think about it. If Alucard needed space, surely he would tell him, right?

Now wasn't the time to be questioning that, though. Even in Eltaria, wizards were formidable beings, and the idea of one being among the crowd of wolves unsettled him, especially because he was worried about Alucard.

The eerie silence of the forest shattered abruptly as a metallic snap echoed through the trees. Flocks of birds scattered frantically from their perches, creating a chaotic flurry of feathers in the air. A chilling yelp, saturated with agony, pierced through the once-tense quiet, and Zalith's mind raced, initially entertaining the notion of a werewolf stumbling into one of the traps he and Alucard had come across. However, any semblance of morbid curiosity vanished when a light breeze wafted the unmistakable scent of Alucard's blood in the demon's direction. Fear seized him in a vice-like grip, and it made each breath feel constricted and suffocating.

As a group of wolves raced into the woods, Zalith moved just as swiftly. He summoned his demon form, adorning his wings and horns, and ascended into the sky.

The demon hurried across the murk in the blink of an eye and headed down into the forest, following the scent of Alucard's blood. When he reached the location where the smell was its strongest, he landed on a tree branch and let his wings and horns crumble to dust.

His eyes frantically searched the ground, and the moment he saw Alucard, his racing heart ached with dismay. Caught in a silver trap was not only a grey-furred werewolf but a small, melanistic fox.

Alucard.

The fox lay there, his front right leg impaled by one of the trap's teeth, his blood oozing from the wound. Alucard was alive—Zalith could sense his demon ethos—but he was clearly playing possum to avoid the jaws of the incoming werewolves. Zalith wanted to help him, but there were a dozen wolves just a few meters away from him, and he felt as though killing them might not be the best idea just yet. Alucard knew what he was doing. He'd appear dead to anyone else; Zalith only knew he was alive because he knew what to search for concerning his life force. No werewolf could sniff it out.

Zalith waited, watching unseen from above as the wolves investigated their dead comrade and the fox. He listened to their muttered talk, and they all assumed that their packmate had stupidly chased a fox out of hunger and hadn't been paying attention. They didn't seem at all bothered that one of their own had died, and soon left both the wolf and the fox and began heading back to the clearing.

Once they were gone, Zalith jumped from his perch, landed on the ground, and rushed to where Alucard lay. "Alucard?" he quietly asked as he crouched beside the trap, trying to work out how to free Alucard from it without making his injury worse.

Alucard didn't respond, so he assumed the vampire was unconscious. He knew that Alucard was a Lucidian demon, and Lucidian demons were susceptible to silver, so he needed to get him out of the trap as quickly as possible. He gripped each side of the trap and carefully pulled it apart, freeing the fox's arm, and then he scooped him up in his arms and started carrying him away.

The demon glanced down at the fox, unsure of what he should do. Alucard's wound hadn't healed, he was still unconscious, and he wasn't sure of the extent of damage that silver did to him. Would he wake up soon? Was his wound going to start healing? Zalith frowned in worry—

Something snapped around his ankle. He deadpanned as he stopped walking and slowly looked down at the ground to see a beartrap clamped around his foot. How could he have been such an idiot? Holding the fox in his right arm, he kneeled, tore the trap from his leg with little effort, and then continued walking deeper into the woods while *his* wound healed.

He kept heading away from the place the werewolves were gathering, focusing on getting Alucard to safety, but when the fox started shuffling around in his arms, he looked down at Alucard and smiled in relief.

When Zalith stopped walking, Alucard pounced out of his arms, and once he landed on the ground, he morphed back to his usual self. The vampire gripped his wounded arm as he turned to face Zalith, who tried to eye the wound to see just how bad it was now that he was no longer a small fox, but Alucard did well hiding it.

"I was chased," Alucard said before Zalith could ask him what happened. "Some wolf. I didn't see the trap, I..." but he gave up, pouted, and looked down at the ground. "Thank you for helping me," he muttered.

Still smiling, Zalith moved closer to him. "Weren't you the one who told *me* to watch out for the traps?"

"I wasn't paying attention," he grumbled. "I thought... I heard something... it doesn't matter. I saw the wizard."

"Me too."

"I gather you got answers from the wolves' minds?"

Zalith nodded as he carefully took hold of Alucard's injured arm and examined it. "The wolves still want to start a war, and before she died, Ada contacted the wizard sitting in that clearing. He came a little too late but decided to remain anyway. He plans to assist the wolves in eradicating vampires from Dor-Sanguis. The wolves want to avenge Ada, but I feel as though the wizard's agenda is different. He looks at the wolves as if they're pests; I suspect he's using them," he said and let go of Alucard's arm as his wound finally started healing—slowly, but surely. "Are you going to tell me why these Selarom wizards might be looking to harm you?" he asked with a concerned frown.

"There could be many reasons," Alucard said with a shrug as he leaned his back against one of the trees. "Ephriel and Damien are enemies, so Ephriel could have asked her wizards to come after me in an attempt to hurt Damien—" he paused and laughed slightly, "—if that is the case, then they are morons. Damien doesn't care about me; killing me would only amuse him," he said, glancing at Zalith, who wasn't the least bit amused. "Maybe Ada made a deal with them and they are honouring it, even after her death. Or maybe that's a rogue wizard who got tired of having nothing to do and decided to intervene here. I don't know. It doesn't matter. All that does matter is the fact that there is a wizard here helping the wolves, and we need to kill him along with them," he muttered as he started leading the way back towards the clearing.

"Would you like me to find out whether the wizard is a rogue or not?" Zalith asked as he followed him.

Alucard glanced at him. "Yes. I want to know if killing him will bring more wizards. We will attack together and kill as many of the wolves as we can until the wizard becomes too large of a threat for us to ignore. We should take out the Betas first and then

I can distract the wizard while you find out if he's alone. Werewolves are cowards without their leaders, so they will most likely flee after we kill a few dozen of them."

Zalith firmly replied, "Understood."

Then, as they got closer to the opening, they glanced at one another and nodded. It was time to get this over with.

Without a moment's hesitation, they both emerged into the clearing and began their attack. Zalith moved to the right and Alucard to the left, simultaneously targeting a small gathering of wolves close by. When Zalith summoned his fire ethos, he watched Alucard do the same. The wolf groups burst into red and white flames, and as they yelped in agony, the rest of the wolves sprang into action.

As his white flames engulfed the wolves and burned away their life force, Zalith turned his attention to those who were now running towards him. He reached out and grabbed the throat of the first wolf; he tore the beast's throat out and set his eyes on the three wolves who followed it. He swiftly held out his right hand and used his telekinesis, forcing two of the wolves to stumble and burst into a red, bloody mess as the third jumped at him. The demon moved out of the wolf's path, and as it landed back down on the ground, he snatched the back of its neck and tore its head from its body before it had a chance to try and defend itself.

Zalith took a moment to glance at Alucard. The vampire hurried forward and crashed his fist into the face of the first wolf to come at him after the wolves he'd set aflame turned to ash; the force of his hit caused the beast's head to explode, and as its blood splattered everywhere, the vampire set his sights on his next target. Zalith watched while he tore one more wolf apart and then snatched another beast's throat, ripped its head from its body, and swung around to catch the jaws of the wolf who had tried to attack him from behind. The vampire tore the creature's body horizontally in half and threw its mangled corpse at the wolf pouncing towards him. As the corpse collided with the animal, it stumbled to the ground, and before it could get up, the vampire mercilessly slammed his foot down on its head, executing it. The vampire's relentlessness made Zalith smirk.

The demon took his eyes off Alucard and tore the head off the wolf he'd just grabbed. Then, while the wolves started to panic, he set his eyes on the white-robed wizard, who had stepped out into the open to prepare for battle. He could sense the wizard's ethos…and it made Zalith feel cautious. Angel ethos was a demon's greatest weakness— any kind of hit from that wizard could kill him, so he had to be careful. He wasn't worried, though; he could handle himself. He was more concerned about Alucard.

But he couldn't get distracted. His sights located Alucard again, who effortlessly slew each wolf in his path. Then, the demon shifted his attention back to the wolves running at him and set them all aflame. As his white fire enthralled all four of them, he hurried over to two more incoming wolves. However, he heard the wizard charging up his attack, so he did his best to move unpredictably.

When Zalith tore the head off one wolf, he abruptly moved towards the next and slew it just as effectively. He set his eyes back on the wizard, who focused his sights on Alucard; panic consumed Zalith for half a moment, but he was sure that Alucard knew what he was doing. He couldn't help but keep checking on him, though.

When he got the chance, Zalith looked over at Alucard again while tearing the head off another wolf. He watched as the vampire broke the neck of a wolf with his left hand and simultaneously pulled a colt from his blazer with his right, which he pointed at an incoming line of wolves. Zalith had to fight the urge to run to Alucard's aid, but when the vampire fired a bullet, it exploded through the head of one wolf, two wolves, and embedded itself in the head of a third. Alucard dropped the dead wolf from his left hand and equipped his other colt. The bullet inside the head of the first wolf exploded, sending a rain of blood into the air, but before Alucard focused on his next targets, Zalith watched the vampire's sights shift in the direction of the wizard.

Zalith dropped the wolf he'd just killed and sharply turned his head to look at the wizard, too. Dread struck him as, in the blink of an eye, the wizard pointed his black staff in Alucard's direction, and sent a blinding, white beam of light towards him.

Angst shot through Zalith as he backed out of the way of a charging wolf; he irritably plunged his hand into the beast's chest, tearing out its heart. He looked back over at Alucard, who dodged the beam and rolled along the ground in time to avoid the wizard's second beam of light. But the wizard didn't attack again after that. Did that mean he could only muster two ethos-charged attacks in rapid succession?

Zalith had a much bigger problem to deal with, though. While he was distracted, he failed to tear the head off of the wolf he'd just executed. Moments later, the corpse of the dead werewolf arose with fire spewing from its mangled body; it darted towards him faster than any lycan, seething and snarling. But it was only a hellhound, nothing he hadn't dealt with before.

He set his eyes on the monster, but wolves were coming at him from every direction, and he only had seconds to think. The demon held out his hand and focused his ethos on the incoming hellhound, but it required a whole lot more of his strength to kill such a creature than it would to kill an ordinary werewolf. Nonetheless, he concentrated, and the hellhound suddenly stopped charging and yelped—but before Zalith could execute the beast, the jaws of a wolf gripped hold of his extended arm. He grunted in annoyance and seized the wolf's jaws with his free hand; he pulled it from his arm and tore the beast in half with both his hands as he stumbled back and out of the path of the hellhound, which immediately charged at him the moment his concentration was broken.

Zalith swung around and set his eyes back on the hellhound as it raced towards him. But there were still *so* many wolves coming towards him. With an irritated snarl, he set as many of them on fire as he could at once, but at least a dozen were seconds from pouncing at him, and the hellhound was even closer. He prepared to fight, claws bared, ethos ready; he knew that he wasn't going to come out of this without several more wounds. However, as the whirring projectile shot from Alucard's colt suddenly collided with the side of the hellhound's head, Zalith turned his attention to the smaller wolves. The hellhound's head exploded, and as it did, Zalith snatched the throat of one of the pouncing wolves, tore its head off, and hastily crashed his fist into the side of the face of his next target. Then, when he removed the last wolf's head, he took a moment to check on the vampire.

A smirk flickered across Alucard's face when Zalith's gaze met his, and then the vampire turned around and pointed his weapon at one of the wolves running toward him. He fired, and the wolf's head exploded on impact; he fired again, executing another wolf, and as he fired the last bullet from his right colt, he tucked the gun into his blazer and wielded his rapier.

But the humming sound of charging ethos snatched both Alucard and Zalith's attention. The wizard fired at Alucard—Zalith sharply turned his head in panic, but when he watched the vampire disappear into vermillion smoke, the wizard's blinding white beam collided with the wolf that had just jumped towards the vampire. The wolf combusted into white ash, which fell to the grass like snow.

The vampire reappeared closer to Zalith. Relieved that Alucard wasn't on the other side of the battlefield, Zalith tried to calm his angst and grabbed another wolf. The wizard fired his second shot at Alucard *again*, but the vampire dodged with ease. The fact that the wizard was aiming solely for Alucard was starting to deeply aggravate Zalith, though.

Now that his arm was healed, the demon reached forward and sent a few of the last remaining wolves up in white flames. With most of them dead, he could focus on getting answers from the wizard. He glanced at Alucard and watched as he sliced another wolf's head off, and then he glanced at the demon with an expectant look on his blood-smothered face. With a smirk of recognition, Zalith hurried forward, leaving the vampire to distract the wizard as planned.

The demon slew as many wolves as he could on the way, keeping his eyes on the wizard, who had seen him coming and retreated into the ruins of Ada's house, most likely to recharge his ethos. The sound of Alucard's firing colts cut through the howls and snarls of the wolves, but as Zalith approached the ruins, he sharply turned his head and set his eyes on a group of ten wolves charging towards him. A blur of white flickered in the corner of his eye at the same time, and as he took his eyes off the wolf to look over at the ruins, he saw that the wizard had emerged back onto the battlefield already.

Zalith grunted as the wolves pounced at him. He skidded to a halt, snatching the neck of a wolf which pounced at him, but as he tore it apart, he caught sight of the wizard… and this time, he was aiming his charging attack at *him*.

Panic consumed Zalith's racing heart. He growled in frustration as all the wolves pounced at him at once, obviously trying to keep him distracted so the wizard could eradicate him. He wasn't going to let that happen. He set two wolves on fire and kicked away another, but a wolf then latched its jaws around his leg and another jumped at him and snatched his arm. He grunted, snarled, and struggled, trying to fight them off—he could see the glowing light of the wizard's ethos, and as *horror* consumed him, he turned his head to see the incoming beam of light—

A powerful force abruptly shoved Zalith aside. The yelping of wolves rang in his ears, and when he hit the ground, he stared up at *Alucard*. The vampire's blood splattered onto his face, and the blinding white light engulfed the area where Zalith had been battling. If it hadn't been for Alucard, that beam would have killed him.

Alucard....

Dread clung to Zalith like a suffocating shroud; the fear of losing Alucard froze him, stricken with terror. Yet, as the ethereal light dissipated, the chilling revelation that materialized before him surpassed even his darkest nightmares, sending shivers down his spine like an icy torrent of trepidation.

Alucard stood there, his body trembling, his blood oozing onto the grass. The wizard's blast had taken the majority of the vampire's right arm, leaving a ghastly, gaping, bloody hole in his side and a look of terror on his face similar to that which clung to Zalith's. But that horrified expression quickly contorted into rage. Zalith watched as the vampire's arm healed back in just seconds but its form wasn't human. Before he could make sense of the scaled, taloned arm, he watched as Alucard burst forward, the ground beneath him erupting under the force of his movement. Zalith got up off his ass as Alucard yelled in anger and grabbed the wizard faster than the white-robed man could react; the vampire pinned him against the wall, silencing his panicked screech as he snatched his neck.

"Do you have *any* idea how long it took me to manifest this fucking body?!" Alucard roared in the wizard's face.

Zalith's gaze fixated on the manifestation that had replaced Alucard's once-human right arm. It resembled a demonic limb, eerily mirroring the shape of a human appendage, yet its composition was an unholy tapestry of blood-red flesh. The majority of the nightmarish limb was ensconced in a macabre mosaic of black and dark purple, resembling armour-like scaled skin, and sinister patterns snaked across its surface.

The demonic arm seamlessly connected to what remained of Alucard's human shoulder, creating a ghastly fusion of the supernatural and the remnants of his original form. The wound in his side had undergone a similar metamorphosis, mirroring the ominous appearance of his accursed arm. The once-raw injury now bore the same blood-red hue and eerie patterns, and the grotesque gave way to a haunting beauty, leaving Zalith captivated by the transcendent allure that had befallen Alucard.

Was this what the vampire's true form looked like?

The wizard, whom Zalith had almost forgotten was trapped in Alucard's grasp, managed a muffled gasp as he stared at the vampire in horror, shuddering and stuttering.

Alucard tightened his grip around the wizard's throat as he glanced back over his shoulder, setting his eyes on Zalith. The demon felt relieved to see that he was okay, and as he made his way over to the vampire, he looked around to make sure no wolves were lurking nearby. It seemed that the last of them had been killed by the wizard's light.

The vampire asked the wizard, "Why are you here?"

He didn't answer.

Zalith stood at Alucard's side, glowering at the wizard.

With evidently no patience left, Alucard leaned his face into the wizard's, glared into his panicked eyes, and threatened with a quiet snarl, "You can tell me yourself, or I'll find out in a way that will be much more painful for you."

The wizard scowled, remaining silent.

Alucard gritted his teeth as the furious look on his face worsened. But before the vampire could execute him, Zalith lightly pulled the vampire aside and snatched the wizard's head in both his hands. *He* was furious, and he wanted to make this man suffer. Without mercy, the demon conjured the darkest of his ethos, turning the blood flowing through the wizard's veins into fire. Zalith watched with a cruel scowl as the wizard screamed, his skin melting, his body withering, and he didn't let go until there was nothing but a skeleton left. That ugly little man had hurt Alucard…and that was something Zalith would never treat lightly. If there were more time, he'd have done far worse, but he wanted to make sure Alucard was okay.

As what remained of the wizard dropped to the ground, the demon turned around and desperately snatched Alucard's right wrist. He pulled the vampire into an almost uncomfortably tight hug, breathing deeply as he tried to silence his anger and worry. For a moment, he'd thought that he might have lost Alucard, and he felt his heart break. But Alucard was okay—he was standing there in his embrace, and he moved his arms around Zalith. The relief that the demon felt was unlike any other; he hated that he'd let those wolves grab him like that. He felt like an *idiot*.

But Alucard had his back, as he always seemed to. It wasn't the first time Alucard had gone out of his way to protect him, and he was sure it wouldn't be the last. However, as thankful as he was, he wasn't at all comfortable with Alucard putting himself in danger to help him. What if the next time he did it, he ended up getting hurt much worse? Or what if…no, he didn't want to think about it.

It was over now. The wizard was dead and so was every wolf who congregated in the clearing. Hopefully, the battle had ended one of the vampire's threats, and hopefully…Alucard would no longer have to deal with werewolves.

Chapter Seventeen

— ⊰ ✝ ⊱ —

The End of Ada's Hatred

| **Alucard** |

Alucard surrendered to Zalith's tender embrace, gently placing the side of his face against his. The demon's skin felt like a caress of warmth and silk, inviting him to lose himself in the comforting sanctuary of their shared closeness. As much as Alucard yearned to be enveloped in this delightful sensation, though, a storm of frustration and anger raged within him.

The softness of Zalith's touch became a soothing balm, a stark contrast to the tempest brewing inside. Memories of a night steeped in sorrow and regret threatened to surface, a night when he lost himself in a maelstrom of emotions and actions he couldn't fully recall. What he *did* remember was that Damien had to pull him from the clutches of that consuming fury and back from the edge of despair.

Determined not to let history repeat itself, Alucard found solace in the arms of his demon companion. The embrace became a lifeline, a source of light that kept him from descending into the abyss of darkness. Here, in Zalith's affectionate hold, he discovered something worth holding onto, a beacon that staved off the shadows threatening to devour him.

He took his eyes off the forest, closed them, and nuzzled the side of Zalith's face. The wizard had been destroyed, the werewolves were dead, and one of his most irritating problems might finally be at an end. He wanted to bask in that relief for a moment, but he couldn't. His arm and a large portion of his body had been eradicated, and it had taken a considerable amount of his ethos to heal the wounds, replacing his missing limb and flesh with that of his true form. But he felt relieved that his *entire* body hadn't suffered. It would still take a rather annoying amount of life force to restore what *had* been lost, though, and that aggravated him a whole lot more.

The vampire didn't dwell on his loss, though. What he did was to save Zalith from a fate he might not be able to come back from. Did Eltarian demons possess true forms?

Could Zalith have done what he did? He wasn't sure, but Zalith's reaction to his sacrifice made him think that the demon most likely *couldn't* have come back from it.

"Thank you," Zalith breathed quietly, still holding Alucard tightly. Then, he turned his head and kissed the vampire's lips.

As Zalith rested his forehead against Alucard's, the vampire frowned and asked, "Did you find out why the wizard was here?" He was eager to know if this truly was the end of Ada's lingering hatred.

With a slight smile, Zalith sighed and placed his hand on the side of the vampire's blood-smothered face. "Are you okay?"

"I'm fine."

Zalith looked down at Alucard's right arm, which he slowly took hold of in his hand. He softly stroked his fingertips down the vampire's forearm, and then he took hold of his taloned hand. "How long is it going to take you to heal this?"

The vampire glanced down at his arm, shrugged, and looked back at him. "A few people."

"And this?" he asked, gently placing his hand on the vampire's waist.

Alucard sighed. "The same," he mumbled, gripping Zalith's wrist. As he made the demon let go of him, he stepped back and irritably pulled off his destroyed blazer, which he chucked to the ground after removing his two colts from inside. He tucked both weapons into either side of his belt; he *really* needed to get holsters that he could wear over his shirt instead of those sewn into his jackets and suits. He huffed and asked Zalith, "Why was he here?"

The demon began to pull off his own blazer. "From what I was able to see," he started, placing his blazer over Alucard's shoulders, "he came in response to Ada's call." He helped Alucard into his blazer and then stood in front of him. "She hired him from what I assume to be a mercenary organization called Blood of Profane. They employ rogue wizards, demons, and probably some other dangerous characters, I'm sure. Do you know them?"

Alucard nodded. "Bottom feeders. This is a good thing. That means no one is going to miss him," he mumbled, looking down at the skeleton which was once a wizard. "The organization got their money…that's all they care about. Ada probably didn't even tell them it was me she was hiring him to work against."

Zalith nodded. "He did look very surprised when he saw you up close."

"*No one* is stupid enough to go against the Nosferatu…so it makes me wonder who or what she convinced them she was paying them to fight." He glanced over his shoulder, making sure that none of the wolves had risen and become hellhounds. "It's over now, anyway. Thank you for helping me."

Zalith smiled and placed his hands on Alucard's arms. "Any time, vampire. And thank *you* for saving my life…again."

Alucard smiled. "Any time."

The demon laughed and rested his forehead against Alucard's again.

However, Alucard was beginning to feel fatigued. Healing his body using his true form exhausted him and he needed to rest. And whether he was willing to give in or not, his body had its own plans. He tried to stop himself, but his tire forced his legs to struggle, and he stumbled forward. Zalith caught him in his arms, and he held the vampire tightly as he stared at him in confusion. Alucard couldn't hear what Zalith was saying...all he heard was his voice murmuring and mumbling, but he was pretty sure that Zalith was asking whether he was okay or not.

"I'm fine," he replied with a deep exhale. "I just need a moment."

The demon fell with him as he dropped to his knees, trying to recover his strangely waned strength. It had all left him so quickly, and he didn't understand why or how—it didn't matter. He just wanted to rest.

"Alucard?" Zalith then asked, his voice finally making enough sense for Alucard to understand.

Taking his eyes off the demon's concerned face, Alucard glared into the woods. "What?"

"What's wrong?" he asked.

Alucard just wanted to sleep. He didn't have the strength to answer.

Zalith lightly gripped the vampire's jaw and turned his head so that Alucard would look up at him.

Alucard frowned and repeated, "I'm fine."

"No, you're not," Zalith retorted with a panicked look on his face.

"I want to go home," the vampire mumbled, looking down at the grass.

"Can you walk?"

"Maybe," Alucard said with a pout.

The demon then smirked. "Would you like me to help you?"

Hiding his embarrassed face, Alucard shrugged. "Maybe."

"Would you like to pretend to be unconscious again so that I'll carry you to safety?" he asked with an amused smile.

Alucard's embarrassment grew. Was he talking about the time he'd carried him away from Ada's ambush wedding? Probably. He kept his pout. "Yes," he grumbled. He liked it when Zalith carried him.

Zalith smiled. "Then, when you're ready, we'll head back."

Alucard didn't waste a moment. He shrouded himself in vermillion smoke and morphed into his melanistic fox form. Zalith then carefully picked him up in his arms, stood up, and began to make his way towards the forest.

The vampire relaxed. In Zalith's arms, he felt warm and safe. It had been a long night, and all he wanted to do now was lay down somewhere and sleep. Ada's era was over—he wasn't going to have to deal with her bullshit anymore. There were still werewolves out in the forests, but they wouldn't be a threat now. He'd be sure to keep an eye on them, though, just in case one of them decided to try and step up and take Ada's place.

While Zalith carried him, he looked up at the demon. He was glad that Zalith was with him...now and every time before. They worked well together and also enjoyed spending time with each other, too; Alucard couldn't think of a better relationship. He just hoped that it would stay this way. In his four hundred years, he'd seen people fall in love, get married, have children...and then someone slept with another person or their feelings faded. He didn't want that to happen...but perhaps it was too early to be thinking about that. After all, he and Zalith had only been together for twenty-four hours. He probably shouldn't be thinking so far into the future.

Zalith looked down at him and smirked. "Are *you* staring at *me* now, Alucard?" he asked.

Alucard looked away and glared ahead, and as Zalith laughed quietly and continued carrying him home, he closed his eyes and let himself get some much-needed rest.

Chapter Eighteen

— ⟨ ✝ ⟩ —

Resignation

| **Zalith** |

A s Zalith carried Alucard—who was still in his fox form—into the main hall of his castle, they both set their eyes on Attila. The ball-gowned man was standing by the table with a bitter look on his face, and he was glaring at Zalith. But the demon had no intention to interact with the dog-faced vampire.

Zalith approached the table, and Alucard pounced out of his arms and onto its surface. He watched with a smile as the fox trotted along the table, and when he reached its end, he leapt off its edge; vermillion smoke surrounded him, and as he emerged from it as his usual self, the vampire set his eyes on Attila.

"Alucard," Attila said, turning to face him with a humble bow.

Alucard ignored him. He turned away from Attila and set his eyes on the door that led to the kitchens. "*Vino*," he called, and moments later, one of the butlers rushed out of the room and approached him.

"Yes, My Lord?" he asked, his voice shaky with fear.

Zalith watched as Alucard wordlessly snatched the butler's throat, pinned him against the wall, and then sunk his fangs into his neck. It might have amused Zalith any time before the moment he came to realize his feelings for Alucard, but right now, seeing Alucard feed made him feel what was undeniably jealousy and discontent. He didn't want *his* vampire feeding on other people; he didn't want Alucard touching these random men. Yes, it was something all vampires did and had to do, but Zalith felt that, in Alucard's case, it was now different. He shouldn't need to sink his teeth into random people; he should be sinking his fangs into *him*.

In an attempt to distract himself from his jealous thoughts, Zalith glanced at Attila. The ugly, dog-faced man stood there with a look on his face so sour that Zalith knew he was moments away from questioning why *he'd* brought Alucard home. Part of him wanted Attila to ask just so he had an excuse to beat the ugly deeper into his face—if that were even possible. However, as Alucard finished draining the butler of his blood, Zalith took his eyes off Attila and set them back on *his* vampire.

"What do you want?" Alucard questioned, wiping the blood from his mouth with the back of his hand as he turned to face Attila.

"I have completed task in DeiganLupus," he said. "King is…ally. You have new task for me?"

"No," Alucard replied.

Zalith smirked amusedly; he remembered that Alucard had told him that he'd have Ben replace Attila once he returned from DeiganLupus, and now looked to be that moment. He was sure he was going to enjoy whatever might be about to happen.

Attila frowned unsurely. "You have…nothing…for me?"

"No," Alucard repeated.

Still staring at him, Attila waited.

"You no longer work for me."

A look of horror slapped Attila's face.

"You will leave my home, my country, and you will do well not to be seen by any of my people. They will kill you on sight once they learn of your resignation. I spare your life because you've served me for a long time. But you will only have this one chance. Get the fuck out of my castle, and don't ever come back."

With a mortified look of disbelief on his face, Attila slowly turned his head and looked at Zalith. A smug smile danced across the demon's face, and Attila scowled and sharply turned his head to look back at Alucard. But he didn't argue. Without a word, Attila took a few steps back, clearly hoping that Alucard might change his mind, but Zalith knew Alucard had made his decision very long ago. With a huff, Attila turned around and stormed out of the castle, slamming the door behind him.

Once he was gone, Alucard sighed and looked down at his right hand, which had returned to its human appearance. Then, he made his way over to the table and pulled his colts from his belt; he placed them on the table as Zalith made his way over and stood beside him.

"I love it when you're angry," Zalith said with a smirk, tucking a loose strand of Alucard's crimson hair behind his ear with his index finger. He then glanced down at the vampire's hand, and he was glad to see that it had returned to normal.

Alucard frowned and huffed quietly. "I'm not angry."

Zalith smiled and placed his hand on Alucard's shoulder. "Was it only one human you needed to heal yourself?" he asked curiously.

"No," Alucard replied. "To heal my arm, yes, but I'll need another to heal the rest of my body."

"Must it be human blood?" he asked, trying to contain his jealousy.

"Yes."

With a hint of disappointment on his face, Zalith smiled slightly and rested his forehead against Alucard's. "Do you feel better now?" he asked as he stared into the vampire's eyes, changing the subject, hoping it would silence his feelings.

"Yes," he answered. He then moved away from Zalith and slumped down into the seat closest to him. "We should discuss tomorrow before we head to sleep," he suggested.

Zalith sat beside him and rested his arms on the table. "Are you sure you won't need to rest?"

"No, I'm fine. Tomorrow, I'll spend most of the day telling Ben about his new job, so that gives you time to head home and get what you'll need for our trip to Avalmoor. We can meet back at my castle...hmm..." he paused and frowned, looking over at the doors to the kitchens. "*Vino*," he called again, and as another butler came hurrying out—stopping for a moment to glance at his dead co-worker—the vampire set his eyes on him and ordered, "Go to the city; find out what time the performance is tomorrow—the opera house."

The butler nodded and bowed humbly. Then, he raced off to do as he had been told.

"I'll tell you a time as soon as I know," Alucard said, looking back at Zalith.

Smiling, Zalith leaned the side of his face on his hand. "Will we do something tomorrow morning before I head home?"

"Like what? We can... walk again?" he suggested quietly, looking down at his lap.

Content with his suggestion, Zalith leaned closer and smiled. "I would very much enjoy that."

"I don't have horses, though. They...perished in the fire that took my house."

Zalith frowned in sorrow—

"I'll replace them, though," Alucard said with a shrug. "Most things that were in that house are replaceable."

Unsure of what to say in response, Zalith smiled and leaned back in his seat. He still couldn't help but feel some responsibility for what happened to Alucard the night Ada burned his house to the ground; he didn't know the full extent of it, but he did know everything that Ben had told him. Alucard killed Tobias, and Zalith was sure Ada had something to do with that, too. He also knew that Alucard cared about Tobias—the vampire might try to deny that he cared for anyone, but Zalith had learned how to read him.

However, he wasn't sure if Alucard had taken the time to grieve yet. As much as he wanted to ask if he was okay regarding Tobias, he felt as though he shouldn't open old wounds if Alucard was still trying to heal them. If Alucard needed to talk about it, Zalith was sure he'd do so in his own time. Alucard knew he was there for him, and he was confident that the vampire would speak to him if he ever needed to.

"Did you replace your violin?" he then asked, having not forgotten Alucard owned one. He was still curious to hear him play if he'd ever grace him with what he suspected was a hidden, beautiful talent.

Glancing at him, Alucard shrugged and said, "No. I haven't really had time to replace much."

"I see," Zalith said quietly.

Alucard then sighed tiredly. "I think I should get some sleep now."

Zalith nodded. He was certain that Alucard must still be feeling exhausted from the night's events; a lot happened, and Alucard had taken a very hard hit for him...*again*. He'd had to keep Alucard from falling asleep in his arms right after their confrontation with the wizard, but now that Alucard seemed to have recovered a little, he felt much more confident about letting the vampire get some rest.

"Do you have a guest room? Unless...we'll be sharing again," the demon suggested with a smirk.

"I have a guest room," Alucard mumbled and pouted as he tried to hide his flustered face.

Still smiling, Zalith laughed slightly in amusement. "Then if you want to show me where it is, we'll call it a night."

Nodding, Alucard stood up. "I don't mean to end the night so abruptly, I just...should rest."

"It's perfectly okay," Zalith said with a smile as he followed him to the door which led to his half of the castle.

The vampire glanced back at Zalith as he pulled the door open and invited the demon to step into the hallway first. Once Zalith headed through the door, Alucard pulled it shut behind him and walked beside the demon as they made their way down the hall.

"And...these clothes you leant me—I can...pay to—"

"No," Zalith said with a smile, "there's no need."

Alucard nodded and stared ahead as they turned right into a corridor Zalith hadn't yet seen. The walls were adorned with red wallpaper with golden floral patterns, paintings of royally dressed animals, and some people he hadn't seen before.

"Who are these people?" the demon asked curiously.

As he set his eyes on the paintings, Alucard shrugged. "Some of these paintings came from the house I shared with Vanessa. Others are pieces I just saw and liked. Although that one," he said, pointing to a painting of a butler feeding a brown shire horse, "is Clarence—he was the groundskeeper at Vanessa's house."

Zalith smiled as he eyed the painting and stopped to admire it for a moment. "And why do you have it?"

"I painted it."

Surprised, the demon looked wide-eyed at him. "You painted it?"

He nodded. "I was in that house for a long time, and I needed something to do. So, I learned to draw and paint."

Zalith smiled at the painting, and when he looked closer, he spotted Alucard's signature. "It's beautiful," he said. "But not as beautiful as you," he added with a smirk and chuckled softly, observing the vampire's flustered reaction as he averted his gaze. "Come on," he then said. "I won't keep you from your sleep any longer."

Alucard nodded and proceeded to guide them down the hall. Upon reaching its end, they turned right and approached a black oak door. When they reached it, Alucard gripped the handle, but before he could open it, Zalith placed his hand over Alucard's.

"Where will you be in the morning?" Zalith asked as Alucard frowned at him.

The vampire looked down at their hands. "Well... I often wake up close to noon; if you wake up earlier, you can just... wander or whatever. If you want something to eat, just ask the butlers—William, the blonde guy, speaks Deiganish, so he'll understand you," he explained tiredly.

"Okay," Zalith said, moving his other hand to the side of Alucard's face. He then gently pressed his lips against the vampire's and rested his forehead against his. "I'll see you tomorrow, then."

With a nervous look on his face, Alucard looked to his right and nodded slightly. "Goodnight," he muttered.

"Goodnight, vampire," Zalith said with a smirk.

Then, he let go of Alucard and headed into the bedroom. He turned to face the vampire, who frowned in fluster again, and as Alucard headed back down the hall and turned left, Zalith smiled in adoration. But it was late, and he should get some sleep, too; he headed into the room and closed the door behind him.

| Alucard |

Alucard sleepily made his way through his castle. He was relieved that he'd done as much as he had tonight; not only had he put an end to Ada and whatever she left behind, but he'd also finally fired Attila, too. He said he'd replace Attila with Ben once Attila got back from DeiganLupus, and that just so happened to be tonight. Alucard was never going to forgive him for insulting Zalith, and firing him was lenient.

He sighed as he headed up the stairs. Tonight, he'd lost a considerable amount of his human body, and he was *really* feeling the consequences. He was glad that Zalith hadn't insisted on examining his wounds, though. Beneath his shirt lay things he didn't want

Zalith to see yet—he didn't want him to see them at all, but if this relationship was going to work, he was going to have to show the demon at some point, wasn't he? He didn't want to think about it. All he wanted to do now was get into his room and go to sleep.

The vampire yawned as he dragged his tired, sore body towards his bedroom door. Hopefully, he'd feel better in the morning. He stumbled into the room, closed the door, and fell onto his bed. And at last, he could finally get the rest he needed.

Chapter Nineteen

In Darkness

| **Zalith** |

In the guest room, Zalith lay on the bed, listening as Alucard got further and further away. Part of him felt as if he was listening because he was fighting the urge to go out there and follow him, and another part of him was convinced that he was listening because he was worried that Alucard might pass out. But he didn't hear a heavy thump on the floor, so he pushed that idea aside and sighed quietly.

As much as he wanted to spend the entire night with Alucard and sleep beside him again, he knew better than to persist. He didn't want to upset or make Alucard feel uncomfortable, despite his own overbearing need for closeness with him. He'd continue to put Alucard's comfort before his own.

Zalith sat up and looked around. The guest room was rather large, and the fact that it was round convinced him that it was inside one of the castle towers. Its walls were a dark purple and patterned with shimmering gold engravings. A large crystal chandelier hung from the centre of the mahogany coffered ceiling, and each candle lit; it was as if Alucard had already prepared for him to be staying in this room. The double bed he lay on was adorned with a beige fur-like blanket and several pillows to match, and some extra blankets sat folded on the couch under the window. It was a whole lot different to the room he stayed in at the vampire's manor, and it looked much comfier, too. But that was probably because Alucard was prepared for guests this time.

The demon stared at the black curtains which concealed the windows. He pulled off his waistcoat and placed it over the back of the chair not far from the bed, slipped off his shoes, and used his ethos to snuff out the candlelight. He then laid back down and stared up at the ceiling.

In his solitude, he allowed himself to sink into his thoughts—but he only had positive ones. Alucard had been back all of two days and he'd already made sure to clear up one of his biggest problems. Zalith admired Alucard's drive, but he wished that the vampire would allow himself some time to rest. Their trip to Avalmoor would give the vampire a few days to relax, though, and then they'd be back to work. There was no one he enjoyed working with more than he did Alucard, and he'd do whatever he could to help the vampire out whenever he could.

But something was wrong with Alucard's ethos. His aura felt different to how it had been the night they'd said goodbye in front of the portal to Eltaria... the night Alucard had tried to cut their contact. The vampire's aura had once been like a raging fire, but now, it felt as though something had dulled his flame—and he suspected that Alucard hadn't even realized it. If he *had* known something was wrong with his ethos, surely he wouldn't still be using it so much... right? From what he had seen, Alucard didn't relent, even if he was hurt.

Zalith sighed and dragged his hand over his face. What could it be, though? A sealing rune would explain what he was feeling in Alucard's aura, but how would such a rune have found its way onto Alucard's body? Could Zalith be mistaken? Or had something happened to Alucard that the vampire didn't want him to know about?

He was overthinking. It wasn't his business. At least... not yet. Just like everything else Alucard was keeping to himself, Zalith was sure the vampire would tell him when the time was right.

With a conflicted sigh, he pulled off the rest of his clothes and made himself comfortable beneath the bed covers. As the night became later, he closed his eyes and allowed himself to drift off to sleep, focusing on the plans that he and Alucard had for tomorrow.

Zalith woke later that night. He wasn't sure what snapped him out of his sleep at first, but when he tried to drift off again, the muffled mumble of Alucard's voice snatched his attention.

The demon opened his eyes as he lay there in the dark, listening. Of course, if it weren't for his heightened sense of hearing, he wouldn't have been able to hear the vampire's distressed mumbles—and if he hadn't been subconsciously focusing on the vampire, either, he wouldn't have woken. But how could he not focus on him all the time? He cared for Alucard so sorely that his worry and need to protect the vampire made it impossible for him not to.

He listened, searching for sense in Alucard's mumbles, but the words the vampire spoke didn't match any of Zalith's understanding. It didn't sound like Dor-Sanguian or any language Zalith had heard before. What he *did* understand, however, was the anguish in Alucard's voice. It matched what Zalith heard last night, the night the vampire had woken because of the thunder. He might be having another nightmare, and after experiencing Alucard's reaction to last night's event, Zalith felt no hesitation in getting out of bed and going to him.

Zalith got up, pulled his trousers on, and hastily left the guest room. He made his way through the brightly lit corridor, effortlessly navigating his way through the castle and up to Alucard's room. He followed the vampire's aura, and it led him to the top of a tower where a dark oak door sat at the end of a small hallway.

He knocked on the vampire's door... but to no avail. *Of course* Alucard wouldn't answer; how could he if he was asleep? Zalith didn't want to intrude, but his worry for Alucard forced him to open the door.

Angst slowly constricted Zalith's heart as he peered into the brightly lit room; he set his eyes on the sleeping vampire, who lay in his bed, tightly gripping the black, fluffy fur covers as he murmured. Every darkly coloured curtain in the room was drawn, all the lights were lit, and something minacious lingered in the air.

"Alucard?" Zalith asked quietly, standing in the doorway.

But the vampire didn't wake. He continued murmuring, the torment in his voice causing Zalith to feel distressed. The demon closed the door behind him and silently made his way along the white fur-carpeted floor. When he reached the vampire, he crouched beside his bed and placed his hand on his arm. Alucard had changed out of the shirt Zalith lent him and was now wearing a black one with long sleeves—of course. Zalith still wanted to know the reason behind Alucard's insistence to cover his arms, but now wasn't the time to concern himself with that.

With his hand on Alucard's arm, he quietly asked, "Alucard?"

This time, he received a response from the vampire in the form of a quiet, confused mumble.

"Are you okay?" Zalith whispered.

But Alucard responded, once again, with a murmur. The vampire then frowned and rolled over, turning his back to Zalith.

That made the demon smile. He stood up and looked down at Alucard, convinced that he might be okay, and his worry was unneeded. However, as he turned around and went to walk away, Alucard sighed quietly.

"Where are you going?" the vampire asked wearily, his voice muffled against the pillow.

Zalith looked back over his shoulder; Alucard lay on his right side, his eyes closed, still and silent as if he were waiting for an answer. "To my room," he told him.

Alucard mumbled quietly and dragged his arm from beneath his blanket, which he pulled up from the empty half of his bed. "*Aici*," he muttered, patting the free space beside him.

The demon didn't need to speak Dor-Sanguian to know that Alucard was requesting he join him. With a relieved smile, he turned around, made his way over to Alucard's bed, and complied with his request. He climbed in beside him, pulled the covers over himself, and rested on his left side so that he could gaze at the vampire as he slowly shuffled closer to him. It was endearing that Alucard's nervous disposition seemed to fade when he was tired; Zalith was sure that Alucard wouldn't have been able to invite him into his bed so confidently if he were completely awake.

While Alucard moved as close as he could get, Zalith wrapped his arms around the vampire and relaxed.

"I want to ask you something," Alucard said quietly.

"Anything."

The vampire fell silent for a moment but then fidgeted around, making himself comfortable. "If there was something about me that you didn't know—something important—and I failed to tell you... and you found out, would you still see me the same way?"

Unsure of what he was asking or trying to say, Zalith frowned and looked down at what he could see of Alucard. "I'm sure there's nothing you could tell me that would change the way I feel. I'm sure there's a lot that we're yet to learn about one another, and we'll come to know them when the time is right," he said, holding him tighter.

"There is *something*."

Zalith didn't know what to think. Alucard was still half asleep, and there was the possibility that he didn't even know what he was saying. Zalith didn't want to take advantage of that and allow Alucard to reveal something he might not yet be ready for him to know. So, he moved his hand to the back of Alucard's head and caressed his crimson hair. "Whatever it is, you don't have to tell me out of fear that it might change the way I feel. *Nothing* could do that."

"Maybe," Alucard uttered.

The demon exhaled deeply. "You were talking in your sleep," he said, changing the subject.

"I always talk in my sleep."

"Why?"

He shrugged. "I don't know."

"Were you having a nightmare again?" Zalith asked.

"I always have nightmares."

A sullen frown clung to Zalith's face. Always?

"But not when you're here," the vampire added. "You make me... feel safe."

"From what?" he asked, a saddened smile on his face.

"The dark. Everything."

Zalith felt reluctant to ask, but what Alucard just said and the need for every light to be on told him that he might be right in assuming. "Are you... afraid of the dark?"

"No. Not the dark—well... maybe. I don't like... darkness inside somewhere."

"What do you mean?"

"Outside is fine," Alucard continued, his voice quiet and weary. "Outside, I can go anywhere. Inside is confined, restricting. I was...raised in pitch-black catacombs for most of my childhood; darkness was where I grew up, and where all the people I used to know died. Ever since then, I find it hard to rest unless there's light somewhere. I guess...that does make me afraid of the dark in one way or another, no?" he asked, a hint of laughter in his voice as he tightened his grip around Zalith. "I guess that's stupid."

Cuddling him, Zalith smiled and rested the side of his face on Alucard's head. "No," he said quietly. "It's not stupid, Alucard. You don't have to feel afraid, though. I'll always be here to keep you safe, no matter what I have to protect you from."

"You can't protect me," he said sullenly. "But you *do* make me feel safe." He buried his face in Zalith's chest. "Don't let them take that from me," he pleaded despondently.

Zalith's smile faded into a frown of confusion. They? Who would take something like a feeling of security from Alucard? Damien? The demon closed his eyes and held the vampire as tightly as he could. "No one's going to take anything from you, and I'm not going to go anywhere, either."

But the vampire didn't reply.

The demon opened his eyes and glanced down at him. Alucard was either too afraid to answer, or he'd fallen back asleep. What could he have meant, though? His words stuck in Zalith's head like pieces of a bullet buried deep inside a wound. Why did he seem so afraid? Who were 'they'? Who could have done something so terrible as to make someone so innocent as Alucard so afraid? His first thought was Damien—it had to be Damien. But what could that creature have done? What was the extent of his tyranny? Was all of this even down to just Damien? Zalith wasn't sure. But he had to know. He had to know so he knew what he had to do to help Alucard feel safe again. There wasn't a thing he wouldn't do to make sure the vampire was happy, and Damien was no exception.

With a quiet, hesitant sigh, Zalith relaxed, trying to silence his thoughts so that he might get some rest. Now that he had Alucard in his arms, he felt he would sleep a whole lot better. And so, with only the vampire on his mind, he allowed himself to drift off to sleep once more—and tomorrow, he'd do what he could to find out more about what Alucard had said.

DEMON'S FATE
Numen Chronicles | Volume Two

ARC TWO

✝

THE HUNT
FOR LUCIOUS

DEMON'S FATE
Numen Chronicles | Volume Two

Chapter Twenty

— ⊰ ✝ ⊱ —

A Morning of Business and Questions

| **Alucard** |

As the morning came around, Alucard woke from his sleep. He frowned and slowly opened his eyes, and his sights fixed on what he could see of Zalith, who was sleeping on his left side with his arm around Alucard's waist. It felt strange to wake up as early as he had...*and* to wake up to find Zalith was still asleep.

He lifted his head from where it was—nearly under the cover of the blankets—and rested the side of his face on his pillow. His gaze slowly wandered to Zalith's face; he'd never be brave enough to stare at the demon's face while he was awake, but he *wasn't* awake, so Alucard had an opportunity to admire it. He wasn't afraid to admit to *himself* that he found the demon attractive. Not only was this demon physically alluring, but everything about him seemed to almost captivate the vampire—his voice, his personality, the way he spoke. But then Alucard frowned and glanced away for a moment, anxious that Zalith might wake up and catch him.

However, Zalith seemed to be in a deep, silent sleep, so Alucard set his hell-fiery eyes back on the demon's face. He wasn't sure why he felt the need to touch what he could see—to place his hand on the side of the demon's face. It wasn't the first time he caught himself wanting to do such a thing; in fact, he often wanted to touch the demon, whether it be his face, his arms, hands—he just wanted to feel him. Would it irritate Zalith if he placed his hand on him while he slept? Alucard hesitated, but he couldn't ignore his need to touch the man who had come to mean so much to him.

He moved his left hand from beneath the blankets and gradually edged it closer to the sleeping demon's face. But as his hand came just a few inches from Zalith's cheek, Alucard's hesitation outweighed his curiosity. He frowned, took his eyes off Zalith, and lowered his hand as a despondent scowl contorted his face. He didn't understand why he felt so nervous all the time or why *Zalith* made him feel so nervous. His confidence was never a problem when it came to things like battle and business, but when it came to this demon, he was unable to find the bravery to speak and do as he wished.

Zalith suddenly gripped Alucard's left wrist; the vampire looked back at him and watched as he smiled. The demon placed Alucard's hand on the side of his face himself, keeping his eyes shut as if he was still pretending to be asleep. Alucard felt as if he might pull his hand away in response to his sudden embarrassment, but Zalith placed his own hand over Alucard's, keeping him from moving it.

"Good morning, darling," Zalith said contently, opening his eyes to look at him.

Staring at Zalith for a short moment, Alucard's face flickered with nervousness, forcing him to look down at the sheets.

Zalith smirked. "I love waking up to your face," he said, taking his hand from over Alucard's, which was still on his face. He then placed his hand on the side of the vampire's neck. "How do you feel?"

Now that his hand was free, Alucard pulled it from Zalith's face and moved it beneath his pillow. "I feel fine."

Zalith took his hand off the vampire's neck and dragged his fingers over his right arm. "And this? Have you healed completely?"

"No," Alucard mumbled, lifting his right hand from beneath the covers. "My hand has healed, but most of the arm hasn't."

"How many more butlers will you need to murder to recover?"

"Two...maybe three."

Still smiling, Zalith guided his hand back to the side of Alucard's neck. "Are we going to make a habit of starting the night in separate beds and inevitably ending up in the same one by morning, or shall we make *this* the norm?"

Lowering his hand, Alucard pondered. He wasn't going to deny that he slept so much better with Zalith beside him *and* that he'd rather sleep next to him as often as he could, so with a nervous shrug, he pouted and answered, "We can just...do this."

As a content smile appeared on his face, Zalith moved his arms around the vampire and pulled him closer.

They lay in the quiet for a short while, and as Alucard felt himself drifting off again, he closed his eyes and sank into the comfort Zalith's embrace gave him.

Zalith started dragging his fingers through Alucard's crimson hair and rested the side of his face on his. "Alucard," he said quietly.

"What?" he mumbled.

Zalith hesitated for a moment. "Last night, you asked me a peculiar question," he started, a casual tone in his voice. "You asked me that if there was something important you hadn't yet told me, and if I found out, would I still see you the way I see you now. I told you that nothing could change how I feel about you because *nothing* can or will. I can't help but wonder, though...what was it you were referring to?"

Alucard frowned in discontent, tensing up as each word came from Zalith's mouth. He felt embarrassed, anxious, and worried—he didn't even remember what he might have been trying to say. Zalith had come to him last night while he was half-asleep; he could have said anything. What he *had* said grabbed Zalith's attention, and he wasn't sure what to say in response to his question. There were a few things he was yet to reveal to the demon, things he feared would change the way Zalith felt about him, and things he still wasn't ready to bring to light.

He shrugged, trying to come up with an excuse, but nothing came to him. He was sure that he knew what Zalith was referring to, though. Last night, when he partially healed his arm back to its human likeness, he hesitated to take off his blazer and shirt. He wasn't ready to show Zalith what adorned the skin of his arm—*arms*… and his back. That must have been what he had been talking about last night. He felt relieved, though, that he had been conscious enough to keep himself from revealing the truth.

With a quiet sigh, he pulled away from Zalith, sat up, and slouched forward. "I don't remember."

Zalith also sat up and edged closer, slowly moving his arms around Alucard as he rested his chin on the vampire's shoulder. "You also asked me not to allow *someone* to take away the fact that I make you feel safe. You asked me not to let *them* take that from you. Who are *they*?"

Alucard frowned uncomfortably as he glared at the floor. "Damien," he muttered, an agitated look on his face.

"And?"

The vampire glanced at him from the corner of his eye and scowled irritably. "Why do you need to know?" he questioned with hostility in his voice.

Zalith frowned slightly. "Because… if someone's hurting you in any way, I'm not going to sit idly by and let it happen. I care about you, and I'll do whatever I can to protect you."

Alucard took his eyes off the demon and stared ahead. He sighed sullenly and took a few moments to ponder; he wasn't ready to have that conversation, to tell Zalith why he feared losing the sense of calm and safeness that he felt while in his presence. While he thought he should tell Zalith the truth whenever prompted, he just couldn't do it this time. Not yet. "Just… Damien," he repeated. "And Lucifer."

Zalith sighed and lightly gripped Alucard's jaw in his hand. He turned the vampire's head so that he could stare into his eyes. "You can tell me when you're ready," he said softly—obviously, he wasn't convinced. "I won't force you to tell me something you're not ready to tell me." The demon then kissed him and rested his forehead against his. "Should we take that walk?" he asked, changing the subject.

Looking down at his lap, Alucard nodded. "Soon. I have to speak to Ben first. You can borrow some of my clothes if you want," he offered, glancing at him.

"Thank you," the demon said with a smile.

Alucard then looked over at the door. "Sabazios," he called.

After a few moments, the door crept open, and the vampire's hellhound scurried in.

"Go and get Ben for me," he grumbled.

The beast whined quietly and hurried back out of the room, and the door closed behind it.

Alucard then sighed and wearily said, "It's going to be annoying teaching someone new how to do Attila's job."

"You shouldn't worry," Zalith said, resting the side of his face against Alucard's again, keeping his arms around him. "Ben's rather eager to please, and I know he's capable of picking it up in no time at all."

"Maybe."

Zalith then smirked and leaned into Alucard's ear. "Just as *I* am eager to please *you*," he said seductively as he moved his right arm from around Alucard.

Alucard tensed up as Zalith slowly dragged his hand up his body until he had hold of his throat. Then, the demon tilted Alucard's head aside—Zalith paused and glanced at his face, probably to see if he was okay with what he was doing…and he was. So Zalith moved his left hand from around him and pulled the collar of his black shirt away from his neck. Alucard began to feel angst pooling in his stomach, his skin tingling as Zalith pressed his lips against his neck. The demon kissed again, gradually making his way up to the side of Alucard's face, but before Zalith could kiss his lips, Alucard sighed and looked away. He'd really thought Zalith might be going for a bite this time, something he sorely craved. But the demon didn't bare his fangs, and that frustrated him.

"Ben will be here in a moment," he mumbled and stood up. He straightened his shirt collar and looked over his shoulder at Zalith, who stared up at him with a disappointed frown. "I keep my clothes in the next room, to the left," he said as he made his way to the door. He grabbed the handle and glanced back at the demon again. "You can come find me when you're ready to go."

Evidently amused by Alucard's response to his teasing, Zalith smirked. "Okay," he replied, watching as the vampire left the bedroom without another word.

Alucard wasn't at all amused. As he closed the door behind him, he rolled his eyes and made his way down the corridor. He walked into the room he kept his clothes in, grabbed a sangria-red shirt, and swiftly changed into it. He then headed back through the corridor, down the stairs, and towards his study.

He wearily slumped down behind his desk and searched for something to fix his eyes on. But all he could do was sit there, stare at nothing, and ponder. He was convinced that Zalith might be irritated about the fact that he didn't want to tell him what he had almost revealed last night, and as much as it upset him to think that the demon might be mad, he couldn't bring himself to tell Zalith what he was hiding. He was confident that once Zalith found out, he'd leave him—he didn't want to lose him, not after waiting so long to be with him. So…as guilty as it made him feel, he was going to try and keep those secrets from Zalith for as long as possible.

With a quiet sigh, he sat up straight and rested his arms on the desk. He watched Sabazios lead Ben into the study; the hound panted excitedly as he set his white-as-snow eyes on Alucard. Ben's scruffy face adorned the same neutral smile as always, but a hint of worry clung to his brown eyes. Clearly, he was concerned about why he'd been summoned so early in the morning.

As the sunlight hit his face, lightening his eyes from hell-fiery to ice blue, Alucard eyed Ben, who sat down in one of the seats in front of his desk. The vampire felt no need to waste time. As Sabazios curled up on the floor beside him, Alucard set his vacant gaze on Ben. "Last night, I fired Attila. You will be stepping up."

Ben seemed surprised. "Of course," he said with excitement in his voice.

"Attila was, for the lack of a better explanation, my right-hand man. He did everything and anything I asked of him, including travelling around the world to meet new allies and clients. You will be doing that. The pay is considerably higher than what you've been earning, and the amount of work is also considerably more."

Listening, Ben nodded.

"Attila kept logs—you will do the same. When you leave Dor-Sanguis, you send correspondence every three days, whether there is anything new to tell me or not. When you return to Dor-Sanguis, you will meet with me the same day, and tell me everything of importance, even if it has been covered in writing. You will work closely with my contacts; you will speak not a word to anyone—not even your wife. There are specific ways of doing everything, so I expect you to do it all as told without deviancy."

Ben nodded again. "Understood."

Alucard then reached into his desk's top drawer and pulled out a few pieces of rolled parchment, a quill, and some ink. "Are you a religious man?" he asked, glancing at Ben as he unrolled the first piece of parchment.

"No," Ben admitted. "Should I be?"

"No," Alucard said with a smirk, stretching out the parchment in front of Ben, revealing a long script of tiny print. "These are forged credentials. To get into most government places these days, you need to be a member of the Lethidian church— humans are stupidly religious; they actually believe the Numen will save them."

Looking down at the parchment, Ben nodded slowly.

"You don't have a foul mouth, so there's one thing covered—cursing is a sin, no?" He smirked, but as Ben chuckled in amusement, Alucard lost his smile. He'd just become pretty sure that the only person he enjoyed smiling and laughing with was Zalith. "You'll need to dress the part, walk the part, and know what to say when it needs to be said. You are not from Aegisguard, so as well as researching my world's religions, you will also need to gain an understanding of each Numen—mainly Letholdus; he's the most popular among prayer."

Ben waited with an expectant look on his face.

Alucard suspected he was either unconfident to ask questions he might consider stupid or was simply so into this new job that he wanted to be told everything as quickly as it could be said. He didn't care which. He just wanted to get this over with.

The vampire dipped his quill in ink and held it out to Ben. "You will sign this, and it will make you an official pastor. You are Attila's replacement, so it only makes sense if you were his student at one point. Attila mentored you and made you the man you are today."

Nodding, Ben took the quill and signed his name at the bottom of the paper. "Where should I do my research?"

Alucard glanced at Ben's signature, reading a very neatly written 'Benjamin Walker'. He then rolled the signed parchment back up and glanced at Ben. "You can study here," he said, looking up at one of the shelves higher on the study's walls. "I have copies of each Book of Lore and non-fiction texts in Deiganish, so you will be able to read them. That shelf there," he said, pointing to the shelf closest to the edge of the second-to-highest platform.

"Thank you," Ben said, setting his eyes back on Alucard.

The vampire tied the parchment firmly with a red ribbon and handed it to Ben. "You vill often need to show this to new contacts, so take it with you wherever you go." As Ben took it from him, Alucard picked up the second piece of rolled parchment and laid it out along the table. "This is a contract of your allegiance to me and the Nosferatu, as well as proof of your new position. Sign," he said, tapping the small space at the very bottom of the intimidatingly-small print.

Ben signed without reading any of it.

Alucard allowed the parchment to roll itself back up and placed it aside. He then unrolled the last piece, which was black, not white. "And this is a contract signing ownership of your soul over to me."

With an amused laugh, Ben gawped at him and then went to sign it—

"You sign this one with your blood," Alucard said, taking the quill from Ben before he could try and sign the black paper with black ink.

With an unsure frown, Ben looked around for a moment and then chuckled. "Are you…that's a joke, right?"

"Is it?" Alucard tested, making Ben stutter in uncertainty. He then handed the man the small dagger left on his desk yesterday and stared expectantly at him.

As he stared at the dagger, Ben frowned anxiously, glanced at Alucard, and laughed nervously. "Okay…" he drawled. He was obviously waiting for Alucard to tell him that it was a joke…but the vampire just glared at him, waiting. When Ben finally worked out that he was serious, he slowly pressed the blade against his right index finger; he paused before he cut, shooting another unsure glance at Alucard again, but still, the vampire remained silent and deadpan.

Ben looked back down at his hand, cut his finger, and then moved it towards the space at the bottom of the black parchment. He pressed his bleeding finger against the paper, and once he pulled it away, he observed as the splodge of his blood soaked into it, soon reappearing and forming his name.

With a nervous laugh, watching as Alucard rolled the black parchment back up and placed it beside the second piece, Ben dragged his hand over the back of his neck. "That uh...that was a joke, right? I didn't really...sign my soul over to you or anything?"

Alucard set his eyes on him once more. "Attila has made all the necessary progress in DeiganLupus; I will write to all my allies and inform them that Attila has stepped down. You will be travelling to DeiganLupus often, so make sure you become accustomed to their way of living. Tomorrow, I leave for Avalmoor; when I return three or maybe four days later, I will take you to meet Cedric. Cedric is from DeiganLupus; he will help you learn what it is to live and work there. He will tell you some of the local language, as they use terms there that wouldn't make sense anywhere else—unless you used such terms back in Eltaria, then the day will go much faster."

Ben nodded and rested his arms on the table, shuffling around uncomfortably. "You said I'll need to dress the part."

The vampire nodded. "You see how Attila used to dress—that will be you."

His pale face turned green, but he nodded obediently. "I haven't toured much of the city. Where can I find the things Attila wore?"

"Go and ask him. You'll find him in the same tavern he always goes to. He knows I'm replacing him, and that I would send his replacement to him. I told him to leave the country, and he will do so tonight when the trade ships leave. Do well to catch him before then, otherwise you'll have to find your own way around."

"I'll go now," Ben said, standing up.

"No," Alucard denied. "Did you bring people for Felix to turn?"

Ben sat back down. "I did. Remont and I found several interesting candidates."

"Good. Put someone else on the prison runs, too. You won't be around to do that anymore."

"Of course."

"On your way out, send one of the butlers to me—not the blonde one, though."

Standing up, Ben nodded again. "And should I go to Attila once I leave?"

"*Da.*"

With a slight smile and yet another nod, Ben turned around and left Alucard's study.

As Ben left, Alucard rested the side of his face in his hand. At least *that* part of his day was over. He'd still have to make sure Ben was up to par before sending him off to do Attila's job, but he felt confident that he was the best choice for Attila's replacement.

Alucard then set his eyes on the door. Zalith made his way into the study in one of the vampire's white shirts and with an amused smile on his face.

"What?" the vampire questioned.

Zalith sat where Ben had been sitting. "Did you actually make him sign ownership of his soul over to you?"

Amused, Alucard smirked and shrugged, sure that refusing to give Zalith an answer would irritate him—the kind of irritancy similar to that which Alucard felt when the demon failed to sink his fangs into his neck. He stood up and took the two rolled pieces of signed parchment with him as he walked over to one of the shelves at the back of the room. "If you still want to walk, we can go soon. I just have something to do first."

"Such as?" Zalith asked as he suddenly appeared and leaned against the wall beside the shelf.

Once he placed the parchment on the shelf, Alucard turned to face him. "I have to heal my arm. If I take too long, the healing process will slow, and I'd rather *not* have to stand around draining the life of a dozen ugly people," he mumbled.

Zalith adorned an intrigued frown. "Out of general curiosity… completely healed: if you were to consume the blood of say… a demon, would it have negative effects on you? Would it cause your true form to begin manifesting?"

"No. I can consume the blood of anything and anyone. I just choose to drink human blood to heal my human likeness because it's a whole lot faster. Drinking demon blood while trying to heal my true form would only make it worse if I was unable to control what the blood does for me," he explained.

The demon moved closer. "What the blood does for you?" he asked as if he didn't already know demons could choose what the blood they consumed did for them and their bodies.

Zalith just wanted to hear him talk, didn't he? Alucard wasn't exactly in the mood to entertain this morning, and as he heard one of his butlers approaching the study, he turned away from Zalith and made his way back over to his desk. When the butler walked in and asked what he was needed for, Alucard gestured his hand, instructing the butler to come closer. However, as he approached, hesitation gripped Alucard. Why had Zalith asked so many times if it *had* to be humans he drank from? It couldn't be that he was curious—Alucard knew how knowledgeable the demon was. Was Zalith going to offer him *his* blood?

Alucard dismissed his frown and stepped forward. He snatched the unsuspecting butler's throat before he could speak another word, and then he relentlessly sank his fangs into the man's neck, pinning him against the wall and denying him the ability to scream.

The vampire quickly drained the man of all his blood, and as he threw the dead body to the floor, Zalith appeared beside him. Alucard leaned against the wall, sighing quietly as the high the blood gave him made him feel content.

"Are you going to run out of butlers, Alucard?" the demon asked.

Leaning his back against the wall as he dragged the back of his hand over his mouth, Alucard shrugged. "No. When one dies, another comes along and replaces them. Anyway, perhaps today we can walk without interruption."

The demon smiled. "Did you and Ben cover everything that needed to be covered?"

"More or less," Alucard mumbled, looking down at the floor. "I told him all I could tell him until he knows what he needs to know from Attila."

"You sent him to talk to Attila?"

"I did. I may have fired and threatened to kill him, but I mean enough to him for him to help his replacement on their way to doing his job."

Zalith smirked flirtatiously and went to say something—

"We can go now," the vampire interjected. He didn't want to fall victim to the demon's unseemly behaviour again.

Smiling, Zalith stood up straight. "Then let's go," he agreed.

Alucard nervously moved away from the wall, and when he was sure that Zalith wasn't suddenly going to grab his arm or stroke his face, he led the way out of the study and headed for the castle's exit.

Chapter Twenty-one

— ⚔ ✝ ⚔ —

Leaving

| **Zalith** |

*Z*alith walked beside Alucard as they strolled along the beach. As they traversed the sandy expanse in a shared silence, the demon's heart swelled with the warmth of newfound joy. Alucard cast a unique spell upon him, weaving a tapestry of contentment he had never known. Each intricate detail uncovered about the vampire became a source of delight, and with each shared moment, the tapestry of their connection deepened.

He was glad that they'd be sleeping in the same bed from now on; he loved waking up to Alucard's face and the delight of just lying in bed with him talking. Knowing he'd get to do that every morning brought a smile to his face.

However, the demon was still curious about what Alucard might have been trying to say last night, but he wasn't going to pressure him to answer. He'd try to be patient and wait for Alucard to tell him in his own time.

He also felt a little irked about what he'd seen this morning. He still didn't like seeing Alucard feed on other people…even though the vampire *had* to do it to heal himself. Zalith would keep that to himself, though; he didn't want to let his jealousy ruin everything.

"What are you going to do until tonight?" he asked curiously, looking at Alucard.

Staring down at the white sand, Alucard shrugged slightly. "I'll speak to Felix about the new vampires I have him making, and then I'll prepare for the evening…and our trip. The show begins at eight—that's what the butler in the hall said to me as we were leaving. We'll also be leaving for Boszorkány rather early if that's okay."

The demon smiled. "That's perfectly fine."

"What will *you* do?"

"I need to tell my friend that I'll be away for a few days, and I have some business of my own to tend to. After that, I'll gather the things I'll be needing for the trip, and then I'll see you tonight," he explained, smiling at him.

The vampire glanced at him. "Remember to wear something gold."

"I will."

Alucard then stared ahead as they came close to the end of the beach where the forest stretched out onto it. "We can head back now," he said, stopping in his tracks.

"Wait," Zalith insisted as he took hold of Alucard's wrist before he could start to lead the way back to the castle. As the vampire looked at him and waited, he asked, "Are you sure you want me to come with you? I don't want to impose or insist upon spending all of my time with you if you'd rather have the time to yourself."

The vampire frowned shyly and glanced at his castle in the distance. "If I didn't want you to come, I'd tell you. I'd much rather have you with me than go alone," he admitted, the nervousness on his face and in his voice making the demon smile.

"I'd not rather be anywhere else, anyway," Zalith said, and as they began to walk back towards the castle, he linked his arm with Alucard's. "I know I need to bring something warm to wear for Avalmoor, but what about Boszorkány? Will it be cold there, too?"

Alucard examined Zalith's curious face. "Strangely enough, no. It's always rather warm there, so bring something for such weather."

"Noted. I'm now aware that you feel the cold, but do you feel the warmth?"

The vampire shrugged. "It depends how hot it is, I guess."

Smirking, Zalith glanced ahead. "So, will I see more of your skin, or will you be dressing as usual, despite the heat?"

Alucard looked down at the sand again. "I don't know. It depends how I feel," he muttered.

Zalith smiled. "Either way, I'm looking forward to our trip," he said as they stopped by the wall surrounding the castle.

"It rains a lot in Boszorkány," Alucard added as he let go of Zalith's arm and stood in front of him.

"I'll remember that, too."

With a slight nod, Alucard looked at the wall. "I'll see you tonight, then."

The demon placed his hands on either side of Alucard's face and kissed his lips. "Until then," he said and let go of him.

Then, Zalith created a rift in the wall. He smirked at Alucard, and without further delay, he stepped through the rift to head back home. As the rift started closing behind him, he glanced back at Alucard again and winked at him. He then grinned as Alucard's face turned red, and once the rift sealed shut, he laughed quietly and headed through the darkness which would take him home.

| **Alucard** |

Alucard sighed tiredly and looked down at the grass once the rift closed. He'd already decided what he'd be doing with the remainder of his day, so he didn't let himself sink into his thoughts and made his way up to the castle.

When he got there, he silently walked through the entrance hall, into the vampires' half of the castle, and up to Felix's room.

Without knocking, he opened the door and stepped into the pitch-black room. Of course, Alucard could see in the dark as if it were daylight, so he set his eyes on Felix, who was sitting on his bed with a small journal in his hands.

Immediately, Felix closed the book, jumped to his feet, and smiled nervously. "A-Aleksei," he stuttered.

Uninterested in making conversation, Alucard leaned against the doorframe and crossed his arms. "Where are the new vampires?"

"In tower," Felix answered, nodding.

"Are they adjusting well?"

"Y-yes. I can't check until night. Sunlight hurt," he said with a nervous laugh.

"Did you use *all* of the blood I gave you?"

Felix frowned, hesitated, and then nodded. "All," he confirmed. "Fifteen people now vampires. Twelve men, three women. Ben and Remont bring them."

"Good," Alucard mumbled. "I will be out tonight, so while I'm gone, I want you to find out who each of them are. Names, occupations, family."

"I will do that."

Then, without another word, Alucard left Felix's room, closing the door behind him.

As he made his way back through the castle, he couldn't help but notice his fatigue. All he wanted to do was sleep, but he couldn't do that until he finished what needed to be done before tonight.

He emerged into the entrance hall—

"Sir," one of the butlers called.

Alucard closed the door behind him and glanced at the entrance to the kitchens. He set his eyes on William, the blonde-haired, blue-eyed butler. "What?" he asked, seeing that the butler had a piece of paper in one of his hands.

"I have the necessary papers for the performance you asked Liam to check the times for. He handed them to me to read, as they are in Deiganish. You need to sign your name in order to reserve a seat," he explained, making his way over as he held the paper out.

Taking the paper from him, Alucard glanced at it. He couldn't read most of it, but what he did understand told him that he did, in fact, need to name himself and if he'd be bringing anyone with him. He asked William, "Do I sign both our names or just mine?"

"If you are taking a guest with you, I believe you just say you will be with someone, sir," he answered, holding a small pencil out to him.

Alucard took the pencil, eyed the paper a few more times, and then signed his name at the bottom. He added '+1' alongside it. If he didn't have to name Zalith, he wouldn't. Then, he handed the paper and pencil back to William.

"I will deliver this back to the opera house for you, sir," the butler said with a humble bow. "Once you arrive, they will ask for your name to confirm you have reserved places. You will also need to pay in advance."

"No, I won't," he said with an amused smile on his face.

William glanced at him and then looked down at the paper. "I'll get this done." The butler scurried away and back into the kitchens, leaving Alucard alone.

The vampire could finally rest. He left the hall, swiftly made his way up to his bedroom, and lazily slumped down onto his bed. There wasn't much else to do with his day, so he might as well sleep until Zalith returned. That was all he was really looking forward to, after all. So, he made himself comfortable, closed his eyes, and allowed himself to drift off to sleep.

Chapter Twenty-Two

— ⊰ † ⊱ —

The Citadel Council

| **Zalith** |

When Zalith stepped through his front door, he sighed deeply and pulled his blazer off. He crossed the hall and headed into his office, and the moment he slumped down, all he could think about was the fact that he missed Alucard already. But despite what Alucard just said, he was still afraid of spending too much time with the vampire. And it wasn't like he had to wait days to see him again; he'd see him tonight. He just had to get today over with.

He leaned back in his seat and started looking through his mail. But before he got through the pile, his door burst open, and he looked up from the letters to see Varana standing in the doorway with a frustrated look on her face.

"Where were you?!" she exclaimed angrily.

"Knocking isn't a crime, you know," he said as he looked back down at his mail.

"Answer me!" she demanded.

Zalith shrugged as he flipped through each envelope. "Nowhere."

"Tell me now!" the woman stropped, stamping her feet as if she were a toddler having a tantrum.

He put the letters down and rested his arms on his desk. "How was your day today?" he asked her, trying to change the subject.

Her scowl thickened. "Sad and lonely. Where were you?!"

"Out," he said. "It's not really any of your business, though," he said with a quiet but irritated laugh.

She crossed her arms and retorted, "Why are you so rude all the time?!"

He frowned. "Wait…I'm *rude*?" he asked amusedly.

"Ugh," she drawled as she rolled her eyes.

Zalith then told her, "I'm going out after my dinner with the council, and I'll be gone for four days, give or take."

Varana's face almost turned red with anger. "And what am I supposed to do for four days?!"

"I don't know. Read a book or something," he said with a shrug.

"Take me with you!" she demanded.

"I can't, sorry."

"Why?!"

"Because I can't."

She scowled skeptically. "Is it because you're going with that ugly vampire?"

Zalith's nonchalant mood withered, replaced by aggravation. "Get out of my office. I have things to do."

But Varana didn't leave. She stayed where she was, even when Zalith started opening and reading his letters. The woman was clearly waiting for him to say anything, but he had nothing more to say to her. And when she worked that out, she groaned and stomped her feet around. "Please just take me with you," she whined.

"No. But maybe I'll bring something back for you if there's somewhere nice to shop."

"I don't want anything," she grumbled.

"Fine. Suit yourself." He put the letter he was reading down and picked up another.

Varana went silent again... but after a few seconds, she said, "If you get me a dress, don't get anything orange or yellow. I'm not interested in those colours this month." And then she left, slamming the door behind her.

Zalith sighed and swivelled around in his seat to face the windows. He stared out at the gardens, watching as one of the gardeners watered the flowerbeds. The fact that Varana was still insulting Alucard and trying to poke her nose into their business irritated Zalith, but he wasn't surprised; she was like this with everyone he started seeing. He just hoped that she'd get over it sooner or later. He also hoped that what he and Alucard had lasted; he really did feel so differently about him than he'd ever felt about anyone else.

And thinking about Alucard made him shift his thoughts to the meeting he had with the Citadel council later. They'd be discussing their plans for the city gangs and knowing that two of them had history with Alucard that might land the vampire in trouble if he happened across the wrong guy made Zalith feel even more motivation to eradicate or chase them out. He wanted this place to be safe not only for the people but Alucard, too.

However, that meeting wasn't until much later. He had other things to get done first.

He left his office and headed upstairs to his bedroom. As he headed into the on-suite, he pulled off his clothes with a deep, heavy sigh. He climbed into the shower, switched the water on, and stood there while it trickled down his body.

All he could think about was Alucard. The vampire possessed every corner of his mind; he missed him so much while he was in Tengetso, and finally getting to spend time with him again filled him with relief and happiness, but he needed more. He craved the touch of Alucard's skin, the feel of his naked body against his. He wanted to experience every inch of him with all of his senses. But he had to wait. He had to be patient.

He exhaled deeply and started washing his hair, but no matter what he did to try and distract himself, he couldn't get Alucard off his mind, and his thoughts were beginning to wander away from simply admiring the vampire's features.

Zalith wanted him *so* bad; his desperation left him feeling frustrated, and he couldn't help but let his hand wander down to his crotch. When he dragged his fingers over his arousal, a shiver of delight spiralled through his body; he closed his eyes and leaned his other arm against the wall, and while he slowly caressed his hardening dick, he let himself imagine that it was Alucard's hand around his shaft.

But the moment he thought about Alucard's hand, he started thinking about his ass. He thought about sliding his dick inside the vampire, he thought about feeling his tight walls wrap around his shaft, and as he started moving his hand faster, he thought about thrusting into Alucard, listening to him moan, watching his body shiver and tremble as Zalith thrusted harder.

The demon's body tensed up. He moved his hand even quicker, sinking into the fantasy that he was finally fucking Alucard. He groaned quietly, and a hushed moan escaped his quickening breaths as delight ensnared him. He neared closer to his peak, but the pleasure didn't get any more intense; it was just enough to push him over the edge, though, and as he climaxed, he moaned contently and rested his forehead against the wall.

However, the second it was over, the fantasy withered, and Zalith cringed *hard*. He felt embarrassed with himself, maybe even a little ashamed. But he didn't want to think about it. He huffed and let go of his shaft, and then he got back to showering. Alucard still possessed every corner of his mind, and as much as he loved thinking about the vampire, all it was doing right now was making him feel frustrated and desperate.

He shifted his attention as best he could to what he had to get done today before he met back up with Alucard. He had letters to respond to, and then he needed to head to the Citadel to meet with the council. *That* was what he should be concentrating on. The gangs terrorizing the city needed to be dealt with, and he planned to purge the Citadel of every single one of them.

The hours ticked by, and when it was time for Zalith to leave and head for the Citadel, he left his office and made his way to the front door. As he grabbed his coat, he saw the butler, Edwin, cross the hall.

"Edwin," he called.

The man stopped in his tracks and turned to face his direction. "Yes, sir?"

"Where's Varana?"

"Oh…she requested not to speak to you ever again," he answered.

Zalith sighed and said, "Okay, thank you for letting me know. Have a good day."

"You, too, sir," the butler said and then walked off.

With an irritated huff, Zalith buttoned his coat up. He wasn't going to run upstairs and give Varana the attention that she clearly wanted; she wasn't a baby. The demon slipped his shoes on and stepped outside. He made his way over to the carriage, and once he climbed inside, he tapped the roof, letting the coachman know that it was time to leave.

He relaxed and stared out the window as the carriage left his estate and headed towards the city. Once he was done with the council, he'd be able to head to Dor-Sanguis and meet Alucard. He was looking forward to seeing an opera performance with him, and to spending more time with him. He just hoped that Alucard didn't get tired of him.

The demon relaxed, watching as the forest passed by outside. When the trees thinned and become suburban roads, he eyed the scattered houses and patches of farmland on the horizon.

When the carriage entered the Citadel, he leaned back in his seat and composed himself. He was about to have a very important conversation, and he didn't want to be distracted thinking about Alucard or how irritated Varana made him feel today. So he dismissed his thoughts and focused on what he knew about the Citadel gangs.

He waited until the carriage reached the Magnolia Elysium restaurant. Once it stopped, an attendant pulled the door open for him. The demon climbed out, emerging into the elegant courtyard paved with white stone; he made his way towards the golden-edged double doors, and when he stepped into the reception area, the black-haired hostess smiled at him and straightened her white uniform.

"Good evening, sir Zalith," she said pleasantly.

"I'll take your coat, sir," another host said as he appeared beside Zalith.

The demon let the man take his coat. "Thank you."

"This way," the hostess then said.

Zalith followed her through the quiet restaurant; he recognized a few faces sitting at the tables, but nobody he felt the need to greet. The hostess took him up a flight of stairs and onto the second floor, which overlooked the first. Sitting around a rectangular table in the middle of the vast space were the city council members, and they all stood up, smiled over at him, and called their greetings as the demon approached.

Benedict Watson, the Citadel Mayor, was the first to shake his hand. The middle-aged man's dull brown hair looked a little greasy as if he'd used too much pomade; his thick, bushy moustache hung over his lips, and as the man said, "Good evening, Zalith," his putrid breath made it hard for Zalith to stifle a grimace. This man hardly ever brushed his teeth, and whenever he ate, food got stuck in his moustache, a sight the demon wasn't looking forward to.

The next council member to shake his hand was Polly Tillman, the uppity city clerk. She was oldest among them, her hair greyed, frizzy, and tied into a bun. Her glasses were at least an inch thick, and her voice was croaky and a little hard to understand. She smiled weakly at him before returning to her seat. Zalith knew that she publicly despised elves, and considering that he was pretending to be one, he was certain that she thought he was disgusting.

Margo Hart, the head of the law enforcement division, shook his hand and greeted him next. The stoic brunette was probably the only person at the table who didn't irritate or revolt him, and it seemed as though she felt the same. "How was your day?" she asked him.

"Good, thank you. And you?" he replied.

"Busy," she chuckled. "But that's nothing new."

Archibald Hornsby then reached past Margo and gripped Zalith's hand. "Glad to see you made it," he said with a grin, baring his yellow teeth. The old, grey-haired man reeked of tobacco, and his balding head had flakes of dried hair products all over it.

"Sit," Benedict then said enthusiastically. "Appetizers will be here momentarily."

Everyone took their seats. To Zalith's relief, there was a seat available beside Margo, so he sat beside her and made himself comfortable.

A waiter then walked over and asked Zalith, "Red or white, sir?"

"Red, please," the demon answered.

The man poured him a glass of red wine and placed it on the table for him.

"Thank you," the demon said.

"So, Margo," Archibald called across the table. "How are the police units working out?" It sounded like he was mocking her.

But Margo kept her calm, nonchalant composure and said, "They've had a tough time dealing with the Imperito and Meshuga, but they'll get their bearings soon enough."

Archibald scoffed. "Soon enough? Those gangs have caused over a cidaris in damages just these past two months!" he exclaimed.

"Now, now," Benedict said. "We're all doing our absolute best to deal with this, so let's be patient with each other." And then he smiled at Zalith. "And let's not forget that if it wasn't for Zalith, we wouldn't even be having this talk. Now, there's actual hope for ridding our city of these scoundrels."

"We would have worked something out eventually," Polly muttered.

Zalith discreetly rolled his eyes as he took a sip of his wine.

The door at the other end of the room then opened, and a group of waiters came out with plates in their hands. They each placed one in front of everyone, and then they left silently.

Zalith looked down at the plate of truffle risotto.

"Have your investigators turned anything up?" Benedict asked the demon before greedily scoffing down some of his risotto.

"They have," Zalith said with a nod. "The Meshuga are pretty much your average band of pirates, only much larger. They operate out of a large, possibly stolen galleon called The Rowdy Barb. It's docked in Royland Shipyard, heavily guarded. Some of them even have dogs."

"How many people are we talking?" Margo asked.

"My men counted at least a hundred and thirty. But their leader, who calls himself Grimclaw Drake—actual name Trent Mills—isn't human."

Polly scoffed rudely.

Ignoring her, Zalith continued. "He's a berserker, otherwise known as a werebear."

"My units aren't prepared to deal with non-humans," Margo said, shaking her head.

"My people can handle him," the demon assured her.

"Have you any ideas as to where we start with getting them out of the Citadel?" Archibald asked and sipped from his wine.

Zalith, who was about to try his food, lowered his fork and nodded. "A few ideas. I suggest that we start with a kinder approach and give them terms, ask them to disband or leave the city, etcetera."

"And if that doesn't work?" Polly questioned.

"Then I'd suggest we use full force," Zalith answered. He then tried his risotto, but it wasn't as good as it looked—it was a little *too* earthy. He'd still eat it, though.

Benedict finished his food *already* and leaned back in his seat. "And what about the Imperito? Any leads?"

"As far as my men were able to tell," Zalith started and took a sip of his wine to wash away the earthy taste lingering in his mouth, "they're all human. Their leader, Don Lorenzo Armani, owns several businesses in the city and has access to trade ships. We discovered that he's smuggling weapons into Nefastus from all around Aegisguard; he's been seen with military-grade weaponry, including ethos-imbued weapons."

The council looked around at each other, clearly unnerved.

"It sounds like we'd need an army to deal with the Imperito," Benedict exclaimed.

"And we don't have the money for that or the damages that'll be left as a result of a full-scale street war," Archibald said, shaking his head.

"I don't suppose you have an army, do you?" Margo asked Zalith.

The demon laughed a little and shook his head. "I'm sure we'll be able to figure something out. We'll find a weakness in their ranks, tear their organization apart from the inside out."

"You sound experienced," Margo flirted.

"I am with many things," he said, glancing at her. He didn't want to outright flirt with her, but if she liked him, things would go a lot smoother in the long run.

"Who do you suggest we start with?" Polly asked, her voice snippy and irritated.

"Well, we have a few options that I've thought about. We could deal with the Meshuga first to get them out of the way, because not only are they incredibly annoying and easier to deal with, but the Imperito aren't going to get involved and might actually help if they see that the local law enforcement is taking a stand against them," Zalith explained.

The council members nodded, waiting to hear more.

Zalith took a sip of his wine and continued, "Or, as I just mentioned, we could plant someone into the Imperito or turn someone already in the gang and get them to feed us information which will help us slowly destroy them." He paused and glanced at them all to see that they were eager to hear the rest. "The third option is a lot messier. We could ignite a war between the two gangs and get them to kill each other off. Whoever is left in the aftermath, the police and my people can deal with." He paused for a moment, giving them a chance to speak, but when none of them did, he said, "However, I think that we should start with option one. Innocent civilians could get caught in the crossfire of option three."

They glanced around the table at each other, all with the same pondering expression.

After a few moments, though, Benedict said, "That sounds like a good plan. Can we rely on the help of your men alongside the police?"

The demon nodded. "Of course."

"All right," Margo said with a sigh. "I suppose we should arrange another meeting with my units and your men," she said to Zalith. "The sooner we discuss a plan of approach, the sooner we can get to work."

"If you send over your schedule, I'll let you know when I'm free," Zalith said.

She smiled and said, "Sounds good."

The door then opened again, and the waiters returned with the main course.

Zalith looked down at the lobster thermidor as it was placed in front of him, and when the waiters left, the council started eating. He tried a piece of his lobster, and to his relief, it was delicious.

"So, how do you plan to fix the damage caused by the Meshuga's latest riot?" Polly asked Archibald.

While the council discussed things that didn't have much to do with him, Zalith finally let himself think about Alucard. He'd be seeing him soon, and he was excited for their date. He was also relieved that the discussion hadn't lasted hours; he *did* have to meet again to formulate a plan with Margo's men, but that probably wouldn't take long, either. But he didn't want to think about that right now. Now, his mind dismissed business and focused on pleasure.

Chapter Twenty-Three

— ⟨ ✝ ⟩ —

Opera

| **Alucard** |

The sound of Sabazios' claws clipping against the floor woke Alucard. He lay in his bed, waiting for the hound's inevitable arrival; through the slightly cracked curtains, he noticed the darkening sky and the light of each moon beginning to stain the warmth of the sunset. It was almost time for him to get up and ready to meet Zalith again.

It felt as though he hadn't slept at all, but he knew that was because of his recovering body. Healing his injuries from the previous night constantly used his ethos and wouldn't cease doing so until he'd consumed enough blood to completely heal himself. He could've fed on all four humans he needed at once, but he felt that if he did that, he might lose himself to all that blood. So, he waited and made sure to spread his healing over a few days.

When he heard his bedroom door creep open, he sighed and watched as the hellhound made his way over. Sabazios sat in front of him, resting his chin on the edge of the bed a few inches from the vampire's face.

"What?" Alucard grumbled, glaring into the hound's white eyes.

Sabazios whimpered quietly, his eyes darting back and forth as he shared the news of Zalith's arrival.

"Right," Alucard said and sat up. He patted the hound's head and told him, "I'll feed you later. Go and fetch my sword—the cane one," he instructed, and as Sabazios left the room, he climbed out of bed and headed into the on-suite. The outfit he'd chosen for the night was already laid out in the bathroom, but he needed to shower first. He took off his clothes, stepped into the shower, and switched the water on.

He didn't like to rush when getting ready for something formal. He thoroughly showered, dressed into his white fitted shirt, black trousers, and black dovetail coat, and tidied his hair. Then, he left his bedroom and made his way through the castle corridors.

He was looking forward to his date with Zalith, and as he thought about seeing the demon again so soon, a smile clung to his face.

| **Zalith** |

In the main hall, Zalith made himself comfortable at the head of the table. He admired what he could see of himself in the golden chair's reflective surface; he eyed his all-black suit, straightened the collar of his white shirt, and fiddled with his black bowtie. He glanced at his black silk high hat, which he'd placed on the table, and wondered whether he should have chosen a different one. He wanted to make sure he looked his absolute best for Alucard, especially since they'd be seen together by the Dargamoor aristocrats.

But almost twenty minutes had passed since his arrival, and as the clock ticked on, he wondered…what could Alucard be doing? He looked around, glancing at the stained-glass windows and the décor lined along the walls. When he heard a door open, he looked over at it, hoping that it was Alucard, but it was just the vampire's blonde butler coming out to clean the floors.

The demon sighed quietly, but just then, the door to Alucard's side of the castle opened. Sabazios led the way out with something in his mouth as Alucard followed behind him. A smile crept across Zalith's face; obviously, the vampire had spent all this time getting ready, and he couldn't look any more alluring—with his clothes on, anyway.

Zalith eyed Alucard as he walked over to the door to the kitchens and muttered quietly to a butler who was carrying Zalith's suitcase away. The vampire was dressed similarly to him—an all-black suit, a white shirt, and he even donned a black bowtie, and in his right hand, he was carrying a black high hat. As Alucard then left the butler and walked towards the table, the demon made sure to let Alucard know that he appreciated just how well he dressed in the form of a suggestive smile.

"I didn't mean to take so long," Alucard said, stopping in front of Zalith as he stood up.

"You can take as long as you need," he replied contently and greeted the vampire with a kiss. When their lips met, a feeling of relief hit Zalith; he felt as if the weight of his day had been entirely lifted.

As Sabazios trotted over and held a cane out to Alucard, the vampire took it and glanced back at the kitchen door. "Your things will be put on the ship," he said, setting his eyes on Zalith again. "The staff will do all of that for us."

"I look forward to seeing this ship of yours," he said as he stroked his fingers over the hand Alucard was holding his cane in. "I assume this is more than what meets the eye?" he asked with a smirk, sure that Alucard wouldn't make a point of bringing a cane without reason.

Alucard pulled the cane's wolf-shaped pommel to reveal that it was, in fact, a rapier-like blade inside a thin sheath. "I always take a weapon wherever I go, just in case."

"Understandable," he said as Alucard concealed the blade once again.

"Unless there's anything you wish to do before we go, we can leave now," Alucard suggested, taking his cape from the back of the chair Zalith had been sitting in.

"I'm ready to go when you are."

Alucard put his hat on and pulled his cape over his shoulders. "Watch the place," he said to Sabazios, and as the beast nodded and wandered off, the vampire looked at Zalith. "The groundskeeper should be waiting outside with the carriage."

The demon smiled and put his own hat on, and then he linked arms with Alucard. "Let's go."

Strolling together, Zalith and Alucard traversed the ornate hallways and emerged into the moonlit courtyard. In the soft glow, Zalith couldn't help but let his gaze linger unabashedly on Alucard. His eyes traced the contours of the vampire's face, each feature illuminated by the moonlight.

A magnetic pull seemed to draw Zalith into the depths of Alucard's mesmerizing gaze, those hell-fiery eyes casting a spell that enchanted his very soul. As they moved, the demon found himself entranced, his attention fixated on the alluring profile beside him. His gaze lingered, unable to tear away from the captivating sight; it was as if the quiet night conspired with Alucard's presence to create an intoxicating atmosphere that enveloped them both.

Their steps carried them towards the black ebony carriage. Just when Zalith thought the enchantment would never wane, Alucard gently withdrew his arm from Zalith's, and with a graceful gesture, the vampire opened the carriage door.

Zalith, reluctantly torn from the spellbinding trance, felt a bittersweet pang. But the night held promises and secrets that he was eager to uncover, and he wouldn't waste a moment. He smiled at Alucard and said, "Thank you," as the vampire invited him into the carriage first. Once he climbed in, he sat down and made himself comfortable.

Alucard got in, too, pulled the door shut behind him, and sat beside Zalith. "I'm not sure how long the performance will last," he started, glancing at the demon's curious face. "If it's not to your liking, we can leave and either find something else to do or head back here," he said, tapping the carriage's wall, letting the coachman know it was time to leave.

As the vampire made himself comfortable, Zalith smiled. "I'm sure it'll be an interesting show."

Alucard nodded as the carriage started moving.

"So, how was the rest of your day?" Zalith asked him.

"Eh." The vampire shrugged. "I checked in on Felix and then I slept some more. What about you?"

"I gathered my things for our trip, cleared up some business, and now here I am." He kissed Alucard's cheek. "I missed you."

Alucard smiled shyly as he looked away. "We'll be together for the next five or so days; hopefully you don't tire of me."

"I don't believe that could ever happen—if it could, it would have happened over a year ago," Zalith said confidently.

"I feel the same," Alucard mumbled nervously.

"So, tell me, what time are we leaving tomorrow?"

Alucard set his eyes on him. "After dawn. It will take the day, night, and a few hours of the next day to get to Boszorkány. Drac will then need to rest, so we'll spend some hours there. Then, we'll travel the rest of the way to Avalmoor—that will take the night and an hour or so of the next day."

"Do you have any ideas for our date in Boszorkány?" Zalith asked with a smirk.

"There are a few things we can do there. I'm sure we'll find something."

"As am I," the demon agreed. "And this ship of yours, are there crew? Or will it be just us?"

The vampire stared out of the carriage window. "There will be crew; it's a large ship. But they will be no bother. Most of them are scared of me so they tend to avoid me unless I need them."

Zalith smirked again. "Good." Then, he turned his head to look outside, too. The gravelled path became cobblestone, and the smell of petrichor lingered in the air. Splatters of rain hit the windows, and as the carriage continued forward, the demon leaned back in his seat and waited for them to arrive at their destination. He was sure he was going to thoroughly enjoy tonight.

| **Alucard** |

When the carriage came to a slow halt, the sound of busy footsteps clattered outside. The rain poured down *hard*, pitter-patting on the roof as the horse snorted quietly. Alucard and Zalith waited as the coachman leapt down off the carriage's front, made his way along the outside, and pulled the right door open, greeting both the demon and the vampire with a humble bow.

"We have arrived, sirs," the man said, stepping aside to reveal the entrance to the opera house a few yards from the curb.

There was a long line of aristocrats waiting to get inside, and although Alucard would usually use his status to barge to the front, he didn't want to deal with the commotion or comments tonight.

Zalith invited Alucard to step out first, and when Alucard climbed out, he felt Zalith squeeze his ass as he followed him out of the carriage. The vampire scowled at him, trying to disguise his fluster with anger, but that made Zalith's smirk grow wider, so he faced ahead and tried to dismiss his embarrassment.

Once they stepped onto the wet sidewalk, the coachman closed the carriage door, climbed back up onto the driver's seat, and headed off up the street.

"What a marvellous place," Zalith said with a pleasant smile as he eyed the entrance of the gold-white marble opera house.

Without answering, Alucard led the way forward and joined the queue. As Zalith stood beside him, he glanced at the demon and said, "It hasn't been around that long but it's become quite popular already."

"And what is this particular opera about?"

Alucard shrugged lightly. "It's called Icarus," he answered as people started to line up behind them. "It's about a man who strives for great achievement, reaches his goals, but tempts fate and pushes for more. He inevitably loses everything he worked so hard for as a result of his greed."

The demon smiled. "Well, it sounds delightful."

Alucard then frowned, unsure if Zalith was being sarcastic or was actually looking forward to the performance. He often found himself questioning whether he was reading Zalith's face correctly, and right now, he wasn't sure if he was able to read it at all. So, he glanced at the demon, examined his somewhat vacant stare as he glared at the people in front of them, and sighed. "Do you not want to be here?"

Zalith frowned as he took his eyes off the annoyingly loud crowd and looked at Alucard. "What gives you that impression?"

Detecting the confusion in Zalith's voice, Alucard shrugged and said, "Nothing."

The demon turned to face him. "I don't want to be anywhere else or with anyone else," he said with a smile. "I'm sorry if I seem bothered tonight; the conversation I had with Varana about my absence over the next few days didn't go well, but nothing ever really does with her—unless she's the centre of attention. I won't let it ruin our evening, though."

That woman's name irritated Alucard—the woman who lived with Zalith; the same woman who made a point of harassing Zalith the night of and morning after they had dinner. Alucard could already tell Varana had an unhealthy interest in Zalith—an unhealthy interest in who Alucard might like to call *his* demon…. He frowned and looked down at the wet ground. He suddenly felt very possessive of Zalith, so possessive that he thought he shouldn't say anything about it in case he said something to upset or offend the demon.

"Are you okay?" Zalith asked in concern, obviously noticing Alucard's silence.

"I'm fine," he instantly replied, glancing at him. "You don't seem bothered."

As the line began moving, Zalith turned to face the front. "Will you be leaving Ben in charge while you're gone again?"

"Probably," Alucard answered as they stepped forward.

When they reached the front of the line, they both eyed the ticket usher; he was a small, tired-looking man dressed in a white suit with a pair of small, circular glasses clinging to his plump, tomato-like face. Without looking at either of them, he tapped his book with his quill and asked with a sigh, "Name?"

Alucard glowered at the man. "Aleksei," he answered, but the attendee hummed to himself and shook his head. "Emeritus," the vampire then suggested.

The man looked down the list in front of him and nodded. "Ah, yes, Monsieur and Madame Aleksei…Emeritus."

"Monsieur and Monsieur," Alucard irritably corrected.

Zalith smirked in amusement.

With a confused frown, the attendee looked up at them both; he stared into Alucard's hell-fiery eyes, and a drop of sweat slid down the side of his round head. He gulped and nodded slowly. "Y-yes, of course…I do apologize, sirs. Please…welcome," he said, holding out his arm, inviting them to enter the opera house.

As they walked in, Zalith leaned closer to the vampire, pressing his shoulder against his. "Are we…married, Alucard?"

Alucard rolled his eyes as he pouted. "No," he grumbled, glaring ahead in an attempt to hide his embarrassment. "The booking form was in Deiganish; you know I can't read it so well. It was a mistake."

Zalith kept his smirk as he and Alucard made their way up a staircase. They followed the hallway, approached a pair of drawn, dull-red curtains, and headed into the suspended booth. Their balcony hung on the left wall of the huge room, overlooking the entire audience, and a black leather loveseat with mahogany cushions sat in front of them. Small tables stood on either side of the couch, and a bottle of wine and two glasses were waiting in an ice bucket on the right table.

Alucard took off his hat and sat on the right side of the couch; he leaned his cane against the couch, placed his hat on the table, and made himself comfortable as Zalith sat beside him. Then, he stared out at the stage; two huge black curtains were drawn across it, concealing whatever waited behind, and the room was quickly filling with loudly chattering people.

"So, what made you choose this particular performance?" Zalith asked curiously as he took his hat off and placed it on the table.

Keeping his eyes on the stage, Alucard shrugged. "I like the idea of a stupid man taking more than he should and suffering for it," he admitted. "It reminds me of... someone."

With an intrigued smile, Zalith asked, "And who might that be?"

Alucard took the bottle of wine from the table, handed Zalith one of the empty glasses and began to fill it. "No one important," he dismissed, filling his glass once he had filled the demon's.

Zalith smiled as he sipped from his wine, watching Alucard with a look of fascination in his eyes. Once the vampire placed the bottle back on the table, the demon moved his free hand closer and lightly stroked the fur on his cape. "Tell me, Alucard, why are you always wearing this? Whenever I see you, *wherever* I see you, it's rare for me *not* to see it on your person... unless you fear it might become damaged. Why is it so precious?"

The vampire glanced at his cape collar and smirked. "Well, the fur is from the mane of the Dragon God I killed and the fabric is woven from the fur of that same Dragon God. He was my first kill as the anti-Numen, a title I actually took seriously once upon a time. I made this as some sort of trophy. I outgrew that part of my life, but I didn't outgrow my liking for this cape," he admitted. "It is... comfortable."

Amused, Zalith smiled and looked out at the stage. "Does it *ever* come off your person otherwise?" he asked, an unseemly tone to his voice.

"No."

"If *I* were to ask you to take it off, would you?"

With a confused frown, Alucard looked at him. It took him a moment to realize that Zalith was flirting with him. *Of course* he was. The vampire stared down at his drink, trying to hide his nervous face.

"Will you let *me* take it off?" he continued, guiding his hand from the fur to Alucard's neck.

"Why?" he asked quietly.

"Because I want to see what it conceals."

Alucard shrugged shyly. He saw no problem in taking his cape off—he *was* inside, after all. "I... guess," he agreed, glancing at Zalith, who immediately smiled.

As they both stood up, Alucard's heart beat a little faster. He hesitated for a moment, but Zalith took the initiative, his fingers gracefully finding the clasp of his cape. There was a tender kindness in the way the demon carefully undid the fastening, and Alucard couldn't help but feel a subtle embrace in that simple act. The weight of the cape lifted, revealing Alucard's form in the soft glow, and Zalith's touch seemed to carry a whispered promise of understanding and acceptance—at least that was what Alucard hoped; after all, what lay beneath the rest of his clothes was still a mystery to Zalith, a mystery that Alucard would continue to enforce.

The vampire sat back down, trying to dismiss the dismay that came with his secrets. A quiet gratitude mingled with the nerves in his chest; he couldn't help but subtly embrace the affection that Zalith had offered, making him feel a little less shy and a little more cherished.

Zalith placed the vampire's cape over the table beside him and smiled at him as he sat back down. "And now for the rest of your clothes."

"What?" Alucard blurted, startled, *horrified*. He sharply turned his head to look at Zalith, his heart racing, his mind attempting to find the words required for an excuse.

But Zalith laughed as he shuffled closer to him. "It was a joke, Alucard—this time, anyway."

Rolling his eyes as he tried to calm down, Alucard turned back to face the stage. To his relief, the curtains then slid open, silencing the crowd. The opera began just moments later; a small and chubby suited man started the performance, and Alucard felt as if he could finally relax. Whenever he was with Zalith, he knew that he should do his best to be on guard; the demon very obviously enjoyed making him feel more or less uncomfortable with both his humour and flirtatious comments. But Alucard wasn't going to deny that he liked it—he wouldn't admit it either, though.

As he sipped from his wine, he watched in silence. But he could feel the demon's eyes on him; he'd suspected that Zalith would find more interest in looking at him rather than watching the performance. He felt nervous—*of course*—and was unsure of what to say or do, something that always happened when he was in the demon's gaze. Did he like the fact that Zalith found *him* more interesting than the show? Yes. But did he like the way he just stared at him without saying a word? He still wasn't sure.

He lowered his glass and found enough bravery to glance at Zalith. "What?" he asked quietly.

Still staring at him, Zalith lightly shrugged, a smirk clinging to his face. He then took his eyes off the vampire and looked down at the stage.

Alucard set his eyes on the performance too, but the moment he did, he could feel Zalith's eyes on him *again*. He did his best to ignore it; however, as he felt Zalith moving his arm around his shoulders, he frowned anxiously…but he let it happen.

Zalith leaned closer to his face. "You have an admirer, Alucard," he mumbled. "The balcony on the other side of the room, directly across from ours. Ponytail. Do you know him?" he asked and kissed his cheek, probably to hide the fact he'd just whispered to him.

As Zalith sat up straight, keeping his arm around him, Alucard waited a few moments. Then, he glanced at the balcony Zalith mentioned. He spotted the man the demon spoke of; his hair was black and greasy, tied into a scruffy ponytail. He was dressed the same way as every other man in the opera house, but what was visible of his neck was smothered in either runes or tattoos; he wasn't able to tell which from this distance.

With an uncertain frown, he looked back down at the stage. "No," he answered quietly.

"Benedict Sier from Elescaster—an accountant. I read his mind. It's quite easy to read a human's mind without having to touch them when they're weak and off-guard," Zalith murmured.

"No," he repeated. "Are you sure he's looking at me, not you?"

"Quite sure. He seems rather fond."

Alucard tried to think of who Benedict might be and why he was staring at him. He'd not seen anyone quite like him before, and he wasn't aware of anyone looking for him at this current point in his life—unless... the Diabolus were on his trail again. Surely, that couldn't be the case; Damien was keeping them at bay, right? So, if not the Diabolus, then who? Elescaster was Dor-Sanguis' second largest city, so the man was local. Could it be werewolves? No, he and Zalith had dealt with them. Members of the Blood of Profane mercenary group, perhaps? They probably had agents everywhere. He wasn't sure, but he *did* want to know.

"I don't know who he is," he said quietly. "But... if he's here for me, I'm sure he'll follow us outside if we were to leave."

"What do you propose we do?"

He thought to himself for a few moments. He didn't want to leave; despite his usual awkwardness when with Zalith, he was enjoying their time together. It was only typical that something would come along and ruin it for them, though. If it wasn't werewolves or Diabolus or Damien, it was some other threat that he wasn't yet sure of. New threats would always present themselves, though, especially in his line of work.

With a quiet sigh, he shrugged and said, "We'll see if he follows."

"Are we leaving?" Zalith asked with disappointment in his voice.

"We are," Alucard confirmed.

He stood up, and as Zalith handed his cape to him, he pulled it on. He snatched his cane and hat and led the way back into the hallway. The last thing he wanted was to cut their date short, but if that man really was watching him, he needed to find out why.

Chapter Twenty-Four

─ ≺ ✝ ≻ ─

A Delectable Night

| **Zalith** |

A s Zalith followed Alucard down the deserted hallway, he frowned in concern. "There could be more than just one man," he said cautiously, glancing at the vampire, who looked irritated. Why wouldn't he be? Their evening had possibly been ruined.

"There could be," Alucard mumbled in agreement. "If he does follow, we'll find out what he wants, why he's here…and then…I don't know, kill him or something."

Amused, Zalith smiled slightly. "You don't sound very enthusiastic."

"I'm not," he grumbled as they reached the exit. "I've been back all of two days and people are on my ass already. I can't seem to catch a break," he complained.

Zalith smirked, but now probably wasn't the best time to flirt. He followed Alucard out of the building and down the empty, lamp-lit street as the rain trickled lightly. "It could also be nothing," he suggested, hoping to relieve the vampire of his stress.

"Maybe," Alucard said with a sigh as he turned into an alley sheltered from the rain. "Or it could be something annoying."

"Perhaps. But either way, at least you have me to help you deal with it," Zalith said when they stopped in the middle of the alley.

However, before Alucard could say anything, both their attention was instantly drawn to the ponytail-haired man who had stopped at the end of the alley. He stood there with a silver stake in his right hand and a small, empty vial in the other. As the rain poured over his suit, he dropped the small vial, and a slither of silver oozed out when it smashed on the concrete.

Zalith scowled, glancing at the man's stake, which had been smothered in whatever was in that vial. Poison, perhaps? Whoever this man was, he was evidently uneducated in demonology and vampirology. Poison wouldn't affect either species. So, this man was either a complete moron, or there was something he knew that Zalith did not. The demon glanced at Alucard, but the vampire didn't seem threatened.

But the stake-wielding man looked confused, his brown eyes darting back and forth from Alucard to Zalith almost as if he had no idea which one of them was his target.

With a weary, lazy sigh, Alucard took a single step forward. "What did they tell you?" he asked as the rain began pouring harder.

The man didn't answer.

Scoffing, Alucard handed his cane to Zalith, who stood there with an intrigued look on his face. "Diabolus," the vampire uttered quietly, informing Zalith.

Zalith smiled as he watched Alucard unbutton his suit; he was sure that he was going to enjoy what was about to happen. Whoever this man was, he was most likely an amateur. Not only did he seem unable to tell which of them was his target, but his entire body was visibly shaking. It wasn't with fear, but desperation; this man seemed to possess a dire need to slay the vampire to prove himself, but today, he would learn that he had made his last mistake.

Alucard burst forward so quickly that the man had no idea he'd been pinned up against the alley wall by his throat until his wrist was already snapped in two. His stake hadn't even hit the ground yet, and he found himself staring into the vampire's hell-fiery eyes, blood seeping from his right, broken wrist. Then, as his stake finally clanged against the concrete where he'd been standing, he tried to yell in horror, but the vampire slammed his other hand over his mouth.

"Who else is with you?" Alucard snarled, glaring into his horrified eyes as he moved his hand from the man's mouth. "How many of you are here?!" he demanded.

Zalith stood there, watching.

The man whimpered, trying to pull free, tugging on Alucard's wrist with his only hand, but he couldn't do anything.

Alucard scowled impatiently. "Speak! Deiganish? Dor-Sanguian?"

"I-I-I'm not telling you a thing!" he insisted.

The vampire smirked. "He's not going to tell us anything," he said, glancing at Zalith.

With an amused smile, Zalith leaned against the wall beside the terrified man. "That would be rather unwise—if you value your limbs," he said, tapping the man's leg and then his arm with Alucard's cane.

Mortified, the man looked at Zalith and then back to Alucard. "I-I...I don't know anything," he said, laughing in panic. "I'm just...I'm just a messenger; you know how it is."

"I do," Alucard said with a calmer tone. "And I'm just a vampire, something that would love to drain you of every ounce of your blood. But you know how it is, don't you?"

As his smile faded, the messenger gulped. "P-please, sir...I-I honestly don't—"

Alucard gritted his teeth impatiently, baring his fangs; the messenger gulped again and frantically glanced around. He looked to Zalith for help, but the demon had his eyes fixed on Alucard, gazing at his angered face.

The man stammered, "N-no, wait, I-I came alone, I swear! I was sent to search the opera house for you. I-I was told you'd be here with a c-c-companion."

Zalith faked an astonished frown. "As a matter of fact, *I* am his *husband*; we are married, are we not, Alucard?" he asked with a grin, looking at the vampire, who slowly turned his head to glare at him. "Monsieur and Monsieur Aleksei Emeritus; I quite like the sound of that—"

Alucard snarled and scowled at him. "I told you, that was a mistake!"

The demon smiled but then tapped the messenger's arm again. "Who told you we'd be here?"

Trembling, the messenger shifted his sights to him but then set his eyes back on Alucard. "It's you... you're *him*."

Alucard scowled—in the blink of an eye, he mercilessly tore the man's left eye out. "Did you think I wouldn't notice this?" he asked amusedly. The man howled painfully and tried to pull free—but that only irritated Alucard more. He pulled the man's jaw open and forcefully fed him his eyeball. "Keep that in there so your superiors can see me tear your insides out, hmm?"

Gagging, the man whimpered and squirmed around.

Zalith laughed as he watched. He *loved* watching Alucard work, and he enjoyed it even more so when he was able to join in. However, he wasn't quite sure what Alucard had discovered in the man's left eye, but he suspected it was some sort of ethos that allowed the guy's superiors to see what he saw; why else would Alucard have made the man swallow his eye and say that his superiors would see him tear him apart?

"Who is feeding your people information?" Alucard growled, tightening his grip on the messenger's throat. "One of my men is conspiring, no?"

The man shook his head.

"It doesn't seem like he wants to talk," Zalith said disappointedly. "Come, darling husband; we should return to our seats. If we leave him here, something far worse will come and pick him off," he said, standing up straight.

With an irritated scowl, the vampire sharply turned his head and glared at Zalith. "Why are you finding this so funny? How many times do I have to tell you that I made a mistake?!"

The demon pulled a fake look of astonishment. "My, where has this attitude come from?"

Watching them, the messenger frowned strangely.

Alucard snarled. "*Prost*," he hissed before looking back at the messenger. "You have five seconds—"

The guy whimpered and shuddered. "Th-the butler—you have a butler! He did it!" he cried, trembling in terror as he turned his face away from Alucard's intimidating scowl.

"I have several butlers," Alucard said with a frown. "Which *one*?"

Gulping once more, the messenger stuttered, "Uh...t-tall...skinny...b-blue eyes...blonde hair." He laughed nervously. "W-we don't know his name."

The vampire then frowned in discontent. "William," he said with a breathy sigh. "He was such a nice man. Well, you will get to see him again soon," he said to the one-eyed man.

He laughed nervously. "S-so...I can go? I h-helped you, right? You don't—"

His fumbling words were cut short when Alucard mercilessly sunk his four fangs into the man's neck.

Zalith frowned sourly. Every time he witnessed Alucard feed, the more irritated it made him feel. At this point, he didn't like it *at all*—it infuriated him so much that he thought it was time to tell Alucard how he felt.

The messenger's stifled groans of horror and agony went silent as the vampire held his hand to his mouth once more, draining the life out of him. In just moments, the man fell still, limp, and lifeless. When Alucard let go of him, the body dropped to the wet concrete ground.

Alucard sighed irritably as he dragged his hand over his mouth, wiping away both blood and rainwater as he leaned back against the wall beside Zalith. "William," the vampire mumbled. "Of all the people, it had to be William."

"What's so special about William?" Zalith asked.

"Eh, he makes the best tea," he laughed.

Amused, Zalith laughed with him.

"Well, we can return to the opera if you like, or we can go back and get drunk. I have no preference."

Zalith, on the other hand, *did* have a preference, but it was neither of what the vampire offered. He leaned the cane against the wall beside him and then moved in front of Alucard; he pressed his left hand against the vampire's chest to hold him back against the wall and rested his right hand on the damp bricks. He then edged his face closer to Alucard's, smirking slyly as the vampire stared in confusion. "Have I ever told you how *charming* I find it when you drain the life out of your victims?" he asked, his face a mere inch from Alucard's. "But..." he then sighed and leaned into the vampire's ear, "be careful what you put in your mouth, Alucard; it might make someone...angry," he warned quietly, his voice something of a murmur.

He then moved his face away from Alucard's ear so that he could see the vampire's face, which adorned an irresolute expression.

But the demon wasn't finished yet. He moved his face to Alucard's neck, and as he breathed against the vampire's skin, he felt Alucard tense up. The vampire leaned his head back against the wall as Zalith pulled his cape and shirt collar away from his neck, and when Zalith placed a soft kiss there, the vampire shuddered in what Zalith could tell was aspiration. He knew that Alucard wanted him to bite him as much as *he* wanted Alucard's bite, and he couldn't help but tease him.

Alucard suddenly gripped Zalith's waist with both his hands and pulled his body closer, exhaling desperately. But instead of giving Alucard what he wanted, Zalith smirked and kissed his neck again. He heard Alucard's subtle huff of disappointment but continued to kiss his way up the vampire's neck. When he came close to his face, though—

"You irritate me," Alucard snarled, pushing Zalith back.

Zalith laughed as he watched Alucard straighten his clothes. But he *still* wasn't done. He lightly grasped the vampire's jaw in his hand. "Be quiet," he said and then silenced the vampire with a kiss.

Alucard didn't lose his irritated scowl, but he did comply with Zalith's instruction. He gripped Zalith's collar in his right hand and pulled him as close as he could get, and they started kissing frantically, almost aggressively. Zalith could feel Alucard's anticipation growing, he could feel his body tensing up against his own, and as his heart started racing in his chest, his desperate desire for more grew—

But Alucard then hesitated and turned his face away from Zalith's.

Zalith didn't want to make him feel awkward, though. "On the subject of irritating," he said, continuing their conversation.

Alucard frowned and looked at him.

"As amusing as it is to see you kill, I don't find satisfaction in watching you enjoy the blood of other people."

The vampire scowled a little and glared into Zalith's eyes.

Zalith wasn't finished. Now he'd started, he might as well tell Alucard *exactly* how it made him feel. He took his hand off the vampire's jaw and slowly guided it to the back of his neck. "I'm not comfortable with you feeding on stray humans—on anyone, to be candid—and I'd much prefer you to feed on me."

Staring at him, Alucard seemed to search his eyes for a hint of sarcasm, but no such thing existed. Zalith was being honest and serious with him, and he hoped Alucard would understand.

"What?" the vampire then asked unsurely.

Looking at his confused face, Zalith frowned. "I understand that you need blood, and I've learned that it doesn't need to be human blood. Stop feeding on random people, Alucard," he said firmly. "You can feed on me whenever you need to."

Alucard took his eyes off Zalith's stern face and glared at the end of the alley—but when a look of surprise struck Alucard's face, Zalith looked over there, too…and set his eyes on a horrified woman. She stood at the alley entrance with an umbrella in her right hand, her entire body trembling as she stared at them and the dead body that lay at their feet.

Before either of them could react, the woman dropped her umbrella and cried hysterically, pointing at them both as she looked to the left and right. She yelled, "Vampires!" so many times that they both rolled their eyes.

Zalith wanted to kill her…but it was Alucard's call.

Instead of silencing her, Alucard picked up his cane and snatched Zalith's wrist, pulling him along as he led the way towards the exit. The woman screeched and raced off down the street as people hung out of their windows and doors, searching for what had terrified her.

Zalith followed at Alucard's side as they made their way out of the alley and down the wet street. They turned onto a deserted road lit by a few flickering lamps and set their eyes on their carriage. Still holding Zalith's wrist, Alucard hurried towards it.

But the demon wasn't content with how they were walking. Instead, he pulled the vampire's hand from his wrist and linked arms with him. "I understand your eagerness, but please, treat me like your—"

"Don't," Alucard snapped as they reached the carriage.

The demon smirked in amusement and let go of Alucard's arm; he opened the carriage door for him.

Rolling his eyes, Alucard climbed up into the carriage and tossed his cane onto the other seat as he slumped down. He then glared out of the window as Zalith climbed in and sat beside him after pulling the door shut. Zalith then gazed at Alucard, who lifted his leg and kicked the carriage wall, letting the coachman know that they were ready to leave.

When the carriage started moving, Zalith frowned in concern. "Why are you angry?" he asked, losing his smirk and amused tone.

Glaring out at the street, Alucard snarled quietly. "Angry," he grumbled. "I'm not angry."

"You are *definitely* angry," he said, smirking.

Alucard rested his feet on the seat in front of him and crossed his arms; a conflicted look clung to his face.

Zalith quickly became worried. He was sure that what he said to the vampire back in the alley had upset him. Had he come off as demanding? Controlling? Maybe. He didn't want Alucard to think that he was there to make him change—to make him do things he might not want to do. So, he sighed, moved closer, and placed his hand on Alucard's. As the vampire looked at him, Zalith smiled softly and started, "Alucard, what

I said back there…I didn't mean to sound controlling. I don't want you to ever think that you have to do what I tell you to do. I may sometimes say something that might make you *think* it's an order, but never have I intended—or will I ever intend—to make you think you have to do what I say. I'm not here to control you, and if you're ever even the slightest bit unhappy with something I've said, something I do, or something I ask you to do, then tell me."

Alucard frowned, clearly unsure of what to say.

Shuffling closer, Zalith moved his hand to the side of Alucard's neck. "I just tried to tell you that it makes me uncomfortable seeing you feeding off random people—people who mean nothing, people who could have been anywhere, done anything. But it's not just the fact that they could be filthy," he admitted. "You're *mine*…and the thought of anyone else touching you…seeing you bite these other people…it upsets me and forces an immutable instinct to attack on me. I'm not going to deny the fact that I feel possessive of you and will do whatever I must to protect you. If you really don't want to stop feeding on humans, I'll try to accept that, but I'll never be comfortable with it. Again, don't feel as though you have to do what I ask; I only want you to do it if you're comfortable."

Alucard pondered for a few moments. Of course, Zalith had no idea and no way of telling what he might be thinking; he still couldn't read his thoughts—he had to remember to ask Alucard why that was. But then the vampire stared back at him, and Zalith waited for his answer, but as the seconds passed, it looked as though he might not get a verbal one.

The vampire edged nearer, his eyes wandering down to Zalith's neck. Could Alucard be thinking what Zalith hoped he was? Had his explanation finally convinced Alucard that it was okay for him to sink his fangs into him as he so sorely wanted?

Zalith smirked excitedly as Alucard moved his face closer to his neck. The vampire guided his hand to the back of the demon's head and lightly gripped his hair; he rather aggressively pulled on his hair, making Zalith tilt his head back. The demon sighed in anticipation, an aspirated smile on his face as he felt Alucard's breath against his skin. Finally, he'd get what he wanted—after what had felt like so long, he'd feel *his* vampire's bite.

But Alucard then scowled and smiled at him. "No." Without another word, he let go of Zalith, moved away, and gazed out of the window.

Astounded that Alucard had just played him at his own game, Zalith frowned, lowered his head, and stared at him. He wanted to ask him why he just did that, but he didn't need to. Alucard had simply done to him what he'd done to Alucard countless times. He knew how sorely Alucard desired his bite, and Alucard now knew how much *he* wanted *his*. Zalith laughed quietly as he looked out of his own window. He deserved that.

Silence fell over them, and in his disappointment, Zalith let the quiet simmer.

But Alucard soon sighed and glanced at him. "I'm sorry."

Zalith frowned and turned his head to look at him. "For?"

"I wanted tonight to be something...well...for us—without distraction. But the fact is, wherever I go, there will always be some kind of danger, something to get in the way. Whether it's werewolves or Diabolus; I don't think I'll ever be free of it."

The demon smiled contently. "I had a wonderful evening. The opera was interesting, but what followed was much more...entertaining."

"We didn't even get to finish watching the opera."

"We didn't need to. As I said, this evening was wonderful. We can always go and see it again another time; we have all the time the worlds have to offer, don't we?"

"You're not...irritated?" Alucard questioned.

"Why would I be?" he asked as an amused smile found its way to his face.

The vampire shrugged and looked back out of the carriage window.

As the castle became visible in the distance, Zalith frowned curiously. "What do you have planned for the rest of our evening?"

"I imagine we can have a drink—or six," he muttered, a look of irritancy returning to his face.

"Please tell me what's bothering you," Zalith pleaded with a concerned frown. "There has to be more to it than what happened at the opera."

He sighed and slouched back. "Nothing," he mumbled.

Zalith donned a skeptical expression as he stared at the vampire. "If you insist," he said and looked out of his window.

The vampire then sighed loudly, rolled his eyes, and glared at him. "Why do you find it amusing to irritate me?" he asked stubbornly.

Looking at him from the corner of his eye, Zalith smirked. "I find you rather...well, I like to see you become flustered. It's...delectable."

As his face reflected his embarrassment once again, Alucard pouted and turned away from the demon. "Delectable," he grumbled.

The demon smiled in amusement once more, watching as Alucard struggled to hide the fact that he had never been complimented so much before. He enjoyed the fact that he was probably the first person to shower Alucard with so many compliments; not only did he enjoy the vampire's reactions, but he also felt as though Alucard deserved such comments. He was, after all, adorable—so much that it had to be made clear to him.

While the vampire continued staring out of his window, Zalith moved his hand to the back of Alucard's neck and pulled him closer. "If you're going to be stubborn tonight, at least let me try to make it somewhat better," he said with a smile, making Alucard rest his head on his shoulder. "There. Does that feel better?"

Still pouting, Alucard scoffed and crossed his arms. "Whatever."

With his arm around the vampire, Zalith smiled in victory.

Chapter Twenty-Five

— ⪜ † ⪝ —

William

| Alucard |

lucard, with his head resting on Zalith's shoulder, stared out of the carriage window as he sunk deeper into the warmth of the demon's light embrace. They weren't far from the castle, and when they got there, he was going to have to deal with his liability. But it wasn't William's treachery that had his attention right now, it was Zalith—of course it was.

The vampire struggled to keep a stubborn pout off his face. For a moment in that alley, he'd become lost in the high of the blood he'd consumed, and it let him ignore his nervousness long enough to pull Zalith closer and await his bite. But Zalith hadn't given it to him; instead, the demon said something that made Alucard feel intimidated... and he was *so* annoyed because he actually *liked* that Zalith made him feel meek for a moment. He enjoyed Zalith's possessiveness and directness, but he also felt a little conflicted. Zalith asked him to only drink *his* blood, and as enticing as that sounded, he felt worried. He needed blood every three days, and was Zalith really going to be around that much? Was he even going to be able to *survive* giving up his blood that often?

But Alucard understood his point. He and Zalith were together now, and he knew that he'd feel the same way if he had to watch Zalith sink his teeth into random people. So, he wasn't going to argue about it; he'd try his best to do as Zalith asked.

Just then, the coachman tapped the top of the carriage, letting them know they'd passed the castle gates.

Alucard sighed in discontent. He enjoyed sitting with the demon's arm around him; he didn't want to get up not only for that reason but also because he wasn't in the mood to kill his liability. Of all people, it had to be William, the one person he might have never expected. But now he knew that someone had been feeding the Diabolus information, and that was, without a doubt, going to come back and bite him in the ass later. He'd have to prepare for that.

When the carriage stopped, he sat up, grabbed his cane from the opposite seat, and unlocked the door. As the demon followed him out into the castle courtyard, he took a moment to stand there and think. First, he had to locate William and find out what he might have told the Diabolus. Then, he'd kill the man and work out what to do with the rest of his night. Zalith was with him, so at least he wouldn't be left alone with his thoughts.

"I assume you're planning to murder your mole?" Zalith asked, walking beside him as he led the way inside.

"Yes," he answered irritably. He frowned in frustration, and his anger increased with every step he took. How could somebody betray his trust? Was William the only one? Did he not pay those pathetic humans enough to work for him? He paid them enough to buy a new home in the city every three months! Or were all humans just disrespectful, greedy pieces of shit? He snarled quietly, ignoring Zalith's gaze as they made their way into the hall.

Alucard stopped beside the table for a moment, trying to calm himself. William would soon come to greet him, and he needed to do his best not to alert the butler that he knew of his transgressions. There was also the possibility that William wasn't the only one to have conspired—for all Alucard knew, *all* his staff could be feeding the Diabolus information.

With a deep exhale, he pulled off his cape and placed it on the table alongside his cane.

"Have you decided how to deal with this?" Zalith asked quietly, helping Alucard take off his blazer, and then he placed it on the table as the vampire turned to face him.

"Yes," Alucard muttered, pulling out his seat at the head of the table. As he sat down, Zalith also sat, staring at him with a curious yet somewhat excited look on his face. Why did he look as though he was looking forward to what was about to happen?

After a few moments of silence, the blonde-haired, blue-eyed butler made his way out of the kitchens and hurried over. He muttered his greetings to the vampire in Dor-Sanguian and waited for his reply.

Glancing up at him, Alucard scowled. "Tea, Earl Grey," he replied in his native tongue. William would be dead soon, so he thought he might as well ask for the tea he made so well one last time.

The butler hurried off and disappeared back into the kitchens.

Alucard and Zalith sat there in silence. The vampire glared at the kitchen door while Zalith smiled at him; he wanted to roll up his shirt sleeve so that it wouldn't become bloody when he slew his butler, but he didn't want Zalith to see what lay upon his skin, so he refrained from doing so. He felt exhausted already and the thought of having to stand there and question yet another man made him wish he could crawl into a corner and die for a while. He didn't have the patience or the motivation to do it, so he'd just kill William. The Diabolus were bound to find him at some point anyway.

William returned carrying a steel platter with two white teacups sitting on it. He handed one to each of them before bowing humbly. He then turned around to head back towards the kitchens—

"Here," Alucard mumbled, holding out his hand, instructing the butler to move closer. As William frowned and moved nearer, the vampire stared vacantly ahead. "Move closer," he instructed.

The butler stepped even closer and leaned forward, waiting. But Alucard had nothing to say. Before William could comprehend, the vampire relentlessly forced his clawed hand into the man's chest and gripped his beating heart. He choked and gasped painfully, and before being given a chance to question why his life was at its end, Alucard tore his heart from his body. When the butler dropped beside him, Alucard let his bloody heart join him on the floor. Then, he glared over at the kitchen door again.

Alucard waited, his bloody hand still held out, and after a few moments, a maid hurried over and handed him a damp, black rag. He took his eyes off the door and glared irritably at his hand as he started to clean the blood from it. Then, he glanced at Zalith, who smiled pleasantly at him; evidently, he'd enjoyed watching that.

The vampire handed the rag back to the horrified maid, who quickly raced off. He made himself comfortable, and when the maid returned, two more butlers followed; they walked over in silence and dragged William's body away. The maid hastily wiped the blood from the marble floor and scurried away, leaving the vampire and demon alone.

With a deep sigh, Alucard slouched back in his seat and stared at the cup in front of him. While he would have usually drained the traitor of his blood, he decided not to after what Zalith told him not long ago. He didn't make a habit of changing to suit other people, but he felt as though Zalith was the single exception—and he had a valid point, too.

Zalith rested his arms on the table. "I love it when you speak in your native tongue, Alucard," he said with a devious smirk. "And I enjoy it more when you're irritated."

"I'm not irritated," he argued, glaring at him.

"I beg to differ."

Alucard rolled his eyes and leaned his arms onto the table, staring down into his tea. "William might have not been the only spy. Killing all of the help has crossed my mind, and I may have to do it."

"Then do it. It's the only way you can be sure, after all. Unless, of course, you want me to find out which of them are conspiring," he offered with a smile.

That would be very helpful. "Yes," he answered.

Zalith smiled...but then frowned curiously. "Alucard," he started, leaning closer as Alucard sipped from his cup. "Not that I've ever tried to invade your thoughts, but when you were unconscious, and I had no idea what to do to help you, I tried to look into your mind, and surprisingly, I couldn't. That's never happened before, and I'm curious to know why I can't see into your thoughts."

Alucard slowly placed his cup back on the table. "Why do you want to read my mind?" he asked with a frown.

"I don't. I'm simply curious."

Alucard was sure that was a lie, but he felt no need to lie or dismiss him. "Hmm... well, I'm Lucifer's son. I'm sure you can't read a Numen's mind, so it would only make sense that you can't read the mind of their offspring—blood offspring. Those created with ethos are significantly weaker, so you can probably read their minds." That wasn't the whole truth... but it was enough.

Zalith nodded as an intrigued look appeared on his face. "What happened the night your house was destroyed?"

Alucard frowned at the sudden subject shift and looked down at the table. "Why does it matter?" he muttered.

"I wasn't there for you. I wish I had been, then perhaps... what happened might not have happened."

Alucard fiddled with his teacup, slowly rotating it on the coaster. "I gather Ben told you what happened."

"He did."

The vampire frowned sullenly. He was sure that Zalith was going to ask at some point, and as much as he might like to avoid thinking about what happened to him—what happened to *Tobias*—he knew that he shouldn't avoid his grief forever. It had been a while since that night and perhaps now was the time to move past it... or at least try to.

He glanced at the demon and shrugged. "I got back from the island, and I... spent some time with Tobias."

Zalith gazed at him, listening.

"I don't know how long we were talking for, but I eventually headed home. My manor was on fire and Ada was responsible. She turned up with a lot of wolves, and I admit at that time I wasn't in the best mind space, so I might not have been myself. They attacked, I killed them, but Ada surprised me. Somehow, she found out that silver was my weakness and attacked me with it. I was... dying," he said with a shrug. "I had nothing to live for, so I just laid there. But then Tobias came out of nowhere and fought them off—he even fought Ada."

"He saved your life," Zalith said, a hint of appreciation in his voice.

"No," Alucard disagreed. He then hesitated as his guilt quickly became overwhelming. Tobias *had* saved his life, but Alucard killed him without so much as an ounce of restraint. He *hated* himself for it. He hated what he did, he hated what he was, and the guilt and anger that he felt when thinking about it was *suffocating*. The vampire looked away, refused to let his grief possess his face, and scowled irritably. "It doesn't matter," he dismissed. "There are more important things to talk about right now."

"Alucard—"

"We should find out which of my workers are Diabolus," he interjected, standing up.

Looking up at him, Zalith frowned hesitantly…but to Alucard's relief, he didn't try to keep the conversation going. He stood up and followed the vampire into the kitchens.

Alucard set his eyes on the two butlers and three maids, who were all sitting around a table. The moment they noticed Alucard and Zalith, they jumped to their feet, dread smothering their faces.

When he stopped in front of them, Alucard glanced at the demon, waiting for him to look through their minds. The vampire watched as Zalith set his eyes on the first butler…and shook his head after a few moments. Then, the demon glared at each maid one after the other, shaking his head each time his eyes shifted. But when Zalith glared at the second butler, the man quivered in fear. The demon moved closer and snatched the man's collar, and before he could utter a sound, Zalith placed his middle and index finger on the butler's left temple and his thumb against his jawline.

The vampire frowned in confusion. "Why do you do that?"

"When someone is trained to withstand mind-reading ethos, or when they know what I'm trying to do, I have to be closer, sometimes I need to physically touch them," Zalith drawled, obviously concentrating as the butler whimpered.

Alucard didn't know that. He nodded in response and glanced at the other staff, who stood there frozen with horrified looks on their faces.

When Zalith was done, he shoved the butler towards Alucard. The man stumbled and cried, and before he could try to fight, Alucard snatched the back of his head and slammed his face down onto the countertop so hard that his head was crushed between the surface and his palm. The vampire then let his body drop to the floor, turned around, and led the way back out of the kitchen as Zalith followed, both ignoring the horrified screams of all three maids.

Amused, Zalith smiled and laughed quietly to himself.

"What did he know?" Alucard asked.

"Not much. The Diabolus are aware that you live in Dor-Sanguis, but he didn't share your appearance with them. And judging from the reaction of the man sent to kill you at the opera house, William most likely failed to do so, too."

"They'll send more now that they know I'm here," Alucard muttered, leading the way over to the door that led to his half of the castle.

"Are you prepared for them?" Zalith asked worriedly as they headed upstairs.

Alucard sighed when they reached the top of the stairs and began walking towards the door to his room. He hadn't dealt with the Diabolus in their entirety before; he had only ever dealt with small groups of them at once—but they had been no threat. He was sure that, whatever the Diabolus might send his way, he could deal with it.

He looked at Zalith and shrugged. "Always," he answered, pushing his bedroom door open.

Zalith followed Alucard into his room. He closed the door behind them as Alucard made his way over to his bed and said, "Well, I'm here to help if you need me."

Glancing back at the demon, Alucard nodded slightly. "I don't know when they might come, but I'll have to find someone to replace Ben's old position and then tell them to watch for them," he said, sitting on the edge of his bed as he pulled off his shoes.

Sitting on the opposite side of the bed, Zalith pulled off his shoes and then his blazer. "Do you have anyone in mind?" he asked, unbuttoning his shirt, which he then took off. When he eased his belt from around his waist, he looked back at Alucard.

Alucard stared at him with a look of confusion on his face. "W-what are you doing?" he questioned nervously, not sure where to stare—his eyes wanted to stare at Zalith's defined body, but his shyness convinced him to look at the floor.

"I prefer to sleep naked, Alucard," he said, smiling. "But if that makes you uncomfortable, I can keep *some* of my clothes on."

Alucard had no idea what to say. He didn't want to make Zalith think he had to sleep uncomfortably because of him; Zalith could sleep naked if he wished to, but Alucard wasn't going to.

With a nervous shrug, he got under the blankets and slowly set his eyes back on Zalith. "That's fine," he mumbled.

Zalith took everything but his underwear off and joined him in bed. He shuffled closer to Alucard and moved his arm around him as he rested the side of his face on his head. "Is this okay?" he asked quietly.

It *was* okay. He enjoyed Zalith's embrace however he might want to give it, so he nodded and gripped Zalith's arm. "I can turn out the lights if you want," he offered, sure that Zalith preferred to sleep in darkness like most people. He didn't like sleeping in the dark inside this castle, but he was confident that he'd feel relaxed enough to do so with Zalith by his side.

"Only if you're comfortable," Zalith replied.

He felt like he should at least try. If he and Zalith were going to be sleeping together from this point on, he was convinced that the demon would eventually ask for darkness. So, Alucard focused on each candle lined around the room and one by one, they flickered out, leaving only the dull, kaleidoscopic light of the moons shimmering in through the cracks in the curtains.

Then, as he made himself comfortable, Alucard closed his eyes.

"Goodnight," Zalith said.

With a content smile, Alucard relaxed and murmured, "Goodnight."

Chapter Twenty-Six

— ⟨ † ⟩ —

Disembark

| **Alucard** |

Morning came fast, and for once, Alucard didn't wake with the same fatigue he always did. The vampire opened his eyes, a feeling of serenity lingering over him as he felt the warmth of Zalith's arms around him. He didn't want to move; all he wanted to do was lay there and enjoy it for a while, but they'd soon have to get up and head for his ship. There was no harm in waiting a little bit, though.

However, as he felt Zalith stir, he frowned and rolled over onto his back so he could turn his head to look at him. The early morning sunlight crept in through the curtains, and as his eyes faded to blue, he grimaced and looked away, pain spiralling through his head.

"What's wrong?" Zalith asked.

"Nothing," he mumbled as the demon leaned onto his arm so he could look down at him. "Just the light."

The demon smiled. "Did you sleep okay?"

Alucard nodded. "Yes," he answered, setting his eyes on the ceiling. "Did you?"

"Always when beside you," he said, smirking. "What's today's plan?"

"Well, we should get ready and then head for the ship. I'm not sure what we can do during the journey, though," he said, glancing at Zalith.

"I'm sure we'll think of something," he mumbled with a smile, moving a loose strand of hair from over one of the vampire's eyes.

With a slight nod, Alucard sat up; he glanced back at Zalith, who remained where he was, and then stared down at his lap as he began fiddling with the crucifix around his neck. "I gather all of the clothes you brought are on the ship, so you can borrow something of mine again to wear now."

"If it isn't too far of a walk, I'll just wear what I have here," Zalith replied, also sitting up.

Alucard let go of his crucifix and climbed out of bed. "I'll go and get ready," he muttered and made his way over to the door.

"Should I wait for you here?"

He glanced back at him, pulling the door open. "I'll only be a moment, so yes."

"Okay."

Alucard left his bedroom and closed the door behind him. He headed down to the room where he kept his clothes; as he entered, he took off his shirt and swiftly pulled on a black one. He changed his trousers and tidied his hair, and then he returned to his bedroom, where Zalith was standing by one of the windows, dressed and ready to go.

"We can go now," he said, and as Zalith smiled at him and made his way over, he began to lead the way down the hallway. "If you want breakfast, I have people aboard the ship who can make whatever you want," he offered.

"Thank you," he said as they walked downstairs. "Will you be joining me?"

"For... breakfast?" he questioned, leading the way into the main hall.

"Yes."

"Maybe," he answered, continuing towards the castle's exit. As he passed the table, he snatched his cape and held it in his right arm. "I'll... see how I feel once we get to the ship."

Zalith nodded and followed him out into the courtyard.

Alucard and his companion strolled along the castle's pathways, making their way down to the docks. There, where his smaller ship had once been anchored, now awaited his grand galleon. The vast, black vessel adorned with golden panels dwarfed his previous craft, built for more extended journeys and accommodating a crew of fifty. As he gazed upon the magnificent ship, Alucard felt a sense of anticipation he had longed for. The sunlight danced off the gold-rimmed windows, and the ship's front featured a bowsprit resembling a sea dragon. Above the windows at the rear of the ship, the name 'Nagarathan,' each letter meticulously crafted in silver, stood proudly, and in the early morning light, the black mooring ropes sparkled, securing the ship in its majestic glory.

The vampire guided the way onto the expansive, empty deck of the ship, and led Zalith into the cabin, which seamlessly blended a bedroom and lounge into a single space. Positioned at the room's far end, a bed rested in front of large arched windows, its covers composed of black, furry blankets. The dark, planked floor possessed the white carpet found in Alucard's castle, and on the left side of the bed stood a mahogany oak changing screen, embellished with hand-painted oriental dragons and darkly coloured fish swimming amidst the intricate details.

Each parted curtain revealed a deep shade of red, casting a dim hue across the room. The windows, when seen from the inside, appeared clearer than they had from the outside. On the room's right side, a fireplace embedded in the wall emanated warmth; the walls were adorned with numerous cabinets, drawers, and wardrobes, and to the left, a table and chairs occupied the space, devoid of any items except for a few unlit candles. A silvery chandelier hung from the room's centre ceiling, and beneath it, a bear's coat served as a rug. Every detail remained untouched, exactly as he had left it.

"My butlers put your clothes in here somewhere," Alucard said as he stopped in the centre of the room. "If you want to get changed, I need to go and tell the captain we're ready to leave," he said as he glanced at Zalith, who was looking around the room.

"Okay," the demon said with a smile.

As Zalith made his way over to one of the dressers in search of his clothes, Alucard left the room, shut the door behind him, and walked up onto the quarterdeck.

Beside the ship's wheel, with a cigarette clamped firmly between his teeth, the ship's captain muttered quietly to himself as he fiddled with a wrench in his hands.

"What are you doing?" Alucard asked as he stopped beside him.

The man, who flinched and almost dropped the wrench in startlement, turned to face Alucard and frowned. "Uh... didn't see you there, sir," he said apologetically.

Alucard gave the captain a once-over, unimpressed by the ordinary features that defined him. His eyes held a dull, unremarkable shade of brown, and his hair, a nondescript mix of blue and black—leaning towards a darker navy hue, perhaps—failed to distinguish him in any notable way. The unkempt stubble that covered his face added an extra layer of mundane mediocrity, and the bandana wrapped around his forehead seemed entirely unnecessary, contributing to the overall unremarkable appearance of just another ordinary human.

"We are ready to go," the vampire muttered.

"Quick question, if that's okay?" the man asked.

"Fine."

"Your uh... Drac," he said, glancing at the ship's edge. "He's not gonna get hungry and chase some sharks or something, is he? She's strong," he laughed, patting the ship's wheel, "but I'm not sure how she'd do when a dragon tolls on her keel."

Alucard shook his head. "Drac is fed enough; he will not be a problem."

"All right. Well, we'll set off right away." He chuckled nervously. "This is my first time sailing a ship pulled by a dragon," he said, dragging his hand over the back of his head. "Anything I should know?"

"Stand there and steer. Drac will do the rest," Alucard muttered.

"Got it."

"Only find me if you really need me; I prefer *not* to be bothered," he grumbled, turning his back on the captain.

"Okie dokes, sir," he called as the vampire made his way down from the quarterdeck.

Alucard headed along the deck and back into the cabin. He set his eyes on Zalith, who was now wearing a new white shirt, and as the demon rolled his sleeves up, he turned to face the vampire.

"We can sit in here while you eat…or out there," he said, pointing back over his shoulder.

Finished with his sleeves, Zalith walked over to Alucard and placed his hands on his arms, smiling. "We can sit outside."

Nodding, Alucard turned around and led the way back out of the room. As Zalith followed, he walked up onto the forecastle deck, where a small table and chairs were. He sat down and watched as Zalith sat opposite him.

Zalith made himself comfortable and asked, "Where did you find Drac?"

Alucard frowned slightly as he recalled the memory. "It was…fifty or so years ago. I was at sea with some of my old subordinates; it was stormy and we had to stop at this small island in the middle of nowhere because Attila wouldn't stop bitching that the ship would be torn apart. So we stopped at this island. I wandered off—I wasn't at all in the mood for conversation with anyone—and I came across this little snake." He smirked, looking out at the horizon as the ship began to move. "Small, pathetic little thing caught up in some fishing line. I don't like to see animals suffer, so I helped him out—the little fuck bit me and disappeared into the sea."

Amused, Zalith laughed quietly.

"Then we set sail once the waters had calmed. One of the crew kept insisting that a monster was following us. We all ignored him until Attila insisted he saw it, too. So, I looked into the water and I saw the same snake that bit me the previous night. He kept following us for weeks. Eventually, he found the courage to come out of the water; I was asleep, so he crept into my bed and decided he was going to burrow inside the pillow opposite me—he actually…got inside the pillow. There were feathers everywhere," he said with a quiet laugh. "I woke up, water everywhere; I had no idea what I was looking at until this quiet hiss came from the torn-up pillow. I looked and I found the snake in there. He wasn't so little anymore but he looked at me as though I was his mother. I tried to send him back into the water, but he wouldn't leave me, so I let him stay."

With a smile on his face, Zalith rested his arms on the table. "You certainly have your way of making an impression on animals, don't you? People, too."

"Maybe," Alucard said with a shrug. "In most cases, I saved their lives and they feel as though they owe me."

A butler appeared beside them. "Can I get either of you anything?" he asked pleasantly.

Alucard asked Zalith, "You wanted something, right?"

Nodding, Zalith looked up at the butler. "We'll have toast, eggs, and bacon. I'll also have some water."

"The same—*parasi*," Alucard said, dismissing the butler.

As the butler left, Zalith kept his eyes on the vampire and smiled curiously. "How many languages *do* you speak, Alucard?"

Alucard took his eyes off the horizon and looked at him. "Six."

The demon looked impressed. "Is that including the one you speak in your sleep?" he asked with a smirk.

Alucard frowned in embarrassment and looked away again. "I don't know what I say when I'm asleep."

Zalith laughed quietly as he leaned back in his seat. "What are these six languages?"

"Lupanese, Aguilian, Boszorkian, Drydenish, Deiganish, and Dor-Sanguian. You know I'm Dor-Sanguian. I learned Deiganish when I travelled to DeiganLupus—I knew *some* before since I had to communicate with Damien. As for the others, I told you that they're similar to Dor-Sanguian and I learnt them on my travels," he explained, setting his eyes on the demon. "Do you know any others?"

"No," Zalith said, shaking his head.

The butler then returned with their breakfast. He placed their glasses of water in front of them and then their plates of food. After bowing humbly, he silently left.

Zalith picked up his glass, sipped from it, and asked Alucard, "Does it bother you when I ask you as many questions as I do?"

Alucard glanced at him. "It depends on the situation and the questions being asked. Right now? It's okay. It's when you ask me about more personal things that I start to feel…hesitant."

"Then, if I were to ask you what you thought about me when we first met, would you answer?" he asked, smirking.

Staring at him, Alucard pondered for a few moments. Despite his dislike for being asked questions, this didn't seem to be bothering him. It was conversation—there wasn't going to be much else to do until they reached Boszorkány, so what harm would there be in engaging in a back-and-forth of asking each other things they wanted to know about one another? He admittedly had something he wanted to ask Zalith, so he complied.

But…what *did* he think about Zalith when they had first met? Should he be completely honest? He was sure that Zalith didn't like him for those first months, and he sure as hell didn't like *him*. So, he shrugged and gained an amused smirk. "I thought you were rude, stuck up, and insufferable. I didn't like your face; all you did was smile and stare at me. I didn't like your attitude or the way you spoke to me as if I was incompetent."

Zalith scoffed in amusement. "Ouch," he said, placing his glass back down.

"You were, though," Alucard said with a slight laugh.

The demon laughed with him. "I was. I hope those opinions have changed now, though."

"Yes," Alucard answered. "What did you think of me, then?"

The demon smiled something devious. "I thought you were slightly abrasive, but I liked that. I admittedly underestimated you—something I won't do again. I liked *your* face; I thought you were very attractive, not to mention the fact that the very first thing I set my eyes on was your ass—when I saw you in the tavern *and* on that tower—and I assume you mistook that for me eying your weapon. That was funny," he said with a smirk and took a bite of his toast.

As embarrassment smothered his face, Alucard looked away and glared at the ocean. *Of course* that had been what Zalith was smiling at the night they met on that tower. He pouted and scowled, unable to believe that he hadn't worked that out, even after Zalith had made it as obvious as he could.

The demon then smiled, gazing at Alucard. "Ask me something else."

Alucard glanced at him and thought to himself for a second. "Do you…have hobbies?"

"I do…somewhat. I don't really have time to do much else than work; however, I like to read a lot, and I admit that I also enjoy buying things. I might also say that I treat my relationships as hobbies, meaning I put a lot of time and energy into the people I see. You above anyone else, of course."

Alucard frowned. He didn't exactly understand what Zalith meant by that. *Could* relationships be treated as hobbies?

"And you?" Zalith asked.

The vampire looked down at his drink and shrugged. "I…used to play the violin, but I haven't got myself a new one yet since it burned in my house. I like to make things— you know that, too. Once upon a time, I worked more with horses—I miss that, but I don't feel there is time for it these days. I don't know if it can be considered a hobby since I don't do it all the time, but I like to travel when I get the chance, whether it be to somewhere entirely new, or somewhere I've been before. I like the feeling of being somewhere that isn't home, but only for so long."

Zalith leaned a little closer. "How did you come to learn to play the violin?"

Alucard didn't think that it was a particularly interesting story, but Zalith had asked, and he felt no need to refuse him an answer. "Well, was…around the time I became a vampire—well…around the time I *thought* I became a vampire. It was hard to deal with everything, so I guess the music was…an escape. It helps me to focus when my thoughts become overbearing or when I don't want to sit there and think about something," he admitted and then tried a piece of bacon, which was rather tasty.

The demon nodded in understanding but then frowned. "If you're *not* a vampire, why do you have to consume blood? And so often?"

"I think…it's because of what kind of demon I am—a sangdevoro. At first, I thought I needed blood to manifest my human form, but once I had that, I still…*needed* it. That sounds like I have an addiction," he said with a pout, looking away from Zalith. "I don't know," he repeated with a quiet sigh. "All I know is, if I don't drink it, I start to feel strange and eventually lose control of myself. It doesn't matter, anyway. I want to change the subject."

Zalith looked a little disappointed, but he sat up straight and continued eating. After taking a sip of his water, he asked with a curious smile, "If there was anything you could change about yourself, what would it be?"

That was a bit of a random question. "Why would I want to change anything about myself?"

"Hypothetically."

"Well…." He pondered, looking back out at the ocean as he finished what he was eating. "The bloodlust," he mumbled. "It's caused me more problems than I would like to admit. Would you change anything about yourself?"

Zalith smiled. "No."

With a slight frown, Alucard looked down at his drink, trying to think of another question to ask. "Do you have… favourite animals? A favourite… colour?"

The demon shrugged lightly. "I like dire wolves… and as for a colour, I'd have to say… green—but red is a close second," he said with a smirk. "I gather horses are *your* favourite animal?"

"Them, and I like… snakes, too," he admitted. "You don't see them in Dor-Sanguis often, though."

A smile crept across Zalith's face—

"I like red, too," Alucard dismissed, looking away from him. "And gold… and black."

"I see that," Zalith said, eying him fondly.

"What about food?" Alucard swiftly asked, sure that the tone in Zalith's voice *and* the look on his face meant that he was going to say something inappropriate.

The demon kept his smile. "I like a lot of foods. But if I had to choose a favourite, it would be red meat. You don't eat much I gather, but do you have a favourite?"

"I can't say I do. I've only tried the things you've given me and the occasional thing in places of social gathering where I had to appear as a normal man. I like… most sweet things, though. I think I already told you that at one point."

"I remember, just as I quite distinctly remember watching you pour half a jar of sugar into your coffee," he said with an amused smile.

Alucard sighed. "Will you ever let that go?"

"No," he answered, and as Alucard rolled his eyes, the demon laughed.

Alucard laughed slightly as he shook his head and looked down at the table. "I feel as though maybe I can try more things now that I'm going to be with you a lot—you eat, so I can try the things you have." Food had never been something that interested him until this point; what Zalith had given him had undeniably surprised him, and he was curious to try more.

"Do you like this?" Zalith asked, glancing at Alucard's almost empty plate.

He looked down at his plate. "Yes," he answered.

"Good. It's my turn to ask you something," Zalith then said. "What are your two biggest pet peeves?"

Pet peeves? Alucard frowned at him. "My... what?"

Zalith laughed slightly. "What two things annoy you the most, Alucard?"

So many things came to him at once; he wasn't sure what might top the list. Humans, werewolves, Ada, Damien, too much sunlight, people who didn't know when it was time to shut the fuck up, people who thought talking to him was a mutual pleasure, humans...humans.... He frowned and shrugged. "Humans. Everything they do makes me want to commit murder. You know that story already, though. And then...maybe when someone wants to persistently talk to me even when I have made it clear is time for them to leave. I enjoy my time and space."

"I respect that," Zalith said, nodding. "And humans—they are one of the most insufferable, irritating things to exist."

"And stupid."

"Brainless."

They both laughed together for a few moments and then fell silent.

Alucard curiously asked him, "What about...are you afraid of anything?"

Zalith shrugged. "Well, I'm afraid to lose those left of the people I care about, yes. And to live an average life—how dreadful that would be," he said, smirking.

The vampire nodded in agreement. "I don't know how humans do it."

"And I assume you're afraid of something?"

Glancing at him, Alucard felt slightly hesitant. He wasn't going to admit his biggest fear...that would turn this conversation into something depressing. So, he shrugged in embarrassment. "Don't laugh," he warned.

"Tell me," Zalith pleaded, his look of curiosity increasing.

Alucard sighed hesitantly. "I am... afraid of...moths," he mumbled so quietly he felt as if Zalith might not hear.

But Zalith heard him. He laughed amusedly and frowned in disbelief. "Moths?" he asked. "Of all things?"

"They're creepy, disgusting little things that fly around in your face!"

The demon shook his head and continued laughing.

"It's not funny," Alucard grumbled, pouting.

Zalith smirked through his laughter. "If it wasn't funny, I wouldn't be laughing, Alucard. Why moths? What could they have possibly done to own the title of Alucard's worst fear?" he asked, grinning.

Alucard rolled his eyes. "If you really must know, when I was a boy, one flew into my room and made its weird little moth noises in my ear while I was sleeping, and when

I woke up, it flew into my mouth and I choked for hours," he explained, but Zalith continued laughing, and Alucard couldn't help but see the hilarity in what had happened. To this day, that one experience clung to him, and he hated the insects ever since. They were harmless, but whenever he saw one, he couldn't stop himself from remembering the terror he felt when it happened. As he looked down at his drink, he shook his head and laughed quietly with Zalith. But as his laughter died down, he glanced at him. "I am... also afraid to lose you," he admitted. Zalith's answer had been a whole lot more personal than some moth story, so Alucard felt he should respond with something just as personal.

"Well," Zalith said with a smile, moving his arm forward. "I'm not going to go anywhere," he said, placing his hand over Alucard's. "And I'll make sure to protect you from the moths, too."

With a slight roll of his eyes, Alucard smiled and looked out at the ocean. "I won't go anywhere, either."

Chapter Twenty-Seven

Antics

| **Zalith** |

After breakfast, Zalith and Alucard moved to one of the ship lounges below deck. The day slowly became dusk, and as the sun set over the horizon, they watched the sea from the window they were sitting beside.

The demon sipped from his tea and set his gaze on Alucard. Today, he'd learned many new things about him, and it only made his adoration for him grow. To think that someone as fierce as Alucard was unsettled by something as small as a moth—it made him smile every time he thought about how the vampire would react when a moth happened to be in the room. Would he panic? Would Alucard ask him to slay it as if it were a creature of darkness? Zalith would enjoy that.

With a smile on his face, he looked down at his cup as he placed it on the table. He was still eager to hear Alucard play the violin but asking if he ever would seemed insensitive right now; he didn't want to remind Alucard once more about his house. Alucard's answer to his questions about blood consumption had him intrigued, too. Of course, Zalith knew there were many different species of demons, but he didn't know much about sangdevoro. They were clearly a powerful species, though; after all, Alucard was able to resist his mind-reading ethos.

That also had Zalith curious. If Alucard was *that* strong, then why did his aura still feel strangely weak? He hadn't yet asked about what might have caused it to change dramatically since they'd said goodbye on that island, but he'd make a point of finding out sooner or later.

He looked back at the vampire, eager to banish the silence that had enthralled them. "When you were a child, what was it you wanted to be?" he asked him, eager to start another conversation so that he could learn more about him.

Alucard took his eyes off the horizon and scowled at him. "Are you thinking about that stupid moth story again?"

The demon smirked. "What if I am?"

Rolling his hell-fiery eyes, Alucard glared back out of the window. He took a moment to think and then shrugged lightly. "I think... at one point, I wanted to be a... the word for it is... pioneer," he said, glancing at him. "I liked the idea of discovering new places, and adventure. I spent most of my younger years in catacombs—hiding, running—I never really had the chance to see the world outside. Then... I grew up and realized that it was a stupid dream. I became... entrepreneur, then philanthropist, and then what I am now."

"Philanthropist?" Zalith questioned curiously. "What have you sponsored?"

Alucard smiled slightly. "Much. You'll find out one day. What about you? I gather you had some sort of dream as a child?"

Disappointed that he'd not yet learned what Alucard had his hand in, Zalith smiled and sipped from his cup. "I wanted to be the ruler of everything," he said, an amused tone in his voice. "The world, maybe."

"Who doesn't want to rule the world? What about... aside from hobbies, what is your preferred pastime?"

A suggestive smile made its way onto Zalith's face. He wasn't going to deny what his favourite pastime was, but he felt as if he shouldn't tell Alucard just yet—he didn't want to make him uncomfortable. So his devious smile became a sweet one. "Spending time with you."

Alucard looked away. "I'm not *that* entertaining."

"I'd not rather spend my time anywhere else or with anyone else."

Glancing at him, Alucard went to say something but was interrupted when the white blur of a bird burst in through the window and crashed onto the table in front of them. They eyed the bird as it stood up, shook its body, and turned its head to look up at Alucard.

"What?" Alucard asked, glaring down at the bird, which had a rolled piece of parchment in its beak.

The barn owl dropped the parchment, snatched one of the cookies from beside Alucard's teacup, and raced off back out the window.

"Business?" Zalith questioned, watching Alucard as he picked up the rolled parchment.

Unrolling the parchment, Alucard shrugged. "Maybe," he answered. As he unrolled the parchment, a sour look plastered itself to his face. He sighed and held it out to Zalith. "I ought to learn Deiganish sooner rather than later, especially since Ben will be writing to me every three days once I send him off on his first task as Attila's replacement."

Smiling, Zalith took the parchment. "Aleksei," he read. "Felix seems to be under the impression that he now has his old job back because of my promotion. I caught him scouring around the dungeon where Detlaff is held and insisted quite firmly that he brought him food—which I had already done. I'm not sure if you've granted him his old job back and thought it best to ask you before I take any kind of action against him. I should also mention that lately, Detlaff has been acting rather odd and looks like he has something he desperately wants to tell me. If you want me to pursue that, let me know, and tell me how to do so. Ben."

As Zalith handed the parchment back to him, Alucard frowned, screwed up the paper, and tossed it aside. Then, he rested his arms on the table with an irritated huff.

"Are you okay?" Zalith asked.

"Fine," he instantly answered. "I'll reply to him in the morning."

"Felix is that ugly little silver-eyed vampire you revived, isn't he?"

"Yes," Alucard confirmed. "He is… a strange man. Always has been. But he does his job; that's all that matters."

Zalith nodded slowly. "It sounds as though he's doing what he shouldn't be."

"He just wants to prove himself, always has. I will sort it tomorrow," he repeated.

Able to tell that Alucard was annoyed and wanted to change the subject, Zalith smiled and asked, "Tomorrow: what time will we arrive?"

"I think… around noon. We'll arrive at the north docks, which are connected to the country's largest city. There will be a lot to do there, so we won't be bored while Drac rests."

"I'm looking forward to it," the demon said.

Alucard nodded in agreement. He then finished his drink and said, "We can head to sleep soon if you want. We'll probably be walking a lot tomorrow, so we best rest."

Retreating to the bedroom and lying beside Alucard sounded very inviting. "I'm ready when you are," he said and finished his tea.

Alucard stood up and led the way through the ship, back up onto the deck, and towards the cabin. As they walked along the deck, Zalith gazed at the array of orange and purple painting the evening sky; the sun had almost completely set, and it would be getting dark soon.

When Alucard opened the door, he invited Zalith to step in first. The demon headed into the bedroom and slipped off his shoes. He then looked at Alucard, who closed the door and took his shoes off, too. The vampire sighed quietly, rubbing his arms in what Zalith assumed to be an attempt to warm himself. The room didn't feel cold to him, but he wasn't as sensitive to temperature, so maybe he couldn't tell just how freezing it was. He watched as Alucard lit the fireplace with crimson flames, and then made his way over to the bed.

"It should be warm in Boszorkány," Alucard said, glancing at Zalith as he sat on the opposite side of the bed. "It does get cold at night, though."

"How lucky you are to have me to keep you warm, then," Zalith said with a smirk as he started to unbutton his shirt.

Alucard took his eyes off Zalith and stared down at the floor. Then, when the shy look on his face faded a little, he shuffled under the bed covers and waited for Zalith to join him.

Zalith didn't want to waste time and hastily stripped down to his underwear before climbing into bed beside him. The demon made himself comfortable beneath the fluffy black blanket as he shuffled closer and moved his arm around the vampire. He hadn't overlooked the fact Alucard that made sure to turn his back to him while he undressed and kept his back to him when they laid down, too; he suspected that Alucard was most likely too nervous to look at him—that made him smile, though. He'd caught the vampire staring at him twice, and he was confident that Alucard would keep looking when he thought Zalith wasn't aware.

The demon, however, felt like he should let Alucard know that it was okay for him to stare at him—the vampire probably thought he had to do so secretly in case it made Zalith uncomfortable. Alucard could never make him feel uncomfortable. So, he smiled and hugged the vampire tighter. "Alucard," he said, smirking.

"What?"

"Why have you started turning your back to me?"

"I just… want to lay like this."

With a doubtful smile, Zalith rolled onto his back and pulled Alucard with him. The vampire rested his head on the demon's shoulder, moved his arm around him, and kept his eyes on the wall opposite them. "Well, *I* want to lay like *this*," the demon argued with an amused smile.

"Fine," Alucard grumbled stubbornly… but as Zalith glanced down at his face, he saw the vampire's sights shift to his body.

"What are you staring at?" he asked.

A look of both surprise and embarrassment smothered Alucard's face as he immediately took his eyes off Zalith. "My eyes are closed," he snarled, closing his eyes.

The demon smirked; he knew Alucard was lying. He moved his arm from his side and reached for Alucard's hand, but the vampire pulled his arm from around him.

"Give me your hand, Alucard," Zalith said with a smile, trying to snatch his wrist.

"No," Alucard grumbled, crossing his arms and concealing his hands.

With an amused laugh, Zalith tried to pry Alucard's arms apart to grab his hand, but Alucard resisted and snarled irritably. Zalith wasn't going to give up so easily, though. When Alucard momentarily freed one of his hands to smack Zalith's away, they playfully fought for a few moments until the demon managed to snatch the vampire's left wrist.

Alucard backed down once Zalith placed the vampire's hand on his abs. The demon then lay there, moving his left arm back around Alucard as a smile of victory appeared on his face.

"You can touch me wherever and whenever you want," he assured Alucard as the vampire rested his head back on Zalith's shoulder, his hand still where the demon had placed it.

Alucard seemed hesitant at first but started to gradually move his hand over and around Zalith's abs. The vampire seemed almost fascinated... but after a few moments, he dragged his hand up to the side of the demon's neck and nuzzled the other side of it.

Zalith then smirked deviously. "My turn," he said as he began to move onto his side.

As Alucard rolled onto his back and adorned a conflicted frown, a mix of anticipation and longing shivered through Zalith. With a subtle smile, he turned to face the vampire, the mischievous gleam in his eyes betraying the desires that lingered beneath the surface. Alucard nervously averted his gaze to the left, attempting to hide his shy expression.

Undeterred, Zalith's hand ventured beneath Alucard's shirt, fingers tracing the contours of his well-defined abs. The initial touch sent a jolt of excitement through him, compelling Zalith to lift the fabric for a more intimate view. However, his impulsive move was swiftly halted as Alucard seized his wrist, a silent plea in his eyes to tread carefully on the edge of desire.

"What are you doing?" the vampire asked, turning his head to look at him.

Zalith frowned. "Do you want me to stop?"

Alucard pondered, the shy look on his face thickening. But when a pout broke through his anxious visage, he shook his head. "No."

With a content smirk, Zalith resumed. He gradually lifted the vampire's shirt, setting his eyes on his abs. He wasn't at all disappointed; seeing them—*finally*—only increased his excitement. Once he'd lifted Alucard's shirt enough to see all six of his abs, he dragged his fingers over each, caressing the defined lines of his body.

Convinced that Alucard was comfortable, Zalith moved closer, gradually edging his face nearer to the vampire's body. He glanced up at him to make sure that he was okay with what he was doing; Alucard *did* glance down at him, but he didn't look as though he wanted him to stop; he just looked curious and confused. So without hesitation, the demon softly pressed his lips against the vampire's skin just below his right pec. He felt Alucard tense up, and as he started kissing his way down the vampire's abs, his own anticipation began to increase. The closer he got to Alucard's waist, the harder it became to ignore his desire to unbuckle the vampire's belt and see what waited below. His heart started beating faster as desperation gushed through his body, which yearned for him to finally satiate the ache of his twitching arousal.

He didn't want to give in to his desires for Alucard's sake, but it had been so long... and he wanted Alucard *so desperately....*

However, when he kissed Alucard's stomach, the vampire fidgetted around and gripped the bottom of his shirt, which he hastily pulled back down over his body.

Although he felt disappointed, Zalith understood that Alucard was nervous. He exhaled deeply, trying to silence the aspiration boiling inside him, and as he laid back beside Alucard, he turned his head to look at him. "Sorry," he mumbled and rested his head on Alucard's shoulder.

As Zalith moved his arm around him, Alucard leaned the side of his head on Zalith's. "It's fine."

"Are you sure?" Zalith asked worriedly. He hated to think that he might have made him uncomfortable.

"Yes. I just want to sleep," the vampire said tiredly.

As he calmed down, Zalith took another deep breath. He waited for his arousal to disappear, and once it had, he turned onto his side and shuffled closer to Alucard, closing his eyes. He was sure that the vampire was flustered, confused, and maybe a little uncomfortable—but obviously not enough to need space; Alucard seemed content enough to lay with him, and *that* made Zalith feel a little better about the fact that he'd almost let his desires take over once again.

He didn't want to let it get to him, though. He wanted to enjoy every moment of this trip with Alucard and wasn't going to spend it overthinking about whether or not he'd upset the vampire. He trusted Alucard enough for him to tell him if he did something that discomforted him.

But it was time to sleep. With a smile on his face, he nuzzled Alucard's neck. "Goodnight."

Alucard made himself comfortable and quietly replied, "Goodnight."

Zalith tried to silence his thoughts, but as he inhaled Alucard's intoxicating scent with every breath, it became harder and harder for him to settle. He wanted him *so fucking bad*; he wanted to touch more than his chest—he wanted to touch, kiss, and *taste* every part of him. But thinking about what he wanted wasn't going to do him any good; it would only make him feel frustrated. He was going to take this relationship at *Alucard's* pace, which meant waiting... possibly for quite a while. However, he knew what he signed up for and he didn't regret it. He could wait. He *would* wait until Alucard was ready.

Chapter Twenty-Eight

Drac

| Alucard |

When Alucard woke the next morning, he still had his head rested on Zalith's shoulder, and the demon had his arm around him. It seemed like Zalith was still asleep, so the vampire slowly looked down at what he could see of the demon's body. He gazed at the demon's defined muscles, and he started to feel a little flustered. Last night, things got a little intense very quickly; he enjoyed getting to touch Zalith's body and loved his affection...but when things were about to get serious, he'd let his nervousness enthral him. A part of him regretted telling Zalith to stop, but it was probably for the best. He wasn't ready yet.

Chatter from the crew echoed outside along with the calming sound of the ocean. Alucard didn't know how far they were from Boszorkány but he was sure that they'd arrive by noon, and judging by the appearance of the sky, which he could see through the small cracks in the curtains, it didn't look as though noon was too far away.

The vampire glanced down at Zalith again. He needed to get up and reply to Ben before they reached Boszorkány, but he didn't want to move and disturb the demon if he was still sleeping. So he slowly moved his right hand to the back of Zalith's head. "Zalith?" he asked quietly. "Are you awake?"

A smile crept across Zalith's face. "Yes. I have been for a little while."

Alucard frowned and stared up at the ceiling. "Why didn't you get up?"

Zalith tightened his grip around the vampire. "Because I like to lay in bed with you, Alucard," he answered quietly.

He'd not deny that he liked to lay there with Zalith, too. The demon's embrace was something he enjoyed so deeply that he'd not turn away a chance to feel it. So, he fell silent, resting the side of his head on Zalith's, but when the sunlight crept in through the curtains, Alucard's eyes ached, forcing him to close them. "I have to write to Ben before we reach Boszorkány," he mumbled.

"Would you like me to write for you?" Zalith offered. "Or do you want me to start teaching you now?"

He wasn't in the mood to be taught anything right now. He shrugged lightly and glanced down at what he could see of Zalith. "We can do that another time. If you could write to him for me, though, I'd appreciate it."

"Of course. Just tell me what to write."

With a slight nod, Alucard exhaled quietly and stared back up at the ceiling. But his feeling of calm was soon interrupted; the ship jolted rather violently, and as the crew began yelling in panic outside, Alucard frowned in both confusion and irritancy. "What now?" he grumbled as he and Zalith slowly sat up.

Zalith smirked when the ship started to slow. "Perhaps we hit a shark."

An unamused look struck Alucard's face as he shook his head and climbed out of bed. Leaving the demon, he headed out of his bedroom, closed the door behind him, and stepped out onto the deck. He watched each crew member as they scurried from one side of the ship to another; he listened to their panicked mumbles, and the word 'dragon' was mentioned at least thirty times in the space of a few moments, which concerned him.

Alucard scowled as he made his way over, snatched the collar of one of the crewmen and turned him to face him. "What's going on?" he asked as the man gasped in fear, his fellow crewmates backing off as they watched the altercation.

Staring into Alucard's cold, ice-blue eyes, the man stuttered. "Th-the dragon, sir, something happened—"

"What happened?" Alucard snapped impatiently.

"Looked like he came up for air but made some weird jolty movements like he was hurt," one of the other men called.

"Wriggling around like a fish," the man beside him added.

Alucard deadpanned. Humans were so stupid; he thought he'd seen them at their worst, but to call a *sea serpent* a *fish?* He snarled, chucked the guy he had in his grip at his crewmates, and then leaned over the side of the ship.

"What's wrong?" Zalith asked as he appeared beside him in the same clothes he wore yesterday, clearly having thrown them on hastily to join him on the deck.

"I don't know," Alucard muttered. He tapped what he could reach of the hull, but Drac didn't emerge from below. With a scowl of concern on his face, he stood up straight and looked over at the mortified crewmen. "Stop the ship," he ordered.

They all glanced at one another before one of them said to Alucard, "If…we stop here—there're sirens around these parts, and we could—"

"Stop the fucking ship!" Alucard yelled.

Horrified, all the crewmen fumbled around and scurried to their posts, preparing to do as they were ordered.

Zalith tried to hide his amused smile as he dragged his hand down Alucard's arm and gripped his hand. "I am sure whatever it is, it'll be fine," he said, moving his other arm around the vampire, embracing him from behind.

Waiting for the ship to halt, Alucard leaned back against him and frowned. "He probably just ate something he shouldn't have."

"Perhaps."

As the ship gradually eased to a halt, Alucard gently withdrew from Zalith's embrace, casting a brief glance before leaning over the edge once more. He tapped the hull with a sense of familiarity, a silent communication between master and his companion; he waited patiently for Drac's response, and within moments, the water below began to ripple and contort. Zalith watched with him as the sea serpent emerged from the depths; Drac's face, adorned with teal scales, ascended through the water, and all four of his sorrow-filled yellow eyes fixated on Alucard. His fin-like ears atop his head flicked with a distinct grace, acknowledging the unspoken connection that bound them.

"What's wrong, Drac?" Alucard asked worriedly.

Drac whined quietly, his tongue flickering as he lifted his head out of the water. Then, with his muzzle just inches from Alucard's hand, the beast frowned in distress.

"Is he okay?" Zalith asked.

Alucard wasn't sure. Drac didn't sound as though he was okay, and it worried him to think that something might be wrong with him. "Come up here," he said, stepping aside.

Zalith also backed off as the creature prepared to leave the water and join them. The demon watched with a dubious frown as the scaled serpent slithered up onto the deck, leaving a thick trail of water in his path as he wriggled around and curled up beneath the mast.

Alucard headed over to Drac, leaving Zalith where he was.

When he reached the sea serpent, the vampire set his eyes on the captain, who was lingering on the quarterdeck stairs. "Sail," he ordered. "We're not far from Boszorkány, no?"

"Twenty minutes or so," the captain confirmed. "I'll get going."

Alucard crouched in front of Drac's distressed face and stared at him. The crew all watched from afar, muttering to one another; Zalith also watched from a distance—Alucard was sure that the demon wasn't one for animals, but that didn't bother him. What *did* bother him was Drac's pained expression.

He sat down and invited the dragon to rest his head in his lap. "Tell me what the problem is."

Drac gazed up at him, responding to him with a series of quiet grumbles. The beast then opened its jaws and waited.

With a concerned frown, Alucard made Drac slant his head so that he could see the beast's top row of shark-like teeth. It took him no time at all to spot the problem. A rotted tooth. Could *that* be why he'd become a rather fussy eater over the past year or so? Most likely.

Alucard sighed, shook his head, and made the dragon close his jaws. "You have three options."

The dragon stared up at him, waiting.

"One: you can let me remove the tooth."

Drac frowned.

"Two: I can go and find you a nice dragon nurse, but that might take some time," he said with a smirk.

The dragon grumbled in discomfort.

"Three: the infection spreads… and you die."

Raising his head, Drac stared at him in dread.

"Well?"

Drac scowled, looked away, evidently thought to himself for a few moments, and then looked back up at Alucard as he rested his head in his lap. The dragon grumbled quietly and opened his jaws.

"Right," Alucard muttered. "Hold still." The vampire reached his arm into the dragon's mouth and gripped the rotting back tooth.

"Are you sure that's a good idea?" came Zalith's voice.

Alucard glanced at him, taking his arm out of Drac's mouth. "I know what I'm doing," he insisted, but as Drac set his eyes on Zalith and snarled in hostility, the vampire looked back down at him. "He's okay," he said, patting Drac's head.

Zalith crouched beside the vampire, keeping a close watch on Drac's jaws.

Without further hindrance, Alucard reached back into Drac's mouth and gripped the beast's rotted tooth. "Are you ready?"

Drac murmured in confirmation.

Alucard abruptly yanked the tooth from Drac's jaw. The beast yelped in pain and jolted violently, but he didn't snap his mouth shut over Alucard's arm. When the vampire took his hand out, Drac slowly clamped his jaws shut and groaned irritably.

Once he dropped the tooth beside him, Alucard placed his hand back on Drac's snout and frowned. "I'll get something for it when we get to Boszorkány."

"Does he have an infection?" Zalith asked.

"It would seem that way. What have you been eating?" he asked, glaring into the dragon's eyes. But Drac looked away. "You did this to yourself."

With a roll of his eyes, Drac wriggled free from Alucard's lap and rested his head on the deck.

As he stood up, Alucard glowered at the beast. "*Prost*," he grumbled, turning his back on the dragon.

Drac hissed in mockery at the vampire.

"We should get ready," Alucard said to Zalith, who was following him towards the cabin. "You can get dressed while I wash my hands, and then I'll get ready; by then, we should have reached the docks. I still need to reply to Ben before we set off, too."

Zalith smiled and turned to face him once they reached the door. "Okay," he agreed. He then disappeared into the bedroom, leaving Alucard on the deck with Drac and the crew of idiotic humans.

| **Zalith** |

Inside the cabin, Zalith changed out of yesterday's clothes. As he heard Alucard wander off outside, he made his way over to the dresser that his clothes were in. He pulled on a new shirt along with a pair of black trousers and a black waistcoat. Then, he slipped on his shoes, tidied his face and hair in the mirror, and headed back out onto the deck.

He made his way over to the edge of the ship and ignored Drac's hostile grumble as he stared out at the docks in the distance. When he heard Alucard emerge from the lower decks, he looked over his shoulder and watched the vampire as he headed to the cabin door; he then disappeared inside to get himself ready.

Zalith set his eyes back on the island in the distance and pondered. He couldn't help but wonder why Alucard was still hesitant about letting him see him without clothes, but he was content with the fact that they had been making gradual progress. As much as he desired to see what lay beneath the vampire's clothes, he knew that he had the ability to be patient for a while longer—if that was what Alucard wanted.

As Alucard emerged from the cabin, Zalith set his sights on him. He was now wearing a fitted white shirt and—as usual—black trousers. His crucifix hung around his neck, shimmering in the sunlight as he made his way over. The shirt complimented his toned body enticingly, and Zalith couldn't help but place his hands on Alucard's biceps when he joined him.

He smiled at the vampire. "Do you want to tell me what to write?"

With a small nod, Alucard reached into his pocket and handed Zalith a piece of folded parchment and a lead pencil. Once he took it from him, Zalith unfolded the parchment, rested it against the ship's fence beside him, and waited for Alucard's instructions.

"Felix knows what his job is—he has *not* been given his old job back. You might have to show this to him, he's weird. If he still persists, make sure he understands again. As for Detlaff, I have no interest in what he might want to say. Ignore him," he instructed.

Writing what Alucard told him, Zalith frowned in concern. "This…Felix character," he mumbled, finishing the note. He stood up straight and handed it to Alucard. "Weird?"

Taking the paper, Alucard shrugged. "Not…right up here," he said, tapping his head. "But I have to put up with it—he's the only one capable of doing the job he does."

"To what extent?" Zalith asked, worried that such a strange man was working for Alucard—the same man he'd seen more or less making out with Alucard's leg the day he revived him.

"It doesn't matter," Alucard dismissed, folding up the parchment. He then held it up, and from the top of the foremast, the same white barn owl that had delivered Ben's note swooped down, took the parchment from him, and raced away into the horizon. "Ben knows he has permission to kill him if he doesn't listen to me."

Zalith didn't know too much about Felix, but from what he had seen and heard, he already knew he didn't like him *at all*. Wandering around Alucard's castle doing a job he'd been fired from? "Perhaps he needs to be replaced," he suggested.

"Do you know how irritating it is to find a brood nurse?" Alucard asked with a slight laugh, but it wasn't one of amusement.

The demon waited; he *was* knowledgeable in the different types of vampires that existed, but he wanted to listen to Alucard explain it to him.

Alucard, however, evidently wasn't going to elaborate. He took his eyes off the demon and glared at the docks as the ship edged closer. "I need to find a herbalist when we arrive," he muttered. "Drac needs something to stop his infection from spreading."

"I see," Zalith answered, also staring at the docks.

"You don't have to come with me; I know you despise animals," he grumbled, an irritated, rude tone in his voice.

Zalith smirked. "I see we've become Mr Grumpy," he said. "Are you in need—"

"No," Alucard snarled, turning away from him.

The demon kept his smirk. At the risk of making Alucard's aggravation worse, the demon gradually edged his extended index finger towards the vampire…and prodded the side of his face.

Confused, Alucard frowned and slowly turned his head to set his eyes on him. The vampire scowled and then glared back at the docks.

But not too long after, Zalith lightly squeezed Alucard's ass with his hand.

Alucard's face turned as red as his hair as he turned away, trying to hide his expression.

The demon didn't stop; he profoundly enjoyed watching Alucard become flustered. With an amused grin, he tapped the pointed tip of the vampire's ear. Alucard swiftly lifted his hand and tried to smack Zalith's away, but the demon had already pulled it back and decided to poke Alucard's side with his index finger—but perhaps a little too harshly. Alucard flinched violently and stepped back in what looked like confusion, so Zalith swiftly grabbed his arm and pulled him closer, wrapping his arms around him before he could try to escape.

"I'm sorry," he laughed quietly.

With a stubborn pout, Alucard stood there in Zalith's embrace… and slowly relaxed. Zalith had thought he might snarl and argue, but he didn't.

But then the ship drifted into the docks as the workers below began preparing to take its ropes and secure it in place.

Alucard pulled himself from Zalith's arms and said, "I'll deal with Drac first and then we can work out what we want to do with the day."

Zalith smiled at him and asked, "Do you know what you need for him?"

"More or less," he said with a shrug.

The demon pulled him back into his arms. "Then we'll go and get what you need for him first."

Nodding, Alucard rested his head on Zalith's shoulder, and the demon hugged him tightly. He was excited to explore a new country and getting to do it with Alucard made it even better.

Chapter Twenty-Nine

— ⟨ † ⟩ —

The Herbalist

| **Alucard** |

Alucard and Zalith stepped down onto the dock, greeted by the captivating sight of the city that lay before them. The architectural tapestry unfolded in a harmonious blend of aristocratic sophistication and elven enchantment. Merlot red and dull white towered brick buildings, adorned with intricate carvings and elven glyphs, graced the landscape. The jet-black roofs, reminiscent of nightfall, added a touch of mystery to the skyline.

The cobblestone streets beneath their feet resonated with a timeless charm, weaving through the heart of the city. The bustling thoroughfares were alive with a dynamic fusion of middle and working-class denizens, creating a vibrant mosaic of daily life. As the duo observed, they witnessed a diverse tapestry of activities—some individuals briskly headed to their workplaces with determined strides, while others leisurely engaged in shopping or exchanged laughter outside charming coffee stores.

A warm, inviting atmosphere carried the essence of both worlds, where elven grace seamlessly intertwined with the *joie de vivre* of a Boszorkian town. Hidden within the details of the buildings, one could discern elven motifs and delicate craftsmanship, while the energy of the streets resonated with the animated spirit of a lively human market. Together, the elements painted a captivating tableau, where the rich history of elven magic met the charm of a quaint human town, creating a city that stood as a testament to the coexistence of two distinct cultures.

Tourists filed off another ship which docked just before Alucard's galleon did, and the workers and tradesmen hurried around as a huge flock of seagulls cawed loudly, swooping down to steal whatever they could from the nearby marketplace.

"It's…not what I remember," Alucard said, watching as a few horses trotted past the docks.

"In a good or bad way?" Zalith asked, smiling at him.

The vampire shrugged and sighed. "Eh. It's a lot busier," he said as he started to lead the way towards the road.

"Do elves live here? A lot of the architecture looks elven," the demon said as he glanced around.

Alucard nodded. "Boszorkány is home to many species of elf. They don't tend to hang around with humans, though—at least not the working class." He set his eyes on a fork in the main road. "When I last came here, there was an herbalist just up that street. I hope he's still there."

"If he's not, I'm sure we can find another one," Zalith said as he followed Alucard onto the main road's sidewalk.

While he led the way towards the street where he hoped to find the herbalist's store, Alucard glanced at Zalith. He wasn't sure whether the demon was irritated with him for snapping at him earlier; it didn't seem as though he was, but it was often hard to read the expression on his face.

Alucard looked ahead again as they walked up the bustling street. "I'm sorry for snapping earlier," he mumbled. "I don't know why I feel so irritated sometimes."

Zalith smiled at him. "You don't need to be sorry. I thought it was funny; it was a rather abrupt comment."

Why was everything so amusing to Zalith? Alucard stopped walking, and as Zalith also stopped to look at him, he glared at the demon. "Why is everything always so funny to you?"

"I find joy in the little things, Alucard—you should laugh more, too," he said with a smirk, nudging Alucard's shoulder with his own as they continued walking.

With a slight roll of his eyes, Alucard sighed. "Right," he muttered. He still wasn't in the best of moods, but at least he didn't feel as irritated as he had before they left the ship.

He set his eyes ahead and spotted the herbalist's store. The street was lined with a whole array of new stores and buildings that hadn't been there during his last visit; opposite the herbalist, on the other side of the wide road packed with shuffling people and whinnying horses, was a curiosity store, a bakery to its left, and a small candy store to its right. A little further up the road was a rather old-looking violin store, and the moment Alucard set his eyes on it, he thought about enquiring within about getting himself a new violin, but the thought of having lost so much in his house's fire kept him from doing so.

Once they reached the herbalist's store, Alucard pulled the door open and invited Zalith to enter first. He then followed the demon into the small, cramped, headache-inducingly potent store lined with shelves upon shelves of items used in everything from potion-making to alchemy. At the very end of the store was tiny a counter, and as the bell above the door rang, the startled face of an albino elf popped up from behind the desk.

The elf smiled as he set his blush-red eyes on Alucard. His hair was platinum white, his skin almost as pale as Alucard's, and his white eyebrows were so unnecessarily long, stretching off his face like single cat whiskers.

Alucard could practically feel Zalith's skepticism emanating off his body, and when he looked at the demon, the hostile glare on his face made it evident that Zalith already didn't like this elf...probably because of the way he'd just looked at Alucard.

With an excited murmur, the elf scurried out from behind the counter, dropping whatever he must have been messing with on the floor; he navigated his way through the maze of shelves, and as he reached them, he immediately held his hand out towards Alucard.

"Do you speak Deiganish?" Alucard asked in Boszorkian.

Nodding, the elf smiled at Alucard—he didn't even spare Zalith a glance. "What is it I help with you?" he asked pleasantly, leading the way forward.

As Alucard walked with the elf, Zalith followed, keeping a watchful eye on him.

"For...a lizard," Alucard said to the elf, who was now walking beside him leaving barely even a few inches between them. Alucard tried to move away, but the elf stuck to his side no matter what. "Tooth," he uttered uncomfortably. "Rotten."

"Yes..." the elf said with a nod, leading them to the back of the store.

To Alucard's relief, there was more room back there, but the elf didn't give him space. He tried to ignore him, along with the overwhelming smell of herbs and spices, and scoured the shelves with his eyes. When he spotted the first thing he needed to create Drac's pain relief, he moved away from the estranged elf and stood in front of a shelf adorned with several differently sized ginger-like roots.

"I will get price list, yes," the elf said with a smile and wandered off.

Rolling his eyes, Alucard crossed his arms and glared at what lay on the shelf.

"Perhaps he can find some respect whilst he's back there," Zalith muttered, standing beside Alucard as the elf disappeared through a door in the far-right corner of the store.

Alucard glanced at Zalith. "Why?"

"He was a little too close, don't you think?"

The vampire nodded as he searched the shelf. He then wandered over to another shelf of jars containing small, ground herbs.

When the elf returned with a piece of parchment in his hands, he stood beside Alucard and smiled at him while he waited to be told what Alucard needed.

"I need this, but fresh," the vampire said, pointing to a small vial of blood vine.

As the elf nodded, he searched down the list he had in his hands. "I have...yes."

"This," Alucard said as he took a small jar of grim root paste from the top shelf. He handed it to the elf, who stroked Alucard's hand when he took it from him. The vampire sharply turned his head as he pulled his hand away and glared at the elf, but he didn't want to snap at him and cause a conflict, so he held back.

"Apologies," the elf said, smiling. "More?" he then asked, nodding at the shelf.

Scowling, Alucard set his eyes back on the shelf. He took a single stalk of lavender, handed it to the elf, and walked over to one of the other shelves.

Before the elf could follow Alucard, though, Zalith snatched the man's shoulder and turned him around to face him. He then grabbed the elf's collar and glared into his confused eyes. "If you lay your hands on him again, I'll tear them off," he warned angrily. Then, he shoved the elf back, snarling quietly before making his way over to where Alucard was standing. "I'm going to wait outside; the smell in this place is atrocious," he said as the vampire turned to face him. With a smile on his face, he kissed the vampire goodbye, and before making his way towards the door, he shot another glare at the terrified elf.

When Zalith left, Alucard turned to face the intricately adorned shelf behind him. An amused, satisfied smirk stretched across his face, lingering as a testament to the profound satisfaction derived from the demon's instinctive need to protect him. Alucard found solace in the possessiveness that enveloped Zalith's actions; it wasn't merely about physical safety—it went beyond that. Zalith's unwavering commitment made Alucard feel wanted in a way he had never experienced before.

In that moment, surrounded by artefacts and trinkets, Alucard couldn't help but revel in the knowledge that he held a special place in Zalith's heart. The assurance that the demon wouldn't allow anything to harm or disturb him created a haven within his world. As he traced his fingers over the elven carvings on a delicate artefact, a warmth filled his being, a sensation of being cherished and safeguarded that only Zalith could evoke.

The store's bell then chimed, signifying Zalith's departure, pulling Alucard out of his moment of enjoyment. He scowled and sharply turned his head to look over at the elf. "I need this, too," he said, tapping the lid of a small jar of gold flower petals.

Nodding, the elf snapped out of his fear-stricken trance and hurried to him.

"Do you have nightshade?" Alucard asked, watching as the elf opened the jar of petals and carefully took out one of the finger-length, teardrop-shaped leaves.

The elf turned his back on Alucard and made his way over to the counter. "Yes," he confirmed. "I get...back here," he said, pointing to the door he had earlier disappeared into.

As the elf wandered off again, Alucard made his way over to a shelf lined with small, beautiful crystals. He didn't need them to create Drac's medicine, but he couldn't resist looking. In particular, a white, wand-shaped crystal caught his eyes; small gold streaks veined through it, almost as if rivers were flowing inside the crystal itself. Alucard knew it was severium, something he was rather familiar with. He took it from the shelf and made his way over to the counter, where the elf was waiting and putting everything Alucard had selected into a small box.

The vampire handed him the crystal, and as he packed it into the box, the elf glanced a somewhat concerned look his way.

"What?" Alucard asked.

"Severium is…strange purchase for—"

"What is all of this?" the vampire interjected, not at all interested in letting him finish what he was about to say.

The elf looked down at the box, sealed it shut with a small wax seal, and then held out a piece of paper with everything tallied on it. "Coronam," he said, giving Alucard the paper.

He wasn't shocked that his small order totalled close to a coronam; he reached into his left trouser pocket, pulled out ten gold coins, and placed them on the counter.

"And crystal…same price as all," the elf said.

With a roll of his eyes, Alucard reached into his other pocket and pulled out a small piece of black card with his sigil on it. "Send the bill here for that," he said, sliding the card across the counter. He didn't have enough gold coins with him.

Looking down at it, the elf frowned and shook his head. "Pay now," he insisted.

"Perhaps you ought to actually look at what I gave you, no?" Alucard said as calmly as he could, but he was quickly losing his patience with this man.

Still frowning, the elf looked down at the card again, but a look of dread quickly plastered itself to his pale face. "Y-yes, I send bill," he said with a nod, his tone reflecting his caution.

Then, Alucard took the box, turned around, and made his way out of the store. All he had to do now was get back to the ship and combine all the ingredients, and once Drac had recovered, they could continue towards Avalmoor.

Chapter Thirty

— ⋜ ✝ ⋝ —

Dragon Medicine

| **Alucard** |

When Alucard stepped out onto the street, he searched for Zalith, but he was nowhere to be seen. The vampire frowned and looked up and down the road, and just as he was about to try and decide which direction to head in, he spotted him crossing the road by a parked horse-drawn carriage.

When the demon reached him, he stopped in front of him and asked, "Did he bother you after I left?"

"No," Alucard answered. "Where did you go?"

"Just for a short walk," he said with a smile. "Would you like me to take that?" he offered, pointing to the box in Alucard's right hand.

The vampire began to lead the way back toward the docks as he said, "No, thank you," with a discreet smile.

Zalith walked beside him. "How do you prepare the medicine for Drac?"

Alucard shrugged. "It won't take too long. Why? Do you want to do something after?"

"I thought it would be nice if we had ice cream together," he suggested as they reached the docks and headed towards Alucard's galleon.

"We can do that," he agreed. He hadn't had ice cream in a long, *long* time.

The demon smiled as they walked up onto the galleon deck and over to where Drac was waiting, still curled up around the main mast with a pained, sour look on his scaled face.

"You," Alucard said with a smirk, setting his eyes on the dragon. As Drac raised his head and looked at him, the vampire tapped the top of the box. "I'll be five more minutes."

Drac nodded and rested his chin back on the deck.

"I don't think he likes me very much," Zalith said as they turned right and walked to the cabin.

Alucard frowned at him. "Who?"

"Drac."

He glanced at the dragon, who was glaring evilly at Zalith.

"See?"

Amused, the vampire smirked and pushed the cabin door open. "He's just cautious." He closed the door behind them and looked around. "There should be a mortar and pestle in there," he said, pointing to one of the cabinets by the door. "Will you get it for me, please?"

"Of course," Zalith agreed and made his way over to the cabinet.

While Zalith looked for the mortar and pestle, Alucard placed his box of items on the table near the fireplace.

"Would you like some help?" Zalith offered when he joined him at the table, placing the stone mortar and pestle beside the box.

The vampire took everything out of the box and then glanced at Zalith. "You can put this in that fancy-looking box over there," he said, handing him the small, wand-shaped piece of severium. He then pointed to the jewellery box sitting on top of the cabinet to the left of the bed.

Looking down at it, Zalith frowned curiously. "What is it?"

"Severium," Alucard replied as he put each ingredient into the mortar. "It forms in the footprints of dragons when elf blood is poured into them."

With an intrigued smile, Zalith leaned back against the table and watched him grind everything up with the pestle. "I assume you don't need this for Drac, considering you haven't added it in," he said, nodding at the mixture.

As he carefully ground everything together, Alucard shrugged and said, "It will be useful for when we reach Avalmoor. There will be dragons there, dragons that won't exactly be too happy to see me... to see *us*. Avalmoor is mostly populated by humans and seers, Letholdus' favourite beings. He's not welcoming of any other race, especially those of us who think of humans as a food source. That's why we must wear the gold; it keeps the dragons from being able to tell that we are demons. As for the severium, it contains gold and is also rather flammable—when demon fire is applied, anyway."

"I see," Zalith said. He then left Alucard to finish preparing Drac's medicine and made his way over to the jewellery box that the vampire had asked him to place the crystal in.

Alucard finished preparing Drac's medicine, placed the pestle on the table, and then turned to face Zalith, who headed back over to him. "Would you like to give it to him?" he offered with a smirk.

Zalith seemed unsure whether or not he was being sarcastic—the frown on his face was thick with confusion and hesitation.

Amused, Alucard picked up the mortar and laughed quietly as he walked past the demon and went out onto the deck. He set his eyes on Drac, who immediately lifted his head to look at him while he walked over to where he lay.

"Are you going to spit it out?" Alucard asked with a frown as he stopped in front of the dragon, who stared up at him in discontent.

But Drac shook his head, followed by a small grumble of agony.

"Open," Alucard instructed, crouching in front of Drac's face.

As he was told, the dragon slowly widened his jaws to reveal his shark-like teeth, which glistened brightly in the sunlight.

Alucard moved his hand into the mortar and scooped out as much of the purple, pasty concoction as he could. Then, he reached into Drac's mouth and carefully placed it over the gaping hole where his rotten tooth had once been.

"Don't lick it," he warned.

But as Zalith crouched beside him, Drac scowled and growled quietly.

As he pulled his arm from the dragon's mouth, Alucard frowned and glanced at Zalith. "I actually don't think he likes you," he said, smirking.

"I can't imagine why," Zalith mumbled.

As Drac closed his mouth, Alucard took Zalith's hand in his own and started to move it towards the dragon. "You need to show him he can trust you or he'll forever look at you as if you want to murder me," he said, slowly placing Zalith's hand on Drac's snout.

With a slightly amused laugh, Zalith said, "I'm not sure how I might have given him the impression that I want to harm you."

Alucard shrugged and let go of Zalith's hand, leaving him to pet the dragon himself. "He's just cautious of everybody. Protective of me."

Nodding, Zalith kept his hand on the dragon's snout, watching as Drac slowly lost his hostile scowl and stared calmly at him.

"Was it rescuing him that made him so loyal?" Zalith asked, glancing at the dragon.

"That, and I raised him. I'm sure he sees me as his... hmm... father, I suppose," he said with a shrug, standing up.

Taking his hand off the dragon, Zalith also stood up. "What's the difference between this type of dragon and the type we might come across in Avalmoor—the same type as Janus? Are all dragons here considered gods, or... are they also fauna?" the demon asked, following Alucard back into the cabin.

Alucard snatched a towel from the bathroom rack, placed it on the counter, and started washing his hands under the tap. "Well," he started, glancing at Zalith, who was standing in the doorway, resting his left arm against the frame. "While Lucifer created Detlaff, Letholdus created the dragons—the... God Dragons. They are known as the Aegis. They are Letholdus' children, I guess," he explained as he dried his hands. "They can speak, but only to certain people, often those born with the gift to speak to them.

They are extremely powerful, too; a lot of mages draw their ethos from these Dragon Gods, similar to how certain cults and species draw ethos from other Numen. As for dragons like Drac, they are…more or less animals. If you saw a Dragon God, you would know right away that they are a god and not like Drac."

"Where did dragons like Drac come from, then?"

"They were already here, just like the fish in the sea and the birds in the sky…and the fish in the sky," he said with a quiet laugh. "Letholdus was fascinated by dragons, so he crafted his children to look like them," he said with a shrug and watched Zalith wash his hands, too. "Some of the dragons—much like demon matriarchs—were made to breed to increase a species' numbers so the Dragon Gods could hide among them if need be."

Nodding, Zalith finished cleaning his hands and walked beside Alucard as they left the cabin and headed across the deck. "And what do the Dragon Gods do for the world?"

As he led the way back down to the docks, Alucard glanced at Zalith and said, "Well, some of them created curses, other species, races—Janus liked to brag that he created vampires, but all he did was use my blood." They headed up the road and into the busy city. "I know that Kardos and his brother, Thalis, created werewolves. Kardos, who created Ada—and later a few other werewolves to start bloodlines—left shortly after I killed Janus. Coward," he muttered.

"It's rumoured among the werewolves in Eltaria that Thalis was the creator of the original wolves—the start of each bloodline," Zalith revealed with an intrigued tone. "The stories also say he left the same day he arrived, almost as if he stepped through the door, dropped off six wolves, and left straight after," he said with a quiet laugh.

"Sounds like something an Aegis would do," the vampire mumbled. He didn't want to speak about the gods, the Numen, or anything like them anymore. He'd tell Zalith what he needed to know later. Right now, he just wanted to enjoy the demon's company. "Where are we getting ice cream?" he asked, changing the subject.

Zalith smiled. "I saw a small place just up the road from that herbalist store."

"Well, I haven't had ice cream in a long time, so I trust you to get me something that you think I'll like."

"I think I know what that might be," Zalith flirted, glancing at Alucard.

The vampire pouted in response and looked away, trying to hide his nervous frown.

Amused, Zalith laughed quietly and moved his arm behind Alucard's back, placed it around his waist, and pulled him closer. "Something sweet, I assume?"

"Preferably," Alucard mumbled as they reached a small ice cream parlour.

"You wait here," Zalith said as he led them to one of the only empty tables. Then, as Alucard sat down, the demon made his way into the busy store.

Alucard glanced around at everyone sitting outside the parlour. Now that he was alone, now that he was busy explaining history or thinking about dragons, his hunger crept up on him. The bloodlust grew stronger as each moment passed, and it forced him to consider which man or woman nearby would be the best prey. Sitting at the opposite, rounded white table were two elves; one woman, one man, and their pet poodle. Alucard managed to shift his attention to the chocolate-brown dog; he'd not seen a dog like that in a long time, and when it set its hazel eyes on him, he smiled, and the poodle excitedly wagged its tail.

The vampire then scoured the other tables. Most of the patrons were elves. Some looked much like the elf who served him at the herbalist store, and others had rather dark, dull auras lingering inside them; they had black hair, strangely grey skin, and eyes as black as night. But he wasn't interested in elf blood. He took his eyes off them and instead stared at one of the only humans who just sat down. Alucard didn't care who he might be; all he could focus on was the fact that he was human and would certainly sate his quickly increasing hunger.

"This is for you," Zalith then said, snapping him out of his trance.

The demon placed a small glass bowl of chocolate ice cream in front of the vampire; it consisted of two scoops of ice cream, both with cherries on top of them and some chocolate sauce.

"*Multemesc,*" Alucard thanked and took a spoon from Zalith as he handed it to him. "What did you get?" he asked, looking at the green-coloured ice cream Zalith placed in front of him as he sat in his seat.

"Pistachio."

"What's that?" Alucard asked curiously, watching as Zalith tasted his ice cream.

Looking at the vampire, Zalith smiled. "A pistachio is a kind of nut."

Nodding, Alucard looked back down at his ice cream, scooped a small bit onto his spoon, and tried it. Despite the fact it was very cold, he found it quite delicious.

"Do you like it?" Zalith asked.

"Yes," he answered.

"Would you like to try mine?"

Alucard took his eyes off his ice cream and looked at Zalith. *Did* he want to try it? Green wasn't a colour he'd associate with something sweet, but Zalith seemed to be enjoying it, so he thought he might as well try. He nodded and watched as the demon used his right thumb to scoop some of the ice cream from his bowl. Zalith then held his thumb out towards him with an amused, unseemly smile on his face. Why couldn't he just use his spoon?

His curiosity to try the pistachio ice cream outweighed his shyness. Alucard irritably snatched Zalith's wrist, pulled his hand closer, and scowled as he dragged his tongue over the demon's ice cream-covered thumb. He ignored Zalith's growing smirk and he let go of his wrist, but a conflicted frown stole his glower; he wasn't sure whether he liked the ice cream's flavour. It wasn't awful, but it wouldn't be his first pick if they were to get ice cream again.

"Do you like it?" Zalith asked him.

"I'm sure *you* enjoyed that a whole lot," Alucard muttered, picking up his spoon.

"As a matter of fact, I did, yes," Zalith confirmed, smiling at him.

The vampire then shrugged. "It was okay, but I like this better," he said, pointing to his chocolate ice cream.

Zalith laughed a little and said, "I suspected as much."

The desperate yells of a man suddenly cut through the noise of the crowded street. Alucard swiftly located him—he wasn't hard to miss with the blinding purples and blues that he was wearing. He was yelling in Boszorkian, and from what the vampire understood, he was spreading the news of a pantomime soon to show in the city centre.

Both Alucard and Zalith watched as the small man hurried up the street with posters and flyers clenched between his arms and chest. He rushed up to people, asking if they wanted to attend, but most of them turned him away or binned the flyers the moment he handed them out.

"What an annoying little man," Zalith muttered as he scooped a pistachio from his bowl and ate it.

Alucard took his eyes off the scurrying man and went back to his ice cream. However, as the man hurried over to the ice cream parlour and began handing out flyers, the vampire didn't turn him away. When the panting guy offered one to him, he took it and glanced down at it.

"What is it?" Zalith asked

"A performance," he replied, handing the flyer to Zalith.

Eying the brightly coloured flyer, Zalith frowned and handed it back to Alucard. "If the man who handed you this is one of the performers, I'm sure it'll be a disaster," he said, smirking.

Smiling, Alucard searched the flyer for a start time. "Well, it could be entertaining. It starts in half an hour."

Zalith smiled at him. "It could be."

"Do you *want* to go?"

The demon nodded as he finished his ice cream and then rested his arms on the table. "We might as well. Unless there's something else you'd rather do with what time we have left here."

Alucard shrugged, tucking the flyer into his pocket. "Nothing comes to mind."

"Where is it?"

"The city centre. It's a small walk from here, so if we are going, we should leave soon."

"I'm ready when you are," the demon said contently.

Alucard ate the last of his ice cream and stood up. Then, they made their way up the street and turned onto a large, vast road lined with towering hotels and bars.

When he noticed Zalith eyeing a few of the taller buildings, Alucard glanced at them and frowned. "There's a lot of tourism here. People come to see the elves and shows, and many people also celebrate Yule here, too. There are legends of a beast that only comes out on the nights of Yule to steal children—there is a rather large bounty on its head, so a lot of people come here each year to try and find it."

"What a strange tradition. Have you seen this beast, Alucard?" Zalith asked with a skeptical smile on his face. "Was that your reason for visiting this place before?"

"No," Alucard said, pouting. "I came for business. Anyway, no, I have not seen the beast. People say it looks like a horned werewolf," he said, leading the way onto another street. "Others say it looks like a man with goat legs—some even say it's a furred dragon."

"And what do *you* believe it is?"

Alucard shrugged. "There are a few species in this world that hunt children and only two that hibernate until the cold season. It's either a sapmarkan or a dorogan," he explained, turning onto yet another street; the city centre was just visible at the end of it.

"I have no idea what either of those creatures are," Zalith said with a quiet laugh.

"Sapmarkan are man-like goats; built like a man but look like goats—horns and all. A dorogan is a species of ice dragon; they just like to snatch children because they are easier to kill than men. They have been hunted to near extinction, though, I'm sure."

"I'm sure there's no question as to why."

Alucard nodded in agreement as they reached the city centre. They both looked around for a few moments, and when the vampire set his eyes on a small gathering of brightly dressed people, he led the way over to a fence standing between two small taverns. The same man who'd been handing out the flyers was standing in front of a gate, allowing people entry so long as they handed him payment.

The vampire and demon made their way over and joined the line of people waiting to reach the front, and once they *did* reach the front, Alucard handed the man a gold coin. With a look of awe on his face, the man pushed open the gate, granting them entry to the performance area.

A stage stood at the end of a large opening in the middle of a huddle of tall buildings. Rows of seats were lined out, and both Alucard and Zalith immediately chose to sit close to the back in the left corner.

"Do you happen to know what this performance is about?" Zalith asked as he sat beside Alucard, who made himself comfortable.

"Something about a...I didn't read the entire thing," he admitted.

With an amused laugh, Zalith moved his arm around Alucard's shoulders and pulled him closer. "I'm sure we'll find out soon," he said and rested his head on Alucard's.

And then, they waited for the show to begin.

Chapter Thirty-One

Rain

| Alucard |

The performance area quickly filled with a loud, chattering crowd, and when they eventually quietened down, the pantomime began. It wasn't at all what Alucard had been expecting, and the performers' acting was so awful that both he and Zalith struggled to keep a straight face for longer than a few seconds. But Alucard felt as if he enjoyed snickering with Zalith more than he would have enjoyed watching something that snatched their attention entirely.

However, the longer they sat and observed, the more the fumbling bard with a god-awful voice reminded Alucard of Elvin. The small, lute-carrying man stumbled over his words, whimpered when the crowd booed, and looked around desperately when he forgot his lines. While everyone else laughed, Alucard frowned regretfully and stared down at his lap. Just as he hadn't allowed himself time to grieve for Tobias, he hadn't thought about Elvin, either. Elvin hadn't deserved to die at all, and if Alucard could have prevented it, he would have.

With a discreet frown of despair, he set his eyes back on the performers as they yelled poetry at one another, trying to speak over the mumbling crowd of disappointed spectators. As much as Alucard might like to forget about what happened, he couldn't, and the longer he denied himself time to grieve, the worse he knew his guilt would become. He took his eyes off the stage and glanced at Zalith, who was watching with a conflicted smile on his face; Alucard was unsure whether it was a look of amusement or disappointment.

He looked back down at his lap. Elvin died because he chose Zalith's life over his. Alucard wouldn't change *that*—he'd do whatever it took to keep this demon in his life— but Elvin hadn't been the first person to die because of Alucard, and he was sure that he wouldn't be the last, either. He couldn't help but wonder, would the day come when he lost Zalith to a similar situation? Would Damien take him, too?

"Are you okay?" Zalith asked, leaning into his ear. "We can leave if you want."

"I'm fine," he denied.

With a content smile, Zalith set his eyes back on the performance.

Alucard tried to focus on the performance. However, his sights soon shifted to the darkening sky. Thick, gloomy storm clouds loomed overhead, and the smell of petrichor drowned out the scent of the snack bar and the flowers lined around the stage. It was about to rain, and Alucard thought that it might be more entertaining to see everyone scream and run in fear of the weather than to sit there and watch the pantomime for much longer.

Small droplets splashed onto his face, and as it got heavier, the crowd began to murmur worriedly, and the performers halted. They stared up at the clouds, and when the light shower abruptly burst into a torrential downpour, everyone started panicking like trapped mice. The actors hurried around desperately, attempting to save their props from the rain, and at the same time, the spectators began rushing for the exit, those with bags holding them above their heads to protect their hair from the quickly increasing rainfall.

Alucard and Zalith were two of the first to leave. With amused laughs, they ran hand-in-hand from the performance area and hurried through the city centre. They navigated the emptying streets and back to the soggy docks, where they rushed up onto Alucard's ship.

With an irritated snarl, Alucard kicked off his shoes before entering the carpeted cabin, and he forbade Zalith from entering until he, too, removed his shoes. Once the demon took them off, he followed the vampire into the room, closing the door behind him.

Alucard stopped by the table and frowned hesitantly. He wanted to change out of his wet clothes, but he didn't want Zalith to see. He glanced back at the demon, who was distracted drying his hair; he then set his eyes on the changing screen in the far-left corner. He could change behind that. He headed over to the wardrobe he kept his shirts in, but before he could, Zalith suddenly snatched his right wrist, turned him to face him, and placed both his hands on his waist.

The demon smiled at him as he stared back in confusion. Zalith had taken his wet waistcoat and shirt off already; his hair was unkempt and a tousled mess, and a suggestive smile clung to his face. Alucard watched as the demon's eyes wandered down from his face to his body, and when Zalith smirked, he frowned unsurely.

"What?" he asked.

Zalith stared into the vampire's confused eyes. "I can see your nipples," he said and grinned as he watched Alucard's pale face redden with embarrassment.

With a look of horror on his face, Alucard looked down to see that Zalith could see pretty much his entire body through his soaked shirt. Utterly flustered, he turned his head away from him to hide his expression and scowled as he used his arms to conceal as much of his body as he could.

Amused, Zalith laughed and gripped Alucard's arms with his hands; he pulled them back down to his sides and said, "It's okay. You can see mine, too."

The vampire scowled harder, reluctant to take his eyes off the floor. *Of course* he'd be able to see Zalith's; *he* had no shirt on. But... he couldn't resist. He slowly glanced at the demon, admiring what he could see of his body from the corner of his eye. However, as Zalith then stepped forward, guiding him back, he frowned in confliction. Where was he taking him? His back hit the dresser behind him, and as it did, Alucard lifted his head and stared at the demon's face in confusion.

Smirking, Zalith moved closer and kissed Alucard's lips. The vampire didn't hesitate; although he was embarrassed, he enjoyed Zalith's affection. He kissed the demon back, and as their tongues gradually entwined, Zalith dragged his hands over Alucard's wet shirt-covered body. Alucard felt a shiver of angst race through him, but he tried to keep his shyness from getting the better of him.

He listened as the rain poured outside, his nervousness starting to wither while he and the demon kissed. The vampire gradually lifted his hands and placed them on Zalith's waist; he'd felt the demon's abs before, and he'd take any chance to touch them again, so he dragged his fingertips over the demon's damp, defined muscles as he moved his left hand around Zalith's body and up to the back of his neck. Alucard then tilted his head aside and guided Zalith's face to his neck, where the demon started softly kissing his skin.

Excitement lingered upon each of Alucard's quiet, subtle breaths, betraying the intensity building within him. Zalith's playfully biting kisses sent shivers down his spine, a prelude to the imminent passion. As the demon's hands began their tantalizing ascent, traversing the contours of Alucard's body, a thrill of anticipation coursed through the vampire's veins.

Reaching the collar of Alucard's shirt, Zalith paused, locking eyes with him as if seeking approval. Alucard, caught in a trance of anticipation, held the demon's gaze, silently inviting him to explore further. With a magnetic pull, Zalith's eyes roamed down once more, and Alucard felt the tremor of vulnerability intertwine with his eagerness as the demon's hands started to unbutton his shirt.

Conflicted emotions surged within Alucard, a maelstrom of desire and apprehension. Beneath his shirt lay a secret, a part of himself that made him hesitate. Yet, the allure of the unknown and the desire for more drew him further into an intoxicating trance. He held back his words, allowing Zalith to proceed, his gaze fixed on the sinuous movements of the demon's hands revealing his bare skin.

As Zalith unveiled Alucard's chest, he placed both hands firmly on his exposed chest, and an excited smirk stretched across the demon's face. Alucard leaned his head back, his heart racing in tandem with the building tension. He wanted Zalith to explore him, just as he had explored the demon's form.

But as moments lingered, Zalith's hand traced a path down Alucard's body, and a wicked smirk played on his lips. "Are you okay?" The question hung in the air, a tantalizing pause in the seductive symphony that echoed through the gloomy room, leaving Alucard on the precipice of surrender, yearning for the next note in the thrilling, intimate composition.

Alucard's gaze lingered on his own body as Zalith's fingers traced enticing patterns over his abs. Anticipation ensnared him, a deep-seated longing surfacing from the shadows, entwining itself around him. In response to Zalith's question, he nodded, his desire burning stronger, further banishing his anxiety. Drawing the demon's face close, their lips met once again, reigniting the flames of their shared passion.

As they kissed, Alucard seized the opportunity to explore Zalith's body. Guiding his hand from the demon's abs, he traversed the contours until reaching Zalith's right arm. His fingers traced the sinewy lines of the demon's bicep, gripping it tightly, and as Zalith's hands moved around Alucard's waist, their bodies drew closer.

In the past, hesitation had lingered, but tonight, Alucard cast it aside. With mounting anticipation, he turned his head to the side, taking a moment to breathe. Zalith's hands ventured past the confines of the vampire's waist and under his trousers, sending a thrill through Alucard's body. When the demon cupped his ass, the vampire's grip on Zalith's arm tightened, his claws threatening to emerge in the intensity of the moment.

A delightful shiver coursed through Alucard's trembling frame as Zalith's hold tightened, the longing for more eclipsing any lingering nervousness. Placing his hand on the back of Zalith's head, Alucard grasped a handful of the demon's hair, attempting to contain the surging desire within. With each passing moment, the intensity heightened. Zalith's lips lightly kissed his neck, the demon's grip on his ass tightening, and Alucard grimaced in a pleasing struggle.

As a smile graced Zalith's face, the demon pressed his lips against Alucard's skin, and the vampire became almost desperate for the sensation of his fangs piercing his neck. Yet, true to Zalith's teasing nature, the moment lingered, frustrating Alucard even as the demon's affectionate touch kept him suspended in the sweet agony of anticipation.

But the moment Zalith pulled his hands from Alucard's trousers and gripped the sides of his shirt, Alucard's intense, consuming lust withered, snuffed out like a candle's flame in the wind. Zalith tried to pull his shirt from his body, but Alucard fearfully snatched Zalith's wrist, and as the demon lifted his head to look at him, the vampire frowned reluctantly.

"What's wrong?" Zalith asked quietly.

Alucard didn't want Zalith to see—not now. He couldn't let himself become so lost in desire that he made such an awful mistake. He was sure that if the demon saw what he tried so hard to hide, he'd leave, and he didn't want to lose Zalith; this demon meant so much to him—he had even once gone so far as to think he loved Zalith. But could he hide it from him forever? Did he *want* to hide it from him forever?

With a distressed pout, he averted his anxious gaze to the floor. He didn't like lying to Zalith, and as much as he wanted to keep this from him, the demon deserved to know. He deserved to know what Alucard was. So he'd show him—he had to—and if it sent Zalith away, well…he was prepared for that. He wouldn't blame Zalith. He'd not blame anyone but himself.

But hesitation snatched hold of him before he could even decide how to tell him. He wasn't ready to show him, nor was he prepared to see Zalith's reaction. He didn't want to watch the kindness fade from his face, he didn't want to see a horrified, disgusted scowl where content smiles and flirtatious smirks once sat.

"I… don't want you to see," he muttered shamefully, his throat tightening as dismay accompanied his despair.

Zalith both smiled and frowned in confusion. "See? Alucard, whatever it is, it's not going to make me feel any different about you."

Alucard wasn't convinced. How could he be? Zalith would react the same way *all* demons did, and he wasn't naïve enough to believe that he wouldn't. But the fact that Zalith deserved to know still remained. Alucard didn't want to lie to him. He didn't want to lead Zalith on and make him feel trapped or tricked when he eventually found the courage to show him. He'd rather do it now before he let himself fall any harder for this man. It was going to hurt like fuck, but who was he trying to fool?

He let out a long, shaky breath and let go of Zalith's wrists. But before the demon could resume pulling his shirt off, Alucard gripped it and said, "Vait." He didn't spare a moment to see what expression was on Zalith's face and turned to face the wall. And then he waited. Dread constricted him tighter as each moment dragged on, and when Zalith gradually pulled his shirt down, revealing the entirety of his back and arms, he closed his eyes and scowled, trying to hold back the tears that were fighting so hard to break free. He was certain that he knew what Zalith was thinking, and he tried his best to be ready for what was about to happen.

Each moment of silence felt like a century; his heart raced frantically in his chest, and his throat became so tight that he stifled a breath. He could feel Zalith's eyes on him, examining every inch of him, but he was far too afraid to look over his shoulder and see the demon's face.

"Who did this to you?" Zalith questioned, his voice resonating with a potent blend of anger and sorrow.

Alucard flinched, expecting a snarl of disgust and a revolted outburst. But as he felt Zalith gently drag his thumb over one of the many raised scars on his back, he opened his eyes and huffed quietly. "I don't…want to talk about it," he uttered despondently.

Zalith wrapped his arms around him and rested the side of his head on the back of Alucard's, hugging him tightly.

The vampire frowned in confliction. He didn't know what Zalith was thinking, but he was still there; although he was silent, he was holding him tightly. However, Alucard wasn't confident enough to let himself sink into the demon's embrace. What if Zalith was trying to decide whether he wanted to abandon him or not? What if he was so disgusted that he was confused about what he was feeling? Alucard's racing heart started aching, and he quickly began to feel as though *he* should leave before Zalith came to his senses.

But then Zalith stopped resting his head against Alucard's, and a jolt of dread surged through the vampire's taut body. Alucard shut his eyes, bracing for the impending outburst; however, to his astonishment, instead of striking him or unleashing a thunderous shout, the demon tenderly pressed his lips to the huge, lingering scar where Alucard's right wing had once been.

Alucard felt confused as Zalith slowly kissed his scarred back... and with each kiss to every one of his scars, he felt his dread gradually wither away. He'd feared how Zalith might react when he saw them, but the demon didn't seem as though he felt betrayed. He tenderly dragged his warm hands up Alucard's sides, gripped the vampire's arms, and nuzzled the side of his neck as he exhaled quietly.

"You don't..." he uttered, his voice shaky. "I—"

"It doesn't make me feel any different, Alucard," Zalith whispered softly.

Alucard's response was preempted, his words silenced by the sudden turn of the demon, who deftly manoeuvred him to face the intensity in his gaze. Before any words could escape Alucard's lips, Zalith claimed them in a fervent kiss. The passion exchanged was undeniable, yet a hint of shadow lingered in Zalith's eyes, suggesting an underlying turmoil as if what he'd seen left him upset. Alucard refused to let it cast a shadow on them, though. His hands traced the contours of Zalith's body, emboldened by the realization that the demon wasn't disgusted by the scars that covered his back. Confidence surged within him, and he surrendered to the enchantment of the moment. As tension melted away, excitement gripped him, and Alucard embraced the allure of the unfolding intimacy. Zalith's kisses grew more aggressive, each touch heightening Alucard's desire.

Once again, the vampire's back hit the dresser; the contact aggravated those of his scars which were more sensitive than the others, but he didn't care. Zalith gripped his ass in his right hand, grasping a fistful of his hair in his left, and as he pulled Alucard's head aside, the vampire exhaled in anticipation. He didn't hesitate, and neither did Zalith. The demon lightly pressed the sharp tips of his fangs against Alucard's neck, and as the vampire eagerly clasped Zalith's hair, the demon bit down.

As Alucard felt the demon's fangs sink into his skin, a surge of exhilaration coursed through his veins, igniting a fire within him that he couldn't extinguish. He clutched Zalith's arm with a desperate intensity, his sharp claws leaving marks on the bicep that held him captive. It was a sensation beyond his wildest imaginings—a potent blend of pleasure and pain that enveloped him, rendering him powerless against its allure.

His body quivered with delight, every inch of his being succumbing to the intoxicating ecstasy of the demon's venom spreading through him. Alucard scowled, a silent battle waging within him as he fought to restrain the subtle groans threatening to escape. The pleasure entwined with his very essence, leaving him yearning for more, aching for everything the demon could give him.

Zalith, humming in satisfaction, reciprocated the embrace, pulling Alucard away from the dresser. With a moan of contentment, the demon withdrew his fangs from Alucard's neck, leaving the vampire in a state of blissful surrender. Guiding him towards the bed, Zalith's touch was both commanding and tender, the perfect contrast that sent shivers down Alucard's spine.

The vampire sighed in delight as he descended into euphoria, succumbing to the enchantment that surrounded him. With a gentle push, Zalith lowered him onto the bed; as his body sank into the plush softness of the covers, Alucard's frown betrayed a hint of uncertainty, a fleeting acknowledgement of the uncharted territory that lay ahead. Opening his eyes, he found himself locked in an intense gaze with the demon who hovered above him, a slow and deliberate approach that narrowed the distance until their faces were mere inches apart.

A subtle smile curved on Alucard's lips as he surrendered to the moment, his hand delicately finding its place on the side of Zalith's face. In the depths of the demon's dark and captivating eyes, the vampire discerned a magnetic pull, drawing him into a realm where calmness, curiosity, and an unexplained eagerness converged. There was a desperation pulsating within him, an urgency that begged to be understood, and yet the object of his desire was crystal clear—Zalith.

His fingers tightened possessively on the demon's jaw, and he drew their faces closer. The rapid thud of his heart echoed his growing eagerness as they kissed frantically, the intoxicating heat of their tongues entwining adding fuel to the fire. Zalith's hands traced down Alucard's body, seizing his belt, yet the demon held back, creating an electrifying pause in their heated exchange. Moments stretched, their kisses momentarily halted, allowing Alucard to meet Zalith's gaze with a smouldering intensity, silently granting permission.

A flirtatious smile stretched across Zalith's lips as he removed the belt, casting a spell of anticipation that hung heavy in the air. Nervousness coiled within Alucard's stomach, a fleeting impulse to pause and savour the moment. But the consuming excitement fuelled his desires. He surrendered to Zalith's touch, the demon skilfully stripping away his trousers until he was left in nothing but his underwear. The cool air gnawed at his skin, sending shivers down his spine, but Zalith's warmth swiftly embraced him.

As the demon's lips traced their way back up his body, locking eyes with Alucard, the vampire shivered in the cold, only to be immediately enveloped in the demon's comforting warmth. The intensity of their gaze deepened, and in that moment, Alucard abandoned himself to the alluring blend of passion and desire that gripped them both.

Zalith dragged his thumb over the wounds his fangs had left in Alucard's neck. "Can I touch you?" he asked quietly, moving his other hand over Alucard's waist.

Alucard stared up at him and nodded, every inch of his being aching for more. Without any further delay, Zalith smirked and moved his hand from Alucard's waist to his crotch. Alucard tensed up, an unfamiliar pleasure electrifying through him as the demon lightly dragged his fingers over the bulge in his underwear. As that delightful feeling intensified, Alucard exhaled deeply and turned his head to look away, closing his eyes as he sunk into contentedness.

Zalith lightly gripped Alucard's arousal, causing him to fidget a little as desperation pulsed inside him. He exhaled quietly, trying to keep himself from uttering a sound while the demon caressed his arousal over his underwear. Anticipation consumed his trembling body—he grew so desperate that if he were braver, he'd tell Zalith that he wanted more, but he couldn't find his voice. He sunk deeper into the pleasure, gripping the blanket beneath him.

The demon then stopped and started slowly pulling Alucard's underwear off. Alucard's nervousness returned like a smack to his face; he lifted his head and looked down at Zalith as he kissed his way down his body...and when he pulled Alucard's underwear off, an amused smile crept across his face. Embarrassed, Alucard went to look away, but when Zalith stroked his fingers over the crimson hair around his crotch, he pouted and rested his head back on the bed with a quiet huff.

But Zalith didn't linger. His warm hand gripped Alucard's hard dick, and as the vampire inhaled sharply in delight, he dug his claws into the blanket. A pleasing, tantalizing sensation ensnared his entire body as the demon gently dragged his hand up and down his shaft, and as he lay there in the dark, listening to the pouring rain, Alucard's contented calm evolved into serenity. Zalith made him feel so many different things, and right now, the demon made him feel utterly euphoric.

However, he frowned when Zalith gripped his shoulder with his spare hand and pulled him so that he would sit up. He complied, sitting so that he was facing Zalith; he placed one of his hands on the side of the demon's neck and moved his face into his. For a few moments, they kissed slowly, but Zalith soon grasped the vampire's jaw in his left hand, letting go of his shaft with his right. He then brought his right hand to his own face, dragged his tongue over his palm, and then lowered it back down to grip the vampire's dick.

The moment Zalith's hand graced his shaft again, Alucard tensed up, an overbearing pleasure enthralling him as he moved his hand from Zalith's neck and gripped his hair. He scowled in struggle, keeping himself from uttering a sound as best he could—but the demon began to move his hand a little faster, caressing the tip of his dick with his thumb every time he pulled his hand back up. Alucard huffed in delight, moving his right hand to the demon's back. He dug his claws into Zalith's skin and nuzzled his neck in an attempt to hide the struggled look on his face, breathing deeply as he fidgeted in Zalith's grip.

But being so close to Zalith's neck enticed him. His heart was racing, his body was trembling, and Zalith didn't stop pleasing him. The demon moved his free hand to the back of Alucard's head, pulling his face closer to his neck as he exhaled eagerly. Alucard's thirst for Zalith's blood was becoming something of a desperate need, and the longer he waited, the longer he tried to remain silent, the harder it became to resist. But the moment he opened his mouth, he knew that he wouldn't be able to keep himself from moaning in response to the rapture.

He wouldn't deny himself what he wanted any longer, though. With a desperate grimace, he widened his jaws and pressed his four fangs against the demon's skin, but he couldn't contain himself anymore. He moaned quietly in delight, and as another wave of pleasure convulsed through his body, he unintentionally dragged the tips of his fangs over the demon's neck, tearing his skin, but it only seemed to make Zalith groan in enjoyment. Alucard didn't hold back. He sunk his fangs into Zalith's neck, a satisfied moan escaping both their breaths as the vampire stroked his claws down the demon's back. The moment Zalith's blood poured into his mouth, the pleasure intensified, so much that Alucard thought he might become the aggressive creature that he knew he was—but he refrained from letting go. He bit harder and groaned quietly, and as the high of Zalith's blood began to consume him, he plummeted into an abyss of pure, unrelenting bliss.

His thoughts quickly dissipated, all but those of Zalith. The only thing he could focus on was his feelings for the demon, on what Zalith made him feel. With a content hum, he pulled his fangs from Zalith's neck and rested his forehead on the side of the demon's face. Zalith didn't stop stroking his dick, sending waves of sheer delight through him. The demon made him feel so many new things, so many things he would have never thought he'd feel. He felt so close, so calm, so…*safe*. He trusted Zalith with more than his life; he'd never let anyone else see this side of him, a side he would have never thought he'd ever experience. But there he was, and there Zalith was. The demon had seen his scars, the very scars that any demon would shun him for, but not Zalith; he didn't care, and why Alucard had thought he might be bothered confounded him. Zalith had never expressed any negativity towards him; he'd never looked down upon him. Why would that change?

Alucard opened his eyes and gazed at the bloody wounds on Zalith's neck. But something wasn't right; there was something beneath the demon's blood, something black, almost like a rune. It spread from the puncture wounds, forking up and down his body like a serpent made of lightning, leaving a trail of branches on his skin. Once the pattern stopped spreading, covering the *entire* left side of Zalith's body, it sizzled into the demon's skin and faded as if it were never there. What the hell did he just do?

He wouldn't get the chance to find out. His tense body stiffened, pleasure *burning* inside him as Zalith caressed his dick a little harder. He was approaching his peak, edging nearer and nearer with each stroke of the demon's hand. He couldn't hold back, and he couldn't stifle his pleased whine as he climaxed, digging his claws into the demon's back, his entire body succumbing to a feverish elation. He pulled Zalith as close as he could, allowing a quiet but greatly satisfied groan to escape his breath as he rested the side of his head on Zalith's. And then…relief.

For the next few moments, they sat there in one another's embrace, listening to the hard-falling rain as Alucard's thumping heart gradually calmed. Zalith then released his right arm and rested the side of his head on Alucard's as he took the towel he'd earlier dried his hair with and used it to clean the cum from his hand and Alucard's dick.

With a smile, Zalith guided Alucard under the blankets, and once he took the rest of his clothes off, he joined Alucard and wrapped his arms around him. "Alucard," he then said quietly as he nuzzled the back of the vampire's head.

Alucard opened his eyes. His current state of euphoria made it hard for him to find words, so he responded with a mumbled, muffled sound.

The demon moved his right arm from around Alucard and began to caress his hair. "Who—"

"I don't.…" He sighed and closed his eyes. "I don't want to talk about it."

But Zalith didn't seem too willing to take no for an answer this time. "Who did this to you, Alucard? Not just the scars, but the runes, too."

In the moment he'd shown Zalith his darkest secret, he hadn't even thought about the runes that accompanied his scars. He didn't even know too much about them; all he knew was that they were there and had been for quite some time. He hadn't looked into them; he hadn't tried to mess with them. He'd just left them and got on with his life, just as he had done with his absent wings.

He didn't know what to say. Was there anything he *could* say? Showing Zalith his back had taken all the strength he could manage for today, and he wasn't yet prepared to tell the demon the story behind each scar. So he remained silent, hoping that Zalith would understand that he wasn't going to answer his questions yet.

"Was it Damien?" Zalith asked.

He didn't answer.

"Lucifer?"

"It doesn't matter," he muttered. "I'll...tell you when I'm ready. Don't try to make me tell you before," he warned with unintentional hostility in his voice. Sure that he might have upset Zalith, he swiftly turned around, rested his head on the demon's shoulder, and frowned sullenly. "I *will* tell you, just...not yet."

"Okay," Zalith said, holding him tightly.

Relieved that Zalith would allow him the time that he needed to work out how to tell him, Alucard relaxed and closed his eyes again. He was tired and overwhelmed by everything that just happened, and he just wanted to sleep. Soon, they'd be on their way to Avalmoor, and he'd have to make sure that both he and Zalith were prepared for what might await them there.

As he lay there, he allowed himself to slowly slip off to sleep, nothing but the contentedness Zalith made him feel on his mind. He felt as if he couldn't feel any more trusting of someone—*ever*. The demon knew so many of his secrets, and he didn't regret sharing any of them with him.

Chapter Thirty-Two

— ⟨ † ⟩ —

Warmth

| Alucard |

Thunder struck as lightning forked through the miserable sky. What was once rain now fell as a combination of snow and hail, hitting the wall of glass behind where Alucard lay. He snapped open his eyes, staring up at the ceiling as the silvery lightning lit up the room once again. The air was bitter, his face almost numb; even beneath the fluffy blanket and beside Zalith, he could feel the cold clawing at his skin. But that was the norm for the seas close to Avalmoor. They had to be near now.

Alucard frowned and tightened his grip around the sleeping demon, listening to the slow, peaceful beating of his heart while he lay with his head on his chest. As much as he might love to lay beside Zalith, he had an abrupt, somewhat eager urge to get out of bed. He wasn't sure whether it was the cold or the fact he felt so suddenly afraid; the storm, the cold, the silence—it all haunted him like a distant memory he once tried to forget.

He closed his eyes, trying to force himself back to sleep, but his thoughts were quick to take over—as was the overbearing headache. At first, he hadn't noticed it, but now that he'd been awake for a few minutes, it became more noticeable. Of course, he knew *why* he had a headache; the combination of a demon's venom *and* blood inside his body wasn't going to make him feel euphoric forever. His high had faded while he slept, and now he felt worse than he had the morning after he and Zalith drank that four-hundred-year-old mystery alcohol.

The longer he lay there, the worse he felt, and it felt as if the only option was to get up and do his best to cure his hangover-like feeling. He didn't want to leave Zalith, but he didn't want to lay there in silence and sink into the familiar depravity that would always grip him in his solitude. He knew how it affected him, and he didn't want to upset Zalith with it.

So, as silently as he could, he shuffled away from the sleeping demon and carefully lifted the covers from over himself. But confusion gripped him when he realized that he was naked. It took a moment, but he *did* recall how he ended up in this situation; the night had been eventful, and he'd enjoyed every moment of it. He'd revealed one of his daunting secrets to Zalith, and the demon had responded in a way Alucard could have only hoped for. Zalith didn't care, and that couldn't make the vampire any happier.

With a discreet, relieved smile, Alucard made his way over to his dresser, pulled out a new pair of black trousers, and slipped them on. He grabbed a black shirt, and as he put it on, he frowned. It was cold. Did he bring a sweater? Probably not. He didn't want to wear his coat, though; he scowled at the coat rack that it hung from alongside his cape. He didn't want to freeze, however—he *hated* the cold. So, he wandered over, snatched his coat, and pulled it on, as well as his cape, and then, before leaving, he glanced back at the sleeping demon. He didn't want Zalith to wake up to the bitter cold, so he glanced at the fireplace, lit it with crimson flames, and quietly left the room.

He made his way along the damp deck, glancing at the horizon, where several large icebergs masked most of the sunlight; some of them had dragons similar to Drac resting atop them, as well as seals and penguins. Drac's dislike for the cold made Alucard smile; his species slept atop the ice, yet Drac would rather spend his time sleeping in a room heated by fire, something Alucard would have to prepare for the dragon once they arrived at Avalmoor.

When he reached the door that would take him below deck, he set his eyes on the crewman on watch. "I want... something to help with a hangover. I will be in my study," the vampire requested, and as the man nodded and made his way down the stairs, Alucard followed.

They reached the bottom of the stairs, arriving in a wide hallway that forked left, right, and straight ahead. The man went left, and Alucard continued forward, setting his sights on the black door which led to his study at the very end of the door-lined hallway.

Once he got to the door, Alucard unlocked it and stepped inside. The room sat at the very front of the ship, below the water level; the back wall was made of thick glass and curved to cover most of the floor beneath where his desk sat. Below, the depths of the ocean were visible, along with Drac's shimmering, streamlined body as he made his way through the water, pulling the ship with him. Comfortable, dark leather reign-like ropes were attached to the ship's hull and the collar around the dragon's body, a collar he could free himself of very easily if he wished.

The left wall had a fireplace with a white-bear rug sprawled out in front of it, and the right wall was made up of multiple bookshelves packed with literature.

As he walked to his desk, Alucard smiled down at the dragon, who glanced up at him with his four shimmering yellow eyes. When he got to his desk, he sat down and lit the fireplace with his ethos. He was *freezing*... and he could only wonder how cold Drac must be. But the dragon was built for this weather, Alucard was not. He sat there, staring at the fire, waiting for it to warm the room enough so that he could take his hands out from beneath his cape.

He waited... and waited .. and eventually, a quiet knock came at the door. The man Alucard had sent to get something to help with his hangover walked in with a white mug in both his hands. He made his way over, placed it on the vampire's desk, and stood there, waiting like a schoolboy.

"What?" Alucard snarled irritably.

The man stuttered in fluster but nodded and left the room, pulling the door shut behind him.

Once he was gone, Alucard leaned forward and peered into the cup to see that he had been given coffee. It helped with his last hangover, so why would it be any different this time? He moved it closer, holding it firmly with both his cold hands; the warmth of the cup was delightful, so nice that he felt he might not even drink it so that he could keep using it to warm his palms.

While the cold slowly withered, Alucard stared into his drink, listening to the storm outside. He let his thoughts wander but managed to keep the negative ones at bay; he was far too relieved to let himself sink into sadness. Instead, he dwelled on his confusion, his *worry*. Last night, so many things happened, so much had come to light, and while they were both devoured by desire and pleasure, Alucard sank his fangs into Zalith. That wasn't what had him perturbed, though; what happened *after* was what confounded him. He saw the strangest thing appear on Zalith's skin for a moment before vanishing soon after. Alucard hadn't seen anything like it before, and he wasn't yet sure what to make of it. He had no idea where it came from, what it was, or where it went. All he knew was that it appeared after he bit Zalith, and in a moment where he felt most serene.

The vampire took a small sip of his coffee. Should he ask Zalith about it? Would Zalith even know what it was? He wasn't sure. What if what he did was dangerous? He didn't have the chance to see much of what it looked like, but he was certain that it spread across one whole half of Zalith's body. He couldn't see it anymore, and he was knowledgeable enough in rune ethos to know that any rune with adverse effects would always remain visible upon someone's body; so, whatever it was, it couldn't be harmful... could it?

He scowled and sipped from his drink again. He didn't want to concern or upset Zalith, so he felt that the best thing to do right now was to find out what it might have been. He *could* ask Zalith, but again, he hadn't seen enough of it to even explain it to him.

With a quiet sigh, he placed his drink down on his desk and swivelled around in his seat. He stared down at Drac as the dragon effortlessly made his way through the water. Alucard still thought about Zalith, but now about the fact that he had accepted what he showed him. Alucard had been terrified that Zalith would leave him after discovering that he was Disavowed—that his wings had been torn from his body; he wasn't yet ready to tell Zalith why it happened, and he knew that the demon wanted to know, but he wasn't prepared to have that conversation.

That was when the despondency took over. He frowned and turned back to face his desk with a sullen look on his face. Zalith had accepted the fact that he didn't have his wings, but what would he think of him once he came to know why it happened? Demons only had their wings removed as punishment, and his crimes were something that he felt Zalith wouldn't accept so quickly. He knew that Zalith didn't think he was incompetent, but he feared that might change if he told the demon why he'd been cast out.

Alucard scowled and glanced around for something to distract himself with; he didn't want to let his worry ruin any more of his time with Zalith. He knew he had to warn his contact in Avalmoor that he would soon be arriving, so perhaps he ought to do that.

He took a piece of parchment, a black envelope, a small wax burner, and a wax stamp from the top drawer of his desk. He placed a few small cubes of crimson wax into the burner, lit the candle inside with his ethos, and then pulled his cape off. While the wax slowly melted, he dabbed his black feather quill into a bottle of ink and pressed the quill tip on the parchment. But his mind was blank. Usually, he'd know what to write, but right now, he didn't have a single word. All he could think about was Zalith, what happened last night, and how he just wanted to be back in the demon's embrace.

As a curious smile claimed his lips, Alucard traced the lingering evidence of Zalith's bite with his fingertips. The twin wounds on his neck, still raw and exposed, were a testament to the intoxicating encounter they shared last night. He revelled in the knowledge that the wounds would persist for another day or so, and he welcomed the sensation of being possessed, marked, and utterly claimed. But the more he dwelled on the allure of this newfound connection, the stronger the undercurrent of arousal surged within him. Zalith had unveiled a deeper layer in their intricate relationship, and Alucard was more than willing to explore the uncharted territories of passion and desire that lay ahead.

While he might enjoy becoming distracted by the memory of last night, he had to get to work. So he dismissed all thoughts about it and focused on his letter.

| **Zalith** |

Zalith woke with a quiet, content sigh. He moved his hand across the sheets in search of Alucard, but when he didn't find the vampire, he opened his eyes and frowned. Alucard was no longer in bed beside him, the fireplace was burning, and a storm was raging outside. The sky was still dark, so it had to be early, and as far as he knew, Alucard never woke up this early. His first instinct was to search for him, but he thought he should probably give him a little space. A lot happened last night, and Alucard must be overwhelmed.

The demon smiled, guiding his hand under his pillow as he turned onto his side so he could stare over at the fire. Last night, he'd seen a whole lot more of Alucard, and he was content that they'd taken that next step. Of course, there were a lot more steps to take, but all in good time.

When he thought about Alucard's scars, though, his heart hurt. Damien's unprompted discussion of wingless demons back in Dor-Sanguis made sense now, and Zalith suspected that it was Damien who tore his wings off... and he must have done it slowly, or the scars wouldn't look so deep, straight, and clean. The rest of Alucard's back was covered in raised, scarred slashes which he was sure had come from a whip, and he believed that Damien was responsible for those, too. It made him furious. How could *anyone* hurt Alucard like that? Such a sweet, beautiful man didn't deserve that, and Zalith's desire to kill Damien increased the more he thought about the pain Alucard must have gone through. And the runes... they were *sealing* runes and were probably responsible for the strange weakening of Alucard's aura Zalith had detected the other day. He wanted to know the story behind everything he'd seen, but he knew it had taken a lot for Alucard to even show him, let alone explain, so he wouldn't pressure the vampire. He'd wait until Alucard was ready to tell him.

He sighed quietly and rolled onto his back. A smile crept across his face as he thought about Alucard's red crotch hair—he was right when he'd assumed it matched the hair on his head, and it made him laugh again. Alucard was adorable, and the more he discovered about him, the cuter he became.

Zalith dragged his fingers over the four puncture wounds Alucard's fangs had left in his neck. He'd finally received Alucard's bite... and it felt unlike anything he'd imagined, just like the taste of his blood. The vampire continued to surprise him, and his venom had done more than that. As it coursed through his veins, it ensnared him in utter delight—burning, intensifying euphoria, and he had to fight with himself so that he wouldn't try to press Alucard for more. He'd wanted to pin him down, kiss him, lick him, *taste him*, and then fuck him, but he had to do his best to ensure that he took things as slowly as Alucard needed.

He was beginning to get aroused just thinking about last night. He sighed in frustration, rolling onto his side. Of course, he could relieve himself, but it wouldn't do him much good. Sure, it would sate his arousal, but it wouldn't fulfil him. And he couldn't stop thinking about Alucard. His blood, his venom…his cum. He'd desperately wanted to drag his tongue over the vampire's shaft last night—he'd wanted to taste his climax, but he didn't want to do something that would urge him to ask Alucard for sex.

With a quiet sigh, he sat up and dragged his fingers through his hair. Lying in bed would only make his thoughts worse, and he was missing Alucard, too. So, wherever the vampire was, he was going to find him.

Chapter Thirty-Three

— ⸲ ✝ ⸱ —

The Bear Rug

| **Alucard** |

When Alucard finished writing his letter, his study door opened. He looked over there and watched Zalith walk into the room in a pair of black trousers and a rather comfy-looking, deep-red wool sweater. Alucard's sights shifted to the four small wounds his fangs had left on Zalith's neck—small might not be the word, though; he'd unintentionally dragged his top fangs over Zalith's skin before actually biting him, and it had left a rather sore, noticeable wound. The demon hadn't made any effort to cover it up, though, so Alucard assumed that he must be as content with them as he was with Zalith's bite.

"Good morning, darling," Zalith said as he reached the desk, which he moved behind, and as the vampire looked up at him, he took Alucard's chin in his hand and kissed his lips.

Alucard smiled and stood up; he wrapped his arms around the demon and hugged him, and as Zalith moved his arms around him, Alucard rested his head on his shoulder. "Good morning," he replied quietly. He then sat back down, and as he did, Zalith leaned against the desk and smiled down at him.

"Are you okay?" the demon asked.

Glancing up at him, the vampire nodded. "I'm fine," he mumbled as he wrote the address on the envelope.

"Are you sure?" the demon persisted with a smirk on his face.

Alucard sighed and glanced up at him. "It's just…the bite," he muttered, trying to hide his nervous face. "And the blood. I've never had either before, so I guess the high hit me worse."

With an unseemly smile on his face, Zalith took Alucard's cup of coffee and sipped from it. "How was everything else?"

Of course he had to ask. Alucard knew his face had turned red, so he pouted and looked away. He'd not deny Zalith an answer, though. "It was…overwhelming," he answered, unable to think of a better word to explain how he felt. "But in a good way."

"Good." Zalith sipped from Alucard's coffee once more before placing it back where he found it. He then glanced at what Alucard was writing. "Who's Luther?"

Alucard finished writing the address and glanced up at him. "An old subordinate," he answered, leaning back in his seat. "He was around the same time as Attila; he and I did much together back when I was younger. He now serves as my Avalmoor contact."

Intrigued, Zalith nodded. "Is he Dor-Sanguian, too?"

"No," the vampire replied. "But he has a translator. I'm informing him of our arrival. He'll prepare anything we might need, and he may also have leads. He keeps an eye on everything and everyone coming in and out of Avalmoor; there's only one main port, and it's in the city he lives in. If Lucious showed up in Avalmoor, Luther would know." He then checked to see if the wax he planned to use to seal the letter was ready, lifting the small spoon-like cup off the burner.

"Would it be easier to send him this message in Deiganish?" Zalith asked.

Alucard sighed quietly. It *would* be easier for Luther. "Will you write it for me?"

"I'll help *you* to write it," he said, smirking. "If you want."

Alucard took his eyes off the demon and looked back down at his letter. He'd already agreed to let Zalith help him learn to better read and write Deiganish, so he felt no need to refuse his offer. He looked back up at the demon. "Okay," he agreed.

Smiling, Zalith lightly gripped his left arm and made him get up out of his seat. Then, the demon sat down and pulled him into his lap. As he sat there, Alucard frowned in confusion and nervousness as Zalith placed his chin on his shoulder and wrapped his arms around him. Once he was sure that Zalith was comfortable, Alucard grabbed a new piece of parchment, placed it over the first piece, and wrote Luther's name once again.

"What do you need to tell him?" Zalith asked.

"That…we'll be arriving in Avalmoor in roughly twelve hours."

"Okay. I don't know what you can and can't write, so use that old piece and write what you usually would, and we'll work off that," he instructed.

As he was told, Alucard placed the old letter he had been writing alongside the blank parchment and wrote what he had said, but in Deiganish. He was certain that there were a whole lot of errors, and he felt rather embarrassed doing it, but Zalith was going to help him with something he knew he'd need to learn sooner or later. He'd managed so far, but it was becoming annoying to have to find translators or scribes to write for him.

Once he was done, he moved his hand so Zalith could read it.

Luther,

I wil be ariving in Helvetes in less than tewlve owers with a frend. We wil need the nesesary meens of transportashun to moove threw the cuntry, and I incurage you to have it redy for when we arive. I allso come in serch of sumwon, so have your records ready.

Aleksei.

"To start, 'will' has two L's," Zalith said, tapping the word 'wil' on the paper.

Alucard glanced at him. "Okay."

"And 'arriving'—it has two R's."

Nodding, Alucard started writing on the blank piece of parchment, following the demon's guidance.

"For 'twelve,' the 'W' and 'E' should be switched, and 'hours' is spelt H-O-U-R-S. It might sound like it should be spelt with an 'O,' but there is a silent 'H' at the beginning of the word."

"Wierd," Alucard grumbled.

With an amused smile, Zalith pointed to the word 'frend'. "Friend is spelt H-U-S-B-A-N-D."

Alucard stopped writing and scowled at him. He wasn't falling for that.

Zalith laughed quietly. "Friend has a silent 'I' before the 'E'."

"Why all these silent letters?" he complained.

The demon smirked and shrugged. "It's just how the language is."

With an irritated huff, Alucard looked back at what he was writing and continued.

"Will, again," Zalith said. As Alucard wrote it correctly, he shifted his gaze to the next few words. "Necessary. It sounds as though it contains two S's, but it is spelt N-E-C-E-S-S-A-R-Y."

"Unnecessary," Alucard snarled.

Amused, Zalith smiled and shifted his gaze to the next words. "Means. There's no double 'E,' but an 'E' 'A.' Transportation—you used 'S' 'H' 'U,' and again, it sounds as though it should be spelt that way, but it is spelt with 'T' 'I' 'O' 'N.'"

Writing the word, Alucard frowned and glanced at him again. "I gather you would be just as perturbed if I were to try and teach you Dor-Saguian, no?"

"Yes," Zalith said, smiling. "Move is a single 'O', and country has a silent 'O' before the 'U'," he said, watching as Alucard wrote. "Encourage—again, silent 'O' before the 'U', and it starts with an 'E', not an 'I'. It's said encourage, not *in*courage."

"Right."

"Ready—silent 'A' after the 'E'. Arrive has two 'R's', not one, and search has a silent 'A' after the 'E'. Someone—once again, it sounds as though it should be spelt the way you spelt it, but it's simply one and some put together. Some is S-O-M-E, and you spelt one right on that invitation you sent me," he said with a smirk.

"I don't know why I thought it would be different in this case," Alucard admitted, finishing the rest of the letter. "Is all zhis vight, zhen?" he asked, waiting while Zalith read it.

Reading it over, Zalith smiled and kissed the side of the vampire's face. "Yes," he confirmed. "I'll teach you more thoroughly when we have more time."

Nodding, Alucard sealed the letter with the wax, pressed his seal into it, and then relaxed. Now, he just wanted to enjoy his time with Zalith. He rested the side of his head on the demon's and stared at the door.

"If we're less than twelve hours from Avalmoor, maybe now's a good time to tell me what I might need to know about Lucious and the country," Zalith suggested.

Alucard felt no need to deny him. "Well," he started.

"Can we move somewhere more comfortable?" the demon requested, looking over at the fireplace. "Such as in front of the fireplace."

The vampire frowned and glanced back at him. "Are you cold?"

"No," Zalith said, smirking. "We can stay here if you want."

Taking his eyes off the demon, Alucard looked at the fireplace. He wasn't going to deny the fact that it would be a whole lot more comfortable if they were to move over there—he could take off his coat without feeling as though he'd freeze to death. So, he stood up. "We can sit over there," he confirmed, pulling his coat off as he led the way.

When he reached the fireplace, the vampire chucked his coat over the nearby cabinet and slumped down onto the bear rug. Zalith sat behind him, making himself comfortable; the demon wrapped his arms around him and pulled him closer so that his back was against his chest, and then they stared at the dancing crimson flames as the combined warmth of fire and Zalith's body graced Alucard's cold skin.

"This bear," Zalith said, resting the side of his head on Alucard's. "Where did you get it? Was it a kill or a purchase?"

Alucard sighed as he leaned back so that he was almost lying with his head in Zalith's lap. "There's no fascinating story behind this one. I simply bought it."

With a small laugh, Zalith began to fiddle with the vampire's hair. "It's fluffier than any bear I've come across."

"Hmm." Alucard nodded. He then glanced up at Zalith and frowned. "I don't know much about Lucious," he started. "All I really know is that he's an angel, one who Damien wants rather desperately. The real danger in Avalmoor is the dragons—the God Dragons. Most of them live there other than Kardos and Thalis, and Janus who I killed a long time ago. They hate everything other than humans, like I said. We wear the gold to keep them from detecting the fact that we're demons."

"What happens if we come across one?"

Alucard laughed slightly as he stared into the fireplace. "It will recognize me immediately—I'm their destroyer, after all. I don't think we'll come across one, though. They might love humans, but they don't make a point of living near their cities. I hope that Lucious will be in a city; I'd rather not travel across the tundra in search of him, but if we have to, we will."

Still caressing the vampire's hair, Zalith smiled. "Destroyer? Tell me more about that."

"There isn't really much to say about it. You know I was sent here to kill Letholdus' children—the Dragon Gods. I killed one, got bored, and never killed another. They were scared of me for a long time, but I don't know if that's still the case. I'm not even sure whether they all think I'm still alive or not. I don't care, though. As long as they don't interfere with my life, I won't bother them."

With a quiet chuckle, Zalith ran his fingers through the vampire's crimson hair. "You're so cute."

Confused about what that had to do with what he was talking about, Alucard frowned and looked up at him. "What?"

The demon smirked. "You're so cute," he repeated, looking down at him.

With a sulky pout etching his lips, Alucard scowled, fixating on the dancing flames. But as Zalith continued to playfully provoke him, tracing teasing patterns with his finger along the side of his face, the vampire couldn't resist a rebellious response. With a swift motion, Alucard lifted his arm and defiantly smacked the demon's hand away.

Zalith's smirk only deepened, and he persisted, prodding Alucard's cheek with the tip of his index finger. A quiet snarl escaped the vampire as he slapped the intrusive hand away once more, but Zalith, undeterred, seized Alucard's wrist in a firm grip. Alucard scowled, attempting to free himself by moving his other arm to dislodge the demon's hold, yet Zalith anticipated the move, catching his hand before it could intervene.

In a whirlwind of playful resistance, Alucard suddenly found himself on his back with his arms pinned above his head. The struggle, laced with confusion and desire, left Alucard both infuriated and tantalizingly intrigued.

Zalith maintained his smirk, looking down at the vampire beneath him, who glared defiantly, aware that any attempt to break free would likely prove futile. A rebellious spark ignited within Alucard, but a curious part of him *enjoyed* his current predicament, revelling in the dominating hold Zalith had over him. As the demon leaned in, bringing their faces inches apart, a hint of nervousness crept into Alucard's frown.

When Zalith's lips met his, a wave of relaxation washed over Alucard, surrendering to the intoxicating allure of the kiss. The demon's exploration extended from his lips to his face and down to his neck, each touch rekindling a familiar desire that began to captivate him. In that moment of vulnerability, Alucard found himself ensnared by the magnetic pull of their connection, his initial resistance melting into a heady mixture of pleasure and anticipation.

He lay there, his heart beginning to beat faster as Zalith let go of one of his wrists and started unbuttoning his shirt. Along with excitement, he felt his anxiety grow—but he'd not let it overwhelm him. He closed his eyes, exhaling in struggle as eagerness raced through him while Zalith unbuttoned the last button of his shirt.

Zalith dragged his fingertips over Alucard's chest, down over his abs, and then to his stomach.

Alucard flinched as a pleasing sensation spiralled through him, his skin tingling.

"Can I suck your dick?" Zalith asked, his voice a murmur as he leaned into Alucard's ear.

The vampire became flustered, angst consuming him. But he'd enjoyed last night so much that he was able to fight through his nervousness and nod. "Yes," he answered quietly.

Zalith grinned excitedly and began unbuckling Alucard's belt. The vampire turned his head to face the right wall, trying to calm himself, but his heart was racing so fast that he couldn't hold back a deep, shaky exhale. The moment Zalith moved his hand into his trousers and lightly gripped his arousal, he felt his anticipation increase. The demon kept both the vampire's arms pinned above his head with his right hand, using his left to please him as he slowly kissed his neck. But a frown found its way to Alucard's face when he felt Zalith kiss his way down his neck and towards his left pec—he flinched in startle when Zalith lightly bit his nipple, which sent a flurry of confusing pleasure through him, and as the demon laughed quietly, Alucard pouted and glared up at the ceiling.

The demon let go of Alucard's wrists and dragged his other hand down his body, kissing his way to the vampire's waist. But as he stopped pleasing the vampire with his hand and instead dragged his tongue over the tip of his hardening dick, Alucard tightly gripped the rug beneath him and grimaced in struggle, holding back a pleased sigh. When the demon slowly took his dick into his mouth, though, Alucard let out a pleased hum, and the pleasure quickly ensnared him.

A stuttered, pleased whimper escaped his breath as he glanced down at Zalith. For a moment, he watched in bewilderment as the demon slowly dragged both his tongue and lips over his dick, provoking his entire body with each gentle stroke. The vampire fidgeted as he rested his head back on the rug, closing his eyes while he moved his hand to the back of Zalith's head. He gripped a handful of Zalith's hair, his body already trembling, the pleasure of Zalith's warm, wet mouth against his shaft enthralling him in delightful bliss.

Alucard couldn't help but groan quietly as each long, pleasing minute passed by. His body became harder to control, and his fidgeted movements grew more frequent as Zalith sucked a little faster. And as the peak of pleasure approached, he tightened his grip on Zalith's hair, gritted his teeth in struggle, and then moaned in contentment, satisfaction electrifying through him as he climaxed into the demon's mouth.

But Zalith wasn't finished; with a hum of both relief and contentment, he licked the tip of Alucard's throbbing dick and groaned as he swallowed his cum. "You taste *so* fucking good," he growled before dragging his tongue over his shaft once more. And then he kissed his way up to Alucard's waist, and without warning, he sunk his fangs into the vampire's right side.

Alucard flinched and winced quietly in startlement, but the shock of Zalith's bite withered just moments later as he felt the demon's venom electrify through his trembling, overwhelmed body. He exhaled in struggle, his heart still racing, his excitement not having waned despite his climax. The vampire smiled and bared his own fangs, sighing in delight as he fell deeper into the tantalizing abyss of Zalith's assertive, possessive grasp.

Zalith slowly pulled his fangs from Alucard's skin and let out a quiet moan of satisfaction. He then kissed his way up the vampire's body, and when he reached Alucard's face, the demon leaned into his ear. "I want to fuck you," he whispered, aggressively pushing his body against Alucard's, and the demon's hardened shaft pressed into the side of Alucard's leg.

Caught in a moment of uncertainty, Alucard frowned nervously, his gaze shifting to fixate on the right wall. The air between them crackled with a palpable tension, and he grappled with the overwhelming question of how to respond. The allure of what lay ahead tempted him, but a sense of unreadiness lingered within.

As Zalith's desire-laden sigh washed over him, warm lips pressed against his neck, leaving a trail of fire in their wake, uncertainty gave way to a heady mix of longing and trepidation. Alucard yearned for the unexplored realms of passion that Zalith offered, aching to delve into the depths of the demon's capabilities. Yet, the timing felt precarious, and he hesitated to fully surrender to the temptation unfolding between them. In the delicate balance of desire and restraint, Alucard grappled with the intoxicating prospect of yielding to Zalith's potent allure.

Zalith clearly understood his confliction. After a few moments, the demon slowly re-buckled Alucard's belt, rested his head on the vampire's shoulder, and lightly nuzzled his neck. "I really like you," he said, smiling.

Alucard admittedly felt a little relieved that Zalith didn't ask him if he was ready for sex. He knew that he wasn't, but his fear of annoying the demon might have made him say something he didn't want to.

He rested what he could of his head on Zalith's and exhaled deeply, his once trembling body calming down. "I really like you, too," he said quietly, conquering his nervousness... even if it were for just a moment.

Chapter Thirty-Four

— ⪡ ✝ ⪢ —

Luther

| **Alucard** |

As the ship drifted towards the Dragonspire docks, Alucard waited on the forecastle deck. The fur on his cape rippled in the bitter wind, but his layers kept the cold from bothering him too much.

The distant city emerged as a vibrant jewel, a stark contrast to the desolation of the snowy mountains that cradled it. Despite the overcast sky, a few feeble rays of sunlight pierced through the gloom, illuminating the resplendent buildings. The gold-silver palace, nestled at the city's rear, gleamed with regal brilliance, and a few shoals of shimmering skyfish circled its tallest tower.

Surrounded by opulence, every structure in Dragonspire stood as a testament to architectural grandeur. Buildings resembling magnificent palaces adorned with twisting towers and resplendent stained-glass windows adorned the cityscape. As if paying homage to the draconic deities the citizens revered, statues of dragons adorned street corners and plazas, their majestic forms captured in stone, metal, and *huge* precious gems.

In the snowy realm of Avalmoor, Dragonspire wasn't just a city; it was the epitome of royalty. The people, devout worshippers of the Dragon Gods, had woven their reverence into the very fabric of the place, turning it into a manifestation of their devotion. In the heart of the tundra, Dragonspire thrived as an attestation to both the elegance of its architecture and the unwavering faith of its people.

Alucard's eyes gleamed ice blue, the frown on his face thickening as he dreaded what awaited him once the ship docked. Avalmoor was full of humans, one of the many things he hated most. At least he'd not be meeting with a human, though, and he also had Zalith with him—he couldn't hope for better company. The demon, however, wasn't at his side and was instead inside the cabin changing into something that would be more suitable for the biting cold weather. The snow may have stopped for now, but it was highly likely to return any moment.

The vampire glanced over his shoulder as he heard the cabin door open and close again. He watched Zalith make his way along the deck in a black turtleneck sweater, which Alucard immediately found he was fond of. It complimented Zalith in many ways; it hugged his body, displaying his thick biceps and defined pecs. Alucard let himself stare for a moment... and when his eyes shifted to Zalith's covered neck, he found that it seemed to entice him—as if the sweater was an obstacle for him to get past in order to get what he wanted. He also thought the demon looked cute, but he didn't have the bravery to tell him that.

When Zalith joined him on the forecastle deck, Alucard set his eyes back on the city as they edged closer. "Will you be warm enough in that?" he asked, glancing at him, eager to take every chance he could to stare at the demon; he also noticed the additional black and gold ring on Zalith's middle finger.

"I believe so," Zalith said, smiling.

"We'll go and see Luther first, and depending on what he has to say, we'll most likely be travelling across the country."

"And what if we meet Lucious?"

"Damien asked me to motivate him to join the cause; he's still trying to create another Daegelus."

Zalith looked a little concerned. "And if he isn't interested?"

"I'm very good at motivating people," Alucard said with a smirk, glancing at him.

"I don't doubt that," Zalith said, shifting his sights to the vampire as the ship slowed into the city docks. "You've been here before, right?"

"Yes, but not in a long time. It's been many centuries, and I'm sure it's changed a lot since then. This city was here back then; I know Letholdus used to live in that palace," he said, nodding in the direction of the gold-silver shimmering palace at the very back of the city. "But once the human population increased, he decided it was time to retreat into the heavens. The land... eh, I don't know if it's changed, but I guess we'll find out."

Zalith gazed at the city as the ship stopped and the crewmen began to dock. "Who owns the palace now, Alucard?" he asked with a suspicious tone.

"Luther's... female friend, who just so happens to be the queen of the humans here."

"So, *you* own it."

"More or less. I own Luther, Luther owns her. If there were not so many humans here, perhaps I would visit more," he said and turned around; Zalith followed him as he made his way down onto the deck.

The demon started, "You control the human population back in Dor-Sanguis—"

"To do so here would cause me unnecessary trouble," Alucard interjected. "Letholdus loves this little island of humans and I'd rather not interfere. I already have enough of the Numen on my ass; I don't need them all on me."

Zalith leaned into Alucard's ear. "Looks like you have *me* on your ass too—well, not just yet," he mumbled and lightly slapped Alucard's ass.

Alucard flinched in surprise and scowled at him but quickly looked away as the demon smirked suggestively. "Whatever," he grumbled, trying to hide his embarrassed, red face as he led the way over to the stairs connected to the dock.

Zalith laughed quietly as he walked beside the vampire. "Did Letholdus not come after you when you killed Janus?"

"Letholdus was mad as hell. He had all of his children looking for me, but most of them didn't try very hard after learning who and what I was. They weren't stupid enough to go looking for the one creature capable of ending their lives forever. They told their father they couldn't find me, so he came looking for me instead. He never found me—obviously—and gave up after a decade; he had more important things to do."

"More important than finding his son's murderer? Interesting," Zalith said as they stepped onto the dock.

"The Numen don't exactly care about their offspring; they created them to lengthen bloodlines and increase species. If one of them dies, so what? They have others and can create replacements whenever they might need. If Janus was born like I was, I'm sure Letholdus would have cared more—is a whole lot harder to conceive a Numen-blooded child than to manifest one with ethos. But that doesn't matter," he explained.

As they walked through the almost deserted harbour, Zalith looked at Alucard and smiled. "It *does* matter. Tell me more."

"It depends what you want to know," Alucard said with a shrug, leading the way to the main port.

"Why is it harder to conceive a Numen-blooded child? I assumed there was a reason the Numen created their children with ethos rather than simply having them with humans."

"Well, I won't go into too much detail—"

"A shame," Zalith said, smirking.

Alucard rolled his eyes. "The Numen couldn't enter Aegisguard for a long time. They worked out that slowly pouring their ethos into this world would increase their influence and eventually give them entry—there has to be enough of their ethos in a world for the world to be able to support them. They are very powerful, and if they tried to enter a world like this without having their ethos here first, the world would tear apart. They *could* enter the world in a mortal form, but they're all afraid to walk around without all that power. Anyway…to conceive a child would make the task of gaining entry to a world so much easier—instant, in fact. But to do so, they have to…eh…mate with a human. But how can you get into the human world and do such a thing if you can't enter the world?"

Zalith smiled. "You tell me."

"You have to pull the human into the Numen world—the Void. It's where the Numen live most of the time; they kind of just... float out there, watch the worlds. However, you can't pull a human into the Void because it would kill them. So, the Numen would have to put themself and the human in a sort of... compromise—somewhere in between. We can call it limbo. It takes a lot of ethos to do that, so much that it left Lucifer weak for hundreds of years—I think he is still recovering now, which is why he has made no attempt to come after me himself, despite having an ethos-created son here. That, and the fact he is currently trapped in Hell—his siblings locked him away to keep themselves safe from him."

With an amused laugh, Zalith kept his eyes on Alucard as they reached the end of the docks and stepped onto the red-brick path that would take them deeper into the lavish city. "There's more to it, I assume?" he asked. "I'm aware of how pathetic some of these Numen are—Damien, for example, who thinks he can climb to what he might consider the pinnacle of existence."

Alucard glanced at him as they stopped at the foot of a long, winding street. "To create me, Lucifer lost half of his ethos, and he will not get it back unless he kills me. The same thing would happen to any other Numen who conceives a child. With each passing day, I grow stronger, Lucifer gets weaker. One day, I guess he expects me to turn up and kill him to take the rest of his ethos, but I have no intention of doing that. I'm... content the way I am. I don't want to become a Numen."

"Become a Numen?" Zalith asked with an intrigued frown.

"That's a long story. Short version: we are two halves of one Numen. I kill him, I become the whole. He kills me, he becomes whole again."

The demon smiled as he stared ahead. "I learn so much when I'm with you. Is there anything else you can tell me?"

Alucard shrugged and said, "Maybe later. It gets busy here, so we are best not to talk about things that might make people think we are... odd."

"Of course."

Alucard led the way up the winding, bustling street, and when they reached the end, he stopped and stared at the palace. It was still a short walk, and the amount of people was starting to make him feel uncomfortable. He glanced at Zalith, looked back at the palace, and then glanced down at the demon's hand; he wanted to take hold of it the moment they stepped off the ship, but of course, his nervousness kept him from doing so. At least now he had an excuse; with a shy look on his face, he slowly slipped his hand into Zalith's and kept his embarrassed expression from the demon's sight.

"It gets busy here," he muttered. "I'd rather not lose each other in a crowd of humans."

"Sensible," the demon said with a smirk, tightening his grip on the vampire's hand. "This Luther man," he then said as they continued up the street. "He's been around since you and Attila were… friends; are he and you familiar these days?"

"Not exactly. If I'm being totally honest, back then, I simply found Attila more interesting. I had to choose which one of them would stay here after I killed Janus, and it was Luther. He doesn't resent me for it, though. He likes being who he is here."

Amused, Zalith smiled. "I think I'd be a little mad if you left me here in the snow, Alucard."

Alucard, trying to hide his face once more, pouted. "I wouldn't leave you anywhere."

Zalith's smile grew as he let go of Alucard's hand and moved his arm around the vampire's shoulders. Ignoring the demeaning stares and mutters of the people around them, Zalith hugged him tightly and kissed the side of his face. He then returned his hand to Alucard's and stared ahead.

The vampire tried to hide his flustered face and avoid the disgusted stares of everyone he and Zalith passed, continuing to lead the way towards the palace's golden gates, where a single guard was waiting.

When they reached the gate, Alucard let go of Zalith's hand as the armoured guard eyed them both strangely.

"I'm here for Luther," the vampire said.

"And you would be?" the guard asked rudely.

"I'm sure he has warned you of my arrival."

With a skeptical stare, the guard looked Alucard and Zalith up and down and then looked back at the palace behind him. "Yes. If you would follow me," he said, turning around, and once the gates opened, he led the way across the grounds and towards the palace's large mahogany door.

Alucard and Zalith followed him inside, through the brightly decorated halls, and emerged into a lounge; the walls were sky-blue and lined with paintings of men, women, children, and family pets. The white marble floors were adorned with red, gold-plaited rugs, and all the furniture was either oak or white.

The guard led them over to one of the couches in front of a glass coffee table and invited them to sit. Once they did, he left the room.

"Have you been here before, too?" Zalith asked Alucard, who made himself comfortable, resting his arm on the side of the couch.

"I have," he confirmed, looking at him.

"Do you visit Luther?"

"No. Would it bother you if I did?"

"No," Zalith said, smiling.

Taking his eyes off the demon, Alucard looked over at the windows. But as Zalith leaned closer, he pouted stubbornly. He wasn't sure whether the demon *was* bothered or not, but he wasn't going to make a huge deal and ask again. He sat there, glaring at the windows while Zalith shuffled as close as he could get and rested his head on his shoulder.

When Zalith reached towards the coffee table, Alucard watched as he grabbed the golden, jewel-encrusted crown sitting beside a half-full glass of wine. Zalith then placed it on the vampire's head. Alucard didn't exactly like it, so he tried to stop him, but Zalith laughed quietly and held it in place.

"It suits you, my darling prince," he said, grinning.

Unsure of what to say, Alucard snarled and rolled his eyes; before he could try and fight Zalith off again, the demon leaned closer and kissed him.

"Suits you a whole lot better than I," came Luther's uppity voice.

With a grumble of irritancy, Alucard pushed Zalith away and sat up straight. He set his eyes on Luther—the tall, broad, silky-brown-haired man who was standing in the lounge doorway with a crooked smile on his pale face. His hair was waist-length but tied and styled to look as though it was only just past his shoulders. He was dressed as though he was the palace's owner—a white blazer with sleeves adorned with light-brown fur, matching trousers, a frilly jabot, and so many jewels on his person that he'd easily drown if he were to fall into a lake.

Luther smirked and crossed his arms as he leaned against the doorframe. "Sorry I took so long to get here."

Snatching the crown from atop his head, Alucard stood up, placed the crown back onto the table, and made his way over to Luther—and Zalith, of course, followed with a hostile glare on his face.

"Did you get what I asked?" Alucard asked.

"It's been a long time since you've come to see me, which has resulted in a list becoming a library. This way," Luther said, leading the way over to a closed door sitting between two huge family portraits. "Who's your friend?" he then asked, glancing at Zalith.

"This is Zalith. He's…hmm…more than a friend."

"Oh?" Luther smiled, looking back at them both as he unlocked the door. "Best friend?" he asked, opening the door. "Boyfriend?"

"That," Alucard confirmed, glancing at Zalith, who smiled in response.

They both followed Luther into a small library packed full of books, papers, and scrolls.

"I assume Attila had much to say about that," Luther mumbled, taking them over to a desk at the back of the room. "I also hear that he lost his job. Might I guess…a connection?" he asked, sitting behind his desk as Alucard and Zalith stood in front of it.

"You can assume all you like," Alucard answered. "I won't tell you."

"Of course," Luther said, glancing up at him. He started flicking through a book and asked, "How is everyone else? Dirk, Tobias, Elvin? The last time I saw them was four years ago."

Despondency attempted to smother Alucard's face, but he scowled and deadpanned. "They are dead. Dirk is alive."

Luther stopped flicking through the pages and looked up at the vampire. "Dead?"

"Find what I came for," he grumbled, trying to ignore his grief. But every time he thought about Elvin and Tobias, he couldn't fight the sadness off. To his relief, though, Zalith gradually moved his hand around his back, gripped his waist, and pulled him closer. He felt a little better in the demon's embrace, so he didn't let his shyness force him to push him away.

"A lot of people have come through here as of late," Luther started, reading over the page he'd landed on. He took his eyes off the book and looked up at Alucard. "Specifics?"

"Angel," Alucard answered.

"Oh." Luther frowned, closing the book. "In that case," he said, reaching over to the shelf to his left. He snatched a scroll and handed it to Alucard. "Coordinates to markings left in a mountain scree, the type left when someone travels down from the Overworld. That might be your angel. I'd be careful, though," he warned as Alucard took the scroll from him. "Dragons have been... vigilant around there. Looks like you're not the only one searching for this guy, huh?"

Tucking the scroll into the inside pocket of his blazer, Alucard frowned. "Which ones?"

"Uh... Boreas mostly. He's been hanging around those coordinates, seen at least once a week. Ourea, too. But mostly Boreas. I had keunsae prepared for you, but these coordinates aren't too far; you could walk if you prefer. I know you're not a fan of those birds."

"Right. I gather everything here is fine?"

"Perfect. Nothing to raise concern about. I'll be marrying the queen this month. That was my crown you were trying on, also."

"The gold is fake," Alucard laughed.

"What?" Luther asked, standing up. "Really?"

The Vampire Lord smirked and turned around. "Until next time," he said, leading the way out as Zalith followed at his side.

Zalith glanced at the vampire as they left the library and made their way back through the lounge. "*Is* the gold fake, Alucard?"

"No," the vampire said, smiling. "It'll keep him on his toes for a while, though. He is a bit of an idiot sometimes, and I do my best to keep him thinking; otherwise, he gets a little lazy. We don't need that."

"You'll have him hunt for the real crown when there's not actually a fake?"

"Yes."

Amused, Zalith laughed quietly and took the vampire's arm in his own. "You're so devious."

"It's just… fun," Alucard said with a shrug as they reached the castle's front door, where the guard was waiting to lead them back into the city.

Still smiling, Zalith looked at him and asked, "These two dragons he mentioned, Boreas and Ourea; will we come across them?"

"There's a possibility," Alucard confirmed as they followed the guard out into the palace grounds and towards the gates. "We'll walk since Luther said it's not far. If we come across either of the dragons, we'll be fine. I know how to deal with them."

"Will it be *my* turn to learn from *you*, Alucard?" he asked with a smirk. "Teaching me to fight a dragon?"

Alucard frowned as they left the gates and walked back down into the crowded city. "It's not so simple to learn to fight a dragon, Zalith," he said sternly. "Luckily, you're not an idiot, so it should be fairly easy."

"Thank you for the compliment," the demon laughed.

The vampire laughed a little, too. "Everyone else I know, I would rather let the dragon eat them before I start fighting it."

Moving his arm around the vampire's shoulders again, Zalith pulled him closer and smiled contently. "I look forward to fighting a god with you, vampire." Then, as Alucard pulled the scroll from his pocket, leading the way down the path, the demon frowned. "Why does Luther know a fair bit about these dragons?"

Unrolling the scroll to read the coordinates written on it, Alucard glanced at Zalith. "He was with Attila and me when I was hunting Janus. The three of us used to work together a lot a while ago."

"Aw. Were you close?" he teased.

"No," Alucard answered, stopping in his tracks. He set his eyes on another street and led the way towards it. "Attila and Luther were good friends, but to me, they were really just subordinates. Anyway, it's this way," he said, leading them towards one of the alleys which led out of the city.

Without another word, they headed towards the exit, and Alucard prepared for whatever might be waiting outside the safety of the walls.

Chapter Thirty-Five

— ⋖ ✝ ⋗ —

Agma

| Ben |

In his new office in Alucard's castle, Ben read The Vampire Lord's reply. '*Make sure Felix understood he didn't have his old job back and ignore Detlaff*—Alucard never failed to get straight to the point.

Ben lowered the paper onto his desk with a quiet sigh and glanced at the barn owl that had delivered the note. The small white bird was perched on the window, and the sun was high in the sky behind it. He'd start by finding Felix and getting him to understand that he *didn't* get his old job back, no matter what it took. Then, he'd feed Detlaff and get on with the rest of his day. He still had to study up for his new job; perhaps he ought to do that once he was done with his current tasks.

He stood up, left his office, and made his way through the silent castle. However, as he made his way down the spiralling stairs, quiet, hushed voices echoed from the hall below. He was quite sure that one of them was Felix, so he scowled and picked up his pace, quickly reaching the hallway that would take him towards the main hall. Immediately, he set his eyes on the door to the dungeon, noticing that it was open.

A growl of irritancy escaped his breath as he stormed forward; he pushed the door open, made his way down the stairs, and glared at the door to Detlaff's cell. Felix's voice was coming from inside, and as Ben got closer, his anger increased. He'd warned Felix once before, and now he was going to have to do it again. This time, he'd not be so kind.

Ben kicked the cell door open, expecting to find Felix muttering away to Detlaff, but what he found instead was a whole lot more confusing. Dead, lying in a pool of blood, was Remont, the new vampire ally Alucard hadn't long employed. His throat had been torn out—and beside him was Felix, but he dropped to the floor the moment Ben stepped into the room and lay still beside Remont.

Confusion gripped Ben as he examined the scene, but before he could catch a glimpse of Detlaff, the demon sprung forward, free of his chains, and gripped Ben's throat, pinning him against the wall.

"Did you miss me, honey-poo?!" Detlaff screamed into Ben's horrified face, his voice a higher-pitched version of Remont's.

Detlaff gripped Ben's throat so tight that he couldn't breathe; the demon's hands were bloody and scaled, and Ben quickly discovered that Detlaff's human-like hands were on the cell floor in a pool of blood. Somehow, he'd torn them off in his desperate attempt to escape. But why was Felix here? Why was Remont here? And what the hell was going to happen now?

Grinning, Detlaff dragged his tongue over the side of Ben's face, giggled in delight, and sighed longingly in his face. "I missed you," he sang. "Your voice was so beautiful; it treated me so well!"

Revolted, Ben tried to escape, but Detlaff was a whole lot stronger than he was.

"Where's my handsome big brother?" he asked, tilting his head to the side.

Ben had nothing to say. He gritted his teeth, trying to pull Detlaff's scaled hands from his throat, but his attempts to get free only made Detlaff grip him tighter.

"Don't struggle, Benny-Ben-Ben-Boo," the insane man said with a sigh, stroking the side of Ben's face with his other hand. "Where is my brother? Is he away with that demon again?" he asked, pouting.

"G-get off me!" Ben yelled, managing to crash his fist hard enough into the demon's face that he stumbled back and let go of him.

Ben moved to attack again, but with an irritated snarl, Detlaff instantly recovered, swung around, and pinned him back against the wall.

"So feisty!" he laughed and snatched Ben's jaw in his hand, glaring into his mortified eyes. "Sadly, I don't need you anymore. If only you weren't a vampire, I'd make you my first little…dampire." He grinned excitedly. "No…that's stupid," he said, looking down at the ground as Ben struggled in his grip. "Hmm…what's a good name for Detlaff's little species of people?" he asked himself. "Vampire…dampire…ampire…a…agmire…hmm…ag…ma!" he yelled, clapping his hands—but before Ben could try to attack, he swiftly gripped his throat again. "Agma!" he exclaimed. "Agma, agma, agma, agma!" he screamed, tightening his grip on Ben's jaw until a loud crack cut through the dungeon's corridor.

Ben's agonized cries were muffled by his broken jaw, and as Detlaff seemed to panic and attempt to fix it, Ben tried as hard as he could to try and escape the demon's grip, but his strength was failing him.

"Oopsie-doopsie," Detlaff giggled, stroking the side of Ben's slowly healing face. "Maybe I should start by removing the ability to feel pain; that would be nice, wouldn't it, Benny-Ben?" he asked, tilting his head to the side. "That would be *so* nice."

As his jaw healed, Ben scowled, waiting for the moment he had enough strength to eradicate the disgusting creature in front of him—and that time didn't take long to come. As Detlaff became distracted muttering to himself about pain receptors, Ben clenched his fist and uppercut the unsuspecting demon so hard that he flew up off his feet, crashed through the ceiling, and landed back down in the bloody cell with a pained wince.

Ben didn't waste a moment. He rushed over to the stunned demon and snatched him by his throat, slamming his fist into his face once more. But Detlaff just laughed—

"Rude!" Detlaff screamed, escaping Ben's grip with ease. He shoved Ben aside and scurried over to the door, but instead of leaving, he swung around and leaned against the doorframe, smiling at Ben, who had just turned to face him. "I'm sorry honey-poo-bear, but now I must take my leave. I have to find myself a nice little place to live, and then I'll come back for you—and maybe I'll see my big brother again," he said with a grin, clapping his hands as he skipped off down the corridor like a child.

But Ben wasn't going to let him get away. He immediately gave chase, and when Detlaff realized he was being followed, the demon burst into a crazed speed matching that of a vampire.

Ben chased Detlaff through the castle and out into the courtyard, where the lunatic stopped, swung around, and tried to snatch Ben, but Ben was fast enough this time to catch Detlaff's hand. He grabbed the demon's wrist, broke it, and snatched Detlaff's throat, but once again, Detlaff just laughed, even as his throat was being crushed in Ben's hand.

With a grin on his face, Detlaff grasped both of Ben's wrists, and as his wings burst from his back, he swung his left one around and impaled Ben's side with its blade-tipped carpal. Before Ben could do anything, Detlaff harshly sank his fangs into his neck, and the moment he felt the demon's venom pour into his blood, he knew there wasn't going to be much else he could do.

He grimaced and grunted, and as the venom inflicted pain unlike anything he'd felt before, he yelled and lost all the strength he once had. Detlaff let go of him; he fell to the ground, and as his face hit the cobblestone, he panted painfully, unable to make a sound, unable to move any part of his body. How could he have been such an idiot? In all the commotion, he'd somehow managed to forget that a demon's bite was one of their most formidable weapons.

Detlaff crouched beside him and pouted, tilted his head to the side, and sighed as he began stroking Ben's face. "Benny-boo-boo-bee…we could have been such good friends, you and I!" he sang. "But…no, you want to hurt me. You want to lock me up back down there? No. No locking up Detlaff anymore. I have a job to do, and so do you," he said with a smile, patting Ben's head.

Ben grunted in frustration, unable to move, unable to speak—all he could do was lay there in dread. What was going to happen to him now? What was Detlaff going to do? The last time he had fallen into this creature's hands, he lost his voice and his ability to heal, and he felt he had almost lost his will to live. He was sure that whatever awaited him this time would be a whole lot worse—so much that he wished he could just die now. But Detlaff wouldn't grant him such mercy, would he?

Detlaff sighed and patted the side of Ben's face. "I'll see you soon, Benny," he said, waiting as his venom slowly pulled Ben into a deep, silent sleep—a sleep that Ben wished he'd not wake up from.

Chapter Thirty-Six

Boreas

| Alucard |

Alucard led the way through Avalmoor's calm tundra. He felt a little cautious, constantly eyeing the snow around them. There was a chance that they might come across a dragon, and he knew Zalith hadn't fought one before.

He looked at the demon and asked him, "Do you know anything at all about the dragons?"

"I know what you've told me; other than that, not much at all. I understand that they're gods in this world, but not in mine," he answered with a smile as they made their way up a snow-covered hill.

When they reached the top of the hill, the vampire took his eyes off Zalith and glared at the mountains in the distance. "Well, Boreas, the first dragon Luther mentioned, is the God of the North," he started. "People believe he creates the wind, the cold, whatever. He's the creator of a lot of ice-class ethos beasts and dragons, and ice is his primary ethos type, which isn't a bother for us because we possess fire ethos. However, the dragons are Numen-blooded, so any injuries that they might inflict on us won't heal as quickly as usual. Against them, our healing powers mean nothing. So, don't get hit, hmm?"

"Noted," Zalith said, smiling. "How do we fight this dragon if he shows up?"

"Well, just as he can fatally wound us, we can fatally wound him. We can hurt him any way we would hurt any other living thing. Fire will be most effective, though."

Zalith frowned curiously. "How big is this dragon?"

Alucard glanced at him to see if he was being sarcastic, but he seemed genuinely interested. "Well, I've seen a few of them, and their sizes vary. They are..." he paused, frowned as he looked around, and set his eyes on a forest of giant sequoia trees. "Some of them can get as big as that," he said, nodding at the two-hundred-and-fifty-feet-tall trees. "And some are as small as those pines," he said, waving his hand towards a tiny gathering of pine trees ranging from ten to fifty feet tall. "Most of them are like wyverns, so they lack front legs, which means they aren't as nimble as six-limbed Aegis."

"Why such a huge size range?" he questioned.

"Some of them are more powerful than others. In most cases, the bigger the Aegis, the deadlier they are."

The demon smirked. "If we find him, will you make a cape out of this dragon too?" he asked, moving his arm around Alucard's shoulders as he pressed his face into the fur of his cape.

"No. Unless you would like one."

"I'd love that."

Alucard smiled subtly. He wasn't sure whether he could picture Zalith wearing a cape, but if he wanted one, he'd make him one. He glanced around as they trailed the sequoia forest tree line; they had to be getting close to the coordinates. "Anyway," he said and grimaced as a bitter, biting breeze swooped past them, "we should be cautious. The dragons can't detect us and we won't be able to detect them, either. If there *is* one out here, it should think we're just wandering humans and ignore us."

"Should?" Zalith asked, raising an eyebrow in concern.

"If we're seen purposely searching for these markings, they will intervene," he said, looking at him again. "If there *is* a dragon guarding what we're looking for, it'll most likely be doing so from above," he said, glancing up, but the dull, grey skies were full of nothing but clouds.

"Once we find these markings, will you be able to determine Lucious' location using them?"

"Depending on how old they are, maybe. I don't usually pry into Damien's business or that of the people he sends me to find, but I do want to know why an angel came to Avalmoor. The only thing of interest here is the dragons; whether the angels are working with them now or not, I don't know, but I would like to know if it's going to cause me problems."

"Why would the angels ally with the dragons?"

"I don't know. Ephriel might be up to something. For all I know, Letholdus and Ephriel could be working together. We know that this world can harbour three of the Numen, and Letholdus has already taken one of those spaces. Perhaps he has decided to help Ephriel gain harbour here. I don't know what Lilith is doing these days; Damien has already secured his place in this world—if he hadn't, he wouldn't be able to enter it, which means there is only one space left. Letholdus doesn't much like Lucifer or Lilith, so I can see him helping Ephriel take that last space to keep those two out."

"Detlaff didn't mention Lilith much when you interrogated him; he said that Ephriel, Damien, and Lucifer were fighting over the spaces in this world."

"I don't know what she's doing," Alucard repeated. "As long as she's not bothering me, I don't care."

"Did she not give you your demon name?" he asked, clearly fishing for information.

This time, however, Alucard wasn't up for giving it. He frowned skeptically at Zalith. "If you suspect there's more to my one-time contact with Lilith, there's not. I don't know her, and I don't care."

"Okay," Zalith answered, still with suspicion in his voice.

As they came closer to the scree of the mountain they'd been approaching, Alucard stopped to face Zalith. "What?"

"Nothing," Zalith answered.

The vampire scowled. "Why are you mad?"

"I'm not mad. I'm curious."

"Right, curious," Alucard snarled, continuing forward.

Following him, Zalith frowned slightly. "I just want to know if I have to be prepared for more than Lucifer and Damien."

Alucard looked back at him. "Prepared for them?" He scowled but didn't care to hear Zalith's response to that. "I don't—"

"From what I've learned, it sounds like every Numen has a problem with you. Lucifer wants to kill you, Damien treats you like a worthless slave, and you killed one of Letholdus' children, so I'm sure he's also out for your head. Ephriel, too—you haven't told me the truth about why she might be after you. Why shouldn't I suspect that Lilith wants you for something, too? And what about Erich?"

Once again, Alucard stopped walking and glared at him. "Why do you care? I've lived this long with them looking for me; I'm sure I can continue to manage."

Zalith frowned in concern. "Because I care about *you*, and I want to protect you," he said sternly as he placed his hand on the vampire's shoulder. "How can I protect you if you won't tell me what I'm protecting you from?"

"I never said I needed protection."

"You don't have to need it for me to want to give it."

With a scowl of confliction, Alucard took his eyes off the demon and walked off. He didn't want to talk about the Numen—not here, not now, maybe not ever. He didn't need protecting from them; he'd managed to keep away from them for four hundred years and he was confident in his ability to continue staying out of their sights. He'd not drag Zalith into it and allow him to risk his life—he cared about him too much.

The vampire made his way over to the scree and set his eyes on the carvings on the ground. Around the markings, all the ice had melted away, and the stone was damp where the snow had tried to set. Alucard crouched, examining them as Zalith joined him and stood beside him.

"Why won't you tell me what they want from you?" Zalith asked, crouching.

With a vexed sigh, Alucard dragged his fingers through the carvings. "Perhaps I'd rather not think about it," he grumbled. But then he huffed quietly and turned his head to look at him. "Maybe there are some things I wish to protect *you* from," he said and glared back down at the markings. "These are a few days old; I can try to find a trace," he said, changing the subject.

Zalith stared at him for a moment… but then looked down at the markings. "I'll try, too."

Alucard focused, dismissing his irritancy as he placed his hand over the carvings. It hadn't been long since he'd traced angel ethos; he had to do so while finding the other angels for Damien. It took him no time at all to find a very faint trace of what could only be Lucious' ethos. He frowned, stood up, and looked in the direction he and Zalith had come from. Could Lucious be in Dragonspire?

Zalith also stood up, staring in the same direction. "Could he be in the city?"

"Maybe," the vampire confirmed. "I don't know how far I can follow this trace, but hopefully it'll take us to him."

"And once we find him, should we expect a fight?"

"Most likely. None of the angels I went to find for Damien took kindly to my appearance; I had to hurt many of them."

With an amused smile, Zalith turned to face him. "I'd say that we should hope he won't resist, but I kind of like the idea of watching you hurt an angel."

"They're very annoying," Alucard grumbled. "Have you had to fight them before?"

"A while ago, yeah, when Damien had me search for one of Erich's children. That encounter resulted in such an irritating fight."

"Which one?"

"Osiris."

Alucard stifled a frown and rolled his eyes. "Oh, right. I remember you telling me about that. Ugly, annoying, boring, and the last person I would want to be sent to find."

"Agreed," Zalith said, smirking.

The vampire then sighed. "We should head back. The more time we spend here, the more time Lucious has to get further away."

Smiling, Zalith nodded. "Okay, lead the w—"

A devastating explosion of ice and rock violently erupted beneath them, unleashing a relentless tsunami of snow that engulfed the landscape in a blinding tempest. The sheer force hurled Alucard and Zalith into the chaotic whirlwind; Alucard, disoriented and separated from the demon, crashed to the ground with a painful thud. As the vampire struggled to regain his bearings, a nightmarish roar, piercing and dreadful, echoed through the tumult, causing the very earth to quiver in trepidation.

Alucard, grappling with the agony of impact, clawed into the unforgiving ice to anchor himself. Despite the urgent instincts urging him to get up and find Zalith, a profound sense of dread crawled over him when his ice-blue eyes beheld the emerging terror below.

The ivory-white wyvern, standing majestically over the disrupted ground as if it claimed the chaos as its nest, had ascended from a concealed, snow-filled abyss. Balanced on all fours, its wings transformed into forelimbs of icy menace, the wyvern seemed to stretch with an eerie lethargy, revealing a colossal, spike-covered club at the tip of its tail. As it lifted its serpent-like neck, adorned with ashen frills, another deafening roar reverberated, resonating with an aura of primal danger that far surpassed Alucard's initial pain and concern.

Alucard scowled and gritted his teeth as he clawed his way back to his feet. The towering wyvern, although a formidable adversary, barely registered in his thoughts. Instead, his gaze fervently scoured the aftermath for any sign of Zalith. In the chaos, Alucard felt a disconcerting connection, a visceral awareness that transcended mere sight.

Despite the uncertainty of Zalith's whereabouts, an unshakable intuition gripped Alucard, whispering of grave injuries befalling the demon. A phantom pain coursed through his own body, wounds that weren't his, yet carried a haunting familiarity. It was an inexplicable tether, an ethereal link that connected him to Zalith's suffering, one that only manifested when he consciously directed his senses and focus towards the demon, attempting to pinpoint his location amid the mayhem.

It took no time at all for him to figure out where Zalith was; he ignored the awakening dragon and rushed to his left, the scent of Zalith's blood getting stronger with each passing moment, but he wouldn't be able to disregard the dragon for long. As he rushed towards Zalith's location, the dragon set its sights on him, and Alucard only just managed to dodge the incoming projectile of flaming ice. He ducked, the ice missing his head by inches, and at the same time, he set his sights on a hint of black lying in the snow.

Zalith.

A macabre trail of blood painted the pristine snow, an ominous guide leading Alucard to where Zalith had fallen. The demon lay sprawled in the scarlet-streaked landscape, his body half-buried beneath the crimson-tainted blanket of snow, consciousness ebbing away. Horror etched across Alucard's face as he rushed to Zalith's side, but the dragon, relentless and undeterred, roared with thunderous fury, wings slamming into the ground, signalling its imminent assault.

Time compressed into a fragile instant, and Alucard's heart raced. He didn't have time to assess Zalith's injuries, but the mere fact that the demon hadn't gotten up spoke volumes about the severity of his wounds.

In that fleeting moment, Alucard seized Zalith, wrapping his arms around him. As the dragon prepared to unleash another deadly barrage, Alucard invoked his vampiric speed. A swirl of vermilion smoke enveloped them, swallowing them whole, a spectral escape from the impending danger. The world outside the crimson haze vanished, leaving only echoes of the dragon's enraged roars behind.

They reappeared a hundred or so feet away behind the cover of a large boulder, but that wouldn't keep the dragon off them for long. Zalith was injured, and the dragon had obviously caught the scent of his blood. But Alucard had fought a dragon before, and he knew exactly how to confuse them.

With time hanging precariously in the balance, Alucard stole a moment to assess Zalith's condition, propping the demon against the rock. Despite the severity of his wounds, Zalith bore them with an eerie stoicism. A vicious gash cut diagonally from his waist to his left arm, staining the pristine snow beneath them with a crimson testimony to his ordeal. The demon, in a desperate bid to stave off the relentless bleeding, clutched at the wound with his hands, yet not a single groan or grunt escaped his lips.

In a moment of realization, Alucard questioned why Zalith hadn't taken the drastic measure of cauterizing his wounds. A renewed focus revealed a more insidious aspect of the injury—it was siphoning away the demon's ethos. The revelation added another layer of urgency to Alucard's mission; not only was Zalith in peril, but the very source of his strength was draining away with each passing second.

Alucard couldn't deal with it yet. First, he had to buy himself and Zalith the time they'd need. With a scowl on his face, Alucard carefully dragged his hand over the blood on Zalith's clothes, and once he'd gathered enough on his palm, he focused his ethos into it. He then held up his hand, and as the blood transformed into black mist, it swiftly ascended into the sky, mimicking the form of long, wispy snakes. The wisps abruptly stretched out and became a thick red and black fog, engulfing the area. It wouldn't last forever, but it would keep them hidden from the dragon's senses for long enough.

The vampire desperately stared at Zalith's dazed face. "I need to see," he said, pulling the demon's hands away from his wounds, which his blood poured from the moment his palms moved. Alucard hastily placed his own hands over the gash and scowled in confliction, trying to work out the best thing to do. He didn't possess healing ethos—not the kind that he could use to heal these sorts of wounds, anyway. He didn't know what would happen to Zalith's species of demon if they were to bleed out; all he knew was that he himself would become comatose, and he didn't want to risk that happening to Zalith.

He took his eyes off the demon's wounds and stared at him, but Zalith didn't look as though he'd remain conscious much longer. The demon looked exhausted and confused as if he had no idea what was going on; Alucard didn't expect less from an injury caused by a dragon. But why had Zalith been wounded and he hadn't? There was no time to wonder. Quickly, he moved his hands under the demon's torn clothes and used his fire ethos to cauterize Zalith's wounds.

The demon flinched and grimaced, but he didn't stop Alucard. The vampire expected him to lash out in response to the pain, but he was relatively calm and quiet throughout the process. Once Alucard was done, he'd still need to help Zalith regain enough strength so that he'd remain conscious while he fought the dragon. The distorting murk of ethos would soon wane, so he had to be swift.

"Zalith," he said, moving his bloody hands from the demon's sealed wounds to his shoulders.

Zalith looked at him, but he didn't respond.

Alucard placed one hand on the back of Zalith's head and used his other to pull his furred collar away from his neck. He guided the demon's face closer, and to his relief, Zalith understood what he was trying to get him to do. The demon sunk his fangs into Alucard's neck and started gulping down his blood. It was the quickest way Zalith would regain his strength.

The vampire waited, focusing on the dragon; it wouldn't be long until its senses cut through the gloom. As each second passed, Alucard's strength slowly decreased as Zalith's increased, and once he was sure that Zalith would be okay, he lightly pushed him back and exhaled deeply.

"Stay here," he said sternly as he pulled his cape from over his shoulders and wrapped it around the demon so that he'd at least be a little more comfortable.

The vampire didn't falter. He stood up, scowled in determination, and made his way out into the snow, taking one last glance at Zalith to ensure he'd stay as he was told, and to his relief, Zalith didn't attempt to get up and follow him.

Alucard set his eyes on the dragon while it aimlessly searched the thinning black-red fog. He knew exactly what he was going to do and how he'd do it. All he needed was for the dragon to set its eyes on him, and then he'd begin.

The distorting fog began to clear, and when the dragon pinpointed the true location of Zalith's blood, it turned to face Alucard...who had to scent on his hands. The dragon fixed its dark blue eyes on him, and Alucard prepared to fight.

With a feral snarl, the dragon unleashed its icy wrath, snapping its jaws and propelling a lethal beam towards Alucard. Unfazed, the vampire advanced towards the monstrous creature, a scowl etched across his face. He swung his clawed hand with a dismissive motion, deflecting the frozen onslaught with casual ease. The beam struck the ground mere feet from him, and as the dragon recoiled in both confusion and anger, Alucard continued his relentless approach.

The dragon, undeterred, unleashed a barrage of successive attacks, each met with Alucard's nonchalant swats that treated the frozen onslaughts as inconveniences. The ground quaked with each impact, a testament to the overwhelming force at play. Surely, the dragon began to realize that Alucard was no mere intruder stumbling upon its lair; frustration smothered its colossal form as it stepped back to charge yet another assault.

With an assured grin, it forced its massive wing forward, preparing for a more formidable attack.

In response, Alucard extended his right hand. A continuous beam of white light erupted from the dragon's wing, colliding with Alucard's arm. The vampire held firm, showing little strain against the onslaught. The dragon, scowling in disbelief, was locked into the relentless assault, unable to cut short the charged attack until it used up all the ethos it had just charged.

Seizing the moment, Alucard raised his left hand, and within it, a blade-like mass of luciferium crystal materialized. With a swift and calculated move, he forced his right arm aside, breaking the connection with the dragon's beam; the unleashed force caused the dragon's beam to veer uncontrollably along the ground to Alucard's right. Seizing his chance, Alucard hurled the luciferium towards the dragon's exposed neck with lethal precision.

As the luciferium blade sank deep into the dragon's throat, an unexpected yelp escaped the beast, resonating like a wounded canine. Swamp-green blood cascaded onto the snow, and despite finally halting its relentless beam assault, the creature found itself defenceless against Alucard's unyielding assault.

Closing the distance with preternatural speed, Alucard leapt into the air, hurling another blade of luciferium into the back of the dragon's neck. Landing on the scaled nape, he executed a swift jump, the rhythmic precision reminiscent of the technique he employed to vanquish Janus. In mid-air, he rained down blades with calculated accuracy, each one finding its mark in the dragon's flesh. The sequence required a meticulous height to ensure the blades gained the necessary momentum to pierce the creature's formidable defences.

As the dragon writhed in pain and fury, it attempted a retaliatory jump, jaws agape, aiming for Alucard. Unfazed, the vampire landed gracefully with one foot on the dragon's snout, locking eyes with the creature in a smug expression of triumph.

Executing a swift kick to disengage, Alucard propelled himself away as the dragon landed back on its hind legs. A palpable horror stretched across its visage as Alucard, suspended in mid-air, brought the tips of his claws together, forming a sphere-like configuration with his hands. Sensing impending doom, the dragon desperately attempted to rid itself of the embedded luciferium crystals, but resistance proved futile.

In a climactic display, Alucard pulled his hands apart, and every crystal embedded in the dragon's body hummed with an ominous resonance before erupting into deafening, brilliant explosions of crimson fire, marking the final symphony of the formidable beast's demise.

The vampire descended and landed on the ground not far from where Zalith, who had been watching with a smile on his face the entire time, was standing, leaning against the boulder Alucard had left him behind. They both watched as the explosive flames consumed the dragon; blood, ash, and fire spewed to the ground, smothering the once-white snow around the creature, and with a loud thump and rumble of the ground, the dragon collapsed.

However, Alucard wasn't yet done.

With a scowl on his face, the vampire made his way forward, setting his eyes on the mangled body of the dragon as it lay in the snow. Huge, gaping wounds sat where Alucard's luciferium blades had once embedded themselves, exposing the creature's spine and wing bones, and most of its skin had burned away.

The dragon glowered at Alucard and tried to get up, but all it could do was struggle.

"Boreas, huh?" Alucard asked, reaching the dragon's face.

Boreas snapped his jaws at him, but he couldn't reach, and Alucard remained exactly where he was.

"Perhaps you will see your brother where you go—or… perhaps not. I don't know how this works."

The dragon attempted to snap its jaws around Alucard, dragging its huge body forward, but Alucard took a step back to avoid its attack.

But Alucard was irritated and didn't want to make Zalith wait any longer than he had to, so he held out his left hand as if he was reaching to grab something. A small black glow appeared in his palm, and the dragon's eyes faded to black; its body went still, and after a few moments, its flesh began crumbling into white dust. Everything around the dragon's skeleton withered into ash and floated towards Alucard's hand.

When there was nothing left of the dragon but its bones, a small, shimmering purple crystal formed in Alucard's palm. The crystal glistened, and with a small flash of black light, it concealed itself inside a dark, hexagonal, rune-patterned talisman. Before the talisman could hit the ground, Alucard snatched it, flipped it over, and glared at the runes on its smooth back. In its centre was a small rune Alucard recognized as the number thirteen—Boreas was the thirteenth of Letholdus' nineteen children. There was no wonder he'd been so easy to defeat; just like demons and vampires, the younger they were, the weaker they were.

But it was over now. Alucard slipped the talisman into his pocket, turned around, and made his way over to Zalith, who kept a weak but typical smirk on his face as he watched the vampire approach.

"Are you okay?" Zalith asked as Alucard reached him.

Without hesitation, Alucard wrapped his arms around the demon and hugged him, but not too tightly in case he agitated his wounds. "I'm fine," he confirmed. Seeing Zalith so hurt terrified him in a way he didn't wish to feel again, but thankfully, the demon was okay, and with a day or so of rest, he'd heal just fine.

Zalith slowly moved his arms around Alucard and rested the side of his face on the vampire's head. "That was hot."

With a roll of his eyes, Alucard smiled and let go of him. "You're fine, clearly."

"All thanks to you, baby," he said with a smirk, and as the vampire frowned in fluster, he pulled Alucard back into a comforting hug.

"We should get back to the ship," Alucard said rather hastily as he glanced down at Zalith's bloody, torn clothes, his cauterized wounds just visible through the tears. Then, with his arms still around the demon, he disappeared into vermillion smoke, taking Zalith with him as he swiftly ascended into the sky and raced back towards Dragonspire.

Chapter Thirty-Seven

— ⟨ ✝ ⟩ —

A Dead End

| Alucard |

When Alucard landed on the ship's deck, he moved Zalith's arm over his shoulders so he could help the demon walk more comfortably. As they headed for the cabin, the vampire set his eyes on the first crewman he saw.

"Be ready to disembark in fifteen minutes," he ordered, and while the crewman scurried off to prepare the ship, Alucard helped Zalith into the cabin and shut the door behind them.

"Why are we leaving?" Zalith asked as Alucard escorted him over to the bed, where the demon slowly sat with a quiet exhale of relief.

Alucard lit the fireplace before sitting beside him. "It won't take long for the other dragons to discover what happened. They'll come looking for me. I'll go and follow Lucious' trace alone, and if he's here, I'll deal with him. You need to stay here and rest," he said sternly as he looked down at the demon's bloody clothes.

But Zalith frowned reluctantly. "I'd rather come with you."

"No," Alucard said, scowling. "Take this off," he mumbled as he started taking Zalith's sweater off. Once it was off, the vampire took it from him and placed it on the other side of the bed—he didn't want to get blood all over the white carpet—and as a smirk stretched across Zalith's face, the vampire frowned and helped him pull his shirt off so he could examine his wounds.

"My, aren't you eager," Zalith said as Alucard eyed his body.

"Be quiet and lay down," he instructed as he lightly pushed Zalith's shoulders so that he'd lay on his back. He then eyed what he could see of Zalith's injury beneath the drying blood. He'd cauterized it well enough and had stopped the bleeding; drinking Alucard's blood would speed up the demon's healing process, but it would still take at least twelve hours. He took his eyes off the demon's wounds and looked at his face. "I will help you with this when I get back," he said regretfully; he'd rather help Zalith clean his wounds right now, but he had just over ten minutes to follow Lucious' trace.

Zalith obviously understood that. "Be careful. I'd come with you, but I'm sure I'll get a lot worse than a 'be quiet' if I try," he said, smirking.

Before Alucard could get up, Zalith struggled but sat up and took hold of the vampire's jaw in his hand. He smiled, leaned closer, and kissed his lips. Alucard carefully placed his right hand on the demon's shoulder, accepting Zalith's struggled affection. But it soon ended when Zalith sighed painfully. Alucard made him lay back down, pulled the blanket over him, and made sure he was comfortable.

"I won't be long," Alucard said, and as Zalith smiled weakly in response, he got up, made his way over to the door, and left the room.

He didn't waste a moment of what little time he had. The moment he was outside, he hurried down off the ship, beginning his search.

| **Zalith** |

Zalith sighed quietly, trying to relax. But a crushing ache lingered inside his body. Alucard's blood helped a little, but he wasn't a species of demon that could effectively use the energy from someone's blood to heal faster. He was an incubus; to heal quicker, he relied on draining someone's energy through sex and intimacy. But he was convinced that Alucard wasn't yet ready for it, and despite the fact that the last two days had been very exciting, he didn't want to ask for more and potentially scare Alucard away.

He was happy with how their relationship was developing, though. Alucard seemed to be growing a whole lot more confident with each day, and he was looking forward to seeing him overcome his shyness. The fact they were heading home soon made him a little sad, but he still had the rest of their journey to spend with Alucard, and he'd make sure to make the most of it.

As he lay there, waiting for Alucard to return, he thought about the day's events. His mind immediately jumped to Luther; Alucard pretty much admitted that he thought Luther was more attractive than Attila, and for a moment, he wondered if Alucard might have been attracted to Luther at some point, but he didn't want to give in to his possessive thoughts, so he dismissed them.

Before Boreas had emerged from the snow, he'd let himself become distracted. Alucard's continuous dismissal of his concerns about the Numen irritated him; he wanted to know why and what they all wanted from him, but the vampire refused to talk about it, and Zalith didn't understand why. All he wanted to do was protect Alucard, but the vampire was making that difficult. How could he protect him if he didn't know what it was he was protecting him from?

Perhaps Alucard would tell him eventually. There were things that Alucard had felt reluctant to talk about before but told him eventually, so he'd just have to do his best to wait and see if that would be the case with this, too.

For now, he'd lay there and try to rest.

| **Alucard** |

Alucard focused on the trace he'd picked up before Boreas appeared. It was stronger in the city than it had been back by the mountain; Lucious might still be there, and if he was, Alucard was going to have to be quicker than ever.

He made his way through Dragonspire, navigating the twisting, turning streets until he came to the front of a curiosity store. *This* was where the trace had led him?

With a confused frown, he looked around, focusing, making sure that this was where Lucious' trace actually ended—and it was. There was no doubt about it. But why? He scowled, sighed, and made his way to the store's front door. He pushed it open, stepped inside, and took a moment to look around at everything. Crystals, metals, glass, stones, trinkets, potions, books—everything an average ethos caster would want. Why? Why would a store like this be in a place packed with ethosless humans? If this place had been seen, it would have surely been burned to the ground.

A silky-blonde-haired man leaned around from behind one of the shelves, setting his brown eyes on Alucard. A curious smile spread across the man's face as he placed a box on the shelf he was behind, wiped his hands with a rag, and then made his way over to the vampire.

"Hello there," he said with a smile, holding out his hand, but Alucard didn't take it. "You are…looking for something?"

Alucard scowled as he looked the man up and down. He wasn't an angel, so he couldn't be Lucious, and he wasn't human because Alucard could sense his ethos aura. A seer, maybe? Mage? He didn't care. All he cared about was finding out why Lucious' trace ended in a store that shouldn't exist in the city it stood in.

"For someone," the vampire corrected.

"Ah, Dor-Sanguian. I watched your eyes change when you came in; see your fangs, your skin—vampire, right?"

"I'm looking for an angel—"

"Aren't we all?" the man laughed.

"Lucious."

"Oh." The man frowned, losing his smile.

"You know him?"

With a quiet sigh, the man turned around, led the way over to the counter, and leaned back against it. "Funny fella. About as tall as you, weird golden-ish skin, yeah?"

"I would imagine so."

"Came looking for uh… a lot of questionable items. Didn't pay for them, either— gave me this," the man said with a scowl, pointing to a scar on the side of his face. "What's he done to you?"

"What did he want and did he say where he was going?"

"Hmph. Dragon's blood, grim root, gold root, human parts. Looked pretty desperate for them."

None of the things the man mentioned made sense to Alucard. Combining such items made no concoction he was aware of, and it made him feel confused. What was Lucious doing?

"Where did he go?" he asked the man.

"I wish I knew. Then I'd give him a piece of my—"

"Where did he go?" Alucard snarled impatiently.

Looking at him, the man shuffled around uncomfortably and crossed his arms. "As far as I'm aware, he left the city a few days ago after taking some random street urchin. Hasn't been seen since."

"Street urchin—human?"

"Indeed."

That was all the information Alucard needed. He turned around and headed for the exit.

"Hey! Aren't you at least going to buy something?!" the man called.

Alucard stopped, looked back over his shoulder, and snarled, "No." He then left the store and made his way back towards the docks.

Lucious had taken a human, and that had to be why his trace ended in Dragonspire. He likely used the human to mask his own aura, leaving no way for Alucard to find him. The angel was smart enough to take a street urchin, someone no one would know or care to look for, so there was no point in asking around for information on the human Lucious had taken.

It seemed that coming to Avalmoor was a total waste of time. Lucious wasn't there anymore, and there was no way to find him. Zalith had been injured, and Alucard couldn't help but feel like it was all his fault. But most of all, how was he supposed to explain this to Damien? To tell him that he couldn't find Lucious? He was sure that Damien would punish him for his failure, but he was prepared. He'd failed, and he'd get what came in response to that. He just hoped Zalith wouldn't be around when that time came.

He scowled irritably and continued forward, setting his eyes on his ship in the docks. It was going to be a long journey home, and all he wanted to do was relax and make sure that Zalith would be okay. The demon was his main priority now, and he felt as if that would be the case indefinitely. He had no objections to that, though; Zalith meant so much to him, and if he had to put his tasks on hold to take care of him, then he would— no matter the consequences.

Chapter Thirty-Eight

Imprint

| **Alucard** |

Alucard arrived back on the ship just as the crewmen were preparing to leave. He headed into the cabin and set his eyes on Zalith, who was still in bed; he seemed to be asleep, but he stirred when the vampire closed the door. Alucard watched as the demon shuffled around, and when he sat up and leaned his back against the headboard, he smiled at Alucard.

"We're leaving now," the vampire told him. "I'll clean your wounds." He went into the bathroom, dampened a face towel with warm water, and grabbed two other towels. Then, he made his way over to Zalith, sat beside him, and placed the towels in his lap. "How do you feel?"

With what seemed to be a despondent look on his tired face, Zalith said, "Lonely."

"Why?" he asked quietly. He was right there with him; how could he be lonely?

"Because you were gone for so long," he replied, the saddened look still on his face, but Alucard didn't fail to detect the amusement in the demon's voice.

Unsure of why Zalith was amused, Alucard frowned strangely. "I wasn't gone *that* long."

"It felt like forever," he replied with a deep, sullen sigh.

Alucard smiled slightly. Zalith had acted purposely clingy the morning he tried to leave him to heed Ben's call, and it seemed as though he was doing it again to either embarrass him or get his undivided attention—but Alucard would give that to him anyway. He looked down at the towels in his lap and sighed quietly. "I'm sorry. I wouldn't have gone if I didn't have to."

"It's okay. Now that you and your ass are here, I feel better," he said with a smirk, forcing a look of embarrassment to appear on Alucard's face.

Keeping his eyes off the demon, Alucard pouted. "Right," he grumbled. "Anyway, I need to clean all that blood away," he said, looking at him. "Does it still hurt?" he asked as he watched Zalith pull the blanket from over his body, revealing the bloody, scorned scarring on his left side.

"Barely. Will it scar?" he asked, watching Alucard as he shuffled closer to get a better look at his wounds.

"No," he answered, glancing at the demon's concerned face. "I gave you my blood; that will stop these wounds from scarring. If I hadn't, then yes, this would have left a rather ugly scar."

With a relieved exhale, Zalith moved his hand to the back of Alucard's head, pulled him closer, and kissed his cheek. "Thank you."

Alucard couldn't keep himself from smiling but did his best to hide his face from Zalith as he picked up the damp towel and began gently dabbing the dried blood on Zalith's side. "What about your ethos?" he asked, carefully cleaning the blood from his skin. "Is it returning yet?"

"Slowly. Although I still feel exhausted. How long will I feel like this?"

"If you rest properly, you'll start to feel better around the time we reach Boszorkány. I can give you more of my blood, but... not yet. I have to heal first."

The demon smiled. "It's okay. You've done enough for me already. I'd rather heal slower if it means you're more comfortable. I'd also like to make a point of stopping in Boszorkány; when we were there last, something caught my eye, and I didn't have the time to decide whether I wanted it or not. I've decided I want it."

"What?" Alucard asked curiously, still cleaning the blood from Zalith's skin.

"Something," he said, smirking.

"Hmm...." Alucard frowned skeptically, taking a moment to glance at the demon's face, but he didn't know Zalith well enough to assume what he might be up to. So, he returned to cleaning the dried blood. "We can stop there. Drac will need to rest, anyway. We should arrive by morning."

"Okay," Zalith said, smiling.

When he cleaned the last of the blood from Zalith's side, Alucard placed the damp towel on the cupboard beside the bed and used one of the dry ones to dry his skin. Then, he stared closely at the slowly healing scars. "They shouldn't take much longer to heal," he said, glancing at Zalith, who was staring at him with a smirk on his face. "Stay in bed," he said sternly, pulling the blanket back over the demon. "I have to go and write a report and get some other things done. I'll be back la—"

"Don't go," Zalith interjected, pouting sadly as he snatched the vampire's wrist.

He was doing it again, acting clingy to amuse himself. Alucard frowned and waited.

"I miss you," the demon said sadly.

"I'm still right here."

"So? I don't want you to go."

"I have to write for Damien."

"Can't you do it in here?" Zalith asked, keeping his forced, sad tone.

Alucard slowly pulled his wrist from Zalith's grip and stood up. "No. All of the things I need are in my study and I don't want to move them. I won't be long. You need to rest, anyway," he denied and made his way over to the door, but when he heard Zalith getting out of bed, he stopped walking and glared back at him.

Zalith struggled to get up as he said, "Then I'll come with you."

The vampire didn't understand why Zalith was acting this way; he wasn't even sure anymore whether Zalith was fooling around or not. Did he genuinely not want to be left alone? Or was he still looking for amusement? Either way, Alucard didn't like seeing him struggle, so he walked back over and helped Zalith stand. "You need to rest, though."

"I can rest in your study," he said, moving his arm around the vampire's shoulders as Alucard helped him up.

With a quiet sigh, Alucard gave in. "Fine. Get dressed, then. It's cold," he said, helping Zalith over to the dresser.

Alucard pulled the top drawer open, and as Zalith took out a shirt and black sweater, he did what he could to help Zalith into them. Then, they both left the cabin and made their way along the deck, down beneath it, and towards the door to Alucard's study.

"What happened with Lucious?" Zalith asked as Alucard pushed the door open.

"I didn't find him," he mumbled as they stepped inside. He led Zalith to the couch in front of the bookcase-covered wall. "He picked up some things from a store, took a human, and disappeared. I won't be able to track him," he said, helping Zalith to lie comfortably. The vampire then made his way over to a cupboard, took a mahogany quilt from inside, and placed it over as much of Zalith's body as he could.

As he rested his head on one of the cushions, Zalith looked up at the vampire and frowned in concern. "Is there no way at all to find out where he went?"

"No," Alucard said with a sigh. "The only reason he would take a human would be to disguise his angelic aura as that of a human. The human was a random street brat that no one cared or knew about, so I have nothing to track him with, either. I'll have to tell Damien that I cannot find him—Damien will…work something out," he said, trying to convince himself more than Zalith. "Rest," he then said before the demon could utter another word. "I will get what I need to do done, and then we can see how you feel."

The demon smiled and nodded. "All right."

Alucard then made his way over to his desk, leaving Zalith to rest.

He sat down and sighed quietly as he got everything he needed to write to Damien. He took a blank piece of parchment from his desk's top drawer, and then a quill, which he dabbed in ink, and started writing. There wasn't much to tell the Daegelus, but he thought that he should mention that Boreas had shown up and been eradicated. Alucard remembered the delight Damien had expressed when he told him he'd killed Janus, so perhaps he would be just as pleased to hear another of Letholdus' children had been killed.

As he wrote, however, he could feel Zalith's eyes on him. He continued writing but glanced over to where the demon was sitting, and just as he suspected, Zalith was watching him with a smile on his tired face. Looking back down at the message he was writing, Alucard frowned and mumbled, "Stop watching me."

"No," Zalith called, smirking.

Shaking his head, Alucard tried to focus on his work. He'd have to hand-deliver the note to one of Damien's people; he'd not send it via one of his own messengers—he didn't want to risk another mishap. A sour frown clung to his face as he thought about such an incident, an incident that caused him to fear sending messages ever since. He didn't want to think about that, though.

Once he finished his message, he sealed it in an envelope and slouched back in his seat. Now that was out of the way, he could take a little time to think about what happened before Boreas—before Avalmoor. He still hadn't looked into the runes he saw appear on Zalith; he *had* to have a book in his study somewhere that might have answers. He owned so many books exploring runes and runecraft, and at least one should contain information on the patterns he saw appear on the demon.

He sat up, glanced at his bookshelves, and frowned. As much as he wanted to know, he still feared he might not like what he would discover. He was already confident that the runes weren't dangerous—they wouldn't have disappeared, otherwise. But that didn't take away the vampire's angst. What if he'd done something that Zalith would hate him for? Something that would anger him, upset him? Alucard wasn't sure, but sitting there without answers wasn't going to get him anywhere.

With a conflicted frown, Alucard stood up and made his way over to a specific shelf. There were seven differently-sized, different-length books on the platform in front of him, all of them covering the study of runes, and he'd most likely have to look through them all. He didn't know anything about the runes he saw, so how could he know which book to look through? The only thing he knew was that it couldn't be a harmful rune, but that only ruled out two of the seven books.

Alucard snatched the largest book first and returned to his desk. He opened the book to its contents page and read the long list of subjects and title pages, scowling in irritancy until he set his eyes on something of interest. '*Love*'. He wasn't sure why his eyes hovered over the word for several long moments, but as he stared at it, he couldn't help but wonder, did he *love* Zalith? The question had come to him before; he'd even thought he'd accepted it upon a time.

Was that what he felt? Was that why he cared so much? Was that why he wanted nothing more than to be with Zalith whenever and wherever he could? Was it love that caused him to feel possessive? To feel a need for his company, his attention, his *affection*.

Was it love that made him feel so nervous? Was that why he'd let Zalith come so close? Was that why he'd shown the demon so many things, told him so many things, and felt as though he would continue to do so?

Realizing that he was drifting from his chosen task, he flicked through the book, opening it to the page with information on the word he'd been staring at. But to his surprise—and confusion—the pages contained words that instantly snatched his attention once more. He found himself reading a shockingly close explanation of what he felt the moment just before the runes appeared on Zalith, and when he saw the word '*imprint*', something close to panic consumed him.

Imprint: *every demon, only once in their lifetime, will unintentionally but instinctually leave a claim on the person they're fated to spend their life with. This connection is sometimes instant, and other times takes a while to develop. The claim never happens unless the demon has felt all the following things, sometimes in the same moment.*

Trust: *it is more or less impossible to obtain a demon's wholehearted trust. But when trust is given, it may never be broken. To feel completely safe and accepted. To unquestionably give oneself to another and to feel accepted.*

Serenity: *all sense of calm, of everything right. To feel as though nothing could destroy the peace a demon feels with the person they are with.*

Possession: *often seen as a negative trait—but demons become utterly, dangerously protective of the people they care about. They won't hesitate to kill anyone or anything they see as a threat to the ones they love. And for the one they imprint on, this trait is much stronger.*

Summary: *demons will only ever imprint once in their lifetime. It occurs when a demon feels all of the above; to feel safe, accepted, possessive—to feel as though the person they imprint on is the person they would give their life to and for. When both demons imprint on each other, they can choose to seal their bond through a marriage-like ceremony. This is the only part of their fated connection that is optional.*

It has often been said in demonology that demons are loveless creatures, damned to search the worlds for eternity for something missing inside them. They search without avail, some doing so openly and consciously, others doing so without realizing.

Demonologists have not confirmed whether this might be what they search for, but it is

highly suspected that 'love' causes an imprint to occur and is what demons yearn for, to

find the one among billions that they can genuinely love. Their soulmate.

[Imprints are not to be mistaken for marks. An imprint is an instinctual, fated bond,

whereas a mark is an ethos trace that demons can leave on each other in cases where they

suspect they might be mates but imprinting has not yet occurred.]

Alucard took his eyes off the page and frowned uncomfortably. Was that what happened? Was what he was reading true? Or was it just some stupid human superstition? Who wrote this book?

He flipped the pages until he came across a small sketch of a rune—a rather *large* rune. The dread in his eyes grew thicker when he recognized what he was looking at; the snake-like rune and the caption '*disappears once applied, can reappear upon the demon's command*'.

Had he imprinted on Zalith?

The vampire flicked back to the pages he'd looked at before and re-read the explanation of an imprint. Did he trust Zalith? Of course he did. The demon had seen his scars, he'd seen the most degrading part of him, and he was still here. Zalith accepted it and accepted *him*, despite the fact that he was Disavowed. And Alucard was sure that he'd pretty much given himself to the demon the night he'd shown him his scars, too, and he felt no hesitation in doing so again—he felt no hesitation in showing Zalith who he was, what he was. He might worry, but he knew he'd tell him eventually. He didn't like to keep the truth from Zalith; sometimes, he just needed time to work out how to tell him.

Serenity? He *had* noticed a similar feeling long before they committed to their relationship. Zalith always managed to make him feel calm, and more recently, completely safe. The things he feared were mute whenever he was with Zalith…*mostly* mute. And Possession—he wasn't going to deny that he felt possessive of Zalith. The thought of anyone else so much as throwing a suggestive look Zalith's way made him angry. And he'd kill anyone that hurt him—he'd very nearly killed Attila just for insulting him.

But love? That feeling hadn't been explained very much on the pages. But surely if he felt all the things he felt, and if he had imprinted on him…that had to mean he loved him, right? He wouldn't deny that he didn't really understand what love meant, but from what he *did* know, he thought that had to be what he felt for Zalith. Demons searched for love? Alucard hadn't been looking, but Zalith had come across his path, and there they now were. When he was with Zalith, he felt complete, despite the depravity of his life.

He felt safe, he felt more alive than ever, and he felt as though there was more to his life than simply working for Damien. And the thought of losing him? It hurt the vampire so much that he felt as if he'd rather be dead than lose Zalith.

The dread, however, didn't fade because…what if Zalith didn't feel the same? An imprint was a one-time, everlasting thing, and he'd placed his on Zalith. It would be there forever, and there was nothing he could do about it. How could he live knowing he felt this way if Zalith didn't feel and hadn't done the same?

He read the writer's summary again. Were they saying that Alucard was fated to spend his life with Zalith because the demon would eventually imprint on him, too, or did it mean that he was fated to spend his life around him no matter what? But in what way? As a casual boyfriend? A business partner? Would their relationship even last? Alucard scowled despondently. Had he ruined everything by doing this? What would Zalith think if he told him, just days into their relationship, that he'd somehow instinctually decided that he wanted to be with him forever?

"What are you reading?" Zalith suddenly called.

"W-what?" Alucard stuttered, quickly lifting his head and looking at the demon.

"What are you reading?" he asked again with an amused smile.

The vampire looked back down at the book, frowned, and then glanced at him. "A…story."

"It must be an interesting, scary story. Flicking back and forth through the pages, those faces you're making," he said, laughing weakly.

Alucard sighed and closed the book. "No." He tried to forget what he'd read, but how could he? Now that he knew what he'd done…now that he knew what it meant, he wouldn't be able to stop thinking about it.

"Will you read it to me?" he then asked, faking a sad frown. "It's rather lonely over here."

"I finished," Alucard lied as he stood up and made his way back over to the shelf. "Are you…hungry or anything?" he asked as he returned the book to the shelf.

"Hungry? No. Anything? It depends on what that means."

Alucard sighed and sat beside him. "Do you want anything?" he rephrased.

With a flirtatious smile, Zalith sat up and shuffled closer to Alucard, moving his arms around him as he rested his head on the vampire's shoulder. "Other than you, no," he said, holding him tightly.

Guiding his arm around Zalith, Alucard relaxed and rested the side of his head on the demon's. He didn't have to do anything else until they got back to Dor-Sanguis, so he could focus on making sure Zalith was okay until he'd fully recovered. If there was nothing Zalith specifically wanted, all Alucard could think of was to get him back in bed where he would be more comfortable.

He glanced down at him. "Then we can go and lay down. I feel tired after having to kill Boreas—and healing you," he said with a smile.

Zalith lifted his head from the vampire's shoulder. "My saviour," he said and kissed the side of Alucard's face.

With an embarrassed pout, Alucard looked away from him. "We can stay here if you don't want to move, though."

The demon pulled the quilt from over himself. "We can go to bed."

Nodding, Alucard carefully helped Zalith to his feet and led him out of his study. "Do you want a drink or anything, though?" he asked, glancing at him. Zalith always had something to drink before he slept on the nights he'd stayed at his manor, so he thought he should ask before they got into bed.

"I'm fine, thank you."

"Okay."

Then, they made their way upstairs, heading for the cabin. The sooner they both got some rest, the better.

Chapter Thirty-Nine

— ⚔ ✝ ⚔ —

Care

| **Alucard** |

Alucard helped Zalith get back into bed, and as the demon slowly pulled off his sweater and shirt, Alucard made himself comfortable beside him. As much as he wanted to lean his head on the demon's shoulder, he didn't; Zalith's left side was still scarred and healing, and he wasn't sure whether leaning on him would cause him pain.

But *Zalith* didn't hesitate; he moved closer and rested his head on the vampire's shoulder but remained lying on his back. Alucard leaned his head aside, resting it against Zalith's, and then sighed quietly. He didn't know where to begin, but now that they'd laid down, he thought he should make sure Zalith was okay. He felt as if the demon's injuries were his fault, and he couldn't seem to let go of his guilt.

"I'm sorry this happened," he said quietly. "I should have been more aware. I knew the dragons were out there, I just didn't think we'd be taken by surprise."

Zalith moved his right arm from his side and placed his hand on the vampire's chest, looking up at him. "It's not your fault, Alucard. I should've been paying more attention, and I don't blame you in the slightest. Please don't think this is in any way because of you."

With a sullen frown, Alucard closed his eyes and tried his best to shroud the strange, confusing sadness that gripped him. He thought that what he was feeling might be relief, but why did it hurt? Zalith didn't blame him for what happened, even though he should. Anyone else would have blamed him... *Damien* would have blamed him. Now, he didn't know what to think or say. He could have done better—he *should* have done better. He wasn't even sure if Zalith had meant what he said or if he just said it to make him happy.

"I'm not angry or upset, either," Zalith added.

Alucard still had no idea what to say. He'd never been in this position; he'd never been forgiven for causing someone's injuries. What should he say? He scowled in distress and buried what he could of his face into Zalith's hair. "Okay," he mumbled; it was all he could think of.

"Are you okay?" the demon asked.

Was he okay? He was confused, but he'd not let it consume him. Slowly, he moved his left hand from his side and placed it over Zalith's. "I'm fine."

"*Are* you?"

"Yes."

Zalith pulled his hand from beneath Alucard's and lightly prodded the vampire's neck with his finger. "What's wrong?" he asked playfully.

Alucard pouted. "Nothing."

The demon prodded Alucard's left cheek.

Still pouting, Alucard tried not to react.

Zalith prodded his face again… and again, and *again* until Alucard's irritancy forced him to smack Zalith's hand away. But Zalith wasn't done yet; he instantly moved his hand back and went to prod Alucard's face once more, but Alucard snatched his hand. Zalith laughed quietly and fought with him, trying to pull his hand free as Alucard struggled to keep hold of it, and once Zalith broke free, he tried to prod the vampire's neck. Alucard, however, quickly moved to stop him but unintentionally slammed his hand onto the demon's right arm in a failed attempt to snatch his left wrist, which Zalith had been moving past his other arm to reach the vampire's neck.

As Zalith grimaced in pain, Alucard immediately moved to look down at him, a horrified look on his face. "I didn't mean that," he said in a panic. "I'm sorry."

But Zalith laughed and smiled up at him. "It's okay," he said but then smirked. "Perhaps… a kiss would make it better."

Staring at him, Alucard's apologetic expression swiftly became a nervous one. He didn't want to disappoint him, so he fought his shyness and edged a little closer to him, his eyes shifting to the demon's lips; however, he became more and more anxious with each passing moment.

The demon smiled, laughed quietly, and moved his hand to the back of the vampire's neck. He then pulled him closer and kissed him a single time before letting go. Alucard didn't immediately move away, but as he went to, Zalith pulled a fake frown of sadness. "Wait, one more," he said.

The vampire kept his nervous scowl, but this time, he managed to fight his nervousness enough to move closer. Zalith guided his hand to the back of Alucard's head to pull him the rest of the way and kissed him again.

"Wait," he said once again as Alucard moved his face from his. "Maybe… one more."

With a slight smile, Alucard moved his face back into Zalith's, and as the demon kissed him, he felt no need to pull away this time—and it seemed as though Zalith had no intention of letting him go, either.

For a few long moments, they kissed, and while they did, Alucard felt Zalith moving his right hand down over his arm, which the demon then gripped and made him place down beside him. Zalith then used his leg to encourage Alucard to move his left leg to the side of Zalith's right leg. It seemed as though the demon wanted him to straddle his lap. Would that be more comfortable for him?

"What are you doing?" Alucard asked as he rested his arms on either side of Zalith's, unsure of where else he could put them.

"Moving you somewhere more comfortable," he confirmed, looking up at him.

Alucard frowned and hesitated to rest the weight of his body on Zalith's. "But... doesn't this hurt?" he asked, glancing down at the demon's left, injured side.

Zalith smiled. "A little, but I like it," he answered. Then, before Alucard could speak another word, the demon placed his hand back on the back of his head and pulled his face back into his, resuming their slow kissing.

As they kissed, Zalith lightly bit the vampire's bottom lip. Alucard frowned; Zalith hadn't done that before, but he liked it, and it sent a shiver of excitement through him. He hesitated, however, when he felt the demon move his free hand to his collar to begin unbuttoning his shirt.

He stopped their kissing and glanced down at Zalith's hand, watching as he untied his shirt's top button. His hesitation withered, though; he wasn't so nervous anymore. With an eager huff, he returned to kissing the demon while he continued unbuttoning his shirt, the both of them beginning to breathe a little faster.

The moment Alucard's last shirt button was pulled free, the demon placed his hand on his bare skin. Alucard's excitement grew with each passing moment, but when Zalith's hand reached his left pec, the demon stopped kissing him to smirk and playfully pinched his nipple. With an exasperated snarl, Alucard flinched and snatched the demon's hand, glaring down at him. But Zalith smiled suggestively, which made him frown nervously; he let go as he looked away, trying to hide his face.

Zalith laughed quietly and placed both his hands on Alucard's body. As Zalith's hands traversed his muscles, a shiver of anticipation coiled within him. The mere touch of those teasing fingers ignited an insatiable desire that threatened to engulf his every thought. Leaning into the intoxicating proximity, Alucard couldn't help but exhale a quiet breath, a subtle admission of the smouldering heat building between them. Zalith's head found a resting place on his, the connection electric and intimate. Alucard's senses were ablaze, his excitement simmering just beneath the surface, threatening to erupt.

When Zalith's lips trailed along the curve of Alucard's neck, a surge of tension coursed through him. His body tensed with a mixture of eagerness and restraint, longing for the familiar sensation of Zalith's bite. Yet, the demon's playful tease, lightly dragging his fangs across Alucard's skin, left him yearning for more, caught in the delicate dance of pleasure and anticipation.

Frustration mingled with anticipation as Zalith's hands traced a path down the vampire's waist. The craving within Alucard intensified, a relentless ache that begged to be sated. Each deep breath and rapid heartbeat from Zalith served as a tantalizing symphony, driving Alucard to the brink of desire. His hand found its way to the back of Zalith's head, his fingers entwining with the demon's dark hair. He urged the demon's face closer to his neck, impatience seizing control; the hunger for Zalith's fangs and the sweet surrender to the demon's touch consumed him, leaving Alucard entangled in a web of lust and longing.

But Zalith didn't comply tonight. Instead of the anticipated bite, the demon's lips caressed Alucard's neck, making the vampire frown in frustration.

With a subtle shift, Zalith reclined, his fingers traversing the path to Alucard's belt. Nervous energy surged within Alucard as anticipation tinged with anxiety took hold. He averted his gaze from Zalith, hiding his anxious face as the demon skillfully untied his belt and removed it from around his waist. The demon's hands eagerly ventured into Alucard's trousers, the vampire's pulse quickening with every movement. He was sure that his face turned red when the demon's firm grip encircled and lightly squeezed his ass, but pleasure mingled with the heat of embarrassment, intensifying his eagerness.

The demon pulled Alucard's body closer to his, and Alucard didn't hesitate. He leaned forward, resting the side of his head on Zalith's as the demon slowly took his hands from his trousers and dragged them over his body once again. Alucard wished to do the same—to drag his hands over Zalith's body—but the demon was hurt, and he didn't want to unintentionally cause him any more pain.

So he waited, allowing Zalith's wandering hands to eventually reach his crotch. He frowned in struggle, trying not to utter a sound in response to his excitement as he felt the demon lightly grip the bulge in his trousers. As he exhaled quietly, his parted lips edged closer to the demon's neck; his desire to sink his fangs into him became something of an immediate desperation, intensifying as each moment passed.

His anticipation was intoxicating—his eagerness was overbearing. It enthralled him tightly as the demon continued caressing his growing arousal, and as his quiet exhales became stifled breaths ensnared with aspiration, he ignored his restraint and pressed his fangs against the demon's skin—but he didn't bite down. He wanted to, but he couldn't. Not only was he worried that he might get carried away, but he felt as if he should show Zalith once more just how it felt to be denied. So instead of biting, he kept his top fangs pressed ever so slightly against his skin, breathing deeply onto the demon's neck as he eagerly awaited what he hoped would come next.

The vampire dug his claws into the sheets, a quiet, unintentional moan escaping his breath as Zalith moved his hand into his trousers and lightly gripped hold of his dick. Alucard nuzzled his neck as each gentle stroke of Zalith's hand sent pleasure spiralling through his tensing body. The demon gripped Alucard's chin with his free hand and guided his face closer to his, and then he started kissing him.

But this time, Zalith stopped a small while after and let go of the vampire's shaft. He gripped Alucard's waist with both his hands, and as the vampire frowned, Zalith made him sit upright. The vampire sat there with a nervous frown on his face; he might have thought something was wrong, but he watched as the demon moved his hands to his own belt, pulled it from his waist, and moved his hand into his trousers.

Alucard observed both nervously and curiously as Zalith pulled his arousal from his trousers. Seeing the demon's thick, hard dick elevated his excitement; he longed to experience it, but not only was he still nervous about taking that next step, but seeing its impressive girth made him feel hesitant. He glanced at Zalith's face, and when the demon smirked at him, Alucard quickly looked away, embarrassed that he'd been caught staring.

"Do you want to touch it?" Zalith asked.

Did he? Alucard quickly took his eyes off Zalith's face and looked away, but both his curiosity and ever-increasing attraction to this demon forced him to glance back down at his shaft. He knew that Zalith enjoyed touching him, and it felt inexplicably delightful when he did. He wanted to do the same for Zalith, and he *did* want to touch him, but would his nervousness allow him to? He tried to fight through his shyness, gradually moving his right hand closer.

Zalith seemed to understand that he was struggling, though, and took hold of his hand. He then placed Alucard's palm around his dick, making the vampire grip it firmly. Alucard's curiosity was sated; he held the demon's shaft, staring down at it, eyeing all he could see. And then he glanced up at Zalith's face again, unsure whether or not the demon was expecting him to say or do something. Should he start moving his hand the way Zalith had done for him last night?

The demon kept his hand over Alucard's and began dragging the vampire's hand over his dick, just as Alucard had assumed he should. He glanced up at Zalith's face once more to see that his smirk had been replaced with a relaxed expression, and started moving his hand on his own. Alucard found delight in seeing the demon's enjoyment; he wasn't sure why, but Zalith's excitement teased him, and he found himself desiring to please the demon as intensely as Zalith had managed to please *him*. But he didn't know what to do; he didn't want to do something that might irritate the demon's wounds, or something Zalith didn't want him to do—he didn't know anything about sex or pleasing someone sexually, and as his confidence waned, so did his curiosity.

But Zalith then let go of his hand. Alucard kept hold of the demon's shaft and waited, watching Zalith as he used his tongue to smother his palm in his saliva before returning it to his dick. In his free hand, he gripped hold of Alucard's arousal and pressed it against his own before holding them both in his soft grip.

The vampire wasn't sure what to do with either of his hands now. He turned his face away from Zalith, trying to hide his pleased grimace as the demon started dragging his hand over both of their shafts at the same time. He frowned, scowled, and struggled, the excitement escaping his frantic breaths as murmured moans. Zalith didn't take long to speed up, and Alucard exhaled in delight when he did; at the same time, the demon gripped Alucard's shoulder in his spare hand and pulled him forward so that his face was just inches from his.

Their lips collided once more, a symphony of deep breaths and quiet moans orchestrating the intensity of their connection. Alucard's body quivered with an intense yearning, an insatiable desire to sink his fangs, to unleash the feral craving within. Yet, he restrained himself, resisting the urge to succumb to the primal instincts that surged within him.

Alucard quickly found himself ensnared in the intoxicating pleasure that Zalith bestowed upon him. Each frantic kiss became a dance of longing and restraint, a tantalizing exploration of boundaries. He surrendered to the intoxicating allure of Zalith's touch, allowing the pleasure to weave its spell around them.

But his restraint almost left him the moment that the pleasure peaked and became exhilarating. He edged nearer and nearer, his shaft twitching in Zalith's grip, and as sheer delight abruptly devoured him, he climaxed with a long, pleased moan, turning his face away from Zalith's. The demon groaned quietly at the same time, climaxing with him; his dick throbbed against Alucard's, and his cum, hot and viscous, trickled down the vampire's shaft. Alucard scowled in struggle as the intense rapture pulsed through him; he leaned nearer to Zalith's neck, ready to give in to his hunger, but as another, unintentionally loud moan escaped his breath, he pressed his face against the demon's skin.

He relaxed, carefully resting his body against Zalith's—he didn't want to risk hurting him, but his shivers wouldn't let him lean comfortably over the demon anymore. And then, they lay there for a few moments, calming down.

Alucard felt Zalith reaching for something, so he lifted his head and watched as he took one of the towels he earlier used to clean the demon's wounds and used it to clean them both up.

Once he was done, Zalith chucked the towel to the floor and placed his hand on the side of Alucard's face. He pulled him closer, kissed him, and then shuffled around to make himself comfortable. At the same time, Alucard climbed off him and lay beside him, resting his head on the demon's shoulder.

But seconds later, Zalith sighed sadly and asked, "When can I fuck you?"

Alucard frowned nervously at his abrupt question. He knew that Zalith would ask at some point, but he didn't know how to respond. He'd already said he was comfortable for them to move forward, and that was what they'd been doing; he just wasn't sure when they'd be moving on to what Zalith evidently desired more. But he had to answer, and he'd be honest.

Resting his hand on the demon's chest, he shrugged. "I... don't know," he said quietly. "I don't know what to do; I don't want to do something wrong or stupid."

The demon moved his hand over Alucard's. "You won't do anything wrong, don't worry; it's just anal. I can talk you through it," he quietly replied.

Alucard frowned harder. He didn't understand—of course he didn't, and it made him feel embarrassed. "What?"

Zalith smiled. "Anal," he repeated.

Still confused, Alucard scowled. "I don't know wh.... What is that?"

Laughing quietly, Zalith gripped the vampire's hand and squeezed it lightly. "Well, because we're both men, in order for us to have sex, we have to do anal, which is when someone puts their dick into their partner's ass. So, in our case, *I* want to put mine inside of yours," he explained with a sultry, amused tone.

With a perplexed frown, Alucard stared aimlessly, unsure of what to say or if Zalith even expected him to say anything. He hadn't heard that term before. But despite Zalith's explanation, he still felt confused, curious, and of course, nervous. But he'd rather lay there and listen to it be explained to him than not know what to expect when the time came—and it would come, he was sure. Not only because he knew that Zalith desired it, but because he also wanted to experience more with him.

"I'm sure it sounds strange," Zalith continued. "But it's completely normal. Some straight couples do it on occasion, too. There's a high chance that it'll hurt at first, but we'll do it slowly, and eventually, it *will* start to feel good. It's helpful, though, for you as the receiver to be relaxed when we do it—it'll hurt less that way, which is why it's important for you to be ready. Don't agree to do it just because *I* want to. Alternatively, if you want, you could do it to me."

Alucard frowned unsurely. He knew what to expect, and that relieved him of some of his nervousness, and his curiosity remained enough to allow him to speak. "We... can do that," he agreed quietly. "I don't know when, though. I don't... you tell me when."

Clearly relieved and excited, Zalith shuffled around so that they were both on their sides and hugged him tightly from behind. "All right. The next time you come to stay with me, I'm going to fuck you," he said quietly, leaning into his ear.

Alucard held Zalith's arms. "Okay," he mumbled, burying his face in his pillow to try and hide his embarrassment. It seemed as though a date had been set—he preferred it this way, though. He had time to prepare. He was sure his nervousness wouldn't leave him when the time came, but that was okay. He felt ready for it.

The vampire exhaled deeply and made himself comfortable beside the demon, who rested the side of his head on his, hugging him tightly. Tomorrow, they'd reach Boszorkány again, and then, they'd be on their way back to Dor-Sanguis. His time away from home with Zalith had been many things, but exciting above all else. He felt like there was nothing he enjoyed more than spending time with Zalith, and he hoped that, once they returned to Dor-Sanguis, their time together would continue to be just as enjoyable—and just as constant.

DEMON'S FATE
Numen Chronicles | Volume Two

DEMON'S FATE
Numen Chronicles | Volume Two

ARC THREE

†

LOVE
AND HATE

DEMON'S FATE
Numen Chronicles | Volume Two

Chapter Forty

— ⊰ † ⊱ —

Nonsensical Motives

| Alucard |

Dawn approached. The imminent ascent of the sun promised to cast its warm glow upon the tranquil morning, saturating the humid atmosphere. The sea lay in serene repose, mirroring the peaceful stillness of the skies, which, although clear, bore a subtle hue of tranquil grey. Drac skillfully guided the ship through the calm waters, effortlessly propelling it forward on this serene maritime journey.

Although he'd been awake for a while, Alucard stayed in bed beside Zalith. He was still curious about what Zalith picked up in Boszorkány, and he was half-tempted to go and peak in the box sitting on the couch; however, not only was he afraid of getting caught, but he also didn't want to stick his nose where it didn't belong. So, he'd just keep wondering.

The crewmen started running around on the deck, their footsteps echoing from every direction. They weren't far from Dor-Sanguis, and soon, they'd reach his castle docks. Their journey had been long and eventful, and despite the appearance of Boreas and the unsuccessful hunt for Lucious, Alucard had enjoyed his time with Zalith.

He lay with his head on the demon's chest; Zalith's wounds had healed, and the only mark that remained on his body was the faint trace of Alucard's bite. Zalith's bite remained faintly on Alucard's neck, too, and as the vampire dragged his hand over his neck, he glanced up at Zalith's face to see if he was awake yet.

But then a quiet knock came at the cabin's door; Zalith stirred, and Alucard grumbled irritably.

With an exasperated sigh, the vampire glared at the door. "What?" he snarled but calmed down when Zalith started stroking his neck.

When the door creaked open, a crewman leaned inside. "We're ten minutes from land, sir," he said with a frown so nervous that it looked as though he was scared he'd be killed any moment.

Alucard rolled his eyes and waved his hand in dismissal. Then, as the door shut, he rested his head back on Zalith's stretched-out arm and sighed quietly. "We should get up."

Zalith smirked in response, still dragging his fingers over the vampire's neck. "Should we? I think I'd rather stay here for a while."

"I would if I could. There will no doubt be things for me to sort out the moment I get back, and I also have to send my message to Damien. I can only contact his messengers from my castle, and I'd rather not wait any longer than I have to," he said, looking up at him.

With a sigh of disappointment, Zalith smiled and kissed the vampire's cheek. "Okay. I'm going to watch you get dressed, though," he said with a grin as the vampire sat up.

Alucard sighed, and as he got out of bed, he smiled slightly. He was still in his shirt and trousers from the previous day; he had to change, and as nervous as he felt about doing so in front of Zalith, he'd do it anyway. He went over to the dresser and grabbed a black, long-sleeved shirt. He then took a new pair of black trousers and sat back down on the bed.

He could feel the demon's eyes on him as he started unbuttoning his shirt; despite the fact that Zalith had seen the scars on his back, he still felt reluctant to allow him to see them again. Alucard despised them; they made him look weak, disgusting, and pathetic. And although he trusted Zalith when he said he didn't care, he still wanted to keep them out of sight.

Alucard looked over his shoulder, setting his eyes on the demon, who smirked at him, watching his every move. The vampire frowned uncomfortably and looked down at his lap, hesitating.

"What's wrong?" Zalith asked.

"Nothing," he answered, unbuttoning the last button.

"Are you sure? You look uncomfortable."

Alucard looked back at him again. "I'm fine," he said, turning so that the demon wouldn't see his back as he pulled his shirt off. He watched as a smile stretched across Zalith's face; the demon watched him pull his new shirt on, and once he was done, he turned his back to him once more and pulled off his trousers. When he changed into his new pair, he buckled his belt around his waist and stood up. "I'm going to go and get my message," he said, looking down at the demon. "I will... meet you on the deck soon?"

Zalith nodded. "I'll see you shortly."

Alucard left the bedroom and made his way down to his study. He snatched the letter he'd written two days ago for Damien, tucked it into his pocket, and headed back up to the deck. Zalith was waiting for him by the cabin door, dressed in a grey, long-sleeved shirt with the sleeves rolled up to his elbows, and black trousers. He smiled at Alucard as he made his way over and handed the vampire his blazer and cape, which he'd been holding over his right arm.

The vampire took his blazer from him and pulled it on, glaring at his castle as the ship drifted closer. "What do you want to do today, then?" he asked, glancing at the demon as he placed his cape over his shoulders for him.

A regretful look appeared on Zalith's face. "I have to go home for now."

Clipping his cape in place, Alucard frowned sadly. "Well...okay," he mumbled and set his eyes back on his castle. He didn't want to part ways with Zalith, but the demon had his business, just as Alucard had his. They were bound to say goodbye at some point, but it wasn't like he wouldn't see him again.

"However," Zalith then said, moving his arm around the vampire's shoulders as he stood beside him. "I'll come and get you later. Perhaps...you should pack some of your clothes, too—to keep at my house. You can bring them with you."

Alucard frowned and nervously asked, "I'm...coming to your house today?"

"Yes, if you like," Zalith said, smiling. "It's...roughly five AM right now, so I'll come back for you around noon?"

As the ship slowed in order to dock, Alucard nodded. He was nervous, of course; he knew what to expect the next time he went to the demon's house, but he didn't want to refuse. He wanted to spend more time with Zalith, and he wanted to sate his curiosity. "Okay," he agreed.

Zalith smiled contently and hugged him tightly.

When the ship finally docked, Alucard and Zalith waited while the crewmen hurried down onto the docks and secured the ship. At the same time, Drac slithered up from the water and curled up under a tree, clearly exhausted from the journey.

"I should find him something to eat," Alucard muttered as he led the way off the ship.

Following him, Zalith asked, "What *do* you feed him? Now that you've dealt with the werewolves."

"He'll eat anything the size of a man. I'll find something for him, or I could let him take to the seas for a while—but the last time I did that, he took down a fishing boat and killed a dozen or so people. He had hunters after him for years." The vampire smirked as he turned to face Zalith once they reached the docks. "Anyway, you don't have to hang around here. I'll deal with all of this unpacking and whatever, and I'll see you later."

Zalith placed his hand on the side of the vampire's face. However, before he said anything, a perturbed frown snatched his smile, and his eyes locked on something behind Alucard.

Alucard heard someone running and turned to face them, but as he did, Felix threw himself forward like a terrified child, crying Alucard's name along with a flurry of words that made no sense…even to Alucard. As Felix collided with him, gripping him tightly, Alucard snarled in utter revolt and immediately tried to pull him off.

The demon growled and snatched the back of Felix's shirt; he tore him off Alucard and threw him to the ground. But before Zalith could do anything else, Alucard stepped forward, grabbed Felix's collar, pulled him to his feet, and harshly pinned his back against the closest lamppost.

"*Taci!*" Alucard yelled, silencing him.

Felix fell silent, a horrified look on his teary face.

In Dor-Sanguian, Alucard spoke to the disgusting little man, "What the fuck do you want?!" Zalith wouldn't understand their conversation, and as guilty as that made Alucard feel, it had to be that way. Felix's Deiganish wasn't great, and it looked as though he had a lot to say—a lot he wouldn't have the Deiganish words for.

Looking up at him, Felix gulped. "B-Ben—he's gone, and-and…Detlaff—he got out, and I tried to stop them, but—"

"What?!" Alucard exclaimed. "How the fuck did—"

"I-I don't know! I-I went down there to feed him and-and-and I—"

"You know that isn't your job anymore!" Alucard snarled, a hostile, evil glare in his eyes.

Felix shuddered and shook his head. "I-I know, yes, but I made a mistake! B-but I went down there, and…and Remy was down there, and Detlaff had killed him and was eating him, and then I tried to scream for help, but he grabbed me and then it all went black!" he insisted, speaking so quickly that Alucard scowled irritably. "A-and then I woke up, and there was blood everywhere, and Remy was dead still, and Ben was gone, and so was Detlaff. So I got up, and I came out here, and there was no one—I looked around for Ben everywhere, but I can't find him, and his wife is gone, and his house is all messed up and I—"

"Shut up," Alucard snapped, letting go of his collar. He then stepped back and stood beside Zalith, who had been observing with a frown on his face. "Detlaff escaped. Ben is missing," he said in Deiganish so that the demon could understand.

Glaring at Felix, Zalith frowned in irritancy. "Again?" he asked and looked at Alucard. "It wouldn't be surprising if Detlaff took him; he appears to have an obsession with more than just you, Alucard."

With a quiet sigh, Alucard took his eyes off Zalith and looked back at Felix, who had just stood up straight, tidying his clothes. "Go to Ascuns, to the faction, and tell the Paladins to get off their asses. They can find Detlaff and Ben—I have other shit to do," he ordered. "Send a messenger to me, too. And be quick…the sun will hit the land soon," he warned, glancing back at the horizon.

Nodding, Felix turned around and scurried away, leaving Zalith and Alucard alone.

"Anyway," Alucard said with a sigh, turning to face Zalith once again. "I'll have my help wash your clothes, and you can take them back with you when you come back later."

Zalith smiled as he moved closer and placed his hand on the side of Alucard's right arm. "I want to leave them here. I'd like for us to both have clothes at each other's homes—if that's okay."

Before Alucard could answer, yet another man appeared before them, but this time, from a cloud of black smoke. He arrived behind Alucard; tall and hooded, with eyes shimmering red on his shrouded face. This was one of Damien's messengers.

"Take this to him," Alucard said as he reached into his trouser pocket and pulled out the letter he'd written last night. Then, as the man took it and disappeared, the vampire turned to face Zalith. "Where do you want me to keep them? In... my room?"

"Yes," Zalith said, smirking.

"Okay," the vampire replied, taking his eyes off Zalith to look down at the ground.

"I'll see you later, then," he said with a smile. Then, he went to turn around—

"Wait," Alucard insisted, snatching his wrist.

Evidently surprised by Alucard's abrupt grab, Zalith smiled and looked at his nervous face. "What is it?"

Alucard frowned hesitantly. He had such a wonderful few days with Zalith that letting him go now felt a whole lot more painful than he would have thought. Yes, they'd see each other again later, but the thought of spending his time without Zalith felt odd. He'd once loved nothing more than being alone, but now, that thought bewildered him. He wanted to spend as much of his time as he could with Zalith, but now that it was time for them to part, he found himself desperate to keep him close for as long as he could.

"I... enjoyed our time together," he said quietly.

The demon smiled contently. "Me too, and I'm sure there will be much more to come for us to enjoy together."

The vampire nodded. Of course, there'd be many more trips and dates; they had all the time in the world, right? They'd only be away from each other for a few hours; what were a few hours compared to forever? He didn't understand why he felt so reluctant to say goodbye, but they simply had to. And all he could think to do to show Zalith just how much he enjoyed his company... was to kiss him. And that's what he did. Despite his nervousness, despite his unbearable shyness, he leaned closer as he placed his hand on the side of the demon's face and pressed his lips against Zalith's.

Zalith seemed surprised—Alucard caught his startled expression as he pulled his face from the demon's, but Zalith quickly replaced it with a smirk. The demon then moved his hand to the back of Alucard's head, pulled his face back into his, and kissed him a few more times.

Alucard, however, felt as if one of them needed to tell the other it was time to go or they'd be standing by the docks forever, and the longer he postponed their farewell, the harder it was going to be. So, with a nervous smile on his face, he lightly pushed Zalith away and stepped back. "Go. I will see you later."

The demon smirked again. He kissed the vampire one last time and stepped back, keeping his eyes on Alucard for a few moments. Then, he turned around, created a rift in the stone wall behind him, and disappeared inside.

Watching him leave, Alucard smiled, and once Zalith was gone, he turned around and began to make his way up to his castle. He'd miss the demon over the next few hours, but he'd see him again later, and they both had work to do. He was sure things had stacked up in his absence, and he was keen to get it out of the way before heading to Zalith's house.

Chapter Forty-One

— ⟨ † ⟩ —

Correspondence

| **Alucard** |

When Alucard got to his study, he wasn't surprised to find a stack of envelopes and scrolls waiting on his desk. His butlers had already organized them, so at least he'd not waste time reading things he didn't need or want to.

As he approached his desk, the sound of clipping claws echoed down the hall, and moments later, Sabazios burst into the room, panting frantically while he made his way over to the vampire. Alucard sat down, and as he did, the hound rested his head in his lap, staring up at him while wagging his tail.

"What?" he asked, smiling.

Sabazios barked and stood up straight, watching as Alucard made himself comfortable and prepared to look through his mail.

The first stack of white envelopes was from Dirk—Alucard didn't care to read them yet. He ignored them and instead took the first scroll from the pile. He opened it, glanced at its contents—a signed partnership with another business he didn't care to know more about than he needed to—and placed it to one side. All the scrolls were the same as the first, and once he'd glanced through them all, he rested his arms on his desk and looked down at Sabazios, who had curled up at his feet.

He sighed in boredom. There really wasn't much for him to do; he had people who took care of literally everything involving his business and life. Right now, he found himself missing his old hobbies—his violin, his horses, his friends. A scowl made its way to his face; 'friends' wasn't a word he'd usually use to describe the people he used to spend time with, but he had just used it…because no other word felt right. Tobias had been his friend. There was nothing anyone could tell that man that would make him turn his nose up, and Alucard missed having such a person around—he had Zalith, but that was different. Tobias was different. He was odd, but the kind of odd Alucard seemed to appreciate.

Despite the amount of time that had passed, Alucard still hadn't come to terms with his death. He still blamed himself, he still hated himself for what happened, and he'd never forgive himself. Zalith was the only exception in his choice to remain distant from every other person around him—he'd not risk the same thing happening again; he knew that it wouldn't and couldn't with Zalith, and that was why he allowed himself to see him after he returned from his mission, and he could be no gladder that he had.

Thinking about Zalith saved Alucard from slipping into his sadness—that demon saved him from many things. But...perhaps not the one thing he had always needed saving from.

A crash of thunder broke the morning's silence—a harrowing, familiar crash. Dread smothered Alucard's face as he shot to his feet, sharply turning his head to stare at the window. He watched in horror as a bolt of crimson lightning hit the grass outside; the Daegelus appeared in the place it struck, materializing as the smoke the collision created cleared, and he slowly turned his head until his eyes met with Alucard's.

Fear surged through Alucard's body the moment he recognized the look of anger in Damien's eyes. As the Daegelus walked towards the castle entrance, Alucard moved from behind his desk; he pulled off both his cape and blazer, threw them over his desk, and waited in the centre of the room, listening, his heart racing as the Daegelus' footsteps echoed louder through the castle walls. Damien wouldn't come to him unless he couldn't express his disappointment through a messenger, and Alucard was never that lucky.

The Daegelus appeared at the end of the hallway, fixing his eyes on Alucard as he slowly made his way forward. He couldn't be as angry as Alucard had first thought; otherwise, he wouldn't have bothered using doors and hallways—he could have simply burst through the walls to reach him. But that didn't exactly relieve Alucard of his fear. He knew what was coming, and there was nothing he could do but stand there and wait for it.

Damien stepped into the room with a cruel, condescending scowl as he prowled towards the waiting vampire. "How was Avalmoor, Aleksei?"

His voice, his appearance, his ashy smell—it all cut each of Alucard's senses like a blade. All of it caused him such discomfort that he couldn't keep a frown off his face. He had forgotten his fear—his dread...the time spent with Zalith had forced him to feel as though he had nothing to worry about, as though he was free. How could he forget?

"I hear it is rather bitter out there this time of year," the Daegelus continued, stopping a few feet in front of him. "Was it bitter, Aleksei?"

He looked up at Damien. "Yes."

Damien smiled and placed his hand on Alucard's shoulder. "I have also heard it has become strangely barren. Was it barren?"

"No," he answered. "There were...a lot of people there."

"Ah, a lot of people." Damien nodded, tightening his grip on the vampire's shoulder. "And... among these people, was there not one that might have known who this boy was? The boy that my angel took—the angel you failed to bring me."

"I asked," Alucard replied. "No one would know who he was; he was just a street rat."

"Right. And *you* would know what it is like to be a rat, wouldn't you, Aleksei? Or have you forgotten that it was I who took you off the streets? The least you could do in return is ask a few hundred people if they have seen the boy Lucious took. But did you?"

Sure that Damien was waiting for an answer, Alucard shook his head. "No."

"No." Damien smiled, his ghoulish teeth glistening in the light of his study. "You didn't. And here we are... here *I* am. You make me come down here *again*," he said with a horrifyingly casual tone in his voice. "To this... disgusting little world, and to see your disgusting little face—" he snarled, snatching Alucard's jaw in his hand— "I told you... the next time you fail to do something so simple, something so stupidly easy... that I'd make sure you *never* disappoint me again," he growled, glaring into Alucard's eyes.

The vampire stared back, waiting for what was about to happen. His heart was racing, and his instincts urged him to fight, but he knew that there was no use. There was *never* any use.

Damien sighed deeply, slowly letting go of the vampire's jaw. "I don't know how many times I have to teach you the same lesson," he mumbled. Then, before Alucard could say anything in response, the Daegelus crashed the back of his hand into the right side of the vampire's face with so much force that he was flung off his feet and smashed into the wall on the other side of his study.

As he hit the wall, Alucard grunted painfully. He dropped to the floor, but before he could try to get up, Damien appeared behind him, snatched his throat, and pinned him against the bricks. He stared into the Daegelus' cruel eyes as a grin crept across his face, obviously noticing the fear in Alucard's once-vacant sights.

"What's this?" the Daegelus then asked, a curious frown on his face as his eyes wandered down to the left side of Alucard's neck.

He'd seen the slowly fading scars Zalith's bite had left, hadn't he?

"Did you have a little fight with one of your disgusting vampires? Or... perhaps—" he leaned closer, glaring down at the scars, and as a scowl of realization smothered his face, he set his evil eyes back on Alucard, "—a demon?" he snarled.

Alucard had no chance to answer. With a repulsed glower, Damien extended two of his claws and began to slowly push them into the scars. Blood oozed from the healing wounds, making the vampire grimace in discomfort, and the deeper the Daegelus' claws went, the harder he found it to remain still and silent. The moment he flinched, Damien dug his claws as deep as they could go, hissing in disgust as he glared into the vampire's eyes.

"Have you defied me on *two* accounts, Aleksei?" he asked, tilting his head to the side. "Have you been messing around with demons?"

"No," Alucard answered, trying to keep a vacant tone in his voice.

"So, where did you get these?" he asked, moving his impaled claws around inside the vampire's flesh.

With a struggled grimace, Alucard frowned. "My... contact in Avalmoor. We had a disagreement."

"And you were so pathetic as to let this happen?" he laughed, yanking his claws from the opened, widened wounds on his neck.

Alucard gritted his teeth and nodded as blood poured from the wounds. "Yes."

Damien's laughter echoed with a malevolence that sent a chill down Alucard's spine. Abruptly, the Daeglus extended his razor-sharp claws, pressing them against the side of Alucard's face just above his ear. "One," he taunted as he slowly drove his index finger's claw into the vampire's skin, blood trickling down in its wake. "You failed to bring me Lucious," he accused, revelling in the tangible pain etched on Alucard's face. "Two," he snarled, malicious intent lacing his words as his middle finger's claw dug into Alucard, a manifestation of his boss's twisted pleasure. "You were lazy," he snarled.

Staring at his tormentor, Alucard felt a cold and distressing shiver coursing through his body. He knew the horrifying ritual that would unfold, and the looming dread paralyzed him.

"Three," Damien hissed with disdain, sinking his ring finger's claw into Alucard's skin. "You're a fucking disappointment—you *disgust* me," he spat out the venomous words, dragging his claws down the side of Alucard's face and over his cheek, narrowly avoiding his eye. "I look at you, and all I see is your father; I wanted to see me in you, but all I see is him... someone I hate, someone I wish I could kill—someone I would kill if I didn't need him."

Alucard grunted in pain, wincing and struggling against the sadistic assault of the Daegelus' claws, a silent plea for mercy drowned out by the ruthless brutality of his cruel boss.

"You're incompetent," Damien growled, his claws carving a path down Alucard's neck, chest, side, and all the way to his waist. The excruciating pain engraved into the vampire's flesh as Damien's sadistic assault continued, culminating in a forceful slam of his fist against the wall beside Alucard's face. "You continue to disappoint me! What are you?" he demanded, a twisted confusion clouding his expression as he peered into Alucard's pained eyes. "Aleksei... what are you?!"

"N-nothing," Alucard replied sullenly, his sore body trembling.

"Nothing," Damien repeated with contempt. "Worthless, useless... pathetic little thing," he snarled, callously shoving the vampire to the ground. "What use are you if you can't even find one man?!"

Remaining on the floor, Alucard looked up at Damien, awaiting the inevitable continuation of the verbal and physical onslaught.

Damien shook his head, scoffing in disdain. "You disappoint me so much that it isn't even worth wasting the energy teaching you a lesson," he declared, crouching in front of Alucard. His hand ascended the vampire's shoulder, and he sighed mockingly. "The only thing that could improve you... is death," he stated cruelly. "And who would remember you? No one."

The chilling words hung in the air, amplifying the horror of Alucard's ordeal as the realization of his utter insignificance reverberated through his tortured mind. He knew that Damin wasn't done reminding him of his place, of who he really was.

Damien's snarl sliced through the air as he seized Alucard's throat, mercilessly pinning him against the unforgiving wall once more. "Find Lucious," he growled, his grip tightening with a threat that resonated through every fibre of Alucard's being. "I don't care where you have to go, what you have to do, or who you have to see. Find my angel, or you'll find yourself in another dungeon, and this time without a friend." With a brutal disregard, he tossed the vampire to the floor.

Alucard's quiet grunt accompanied the sickening thud as he collided with the ground, blood oozing from his wounds, the pain coursing through his battered body. He lay there, enduring the agony, unwilling to move until the Daegelus had departed. The weight of dread pressed upon him; he dared not rise before Damien's malevolent presence had retreated.

Listening intently, Alucard traced the Daegelus' departure through the echoing halls, marking the ominous sounds of Damien's progression into the courtyard. As the distant crash of thunder and the accompanying flash of lightning signalled Damien's departure, Alucard painfully sat up, his back leaning against the shattered, blood-stained wall. The residual echoes of torment lingered, and he couldn't shake the harrowing aftermath of his encounter with the merciless Daegelus.

Sabazios—who had known better than to intervene—made his way over, whining quietly as he set his eyes on the vampire's wounds. The hound frowned and whimpered, nuzzling Alucard's hand as he held it out towards him.

Alucard sat there, a heavy blanket of despair and dismay enveloping him, his mind echoing with the relentless mantra of his perceived worthlessness. He felt like nothing, no one—a mere vessel of inadequacy. Useless, worthless, and pathetic were the cruel labels etched into the fabric of his very existence. The throbbing of his wounds served as a rhythmic reminder, each agonizing pulse reinforcing the conviction that his rightful place was on the cold, unforgiving floor, where he lay in a state of bloody defeat.

Sabazios, ever loyal, whined again, a plea for Alucard to tend to his wounds. But Alucard knew better than to disrupt the lingering punishment Damien had inflicted upon him. The wounds were a testament to his failure, and the lesson, he believed, wasn't complete until they healed on their own.

The urge to contact Zalith and ward him away from the aftermath clawed at Alucard's conscience. He didn't want the demon to witness his pitiful state, but the weight of his despair rendered him motionless. In the recesses of his tortured thoughts, a persistent question gnawed at him—why could he never satisfy Damien? Why couldn't he demonstrate that he wasn't as incompetent as the Daegelus believed him to be?

But in the cruel solitude of his mind, Damien's words echoed with a chilling truth. Alucard believed he was truly incompetent. The inability to find Lucious, a fallen angel who should have been within his grasp, haunted him. He knew the angel's potential hiding places in Aegisguard, but his search had faltered at Avalmoor, leaving Lucious undiscovered. The weight of his perceived failure hung heavy, and self-loathing intertwined with every thought. He felt stupid, disgusting, incapable of doing anything right. The pain he endured seemed just, a deserved punishment for his perceived sins. In his own distorted view, he convinced himself that he deserved the suffering, the painful reminders, and the relentless torment that Damien cast upon him.

Chapter Forty-Two

Strategy

| Zalith |

The moment Zalith got home, he heard Varana's heels clicking down the hall. He sighed quietly and slipped his shoes off, preparing for the inevitable storm of questions. But he didn't wait for her to find him; once he took his blazer off, he crossed the hall and headed upstairs—

"Where were you?!" Varana demanded, following him up.

"I told you already," he lied, laughed a little.

"No, you didn't!" she insisted as they reached the top of the stairs.

"I didn't?" he questioned with fake surprise, heading for his bedroom. "Are you sure? Because that doesn't sound like me."

Varana's aggravated glare thickened. "Drop the act and tell me where you went! Or at the very least who you were with!"

Zalith smiled as he pushed his bedroom door open and turned to face her. "Life isn't very fun without a little mystery, V. I think I might drag this out for a while," he said amusedly.

"Why can't you just tell me?!" she stropped.

"I don't want to," he said, smiling wider. Then, he closed the door on her before she could say another word. He was admittedly disappointed that she didn't start hammering on the door because he enjoyed bugging her, but he was also relieved that she'd chosen to leave him alone.

With a quiet sigh, he pulled off his shirt and tossed it into the laundry basket. He'd had a long few days, and he wouldn't get any rest today, either. He had to go and see Margo once he was done cleaning up. But knowing that Varana wasn't going to give up on her quest to find out who he was seeing relinquished some of his fatigue; he wasn't going to give in because it was funny, and he'd continue to enjoy it for as long as he could.

He undressed and headed into his bathroom. Once he got into the shower, he stood under the hot water and stared down at his feet. He watched the water wash away the blood Alucard hadn't been able to clean from his body, and his healed wounds, which still felt a little sore, began to feel better.

Despite only leaving him ten minutes ago, he missed Alucard already. A part of him wanted to cancel his meeting with Margo so that he could head back to Dor-Sanguis much sooner, but he needed to be responsible. Not only did he need to get this Meshuga and Imperito business dealt with, but he also didn't want to spend so much time with Alucard that the vampire started to feel uncomfortable; that was the last thing he wanted.

With another quiet, deep sigh, he stood up straight and grabbed the shampoo. He washed his hair, cleaned the rest of the blood from his body, and checked his healed wounds. Once he was content that he was clean and comfortable, he switched the water off and pushed the glass door open—

The demon halted, a little surprised to see Varana leaning against the counter in front of the shower with a frustrated glare on her face.

"Can you just tell me what's going on, please?!" she pleaded angrily as Zalith walked past her and grabbed a towel. "You're making me angry!" But then her scowl turned into a confused frown. "And why do you look like a used scratching board?!" she questioned.

Zalith was certain that she was referring to the visible, healing scar on his neck left by Alucard's bite and the fading marks left by his healing injuries. He rolled his eyes and wrapped his towel around his waist. "Well, you're just being a little rude," he answered, ignoring her latter question.

"*I'm* being rude?!" she exclaimed.

"Yes," he said and grabbed another towel for his hair.

"*You're* the rude one!" the woman shouted.

The demon sighed and started drying his hair. "If you think waiting for me to get out of the shower is going to coax it out of me, it's not working, V."

She glared at him while he dried his hair and body, and when he started combing his hair, she asked him, "What if I buy you something?"

He deadpanned and put his comb down. "No."

Varana screeched frustratedly and gave up. She stormed out of the bathroom, yanking a towel off the rack in the process.

Zalith rolled his eyes again and went into his bedroom. He knew that she was going to get more sneaky with her little mission, and since Alucard was coming over later, he'd need to make sure that he kept his guard up. Not only was it fun to hide who he was seeing from her, but he also *had* to. There'd be a right time to introduce them, but that wouldn't be until he'd told Alucard that Varana was his sister, and until he'd made Varana promise not to sell Alucard out to Lucifer. But both of those conversations were going to take a while to happen, and they'd be *very* difficult.

He went into the dressing room and picked out a new suit and tie. Once he got dressed, he headed downstairs and across the main hall.

"The carriage is ready and waiting, sir," Edwin said as he stepped into the hall.

"Thank you," the demon said, pulling his overcoat on. "I'll be having a guest coming over tonight; could you make some space in my dressing room for some of his clothes?"

"Of course, sir," he said with a nod.

Zalith then left the house and closed the door behind him. He headed over to the carriage, climbed inside, and made himself comfortable. When he tapped the roof, letting the coachman know that he was ready to leave, the carriage began moving.

As it took him to the Citadel, he watched the forest and country pass outside the window. He thought about who he'd take with him when it was time to deal with the Meshuga, and he hoped that Margo and her men wouldn't hold any prejudices against them for being demons. But Margo didn't seem discriminating to him; he couldn't speak for her subordinates, though.

But his thoughts quickly shifted to Alucard as they always did. Despite getting mauled by a dragon, he'd had a really nice time; he and Alucard took new steps in their relationship, and the mere thought of it made him brim with happiness. He smiled to himself, thinking about the sensation of Alucard's intoxicating bite, the feeling of his soft skin against his, and the taste of his cum. But the latter started making him feel aroused, and he couldn't let that happen right now. So he dismissed it as best as he could and attempted to focus on what he had to get done today before heading to Dor-Sanguis to pick Alucard up.

When he arrived at the Sheriff's Office, Zalith climbed out of his carriage. The building was constructed from sturdy brick and adorned with ornate architectural details; tall arched windows with intricately crafted wooden shutters lined the front, allowing a glimpse into the bustling activity within. The entrance door, solid and imposing, was made of heavy oak, with a well-worn brass handle that had witnessed countless comings and goings. A small, covered porch offered shelter to those waiting to conduct business or seek justice, and the three men and single woman waiting outside eyed Zalith as he approached.

Zalith smiled at them in greeting and stepped into the building. The reception area featured a polished wooden desk, wanted posters, and a large map. Dimly lit by hanging oil lamps, the space exuded a vintage cosiness, and the clacking of typewriters and shuffling of papers added to the ambiance.

Sturdy benches provided seating for those awaiting assistance, but Zalith didn't sit with the men and women waiting. Instead, he headed deeper into the building until he found the sheriff's private office; it was adjacent to the lobby, reflecting professionalism with polished furniture, leather-bound ledgers, and a prominent desk.

And waiting inside was the sheriff himself. The middle-aged man was sitting behind his desk with his legs rested up on it and a cigar in his mouth. When he saw Zalith, he sat up straight and waved him in.

"On time, as always," Sheriff Reed said with an enthusiastic smile. "Margo'll be right in," he then said, gesturing to one of the seats in front of his desk.

Zalith unbuttoned his coat and sat down. "Have the Meshuga caused you any new trouble lately?"

Reed sighed and inhaled from his cigar. "It's every other day now that they're causing some kind of problem for us. Just last night, they robbed a trade ship."

"What did they take?"

"Food, ammunition, medical supplies. Everything," he said irritably.

"Well, don't worry," came Margo's voice. "They'll be out of our city soon enough."

Zalith turned his head and looked over at the door. Margo was standing there with several officers behind her, and when she shifted her gaze from Reed to the demon, she smiled in greeting.

"Good morning, Zalith," she said.

The demon stood up and said, "Good morning, Margo."

She looked a little confused. "Where are your men?"

"I'll discuss the plan with them once we've decided," he answered.

Margo nodded. "All right. Are you ready to get down to business? My men are as eager to get a plan set in motion as the council."

"I'm ready when you are." Zalith agreed.

Reed snuffed his cigar out and stood up. "I've set aside one of the larger interview rooms for us," he said as he walked past Zalith and then squeezed out the door past Margo.

They all followed the sheriff across the station lobby and into an empty interview room. As they each took a seat around the table, Margo pulled out and unfolded a map of the Royland Shipyard.

"So," she said as everyone made themselves comfortable, and she remained standing. "This is where The Rowdy Barb is docked," she said, pointing to one of the three docks. "Lucky for us, there's a lot of cover in this area, so we'll be able to get pretty close before we're seen."

"They have two spotlights," Zalith said, looking around the table at Margo's men. "One here—" he pointed to two locations on the map— "and the other here." He then pointed to an area near the shipyard gates. "The guards here have rottweilers. They're trained only to smell humans, so we can use an old elven herbal mix to disguise everyone's scents."

"Ooh, elven herbs," one of the men mocked.

There it was. The discrimination Zalith had been hoping he wouldn't have to hear from anyone but Polly. He might not actually be an elf, but humans who were prejudice to one race were often prejudice to every race other than their own.

"Shut up, James," Margo warned him.

The man went silent.

Margo then looked at Zalith. "What about Grimclaw? Won't he be able to sniff us out?"

"No," the demon assured her. "But he *will* still be able to hear extremely well, so the slightest disturbance might set him off, especially since berserkers are very volatile."

"Don't worry," Margo said, glancing around the table. "The men I have selected and their units are specially trained to deal with stealth situations."

"They won't know we're there until *we* want them to," Sheriff Reed said.

That was a relief to hear. Zalith didn't want to have to deal with amateurs. "My men will work on taking out as many of the off-ship pirates as possible, clearing us a path to get up onto the galleon. There aren't a lot of places to hide on a boat like this—" which he knew thanks to spending a few days on the same type of ship with Alucard— "so once we board, the stealthy part of the op will be over."

"You'll all be provided with rifles," Margo told her man. "As well as a sidearm. It's likely that the Imperito will hear the gunfire, but we're confident that if they *do* decide to get involved, they'll assist us."

"And then we take them out too, right?" one of the men asked.

"Two birds, one stone?" James agreed.

"We won't be firing the first shots," Margo said, shaking her head. "This op is to deal with the Meshuga; we're not yet equipped to deal with the Imperito."

"If they do decide to attack us," Zalith said before anyone could reply, "then it'll be my men's job to get you all out."

"Why can't we just gear up to deal with them all?" James questioned.

"Because we don't know enough yet," Sheriff Reed said firmly. "Zalith's been working hard to gather intel, but the Imperito aren't as easy to investigate as the Meshuga."

James scoffed. "Right."

Zalith frowned irritably but then smiled condescendingly. "By all means, if you think that you can do a better job, please, be my guest, but these people are *extremely* careful. They'd sniff you out in a matter of seconds."

For a moment, James glared across the table at him, but he decided not to retaliate and slouched back in his seat.

"What about Grimclaw?" a man who'd been silent until now asked. "How do we deal with him?"

"That's my job," Zalith answered. "I've fought many different kinds of lycan before, so while you and my men deal with the pirates, I'll keep Grimclaw off your backs."

"Are we taking him in?" Reed asked. "I'd prefer him alive rather than dead."

"I'll deliver him alive," Zalith said with a nod.

"And then he hangs, right?" James asked.

"And then he hangs," Reed agreed.

Margo then placed a folder on the table and took out several wanted posters. "These are all the members of the Meshuga that we'd prefer to take alive," she explained, looking around the table. "Of course, there are bound to be incidents, and I don't want any of you or your men putting your life on the line to arrest them. Only arrest when you're certain that you can grab them without anyone getting hurt. Understood?"

Her men nodded.

"All right. This is Jaq Franco," she said, pushing the first poster to the middle of the table.

That was when Zalith zoned out a little. The important part was out of the way, and now he just wanted to head home and get ready to head to Dor-Sanguis, but even if the meeting ended now, he still had to share the plan with his chosen fighters.

He still had a *long* day ahead of him.

Chapter Forty-Three

Hurt

| Zalith |

The day had been long, but Zalith made it through, and as he stepped out of the rift he'd opened in the wall surrounding Alucard's castle, he let out a relieved sigh. Despite his annoying morning, knowing that he was just moments from seeing Alucard banished all the discontent.

He smiled as he moved forward, glancing over his shoulder at the silhouette of the vampire's castle against the horizon. However, the dismaying scent of Alucard's blood instantly infiltrated his senses, transforming his smile into a deeply concerned frown. A foreboding shiver ran down his spine as he picked up on the unmistakable aroma of Alucard's life force in distress. All manner of dread and confusion entwined within him, casting a dark shadow over his initial sense of ease.

Without hesitation, Zalith hurried into the castle, his usually composed demeanour now tinged with urgency. The unfolding scent of Alucard's blood stirred an unsettling fear in him, the unknown circumstances surrounding its presence intensifying his worry. The air within the castle seemed charged with ominous tension, and as he ventured deeper into the darkened halls, a sense of foreboding clung to him like a haunting spectre, leaving him uncertain of the chilling truths that awaited him.

Had someone hurt him? What could have happened between the time he'd left and now? Maybe Alucard had got into a fight—more werewolves? Vampires? No…his own people wouldn't hurt him. Had the Blood of Profane turned up to avenge their fallen comrade? The demon hurried through the halls, trying to silence his worries and prepare for whatever might lay ahead, but knowing Alucard could be hurt upset him so much that he couldn't disregard his panic.

When he reached the vampire's study, a growing unease tightened its grip on Zalith's senses. Alucard's hellhound, normally vigilant, lay asleep by Alucard's desk, surrounded by the vampire's dishevelled belongings—cape and blazer tossed aside. It appeared as though Alucard had been immersed in his work, abruptly halted; a red-feathered quill rested on the desk, an unsealed pot of ink, and several unopened letters scattered about. Papers littered the floor, and even the dog, as it lifted its head, seemed to wear an expression of distress.

Zalith's worry deepened, and his gaze shifted to the right of the room, where an ominous mass of cracks marred the wall. The violent impact suggested someone had been thrown against it, and the sight of Alucard's blood splattered across the wall and floor beneath intensified the dread. Fearful thoughts raced through Zalith's mind—where was Alucard?

"Alucard?" he called worriedly.

There was no verbal response, but a subtle shuffling emanated from behind the bookcase on the other side of the room.

Instinctively honing his senses, Zalith discerned that Alucard's scent came from the source of the noise. Hurrying across the room, he rounded the bookcase, and the sight that met his eyes shattered any semblance of composure. Alucard huddled in the back corner, surrounded by a pool of blood, and a wave of horror and dismay surged through Zalith, gripping him in a tight, suffocating embrace. The demon couldn't fathom the depths of the torment Alucard had endured, and the disheartening reality unveiled before him left Zalith reeling with a profound sense of dread.

"Alucard?" Zalith asked again, cautiously edging a little closer.

The vampire remained silent, turning his head away as if to conceal what little of his face wasn't shrouded by the gloom.

"Are you okay?" Zalith questioned softly, attempting to contain the growing worry that clawed at him. "What happened?"

"N-nothing," Alucard finally answered, his voice laced with struggle and pain. "I... want you to go."

Zalith wasn't prepared to comply, not when he could sense something was amiss, not with the disconcerting sight of so much of Alucard's blood. With a despondent gaze, he carefully moved his hand closer to Alucard and placed it on his right shoulder. "Are you—"

Alucard flinched the moment the demon's touch grazed him. Zalith couldn't discern if it was due to unintentionally aggravating an injury or the vampire's startle at the sudden contact.

Swiftly retracting his hand, Zalith frowned. "I'm sorry," he uttered quietly. "Did I hurt you?"

Alucard's response came in the form of a slight shake of his head and a dishearteningly quiet, sad huff. "No."

The demon sensed otherwise; he caught Alucard's hushed gasp of pain, and the vampire stubbornly refused to turn and meet his gaze. It wasn't nerves or embarrassment this time; it was different—the blood, the haunting emptiness in his voice, and the agony threaded through his quiet breaths. "Why won't you look at me, Alucard?" Zalith asked, a tinge of sadness lacing his tone.

Alucard remained silent, keeping his face hidden, his body trembling as if gripped by an unseen chill. His stifled breaths quickened, and with a gradual turn of his head, he winced painfully.

Zalith's eyes widened in dismay. Three deep, long gashes marred the left side of Alucard's face, stretching from temple to jawline, trailing down the side of his neck, shoulder, chest, and all the way to his waist. The wounds, no longer bleeding, remained open and sore, as if freshly inflicted. Two small wounds on his neck still seeped blood— ominously positioned where the marks from the demon's bite had been.

Anger simmered within Zalith, threatening to consume him, but he fought to contain it. Crouching beside Alucard, he momentarily averted his gaze from the wounds to peer into the vampire's sullen eyes. "Who the fuck did this to you?" he demanded, the intensity of his words reverberating with a mix of concern and rising fury.

Alucard remained silent, his gaze fixed on Zalith as though words failed him— perhaps because he couldn't bring himself to speak of the unspeakable. His torn shirt was a gruesome canvas, drenched in blood, the side of his face and body beneath the clothes smeared with the crimson evidence of torment. Unhealed, the wounds bore witness to the cruel artist behind them, and Zalith, familiar with these claw marks, felt a sinking realization settle within him. He had seen the scars left by similar wounds on Alucard's face before, and he understood the vampire's reactions when Damien visited. The pieces fell into place, and he already knew what had transpired.

"Did Damien do this?"

A flicker of dread distorted Alucard's agonized face, but no words escaped his lips. He turned away, exhaling painfully.

The sight struck a dismaying ache in Zalith's heart. He longed to hold Alucard, assure him that he was safe now, promise to find the one responsible and deliver justice. However, succumbing to anger wouldn't serve Alucard's well-being at this moment. Zalith didn't want to see him suffer any longer. Despite the obvious agony, Alucard persisted in concealing his pain—a fact that intensified Zalith's distress. Alucard shouldn't bear this silent burden. He didn't deserve the torment, and as enraged as Zalith felt, he needed to let go of the anger to be the support Alucard desperately needed.

He stood up and ever so lightly gripped Alucard's arms in his hands. "Let's go," he said quietly.

Alucard frowned and glanced up at him. "What?"

"We're leaving," he said, helping the vampire to stand up. His home in Nefastus was probably much safer than here. "We'll come back for whatever you need later."

The vampire didn't fight him. He let Zalith walk him to the closest stone wall, where the demon opened a rift. Zalith's anger simmered, pleading that he let it loose, but what would he do with it? It wasn't like he could call Damien down to Aegisguard and scream at him for hurting Alucard. And in all honesty, all he wanted to do right now was focus on helping Alucard get and feel better. His fury could wait.

"Come on," he said quietly, guiding Alucard through the rift.

And then, as the rift closed behind them, Zalith led the way through the darkness, holding Alucard's hand tightly. He wasn't ever going to leave him alone again.

Chapter Forty-Four

— ⋖ ✝ ⋗ —

Attentive

| **Alucard** |

Alucard waited, sitting on the edge of Zalith's bed. The black covers were soft and comforting, and although the sunlight shone in through the windows on the walls behind him and to his left, he didn't feel its usual sting; the pain of the wounds Damien left on his face was far too painful for him to notice anything else.

It felt a lot warmer than Dor-Sanguis, and a whole lot calmer, too. The scent of bergamot and oak gave the vampire a little relief as his eyes wandered around the room, eyeing each piece of antique furniture, the light grey walls and the dark oak panelling lined along them. He sat in just his trousers, dried blood smothering the majority of the left side of his body. Close to half of it had been cleaned away—mostly from his face— and there he sat, waiting for Zalith to return with a new, clean towel to continue his work.

The sound of movement from the room across didn't startle him, nor did the sound of running water and approaching footsteps. He felt so misplaced that he couldn't seem to work out how he should feel right now; all he could do was set his eyes on the demon as he walked out of the bathroom and over to the vampire.

"I have the staff preparing a bath for us," Zalith said, sitting beside him.

He gazed at the demon, his voice held captive by the weight of Damien's punishment. No words dared escape his lips; all he managed was a solemn nod. Hours had passed since the ordeal, yet the echoes of Damien's cutting words and damning actions still reverberated in Alucard's mind. This wasn't the first time—of course it wasn't—but the difference lay in the depth of disappointment and repulsion that dripped from Damien's voice.

The Daegelus' haunting tone lingered in Alucard's ears, a constant reminder of the profound letdown he had become. He grappled with the aftermath, unsure of how to mend the shattered trust and rectify his grievous missteps. The decision to divert his Paladins from the mission to find Ben and redirect their efforts toward locating Lucious weighed heavily on him. As he sat in the aftermath of his actions, there was an overwhelming sense of helplessness, with only the hollow solace of waiting and hoping for a resolution that might salvage what remained of his fractured alliances.

"Alucard?" Zalith asked quietly as he stopped cleaning the dried blood from the vampire's body.

Snapping out of his thoughts, Alucard looked at him and frowned. "What?"

For a moment, Zalith just stared at him; the look in his eyes was heartbreakingly sad, but after a few moments of what might be contemplation over what he wanted to say, the demon banished his despondent expression and managed an attentive smile. "How do you feel?"

Alucard took his eyes off the demon and stared down at the floor. "I'm fine," he lied.

Zalith, who obviously wasn't convinced, placed his hand over Alucard's and sighed quietly. "Is there anything I can do…to make you feel better?"

"No," he mumbled.

With a sullen frown, Zalith finished cleaning the vampire's waist and placed the damp towel aside. Then, he carefully moved his hand to the back of Alucard's head and stared into his eyes. "Let me help you," he said, pulling him closer, and as the vampire hesitated, he frowned in dismay. "You should drink some of my blood so that you can heal, Alucard. These are very deep, and I don't want you to be in pain."

Alucard hesitated. He knew that Damien wanted him to sit with his wounds and suffer, so he pulled his head from Zalith's hand, looking away.

"Please," Zalith pleaded, sounding almost distressed.

Alucard stared at the floor, his conflicting thoughts beginning to overwhelm him. He didn't want to remain in pain—it was agonizing, exhausting, and he felt as if he'd pass out at any moment. But he held on because he knew that it was what Damien wanted. To drink Zalith's blood and heal faster would be to defy Damien, and he didn't want to do that—not again.

But the pain…he *could* sit there and bear it, and as much as he wished not to defy Damien, his wish to take away *Zalith's* pain was greater. The demon didn't like seeing him suffer—he knew that. Not only did he know that, but he could feel it. Ever since he imprinted on him, he'd been able to feel what Zalith felt whenever he wanted to know. Right now, he could feel the demon's anger—his quiet, simmering anger—but it wasn't aimed at him; he could feel his distress, sorrow, and pain, and he didn't like it. He didn't like knowing that *he* was causing Zalith such distress. And it was because *he* was suffering. It was because *he* didn't want to heal faster because *he* didn't want to let Zalith help him. But he would…because how Zalith felt mattered to him more than anything else ever would.

Alucard slowly took his eyes off the floor and set them back on Zalith. Hope glimmered in the demon's eyes, and Alucard knew it was because he thought he may have changed his mind. He had.

He moved a little closer, as close as his aching body would let him, and allowed his eyes to wander down to Zalith's neck. The thought of his blood, the idea of relieving his pain, and the thought of banishing Zalith's sadness—it all encouraged him. His fear of Damien lingered, but his concern for Zalith outweighed it. And so, he slowly moved his left hand to the back of Zalith's head, and as the demon tilted it to the side ever so slightly, Alucard moved his face closer until his lips were but inches from his skin.

But then he hesitated. What if Damien showed up again soon enough to see that his wounds had healed faster than they should? Did he want to risk that? He'd have to…because he couldn't resist biting down as Zalith placed his hand on the back of his head and pulled him closer. He slowly sunk all four of his fangs into the demon's neck, and his aching body began to relent the moment Zalith's blood touched his tongue; as the euphoric high swallowed him, he lost all sense of pain and worry.

Zalith exhaled in both relief and satisfaction. He took his hand off the back of Alucard's head and lightly gripped his throat, making Alucard frown as he swallowed the demon's blood. He wasn't sure if Zalith was holding his throat to ensure that he didn't take too much, or because he liked feeling him drink him. Either way, it didn't matter right now. The demon's blood quickly consumed him, blessing him with a high so pleasing that he exhaled quietly in delight.

Alucard smiled in contentment as he pulled his fangs from Zalith's neck. He licked the blood from his lips, exhaling deeply as he let the contentment ensnare him tighter and tighter, and as he lost himself, the words, "I love…" slipped from his mouth, the high swirling around inside his head. He caught a glance of Zalith's face through his distorting vision, and what looked like a stare of *dread* clung to it…why? Alucard couldn't focus enough to wonder for long. "I love your blood," he drawled with a content sigh. Then, he laughed quietly and rested the side of his head on Zalith's shoulder.

The demon's look of dread faded as he smiled, moving his hand to the back of Alucard's head. "You do?" he asked with a smirk, caressing the vampire's hair.

Closing his eyes as he relaxed, Alucard nodded slowly. "It tastes…different. I like…that it's different—that *you* are different. Everyone else is…the same. All the people I've met and ever will meet are the same. But not you," he mumbled, moving his arms around the demon to hold him tightly.

"You're right," he said confidently, glancing down at him. "I am rather unique, aren't I?" he laughed, and as the vampire lifted his head to look at him, he smiled. "As are you." He kissed him, and then he shuffled to the pillow end of his bed; he pulled the vampire with him as he fell back, and once they lay side by side, the demon stared into Alucard's ice-blue eyes and placed his hand on the side of his face.

Alucard stared at Zalith; he could feel the high from the demon's blood already waning. He wasn't sure how long it might last, but he'd bask in it for as long as he could. His body had stopped aching, his wounds were slowly healing, and his sadness left him.

But it wasn't just the high that did that for him; being with Zalith helped him forget the depravity, and he felt as if there was nothing that could or would ever take that from him. He shuffled closer, resting his forehead on Zalith's as he closed his eyes and relaxed as well as he could; he could lay there with him forever.

"Sir, your bath is ready," the butler suddenly called.

Alucard opened his eyes and exhaled quietly.

"Thank you, Edwin," Zalith replied, keeping his eyes on the vampire, their gazes locked. Once the butler left, he tucked a strand of the vampire's hair behind his ear. "Do you want to stay here instead?"

"No," he said as he sat up. A bath sounded relaxing, and he felt as if it would help with his wounds. So, despite the nervousness that he felt about being utterly naked in front of him again, he got out of bed and waited for Zalith to get up and lead the way.

With a devious smile, Zalith got up, took hold of Alucard's hand, and led him towards the on-suite.

Alucard followed him inside, and as Zalith shut the door behind them, he took a moment to glance around. The marble floors sprawled beneath in an elegant dance of black and white, adorned with subtle touches of gold that shimmered near the claw-footed quartz bathtub to the left.

Opposite the bath, a vast wall stood adorned with a large, arched window that framed an artful view of the surrounding forest. Mirrors, grand and reflective, graced each corner on the right side of the room, each paired with a white basin below. The countertops mirrored the style of the flooring, seamlessly tying the elements of the room together.

Between the mirrors, a glass door beckoned, leading into a shower, and another led to the rest of the bathroom. Adjacent to this portal, a small cabinet nestled discreetly, presenting an assortment of black towels of various sizes and two plush bathrobes. The meticulous arrangement of the space unfolded before Alucard, a blend of opulence and functionality, casting an impression of both refinement and comfort.

The room was lit with both the afternoon light and the orange glow from the white candles lined around the place. But as elegant as the bathroom was, Alucard's focus was quickly stolen by his nervousness. He wasn't sure whether Zalith was planning to live up to what he said two nights ago; the demon told him that the next time they were at his house, they'd have sex, and he wasn't exactly confident for that to happen right now. *Was* that what was happening?

When he heard Zalith undressing behind him, he looked over his shoulder and set his eyes on the demon.

Zalith smiled at him as he pulled his clothes off. "What?"

Alucard looked away, trying to hide his nervous, embarrassed face.

Once Zalith was done undressing, he moved closer to Alucard and wrapped his arms around him. He then rested his chin on the vampire's shoulder and glanced up at him. "Are you okay?"

"I'm fine," he answered, and as his response prompted a smile to appear on Zalith's face, he looked away once again. His anxiety increased when Zalith began to unbuckle his belt for him, but he let it happen—his trousers needed to come off anyway.

Once Zalith pulled his belt from his waist, Alucard took off his trousers and shyly stared ahead, unsure of what to expect next as he stood there with nothing but his crucifix around his neck.

Zalith placed his hands on Alucard's shoulders and escorted him towards the bubble and water-filled bathtub. The vampire hesitated and frowned as he glanced back at Zalith, unsure of what was coming next.

"Are you sure you're okay?" Zalith asked, something of an amused smile on his face.

Alucard nodded and climbed into the bath; Zalith followed, and as he sat at the right end of the tub, he lightly gripped Alucard's arms and turned him around.

"Come here," the demon said as he leaned back and relaxed; he pulled the vampire closer so that he could lean his back against his body, and as Alucard rested his head on Zalith's shoulder, the demon smiled down at him.

But Alucard couldn't shake his nervousness.

"What's wrong?" the demon asked.

"I'm fine."

"You look uncomfortable."

"I'm not," Alucard said with a pout.

"Then why are you making a face?"

With an uncomfortable shuffle, Alucard shrugged. "I don't..." he hesitated.

"You don't... what?"

Still pouting, Alucard scowled in struggle. "You said... that the next time we come here, we... I don't—"

Zalith laughed quietly and hugged him. "I just want to have a relaxing bath with you, Alucard. I'm not going to ask you to have sex with me," he said and kissed his head.

Alucard felt like an idiot. He'd been so nervous for no reason. He was still anxious to be seen naked but not as nervous as he had been when he was expecting Zalith to initiate sex. But now, he knew that wasn't what Zalith was aiming for, which relieved him. He calmed down and relaxed, trying to enjoy his time with Zalith in the bubble bath as much as his wounds would allow him.

Still hugging him, Zalith rested the side of his head on top of Alucard's. "You're so cute," he teased.

Pouting, Alucard glared at the bathroom door. "Whatever," he grumbled.

"Your pretty face," he said with a smirk, prodding the vampire's right cheek with his finger. "And your beautiful hair."

Alucard mumbled quietly in response and rested the side of his face on Zalith's shoulder once more, staring at the wall opposite them. "My face isn't pretty right now."

Zalith sighed as he started fiddling with his crimson hair. "Your face is always pretty, Alucard," he said, smiling. But then he firmly asked, "Are you going to tell me what happened?"

The vampire remained silent. He didn't want to tell Zalith what happened; if he told him that Damien had done this to him, he was sure that Zalith would start to piece things together, things Alucard wasn't yet ready for him to piece together. He felt awful about leaving him in the dark—he didn't like lying to him, hiding things from him...but he couldn't force himself to be ready to talk about something just to satisfy Zalith. As much as he cared for him, as much as he wanted to make him happy, he just couldn't speak of *that* yet. So, instead of speaking, he sat there, staring at the wall, trying to keep himself from sinking into his sadness.

"If you really don't want to tell me about it, it's okay. I just want to know if you're in any kind of danger or not," Zalith said quietly, worry in his voice.

"I'm not...in danger," he said, glancing up at him.

Zalith frowned. "That doesn't sound at all convincing."

"I'm not," he irritably repeated, glaring ahead at the bath taps. "I'm fine." He *was* fine. He wasn't in danger—Damien might hurt him, but he'd never kill him...would he? He frowned, distress and confusion starting to consume him. He didn't want to think about it—he didn't want to remember. With a distressed sigh, he turned his head and glared over at the door. "I'm not in danger," he repeated, but he was sure that he wasn't only trying to convince Zalith, but himself, too.

The demon, however, laughed quietly and hugged him once again. "That's all I wanted to hear," he said, but Alucard knew that he wasn't very convinced. The demon then sighed and rested the side of his face on Alucard's. "I'm sorry if my desire to help you is annoying; you're just very special to me, and I want to do whatever I can to make sure you're safe," he said softly.

Alucard relaxed and sighed quietly. "It's not annoying."

"Good," Zalith said, smirking, "because I'm not going to stop."

Glancing up at him, Alucard smiled slightly before looking back at the wall.

The pair sat in the bath for a long, relaxing while. Alucard enjoyed the warmth of the water and Zalith's body; he began to feel a lot better than he had before, and he let himself relax so much that he started to drift off to sleep.

But when the last of the bubbles began to wither, Zalith sighed quietly and looked down at the vampire. "I think we should get out now. I have some of my clothes over there that you can borrow," he said, glancing at the basin countertop, where two sets of clean clothes were folded. He then reached over to the cabinet close by, took one of the towels off, and offered it to Alucard.

The vampire took the towel, and of course, he hesitated shyly for a moment, but he pushed his nervousness aside and stood up, wrapped the towel around his waist, and stepped out of the bath while Zalith watched his every move with a devious smile.

Zalith grabbed a towel for himself; he stood up, wrapped it around his waist, and followed the vampire over to the basin.

Alucard glanced into the mirror, eyeing what he could see of Zalith through it; he watched the demon take off his towel to dry his legs, but when Zalith glanced over at him, Alucard looked away and tried to hide the fact that he was watching. But after a few moments, he looked into the mirror again and saw Zalith put his trousers on. He looked at the clothes Zalith had said he could borrow, and while the demon was distracted pulling his belt on, Alucard swiftly grabbed the trousers and put them on.

Once he buckled his belt, Zalith began drying his hair with a different towel. But as Alucard looked at him again, the demon moved closer, carefully gripped the sides of his arms, and pushed him back against the countertop. He then placed his hands on either side of the countertop behind Alucard and leaned closer. "I see I'm not the only one with a staring problem," he said with a grin, gazing into the vampire's confused eyes, watching as his confusion became embarrassment.

Alucard turned his head and looked away, trying to hide his flustered expression. But Zalith lightly gripped his jaw in his hand and turned his head back to face him. He then kissed the vampire's lips, pressing as much of his body as he could against Alucard's.

After a brief hesitation, Alucard summoned the courage to defy his nerves, trailing his hand up the demon's damp body. Gently pushing him back, he stared at Zalith's face, his gaze intense and fixated. Despite the dismaying events that had transpired, one undeniable truth persisted—his focus was solely on Zalith. The enigma of his profound connection and undeniable attraction remained elusive, but in this moment, all that mattered was the proximity of their bodies.

His hand, having traversed Zalith's chest, glided to the side of his neck. Alucard's eyes wandered every contour of Zalith's face, an alluring force drawing his attention. He found himself unable to maintain prolonged eye contact, the intensity inducing a welcomed nervousness. Yet, as Zalith leaned in for a kiss, a smile graced Alucard's lips, and he moved his hand to the back of the demon's head.

Their lips met once again, and as their tongues entwined, Zalith's right hand descended along Alucard's body, eventually reaching his crotch. A surge of excitement and trepidation coursed through him as the demon's firm grip seized his bulge. Alucard frowned anxiously, tilting his head in a mixture of anticipation and curiosity, while

Zalith's kisses traced a path down to his neck, his hand venturing into the confines of his trousers.

Zalith didn't seem to want to waste any time at all. He swiftly kissed his way down the vampire's body, and as Alucard exhaled in aspiration, the demon got onto his knees, pulled Alucard's arousal out of his trousers, and took hold of the tip of his dick in his mouth. Alucard sighed deeply, moving his hand to the side of Zalith's face as he tilted his head back and hummed pleasurably. His body started to tense when Zalith slowly took each inch of his shaft into his mouth and throat, but as pleasure surged through his body, his wounds began to ache.

With a conflicted frown, he glanced down at Zalith, observing as the demon pleasured him. He gripped a fistful of Zalith's hair in his hand, a struggled, hushed groan escaping his breath while he lifted his head to stare at the ceiling. He didn't want to tell him to stop. Each stroke of his tongue sent a shiver of delight through his aching, trembling body, and the pleasure quickly outweighed the pain.

But that was when the bathroom door abruptly swung open in a violent motion, followed by an estranged, victorious, "Hah!"

Alucard—who didn't recognize the voice—with a look of startlement on his face, sharply turned his head and stared in horror at the black-haired, crimson-eyed woman dressed in a scarlet, off-shoulder dress standing in the doorway with a wide, proud grin on her pale face—a grin that quickly contorted into a look of horror much like Alucard's.

She set her eyes on Alucard, ignoring Zalith, who had stopped and turned his head to glare at her with a, "Do you fucking mind?!"

"You!" she accused, pointing at Alucard, who stared back in utter confusion.

But before she could say anything more, Zalith sprung to his feet and slammed his hand over the woman's mouth, silencing her. Then, without a word or even a glance at the vampire, he dragged the woman out of the room and pulled the door shut, leaving Alucard alone.

Chapter Forty-Five

Varana

| **Zalith** |

Zalith pulled Varana over to the spacious linen closet beside the bathroom, shoved her inside, and slammed the door behind him. She instantly tried to push past, flailing her arms, hitting him, trying what she'd like him to think was her best to move him out of the way so that she could escape.

"Would you move?!" she insisted. "I have to tell my—"

"You're not going to be telling anyone anything," he interjected sternly, glaring at her.

With a huff of irritancy, she scowled at him. "Be quiet and let me past!" she insisted, once again trying to squeeze past him and get to the door.

He knew that if she really *did* want to get past him and leave the room, then she could do so very simply and without the show she was putting on. He knew that she enjoyed the attention she was currently getting, and a part of him entertained the idea that perhaps she'd grown a heart while he and Alucard were out at sea. But it was most likely…no, it was *certainly* the former.

She continued trying to get past him, and he didn't know what to do. He didn't want to threaten her, but he might have to; he couldn't let her inform Lucifer of Alucard's location…his identity, even. He wouldn't risk that. It wouldn't bode well, but he didn't have much of a choice in this case.

Varana stopped flailing her arms and hitting his body and tried to *climb* over him as if he were some sort of shelf.

With an irritated grunt, he pushed her off—

The woman screeched in frustration and yelled, "What the hell is wrong with you?! Let me through!"

"I'm *not* letting you through, Varana," he denied.

As the look of anger in her eyes grew into something furious, she gritted her teeth in revolt. "You don't even know whose dick was in your mouth! Shut up and let me do my job!"

Zalith grimaced in annoyance. "Do you really think we'd be in this closet right now if I didn't know what was going on?"

Varana blinked in bewilderment. "Is *this* why you wouldn't let me meet him?!" she exclaimed, her voice shrilly and confused.

In response to her loud, irritating voice, Zalith closed his eyes and sighed quietly. "I need you to calm down so that we can talk about this," he said, opening his eyes again to look at her angered face.

She clearly didn't care about what he had to say. She snarled quietly and pushed him with enough force that he was moved away from the door, but before she could reach it, Zalith snatched her arm, and as she struggled and yelled, he pushed her back to where she'd been standing. Varana screamed in anger and frustration and lifted her hand to slap his face, but he snatched her wrist before she came close. Her anger was now something catastrophic, and surely enough, she'd soon put up more of a fight. But she stood there, seething, panting, exhaling angrily through her gritted teeth.

"Are you ready to talk?" he then asked.

With yet another nasty snarl, Varana abruptly sunk her teeth into his hand.

Zalith had no patience left. He snarled and pulled his hand from the grip of her teeth; he then grabbed her shoulders and harshly slammed her back against the closest wall with such force that the room shook, causing dust to float down from the ceiling. He kept his hands on her shoulders, keeping her against the wall, an angered glare in his eyes as he glanced at his hand. His knuckles were bleeding as a result of yanking his hand from her teeth. He scowled in irritancy but then set his eyes on her.

"Look into my eyes and listen to me *very* carefully, Varana. I don't care how long you and I have known each other, and I don't care about what your father told you to do. If you do anything to endanger Alucard, believe me when I say that I will hurt you irreparably," he stated.

Varana stared back at him, a look of both shock and heartbreak on her frustrated face. As she stared, waiting for anything else he might have to add, tears began to spill from her crimson eyes. "So, I'm just supposed to turn my back on my family?!"

"Am *I* not your family?" he asked calmly.

She pouted angrily and took her eyes off Zalith to glare at the door behind him, a look of pondering on her face.

"You have to promise me, Varana," Zalith said.

Taking her eyes off the door to look up at him, she scowled in discontent. "Ugh, God," she uttered in revolt. "Wait…did you imprint on him?"

"No."

She scoffed. "Well, you're certainly acting like you did—"

With a tired sigh, Zalith kept his hands on her shoulders. "Can you just promise me, Varana? Please."

Taking another moment to ponder, she glared down at the floor beneath them. A sour look plastered itself to her face, but after a few moments, she looked up at him again. "Why do you even like him so much?"

Zalith smiled. "Because he fills my heart with joy."

Disgusted, Varana rolled her eyes. "Eugh…. He's really *this* important to you?"

"He is *extremely* important to me."

One last time, she took her eyes off Zalith and glared to her right. He watched her sour frown fade into a sad one, and she set her eyes back on him and stubbornly said, "Fine. I won't tell my father."

Relief washed over him, but he wasn't ready to let Varana out. "What about your sister?"

"What about her? Are you fucking her, too?"

He rolled his eyes, not at all in the mood to answer her ridiculous question. "Are you going to tell her about Alucard?"

Varana frowned in defeat. "No."

He didn't believe her; he knew too well that she told her sister *everything*, and this was one thing he had to make sure she didn't tell her. "*Are* you?"

"No!" she insisted angrily.

"Good. What about your ridiculous goblin of a younger brother?" he grumbled with revolt—even the thought of Detlaff made him angry.

She shared the same look of disgust. "No," she mumbled.

He took his right hand off her shoulder and held it out to her so that she could shake on their deal. "You have to promise me, Varana."

With a roll of her eyes, she irritably placed her hand in his and sighed. "I promise."

For now, he could say he was satisfied. He knew that he would most likely have to have this conversation with her a few more times later on, but for now, he felt it was at an end. He took his grip off her shoulders and stepped back. "Thank you."

Tears instantly burst from Varana's eyes as she flung herself forward and hugged him as tightly as she could.

He sighed unenthusiastically and hugged her in return.

"I'm sorry I bit you," she mumbled sadly as she stepped back to look at him.

"No, you're not."

She nodded. "I know."

He then smiled, a little amused.

Varana frowned strangely. "You know, for a moment, I thought you were with my father. I wouldn't put it past you, though."

With nothing to say in response, Zalith stepped back. "I have to get back, V," he said, reluctant to leave Alucard alone for a moment longer.

"Okay," she said with a sad little frown. "Will you introduce me to him *now*?"

He deadpanned. "Varana," he grumbled.

She glared up at him with an insistent glower on her face. "Please?!" she asked loudly. "It's the least you could do!"

Zalith was reluctant, but the fact that all of this was very clearly not easy for her seemed to make him feel as though he should be a little lenient. So, he sighed and said, "Fine," and as she grinned, he rolled his eyes and turned around to open the linen closet door. "Be nice," he warned, glaring back at her as he began to lead the way.

She smiled, following beside him.

He was certain that Alucard was going to be extremely pissed off. He knew just as well as the vampire did that Lucifer's other children were probably the biggest threat to his existence, and Zalith was living with one of them. But he'd try his best to explain that Varana wasn't like Detlaff—she wasn't going to sell him out.

But that wasn't the only thing worrying him. Earlier, before their bath, Alucard said two of the three words that Zalith dreaded most. '*I love*'. Zalith wasn't sure if Alucard really was going to tell him he loved him, but it felt like he was, and it brought pain to his heart. Did *he* love Alucard? Yes, he did—without a doubt. But he wasn't ready to say it, nor was he ready to hear it, either. His track record with love and relationships wasn't great, and he still feared he and Alucard might be headed down the same road he'd been to thousands of times before.

He'd try his best, though, to focus on the here and now. Things were about to get intense… and he needed to prepare for that.

| **Alucard** |

Alucard sat on the end of Zalith's bed in the clothes the demon had given him, fiddling with his crucifix while he waited for him to return. He was convinced that the woman who burst into the bathroom was the same woman Zalith told him he lived with, the same woman he'd heard twice muttering to Zalith about *him*. He wasn't sure what might be going on right now, but he was pretty sure she was trying to convince Zalith to let her meet him again. Why did she want to see him so badly? Was he missing something here?

When the sound of approaching footsteps snatched his attention, he took his eyes off the wall he'd been staring at and instead watched the door, waiting for it to open. Zalith was coming, and he wasn't alone. The door opened, and in came Zalith with his estranged woman-friend at his side, who immediately set her crimson eyes on Alucard.

The vampire stopped fiddling with his crucifix and stared at them both.

"I figured it's about time I introduced the both of you," Zalith said as he led the way over to Alucard. "This is Varana," he said, looking down at the vampire and then back at the woman.

She smiled so very sweetly—so much that it looked fake. "It's nice to meet you," she said, staring down at him.

Alucard glanced at Zalith, who didn't look the least bit happy. He then set his eyes back on Varana and frowned. "Right…" he said, unsure of what he should or even *wanted* to say. He was already confident that he wouldn't like this woman; seeing her up close, and her previous entry into the bathroom… and there was just something about her that told him he'd dislike her, that he should do his best to keep away from her. He wasn't sure what it might be—instinct, maybe—but he'd not let it cause this situation to boil into something else.

"And… you," he replied.

Varana's kind smile soon faded into a disgusted frown as she eyed the vampire's wounds. "What happened to your face?" she asked rudely.

With an exasperated sigh, Zalith grabbed the woman's shoulders. "Okay," he said, escorting her over to the door as she tried to escape his grip. He then pushed her out of the room and closed the door behind her before she could try and get back in.

"Idiot!" she yelled from outside before storming off down the hall.

Zalith then huffed as he turned around and made his way over to Alucard, who watched him closely. "I'm sorry for all of this," he said quietly. When he sat beside Alucard, he frowned and placed his hand on his left thigh. "We need to talk about her."

Alucard, who didn't know what to say or think, waited.

"I regret not telling you earlier, and I'm sorry I left it so long, but… Varana is actually your sister," he revealed, watching Alucard's face for a response.

The vampire felt a nauseating concoction of confusion, anger, anxiety, and worry surge through him. His *sister*?

"She isn't your sister biologically, but she is through *ethos*, in the same way that Detlaff is your brother," the demon continued slowly. "She also has a twin sister, Ysmay. But she won't be any trouble. Varana is harmless; she and I have known each other for centuries, and I trust her completely. If you want to talk to her, then you can—and again, I'm sorry it took me this long to tell you."

Staring at him, Alucard couldn't figure out how he should react. He wasn't completely astonished about the fact another of his technical siblings had revealed themselves; thanks to Detlaff, he already knew that he had two sisters out there somewhere. What *did* perturb him was the fact that one of them was living under the same roof as the single person in his life whom he trusted without question. It felt like an unnecessary coincidence—or was it? There *was* the possibility that Damien had made him work with Zalith because he knew that this demon lived with one of Lucifer's ethos children, a creature that posed a significant threat to him. Had this been some sort of game for Damien?

He took his eyes off Zalith and glared down at the floor for a few moments. Whether this was a coincidence or because of Damien, he'd probably never know, and he couldn't sit there and try to work it out. Zalith should have told him the moment they started growing closer, but he hadn't, and Alucard wasn't yet sure what to make of it. Perhaps Zalith just hadn't found the right time, maybe he was hesitant, or maybe he simply forgot. Whichever it was, once again, Alucard wouldn't sit there and try to work it out. Zalith had told him *now*; at least he hadn't waited until Varana found him alone and began something he dreaded might one day happen.

Was he safe here? That woman had seen his face, she'd most likely heard his name, and it would take her but a second to tell Lucifer. He stared at Zalith, still unsure of how he should react. His eyes shot to the door—it would take a mere moment for her to tell Lucifer, a mere moment for his somewhat comfortable life to become hell. And it would take but a moment for him to silence that woman forever. But... could he do that? Would he do that? She was very clearly important to Zalith, so important that Zalith was in front of him right now trying to convince him that she didn't pose a threat.

Once again, he set his sights on Zalith. If he stayed here, there was a chance that woman would tell Lucifer where he was. If he left, that woman would still reveal his identity to Lucifer. If he eradicated her, Zalith would never forgive him—that much was clear. Zalith might be convinced that she'd not inform Lucifer, but Alucard was *not*. He knew how much of an influence Lucifer had over his followers, his children, his creations. They physically could not defy him, lest they suffer—a safety measure he'd crafted into them after all the mistakes he made with Alucard. Would Varana really endure the pain that would come if she defied her father? Did she care about Zalith *that* much? Alucard wasn't convinced.

He stood up—he thought he might leave, but then he stopped before he could move, his confliction so overbearing that he had no idea what to do.

Zalith stood up with him and placed his hands on his shoulders. "She's barely loyal to Lucifer at all," he tried to convince him. "I honestly and truly believe that she isn't going to say or do anything, Alucard," he said sternly as he stared into Alucard's confused, conflicted eyes. "If it helps, we can talk to her—if there's anything I can do to help assure you, please tell me."

Staring at him, Alucard finally found his voice. "I... don't want to talk to her," he denied, taking his eyes off Zalith's face as he gripped his arms and tried to pull him off, but the demon wouldn't let go.

"I'm sorry I didn't say anything sooner," Zalith repeated, but with a saddened look on his face. "There was never a good time. I understand if you're mad at me, but if I weren't confident in what I've just said, then I wouldn't have you over here with her around."

Alucard slowly set his eyes back on the demon and frowned unsurely. He knew that Zalith wasn't an idiot and definitely wasn't stupid enough to expose him to one of Lucifer's children if he really didn't trust that she wouldn't tell Lucifer where he was. He trusted Zalith, but his confliction would always linger. He felt he could set it aside, though, for the sake of Zalith and for the sake of what he felt for him. If that woman was going to tell Lucifer, she would have done it by now, and Lucifer's ugly little henchmen would already be busting down the door to get to him. *They weren't.*

He looked down at the floor and scowled. "I don't know why you couldn't tell me the first night she made herself known," he said, slowly looking back at him. "Or when Detlaff told me I had sisters or any other time I spoke about Lucifer and the Numen *and* their children."

Zalith sighed regrettably and moved his hand to the back of Alucard's head. He rested his forehead on Alucard's and said, "Because I was afraid. Before, I was scared that you might take it awfully and leave, and that you'd never want to see me again. I didn't want it to cause us to lose each other."

The vampire stared at Zalith's distressed face. He still didn't know what to do, what to say, where to go—he *was* frustrated that Zalith hadn't told him before and waited so long to tell him that he shared a house with someone who posed a great threat to him. Zalith couldn't have been completely sure that she wouldn't have told Lucifer where he was, and that angered Alucard. But what could he do? Zalith clearly liked to think he knew what his friend would and wouldn't do, but Zalith didn't understand how Lucifer worked—he didn't understand how deep that creature dug his claws into all of his children. Alucard had barely escaped, and that was because he was only half of his father. Detlaff and his sisters were utterly Lucifer, and there was no way they could escape him.

But what would be the point in telling Zalith that? What would be the point in trying to convince him that, despite his trust in that woman, she would eventually do as her father willed? He took his eyes off Zalith and glared at the door. There *was* no point. For now, things seemed fine—as fine as they could be, given the circumstances. He wouldn't lose Zalith because of her—because of Lucifer. So, he'd stay quiet, he'd watch, he'd wait, and he'd make sure that he was ready to do what he had to do when the time eventually came. But he still couldn't accept the fact that Zalith had waited as long as he had to tell him.

"Right," he muttered as he lightly pushed Zalith away, trying to bury his frustration.

But Zalith then scoffed in what seemed to be astonishment. "Right? I'm speaking honestly. What else would you like me to do?" he asked, an argumentative tone in his slightly raised voice.

Alucard instantly scowled—was *he* angry? The last thing the vampire wanted to do was lose his temper with Zalith, but it seemed as though Zalith himself was already on his own way down that path, and Alucard felt no motivation to stand there and keep his thoughts to himself for a moment longer. "I don't know," he said, stepping back. "Perhaps tell me that you live with someone who could possibly be the end of my life the moment I became important to you rather than a year later when she bursts into the room?"

Zalith frowned. "Alucard, if I genuinely thought that she was a threat, I would have said something long ago—but she isn't. Why would I keep someone around who's a danger to you? Why would I put effort into taking care of you as much as I have just to turn around and purposefully let someone harm you?"

"I don't know." Alucard shrugged, trying to keep himself as calm as he could. "You probably thought it would be amusing," he snarled.

"Why in the world would I think that?"

"You tell me. Everything is some kind of game to you, isn't it?"

"You are *not* a game to me, Alucard, and you never have been," Zalith insisted, still with a calm tone—and Alucard didn't understand why that was. Why wasn't he yelling? Why wasn't he raising his voice anymore? He was frustrated—Alucard could feel it—but why was he so calm? Anyone else would be yelling in his face right now.

He scowled in response to his distress and took his eyes off Zalith. He didn't want to fight with him.

"I'm sorry," Zalith then said as he slowly reached forward and placed his hand on the vampire's right arm. "If there was any way I could go back and tell you sooner, then I would," he said as Alucard looked at him. "The last thing I want is to argue with you," he said, using his free hand to move a strand of Alucard's hair out of his face, and as he tucked it behind the vampire's ear, he sighed quietly. "I'm sorry," he repeated one last time.

Alucard didn't want to argue, either. He'd already made his choice, and he might not completely understand why Zalith had chosen to wait, but he'd try to. The demon had said sorry so many times that Alucard couldn't stand there and tell himself that Zalith wasn't serious. There wasn't really much else that could be done, was there? Varana was his sister, Zalith's friend, and lived in the same house that Alucard would often be visiting. Zalith was convinced she wasn't a threat, so Alucard would have to do his best to believe that. He trusted Zalith, so he'd have to take his word for it.

Losing his conflicted frown, he looked down at the floor and nodded. "At least I know now, I guess. We don't have to talk to her, and we don't have to talk about this anymore, either. It's... fine."

With a sullen frown, Zalith moved closer and wrapped his arms around the vampire. "I'm sorry I upset you," he said as he hugged him tightly.

"I'm not upset," Alucard mumbled and wrapped his arms around the demon.

He felt Zalith smile against the side of his face, but he didn't ask why. Nor did he want to stand there and think about the things Varana might do. Right now, he just wanted to enjoy the demon's embrace.

Chapter Forty-Six

— ⟨ ✝ ⟩ —

Dinner

| **Alucard** |

Seated at the table with a spread of food before him and Zalith to his left, Alucard found himself lost in a trance. His gaze, devoid of focus, drifted into the distance as he grappled with the tangled web of conflicting thoughts that held him captive.

His thoughts were trapped on Varana—*that woman*—and the father they shared. She may not have told Lucifer anything *yet*, but he still couldn't shake the feeling that she might eventually say something. Whether it was out of loyalty or simply in search of affection from Lucifer, he knew that one day, she'd say something. Zalith didn't believe that she would, but Alucard, in this case, knew Lucifer's children better than he did; he knew exactly how they worked.

As the clink of Zalith's fork against his plate snapped him out of his thoughts, he took his eyes off his glass of red wine and picked it up. He took a small sip, still staring aimlessly. He already had a lot to deal with; Damien, Lucious, Detlaff, his business, his life—if Lucifer were to be added to that, he was sure he'd lose what little sanity he may have left. But…Zalith seemed sternly convinced, and for now, that would have to be enough. He still trusted Zalith, so he'd trust him when he said that his friend wouldn't run to Lucifer and give away his location.

"Is there anything you want to do tomorrow?" Zalith asked as he topped up their glasses.

Alucard glanced at the demon. *Was* there anything he wanted to spend tomorrow doing? Nothing came to mind. He looked down at his plate, eying the spaghetti on it. "I don't know."

Zalith sighed quietly and leaned a little closer to the vampire. "How are you feeling?" he asked with concern in his voice.

Looking at Zalith once more, Alucard shrugged lightly. "I'm fine."

The demon waited with an expectant expression. Obviously, he was waiting for a more elaborate answer, and Alucard felt no need to dodge his question.

"Just... tired," he mumbled, looking at his wine glass. "I feel fine, though. This will be healed by this time tomorrow," he said, waving his hand towards his face as he picked up his glass in his other. "It doesn't hurt anymore," he added, sure that that was what Zalith wanted to hear.

"Good," Zalith said with a smile, returning to his food.

Alucard looked down at his dinner again and twisted some of the spaghetti onto his fork. He was pretty sure that Zalith must still be wondering what happened before he'd found him in his study, and he couldn't help but fear that he might insist he told him. He also feared that Damien might find out he'd taken someone's blood to heal his wounds faster, and if he did, the consequences would be far worse than the punishment he'd already received. Maybe he could just stay here for a few days until his wounds would have healed by themselves. Damien thought he was out looking for Lucious; he had his Paladins searching, so it wasn't like he wasn't doing as he was told.

"Are you okay?" Zalith suddenly asked after sipping from his glass.

The vampire nodded, eating the food on his fork. Then, when he glanced at Zalith, he watched a smile appear on the demon's face.

"I won't be a moment," the demon said as he stood up.

Alucard opened his mouth to speak; he wanted to ask him where he was going, but Zalith left the room rather quickly. Had he said something to annoy him? Or had Zalith heard something he hadn't? Varana, for example....

He frowned and looked down at what was left of his food. He had no idea what to assume—perhaps Zalith had some sort of business to see to. So, he finished his food, moved his plate aside, and rested his arms on the table as he stared sullenly into his glass.

In the anticipation-laden silence, Alucard battled against the descent into the depths of his own contemplations. Just as the tendrils of confliction threatened to envelop him, the door swung open, and Zalith reentered the room. Clutched in the demon's arms was a box of deep, velvety purple, its hue intensifying under the warm embrace of candlelight. The box, nearly the length of one of Zalith's arms, exuded an air of mystery, leaving Alucard to wonder about its enigmatic contents.

Zalith made his way over and smiled. "Here," he said, placing the box on the table in front of Alucard. He then sat down and watched Alucard examine the box.

The vampire frowned unsurely and set his eyes back on Zalith. "What is it?"

"Open it and see," Zalith said, smirking.

Taking his eyes off the demon, he looked back down at the box. He felt nervous about opening it in front of Zalith, but he didn't want to make a fuss about it. So, with a stubborn pout on his face, he sat up straight and carefully pulled the lid off, revealing something inside wrapped within the confines of black, ribbony silk.

He'd not glance at Zalith—he was sure the demon was smiling, and if he caught sight of it, he knew his face would become as red as his wine. So, he reached into the box and began to slowly pull away the ribbon keeping the silk in place. When the ribbon came away, and the silk unravelled, it revealed a violin case, inside which Alucard was sure sat a violin.

He didn't take his eyes off it, despite his abrupt curiosity. Why had Zalith got this for him? When? Where? There'd be time to ask after. He reached into the box with both his hands, carefully pulled the case out, and placed it on the table. He ignored his nervousness and unclipped the case, opening it to reveal the violin inside; it was as black as its case and made of ebony wood, as was the bow sitting beside it.

An appreciative smile banished the nervousness from his face. Unsure of what to say, he glanced at Zalith to see that he was indeed smiling, which immediately flustered the vampire. He looked back down at the violin and asked, "Is it…tuned?" But then embarrassment struck him like a fist. Why was *that* the first thing that he said? Why couldn't he have started with thank you?

The demon laughed quietly and sipped from his glass. "Probably not."

"Where did you get it?" he asked curiously.

"I placed an order for it when we were in Boszorkány; I picked it up on our way back. That was why I wanted to stop off there again."

Alucard looked back down at the violin and frowned slightly. Zalith had gone out of his way to get him yet another gift, and Alucard couldn't help but wonder why. Why did Zalith feel the need to give him gifts? Was he supposed to return this kindness? He had no idea, but he wanted to.

He glanced at Zalith again and asked, "Why?"

"Because—" Zalith sighed sadly, placing his empty glass back down— "you lost yours in the fire that took your house, and I still feel awful about that and what happened with Ada. Not just that, but you also deserve it."

The mention of Ada's name brought back a whole lot of memories and feelings Alucard wished to keep buried. He took his eyes off Zalith and looked back down at the violin, trying to keep his sadness from enthralling him. "Thank you," he said quietly, smiling. He then thought that he should try to keep hold of the happiness this gesture made him feel, so he glanced at Zalith and smirked. "I would try it out, but I don't think you'd like to lend me your face, hmm?" he asked, waving his hand towards the healing side of his face; he couldn't possibly play in his current state.

Zalith smirked suggestively. "You can use my face for whatever you like," he said but then laughed amusedly. "It's okay. You don't have to try it out now. I'm glad that you like it, though."

With a conflicted smile on his face, flustered because of Zalith's comment, Alucard looked back down at the violin. "I'll try it once I've healed."

"All right," Zalith said with a smile.

Alucard took a sip of his wine and then asked him, "Why... do you feel awful about Ada?"

Regret smothered Zalith's face. "Because I assumed she was dead and I didn't think to make sure. Because of my choice, your house was destroyed, as was everything inside. If it wasn't for my mistake, what happened the night your house burned may not have happened, and I feel as though most of the blame is mine."

Alucard laughed sadly, but he was admittedly amused, too. "No, it wasn't your fault," he said, staring into his wine. "You didn't know what she was, so you couldn't have known to make sure she was dead. I don't blame you if you think I do. I don't blame anyone but her and myself. *I* shouldn't have assumed she was dead; I knew better than to do that. But I assumed she was, and because of that, everything that happened happened. It was in no way your fault," he said, trying to assure Zalith, who he could see wasn't much alleviated.

But Zalith smiled and looked down at his drink. "Thank you."

The vampire wasn't sure whether Zalith was convinced or not, but he felt as if he'd said all he could to try and let him know that it really was not his fault. Alucard should have told Zalith that Ada would be able to resist ethos and injuries that would kill most others. The demon had no idea back then, so how could it be his fault?

His gaze faltered, diverting from Zalith to his drink as guilt and shame coiled around him like a constricting snake. The memory of surrendering to despair haunted him; he gave up the moment Ada stabbed him because he thought he'd lost Zalith forever. In that desperate moment, he'd embraced death as a solace, a morbid companion. The realization of his own perceived weakness gnawed at him, intensified by the knowledge that Tobias paid the ultimate price for his lapse.

Alucard couldn't escape the weight of responsibility that hung heavy on his shoulders. Tobias' death rested solely on him, a consequence of his momentary vulnerability. He refrained from laying blame on Ada, understanding her twisted obsession that painted a grim picture—a belief that if she couldn't have him, no one could. The toxic tapestry of their entangled fates had unfolded under his passivity, a failure to dissuade her from the dangerous path she pursued. Alucard grappled with the damning truth that he had inadvertently played a part in the chaos that ensued, a painful acknowledgement of his own shortcomings.

Everything was his fault, wasn't it? The burden of culpability settled permanently on his shoulders, an unwavering companion through the twists and turns of his tumultuous existence. Damien, with cruel precision, had guided him through the maze of self-blame, ensuring that he comprehended his role in the unfolding tragedies. The weight of responsibility, both historical and current, pressed upon him relentlessly.

Anger found no foothold against Zalith or Tobias; it was Ada who bore the brunt of his ire, yet the true tempest raged within him. The frustration wasn't directed solely at her; it was a reflection of his own perceived failures. In the pivotal moments, he faltered, unable to mount a resistance, unable to shield Tobias, and unable to preserve his own sanity. Even after Ada's demise, it took Damien's intervention to quell the chaos, and Alucard couldn't help but wonder what might have transpired if the Daegelus hadn't intervened. The echoes of his shortcomings reverberated in the chambers of his conscience, haunting reminders of his perceived inadequacies.

He scowled down at his hands. His scars ached, and as much as he resented the wounds they once were, he began to accept them. Damien was only trying to help, wasn't he? He punished him so that he would learn—he *needed* to learn. If he didn't, he'd continue to make the same mistakes. He couldn't be angry at Damien, and he couldn't be upset that he'd punished him for failing to find Lucious. He couldn't be upset about any of it. He deserved it.

"Alucard?" Zalith then asked, snapping him out of his thoughts once again. "Are you okay?"

Alucard took his eyes off his hands and looked over at him. "What?"

The demon frowned, something of a confused smile on his face. "You're making faces."

There would be no use in trying to hide his sadness. He sighed, shrugged, and looked back down at his drink. "I'm fine. I just... a lot happened that night, and I haven't really thought much about it."

Zalith frowned sympathetically and slowly moved his hand over Alucard's. "Do you want to talk about it?" he asked quietly.

"No," he immediately answered. He didn't want to revisit that night; it would only make his sadness heavier and would ruin his time with Zalith.

But the demon didn't seem to accept that. "Are you sure? Sometimes, talking about things helps us cope with them."

Looking back at him, he felt hesitant. He didn't want to talk about what happened, but... he knew that he couldn't bury it forever. He tried to conceal his pain, but it always found a way to break free and torment him at the most unprecedented times. If there was ever anyone he might talk about his pain with, it would be Zalith. Not only was he understanding, but he listened, he cared, and with him, Alucard felt safe—so safe that one day, he knew he'd tell him why he'd lost his wings and why he was so alone.

With a quiet sigh, the vampire averted his gaze and said, "I guess... I got back," he started, staring into his wine, "and I didn't exactly want to be by myself, so I went to see Tobias for a while—he asked me if I wanted to have a drink with him before I came to meet you, and I said no at first, but changed my mind—he was... good company, and I didn't really appreciate that until that night. We sat there, we talked about his past, and I told him what happened with us, and then I went home."

Listening, Zalith made himself a little more comfortable, keeping hold of Alucard's hand.

Alucard sighed deeply and shrugged. "On my way back, I saw the smoke—it was coming from the direction of the city, and that's where I thought the fire was, but when I took to the skies, I saw that it was actually my house on fire. I got there, the werewolves came, surrounded me, and clearly thought their numbers would help them. It didn't. They came at me, I killed them, but eventually, Ada showed up, and somehow, she knew my weakness. She stabbed me before I even knew that the stake was silver—if it were any other time, I'm sure I would have fought back, but... I just... didn't," he said, glancing at the demon.

Zalith frowned. "Why didn't you fight back?"

He laughed slightly. "A moment of weakness," he admitted. "I thought I'd lost you, and with that came the feeling of loneliness, one I haven't felt in a while—it hurt a whole lot more than my usual solitude. And I thought that... I would rather die and be done with the pain of my life than live without the one person who actually made me happy. But—" he said before Zalith could say something to accompany his scowl— "as I was dying, Tobias came out of the smoke and fought off the wolves that would've ended my life for good. He even fought off Ada so I could have a chance to get up. But... I lost blood, and when I lose too much and remain conscious, my body just... I don't know how to explain it, but I lose myself for a moment, and sometimes for too long. In this case, was too long. I attacked Tobias without even realizing, and even when I knew it was him I was killing, I couldn't stop. Hunger, I guess—and instinct. I didn't learn how to control that part of myself, so I couldn't have stopped, no matter how much I wanted to.

"Anyway, once I *could* let go, Tobias was already dead. Once I saw what I had done, once I came to terms with what I had lost, something just... I don't know. A part of me changed—woke up, maybe. I could only focus on my rage, and it was directed at Ada. I left Tobias, I left my house to burn, and I searched for her like some sort of starved creature. I can't remember much of it, but I do remember finding her and her family; I think she was expecting me to come since it looked as though she was preparing to flee with them. I didn't let that happen. I subjugated her and made her watch as I killed her family, and then I did something to her—I don't know what it was, but it was worse than death. I think... I sent her somewhere... Hell, maybe... or something like it.

"After that, I don't know how long I was standing out there, but Damien came. I woke up in his castle a few days later with that rune on my back—I'm sure you've seen it."

Zalith nodded. "I saw it."

"Well, Damien said it will stop that from happening again—stop me from losing myself in a... fit of rage. I'm glad, though," he said, glancing at Zalith again. "I don't want that to happen again. My anger is... well, I do my best to keep as calm as I can. I don't like to anger; when I do, things like that happen—not as bad, but still things I might not do if I wasn't angry. I gather that is another thing I haven't learned to manage—being a demon. Damien didn't teach me much in that regard, since he is not...well...a full demon. I'm sure he tried, but I struggle with some things still. So, now that you know that, if it ever does happen, hopefully you will not be too surprised. I won't kill you, though; Tobias was...not so strong. I feel like if I knew how to stop things like that from happening, then maybe he wouldn't have died. But I didn't know what to do, so he died, and I will never forgive myself," he said despondently, glaring into his drink.

Zalith tightened his grip on Alucard's hand and frowned sadly. "I'm so sorry that you had to go through all of this, Alucard. I know how it feels to lose somebody close to you because of something you've done, and I would never wish that feeling on anyone, least of all you."

Alucard took his eyes off his drink and looked at him. "You lost somebody, too?"

With a hesitant sigh, Zalith looked down at his hand while he held onto Alucard's. "Yes, I have."

"What happened?"

He shifted his saddened gaze to Alucard. "Would you like the short version or the long one?"

Alucard frowned, glancing down at their hands. "Whatever you want."

"Well, the humans and their allies killed my entire family...but when they got my brother..." he paused and frowned painfully.

Alucard watched him take a shaky sip from his wine. The vampire felt guilty for asking and wanted to tell him that he didn't need to talk about it, but before he could speak, Zalith cleared his throat, sighed, and smiled.

"Xurian was my very best friend. He was about four years older than me and almost like an idol of mine while I was very young. There was absolutely nothing that could tear us apart—and believe me, my mother tried at various points in our lives, but we were inseparable.

"My parents had very high expectations for Xurian and me, but because Xurian was older, they were much harder on him. I watched them push him over and over to live up to their standards, but he always had a way of rebelling against them, and when I was young, it was very inspirational for me," he said with a smile. "Eventually, he deviated from their plans and began to follow his Passion. He was a musician, but...he was horrible. Xurian could *not* sing, barely had any sense of rhythm, and there was not a single instrument that he could effectively play—but he didn't care. He loved music. He would write these horrendous little songs, and even though he tried and failed to make them sound pleasant, he never quit, and I always thought that it was admirable."

Alucard smiled. Not only did he love listening to Zalith speak, but he was also enjoying learning more about him and his family.

Zalith sipped from his glass again, a distressed frown fighting to steal his calm expression. "Anyway," he said with a slight shuffle of his shoulders as he turned to look at Alucard. "I don't want to bore you with any further details, but I will say that my side was winning the war with little to no contest, and we could've settled with what we had done, but I was foolish and decided to escalate the situation further because humans never really seem to learn, and they continued to act unreasonably. Eventually, in an act of rebellion, the humans somehow desperately came together and collectively manifested their own deity. They wanted to scare me and Varana with their new friend, I suppose, so they decided to hit us both where it hurt just to announce his arrival," he explained, his frown growing thicker with torment with each word he spoke.

"Unbeknownst to me," he continued, "they found where my brother was located; they made him and his wife watch as they viciously mutilated their two young daughters. Once they were dead, they killed his wife... and then they dropped Xurian off at my doorstep." He then hesitated again, his painful expression deepening.

Alucard stared at him in concern. "You don't... have to tell me any more," he said. "I think I—"

"It's okay." He took a quiet, deep breath before setting his eyes back on their hands. "As the humans willed it, their new deity called himself an angel, but he wasn't. Still, he felt the need to make his mark. They poisoned Xurian somehow, just enough so that it wouldn't allow him to heal properly, but his healing would keep him alive long enough for me to bear witness to what they did. Not only had they beaten him to the point where he was barely recognizable, but they tore the skin and muscle from his back on each side, cracked his ribcage, and pulled out his lungs. They crafted a wooden frame and nailed him to it so that he appeared to be standing with his arms raised, the lungs positioned along with the cut skin to look like feathered wings...." He grimaced, looking away to hide just how upset he was—Alucard wanted to tell him he could stop again, but he continued. "He was still breathing when I reached him, but... he didn't pull through," he explained. He then took his glass and drank what was left of his wine before looking back down at his hand.

Alucard stared at Zalith's hand as the demon gripped his a little tighter throughout the short silence. He had no idea what to say—to lose a brother was worse than to lose a friend, he was sure, and he was also sure that a simple '*I'm sorry that happened*' wouldn't help Zalith feel any better. He could see just by the look on his face that he was struggling with his sadness, so much that Alucard had to refrain from allowing himself to feel what Zalith was feeling the same way he had recently discovered he could.

What else could he say, though? '*Oh...*', '*that's awful...*', '*I'm so sorry...*'. He scowled in sorrow and set his eyes on the demon. "I... suck at this," he admitted, looking away. "I don't know what to say that might make you feel better. No one deserves to have that happen to them, and no one deserves to see it. I don't... I'm sorry."

Zalith moved his hand up the vampire's arm and gripped his bicep lightly. "You don't have to say anything," he assured him.

The talk of war revived yet another memory deep within Alucard's mind. Zalith was once a warlord, and perhaps…the demon might understand his guilt. "You had to do things you didn't want to, right?"

"Yes," he confirmed. "There were many things I did that I would have liked to do differently. Some things I regret to this day, too."

"Then…to kill people that you don't want to kill…does that…has that stayed with you?"

Zalith frowned ever so slightly. "In a way, yes. But some things have a way of feeling less….impactful as time passes."

Alucard sighed and looked down at the table. Now he had started, he felt he might as well continue. Speaking about Tobias' death had given him some sort of small relief, and perhaps speaking of his own wartime experiences would do the same. "I told you before that I've been in many wars; I've had to lead wars I had no involvement in, no interest in; I've had to do so many things I didn't want to do, and I had no choice in the matter. I've had to kill people—thousands…hundreds-of-thousands, in fact, all because…well, for the Numen. Because of them. They don't care about this world—about Aegisguard, but *I* do. It's where I live, where my people live, and where I want to stay, so I have to do what I can to protect it.

"The Numen start fights with each other, and this world is what suffers. The people here follow different religions, different Numen, and wars break out when a disagreement happens. The people fight for their gods, gods that don't care to intervene. Damien gets me to intervene for them; he picks the side of whichever sibling he currently likes the most and gets me to fight on that Numen's followers' side. They win, that Numen gains more followers, more influence, and so does Damien for helping."

The demon frowned. "And what do you get?"

Alucard laughed slightly. "Nothing. I don't expect anything, though. It's work. I work for Damien, so I do what he tells me. It often means I'm doing things I don't want to do, killing people I don't want to kill, but…I have to."

Zalith slowly shook his head…but as Alucard looked at him, a smile crept across his face. He moved his hand back down Alucard's arm and lifted his hand, resting his elbow on the table. "Perhaps…one day, you and I should make the Numen do things *they* don't want to do—so they can see how it feels."

Staring at him, Alucard felt a little perturbed. He wasn't sure what he meant by that, but the idea was amusing. "Maybe," he said quietly.

Zalith then smirked deviously. "Would you like to know what *I* want to do?" he asked, placing his other hand on Alucard's leg; he slowly dragged his hand closer to the vampire's inner thigh, and as Alucard stared at him with a growing look of embarrassment on his face, the demon smiled.

"What?" he asked, trying not to let his anxiety consume him.

"You," he said with a grin.

Alucard was sure that his face turned bright red as he looked away, trying to hide his embarrassment. He'd fallen right into that one. But he didn't object to the subject change. He'd rather feel flustered and shy than depressed and guilty.

"Would you prefer to wait?" the demon asked.

The vampire hesitated for a moment. He tried to ask himself what he wanted, but he felt conflicted. He *did* want to be closer to Zalith right now—he wanted to kiss, hug, and lay in bed with him. But did he want *more*? He shrugged, glancing at Zalith. "I don't know," he answered.

With an amused smile, Zalith laughed slightly before moving his hand from over the vampire's and to the side of his face. "Would you like to continue where we left off earlier?"

That *did* sound inviting. He didn't let himself overthink it. With a shy nod, he glanced at Zalith.

A look of relief and excitement appeared on the demon's face. He leaned forward and kissed Alucard's lips; Alucard kissed back for a few moments, and then, Zalith rather eagerly gripped his hand and pulled him with him when he left the table.

Alucard's excitement was growing, too. As the demon avidly led the way, he followed him out of the dining room and through the house. Whatever was about to happen, he was sure it was going to be a satisfying end to this awful day.

Chapter Forty-Seven

— ⟨ ✝ ⟩ —

Disposition

| Alucard |

Alucard followed Zalith upstairs. The demon lightly squeezed his hand as he pulled him along, glancing back at him with a smile on his face. Despite this not being the first time they'd been sexually intimate, Alucard still felt as though it was. His heart was racing, he felt anxious, but he wanted to keep walking. He might be shy, but that hadn't stopped him before. He knew what to expect, and it excited him.

When they reached the bedroom door, the demon pushed it open and invited him inside. The vampire let go of his hand and walked past him into his bedroom, which was lit only by the kaleidoscopic moonlight. He stopped in the centre of the room, waiting as he listened to Zalith closing and locking the door behind him, which he suspected was to keep Varana from bursting in again. Then, once the demon made his way over, he wrapped his arms around Alucard from behind and rested the side of his face on his.

"She won't be getting in this time," Zalith mumbled into Alucard's ear and started softly kissing the right side of his neck. At the same time, he moved his hands to the collar of Alucard's shirt and began unbuttoning it.

The demon turned Alucard around and kissed him. Lips melded, they embarked on a slow, sultry dance, guided by the tempting pull toward Zalith's bed. As the last button of Alucard's shirt succumbed to Zalith's touch, a gleeful excitement flickered in the demon's eyes. With a swift motion, the shirt relinquished its hold on Alucard's body, leaving his bare skin in its wake.

Their kisses, once languid, now bore the imprint of heightened desire and anticipation. Zalith's tongue rekindled the intoxicating rhythm, and the air thickened with the fervour that hung between them.

Alucard's desire and desperation began to consume him. When Zalith pushed him down onto the bed, he reached up and gripped the collar of the demon's shirt, pulling his face back into his own to continue to kiss him. Despite his already increasing arousal, he didn't yet want to let Zalith tend to it. Instead, he started to unbutton the demon's shirt, and once it came away from his body, Alucard slowly placed his hands upon the muscles that lay beneath. He loved to stare and touch, and right now, he'd not let his nervousness keep him from doing either.

As Zalith's tantalizing kisses traversed from his mouth to the sensitive expanse of his neck, Alucard couldn't help but let out a deep exhale, attempting to anchor himself amidst the rising waves of desire. His hands, a testament to his own exploration, guided along the sinuous terrain of the demon's body, each touch a revelation as they ascended over chiselled abs and sculpted pecs, and when his fingertips found Zalith's arms, ardour took a firm hold of him.

A momentary pause in Zalith's advances heightened the suspense, a smirk playing on the demon's lips as he took his shirt off, casting it aside to join the discarded garments on the floor. Zalith then returned to claim Alucard's lips, reigniting the desperation between them. The vampire's hands, now reacquainted with the heated canvas of the demon's skin, continued their exploration, revelling in the tactile symphony of each defined contour.

But he soon slipped his hands down the demon's arms as Zalith's right hand wandered to his crotch. Alucard knew that when he became this excited, he'd not be able to stop himself from digging his claws into Zalith's skin, but he was convinced that the demon enjoyed it.

The vampire tightened his hold on Zalith's forearm as the demon lightly gripped his growing arousal over his trousers. His excitement grew with each subtle movement of Zalith's hand, as did his eagerness. He started to wish that Zalith would pull his trousers off, and he even considered doing it himself, but he was too nervous. Instead, he moved his hand to the back of Zalith's head, gripping his hair as they continued to kiss aggressively. Alucard enjoyed Zalith's assertiveness, though—and his aggression… but he was sure that Zalith was holding most of it back, and that only made the vampire yearn for more.

He tightened his grip on Zalith's hair, kissing him, his anticipation becoming an overwhelming quiver of exhilaration as the demon continued caressing his hardened shaft. When Zalith guided his hand into Alucard's trousers, the vampire turned his head aside, halting their kissing as a deep, eager sigh escaped his frantic breaths. His body felt strange; he felt excited, he felt the pleasure travel through him like a cold shiver, but as it surged past his healing scars, he felt uncomfortable. He wasn't sure why, but as odd as it felt, he didn't want to stop.

So he lay there in the heated gloom, gripping Zalith's hair in his hand as the demon slowly pressed his lips against his neck, kissing his skin, inviting his desperation to become something he couldn't keep silent much longer. He ached for more—for what he knew would come—and as much as he could enjoy Zalith's teasing, he felt that it was time he let the demon know he wanted more.

He lightly pulled on Zalith's hair and exhaled frustratedly as he pushed Zalith's head away from his neck, insisting—and Zalith complied. The demon kissed his way down Alucard's body and to his waist, where, with an excited smirk, he gripped the vampire's trousers and pulled them off.

Zalith didn't seem to be done teasing, though. Alucard waited, a longing sigh accompanying his quiet exhale, and as he felt the demon slowly dragging his tongue from the base of his shaft and to its tip, he felt his entire body tense up with restless anticipation. He gripped the blankets with both his hands, a struggled grimace making its way to his face as he tried his best not to fidget too much.

But how could he not? The moment he felt Zalith move his mouth over his tip, his subtle sigh became a quiet, pleasured moan. He gritted his teeth, his body tensing as each moment passed, and when the demon took his shaft deeper into his throat, the vampire huffed quietly, his excitement becoming overbearing, and his body felt feverishly agitated. The vampire moved his hand to Zalith's head, gripping his hair, humming in content as Zalith slowly and skillfully sucked his dick.

Alucard frowned through his delighted smile when he felt Zalith grip his right leg. He didn't feel the need to question him; he lay there, enjoying the pleasurable feeling of the demon's warm, wet tongue against his shaft. But Zalith soon took the vampire's shaft from his mouth and kissed his way to his inner thigh. He caressed his chosen place on the vampire's leg with a kiss, but then he sunk his fangs into his skin. Alucard jolted in both startlement and confusion, he even let a wince of pain escape his voice, but that only seemed to make Zalith smile through his bite.

The vampire's frown soon faded as the demon's venom ensnared his body in euphoria. He felt Zalith bite harder, but it only made Alucard hum blissfully. The demon sighed simultaneously in satisfaction as he consumed the vampire's blood, but he soon stopped, taking hold of Alucard's shaft in his hand once more, and hastily returned it to his mouth.

It didn't take much longer for Alucard to become enthralled; he groaned quietly, tightly gripping Zalith's hair in his hand, grasping the blanket with his free hand. He fidgeted, he exhaled in struggle, and as the most intense climax he'd ever felt convulsed within him, his shaft erupted, and he moaned pleasurably in response.

He lay there, relaxed, enjoying the euphoria he received from both his peak and the demon's venom. A smile found its way to his face as he felt Zalith kiss his way back up his body and to his neck, which he began to kiss and playfully bite. Alucard's hand remained on the back of Zalith's head, but he kept his eyes shut, sinking deeper into his bliss. He opened them, however, to stare at Zalith as the demon lightly gripped his jaw in his hand and turned his face so that he'd look up at him.

Zalith smiled, staring into the vampire's tired eyes, and then he started to kiss him once again. As they kissed, he took hold of Alucard's hand, pulling it from the top of his head and placing it on his crotch. Alucard didn't shy away; he gripped the demon's arousal over his trousers. He felt curious, and he felt as though he wanted to please the demon the same way Zalith had just pleased him.

But Zalith clearly had something else on his mind. He kissed Alucard for a few more moments but soon pulled his face from the vampire's and leaned into his ear. "Can I fuck you?" he whispered, desperation in his voice.

A nervous frown broke Alucard's content smile. He waited, staring up at the ceiling, and as Zalith lifted his head to look down at him, he looked to his left and thought to himself for a few moments. He knew what to expect, so he wasn't as nervous as he thought he might be, but…was he ready? He'd agreed that they could have sex when he stayed with Zalith next, and now was that time. He was curious, nervous—but mostly curious, and he found that he liked the idea of Zalith feeling pleasure because of him.

His nervous frown became something of a meek stare as he turned his head to look back up at the demon, and in response, he nodded.

The demon smiled excitedly. He kissed Alucard slowly and passionately for a few moments, but then stopped and smiled again. "One moment," he said before moving to the edge of the bed.

Alucard slowly sat up, watching as Zalith headed over to one of the cabinets. The demon searched for something inside the top drawer, and once he found whatever it was, he put it in his pocket and made his way back to the edge of the bed, which he then patted with his hand.

"Come here," he instructed, smirking.

The vampire didn't ask why, nor did he shy away; both his high and curiosity kept him from hesitating. He moved from the centre of the bed and to its edge; Zalith gripped his left arm and made him stand, and then he kissed him for a few moments before turning him around so that his back was against his chest. That was when Alucard's nervousness broke free of his euphoria. He was excited—nervously, curiously excited. He waited as Zalith dragged his hands up his back, kissing his neck.

When Zalith stopped kissing him, he leaned into his ear. "Bend over," he said quietly, a low, seductive tone in his voice. "You can rest your knees on the bed if that's more comfortable for you."

Alucard did as he was told. He leaned forward, supporting himself on his hands; the subtle discomfort that pulsed through his wounds served as a reminder, but he remained steadfast in his resolve not to draw attention to his physical vulnerabilities. Following Zalith's guidance, he gently rested his knees on the soft expanse of the blanket. Despite the twinge of nervousness that lingered, an undercurrent of relaxation enveloped him.

Euphoria, a potent elixir, coursed through his veins, and anticipation hummed in the air as he eagerly awaited the revelations that Zalith was poised to unveil.

His frown faded into a small smile when Zalith lightly dragged his fingers from the back of his neck, down his back, and to his thigh—it caused a pleasing shiver to surge through his body once more, but as the demon gripped his thigh, he waited anxiously.

"This may feel strange; tell me if it hurts or makes you uncomfortable, okay?" Zalith told him quietly.

Alucard nodded, staring at his right hand as he gripped the blanket in angst. He waited, his heart beginning to race in trepidation. Then, he felt something cold and viscous on the two fingers Zalith pressed against his hole. He frowned as his heart raced faster, and when Zalith gently eased his fingers into his ass, he felt conflicted. At first, the sensation of him slowly massaging the inside of his ass was a little strange— discomforting, in fact—but when Zalith pulled his fingers from him, he felt relief.

And then he heard the clink of Zalith's belt. He tensed up again, his heart *pounding* in his chest. He tried to calm his nervousness, which quickly enthralled him, but it wouldn't settle. He shivered anxiously as Zalith pulled his trousers off, and when the demon gripped his waist with his right hand, the vampire exhaled deeply and quietly.

"Are you ready?" Zalith asked.

The vampire nodded immediately in response; he knew that if he let himself overthink, he'd worry himself and ruin the moment for the both of them. He wanted this. So he focused on his curiosity and waited.

"Okay. Try to keep yourself and your muscles relaxed; tell me if it hurts. I'll be slow and gentle," Zalith assured him.

Alucard nodded again, concentrating on the lingering euphoria from the demon's bite and his recent climax. Both sensations made him feel calm and relaxed, and he was sure that what he was about to experience would make him feel even more so.

But when he felt the tip of the demon's dick against his ass, he frowned again. He was nervous—of course he was—but he did his best to ignore it; he relaxed, focusing on the fact that this was something *he* had been curious about, and something he knew Zalith sorely desired. He wanted to please him, so he'd not let his anxiety take that from either of them.

To his discontent, however, it *did* hurt. The moment he felt the demon's hard, thick shaft moving into him—despite being relaxed, despite his curiosity and willingness—it felt *extremely* uncomfortable. But Zalith said that it might hurt at first, so he waited, tightening his grip on the blankets as Zalith gradually eased his tip deeper inside him.

Zalith stopped and stroked the vampire's back with his free hand. "Are you okay?" he asked.

Alucard, with a look of struggle on his face, frowned and nodded. "I'm fine," he uttered, trying to keep calm, but all he wanted to do right now was tell Zalith it was too uncomfortable. He wanted it, though... he just didn't understand why it had to feel like this.

The demon, who surely knew that wasn't the whole truth, leaned ever so slightly to the side in what might be an attempt to glance at his face. "Do you want me to stop?"

"No," Alucard said with a pout, denying the demon a glance back.

Zalith waited for a moment, dragging his fingertips down Alucard's back. He then started ever so slightly moving the tip of his dick back and forth. At first, it felt very strange; Alucard gripped the sheets and huffed quietly, trying to stay relaxed, but after a few moments, it actually began to feel pleasing. He calmed down, the tip of Zalith's shaft teasing his ass, and when he relaxed a little more, Zalith gradually moved deeper.

Alucard exhaled in struggle, his frown becoming thicker as each inch of the demon's girth buried itself deeper inside him. It still felt a little painful, but after a few slow thrusts, it began to feel strangely good. The demon went a little deeper with each slow thrust, and when quiet, pleased sighs carried upon Zalith's breath, a shiver of satisfaction spiralled through Alucard.

After one final slow thrust, Alucard felt Zalith's thighs press against his ass, and the pleased groan escaping Zalith's breaths assured Alucard that the entirety of the demon's dick was inside him. It still felt curiously enjoyable, but something of a discomfort at the same time. He focused on the pleasing aspect of it, though.

"Is this okay?" the demon asked one last time.

Alucard nodded. "Yes," he said, sure that if he said he was fine, it would prompt Zalith to doubt him once again. His answer instead assured the demon that he was comfortable, and that was when Zalith started to slowly pull his shaft back out of him, but once his tip came close to leaving Alucard's ass, he gripped the vampire's waist tightly in both his hands and pushed back inside, a quiet, satisfied hum upon his exhale.

The twinge of discomfort intensified, etching a momentary grimace on Alucard's face. Yet, the allure of the sensations propelled him forward, a willing participant in the pleasure that unfolded. With each rhythmic thrust from Zalith, waves of ecstasy surged through the vampire's body, gradually erasing the lines of discomfort, and as the demon's pace quickened, a transformative smile displaced his frown.

A gratified whimper slipped past Alucard's lips, an unwitting acknowledgement of the pleasure surging through him. His body, a canvas of delight, quivered in response to every nuanced movement, orchestrating a symphony of sensations. Zalith's contented moans, a sultry melody, seamlessly melded with Alucard's own, intensifying the vampire's burgeoning satisfaction, and in the fusion of shared ecstasy, Alucard found elation in the realization that his body could bestow such immense pleasure upon Zalith.

But then a sensation almost like what he felt upon climax began to enthral him. His limbs trembled, forcing him to find comfort in resting the weight of his body on his elbows and forearms, arching his back inwards. He groaned and exhaled deeply, gritting his teeth in pleasured struggle as he felt the demon moving his dick deeper, faster, *harder*.

He gripped the blanket, resting his forehead on his arm as he hummed into the sheets. His body began to ache and waver like it was struggling to reach its peak again so soon. But Alucard also felt as if the demon might be losing the control he had over himself; he tightened his grip on the vampire's waist, his thrusts becoming increasingly assertive, *aggressive*. Alucard didn't struggle, though—he complied. He liked this new feeling of serving to satisfy Zalith, and he enjoyed allowing the demon to control everything.

But the demon moved even faster, moaning desperately with each eager thrust. The discomfort was beginning to outweigh the pleasure, and Alucard grimaced again, worried that he might have to tell Zalith to stop. The demon thrusted harder and harder and *harder*, forcing Alucard to whine in a conflicted mix of sheer delight and nervous discomfort. When his body finally broke past that barrier keeping him from his peak, the discomfort withered, and Alucard was quickly overwhelmed with anticipation. His body trembled, his dick throbbed, and when Zalith aggressively pulled the vampire back, burying his thick shaft as deeply into Alucard's ass as he could, they both whined in contentment and relief.

As Alucard climaxed, Zalith gripped his shoulder and pulled him up, making him lean his back against the demon's chest. But as a quiet, pleased, "Fuck," escaped Zalith's deep breaths, Alucard felt a new sensation. The demon's dick pulsed inside him, and a strange but soothing warmth pooled in his ass and spread through his body, enthralling him in delight.

Alucard closed his eyes and exhaled in content as the demon nuzzled the side of his face. "What are you doing?" he asked quietly, his voice a tired, pleased murmur.

"Oh…I came in you," he said apologetically. "Sorry. I should've asked first; I got carried away."

The vampire smiled again and said, "No, it's okay. It feels good."

Zalith kissed his cheek and said, "If you ever change your mind, let me know—if you want to do it again, that is."

Alucard reached back and ran his fingers through Zalith's hair. "I do," he told him.

"Okay, good," the demon murmured, smiling against Alucard's cheek.

Zalith then carefully pulled his dick from the vampire's ass; he let Alucard get into bed while he cleaned up, and then he crawled under the covers and cuddled up beside him, wrapping his arms around the vampire.

"Thank you," he said quietly, nuzzling the back of Alucard's head.

Alucard smiled tiredly but didn't have the energy to respond. The moment he laid down, fatigue struck him abruptly, and he was struggling to keep himself from drifting off. He wanted to lie there and talk, but he knew that he wouldn't win the battle against his body's need to sleep and heal. But he felt safe, satisfied, and content, and he let himself sink into the comfort of Zalith's warm embrace. It had been a *long* day, and all he wanted to do now was sleep.

| **Zalith** |

As the night deepened into the quiet hours, Zalith lay wide awake beside Alucard. Having allowed the vampire to succumb to the embrace of sleep, the rapidity of Alucard's slumber didn't catch him off guard. Zalith understood the energy-draining aftermath of their intimate connection, a phenomenon he experienced and observed countless times. Despite his attempts to hold back with Alucard, he couldn't help it. He hadn't had sex in so long; it had been a craving left unfulfilled for far too long, and finally satiated in the warmth of Alucard's presence.

Yet, despite the satisfaction coursing through him, an hour later, sleep eluded him. Why?

He frowned in the dimly lit room, resting his head beside Alucard's as the vampire slept peacefully. Immersed in the quietude, Zalith allowed his thoughts to drift, a majority of them tinted with the hues of bliss. The contentment derived from sharing that intimate moment with Alucard lingered, and as he raised his head and gazed down at the serenity gracing the vampire's sleeping visage, a soft smile claimed his lips. The vampire was so cute, even when he slept, an endearing quality that stirred warmth within Zalith.

But as Zalith stared, realization smacked him so hard that he stifled a breath. He'd just fucked Alucard and he still liked him just as much as he did before; it was a feeling that had never clung after he'd had sex with *anyone*—he grew bored of his other sexual partners fairly soon after sex, but not Alucard. He still felt so happy with him, so content, and something he might even describe as complete…and it unsettled him. He couldn't stop himself from wondering: what would happen the next time they had sex? Would he begin to enjoy Alucard's company less? Would he start to lose the feelings he had for him each time they were intimate? No…with Alucard, it was different. It had *always* been different. He wasn't just some man he'd pursued for fun. Alucard was more than a simple lay.

Zalith couldn't imagine not being with this vampire…*his* vampire. That was what Alucard was—*his*. The time he'd spent away from Alucard had been so painful; it had been such a struggle, and to imagine having to go through it again, even for a time shorter than a year…it hurt, and he felt as if it was because…he loved him.

He *did* love him, didn't he? And the fact that he did caused fear to grow within his heart. He knew why he was afraid, though. It didn't confound him. What if Alucard left? What if this vampire grew tired or resentful of him and walked out of his life? What if Alucard didn't love him back? What if this love would change their relationship?

The demon stared at Alucard, his smile fading into an upset frown. He wasn't at all used to loving the men he had sex with, and it scared him. What if…he *didn't* love Alucard? What if he simply liked him a whole lot and wanted to keep spending time with him to see where they might end up? He scowled at the thought of that. He knew that he *never* wanted to live without him, but the idea of committing fully to him right now…frightened him. But right now, at least he had Alucard, and Alucard had him, and they could simply enjoy their time together. It wasn't like they were getting married, was it?

Was it? He took his eyes off the vampire, fighting with his thoughts. He had a lot to think about, clearly. But not now. Now, it was time to rest. It had been a long day and an eventful, pleasing night, and he was sure that tomorrow would be just as enjoyable as any other time he got to spend with his vampire.

With a content smile on his face, he carefully pulled Alucard so that he was lying on his back. He then kissed the side of his face, rested his head on the vampire's shoulder, and closed his eyes, disappearing into a deep, calming rest.

Chapter Forty-Eight

— ⸲ ✝ ⸲ —

A Serene Start to A Despairing Day

| **Alucard** |

Alucard woke to what were surely the consequences of last night. His entire body ached; his old and new wounds were sore, his head was pounding, and pain shot through his eyes as he slightly opened them to see what time of day it might be.

His eyes faded from hellfire to ice, the sunlight breaking in through the room's drawn curtains to greet his tired face. Despite having slept through until what looked to be close to noon, the vampire felt like he hadn't slept at all. None of his discomforts bothered him, though; the weight on his right shoulder, however, perturbed him, so he took his aching eyes off the curtains and looked down at his shoulder to see that Zalith had his head rested on it, sleeping soundlessly. The demon also had his right arm around him, holding him tightly in his sleep.

The vampire smiled slightly, resting his arm on the pillow above him so that he could bring his hand to the demon's head. He hesitated for a moment but wouldn't miss the opportunity to caress Zalith's unkempt, messy hair. Alucard found that he loved seeing his usually neatly combed hair in its natural state, and he'd not waste his chance to admire it. He ignored the ache and pain and lay there, enjoying the comfort of being beside Zalith in the silence of the late morning. He found that waking up beside the demon was something he adored so much, and he didn't want to wake up another morning without him.

But Zalith soon smiled and opened his eyes to glance up at him. "Hi baby," he said, lifting his hand from the vampire's arm to stroke the side of his face.

A nervous smile found its way to Alucard's face as he took his eyes off Zalith, but the demon didn't give him much time to respond. Zalith moved onto his back and pulled Alucard closer; the vampire complied, of course, and rested his head on the demon's chest as he sighed quietly, making himself comfortable.

"I love waking up next to you," Zalith said quietly as he started to caress the vampire's hair with his fingers.

Alucard, who felt the same, dragged his hand up the demon's body and to the side of his neck. "Me too."

The demon smirked. "You're so handsome," he said, guiding his fingers down from the vampire's hair and to his face.

With an embarrassed frown, Alucard pouted and tightened his grip around the demon.

"How are you feeling today?" Zalith asked, moving his caressing hand back to the vampire's hair.

Alucard assumed he was asking about his healing wounds; they ached, but they were almost entirely healed thanks to Zalith's blood. Or could he be referring to his feelings? He knew that he probably hadn't been in the best of moods over dinner yesterday. Or…was he asking how he felt about last night? He wasn't sure, but whatever the question was aimed at, his answer was, "I'm okay."

"Does your body still hurt?"

He shrugged and glanced up at Zalith. "No," he answered as he looked over at the wall. "It just aches. I'll be fine, though."

Zalith sighed quietly in what sounded like concern as he continued to fiddle with the vampire's hair. "Would you like more of my blood? I want to help you to feel better."

The demon's blood *would* help him feel better, but it would also force a high upon him, something he didn't feel like experiencing right now. Besides, it would only take around half this day or so for the remainder of his scars to heal. Zalith's bites would take longer, but they didn't cause much of an ache at all—at least not while he was lying there, anyway. There was a bite on his leg, and he wasn't sure how that might make him feel once he tried to stand. But he was sure he'd find out soon; he wanted a shower.

"No," he responded quietly. "Thank you, though. I feel fine; I think I just want a shower…if that's okay."

"Of course; you can do whatever you like," Zalith said, smiling. "However," he then said as he sat up, pulling Alucard so that he sat up to look at him. "First, I want you to take some of my blood," he said sternly.

Alucard still felt hesitant. *Should* he? Yes, but he didn't *want* to. He'd lost a lot of his blood because of Zalith's bites, and he'd heal a whole lot slower if he had to heal his blood back too, but he just didn't feel like he wanted to experience the high that came with drinking Zalith's blood. It had a way of making him feel strangely euphoric, a type of euphoria that left him feeling oddly dissociated for a while after the high had started to fade. He'd noticed it the first time he'd bitten the demon; he'd woke up feeling odd and had to wander around by himself for a while before he found his ground. The second time—last night at dinner—he'd once again felt a little less like himself. He'd spoken so openly without so much hesitation, and he was sure that was because of how Zalith's blood made him feel. He wasn't sure what might come of it today, and he wasn't exactly confident to let himself find out.

He looked at Zalith, trying to work out how to say no again.

But the demon frowned sadly. "I got a little carried away last night. I drank a lot of your blood; you should at least take back what I took from you."

The vampire frowned reluctantly as he stared at Zalith. The longer he took to leave for his shower and the more Zalith tried to convince him to bite, the more he found himself feeling compelled to do so. It *would* help, it would make him feel better, and it would make him feel a whole lot less dead... but he couldn't. Not only did he not want to feel the effects, but he also didn't want to risk addiction—for himself or Zalith. He knew that demon venom was addicting, as was their blood, and the last thing he needed right now on top of everything else was an addiction to clear up, and he was sure that Zalith didn't exactly want to deal with it either. Surely he knew those facts, so why was he insisting?

Alucard took his eyes off Zalith, frowned, and shrugged. "I don't need to. I feel fine. If I didn't, I would say yes, but I really don't need it right now," he said, trying to convince him.

"Are you sure?" Zalith asked, placing his hand on the side of Alucard's face.

The vampire nodded. "Yes," he confirmed. "I just want to shower."

Zalith smiled. "Okay," he said as he nodded over at the door that led into the bathroom. "It's just in there. I'll bring you some clothes soon." He then kissed the vampire before letting him turn around and shuffle to the end of the bed.

When Alucard reached the end of the bed, he took a moment to pull the blanket from his lap so that he could stare at the wound left on his inner thigh—the wound that had begun aching the moment he moved. Zalith had left two small but deep punctures on his leg where he had sunk his fangs into him; they were smothered with dried blood and bruised, and he was sure that was because he had bitten rather harshly. He didn't resent that, though. He liked it.

"Are you okay?" Zalith asked with a slight laugh.

"What?" Alucard frowned, looking back at him to see that he was smiling curiously. "I'm fine," he said, snatching his trousers from the floor. Then, he pulled them on, stood up, and made his way over to the bathroom, sure that Zalith was watching his every move.

He went into the bathroom and closed the door behind him. Now alone, he allowed himself to grimace in response to the growing ache in his body—an ache that he hoped would pass once the warm water hit him. He walked over to the shower, pulled off his trousers, and stepped inside, closing the glass doors. To his relief, the technology was much like that of his castle's shower, so at least he wouldn't have to make a fool of himself and go back outside to ask Zalith how to work it.

Gripping the shower's tap, he twisted it ever so slightly so that the water didn't come at him too fast or too hot and slowly adjusted it until it was just right. Then, he stood there for a short while under the pouring water as it hit his head, ran through his hair, and down his body, hitting the white marble floor below. The vampire then lifted his face towards the water, a refreshing feeling outweighing his ache as the water trickled down his face.

Solitude for Alucard usually meant that it was time for his thoughts to wander, but right now, they were calm, quiet, and strangely relaxed. He had nothing to dwell on, nothing to overthink. Despite what happened yesterday, he didn't feel despondent. Zalith so easily cured his sadness, and he'd hold onto that for as long as he could. He didn't care about Damien or Lucifer or the woman that the demon shared his house with. All Alucard cared about was Zalith—*his* demon—and as Luther had recently referred to him, his boyfriend. He liked that, and he felt no hesitation or shyness to think of him as such a thing.

| **Zalith** |

In his bedroom, Zalith carefully selected fresh attire for both himself and Alucard. The emotions swirling within him, far from diminishing since the previous night, seemed to have taken root and gotten stronger. The admission of love—although only to himself—had been a vulnerable confession, and he'd admitted it not once but twice; but it was an emotion that resonated within him, mingling with the threads of anxiety that the vampire might not reciprocate.

Yet, far from succumbing to apprehension, Zalith harboured a determined resolve. His burgeoning feelings for Alucard, tender and profound, fueled a determination to convey the depth of his affection. He'd do what he could to try and get Alucard to understand how he felt about him.

He took out two shirts and pairs of trousers, as well as some socks and underwear. At first, his eyes wandered to a selection of jockstraps to the right of the drawer; he smirked and laughed quietly, but as much as he'd like to try and get Alucard to wear one, he thought the vampire might be too shy. That didn't mean he wouldn't suggest it some other time, though.

When he closed the drawer, he headed for the bathroom. He quietly pushed the door open, and as he set his eyes on Alucard, who stood under the shower's falling water, he smiled. His eyes, however, wandered to the sealing runes on the vampire's back. The conversation they'd had last night came to mind; he'd had no idea that Alucard hadn't learned to control some of his demon traits, and it was no surprise at all that Damien had failed to teach him. The fact that Damien was only half demon didn't matter—he was a *Daegelus*, both demon and angel, which meant he had all the traits of both creatures; he had no excuse not to teach Alucard to take care of himself. So why hadn't he?

Now wasn't the time to think about Damien. No. Today was about him and Alucard, and so was every other day they'd be spending together.

He went to say Alucard's name but then saw that there were no towels on the rack. Had the staff not replaced them yet? He sighed and put the clothes on the closest cabinet before leaving the room, heading for the linen closet himself.

| **Alucard** |

With a deep sigh, Alucard ran his fingers through his hair and looked down at the floor. The water no longer ran red with dried blood, and the heat had eased his soreness. He felt a whole lot better already.

But then Zalith entered the bathroom, snapping the vampire out of his thoughts. Alucard sharply turned his head to stare at him, and the moment he realized that Zalith was utterly naked, standing with a few folded towels in his arms, Alucard's face surely turned red with embarrassment as he looked away from the demon, who smirked in response. It seemed as though Zalith would be joining him, and it wasn't much of a surprise to him when he felt the demon's hands grip and slowly move around his waist.

"Hi again," Zalith mumbled into the vampire's ear as he hugged him from behind.

Trying to ignore his embarrassment, Alucard smiled and lifted his hand to the side of Zalith's face; the demon then kissed his cheek as he pulled the vampire's wet body against his.

"How was last night for you?" Zalith asked quietly, a flirtatious tone in his voice.

His question instantly flustered Alucard. He tensed up and looked down at the wet floor, trying to hide his face despite the fact that Zalith couldn't see most of it. He shrugged slightly and shyly replied, "It was…really good. I enjoyed it."

Zalith smirked against the back of Alucard's neck as he dragged his hand down the vampire's wet body, caressing the lines of each and every defined muscle on his way down to grip his ass. "Good," he said, leaning into his ear once more. "Because I want to fuck you again."

"Right...now?"

The demon tightened his grip on Alucard's ass. "If that's okay."

Alucard pondered for a moment. He *had* enjoyed last night—all the grabbing, kissing, and touching, *and* the enthralling pleasure. He didn't need to think about it. "Okay," he agreed.

Zalith kissed the vampire's neck and turned him to face him. He lightly pushed Alucard back so that he was against the wall and stepped through the falling water to start kissing the vampire.

Alucard smiled contently, and with each kiss, his excitement grew. But after just a few more gentle strokes of their tongues, Zalith stopped kissing him and stared at his face. The vampire frowned, not sure why he'd stopped, but as Zalith smiled and rested his forehead against his, Alucard smiled back at him.

As Zalith's dark, alluring eyes stared into his, he started to feel nervous. He looked away, glancing down at the demon's arousal, but he immediately looked elsewhere when Zalith moved his arms around him and pulled him closer, resting the side of his head against Alucard's.

Zalith didn't say anything.

The demon's silence confounded Alucard, as did his hug. But he felt no need to question him; if he'd changed his mind, that was okay. He stood there in the demon's embrace, a smile on his face as he relaxed. *This* was something he enjoyed so very much, just standing there and hugging him, to be held by him. He could stand in Zalith's embrace until the very end of time; he didn't even feel stupid for admitting such a thing despite the fact that they'd only known each other a little less than two years. In that short time, Zalith had introduced him to a world he didn't want to let go of.

Before Zalith, Alucard hadn't known what love was or what it might be. But now, he felt as if he *did* know, and that was because of Zalith. It *was* Zalith he loved. After four hundred bitter long years of sorrow, pain, and loneliness, he stumbled across this demon, and within him, he had found a part of himself that he thought he'd never find. He found something that felt like home; he found safety, trust, and love. Three things he thought he might never feel, especially not all within *one* person. But in Zalith's arms, everything felt right. Nothing would take that from him.

While he stood there, he soon felt the demon's hand move up his body and to the back of his head. At the very same time, his once silent hunger was beginning to grow— of course it was. Zalith's neck was just inches away, and despite his earlier hesitation, right now, he felt like he might not feel as reluctant. The demon obviously still wanted him to take his blood so that he could feel better, but Alucard's reason for wanting it was simply out of desire. He didn't care that it made him feel euphoric or that it would cure his pain; he desired to have Zalith inside him in whatever way he could.

Zalith pulled Alucard's head closer to his neck, and as he did, Alucard complied. He widened his jaw, and without hesitation, he sunk his four fangs into the demon's neck. The moment Zalith's blood touched his tongue, he sighed in relief, moving his hand to the back of the demon's head, which he then used to grip a fistful of his wet hair. He felt Zalith grip his throat with one of his hands, a satisfied sigh escaping *his* breath as the water poured down to the floor behind him.

The demon, who obviously couldn't help himself, then sunk his own fangs into the left side of Alucard's neck, and both of them sighed quietly in contentment. But Zalith was quick to pull his fangs from Alucard's skin, clearly worried that he might be causing him discomfort, but the vampire felt no such thing. For a few more moments, he downed the demon's blood, and once he was satisfied enough, he pulled his fangs from his neck and leaned against the wall, tilting his head back to sigh and smile in gratitude.

As Alucard sighed, Zalith smirked, staring at his bloody fangs. He moved closer, gripping Alucard's jaw in one hand; he then dragged his left thumb over one of the vampire's fangs, wiping the blood from it, cutting his skin at the same time so that it would bleed for a few moments. With an unseemly smile on his face, he then placed his bloody thumb on the vampire's tongue. Alucard didn't hesitate and slowly closed his mouth, keeping the demon's thumb within.

Zalith watched him as he gripped the demon's wrist and slowly pulled it back so that his thumb was dragged over his lips. He swallowed the blood with a content groan, and once he pulled the demon's thumb from his mouth, he leaned closer to kiss him.

But then a knock at the door ended their pleasured trance.

Zalith scowled in the direction of the door that led out to the hall. "What?" he called irritably.

"Danford is calling, sir," answered the butler.

The demon rolled his eyes and sighed as he looked back at Alucard.

"Who is Danvord?" he asked with a curious frown.

"Someone who works for me," the demon replied as he moved his face back into Alucard's and kissed him a few more times. But then the demon stopped and frowned regrettably. He pressed one last kiss upon the vampire's lips and stepped back. "I have to go and take that call. I'll find you shortly." He then smirked, dragging his thumb over Alucard's bottom lip. "There are clothes for you on the side with the towels. If you want something for breakfast, you'll find staff in the kitchen," he said and kissed him *one* last time before turning around to get out of the shower.

Watching him leave, a sad frown clung to Alucard's face. He didn't want Zalith to go, but he clearly had business to see to, and he'd not interfere with that. So as Zalith dried off and got dressed, Alucard turned back to face the water and leaned his right hand against the wall in front of him.

The water hit his new wound, making him grimace lightly; it ran red as it trickled down his body and to the floor but cleared after a few moments. A smile found its way to his face, however, as he basked in the thought of having *three* of Zalith's bites on his body—although one had almost healed entirely. But so many at once made his headache worse. He scowled, bringing his hand to his head as he did, but thanks to Zalith, he'd discovered a remedy for these pains.

He twisted the tap, cutting off the water. He then stepped out of the shower and took one of the two black towels that had been left for him in front of the large mirror; beside them sat a neatly folded white shirt and pair of black trousers. He'd get dressed and head downstairs to find someone who could make him some coffee. The taste might not please him, but it did help calm the headache that came after the high of Zalith's blood and venom.

Grabbing the second towel, he used it to dry his hair as well as he could. He then set his eyes upon several combs and brushes beside the basin and frowned unsurely as he tried to decide which one he should use. He couldn't locate the comb Zalith lent him the first night he stayed, so he grabbed the one that looked the closest. He tidied his hair, dried the rest of his body, and got dressed. Then, with a nervous frown on his face, he left the bathroom in search of the kitchen.

He just hoped he didn't cross paths with Varana.

Chapter Forty-Nine

— ≺ ✝ ≻ —

Poison

| **Alucard** |

If Alucard were to find the kitchen, he thought that he should search for a room that had more than a single life force inside. It took him a moment to locate one, however, as his ethos was slow to respond due to the amount of blood he'd lost and the demon venom currently raging through his body. It didn't bother him, though; it wasn't like he had anywhere to be today, was it?

Once he located a room, he turned around and navigated through the hall, descended the stairs, and explored uncharted sections of the house. Before long, he stumbled upon the kitchen, distinguished by its black tiled flooring and dark ivory-green tiled walls adorned with white panelling along the top. The back wall boasted expansive windows, offering a captivating view of the extensive garden outside.

At the heart of the kitchen stood an island counter space, surrounded by counters on the back wall and half of both the left and right walls. This arrangement left ample room for a tall pantry and two doors adjacent to it on the left, with another door leading to a wine cellar on the right. Considering the layout of Zalith's house, Alucard deduced that one of the doors on the left likely led to the lounge they occupied the previous night—a practical choice for the staff, ensuring they didn't have to traverse great distances with piping-hot meals.

He set his eyes on two kitchen staff, who were all tending to tasks, and the butler, Edwin. The first man—tall, dark, and rather skinny—was washing the dishes. As he put them into their correct cupboards, the second man—who was smaller than him—was seemingly making sure that everything within each cabinet was accounted for, his green eyes scouring everything very carefully. The butler, Edwin, stood with his back against the pantry, a watchful look on his face as he observed the others' work.

The vampire made his way into the kitchen, and as he did, all three staff members glanced at him as though they were unsure who should address him.

"Can I help you, sir?" Edwin asked.

Alucard stopped beside the island and looked at him. "Yes," he said with a matter-of-fact tone. "I would like a coffee."

The butler nodded as he stood up straight. "How would you like it?"

He'd never been asked such a question. There was more than one way to make coffee? He thought to himself but then shrugged. "However Zalith has his."

However, Edwin didn't begin his task. "He often has it different depending on the time of day, sir."

A sour glare clung to Alucard's face. "Do it however, then," he grumbled, and as the butler nodded and moved to do as he was told, the vampire set his eyes on the garden through the windows to his right. He waited, watching as a flock of birds flew over the tops of the trees in the distance.

The other two staff soon left, and as the smell of coffee filled the kitchen, Alucard looked over at the butler to see that he was almost done.

That, however, was when he realized that it wasn't just him and the butler in the kitchen.

"Oh," came a woman's voice.

Alucard turned his head to stare in Varana's direction, the woman he'd not long come to learn was not only Zalith's best friend but also Alucard's own sister. She stood in the doorway in an emerald green off-shoulder dress that reached her ankles, and as he set his eyes on her, she smiled and made her way into the kitchen, her heels clicking on the tiled floor.

"Good morning," she said with a smile as she pulled out a chair from the island and sat down. She then looked at Edwin, who was preparing the vampire's coffee. "You, bring me some wine."

The man obediently did as he was told. He abandoned the boiling coffee, took a bottle of wine from a cabinet, and poured a glass for the woman. He made his way over, placed it in front of her with a skittish, "Here you are, ma'am," and returned to his previous task.

As she took a sip—maintaining eye contact with the frowning vampire the entire time—she smiled again. "So, it would seem that you are Z's latest pet," she said, sounding condescending.

Unsure of what she meant, Alucard frowned harder. However, he was sure that she was talking about Zalith. At first, he'd thought Zalith's name started with an X—such a spelling would make more sense to him, but hearing this woman say Z told him that he was wrong. It made more sense now, though; Zalith...Z...why had he thought it might be spelt with an X?

He was drifting. He stared at the woman, waiting for her to elaborate—she was clearly going to. Why else would she have sat down?

"You know, it's funny," she started. "When he refused to let me see you, initially I thought that you might have been somebody that I knew—and it frustrated me deeply because he usually at least gives me a name, like Gabriel or Colin..." she paused, thinking to herself for a moment as her eyes wandered up to the ceiling. But she then smiled and looked at him again. "And there was Danford, Geoffrey, Jack, Victor, Marius, Sinclair—who he really enjoyed for *quite* some time—and there was Jacob, Frederic, another Jacob, Isaac...you get the picture, I'm sure," she said with yet another sweet smile.

But all Alucard saw was the sour hue smothering her face. He could see her eyes darting from his face to his neck; the bite Zalith left there was surely visible, and she seemed awfully irritated by it. He kept her eyes on her, though, and when he thought about what she'd just said, his mind started racing, and confusion consumed him. Pet? *Latest*? Danford? The Danford Zalith hadn't long left him to go and speak to? He wasn't yet sure what she was talking about, but he was certain that he was going to find out.

"But anyway..." she continued. "As it turns out, you're just my brother." She then sighed loudly. "Surprise, surprise. Leave it to Z to find a way to nearly seamlessly involve himself in something he has no business being involved in. And so...now he's with you, I suppose," she said with a shrug and took a sip of her wine.

She then stared at him for a few moments, clearly waiting for him to say something. But he had nothing to say—he didn't know what he was supposed to say. She tilted her head, he scowled slightly, and as she glanced down at her wine, she slowly lost her smile before looking back at him.

"You look just like Lucifer; has anybody ever told you that?"

His light scowl became thick with anger. Had anybody ever told him that? Only everyone that had ever raised him, only every thought in his head every time he saw himself in a mirror.

Varana then rested her arms on the countertop. "You know, Alucard—I *can* call you Alucard, right?"

"No," he snarled.

A flicker of amusement glimmered in her eyes. "You know, Aleksei, I'm so sorry for what happened yesterday. I feel so ashamed. I really should have apologized to you for the interruption and what I was about to do to you..." she said with a tone in her voice that Alucard couldn't quite understand—sorrow, regret...patronizing, even.

The vampire wordlessly glared at her, waiting. He was already tired of this woman's face, her voice, her presence, but he'd not be rude. This was Zalith's friend, after all. But...he couldn't help but wonder...how did she know his name? *Names.* She knew to call him Alucard and then Aleksei when he disapproved. Had Zalith told her? If so, that irritated him—Zalith should know *not* to expose his names to anyone, especially someone like Varana, someone who could sell him out to Lucifer in the blink of an eye. However, he trusted Zalith, so he assumed that she must have heard them elsewhere...but where?

Varana continued. "I know that we don't know each other very well, and maybe this is a one-way feeling, but I'm sure that you can agree that there's a certain...*something* that you and I share between us. Not a spiritual link, but...well, I suppose whatever connection it is that comes from sharing a father, in one way or another. So, as your *sister*, I believe that it would be deceitful and negligent of me *not* to warn you about something that might hurt you—and there *is* something that I think you should know about. In fact, I've been near sick about it since the moment I set eyes on you," she said with a sorrowful frown.

With a look of disinterest, he blinked slowly. "Okay," he mumbled, waiting for her to continue.

"So, Z and I have been very close for centuries, and I've seen every single side there is to that man," she started with a pleased tone in her voice. "I know he's captivating, and I know how it feels when he smiles—that little smile of his," she said with a sigh. "And when he accepts you into his little circle, and how he has this ability to make you feel safe and warm and fuzzy inside. I know him, big brother, and I am begging you from the bottom of my heart to be careful," she said, her tone changing from stern to worried.

Alucard stared at her, his frown of confoundment growing as each word left her mouth.

"He takes good men, uses them, and throws them away like useless trash. It's horrible to watch, it really is—especially when he takes his time. And he's *so* good at what he does. He makes them trust him...love him..." she paused to sigh sadly. "He makes them feel like they're protected, like they're a part of his world...but they're *not*. They *never* are. How could they be? He's a narcissist; everything he does is for his own entertainment. Z doesn't have room for anyone in his heart other than himself. It pains me to say this to you, but men like *you* are nothing more than a way for him to pass the time. It's all just a silly little game to him." She then shook her head, a sympathetic look on her face as she stared at Alucard, waiting for him to answer.

He didn't know what to say...or what to think. He wasn't even sure if what he was hearing right now was actually being said or if his thoughts were toying with him again. The words she spoke sounded so much like what Damien said, and that only made him feel worse.

"He usually drops everyone soon after he's had sex with them a time or two; maybe three or four times—once the thrill of the chase is gone...or once he gets what he wants. Nothing ever lasts more than a year or two. And...well, I assume he's fucked you already, hasn't he?" she asked, glancing at the bite on his neck.

Alucard frowned uncomfortably, her words beginning to dig their way past his happiness and into the depths of his anxious mind.

Varana then sighed again and frowned sadly. "The clock's ticking, I suppose. He chases power, Alucard; he can't help himself. It's almost like it was bred into him... and who out there is more powerful than Lucifer's very own son?"

A dreadful, suffocating anguish pierced Alucard's heart, transforming his once perplexed frown into a visage of sheer horror. As his heart quickened its agonizing rhythm, ensnared by the relentless thorns of despair and dismay, he helplessly observed the woman rise from her seat and slowly traverse towards the door, each step echoing the melancholy cadence of his shattered emotions.

She stopped to look back at him. "You've known each other for two years, and you don't really know him very well at all, do you? I'm sorry," she said with a sigh, and then she left the room.

Alucard's thoughts hit a wall. His body tensed, his heart ached, and everything within him told him that he'd fallen into a trap—that he should have listened to Damien, to his doubtful thoughts... to *Elvin*. So many names, so many people.... Pet? He wasn't the first person Zalith had been with, that was obvious, and he clearly wasn't the first he'd broken, either. *That* was how he felt.

Broken.

Utterly destroyed.

Empty.

Used.

It was the worst feeling he'd ever been forced to feel.

Everything Varana said made sense, and as much as he wanted to ignore it, he couldn't. He did trust Zalith; he did *love* him. He felt safe with him; he felt like he was a part of his world, and it had taken Zalith such a long time to make him feel these things. Now that he thought about it, it seemed like Zalith knew exactly what to say and do, and just at the right time, too. The demon had tried so many different approaches, almost as though he'd been through them all a thousand times before—like Alucard was a lock to which he simply had to find the right key.

A game.

Entertainment.

Things he knew Zalith chased.

And sex? Zalith tried so many times to get it, and finally, he got what he wanted. Just a small while ago, he'd asked for it again... but he changed his mind. That all but confirmed what Varana said, right? Zalith was probably already bored of him. And what now? Would Zalith throw him away like he did all those other men? Would he brush him off like some used, out-of-date tool and forget about him?

Alucard wouldn't blame him. Who was he to think that he might be different? He didn't even consider it for a moment. He'd fallen into a demon's well-laid-out trap, and he deserved the consequences. The pain he felt was of his own doing. *He* had fallen in love with Zalith—the demon hadn't forced that, he simply... caused it. He invited Alucard into his game, and Alucard had accepted, only to end up another loser on a list of countless others.

Gabriel, Colin, Danford, Geoffrey, Jack, Victor, Marius, Sinclair, Jacob, Frederic, Jacob, Isaac... Alucard.

He was simply another name for Zalith to add to his collection, wasn't he? And Danford? Zalith was talking to a Danford right now, a Danford he'd left him alone in the shower for. Business? Was that really what it was? Or was Zalith playing two men at the same time? Alucard wouldn't blame him if he was, either. He wasn't enough—he was told that far too often by Damien, so why would that not also be the case with Zalith?

He stood there, staring at the floor, unable to silence his thoughts, unable to disregard the agonizing pain he felt in his heart. Of course this would happen. Why wouldn't it? He was a fool to think it wouldn't, a fool to believe that he could be happy. Damien was right; who could love him? Who would spend their precious time with a miserable, boring, unlovable creature like him? All he was good for were games like those Zalith played because he'd play along so well. The slightest bit of attention had reeled him in like a fish on a hook, a hook that he just wouldn't let go of despite the ghastly tear it made in his body.

He'd not hold on anymore, though. Now that he knew what happened... what *was* happening, he'd not disrespect himself so much as to continue to participate in a game that belittled who he was. It hurt—it hurt *so much*, but what choice did he have? To stick around and let Zalith fuck and toy with him until he was tired? To pretend he didn't know what was going on so that he might feel loved just a little longer? No. He'd not be laughed at a moment more—he'd not be seen as stupid, easy, and meek. He was within this trap willingly, and he'd escape as easily as he'd fallen in.

However, Zalith then walked into the kitchen, a smile appearing on his face as he made his way over to the vampire. But Alucard glared at him with so much hostility that he saw the confusion flicker through Zalith's eyes.

"I'm sorry about that," the demon said, obviously assuming that Alucard was upset because he left him to take Danford's call. Then, as the butler made his way over with the vampire's coffee, Zalith took it from him and dismissed him. He smiled, glancing down at the coffee. "Are you okay?" he asked, looking at Alucard as he held the cup out to him.

Okay? No. His sadness boiled into anger—sad, confused anger, and it was a combination of feelings that he couldn't retain for very long. He held up his hand to take the coffee, and as Zalith placed it in his hand, he failed to clasp the mug. Instead, as

Zalith let go, it fell to the ground, smashed, and sent the boiling liquid across the floor. Immediately, before Zalith could question him, he snatched the demon's throat and harshly pinned him against the wall, glaring into his confused eyes with such *hatred*.

With a confused, somewhat frustrated look on his face, Zalith stared at him. "Alucard, what are you doing?" he asked in utter confoundment as he gripped the vampire's wrist.

Alucard glared at him, his anger raging, his intent to harm increasing... but... he didn't want to hurt him. After all, he couldn't blame Zalith; the demon was just playing his game, and Alucard had been the one to wilfully walk in and take part. It was no fault but his own, and the heartbreak was his own fault, too.

And it hurt. It hurt so fucking bad; seeing Zalith in front of him, gripping his throat in his hand, knowing he could tear it out in half a moment... and that he *would* if he didn't love him so much.

Slowly, as his angered scowl faded, he loosened his grip on Zalith's throat and eventually let go and backed off. He took his eyes off Zalith, who dragged his hand over his neck and stared at him, waiting for an answer.

With a breathy, shaky huff, Alucard said, "I'm... leaving."

Zalith frowned in confusion. "Why?"

The vampire scowled—as if he didn't know. "You know why," he snarled before turning around to head for the door.

Zalith grabbed his wrist and stopped him from walking off. "Actually, I don't," he insisted. "Is... this because I had to take a call?"

With a hostile snarl, Alucard hastily yanked his wrist from Zalith's grip and shoved him back. "Don't touch me!" he snapped, glaring at him with as much anger as he could muster through his sadness. Then, he headed for the door once again.

Perplexed, Zalith swiftly snatched his arm and prevented him from leaving. "What the hell happened?" he questioned, and as Alucard pulled away from him once again, he frowned worriedly. "At least give me an explanation," he requested calmly.

"Explanation?" Alucard snarled, beginning to feel distressed. "What is there to explain? I know what you're doing—what you want to do. I won't stick around and remain one of your little pets," he snapped. "You got what you wanted; don't act like you're worried or upset—it's all just part of your game." Then, he turned his back on the demon and left the kitchen. He didn't care about the upset expression on Zalith's face; he was sure that was as fake as everything else he'd ever said to him.

"Pets?" Zalith asked in confusion as he chased after the vampire. "Where is this even coming from?!" he called with distress in his voice.

Ignoring him, Alucard made his way through the hall and towards the stairs that would take him back to Zalith's room.

"Alucard?!" Zalith called as the vampire stormed up the stairs. "What's going on?!"

But the vampire continued to ignore him—

Then came Varana's voice, "Oh. What's happening?"

"Fuck off," Zalith instantly snarled as he hurried up the stairs after Alucard.

Alucard went into Zalith's bedroom, grabbed and pulled on his shoes, and then headed for the door, but he wasn't fast enough to get out before Zalith stepped inside.

Zalith stood in the doorway and stared at Alucard, who stopped in his tracks. "Can you *please* tell me what happened so we can figure this out?" he pleaded calmly.

"There is nothing to figure out," Alucard said with a scowl. "Get out of my way."

But Zalith didn't move. "I don't know where you got such an impression, but I'm not playing any sort of game and never have been!" he insisted. "I understand that you're upset, but you could at least dignify me with an explanation."

Alucard's confliction seethed through his anger. He didn't know if he could trust him anymore. He didn't know what to think; all he knew was that he had to leave. If Zalith really didn't know why he was insisting upon doing so, then he'd tell him.

As his scowl reflected his pain, he glared at the confused demon. "How can I believe you? How can I trust anything you say? I don't know anything about you, Zalith; I don't even know your full name," he said with a pained laugh. "You know so much about me, yet when I think about it, I really don't know you. But what I do know is that I would rather leave myself than stick around for you to get tired of me and throw me out like some used, unwanted toy," he said, his voice weakening.

With sadness both on his face and in his eyes, Zalith shook his head. "Alucard, I'm not going to get tired of you, and if there's anything you'd like to know, I'm more than willing to share it with you," he persisted with a despondent tone in his voice.

Alucard didn't answer. He took his eyes off the demon and stared down at the floor.

"If that call had anything to do with this, Danford is just a colleague—he means very little to me. If you'd rather me kill him, then so be it. I'll kill him."

The vampire glared at him. "Have you fucked everyone that works for you?" he asked, watching as Zalith's saddened frown was accompanied by a confused, conflicted stare. "Did all the others work for you, too? Do they still work for you? Will I tomorrow hear that Sinclair is calling? Or Jack or some other man you just used? How long until I'm on that list, too? How long until I'm just someone you work with that means very little to you?"

Zalith scowled angrily. "Did Varana tell you all of this?"

Dismay smothered Alucard's face as he looked down at the floor once again. Zalith didn't answer, and he was avoiding it. That pretty much confirmed his suspicions.

"Alucard, she's a bitch," he said, stepping forward—but Alucard stepped back, not at all interested in allowing him to touch him. "She's borderline obsessed with me and has been for a very long time. She's trying to tear us apart because she's jealous, and this is a large part of why I didn't want you two to meet right away—she's crazy!"

"You didn't answer my questions," he uttered, and then he growled, " I want to leave. Either get out of my way, or I'll move you myself."

He didn't comply. "Can you please stay so that we can sit down and have a proper conversation about this?" he pleaded sadly.

Stay? Alucard wished he could. Despite his anger, despite his sadness, he still wanted nothing more than to stay with him. But he couldn't. He wouldn't allow himself to stay in a situation that would ultimately end with him feeling a whole lot worse than he already did. He felt selfish for denying Zalith's constant pleas, but if he stayed, Zalith's words would infect him like poison. He always knew exactly what to say and how to say it, and Alucard wouldn't let him drag him in deeper.

"Some of them *did* work for me, yes, but a large majority of them didn't," Zalith continued, answering Alucard's previous questions. "Most of them died; however, those who are still alive, I will get rid of them without a moment's hesitation if that's what you need to feel secure. They didn't mean anything to me, Alucard—*nothing* close to what you mean to me. If this were any of them right now in this situation, I would most certainly *not* be fighting for them like this."

He didn't care. He'd made his choice. "Move," he growled with animosity one last time.

Despair smothered the entirety of Zalith's face. "Please, don't do this," he begged as he stepped closer and slowly placed his hand on the vampire's chest. "Please."

Unable to look at his face for a moment longer, Alucard glared down at the floor. He didn't know whether Zalith really was upset or if this was just another façade. He could never tell—would he ever be able to tell? It didn't matter. Today was the last day he'd ever see him.

He tightly gripped the demon's wrist, pulling his hand off his chest, and as he harshly threw it away, he scowled at him. Then, with a look of distress, he shoved Zalith aside so harshly that the demon stumbled to his left and collided with one of the dressers.

Alucard couldn't allow himself to remain inside the demon's house or in his company anymore. He left the room, made his way downstairs, and ignored Zalith's pained call.

"Wait!" he shouted desperately, chasing after Alucard.

The vampire reached the bottom of the stairs and walked into the hallway, setting his eyes on the front door. Zalith abruptly snatched his wrist, but Alucard shoved him aside once again, and as the demon hit the wall, the entire hall shook. He continued on his way out, reaching the front door, which he pulled open so he could storm through the courtyard and towards the ground's exit.

As he prepared to morph into vermillion smoke, however, the demon caught up and wrapped his arms around him so tightly that escape in his chosen way was no longer possible.

"Alucard, please," he sorely begged, holding him tightly. "Don't leave—"

"Get off me!" Alucard yelled, losing what hold he had on his anger. He tore Zalith from him and shoved him away. "I won't be used by someone else who is supposed to care about me!" he insisted, his anger and pain infecting in his breaking voice.

"Alucard, I'm not using you—"

"Shut the fuck up!" he yelled in outrage, but then exhaled deeply and tried to calm himself. "I'm...so...*tired* of this—of everything," he breathed, his anger outweighed by sorrow as he backed away from Zalith, who stood there, staring at him with a dismayed frown. "I just...want...*something*," he said, the ache in his heart burning like fire. "Something real—something where I don't suffer, something where I don't end up losing. I can't...I won't stay here and pretend like it's fine. As much as I want to, as much as I...." He hesitated, his breaths becoming faster as his pain increased. He'd not say it. There was no point. He scowled harder and shook his head. "I let myself fall for your game, and I'm the one left feeling like a fucking idiot—but I don't blame *you*. I just won't let you keep playing with me." He then laughed painfully. "The *one* time I let myself fall in love, and all it did was cause me misery—all anything ever does is cause me misery. I guess you're just another name on *that* list, no?"

Zalith shook his head and tried to step closer, but Alucard backed off. "There is literally *nothing* going on, I promise!" he lamented. "Let me prove it to you—tell me *how* I can prove it to you...please."

"Goodbye, Zalith."

"Alucard, wait!" the demon insisted, reaching out—

But Alucard disappeared into vermillion smoke before he could reach him. Then, without looking back, he raced over the forest, leaving behind everything he had thought would be the long-awaited escape from the depravity which was his life.

It was over...and now everything would go back to how it was before, wouldn't it?

| Zalith |

In half a moment, Alucard was gone, and Zalith was left with a hundred different thoughts and emotions. He felt terribly, awfully sad; he felt angry as all hell and instantly set his fury upon Varana—*where* was she? He knew she had something to do with this, and he'd not let her off lightly—he'd not let her off *at all*.

But Alucard...where was he going? Zalith hadn't even done anything...and all he could think about was how he could make this up to him. He couldn't let him go—

he *wouldn't*. Alucard meant so much to him that watching him leave in such agony caused him so much pain of his own.

He buried his anger—for now—and focused on Alucard. *He* was what mattered right now. Zalith would interrogate Varana later. He had to find Alucard; He'd not let him go; he could never let him go, especially not over something that was neither of their faults. If there was anything Zalith would hold himself accountable for, it would be leaving Alucard alone, knowing that Varana would most certainly take the opportunity to try and get to him—and that was what she had clearly done.

With worry and sorrow in his eyes, he focused on Alucard's weak, far aura, and began his chase.

Chapter Fifty

— ⟨ † ⟩ —

The Slow Descent into Something Quite Like Death

| Alucard |

Alucard found himself adrift in an endless flight, the passage of time slipping through the cracks of his wearied consciousness. His once formidable body now faltered, aching for respite, its strength waning as an urgent plea for rest echoed within. The looming spectre of unconsciousness loomed, a threat he couldn't afford. Fixing his gaze on the sprawling forest beneath, the vampire contemplated the unknown expanse ahead. The distance from that accursed demon's abode remained a mystery, the uncertainty gnawing at him with each passing moment. Were it not for the relentless grasp of fatigue, he would have traversed oceans by now.

He descended to the forest, and when he landed and rematerialized from his vermillion smoke form, he stood there, heart racing, legs shaking, and staring at the endless forest that lay ahead. He didn't want to let himself sink into his thoughts, but he couldn't ignore them for much longer. Zalith—*him*…he'd caused him so much pain, so much *agony*. To make him trust him, love him…all for a stupid little game.

Alucard felt so, *so* ashamed of himself for having fallen so easily into Zalith's trap. Every instinct within him had told him to be careful the moment he'd been forced to work with that creature; *everyone* he knew back then warned him—even *Damien* had warned him. But had he listened to any of them? No. He'd disregarded their warnings and followed his heart—his stupid, pathetic, useless heart, a heart that only ever brought him pain and suffering. He'd stupidly allowed himself to fall in love—love…*love*…such an ugly feeling. Such a horrible, despicable, awful feeling. That feeling had caused him so much torment, so much horror; it led him blindly into a web of lies that would stay with him forever. He'd been used in the most horrid way; he had given himself completely to that demon, and all for nothing. All so Zalith could have a little fun without caring how it would leave Alucard feeling once he was done.

He began an aimless walk, unsure of where he was going. Home, maybe…home was where he wanted to be. Home with everything he knew, everything he understood, and no Zalith—no demons. He wanted to forget *everything*. He wished he'd never let that demon into his life, into his heart. If only he could forget…if only he had listened, if only…if only he was the loveless creature everyone seemed to believe demons were; if he couldn't feel love, none of this would have happened. But how could he forget? How could he ignore it? His imprint was on that creature…that terrible man, that awful, selfish…no. He couldn't think of Zalith like that, and that made him angrier. He hated him—he *resented* him—but he also *loved* him. It didn't matter, though. It would never matter. Zalith didn't love him. Zalith used him, and he should have known. He had no one to blame but himself.

Alucard pressed on, the landscape blurred by the tears that welled in his eyes. The physical pain he endured seemed inconsequential compared to the searing ache that radiated from his chest, a relentless agony that mirrored the torment of his shattered emotions. As he moved forward, his limbs protesting with each reluctant stride, he felt his wounds slowly reopen, but he didn't care. He couldn't stop.

He grappled with the shattered fragments of his once-boundless happiness. The abrupt and heart-rending conclusion to his time with Zalith left him adrift in a sea of despair, an ocean of sorrow that threatened to drown him. Would joy ever find its way back to him, or was he destined to navigate the stormy waters of heartache indefinitely? The further he distanced himself from the place where Zalith's false affections had played out, the more suffocating the grip of desolation became.

The prospect of a life without Zalith, once an unbearable thought, now weighed upon him like an anchor, pulling him deeper into the abyss of sorrow. The night he believed he'd lost Zalith forever paled in comparison to the reality of this final separation. Zalith was no longer within reach, and the mere idea of retracing his steps was a futile endeavour. What awaited him back there? Only the remnants of a fabricated connection, a painful reminder of love that was never genuine. Alucard couldn't—he *wouldn't*—subject himself to that deception again.

So he walked, and walked, and walked, each step more painful than the last; he moved through the world as if trying to outrun the haunting echoes of his shattered heart. His feet, heavy with fatigue, protested each advancement, and the numbness that crept up his legs seemed an apt reflection of the emotional void that now enveloped him. The pain in his heart, once a sharp and acute ache, now melded seamlessly with the weariness that pervaded his entire being.

Eventually, he could walk no more. His body rebelled against the relentless march, his feet throbbing with an ache that resonated deep within his bones. Leaning heavily against the nearest tree, he sought refuge, transferring the burden of his weight to the sturdy trunk. As he pressed his hand against the bark, a shaky exhale escaped him, a feeble attempt to contain the despair threatening to engulf him. He wouldn't shed tears or scream like a wounded child, especially not over someone like Zalith, someone who perceived him as nothing more than a jest. He channelled the stern resolve that Damien had clawed and beaten into him for hundreds of years, and just as Damien would tell him to, he'd get the fuck over it.

What other choice did he have? Zalith didn't love him. To Alucard, that demon had been his world, a profound mistake that now echoed in the emptiness surrounding him. He realized, with a bitter clarity, that his true world was the one he had abandoned—the world of his work. His craft, his purpose, and his identity were intertwined with the pursuit of his duties, and in deviating from that path, he'd courted heartbreak. It was a lesson learned through pain, a reminder that his worth transcended the fleeting illusions of affection.

With a scowl on his face, he stood up straight and moved forward. But the vampire's emotions were clouding his focus... his ethos was dwindling, as was his strength, and when he heard rushing footsteps, he was too slow to react—

"Vlady-poo!" came Detlaff's sing-song, cheery voice. "I found you!"

Before Alucard could lift his arms to defend himself, Detlaff crashed into him with so much force that the vampire stumbled back, but Detlaff wrapped his arms around him and abruptly greeted him with a disgusting kiss to his mouth—if slapping his widened mouth over his could be called a kiss.

The vampire gagged and scowled in revolt, but he refused to let the repulsion deter him. Engaging his teeth, Alucard seized Detlaff's tongue. In the midst of the demon's attempted scream, Alucard ruthlessly tore the appendage from his mouth, causing a violent spray of blood to splatter in all directions. Yet, Alucard's relentless pursuit persisted.

Undeterred, he continued his macabre actions. Swiftly, before Detlaff could attempt to pull away, Alucard relinquished his grip on the demon's arm, seizing the severed tongue and forcefully thrusting it back into Detlaff's gaping mouth. He then clamped Detlaff's mouth shut, leveraging his strength to press the demon back against a nearby tree. The vampire covered Detlaff's mouth and nose with his palm, depriving him of breath. As Detlaff struggled, swallowing his own tongue, a snarl of amusement curled across Alucard's lips, watching with a dark satisfaction as Detlaff succumbed to the forced silence.

But despite just having his tongue torn out, Detlaff smiled in glee and laughed through Alucard's hand. It was then that Alucard realized the smear of silver on Detlaff's cheek.

Alucard's entire body convulsed, but not in fear or shock... it did so in response to something happening inside him. He stumbled back as Detlaff lightly kicked his shin; with a painful cough, he brought his hand to his mouth and wiped what he thought was just Detlaff's blood from his lips, but among the red was silver—silver that sizzled and burned the skin on his fingers.

"Uh-oh," Detlaff giggled as he skipped over to the vampire, who lurched back in confusion. "Looks like *little* brother knows how to get *big* brother all droopy," he said with a smile, clapping his hands as he stopped in front of Alucard, whose back hit a tree.

When it felt like fire burned through his throat and body, Alucard groaned painfully and gritted his teeth as he gripped his neck in his hands. Silver—one of his only and deadliest weaknesses—to stab him with it was one thing, but for him to swallow it? Detlaff was clearly smart enough to know that there really wasn't anything he could do about that. A stake could be torn out, and his body would heal, but a liquid? He could only try to throw up, but Detlaff wasn't going to give him the chance.

With his grin fading from excited to frustrated, Detlaff snatched Alucard's throat and wrist before he could ram his fingers down his throat. "You left me down in that dark, horrible little cage for a year!" he yelled, glaring into Alucard's horrified eyes. "A whole year! *YEAR*!!!" he screamed, stomping his feet on the ground. "I could have DIED down there! What kind of big brother does that to poor little Detlaff?!"

Struggling, Alucard snarled and slammed his fist into the demon's stomach, sending him flying back fifty feet before he hit a tree and crashed down to the ground. He was *so* slow to do so, but Alucard managed to put a small distance between himself and the demon by disappearing into vermillion smoke and reappearing a mile or so away. But Detlaff was a whole lot faster than he remembered, and Alucard had used pretty much the last of his ethos in his attempt to get to a safe enough distance.

Before he could attempt a second time to force himself to throw up and remove the silver from his body, Detlaff reappeared, snatched his neck, and pinned him down on the ground with a playful grin on his face.

"Where are you GOING?!" he yelled crazily, laughing as he pinned Alucard's arms above his head so that he couldn't attack. "You're not going anywhere this time, big brother. I've got you now...and Daddy's gonna be so proud!" he sang gleefully. "Daddy...he bred all of big brother's weaknesses out of us and gave us all your strength—and more! Detlaff's not weak to silver, no, no...no. Detlaff's not weak to anything!" he insisted with a scowl as he stared down at Alucard, who struggled with a pained grimace on his face. "Daddy made us perfectly...just to fight you," he said, smiling as he tilted his head.

Alucard went to speak, but Detlaff interjected—

"Shhh," he denied, shaking his head as he leaned his face closer to Alucard's. "Don't waste your strength, big brother. You'll need it when you come and see what I did to your favourite little vampire, Benny boy."

The vampire glared up at him, collecting whatever strength he had left to unleash a desperate attack on the disgusting creature that stood over him. He'd lay there, he'd play his little game for a while longer, and then he'd teach Detlaff that ethos-created children were *nothing* compared to blood offspring.

With a sad sigh, Detlaff pouted. "How are you feeling, Vlady-poo? Does it hurt? I'm so sorry if it hurts."

It hurt like fuck, but he'd not express his pain; he knew that was what Detlaff wanted. He'd spent four hundred years of his life hiding his pain, so he was sure that he could do it for another few minutes.

Detlaff gradually let go of Alucard's wrists, obviously sure that the vampire had begun losing control of his body. He then stroked the side of Alucard's face and sighed once more. "I wanted to kill you... so bad. After you left me in that dungeon, it gave me time to think about Detlaff and big brother's relationship. I don't think you want to spend time with your little brother... so I take back my offer. I'm going to take you back to my home, I'm going to remove all those ugly little pictures Damien drew on your back, and then, once the other Numen can detect you, they will all come running like moths to a flame!" he sang, clapping his hands as he wriggled around excitedly, straddling the vampire's lap.

Alucard glared up at him in revolt. Just a moment longer.

"Who will come for you first, big brother? Ephriel? Lilith? Erich? Letholdus? Which one of them hates you the most? Which one of them will first jump at the chance to kill big brother? You know... Daddy never told me *why* they all want to kill you.... Why *do* they all want to kill you, Vlady-poo?" he asked but then laughed. "Don't worry, big sister told me. But I won't tell anyone—shhh!" he insisted, looking around as though there were people to listen. He looked back down at Alucard. "I'll use you to draw them all in, and when they come, Daddy will kill them all for what they did to him."

Now that Alucard had heard that information, it was time to kill Detlaff. He had about a minute before the silver paralyzed his body, but he didn't even need *that* to end this creature's life. As Detlaff cackled into the air, Alucard crashed his fist into the demon's chin, sending him flying up.

Alucard shakily but quickly climbed to his feet, and before Detlaff could hit the ground on his way back down, the vampire crashed his fist into his side, sending him racing forward and through several trees that fell upon collision, and when he hit the last tree in his path, he dropped to the ground like a lifeless corpse. Alucard wasn't yet done, though. He watched Detlaff try and struggle to his feet, so he burst into action, reaching the demon in the blink of an eye. Before Detlaff could fully turn to face him, Alucard snatched his face in his hand and smashed the back of his head into the tree.

He moved his hand to the back of Detlaff's head, turned him, and relentlessly smashed his face into the tree over and over and over. The demon's blood splattered everywhere as he tried to cry through each collision, and after a few seconds of continuous hits, Alucard pulled him back with enough force that Detlaff went crashing back the way they had come from. The vampire instantly appeared over him, grabbed his ankle as he tried to crawl away, dragged him for a second or so, and then flung him through the air once again.

As Detlaff hit the ground, he coughed, whimpered, and cried like a child; he held his hands up in surrender when Alucard reached him once again, and as the vampire grabbed him by his collar and pulled him to his feet, he cried and shook his head like a whimpering baby.

Alucard widened his jaws and prepared to end Detlaff's, but he was out of time. His heart convulsed, his body shuddered, and the silver constricted him in a tight, suffocating grip.

Detlaff didn't fail to notice Alucard's time was up. He seized Alucard's throat and forced him back until he hit a tree, which cracked against the collision. The demon grinned in his face, watching as blood began to seep from the vampire's mouth.

"Too slow, Vlady-poo. Like always," he said cruelly, scowling.

Alucard snarled and tried to attack, but the silver had enthralled his entire body. His limbs were becoming entirely numb, his ethos wasn't responding, and he struggled just to remain conscious.

"We're going to be *so* close, big brother," Detlaff whispered. "Not only am I going to see what makes you tick, I'm going to find out how you work... I'm going to cut you, I'm going to feed you, see you, maybe even *be* you. Would you like that? How close we can be... Vlady... poo?"

The vampire grimaced and stuttered painfully. But just as the victorious smirk on Detlaff's face stretched to its peak, Alucard's slowly blurring eyes located a faint blackness moving quickly towards them both.

Alucard had no chance to see what it was—the second it reached them, it collided with Detlaff, who screamed hysterically when he was ripped from Alucard and carried away in the grip of whatever had attacked him.

The vampire dropped to his knees, watching the blurred commotion. But the moment he saw wings and heard ferocious snarling, he knew that it was Zalith who'd found him. The demon slammed Detlaff against a tree, but Detlaff disappeared into nothing, and he started running like a coward.

Alucard's body started shutting down. He panted, grimaced, and tried his best to keep his eyes open. He struggled to bring his hand to his mouth, but as he did so, he wiped it to see that silver was seeping from it. He needed to get the silver out of his body, but he didn't have the strength. Before he could try to move his fingers into his throat, he fell forward, and as the side of his face hit the ground, he exhaled in agony.

He wasn't sure of where he might end up now. What even happened when he died? Would he be sent to purgatory like everyone else? Would he be sent to wherever Lucifer was banished to when his siblings killed him? Or would he just... disappear?

Surely, *that* was the best of all options. He didn't want to spend his life in prison, alone and suffering; but that was his life anyway. No. He'd rather just cease—vanish…end. After all, what more did he have to live for? He'd had these thoughts before, and it tired him. But he was dying, and when people died, did they not think of their fondest memories? Did they not think about the people they loved? The people they would leave behind?

Alucard would leave behind a man who didn't love him, a man who *he* loved, a man he'd spent the best year of his life with—his long, four-hundred-year life, and only a single year had been a good one. One…single year. How stupid was that? To live that long and only be happy for such a short time? It couldn't be a more fitting end, to die the day he lost his reason for living. He felt almost thankful that Detlaff had found him, *grateful* he had come with the one thing that could end his existence and used it in a way that was impossible to be saved from.

The pain couldn't be worse than what he'd been feeling before Detlaff's attack. The pain of dying…and the pain of seeing Zalith hurrying towards him a phantom. Did people see the one they loved before they died, too? Was this some mirage to make his death easier? More painful?

But then…Zalith spoke. His words were murmurs, mumbles, distorted, things he couldn't understand, but what he *did* understand was that this was surely *not* a mirage because Zalith grabbed hold of him and pulled him into his lap. Did mirages feel real as well as appear visually real?

Alucard's eyes started closing while he stared up at the demon, who insistently spoke to him in what looked like panic. Alucard didn't know what he was saying, but…if this was real—if Zalith really was here—then it was possible that he was asking Alucard what the hell happened and what he could do.

Alucard felt conflicted. He didn't want to live with the heartbreak, but he felt as if he'd rather live to hate Zalith than die and give him the satisfaction of knowing that he'd literally caused someone to die for his love. But was that pathetic of him? Did he really want to live or were his instincts telling him to fight for his life? He didn't know what he truly wanted, but *something* was urging him to tell Zalith how to save his life.

He had his ethos reserve—that small amount that would allow him the strength he'd need to feed when in a dying state. He couldn't use it to save himself this time, though; his body wouldn't move even with *that*. But what he could use it for was to show Zalith what happened. He struggled, grunting painfully as he gripped the demon's shirt; his hand gradually climbed to Zalith's face, where he placed his fingers in the correct position to share his thoughts. Then, he grimaced, urging his reserved ethos to wake up and do what it was supposed to do. And although it was slow to wake, it gave him a little—but enough—ethos to show the demon what Detlaff had done to him, and once the memory was in Zalith's mind, Alucard lost his sight, his touch, his everything. The world around him faded to black, he slipped away into the darkness of what might just be death.

Chapter Fifty-One

— ⊰ † ⊱ —

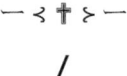

| **Alucard,** *Somewhere in his subconscious* |

Alucard brooded in the solitude of his chamber—a sombre sanctuary that mirrored the cold detachment within. Damien's fortress, though imposing from an external standpoint, lost its grandeur once one stepped beyond the majestic walls. Externally, it projected regality, a structure befitting a monarch. The obsidian crystalline walls, meticulously maintained, radiated an eerie beauty. However, inside, the grandeur dissolved into a stark reality.

His dimly lit room was encased in foreboding dark stone bricks, riddled with fractures and ensnared by webs spun by unspeakable creatures, giving the semblance of blood-like moss. The contrast between the exterior opulence and the interior decay served as a haunting reflection of the dual nature of Damien's castle, a dichotomy not lost on Alucard as he grappled with the shadows lurking within its very walls.

He rested on his bed, staring at the red world out through his small window, which was actually just a few chunks of missing wall. Despite the Underworld being above Hell, it was cold, silent, and empty. Alucard held his arms around his small body as a shiver ran down his spine, forcing him to pull tighter on the sheets he'd been given. But as a boy of seven, he didn't know what to expect from this new place he found himself in. Just a week ago—was it a week? He wasn't sure. Time didn't seem to work the same way there as it did back up in Aegisguard. But he did his best to keep track. A week ago, maybe, he lost his home. The cathedral in which he had been born and raised was gone. The people he knew had been killed right before his eyes by cultists sent by his own father.

Who did he have now? Someone had come. Damien: that was what the strange man had called himself. Alucard had never seen someone so peculiar; half his long hair was white, the other half black. One eye red, one eye blue, and a face so terrifying that Alucard wished not to see it again. But he would. The man had called himself his uncle and claimed he'd be taking care of him now. Alucard wished the woman who had named *him his third name would be the one to take care of him, but she disappeared the moment they left the cathedral.*

He stared aimlessly at the redness outside, unable to make out much through the thick fog. The cries of demons and damned souls echoed around him, creatures his carers had once told him he'd soon be very close with. He knew that he was meant to be royalty, some sort of prince or king or something that would one day be telling those creatures what to do, just like his father before him. But he had no interest. Why should he? Lucifer didn't want him. All his father wanted was his death, and Alucard didn't want to die—why would he want to die?

Die.

He *was* dead.

Right now, he wasn't in his old room; he was trapped inside his own mind. He was reliving his life through memory as it slowly slipped away from him in the real world. He couldn't do anything about it—did he even want to do anything about it? He felt the answer to that was 'no'. Why would he? What did he have? Back then, when he was just a boy, death scared him like a monster in the night, but now, it felt like a sweet, long-awaited relief to escape something so sour as life.

As love.

As pain.

To die was to be free.

Free—something he had never been.

Alucard stared at his uncle. Damien sat there on that same throne he loved so, upon the stage within his castle's huge, crumbling hall. Hundreds of thousands of men and creatures cramped in to see him as he basked in his glory—a dead dragon at his feet, one so very treasured by his brother, Letholdus. Damien had always hated his siblings, and Alucard had never really understood why. His uncle had insisted that it was because he was better than them all, and they refused to see it... and Alucard believed him. What reason did he have to doubt the man who saved his life a month ago?

He stood at the very front of the room among a group of other children, all of whom he knew weren't Damien's. They all looked just as cold and confused as he felt, but not one of them dared speak a word. They stood as he did, staring at their uncle, waiting for his sights to be set upon them.

Yesterday, there were nineteen of them, and today, just eighteen. They all knew where the nineteenth had gone, but no one would say. No one would even dare think it.

Most of the children were older, scarred, and looked as though war had scorned them all several hundred times. Alucard thought about what the nineteenth boy had said before he disappeared: kids this age should be playing; they should be happy, adventurous, and they should be with their parents.

Play? Adventure? What strange words were they?

Alucard never learned what that boy was talking about until he first escaped Damien. And he'd never experience anything like that again...unless he woke up.

So soon, it was only he and four other children remaining. As the nineteenth had done, the rest had fallen out of line, disappearing overnight. Damien didn't tolerate disobedience and awarded it with a terrible cut to the perpetrator's face. Alucard had received many, but he understood why. Damien was their protector, and if they continued to defy him, they'd only be making his life difficult. Damien didn't need that. To protect them, he needed an easy life. He needed them to give him an easy life. To listen, to obey, and to do as they were told when they were told. They all knew what would happen if they pushed too far. Of course, they did. They were the remaining five of nineteen. They wouldn't still be standing in front of their uncle if they didn't understand.

But... when dangled in his face, Alucard chose to seek freedom. He followed when the children tried to escape their uncle's agonizing, bloody rule. However, all that resulted in was Alucard being the last of nineteen. He didn't know why his uncle didn't kill him, too, but he assumed that it was because he cared about him. Why would he think otherwise? Damien had come to collect him himself the night his carers died. All the other children were brought by messengers.

Damien cared. Damien was his family, and as much as Alucard disappointed him, he didn't end his life. A scar or two, sure, but it was only to teach him a lesson.

So many lessons, so many years. Alucard still hadn't learned, had he? He still fucked up, he still let everyone down, and he still got people killed. Dying was the only way to escape all of that, to escape the pain and guilt of his failures, and to escape the heartbreak that he was rewarded with for choosing to ignore Damien's warning.

Alucard, now sixteen, felt as if he was more than capable of pleasing Damien. His first task—he'd not fail. To bring a demon to his uncle's castle; how hard could it be?

A lot harder than he thought, told him the slash across his face. He took too long, Damien said. Of course he did. He should have been faster, more efficient. To take two days instead of one—how stupid of him. He'd not wallow; tomorrow was another day to try and please, and tomorrow would be the day he proved to his uncle that he wasn't the boy who had failed him so many times before.

But years passed. So many years. Four hundred.

Never once had Damien seen he'd grown, and who was Alucard to think otherwise? Would he ever learn? Would he ever realize that Damien was right and always would be? He knew that now. To deviate from Damien was to curse oneself. Damien knew the way, and Alucard knew to follow. Sometimes, he just wanted to wander, but he wouldn't wander anymore. He'd learnt his last lesson. If the loss of his wings wasn't enough to teach him, the loss of his heart was.

Love—such a pathetic waste of time, Damien had said. Don't fall in love, Alucard; it will only destroy you. To love is to be weak. Are you weak, Alucard? You are. You always have been. You tried to live—that failed. You tried to run—that failed. You even tried to fly. Where did that get you? And now, you try to love. Such a pathetic boy. So worthless, so useless, so stupid, so small, so... alone. But to be alone is to be strong. To be strong is to be useful, and to be useful is to please.

That was all that mattered.

Death gripped so tightly. It strangled. It suffocated.

Alucard had never met Death before. But there he was, standing before him. Tall, sleek, and dressed much like the man he'd let himself love. Suit, tie, glasses, and a smile to match his devious aura. He held out a pale, bony hand, inviting Alucard to take it.

But unlike most, Alucard had a choice.

A choice. His *first ever* choice.

But was it? Was it *really* his choice to choose whether he lived or died? It wasn't, was it? Damien would want him to live. Damien would tell him to live. Damien would fight Death so that he would live. He would force him to live so that he could continue to teach him. To weave him into the man he might one day become. Alucard wanted to live for that day. To live for the day that Damien would see him as not a boy but a man who had learned. He just wanted... to feel something.

Something.

Something real.

Something other than shame and failure.

Would he ever feel that? From Damien... from anyone?

What would he feel if he took Death's hand? Would he feel relief? Joy? Release? To be released from the pain that he had long suffered but buried in an attempt to have Damien see just how competent he was. It would be so wonderful. To lift the heaviness of his struggle, of his silence. If he took Death's hand... would he feel that relief?

No relief would come. Never. Not ever.

Death was pulled away from him just as everything else he felt he might take hand in hand was. He stood within darkness. He watched as the suited man vanished like smoke in the wind, a flame snuffed out in a cold, gnawing breeze.

He wasn't really there. Death was never really there.

To die was to wrong Damien.

To die was to be a coward.

To die... it would only please Damien if it were by his own hand. Alucard wouldn't take that from his uncle.

He denied the offer. He denied his chance of freedom. But would he wake? Where he stood was nowhere. Where he felt was nowhere. Where was he? What was this place full of dark and emptiness?

Where was Zalith?

Chapter Fifty-Two

— ⋖ ✝ ⋗ —

Removal

| **Zalith** |

Zalith sat beside Alucard, staring down at him. The vampire lay there, tucked comfortably into his bed, unconscious. But for how long? He didn't know, but he assumed that it would last as long as the last time Zalith took care of him. He'd removed the silver from Alucard's body, as Alucard had instructed, and now all he could do was sit there and wait.

His anger was simmering, boiling past his pain and dismay, soon to unleash itself. But not yet. Before he allowed himself to show Varana exactly where her involvement in Alucard's current predicament had got her, he wanted to make sure that his vampire was comfortable. How could he know, though? He couldn't stare into the vampire's mind, he couldn't feel much of his aura, and if he didn't know better, he'd think that Alucard was dead. But he *did* know better and knew that Alucard was simply healing in the comatose state that Zalith knew his body adopted when he suffered great injury.

Dread tightened its suffocating hold around him. He'd come *so* close to losing Alucard, so close that something inside him had woken from a slumber he hadn't been aware it was in. He really did love Alucard—*so much*—and almost losing him the way he did brought him a horrible, crushing feeling of pain and despair. He didn't want anything like that to ever happen again—he'd do whatever he could to protect him.

However, with the dread came relief. Alucard had said he loved him—more or less. *That* shook him awake him, too. He'd make sure he did his very best to protect his vampire from whatever might come either of their ways, and his very first step in doing so was to deal with Varana.

He'd not wait a second longer. Allowing his impatient anger to break through the hold he'd had over it, he stood up, left the bedroom, and made his way through his house. His anger quickly became a sinister rage as he thought about what he saw in Alucard's memory transfer, when he saw what that woman had said to him—the things she had made him feel with her words, and he wasn't going to let her think she'd gotten away with it. He was tired of her jealousy, her desirous need to ruin his relationship with Alucard. But it wasn't just that. Alucard was hurt—he could have *died*—and she may have something to do with that, too. How the hell had Detlaff known where to find Alucard? Zalith suspected Varana might know, and he'd not falter in showing her just how dangerously angry that made him.

His fury grew as he stormed toward her room. He could hear her voice coming from inside, chattering away to her creature of a sister, who Zalith suspected might also have something to do with what happened. It wouldn't surprise him if all of Lucifer's wretched little children were involved, and if he had to hurt them all to protect Alucard, then he wouldn't hesitate. Detlaff may have escaped, but there was nowhere he could go where Zalith wouldn't find him.

The moment he reached Varana's bedroom door, he kicked the door open with an enraged snarl, and as it slammed against the wall it clung to, he stepped in and set his eyes on the revolting little woman sitting at the vanity. Propped up on the table was her hand mirror—the same mirror she used to speak to her sister, and as suspected, Ysmay was inside the mirror, watching Varana.

As the white curtains flew around violently, caught in the force of the opening door, Varana flinched and dropped the eyeliner pencil in her hand; a look of horror smacked her face as she turned to face Zalith, and her sister giggled in amusement from inside the mirror, but Varana was clearly far too terrified to tell her to shut up.

"What's wrong?" Varana asked, a look of unsettled confusion on her face.

Zalith, glaring at her, didn't hold back. He was certain that she knew *exactly* what was wrong, and the fact that she felt like she could plead ignorance *infuriated* him. He stormed to where she was sitting and grabbed hold of her; she squirmed around and flailed her arms, and in their struggle, they hit the floor as Varana's witch of a sister laughed amusedly. The pair wrestled for a few moments, Varana trying to escape, Zalith trying to pin her down, and through her kicks and screams, he eventually arose victorious, pinning her on her back.

"What the hell is your problem?!" Varana shouted, trying to escape.

"What do you fucking think?!" he yelled but turned his attention from the struggling woman to her identical twin cackling in the mirror—he didn't want her witnessing what was about to happen. "I thought I told you *not* to talk to your fucking sister," he growled.

Varana stared in astonishment. "Ever?!"

Ignoring her, he snarled in anger, snatched the hand mirror from the table—

"What's wrong, Z?" Ysmay giggled from inside. "You look mad."

He scowled in revolt. "Shut the fuck up!" He slammed the mirror into the desk's corner, shattering it into pieces.

"That's an antique, you asshole!" Varana screeched as she threw her claw-bared hands towards him, but he snatched her wrist and pinned it back above her head. "Let me go!" she insisted, a stutter of desperation upon her shrill voice.

"You *promised* me, Varana; you shook my fucking hand—"

"Let go!" she yelled, pulling her hand free to try and swipe at him again.

Zalith snatched her hand and held it where he caught it. "And you promised me that you wouldn't tell anybody about Alucard—"

"I didn't!" she insisted.

"Then why the fuck did your ghoul of a younger brother just *happen* to make an attempt on his life not too far from here?! *Coincidence?*" he snarled—he didn't give her time to answer. His anger was almost painful, burning and tearing inside him, and it was *so* intense. He snatched her neck in both his hands, his rage burning through his skin and onto hers. Varana clasped his wrists and tried her best to escape his scorching grip, crying painfully as her skin sizzled beneath his palms.

Struggling, choking, and whining painfully, Varana scowled and insisted, "I didn't tell anyone! I promise!" Her voice broke as the burn of Zalith's hands seethed deeper into her skin. "S-Stop!" she cried. "You're hurting me! I didn't tell Detlaff!" She struggled, still trying to pull his hands from her sizzling throat. "I'll show you everything!" she then pleaded, taking one hand off Zalith's wrist and positioning her fingers on his face.

Zalith saw everything Varana's day consisted of…everything but the time she spent in the kitchen tormenting Alucard. He'd already seen that conversation in Alucard's memory and knowing that Varana had just tried to hide it…words couldn't describe his anger well enough. But he wasn't done just yet. Her mind was open, and he'd not let that go to waste. He placed his hand on her face, still gripping her throat with his other—he searched, he witnessed, and he felt no less enraged. She may not have told Detlaff anything, but that gave him no relief.

He stopped scorching her skin, but he didn't let go of her neck. Seeing her and Alucard's interaction from the vampire's point of view was one thing but seeing it from Varana's was a whole new level of horrifying. He saw just how upset Alucard had looked, the tormented look on his face, his stuttered answers. And the satisfaction Varana had felt in seeing just how hurt he had become. Alucard didn't deserve any of it, and Zalith couldn't blame him for his reaction. It only made him a whole lot more furious at the revolting woman in his grip.

With an exasperated snarl, he smacked Varana's hand away from his face in utter disgust. "After all I've fucking done for you," he said, gritting his teeth.

Varana—of course—burst into tears and shook her head. "I'm sorry!"

He didn't care; he didn't give a single shit about what she had to say. He growled as he stood up, letting go of her. Wordlessly, he stormed over to her walk-in wardrobe and made his way inside.

"What are you doing in there?!" Varana called shakily.

Zalith snatched two large suitcases from one of the shelves, moved back into the room, and chucked them onto her bed. He opened them both with a huff and returned to the closet. He snatched whatever clothes of hers he could see, pulling them off their hangers and out of drawers. Then, he threw them into the open suitcases. Some of the clothes didn't even fall inside and landed on Varana's bed; some hung over their edges, and some hit the floor.

"W-what are you doing?!" Varana shrieked, watching him with a horrified look on her teary face.

He returned to the closet, grabbing more clothes.

"Hello?!" she insisted. "Can you answer me, please?!"

"I'm doing what I should have done a long time ago," he angrily mumbled, throwing more of her clothes on top of the piles that had formed over the open suitcases.

With a desperate frown, she stared in confusion. "What?!"

Ignoring her, Zalith started packing the clothes into the suitcases and then headed back into the wardrobe for one final armful of her stuff. And that seemed to be when she realized what was happening.

"W-wait!" she pleaded, trying to stand in front of him as he came back out of her closet. But he irritably shoved her out of his way. As her back hit the wall, she huffed in terror. "Z, can we talk about this first?!" she insisted, tears trickling down her face.

Talk? Zalith exhaled loudly and smiled at her, twisted and seething with rage. "Okay, let's talk," he said as he chucked the clothes he had in his hands onto the bed and turned to face her. He could see the fear in her mascara-smothered eyes, but he didn't care. "What would you like to talk about first? The little meeting you had in the kitchen this morning or the perverse sense of ownership that you feel over me?"

"I..." she stuttered, staring at him. Clearly, she had no idea what to say.

"You're so *very* quiet for someone who wanted to have a conversation," he said, keeping his smile, his smile a narrow thread between rage and the near loss of his mind.

She stuttered and gulped. "....I-I'm sorry—"

Disgusted, Zalith shook his head, snarled, and turned away from her. He hastily closed the suitcases he'd very messily filled with her clothes, some of them remaining outside the boundaries of the cases. "I want you to get the fuck out of my house—immediately!" He scowled, picking up one of the suitcases as he turned to face her. Ignoring her desperate little whimper, he stormed over to the window and threw the suitcase out into the garden.

"Stop!" she wailed, watching as he snatched the other suitcase, launched it out of the window, and then returned to the closet.

He tore more of her clothes from the racks while Varana tried desperately to snatch them from him, but he aggressively pushed her away. She hit the floor, bawling as he stormed over to the window and began throwing her precious outfits outside.

"Hey!" she screamed, scrambling to her feet. She hurried over to him and managed to snatch some of her dresses from his grip before he could throw them and cradled them as Zalith stormed away from her.

But he then pulled an entire drawer from the dresser closest to her bed. As she screamed and tried to fight him, he chucked the underwear-full drawer out of the window. It smashed against the cobblestone ground; the woman's clothes were everywhere, clinging to the cypress trees, caught in the rose bushes—a blue dress had even managed to get caught on one of the parked carriages.

Varana was clearly done pretending that she could talk and cry her way out of it. With a furious shriek, she pounced at him, screeching as she latched her claws into him. They struggled again, and the woman was using a lot more of her strength than she had before, but Zalith didn't feel the slightest bit concerned. He pinned Varana against the wall, snatching her healing throat in one of his hands as she wailed in frustration.

But she soon began to sob. "Why are you doing this?!" she cried, staring into his eyes.

"Why?" he snarled. "Are you fucking stupid?!"

"I didn't do anyth—"

He scowled and bellowed, "Varana, you had no right to say ANY of that shit to Alucard—"

"I was just telling him the truth!"

"It's not your fucking truth to tell!"

Staring at him, Varana sniffled and shook her head. She placed her hands on his wrists, tears streaming down her face. "I-I'm so sorry, Z," she insisted. "I-I love you, I'm sorry. I don't want you to be with anyone else."

Revolted, he snarled at her, ignoring the pity that he often felt for her. His anger outweighed anything else that he might feel, and he'd not let her try to slither out of it. "Pack up the rest of your shit," he said coldly, a vacant glare on his face. "And then get the fuck out of my house." Then, he let go of her and backed off, heading for the door.

Stepping away from the wall, gripping her sore neck, she cried in desperation. "Where am I supposed to go?!"

"I don't care," he dismissed. "If you're not gone in an hour, I'll remove you myself." He pulled the door shut, slamming it behind him, leaving her to cry, sob, and do whatever the hell else she did. He didn't care—she'd crossed a line; she'd hurt someone he cared very deeply about and had even played a part in Alucard's current predicament. She might not have told Detlaff where Alucard was, but it had been her fault that the vampire fled the house, and seeing Alucard try desperately to get away hurt Zalith so much. But Varana would soon be gone, and that would be one problem out of the way.

Now, all he wanted to do was return to Alucard, and that was precisely what he did.

He made his way back through the house, his anger slowly withering into worry. He knew that when Alucard woke up, he'd have to do his very best to try and help the vampire understand the things that Varana had said. He'd not risk losing him, especially not because of something that woman had done. He would have liked to tell Alucard about his past himself at a more suitable time, but Varana had taken it upon herself to do so, destroying Alucard in the process. That had obviously been her goal, but Zalith wouldn't let her win. The vampire meant far too much to him for him to *not* want to fight for him, and he didn't care how hard he had to do it... he *would* fight.

All he had to do was wait for him to wake up. But when would that be?

Chapter Fifty-Three

— ⋖ ✝ ⋗ —

Burning, Waning

| Alucard |

Alucard thought that Damien would be the one to come for him, but the faint scent of sandalwood and bergamot told him otherwise. The new but familiar comfort of one certain bed left him feeling relieved of his pain, pain that would surely grip him tighter the moment he opened his eyes to face the world.

Something embraced him. As he lay there in the warmth and the calm, he felt an arm resting over his chest and a hand gripping his left arm tightly. He could feel the weight of someone's head on his right shoulder and a body pressed against his. And quiet, calm breathing.

The vampire slowly opened his eyes, greeting the dark room, and he wasn't alone. Beside him was Zalith; the sight of the demon teased a feeling of serenity to break through Alucard's simmering anger, but he wouldn't let it. However…it was selfish of him to still hate Zalith, wasn't it? Was hate even the word? Did he despise him so much that he felt as if he'd rather berate and upset him? No. Alucard didn't hate Zalith. The demon was the one who saved him from the grotesque grip of Detlaff's claws and whatever that creature of a man had planned for him.

Detlaff. Where had he come from? How had he known exactly where Alucard was? Had someone told him? Could it have been Varana? Was setting her brother on him one last stab after she'd wounded him with her sharp, dismaying words?

His mind shifted back to Zalith. He'd heard so many things, so many upsetting, worrying things about the man he couldn't deny he loved. Names…so many names. But now that he had nothing but time to think about what happened, he felt like a complete ass. He'd disregarded Zalith's attempts to explain—after all, who was Alucard to think that Zalith hadn't been with other people before him?

He glared up at the white ceiling as though it were his enemy. He'd not wake the demon, and he'd not attempt to move his aching, struggling body. He'd lay there…and think. The silence would help him to do so. He really didn't know much about Zalith at all, and it never bothered him before. Why should it bother him now? Just because some woman who clearly had a strange obsession with this man had said a few things? Things so perfectly said that it was almost as if she had spent a lot of time preparing her words.

Zalith was older than he was—he knew that. And he was a demon, too. Alucard knew very little about demons but had read a fair bit in the past few days. Demons searched forever until they found the one person they could love truly, until they found their *soulmate*. Zalith had evidently been on that mission—whether he knew it or not, he'd been searching—Alucard was sure of it. And it hurt him to think that Zalith had spent so long looking and hadn't found his love.

Was *he* this demon's love? He didn't know, and he might not know. But he didn't want to stress himself out by wondering. Instead, he focussed on the fact that they were both still alive, still beside one another, and although in his moment of upset, the vampire had insisted that he was leaving, he knew that he wanted to stay. With Zalith was where he wished to be, no matter what might reveal itself, no matter what might come his way. He loved him, and he'd not let go so easily.

His attention shifted to the lingering ache in the left side of his body. He wasn't sure what happened after Zalith had come to his rescue, but he was certain that the demon had done what was necessary to save him. Somehow, Detlaff managed to fuse blood into liquidated silver; Alucard's body absorbed blood when he consumed it and would use it to sate his hunger, regenerate his ethos, or heal his wounds and lost blood. He'd lost a lot of blood over the past few days, and the concoction Detlaff had forced down his throat had clearly made its way into his bloodstream. There was nothing he could have done himself, and to some miraculous relief, Zalith had come for him, despite what Alucard said before leaving. And...he was *still* there.

With a confounded scowl, Alucard slowly lifted his left hand, bringing it to the side of his neck. His fingertips met with two small scars unmistakeably left by a pair of fangs he hadn't long come to desire. But...the rest of his scars were gone. Those left by Damien, and those from each time Zalith had bitten him the night of and the morning after they had sex. How long had it been since then?

"Alucard?" came Zalith's quiet, calmingly familiar voice. The demon sat up, leaning on his left arm as he stared down at the vampire. "Hey," he greeted, a worried yet warming smile on his pale face as his eyes met with Alucard's.

But their stare didn't last long. Alucard took his eyes off Zalith as he lowered his hand from his neck. He stared sullenly up at the ceiling, his discombobulated thoughts swirling around inside his head like a thousand leaves caught in the wind—a cold, bitter wind. But...answers would perhaps help him feel calm and ease his thoughts. "What happened?" he asked quietly.

Zalith frowned sadly. "I arrived intending to kill Detlaff, but he started running, and I didn't want to chase him and leave you. I don't know where he is or what he wanted, but that didn't matter at the time. My priority was *you*; I did as you instructed and removed the silver from your blood. I didn't know whether this was the same case as when you passed out after travelling through the portal, so I fed you my blood, too."

The vampire glanced up at him. "All of my wounds are gone. How long have I been here?"

"Four days."

Alucard closed his eyes with a quiet sigh in an attempt to keep himself from panicking. Four days? Anything could have happened while he was unconscious; Damien could be looking for him—but the Daegelus always somehow knew exactly where to find him, so he was sure that wasn't the case. His contacts...they also knew how to reach him if they needed him. Zalith hadn't mentioned any owls or crows or letters, so he was sure that everything was fine.

He opened his eyes to look up at Zalith's despondent face. Four days? If four days had passed, and Zalith had been feeding him his blood, why were there still scars on his neck? Scars left by a demon's bite should have healed by now. Perhaps his healing abilities were still recovering, and that didn't exactly matter right now, anyway.

He shifted his sights back to the ceiling and adorned a conflicted stare, unsure of where to begin. So much had been said to him; he'd heard things about Zalith that had made him overreact, he hadn't given the demon room to explain, and he didn't know whether discussing it so soon was a good idea or not. He wanted answers, of course, but did he really want to hear what Zalith might have to say? He wasn't sure. He already understood the fact that Zalith had been with other men before him, but...did Alucard *really* accept it?

Silence lingered between them for a while. Zalith stared down at him, and every time Alucard glanced at his face, he saw a pondering expression. What was he thinking about?

But then when Zalith's eyes met his, the demon exhaled sadly. "My name...is Zalith Valerian," he stared. "I was born January eighteenth—Primis eighteenth in Alvenguard terms. My parents were never given last names; they were so highly regarded that they didn't really need them, so everybody just called our family the Valerians after the palace we lived in. I'm six hundred and twenty-six years old; both of my parents were two of Lilith's ethos creations, and I'm gay, although I'm sure you already know that," he said with a smirk.

The vampire slowly took his eyes off the ceiling and stared up at him. Evidently, Zalith had been thinking about what he'd said about not knowing anything about him.

Zalith continued, "I was smart as a child, but even so, I was very shy and very sensitive. I would spend a lot of time on the sidelines watching my brother play with his friends because I wasn't confident enough to consider myself one of them. I attribute most of this to my mother and her tendency to put us down all the time when we didn't perform to her standards, which was something that happened very often. At around age eleven, I got in a bad fight with my cousin over something silly, and I lost. After being belittled by my parents, I decided that I was going to learn how to be the opposite of what I was.

"My parents were positively thrilled when I told them that I wanted to learn how to fight; they hired me the best teachers and continued to do so for many years. I was around... twelve, I believe, when I realized that I was gay, and it wasn't until I was about sixteen that I felt confident enough with myself to pursue anybody. I fell in—well, what I *thought* was love at the time—with one of my brother's friends, and it didn't end well. It was around this time that I noticed that I had problems regulating my anger; of course, many people told me so over the years, but I didn't agree. Anyway, he broke my heart, so in return, I broke his arms," he explained, his eyes drifting to the vampire's hair which he started to fiddle with.

Alucard took his eyes off the demon and looked up at the ceiling once again. At least there was something he and Zalith could relate to—the anger. But that was something all demons struggled with. He'd not drift into his thoughts right now, though. He waited, lying there as the demon fiddled with his hair while he spoke.

"The older I became, the more I started to fall into the pattern of using men. It started off as a desire for companionship, I'm sure, but then it became something like a habit, and then somewhere along the way, it turned into a hobby, I suppose. Serial promiscuity was fun, and it's not often that I like people for very long, so jumping from person to person worked for me."

Staring, Alucard managed to remain deadpan. He didn't want to react—not yet. He dreaded what he might say next, but he'd not cower from whatever he was about to hear.

Zalith sighed as his fingers wandered down from the vampire's hair and to the side of his face. "If you look at it objectively, it was all just an escape from the stress of having a family like mine and a job where thousands of people are constantly looking to me for answers. I've done and said some cruel things to many people, but there's nothing that can be done to undo any of it; all I can do is be a better person." He paused for a moment, and then he continued, "Eventually, hundreds of years later, the war came, and I grew up a little. I didn't stop entirely, but I slowed down, and then at long last, I met you and decided I wanted to give it all up," he said, caressing Alucard's face.

As much as Alucard wanted to smile and believe that, he couldn't. Six hundred years of using men; how many had there been? Hundreds, thousands? Alucard wouldn't know, and he wouldn't ask. Was he being selfish to feel so... ill at ease, so anxious—so uncomfortable? The thought of being just another name on Zalith's list... it made him feel so many strange, upsetting feelings that he didn't fully understand. How could Zalith meeting him make him want to give up a life lived so long? Desire—addiction, maybe. Alucard couldn't begin to make sense of it, but he could at least try. So, he remained silent and waited, listening.

"As for Danford, I met him about six years ago. He's a werewolf, but his life has been plagued with horrible luck, and he hasn't been in a pack for about nine years. I've had sex with him three or four times, the most recent of which was around three years ago. He's just an employee, and I promise you that I have no feelings for him—or anybody else that I work with whatsoever."

Alucard couldn't hide how *that* made him feel. He didn't want to think about what he'd been told by Varana, or what Zalith had just said; if he did, he'd only fall deeper into dismay. He turned his head to glare sullenly at the windows so that Zalith's touch was no longer on his face. It was starting to make him feel worse.

But the demon didn't stop to question his response. "And then there's Varana, who I kicked out not long after getting you back here. She's been in my life for a very long time. She's a queen of the highest regard in Eltaria, and my father was one of her advisors. Varana and I quickly hit it off, and she spent a lot of time with my brother and me. It wasn't until years later that we learned that she'd been sent to Eltaria by her father to produce offspring with a powerful demon of her choice, and the options were Xurian and me. Neither of us was interested, though, and Varana kind of just gave up and focused on her duty as queen. But she's always been obsessed with me, no matter how many times I tell her it's not going to happen.

"Anyway, eventually, after shadowing my father for a few years, I was given a role in her council alongside him, which is how I eventually came to lead a war that ended up killing my family and displacing Varana and myself. She lives with me because we've always been together—platonically—and I can't imagine a life without her in it. I think...that we need each other, in a way," he said with a slight smile. "She's horrible, though. She's picky, unfriendly, a snob, argumentative, and about a thousand other negative things, but she's my dearest friend, and there is very little that I wouldn't do for her."

Alucard lost his battle with his protruding emotions and sunk into his despair. It all made sense, though; of course Varana had been created to produce new demons to begin bloodlines, and *of course* it was Zalith whom she'd chosen to attempt to do so with. After all these years, was she *still* trying to get him to have sex with her? Did she feel like she *owned* Zalith just because they'd become such close friends?

With a deep sigh, Zalith returned his hand to the vampire's hair, caressing it slowly with his fingers. "What else?" he asked himself aloud. "I love to read mystery novels. Both autumn and summer are my favourite seasons. I'm starting to love the colour red more and more," he said, tucking a loose strand of the vampire's hair behind his ear. "And in all my life, I've never wanted anything more than I want you, Alucard."

"How long do you want me for?" he abruptly asked sullenly, turning his head to look up at him. How could he not ask? He'd been told to expect this little relationship of theirs to run out of time, and he wondered...how long did they have left?

A sad stare clung to Zalith's face. "As long as you'll have me," he answered. "And longer than that, even."

Alucard still didn't know how to feel, what to do, or what to say. All he could do was turn his face away from Zalith. He'd like to believe what the demon was telling him—that he was going to be the one whom Zalith wanted to be with forever. But... six hundred years was a long time, a long time to spend looking for something like love. Why would it be Alucard? Why would he be so special? He wasn't. He couldn't lay there and think that maybe he wasn't just another mistake. There wasn't a thing about him that could make him remotely different from anyone else Zalith had been with.

He closed his eyes for a moment, trying to stay afloat in a sea of horrible, drowning emotions. He felt so sad—so alone despite the fact that Zalith was right beside him. Although the demon just told him a lot about himself, although he had explained the things Varana had spoken about four days ago, Alucard just... didn't feel the same. He felt anxious. Nauseous. He wanted to believe him—he really did. But how could he? How could he trust that Zalith wouldn't tire of him the same way he had Danford and everyone else who came before him? How could he believe that he was any different to everyone else Zalith had pursued?

And love. It hurt more than any wound. If this was what love was, he didn't want to feel it anymore. He didn't want the ache in his heart; he didn't want the painful stabbing in his chest when he thought about what life might be like once Zalith grew tired of him. The struggle to breathe, the struggle to think that maybe... maybe this was what he deserved. He didn't deserve to be loved, Damien had said so many times, and he was a fool to think that Zalith would be the one to prove the Daegelus wrong.

While their time together lasted, it had been such a relief. But it was like a candle on a wall, burning and edging closer to its end as time passed, and once its wick flickered out, it would never light again. How much longer would their time burn? How much longer did he have before Zalith realized that he was just another distraction? Could he do that to himself... could he stay until the flame burned out just so that he could be happy for a while longer?

Zalith was his light—his escape from the dark, empty world his life had become four hundred years ago. It might be weak and stupid to hold onto something that would soon turn to dust, but he *was* weak, he *was* stupid, and he was tired of losing. Zalith was the only positive thing to come of his life, the only thing that allowed him happiness, and he'd not let go of it—as much as it hurt to know that one day he'd mean nothing to the man he loved, he'd hold onto him for as long as he could, and once it was over, he'd deal with the pain he knew it would cause. Because... it was worth it. To feel happy, to love, and to spend his time with someone who made him feel alive—it was worth the suffering its imminent end would bring.

"Do you need time alone with your thoughts?" Zalith asked. "I can leave—"

But the vampire rolled over onto his right side and rested his forehead against the demon's chest, moving his left arm around him. "No," he mumbled sadly.

Zalith wrapped his arms around him. "Okay."

"Why are there scars on my neck?" he asked, eager to change the subject.

"I thought *you* might have the answer to that," Zalith admitted. "I thought that they would disappear after three days, and when they didn't, I assumed it might be because of your current state."

"Maybe," Alucard muttered.

"Are you okay? If you want to know more, I'll do my best to explain whatever you—"

"I'm…" he hesitated. He was sure that if he claimed he was fine, Zalith would interrogate him until he told the truth.

"If there's anything I can do to make this easier, please tell me," the demon pleaded quietly, holding him tightly.

"It doesn't matter," Alucard replied, trying to shroud the sadness in his voice with irritancy.

"Of course it matters, Alucard. The last thing I want is for you to feel stressed or worried because of this."

The vampire tightened his grip around him. "I'm not stressed or worried," he denied quietly. "I'm just…I overreacted. I don't know why I expected to be the only person you've been with, and I don't know why I got so angry when I learned I wasn't. I guess…it's just because all of this is new to me. I haven't been with anyone before, so I wasn't sure what to expect. But it doesn't matter."

Zalith sighed as he nuzzled the vampire's hair. "Anyone would have been upset about it, especially with the way Varana put it. I'm sorry that this happened, Alucard."

"It's fine. You explained it, and I understand it. We…don't 'ave to talk about it anymore. Now, I think I just…want to sleep some more. I guess I've been asleep for four days, but it doesn't feel like it," he said with a tired huff.

Smiling, Zalith made himself comfortable beside the vampire. "Sleep for however long you need; I'll still be here when you wake up," he assured him quietly,

Alucard made himself as comfortable as he could and closed his eyes. He didn't want to think about anything anymore. All he wanted to do was rest. And as Zalith held him a little tighter, he exhaled in relief and let himself drift off. Zalith's embrace still made him feel safe, and he'd make the most of that.

Chapter Fifty-Four

— ≺ ✝ ≻ —

To Accept Fate Is To Feel Its Harsh Sting

| **Zalith** |

In the stillness of the night, Zalith woke intermittently to check on Alucard, his beloved vampire. Amid the hushed darkness, Zalith's gaze lingered on the vampire's peaceful slumber at midnight. Despite Alucard's assurance that everything was fine between them, a subtle ache lingered in the demon's heart.

The usual rhetoric that Zalith possessed when navigating relationships seemed to falter. Alucard, enigmatic and complex, defied the simplicity that characterized Zalith's past connections. Yet, it was precisely this complexity that drew Zalith closer because he discovered a love that surpassed the familiar patterns of his previous encounters. With Alucard, every nuance was a deviation from the ordinary, and the demon cherished the unique and profound nature of their connection.

But he sunk deeper into his worry the longer he waited for Alucard to wake up. Varana told him so many things that he wouldn't understand; to tell someone like Alucard—a man who trusted no one—that he'd been used and betrayed…Zalith wouldn't have expected the vampire to react in any other way. Alucard had tried so desperately to run from the pain it evidently caused him, and it hurt Zalith. He didn't want Alucard to be upset, nor did he want his vampire to worry, fear, or wonder. Alucard deserved nothing but the truth from him, and he'd continue to do his best to give him that. It might not fix what happened, but it *would* help their relationship, right? He'd told Alucard some of the more important things about himself, and if the vampire had any questions, he'd answer them.

What he needed to focus on right now, though, was the fact that Alucard said he understood. Alucard was there, he was alive, and he was healing. For a moment, Zalith feared he'd lose his vampire—the vampire he loved. But he hadn't, and he was going to do whatever it took to ensure that neither of them went through anything like that ever again.

With a quiet sigh, he rested his head on the pillows and gazed at Alucard's peaceful face. He wasn't going to move until the vampire woke.

| **Alucard** |

Alucard woke to discontent, to sadness. He lay there in Zalith's arms, but his embrace didn't warm him the way it once did. He'd thought sleep would banish this awful feeling of dismay, but it didn't. To lay there and know that one day someone else would be in his place…. It hurt.

He stared at the curtains, the early morning light from the world outside peeking through the cracks. Birdsong carried upon the light breeze, and while Alucard might usually find comfort in waking up beside Zalith, he found…heartache. Each morning that came was a day closer to the morning Zalith would wake up and realize that he didn't want Alucard anymore. But it was a harsh fate that Alucard had accepted. It might break his heart, it might make him feel as though he was on the verge of tears every time he thought about it, but he'd rather that than give up whatever time he had left to spend with this demon.

His choice had been made, and he'd not think about it more than he had to. He wanted to enjoy his time with Zalith—he wanted to love him until he meant nothing to him, and even after that time had come.

Taking his eyes off the curtains, he stared down at his arm, which was resting beside him with his hand nestled under the pillow. Zalith lay behind him, his head rested on the side of his; the demon's right arm held him so tightly, and his left was stretched under his pillow, his hand just visible as Alucard took a moment to glance up at it. It was a hand he wished to hold forever…but he wouldn't get to. That was okay, though. He could hold it now, and for however long he had left to spend with Zalith.

With a sullen stare, the vampire moved his hand from beneath the pillow and slowly slipped it into Zalith's. He'd grip it perhaps in desperation, in hopes that if he held tight enough, maybe it would last forever. But whether it was because of his wounds or his sadness, he couldn't seem to grip. He couldn't move much at all. The only thing he could do was lay there and stare, his despondency choking him as the heartache tightened a forceful grasp around his throat. He hated it.

He shifted his focus to Detlaff in an attempt to ease his pain. That creature of a man…how had he found him? How had Detlaff known exactly where he would be? In the middle of some forest miles away from civilization—how could Detlaff have known?

Had Varana told him? Was there something he was missing? He didn't know, but he'd be sure to put his mind to work, and his people.

He'd sent his Paladins to search for Lucious, so they'd be of no help; Attila had been fired, Felix was too much of a strange little man, and Ben—well, Ben was a part of the Detlaff predicament. He needed to find Ben, too; he'd given him Attila's old job and he needed the position to be filled. Right now, his path of communication with DeiganLupus was cut off, and Ben was supposed to walk it, but he was gone. Alucard wasn't sure how much longer he could leave the silence between himself and DeiganLupus until it became a problem—a problem he didn't want to have to deal with. Someone needed to fill Ben's place, and someone needed to be put in charge of finding Detlaff.

Who? He scowled and carefully rolled onto his back, waiting as Zalith stirred and moved his head onto the vampire's shoulder. There weren't many people qualified for such a high-risk, delicate mission. Felix *did* have age on his side, but Alucard wouldn't put that boy in charge of anything, especially not something as precarious as a search for Detlaff. No, he needed someone who knew what he was doing, someone who wasn't a stranger to command—and a name came to him.

Luther.

Alucard had long abandoned his old 'friend' in Avalmoor to marry each generation of royalty to ensure he had control of the country. To his surprise, Luther didn't resent him for that—as far as he was aware, anyway. He felt as if it might just be time to relieve Luther of that tiresome task and give him something more important to do. Anyone could marry a Princess—as long as they were pretty enough. He was sure that he'd find someone else to marry whoever came after Avalmoor's current monarch, but he'd have to find someone like Luther, someone who wouldn't fall in love and compromise the arrangement.

He had to contact Luther, and the sooner the better. The quicker he could get someone to find Detlaff, the swifter he'd get results. But he didn't want to go back to his castle. He was sure that he'd feel a whole lot more alone there than he did here. Would Zalith be open to allowing Luther into his home, though? He didn't expect the demon to agree, but he'd ask. He'd not invite him without warning Zalith.

He stopped staring aimlessly and glanced down at Zalith. But his words were silent. He had no idea what to say, and he didn't understand why it was such a struggle. All he had to do was ask him if he was awake; how hard could it be?

But then Zalith smiled and slightly opened his eyes to glance up at him. "Good morning, baby," he said, bringing his hand from the vampire's left shoulder and to the side of his face. He tucked a loose strand of the vampire's hair behind his ear and closed his eyes. "How are you feeling?"

"Concerned," he answered.

With a perturbed frown, Zalith lifted his head, moved his arm from beneath the vampire's pillow, and rested the side of his face on his hand. He then looked down at Alucard, leaning his arm into his pillow. "What are you concerned about?"

"Detlaff," he replied, looking up at him. "I need to find him."

A worried expression possessed Zalith's face as he took his hand off the vampire's face and placed it over the side of his neck. "You should rest, Alucard. We can find him once you—"

"I don't need to look for him myself," Alucard interjected, taking his eyes off Zalith to look over at the windows. "I just need to contact one of my subordinates and have them do it. I want to bring Luther here and talk to him if that's okay."

With a relieved sigh, Zalith smiled. "All right. You can invite Luther here, yes."

He looked up at him again. "Do you… have things I can use to write to him?"

Zalith smirked. "I do. You can use my office."

"Thank you," he said, taking his eyes off the demon again. "I would… also like a shower, too."

The demon rested his head back on Alucard's shoulder. "You can use the shower. I'll bring you some clothes again. But Alucard—" he said, gripping the vampire's arm a little tighter— "are you okay?"

"I'm fine," he said, placing his hand over Zalith's. "I just want to get this out of the way so I don't have to risk running into Detlaff again when I leave."

He sat up again, leaning on his arm. "Okay. If you want to shower, I'll get myself dressed, and then I'll bring you some clothes and show you to my office."

Alucard nodded. He then sat up but grunted painfully when pain surged through his left shoulder—

"Maybe moving isn't such a good idea right now," Zalith said, placing his hand on Alucard's arm as he sat up, too.

"Maybe," Alucard agreed quietly. "But I have to. I'll be fine," he dismissed as he slowly stood up and began to make his way towards the bathroom. Without another word, he headed inside, pulling the door shut behind him.

He pulled his trousers off, climbed into the shower, and turned it on. Then, as the water ran over his face, he sighed deeply and waited for the heat to relieve some of his discomfort.

| **Zalith** |

Zalith remained sitting where he was, staring at the door as if he couldn't quite yet understand that Alucard had left. It was as clear as it could be that he was distant and upset. Of course he was. Why wouldn't he be? To learn the things he had learnt, and from such an awful woman, Zalith could only try to understand what he must be thinking.

But...Alucard told him everything was okay. Perhaps he shouldn't have believed him so quickly. Part of his abrupt acceptance of Alucard's answer was probably out of worry; he wanted to think that Alucard was okay, but he clearly wasn't. Time, however, was probably what Alucard needed. The vampire was most likely still recovering from everything that happened, and Zalith hoped that he'd soon be back to his usual self.

What if he wasn't, though? What if the things Varana said caused permanent damage? Alucard was a finicky, complicated man, and even more so when it came to understanding relationships. Perhaps it would just take Alucard a little longer to understand completely than it would someone else. If Zalith had to explain himself again and again to help Alucard get it, then he would. There was *nothing* he wouldn't do for Alucard.

For now, all he could do was wait and try his very best to dismiss his worry. Alucard would surely understand...right?

| **Alucard** |

The hot water poured over Alucard's aching body as he leaned the majority of his weight onto his right arm, which he pressed against the wall. He stared down at the marble floor, watching the water as it hit like rain. He'd made his choice, but he couldn't stop thinking about it, and that irritated him more and more with each passing moment.

He scowled, glaring at the floor. The same questions circled inside his head like a persistent enemy; how long did he and Zalith have left? Was his love nonsensical? Should he say something? No. Why would he tell Zalith that he knew he'd tire of him? That would probably take away whatever time he had left with the demon. Whether Zalith was using him as Varana had said, or whether he simply thought Alucard would be the person he stayed with forever only to soon discover that he wasn't, Alucard wasn't sure, but he'd chosen to stay with him for his own selfish needs. He loved him, and he wanted to keep loving him—he wanted to stay with him for as long as Zalith would have him, but the unknowing of how long that might be scared Alucard—it terrified him, and fear was something he didn't wish to feel when it came to Zalith.

Taking his eyes off the floor, he leaned back against the wall and sighed quietly. The more he thought about it, the more it hurt, and it seemed as though the only way to avoid the pain was to occupy his mind with anything else. He'd been trying, and he felt like he needed to try a little harder. Once he was done showering, he'd send Luther a message; his old friend would take roughly an hour to arrive, he suspected, and once he was here, he could talk business with him. *That* would take his mind off his pain for a while.

When a quiet knock came at the bathroom door, he stared at it and watched as Zalith made his way in. The demon had combed his hair and was now dressed in a light grey shirt and black trousers; he placed the clothes he'd brought for Alucard onto the countertop and walked back over to the door, but he didn't leave. He stopped and looked back over his shoulder at Alucard.

"Do you need anything else?" he asked.

"No," Alucard said as he looked away, having seen the smile making its way onto Zalith's face. "Thank you."

"I'll wait for you in here; I'll take you to my office once you're ready," he said, and then he left and closed the door behind him.

Once Zalith left, Alucard lost all interest in what he was doing. He'd been in the shower long enough—either that or he didn't want to be without Zalith's company any longer. He switched off the water, snatched a towel, and hastily dried off before beginning to dress. He pulled on the black trousers and white shirt, dried and tidied his hair, and left the bathroom, stepping back into the demon's bedroom.

Zalith was sitting on what Alucard liked to think was his side of the bed, leaning against its headboard with a book in his right hand. He immediately took his eyes off the pages to look over at the vampire, who took a few steps out of the bathroom but then stopped moments later, confliction gripping hold of him. He so sorely wanted to be closer to him, but his fear constricted him.

Lowering his book, Zalith smiled. "Hi," he said, placing his book on the bedside cabinet.

Alucard couldn't seem to work out where to look. At first, he stared at Zalith, then his eyes darted to the book he placed down, and then to the floor when a conflicted pout stole his vacant expression. He didn't hesitate when Zalith stood up, walked towards him, and embraced him tightly once he reached him. He wrapped his arms around the demon, and as they stood there for a few minutes, he rested his head on Zalith's shoulder and closed his eyes.

And in that moment, everything felt okay. But he knew that feeling would soon wither.

Zalith placed his hands on Alucard's shoulders and smiled at him. "Do you feel better?"

The vampire nodded, placing his hand against the demon's chest as he stared at him. "I do now," he said quietly, turning his head in an attempt to hide his nervous face.

"Good," Zalith said, pulling him back into another hug. "I do, too."

Alucard relaxed, but a despondent smile danced across his lips as he held onto Zalith in what might be desperation. The demon lightly moved him back, and as Alucard's back hit the wall, Zalith slowly and lightly gripped his jaw in his hand, stared at him for a few moments, and then moved his face closer, kissing him. Alucard allowed himself to become lost in the moment just as he would before, gripping Zalith's arm in his right hand.

But the sadness hit—of course it did. Knowing that this wouldn't last forever cut like a searing, serrated knife. He turned his head to the right, abruptly ending their kissing as he scowled in distress. Zalith was surely going to ask why he'd stopped, and he didn't want to talk about it. So he turned his head back to face him and said, "I should contact Luther soon."

"Of course," Zalith said with a smile, letting go of his jaw. He dragged his hand down his arm, and with a smirk on his face, placed one last kiss upon the vampire's forehead before stepping back so that Alucard could move away from the wall. "I'll show you to my office," he said and began leading the way towards his bedroom door.

Alucard silently followed the demon through the house. Zalith glanced back at him a few times with a smirk, which made Alucard frown shyly; despite everything, Zalith still had a way of making him feel nervous.

Entering the main hall, Alucard followed the demon to the left, venturing into the room directly beneath Zalith's bedroom. Having glimpsed Zalith's office through mirrors and during his initial visit, the space unfolded before him as expected. The desk stood prominently ahead, flanked by a substantial wall lined with books. Behind the desk, tall rectangular windows commanded attention, extending to the left wall. Despite the drawn black curtains, the expansive grounds outside were visible, with the forest lying just fifty feet beyond the house.

In the forefront of the room, a trio of sleek black leather seats were arranged before the desk, inviting conversation and collaboration. To the left, a black couch nestled beside an oak table, creating a cosy enclave for relaxation, and positioned to the right of the desk was the mirror through which he and Zalith communicated.

Zalith walked to his desk while Alucard waited by the door, unsure where he should stand. He watched, observing as Zalith pulled one of the desk drawers open and pulled out everything Alucard would need to write and send a letter. He then set his eyes back on the vampire and smiled. "Come over here," he invited, patting his desk chair.

Alucard wandered over and sat down.

"I'm going to get breakfast brought out on the patio for us, so meet me out there once you're done here," Zalith said and kissed the top of Alucard's head.

"Okay," Alucard agreed, watching the demon as he walked towards the door.

"You can also just leave all of that there once you're done. I'll put everything back later." Zalith smiled, looking back at him one last time.

"*Multemesc*," Alucard thanked, and as the demon left the room and closed the door behind him, the vampire sighed quietly and picked up the quill.

He didn't waste time; he knew what he had to write, and he didn't need to give Luther an address. Any vampire could find him through their connection to him as their sire....

Any... vampire.

Alucard stopped and stared at the blank paper as the ink dripped off the end of the quill. As it splashed quietly, realization struck him like a sudden burst of lightning, soon to be followed by a raging storm. How could he have been so blind?

Detlaff had Ben.

Ben was a vampire, one so old that finding Alucard through his sire link was *easy*. Was it possible that Detlaff had found a way to use that to find him? That creature had learned to bond silver and blood, so it was very likely that he'd worked out how to use the link all vampires had to their creator to find him.

But there wasn't anything Alucard could do about that other than up the security in his castle. Even then, though, not all vampires lived in Dor-Sanguis; some had moved on, living all around Aegisguard. Detlaff could find and use *any* one of them.

Alucard needed to find him before he spread the word of such a dangerous weakness in his defences.

With a deep sigh, he pressed the quill's tip against the paper and began to write in Dor-Sanguian:

Luther,

Recent events have caused me to need someone to take up a position I long outcast. Attila has been removed, and his replacement has been stolen from me.

I need you to make your way to my location immediately. Tell your current wife you may be gone for some time, as I have work for you here and wherever else the job may take you. We will discuss this further once you have arrived.

Make haste. It is of the utmost importance.

A.

Alucard waited a few moments for the ink to dry and then folded the message into an envelope. He sealed it with wax and then held it out in his right hand. A few seconds later, a crow flew in through the open window and took the letter from him. Then, the bird raced out of the window and towards Avalmoor. Now, all he had to do was wait— wait…and spend more time with Zalith.

With a quiet sigh, he got up, headed over to the door, and left the room, following Zalith's aura in search of the patio.

Chapter Fifty-Five

Old Friends

| **Alucard** |

Alucard stepped outside onto the patio and set his eyes on Zalith, who was sitting at an oak table with an assortment of breakfast foods laid out; Alucard had no idea what any of it was apart from the bacon, eggs, toast, and pieces of fruit.

The demon smiled at the vampire, waiting for him to join him. "Did you send your message?" he asked, watching Alucard as he wandered over and sat across the table from him.

Making himself comfortable, Alucard nodded. "He should be here in around an hour, maybe less, depending on what he's doing."

"You can use my office again to speak with him if you would like," Zalith offered and sipped from his coffee.

Glancing at him, Alucard nodded again. "What is that?" he asked, gesturing with his hand to what looked like syrupy toast.

"That's Boszorkian toast," he said with a smirk and reached over to grab a piece. He then offered it to Alucard and said, "I thought you might like it since you have a preference for sweet things."

Taking it from him, Alucard eyed the syrup-smothered toast with two halved strawberries on it.

"Tell me if my assumption is correct," Zalith said.

Alucard tried the toast. At first, its texture felt a little strange, but its taste was rather delightful. He smiled ever so slightly at the demon, confirming that he was right to suspect that he'd enjoy it, and as Zalith began to eat his own breakfast, Alucard continued enjoying the toast.

He quickly grew curious, though. "Did you...really kick out your friend?" he asked, shifting his gaze to the demon.

Zalith finished what he was eating, sighed, and looked at Alucard. "I did," he confirmed. "I heard the things she said to you, and I felt how it made her feel. She has some evil little vendetta to keep me for herself. You don't need to worry, though," he said, smirking suggestively. "I'm all yours."

"She...does understand what gay means, right?" he asked with a perturbed frown.

"Yes, but I imagine she believes she might be able to change me. I pity her for it; she's like family to me, but to her, that simply isn't enough. And just as she tells herself that one day she hopes she'll change me, I hope that one day she might learn to understand that she and I will never be together the way she wants."

Alucard nodded and looked down at his coffee. "At first, I thought she might have something to do with Detlaff showing up, but she didn't, did she?"

"No."

He took another bite of his toast and then said, "I think Detlaff has worked out how to use Ben to find me."

Zalith leaned his arms onto the table and frowned in concern. "How?" he asked, sounding a little intrigued.

"Well...long version or short version?"

"Give it all to me," he said, grinning.

Alucard pouted, trying not to let the demon's flirting fluster him too much. "All vampires are linked to me, their sire," he began.

Listening, Zalith nodded.

"And we all know that the older a vampire, the stronger they are. When a vampire is strong enough, they can...come to me using that sire link. They can find me no matter where I am. Some younger vampires need guidance, but older ones like Ben wouldn't struggle at all. I think Detlaff found a way to use that to find me. How else would he have known exactly where I was? Even if your friend had told him, I was miles away from your house when he found me."

"I didn't know a link like that existed. Detlaff will probably do it again; is there a way to stop vampires from being able to use that link to find you?"

"Not that I can think of. It's blood magic—a vampire's entire existence is blood magic. If I want to stop someone from using that link, I have to kill them. I would have thought that by that age, a vampire would be strong enough to defend themselves from anything or anyone that might want to find me—but then I wasn't prepared for Detlaff. I don't exactly blame Ben for getting snatched, but...if it were Attila, the man would have killed himself before Detlaff got away with him. Either Ben doesn't know how a vampire executes one's self, Detlaff didn't give him a chance, or he didn't want to kill himself to protect me."

"Ben worked for me for a long time," Zalith said. "I know that if it were the only option, he'd do it, so perhaps Detlaff has done something to make that impossible." He sighed, finished off his coffee, and looked back at Alucard. "But what matters now is that Detlaff knows how to find you, and he *will* come again."

"I know," Alucard mumbled and sipped from his coffee. "I'm confused as to why he hasn't yet."

"Perhaps…well, I'd say definitely that he's a coward. He thought you were alone when he attacked you five days ago; now, he knows that you're *not*, and clearly, he's somehow smart enough to know that I'm with you and will be with you until we kill him."

"Perhaps," Alucard agreed quietly, taking the last piece of Boszorkian toast. "Luther will find him; he can be a lazy piece of shit, but he does his job when told."

Amused, Zalith laughed quietly and smiled at him. "You and Luther were friends, yes? I do remember you telling me that he was with you and Attila when you were hunting Janus."

The vampire shrugged, staring down at his toast as he slowly ate it. "I don't know. There was a time when I felt as if I didn't have or need friends. But ever since Tobias, I've been coming to realize that…maybe I have unknowingly had friends and failed to appreciate them when I should have. It's…a long story—for another time," he mumbled sadly.

Zalith nodded understandingly. "And I assume Luther was someone you felt you didn't appreciate?"

"Maybe." Alucard sighed, finishing his food. "Luther and Attila were always…nice. Despite my harsh snapping and dismissal of their wish to socialize, they never looked at me as though I was awful—even though I was," he said, a slight smile on his face. "A time when I didn't have so much weight on my shoulders—a time I had the space in my life to wander the world with those two seeking entertainment. I could do better to hang out with them—well, Luther at least, now that Attila is gone. But I find that my spare time belongs to you," he said quietly, keeping his eyes on the table.

The demon smiled brightly. "I enjoy every second of our time together, and I wouldn't give any of it up for the world," he said as he leaned closer. He moved his hand to the back of Alucard's head, pulled him closer, and kissed him.

But that was when the door knocked.

Zalith didn't seem to care. "One of the staff will get it," he said as Alucard turned to stare into the lounge they were sitting outside of. As the vampire shifted his attention back to him, Zalith continued kissing him.

For a few more moments, they enjoyed their solitude with one another, but as Edwin stepped out onto the patio, Zalith sighed and looked at him.

"There is a Luther at the door, sir…asking for Aleksei," the butler told them.

"Right," the demon said. "Tell him we'll be with him shortly."

Nodding, the butler disappeared back into the house, leaving them alone.

Alucard frowned as Zalith set his sights back on him. It hadn't even been half an hour, and Luther had already arrived? He clearly took 'make haste' a little too seriously—either that or the hopes of a new job that didn't involve marrying princesses had excited him so much that he used up an unnecessary amount of ethos to fly there so quickly.

"I guess…I should deal with that," the vampire muttered.

"*Or* we could make him wait a few more moments," Zalith said with a smirk, leaning in to kiss him again.

But Alucard sighed and looked away. "The sooner I talk to him, the sooner he can search for Detlaff."

With a saddened frown, Zalith sat up straight and nodded as he took his hand off the back of Alucard's head. "Of course. If you'd like to head back to my office, I'll go and greet him for you. I'll have to be the one to invite him in."

Standing up, Alucard nodded. Then, he headed back into the house and towards Zalith's office.

| **Zalith** |

As Alucard went back into the house, Zalith sighed and finished his croissant. Then, he made his way inside; he didn't exactly rush to the door, but once he reached the entrance hall, he set his eyes on Alucard's vampire friend while he waited outside, leaning against the porch.

Noticing him approaching after a few moments, Luther smiled and stood up straight. "Zaliv, right?"

"Zalith," he corrected unamusedly as he watched Luther's smile slowly wither.

"Right. Alucard's accent, huh?" he laughed.

Zalith stood in the doorway, eyeing Luther with a scornful look on his face. He'd come dressed in clothes similar to what he'd seen him wearing the first time he saw him, but his hair wasn't styled and tied; it hung loose, reaching his waist, and if this weren't Alucard's friend, he'd warn Luther not to shed it all over his house.

He took his condescending stare off the man and nodded with a vacant expression. "This way," he said, turning around. He walked for a few moments, smirking amusedly as he pictured the look on Luther's face, but then he stopped and looked back at him. The man was still outside, looking uncomfortable. "What's the matter?" the demon asked.

Luther, with a vexed grin, laughed slightly—he was obviously irritated but was doing his best to remain calm. "You need to…invite me in."

"Oh, how silly of me. Do come in," he said, smiling.

With a slight frown, Luther stepped past the threshold. He closed the door behind him and then followed Zalith through the house.

| **Alucard** |

Alucard, waiting in the demon's office in front of his desk, turned to face the door as it opened. He watched as Zalith made his way in with Luther following closely behind.

Luther immediately moved past Zalith and approached Alucard. "How strange to see you so soon after your recent visit," he said with a smile, moving in for what looked like a hug, but Alucard scowled irritably. Luther clearly understood he wasn't interested and stopped walking to remain where he was. "I'd have uh…got here sooner, but the new woman you had me marry is overly clingy."

"Then a relief it will be for you to spend time away from her, huh?" Alucard said with a smirk.

"Such so," Luther agreed.

When Zalith stood beside him and slipped his arm around Alucard's shoulders, the vampire looked at him.

"Do you want me to bring you anything?" Zalith asked, smiling at him.

"No, thank you," Alucard answered.

"Then I'll see you when you're done," he said, hugging him tightly as he kissed his head. His hand then wandered down from his shoulder, however, and as the demon smirked, he lightly squeezed the vampire's ass. Alucard scowled at one of the shelves in response, but Zalith smiled and walked off, heading for the door. He made sure to stab Luther with one last hostile glare but then left the room, pulling the door shut behind him.

Once Zalith's footsteps faded away, Luther sighed and relaxed. "You look like shit, just saying."

Alucard rolled his eyes and sat on the couch. "I've had an interesting week," he replied, watching Luther as he sat beside him on the other side of the couch.

"Interesting doesn't look to be the word. What happened there?" he asked, pointing to Alucard's left shoulder.

With a frown on his face, he lightly dragged his fingers over the scars that had been left by Zalith's fangs—scars that should have healed by now, but they were exactly as they had been yesterday. He'd not think much of it; he'd consumed silver, so he was sure that it might take a little longer for the wounds to heal. "That's why you're here," he started.

Luther waited.

"There have been… developments in the light of Lucifer."

"Oh, him," Luther muttered, resting the side of his head on his hand as he leaned his arm on the top of the couch. "Can I guess?"

Alucard shrugged lightly as he rested his arm on the arm of the couch, leaning back ever so slightly so that he was comfortable.

"Diabolus," Luther started.

"No."

"Ada?"

"No," Alucard muttered.

"Hmm… demon things?"

"In a sense."

"Interesting. Organisation or single person?" Luther asked, tapping his chin.

"The former," Alucard answered.

"Your… boyfriend?"

"No—well… that is another conversation."

Luther nodded slowly and thought to himself. "Damien?"

Tiring of Luther's guesses, Alucard sighed and looked over at the window. "I've learned that Lucifer created other children—not the same way he created me, but in the way the other Numen have created children. Three exist—two females and a male. The male is the one causing me problems, and it's going to be your job to find him."

With a nod, Luther slouched back. "It was only a matter of time, I guess—for Lucifer to create scions, if that's what we still call them."

"Yes," Alucard said with a tired sigh.

"Well, let us be thankful he made those and not offspring."

"I will be thankful when the annoying little shit is dealt with," he grumbled.

Luther smiled nervously and looked around the room. "Uh… so, what do you want me to do? Find him and kill him?"

"If only it were that simple Damien wants him; I had him locked up in a dungeon and was planning to bleed him dry of everything he knows about Lucifer before handing him over to Damien. But he escaped while I was visiting Avalmoor. I don't really know how, and I don't care to know why. I know that he has some disgusting obsession with me and that is all that matters. You will find him, sedate him, and bring him to my castle. If I'm not there, you'll throw him into the dungeon and keep a *very* watchful eye on him until I get back."

"Understood."

"There is also the matter of Attila's replacement. Detlaff stole him and I need him back, too. His name is Ben and he knows *a lot*. I want to find out what Detlaff has got from him."

Luther nodded.

Alucard then said, "The Paladins are currently searching for someone else for me, so if you want a team at your disposal, you will have to talk to Felix."

"Him," he muttered with a grimace. "You really ought to find yourself a new Felix, Alucard," he said, smiling. "That little man will one day do something even *you* can't ignore."

With a roll of his eyes, Alucard scowled at Luther. "You are the second person to suggest that. Mind your business."

"Sure." Luther nodded in apology. "I think I can manage alone. What does he look like? Do you know where I should be searching?"

"Ugly little man," Alucard snarled. He then lifted his hand and placed his fingers on Luther's face, transferring Detlaff's appearance into his mind. "Stupid, pathetic, annoying, but he knows what he's doing," he explained, placing his hand back into his own lap. "I don't care how you do it, just find him. He's a scion, as we know; he's not weak to silver, he's quick, and he probably possesses things I don't yet know of. I trust you are prepared for that."

"He's not the first one we've killed, Alucard," Luther said, smirking. "You know I know what I'm doing."

"Right," Alucard mumbled, setting his attention back on the window. "How are things in Avalmoor?"

"Calm... boring. Did you find the angel you came looking for?"

"No. That's who I have the Paladins hunting."

"Might I ask why this angel is of interest?"

"No."

Luther nodded and took his eyes off the vampire. "And... you and this demon? I must say I'm rather surprised to have learned that you've left the life of loneliness, Alucard. He seems... peculiar."

Glancing at him, Alucard frowned slightly. "When will you do the same, Luther?"

"When you stop telling me who to marry," he said with a grin.

Alucard rolled his eyes.

"When did it happen?"

Glancing at him, Alucard hesitated for a moment. He didn't like to share his personal life with those he worked with, but then again, he'd shared things with both Attila and Tobias. Luther was nothing like Attila, but he wasn't as laid-back as Tobias. However, Alucard had found comfort in talking about Zalith to Tobias, so perhaps he might alleviate some of his stress if he were to speak to someone else.

He looked down at his hand, which he had rested on the arm of the couch. "Well, we met nearly two years ago. Damien had me transferring vampires from...where Zalith lived to Dor-Sanguis. At first, we sort of...hated each other, I think. We weren't exactly best friends. But then, long story short, we sort of just...became friends, and then this," he said with a shrug.

"Elvin tried for years to get your attention, among others. How did this guy manage to do it?" he asked with an amused laugh.

Alucard frowned, still staring at his hand. How *had* Zalith managed to get his attention? He felt as if he'd always had some sort of liking for Zalith before he'd realized he had feelings of adoration, but when exactly had he realized Zalith was someone he wanted to hold onto forever? He knew when he was sure. It was the moment Zalith defended him in front of Damien. No one had ever done that. No one was brave enough. But Zalith was brave, and that made him very alluring. Not only did Alucard find his appearance, voice, and personality attractive, but he also felt safe with Zalith, and safe was something no one had ever been able to make him feel—especially not from Damien.

He took his eyes off his hand and looked at Luther. "Zalith is...otherworldly," he said, smirking.

"Otherworldly? Well, I guess there's no beating that. I imagine Attila was in your ear like a mother when he found out."

"Actually, when he found out, he tried to convince me that it was every kind of wrong. I told him to shut up and I thought he had listened until I found out he approached Zalith and said the same thing, but with much more vile terms. Zalith taught him a lesson, I taught him a lesson, and now he's probably sulking in some tavern off the coast of Samayō-Akuma."

Luther laughed and shook his head. "He's probably waiting for your forgiveness."

"He won't get it. He insulted and upset Zalith. He is lucky I didn't take his life."

"You care about him a lot, then."

Alucard didn't even think before he answered. "He means more to me than my own life," he said, staring down at the floor. "He's...able to make me see that there's more to life than my work and hunting dragons."

"Ah." Luther nodded, looking down at his own hand. "Dragons—the good old days. I saw the remains of your visit; Boreas wasn't so fortunate."

"Boreas is just another idiot who hurt Zalith and suffered the consequences. Anyway," Alucard then said, looking at Luther. "Detlaff has Ben. Go into my study; there's a blood contract that I had him sign a while ago. Use it to locate him, and where Ben is, Detlaff will hopefully be," he explained. He then stood up, watching Luther as he did the same.

"Well, I'll do my best to have this Detlaff creature back in his cage as soon as possible," Luther said as he followed Alucard over to the door.

Once he pulled the door open, Alucard led him across the hall and towards the front door. "Once you've dealt with that, you'll be serving as my vice—the job Attila had before the one I fired him from."

A delighted smile clung to Luther's face as Alucard pulled the front door open. He stepped out onto the porch and turned to face The Vampire Lord. "I suppose you'll be sending someone to do *my* old job, then? My current wife might not take so well to that."

"You'll die and your brother will replace you. It's not hard to find someone to replace you," he said, smirking.

Luther scoffed in amusement and took a few steps back. "I'll be seeing you again fairly soon."

"Don't die," Alucard said with a frown.

"You got it," Luther said. Then, he morphed into a small black bat and swiftly raced away into the sky, leaving Alucard alone.

Chapter Fifty-Six

— ⚔ † ⚔ —

By the River

| **Alucard** |

As Alucard firmly shut the front door, a soft exhale escaped him, and he turned around. His gaze promptly locked onto Zalith, who was traversing the hall towards him. The demon had his characteristic smile, but there was a subtle nuance to it—a hint that bespoke an impending revelation, one that hinted at a conversation that Alucard might find challenging to navigate.

"Let's go," Zalith said as he reached the vampire and placed his hands on his shoulders, turning him to face the door.

"Where?" Alucard asked as Zalith began to escort him back towards the front door.

"Somewhere," he said, stopping at the door.

Alucard frowned, watching as Zalith slipped his shoes on. He'd like to know exactly where it was they were going, but he like felt Zalith wanted to keep some mystery to it. He'd play along; he put his own shoes on, and once Zalith opened the front door and took hold of his hand, he followed the demon through the courtyard and towards the stables.

However, while he followed, a shimmer of blue in the corner of his eye caught his attention. He turned his head towards it, and when he saw that it was a pair of women's underwear caught up in one of the trees, he frowned confusedly and looked at Zalith. "Why is there underwear in that tree?"

Zalith glanced around until his eyes found the tree in question. He then sighed and said, "A lot of Varana's clothes left the premises through a window."

Acknowledging with a subtle nod, Alucard suppressed any trace of amusement that might show itself on his face. His focus shifted toward the stables, and he trailed behind Zalith as they entered. Inside, he saw that two of the three horses were in the midst of a shoe-changing process, while Zalith's horse appeared ready with its newly fitted shoes. The vampire frowned in realization—was Zalith contemplating another horse ride, but with only one horse?

Alucard stopped in the stable doorway as Zalith made his way past the stable workers and towards his horse. "Will we...wait for one of these other horses to be ready?" he asked, watching as Zalith took his horse's reins and guided it back towards the door.

"No," the demon said with a smirk, taking Alucard's hand in his other and leading the way out of the stables. He led the way through the grounds, smiling back at Alucard, who stared at him with a look of shy confliction. But he then stopped not too far from the gates and turned to face him. "Would you like to steer, vampire?"

With a nervous frown, Alucard took his eyes off Zalith and stared at the horse. He didn't feel any need to protest about sharing a horse; he'd most definitely feel flustered the entire time, but he'd be closer to Zalith, and that was something that he found himself wanting more lately. So, with a quiet sigh, he approached the horse and mounted it.

Zalith then climbed up and sat behind Alucard as he took the reins in his hands. The demon wrapped his arms around the vampire, rested his chin on his shoulder, and sighed contently, hugging him tightly.

Alucard smiled discreetly, and once the groundskeeper had opened the gates, the vampire tapped the horse's side with his foot. As the horse walked forward, following the country road, Alucard relaxed and stared ahead. He didn't do much steering at all; the horse seemed to know where it was supposed to go.

"How did everything go with Loser?" Zalith asked.

Loser? Alucard frowned and glanced back at him. "What?"

Zalith laughed quietly. "Your friend."

"Oh." Alucard looked down at the horse's mane. "It was fine. I sent him looking for Detlaff. I have a contract with Ben's blood on; Luther can use it to find him, and wherever Ben is, I'm sure Detlaff will be. Luther will bring him back to my castle, where I'll keep him until I'm sure I've learnt everything I can from him."

"What more are you hoping to learn?" Zalith asked curiously.

Alucard shrugged while the horse guided itself off the path and into the forest, following a narrow dirt path. "What exactly Lucifer is planning—with his scions, with the Diabolus, with me. Damien has managed to keep them off my ass for a while, but I feel as though something isn't...well...right—like I'm missing something. Lucifer suddenly sends Detlaff after me after so many years of forgetting that I exist, and the fact that he specifically made Detlaff to find me...something is happening, and I want to know what," he said, glaring ahead.

Zalith rested the side of his face on Alucard's and smiled slightly. "I'm positive that we'll figure it out together. And I have your back," he said with a smirk, playfully pinching the right side of Alucard's waist.

The vampire flinched in startlement but then snatched Zalith's wrist before he could wrap his arm back around him again. "Where are we going? This horse seems to have a location in mind."

Smiling, Zalith hugged Alucard tightly. "You'll see," he muttered into the vampire's ear before kissing his cheek.

Perturbed, Alucard stared ahead, waiting as the horse continued forward. He had no idea where they could be headed, but it was Zalith's doing, and that made him believe that wherever they were headed had to be something spectacular. So, he didn't question him further. He sighed, leaning back against Zalith as he let go of the horse's reins—he clearly didn't need to be holding them, did he?

Enveloped in Zalith's embrace, he deliberately focused on the prevailing sense of contentment, safeguarding his mind from stray thoughts that could unravel it. His gaze remained fixed, observing each tree that swept past, the rhythmic progression of their journey unfolding for another twenty minutes until the dense forest ahead began to thin. He frowned as the once-impenetrable curtain of trees revealed something beyond—was it a lake?

The translucent water glistened under the afternoon sunlight, its bed adorned with tall, luminous reeds. A golden sea of grass encircled the water, and a lone oak tree stood a bit farther into the clearing, not too distant from the lake's edge. It became evident that their destination lay there—the prearranged white sheet-like blanket and wicker basket positioned between two of the tree's exposed roots made that clear.

He glanced at Zalith, who sat up straight, but he didn't know what he wanted to say, so he set his eyes on the lake and waited as the horse traversed the yellow grass.

When the horse stopped a few feet from the tree, Zalith dismounted it. He then held his hand up to Alucard, offering to help him down. With a curious frown, Alucard took the demon's hand and dismounted the horse, which wandered off and lay down in the grass not too far away.

He followed Zalith towards the tree, and when they reached it, Zalith invited him to sit. He did as he was told and watched the demon as he picked up the basket, sat down beside him, and placed it between them.

"I thought that some time away from either of our homes would be nice," Zalith said as he opened the basket. He pulled a bottle of red wine from inside, along with two glasses. "I hope you don't disapprove of my kidnapping you," he said with a smirk, placing the wine and glasses down.

Watching him as he took several food items from the basket and placed them on the blanket, Alucard looked down at his lap and smiled slightly. "No," he answered.

"Good," Zalith said with a smirk, placing the empty basket on the grass behind them. "It certainly won't be the first time."

The vampire's smile faded. Any mention of time upset him. Despite his acceptance, he still couldn't stop thinking about the inevitable end that would come of his and Zalith's time together.

"I wasn't sure if you've ever tried any of this, but don't feel compelled to do so if you don't want to," Zalith said, taking a single green grape from the platter he'd laid out in front of them.

Alucard took his eyes off his lap and stared at the platter. It consisted of many different crackers, cheeses, and meats that he hadn't before seen; all he recognized were the grapes. He took his eyes off the food, picked up his wine glass—which Zalith had just filled—and took a small sip. "I will... try some."

Zalith smiled as he finished his grape and then picked up another, which he held out to Alucard.

Staring at Zalith, Alucard frowned and slowly set his eyes on the fruit. He was sure that the demon was expecting him to eat it from his fingers, but he didn't feel like doing that. Instead, he took the grape from him with his fingers. Zalith frowned in disappointment, but Alucard didn't feel like entertaining him. He didn't immediately eat the grape, either. For a few moments, he stared down at it, trying to decide whether or not he wanted to bring up his concerns to Zalith. The longer he held onto them, the worse he was surely going to feel. But... if he told Zalith about his fears, would that ruin whatever time they may have left?

He sighed quietly and placed the grape back down onto the platter. "I'm not... hungry for fruit," he mumbled.

Zalith sat up straight and leaned forward so that he could see the vampire's face. "Are you okay?"

"Yes," Alucard immediately answered, taking another sip of his wine.

The demon frowned unsurely but leaned back on his arm again.

"What is that?" Alucard then asked, pointing to one of the crackers.

Taking his eyes off the vampire, Zalith looked down at the cracker he was pointing to and smiled. "A cracker, but with dried pieces of berry in it. They're best with this cheese," he said, taking one of the crackers and a slice of orange cheese. He placed them together and then held them towards Alucard. "Try it."

Alucard took it from him and eyed it for a few moments, but then bit into it—and it wasn't at all bad. The cracker was rather salty, but he didn't care. As he watched Zalith take a few more of the grapes, he finished the cracker before reaching for another.

"Are you still making your own wine, Alucard?" Zalith asked, staring at him curiously.

As he took a bite of his food, Alucard glanced at him. "It's one of my favourite hobbies, so yes. It was fine while I was away for that year; my butlers keep an eye on it when I'm not there."

"It'll soon be time to venture to your vineyard, won't it?"

"Yes. Why?"

"I'd still like to see it," he said with a smile.

Finishing his cracker, Alucard shrugged slightly. "You can…come and see when I have to go there. Maybe sometime next month."

"It's a date," Zalith said with a smirk, picking up his glass.

As the demon sipped from his glass, Alucard nodded slowly. "It really isn't much to see, though."

"I beg to differ," Zalith said, watching the vampire as he set his eyes back on the platter.

Alucard picked a different cracker, and when he glanced at Zalith, the demon smiled as he watched him try to decide what to put with it.

The demon picked one of the cheeses for him and leaned back on his arm. "I'd also like to help out." He smiled, watching as Alucard took a bite of the cracker. "Winemaking has always intrigued me."

Alucard glanced at him. "Will you need me to teach you?" he asked, a slight smirk on his face.

"I believe you will, yes," he replied, refilling both their glasses.

Nodding, Alucard finished eating his cracker. "Then what? Will you start making *your* own wine?"

"Would you be mad if I did?"

"No."

Zalith took another sip of his wine and smiled at the vampire before taking a few more grapes from the platter.

Alucard stared at the lake, trying to keep himself from sinking into his worry and sadness the moment silence fell over them. As the sun's rays crept through the leaves of the tree above and hit his face, his eyes slowly faded to blue, and as the pain it brought surged through his head, he scowled and turned his face away from the light.

"Alucard," Zalith abruptly said, a stern tone to his voice.

With a perturbed frown, he turned his head and looked at him.

"Are we okay?"

The vampire's frown became thick with dismay as he stared at the demon's concerned face. He couldn't immediately answer, nor could he lie; he took his eyes off Zalith and looked down at his lap, unable to keep himself from sinking into his thoughts. *Were* they okay? He didn't have a simple answer. His constant distressing worry wasn't okay, he was sure, and Zalith had clearly noticed that he wasn't coping so well after hearing what Varana said. Either that or Zalith was just generally asking—the concern on his face told Alucard it was the former, though.

He scowled in distress, trying to work out what to say. If he told Zalith about his fears, he was afraid that it might take away whatever time they had left. If he didn't speak up, though, he might never hear the things he felt like he needed to hear. But…what if he told Zalith and the demon told him things he *didn't* want to hear? However, if he held onto his pain, he was sure that he'd feel a whole lot worse over the coming days. He felt that, for once, he had to stop holding back and tell Zalith *exactly* how he felt.

Alucard slowly set his eyes back on him. "We…are okay," he answered.

Zalith sighed in relief—

"But," Alucard said.

A look of dread warped the demon's face—

"I don't…I can't stop thinking about how long that might be the case for."

Staring at him, Zalith frowned in both sorrow and worry. "Alucard, I'm so sorry you had to find out about my past like that. I really wish I could have had the chance to tell you myself, but the time just never came. But that's exactly what it is: the *past*. You're nothing like any of the people Varana spoke of, and I'm not going to tire of you. You already mean so much more to me than anyone else, and nothing will change that," he said sincerely.

Alucard frowned sadly and looked down at his lap. "I imagine you said the same thing to the people who came before me. But how can you be sure that this isn't the same? I don't…want to lose you, but if you're going to eventually tire of me, I'd rather just…I don't know," he muttered despondently, turning his head to hide his face from him.

"Alucard.…" Zalith frowned, placing his glass down before shuffling closer to him. "If I was going to tire of you, it would've happened already, especially during that year when I couldn't even see you, when I couldn't even be with you *at all*. I'm not going to deny that I'm very physical, but that didn't keep me from waiting for you. I would *not* have waited for anyone else—but I waited for *you* because you're very special to me," he explained as he placed his hand on the vampire's shoulder.

The vampire pouted and scowled sadly, still denying Zalith a look at his face. "I'm here now," he said quietly, his throat tightening as his distress grew. "You have me, and you can do whatever you want—the wait is over, and now that you can touch me, who is to say that you won't eventually get bored of that? Of *me*."

Zalith fell quiet for a moment. But just as Alucard was about to look at him, he said, "I…Alucard.…" He sighed heavily. "I can't sit here and pretend like I know where we might end up together. I can't tell you that what we have will last a lifetime, but what I *can* say is that I want it to. I've not once felt this way for anyone—to want an actual future. But I want that with you, and all we can do is try to make that happen…*together*," he said, moving his hand to the back of the vampire's neck.

He shook his head. Zalith's words weren't much of a comfort. "You want that *now*, but—"

"Alucard—"

He didn't want to hear it anymore. His heart ached, tears threatening to spill, and the desire to escape overwhelmed him. Wincing in emotional pain, he attempted to rise, eager to depart before his tears betrayed him. However, a scowl etched with agony marked his face as Zalith swiftly seized his wrist, thwarting his attempt. Alucard strained to break free, using his other hand to push Zalith away, only to engage in a brief, futile struggle. True to form, Zalith effortlessly subdued Alucard, pinning him to the ground and fixing his gaze upon the distressed contours of his face.

Before Alucard could speak, Zalith placed his index finger against the vampire's lips, silencing him. He glared up at the demon—he could see a smile trying to steal Zalith's stern frown, but with a quiet huff, the demon gazed into his eyes and moved his hand to the side of Alucard's face.

"I love you, Alucard."

The ache in Alucard's heart retreated. Relief, among many things, swarmed him. If he could pause time, he'd wish to do so now so that he could bask just a little longer in the new kind of happiness that flooded through him, casting out the distress and the dismay. That was the first time he'd *ever* heard someone say that to him, and he couldn't have wanted it from anyone else.

Zalith's words banished his worry, despair, and pain. He couldn't explain what he felt other than a relief he had waited so, *so* long for—words he thought he'd never hear, words he'd wanted to hear from no one but the man *he* loved. To know—to *hear* that Zalith *did* love him… and to have heard everything he just said, too. How could he have allowed that witch of a woman to make him think otherwise? He didn't want to think about her or anything she said. All that mattered right now was Zalith and the words he had spoken.

His happiness sent his confliction and fear running, and as nothing but contentment enthralled him, he smiled and placed his hand on the side of Zalith's face. As the demon then moved his finger from his lips so that he could speak, Alucard frowned in response to his overwrought happiness. "I love *you*."

The demon smiled brightly and exhaled in relief, resting his forehead against Alucard's. "Good," he said with a smirk, and then, he passionately kissed the vampire, keeping his hand on the side of his face.

In a lingering embrace, their tongues met, and the world around them seemed to dissolve. The kiss, a fusion of desire and sheer relief, enveloped them in a fleeting sanctuary of profound contentment. Yet, as the once-pleasant breeze turned bitter around them, the ethereal connection waned. Reluctantly, they broke their kiss, casting a brief yet intense gaze at each other, savouring the residue of the shared moment on their lips.

"I don't ever want to lose you either, Alucard," Zalith said as he began to fiddle with the vampire's hair.

Staring up at him, Alucard lowered his arms to his side and looked away shyly. "You won't."

With a content smile, Zalith kissed the vampire's forehead and pulled him with him as he sat upright. "Do you want to head back?" he asked, placing his hand over Alucard's.

Alucard took his eyes off Zalith and stared out at the lake. "We can... finish this," he said, looking down at what remained of their food and wine. "Then we can go back."

"Okay." Zalith leaned back on his arm again, keeping his eyes on Alucard.

With nothing but content thoughts to sink into, Alucard reached back to the platter and selected another of the crackers he hadn't yet tried. "What... should I have with this one?" he asked, looking down at Zalith, who was smiling up at him.

Zalith reached towards the platter, placed a piece of cheese on the cracker Alucard was holding, and then shuffled closer. He rested his head in the vampire's lap, staring up at him as he took a bite of his food. "You look very handsome from down here." He smirked as he lifted his hand and flicked the crucifix hanging around the vampire's neck.

Alucard glanced down at him, a nervous look on his face. But he allowed himself to smile in response—how could he not? He felt so happy—more happy than he had ever felt in his entire life. But... his smile faded when he swallowed the cracker.

"Alucard?" Zalith immediately asked in concern.

As Zalith sat up and placed his glass of wine aside, Alucard stared at him and then looked down at the cracker in his hand. "What... is there... garlic in this?"

Zalith looked stumped for a moment, and a look of angst struck his face. But then he snapped out of his confusion, setting his eyes on the cracker Alucard had in his right hand. "There is," he confirmed worriedly.

Alucard grimaced in revolt and placed the cracker down, looking around frantically as he gripped his throat with his left hand.

With a panicked stare, Zalith moved closer, and as Alucard started breathing frantically, the demon gripped his wrist. "Alucard? Alucard?!"

But Alucard didn't respond. He struggled, trying to pull away from the demon, but when Zalith fought with him and tried to turn his head to get him to look at him, Alucard couldn't stop his struggled breaths from becoming laughter.

Zalith stared at him in utter confusion.

As his laughter slowly died down, Alucard said, "For a moment, you thought I was actually allergic to garlic, no?"

At first, a look of disbelief sat on Zalith's face, but it quickly evolved into an amused smile. "You might have been. You had me fooled for... two seconds, though."

"Two seconds is better than none," Alucard said as he also leaned back on his arm, picking his glass back up to finish his wine. He wasn't allergic; the coarse cracker had just scratched his throat. As he took a sip of his wine to soothe his throat, he glanced at Zalith. "Are *you* allergic to anything?" he asked curiously.

Still staring at him, Zalith smiled. "No. Are you—truthfully?"

"No," Alucard said and finished his wine. "Well…people," he grumbled. "Too many of them make me want to snap."

Zalith nodded. "Humans."

"Eh." Alucard shrugged, sitting up straight. "One day, they will be less in numbers here, I'm sure. They don't last very long in the wars that break out here, and one day, one war will see to their endangerment."

"If only the same could be said for humans back in Eltaria; they continue to multiply like rats."

"Do you know what they did when rats were spreading a plague through a city in DeiganLupus two hundred years ago? They burned them all, and the city with them. Maybe you can take inspiration from that," Alucard said, smirking.

Zalith laughed and finished the rest of his wine. "I should, shouldn't I? Would you care to help me burn them, Alucard?"

Alucard smiled amusedly "It would be an enjoyable day, I'm sure."

Still smiling, Zalith placed his glass down and shuffled closer to Alucard. He sighed quietly and rested his head on the vampire's shoulder as he stared out at the lake. "Any day with you is enjoyable," he said quietly. "I wouldn't rather be anywhere else."

Glancing down at him, Alucard smiled slightly. "I don't know how long my people will take to find Lucious and Detlaff," he started. "But once they do, I'll have a lot to do. I don't want to take you away from your work, but…if you want to come with me, you can," he said. He was sure that he'd have new tasks to complete once Damien had Lucious, and he didn't want that to affect the amount of time he got to spend with Zalith.

The demon smiled and placed his hand in Alucard's. "I'd love that," he said. "You also still need to bring some of your clothes to keep at my house. I think we should do that…tomorrow—once you're completely healed," he said, moving his hand to the vampire's neck and slowly dragging his fingers over the scars left by his fangs after he removed the silver from his blood. "How does that sound?"

Alucard nodded as he rested the side of his face on Zalith's head. "We can do that. I will…also tune the violin later."

An excited smile appeared on Zalith's face. "Are you going to play for me?"

"Maybe," Alucard said quietly.

"I'd love that, too." Zalith lifted his head, and as Alucard turned his head to face him, the demon kissed him.

When Zalith smirked at him, Alucard tried and hide his embarrassed face, but he smiled, too; it felt strange to feel so happy and without worry, but he liked it. He knew that the man he loved also loved him, and he felt a whole lot more confident that Zalith wasn't going to tire of him. The demon told him that he wanted them to share a future together, and Alucard knew that was what *he* wanted, too. He wanted to spend every day with Zalith and knowing that Zalith felt the same—*hearing* him say it banished his worries. He thought that, right now, nothing could steal his contentedness. Zalith made him happy, and he wasn't going anywhere.

Chapter Fifty-Seven

— ≺ ✝ ≻ —

Sister

The heart of Avalmoor languished beneath the oppressive shadow of a towering, jagged mountain range—a desolate expanse of tall, obsidian-hued rocks that clawed at the heavens, their summits shrouded in an eerie embrace of snow and ice. The menacing hills pierced through the clouds, creating an intimidating silhouette against the sky. A warning echoed among humans, urging them not to venture too near, for the common belief held that dragons lurked within. However, the reality was far more malevolent. It wasn't the domain of godly creatures but a sinister force that surpassed the dread inspired by the Aegis.

A narrow, murderous path that had claimed the lives of many stretched from the snow-covered ground and deep into the depths of black rock. At its very end, clinging to the face of one of the tallest, fang-like mountains, sat a beguiling fort made up of the same rock it was gripping onto. Graveyard was a word better used to describe the courtyard, warped in dark fog not even the shivering snows of Avalmoor could puncture. Corpses—ashy flesh clinging to their twisted bones—were scattered through the grounds like sentries frozen in time. Not one possessed a look on its face that might say it had willingly become the creature it now was, and the grass—there was none. No snow, only the ash of corpses that had long lost their strength to pose upright. But the corpses out front weren't the castle's most concerning décor.

A messenger made his way past, heading towards the front door; he kept his dark eyes ahead, ignoring the thousands of crimson dots watching from the mountains surrounding him. Fear clung to his pale face, most of which was hidden beneath his hood, and as he made his way up a steep staircase to reach the door, he lifted a pale hand from the inside of his cloak and knocked loudly.

His short, ominous wait ended when the attendant answered the door, a tall, dark man with eyes as red as human blood. A gust of warm air burst out of the building as the door opened, hitting the messenger like a smack to his face, and he grimaced as it greeted him. He'd not falter, though; he reached into his pocket, pulled out a carefully rolled scroll tied with a navy-blue ribbon, and handed it to the man.

With a nod, the attendant stepped back and closed the door, shutting the messenger back out in the cold. Little did he know that his final journey had been made. As quickly and cautiously as he approached, he hurried away, but the red that had been watching soon descended from their nests of darkness and prowled through the thickening fog. Snarls and grumbles tore at the messenger's soul as he realized he'd not see the light of another day, and this dark, dismal wasteland was where he would finally rest.

| **Ysmay** |

The piercing scream of a man sent a macabre thrill across the wicked countenance of the woman perched at the helm of a long, obsidian table. Her lips, stained a hue as vivid as blood, contrasted sharply with her pallid skin, while her bone-straight hair cascaded like an abyss of darkness. Claw-tipped fingers delicately toyed with the dark fur of a rat-like creature sprawled before her, emitting a contented purr akin to a cat, its fuzzy tails swaying in rhythmic harmony.

Crimson eyes, vibrant and predatory, shifted from the creature to the attendant entering the hall, a scroll clutched in his left hand. Unfazed by the unsettling landscape, he traversed floors strewn with the naked bodies of sleeping men and women, entwined together for warmth before a solitary fireplace in the nearly lightless room.

The woman's attention shifted, withdrawing her hand from the creature's belly as the attendant neared. With black-painted nails, she flicked a wiry hair from her white satin dress, crimson eyes locking onto the approaching figure. "Thank you," Ysmay's voice, silvery and soft-spoken, carried an undercurrent of threat.

He extended the scroll, his gaze steady but clearly strangled by the eerie quietude of the surroundings. Ysmay accepted the scroll, dismissing him with a languid wave as a nearby sleeper stirred. The attendant retreated, liberated from the palpable tension that had threatened to overwhelm him.

Ysmay's smile remained on her face as she returned one hand to her pet and used the other to open the scroll. But as her eyes met with the words on the parchment, she scowled irritably.

Her creature of a pet opened its snake-like eyes, setting them on the woman.

With a quiet sigh, she placed the scroll aside and looked down at the creature as it shuffled around to sit much like a cat, but a cat with six scaly legs. "Why my haughty little sister needs so many ugly gowns, I'll never know," she hissed, glancing down at the scroll, which was a notice of delivery—a delivery *someone* would have to go and pick up from the city.

Her little sister—who had been with her for the past five days—was holed up in her room and hadn't left at all since her arrival. How that woman had a way of irritating Ysmay. With an exasperated sigh, the red-lipped woman stood up and left her table. She elegantly glided forward, her bare feet silent against the mahogany carpeted floor, the long, drapey end of her dress dragging behind her as she walked past the sleeping guests she had spent most of the previous night being entertained by.

Silently, and as her pet followed, she made her way through the gloomy, candlelit halls of her home, up a staircase, and along a narrow walkway until she reached the door at its end. She didn't knock and entered the room as if it were her own. Immediately, she set her eyes on the black-haired woman curled up and enthralled in the white sheets of her bed at the very end of the room.

Weeping, makeup smothering her pale face, tears seeping from her crimson eyes; Varana wailed like a woman in mourning, gripping her sheets as if they were all that was left in the world.

Standing in the doorway, Ysmay shook her head in pity for her twin sister. "Are you actually still crying?"

"Of course I'm still crying!" Varana cried, keeping her back to her sister. "If you were capable of understanding something as complex as love, then you'd be crying too in my situation!" she yelled as she swiftly sat up and launched one of her pillows towards Ysmay.

With an irritated tut, Ysmay stepped aside to avoid the pillow. She then crossed her arms and leaned against the door frame. "I know how to love," she said, shrugging. "And I know that loving the king of gays isn't going to get you anywhere other than back here once every couple of months crying into my linen—much too often for my liking."

Varana scowled and gritted her teeth in anger. "Well he's never disowned me like this before, so shut the hell up! You don't know what you're talking about!" she insisted, tears of both anger and dismay streaming down her face.

Ysmay scoffed. "He probably got tired of your bitchy attitude. God knows I have," she muttered as her pet wandered into the room.

With an overly frustrated glare on her face, Varana pointed at her sister's bulldog-faced pet. "Get that disgusting thing out of here!"

The creature frowned and whimpered sadly as it stopped in its tracks.

"Aww, don't listen to the mean lady, Pickles; it's just her time of the month," Ysmay said, wandering over to pick her pet up as it sniffled sullenly. "I got *another* pickup form for you downstairs; you've been here all of five days and there are enough clothes waiting in that city for you to clothe all the people in my hall," she grumbled with a scowl, setting her eyes back on Varana, who glared up at her.

Varana took her eyes off Ysmay and glared at the suitcases by the dresser at the end of her bed. "Maybe if you actually got someone up here to clean my clothes, then I wouldn't have to order new ones."

Rolling her eyes as she slowly stroked her pet, Ysmay made her way over and sat on the end of Varana's bed. "Maybe if *you* came out of this damn room, I'd send someone up here to clean whatever needs cleaning. The last guy I sent up here came back looking like he'd seen the end of the world."

"He looked at me funny," Varana said with a pout.

"Probably because you're the only person he's seen here wearing clothes," she said amusedly, picking a loose strand of hair off the front of Varana's nightgown. "Are you ready to tell me what happened?"

Varana smacked her hand away and scoffed. "Don't act like you care. You're just nosey."

With a theatrical scoff of offence, Ysmay held her hand to her overly-sized chest. "Excuse you," she said, astounded. "I care very much for my darling little sister," she claimed as her pet snickered in her lap. "But I would also like to know why that animal kicked you out like that—and broke a family heirloom, I might add," she said, a bitter tone in her voice.

"He's not an animal," she said, frowning. "He was just angry. And stop calling me your little sister—you're no more than a second older than me," she complained, scowling.

"Bursting in your room, flying at you. You call that angry? He looked like he was about to kill you, Varana, and you still sit here and defend him. You honestly have a problem, and I'm tired of trying to figure out why you can't understand that—"

"I don't need you to lecture me!" she interjected, glaring at her sister. "And Z would never kill me! He'll calm down soon, I know he will," she insisted sadly.

"No, Varana, you need me to remove that ingrate from your life so you can move the fuck on," she said, a threatening smile on her face. "You've wasted…how long sucking up to him? It's time to get over it and live your own life."

Glaring at her, Varana scowled in hostility. "You stay away from him, witch!" she screeched, reaching out to grab her sister's hair, but Ysmay leaned back and hissed irritably, revealing a mouth full of razor-sharp teeth. Varana grimaced, frowned, and calmed down. "Regardless of what happens, he's still my friend and is always there for me when I need him; I'm not just going to cut him out of my life!"

"All right.…" Ysmay sighed, making herself comfortable again. "Maybe if you told me why this even happened—"

Varana scowled. "Why do you want to know so bad?"

Her sister scoffed and frowned. "You're not usually *this* reluctant to tell me anything, and it just makes me curious. Tell me."

She shrugged and pouted sadly. "Z just came in all mad, and I barely even did anything bad—I didn't even do *anything*!" she insisted. "He just threw himself at me and started attacking me like I did something awful! And then he started just throwing my clothes outside and told me to leave in an hour! I didn't do anything, and I was so confused, but he wouldn't tell me why he was doing any of it!" she cried, tears streaming down her face.

Slowly, Ysmay nodded, a doubtful frown on her face. "Even *he* doesn't just burst into your room and threaten to kick you out if you didn't do anything, Varana. I bet it had something to do with that little stunt you pulled in the kitchen." She smirked amusedly. "Did his new boyfriend tattle on you?"

With a revolted snarl, Varana glared over at the door. "Because he's a little bitch," she growled.

"Such anger, sister," Ysmay laughed.

"Well, obviously I'm mad, Ysmay!" she yelled. "I'm being replaced by some guy, and Z doesn't even want me living with him anymore!" she cried, burying her face in her hands as she wept like a widow once again.

Ysmay slowly shook her head. "I could point out multiple errors in that statement, but for the sake of my ears, I shan't. This new guy, though—you've told me a strangely minuscule amount about him. All I know is that you've walked in on him with his dick halfway down your imaginary husband's throat, you've upset him in the kitchen—which you were very proud of, and that you can't stand his accent—an accent you've only heard from eavesdropping like a desperate little housewife," she said, watching as Varana's anger quickly increased into something devastating, sure to explode any moment now. "Is he the same guy Z got depressed over, the same guy he's disappeared with for days at a time? You never told me his name, unless 'Z's new boyfriend' is what he's actually called."

"I'm not a desperate little housewife!" she snapped. Clearly, she had no intent to answer her sister's questions.

Looking at her sister, Ysmay frowned skeptically. It wasn't hard at all for her to notice her sister was deflecting and avoiding answering. "Who is he, Varana?" she asked firmly.

Varana tutted irritably and looked away from her sister. "Just some guy he met while doing that job for Damien," she mumbled. "Just some random guy in some random place doing nothing important."

"And what's this random guy's name?"

She paused, clearly thinking to herself for a moment, but she then shrugged. "Lu...Luca, or something—he fucks so many guys I lose track."

Amused, Ysmay laughed and looked down at her pet. "And what's so special about this Luca? Last I heard, your precious Zalith drops his boyfriends after a few weeks; how long's it been? A year...two?" she asked, watching as the look on her sister's face became sour once again.

"There's literally nothing special about him at all!" she exclaimed, her anger returning. "Don't even say anything else!" she then snapped, holding her hand towards Ysmay to silence her before she could say something to accompany her smirk. She then sighed, rested her hands in her lap, and frowned sadly. "I wish he'd just love me the way I love him. Maybe if I can just talk to him and tell him I'm sorry, then he'd let me come home. It's just so weird not being with him; we've been inseparable for so long," she said despondently, her voice breaking.

"Yeah, until lover boy Luca came along and separated you. I mean, isn't it a good thing? You two were joined at the hip like one of Detlaff's gross little experiments—"

"Shut up!"

"No! I'm tired of hearing 'Z's done this', 'Z's done that', 'he's fucking this guy', 'but one day he'll love me too'—it's about time you woke up, V," Ysmay scolded her, watching as her sister's anger increased. "He's *not* going to love you the way you want him to, no matter what you do or what you say. He's a manipulative, obnoxious, selfish little man, and you need to stop telling yourself that he isn't. You're wasting your time like time is nothing. Father could order us back home at any given moment; we can't say no, and you can't take your precious Z with you, and to be honest, I don't think he'd want to go with you, especially not now he has this Luca guy to ignore you for. You're here with me now, and I'm not going to watch you scurry back to him like a lost lamb," she stated.

"You don't even know him! You only know what I've told you! He's *none* of those things at all!" Varana insisted, gripping the blankets beneath her as she yelled in her sister's face. "If you think you're going to keep us away from each other, you're an idiot!"

With an entertained smile on her face, Ysmay dragged her hand over the back of her pet as it remained in her lap. She felt a familiar aura approaching, and she knew that things were about to get a whole lot more frustrating. "I think you'd find that there's only *one* idiot in this family, and he's making his way up the tower right now," she said with a sigh.

Varana's anger faded into utter disgust. "Ugh, why?!" she exclaimed.

"He's enjoying his freedom, little sister. Perhaps he wants to come and tell us how much he loves the mayflies in the city."

"I don't care what he has to say. I'd rather have that ugly thing in here than him!" she insisted, waving her hand towards Ysmay's pet as it whined sadly.

"Now, now...." Ysmay tutted, shaking her head. "That's no way to treat your precious little brother, Ronnie." she said, smirking.

"Don't call me that, you bitch!" Varana screamed as Ysmay stood up.

Laughing, Ysmay took a few steps away from her sister's bed and stared down the hallway, listening as the loud thumping of rushing footsteps made their way up the stairs. Her pet wriggled around and escaped from her arms, scurrying for cover as Detlaff reached the top of the stairs. He had a crazily excited smile on his face, and as he rushed forward, skipping and laughing like a child, Ysmay and Varana groaned in displeasure.

"Yayay!" Detlaff squealed as he sprung forward, trying to wrap his arms around Ysmay, but she grunted in revolt and stepped aside. Pouting sadly, Detlaff stumbled forward and set his eyes on Varana. "Vivi!" He clapped his hands excitedly—

"No," Varana warned, glaring at him from where she sat.

Detlaff stropped sadly and slouched forward, his arms dangling in front of him. "Is no one happy to see Detlaff?"

"I'd be happy if you brought me something to eat." Ysmay sighed, picking up her pet from the basket it had cowered behind.

Seeing the pet, Detlaff squealed excitedly and clapped his hands. "You kept him?!" he asked happily.

Ysmay nodded, stroking the creature's fluffy mane. "Pickles serves me well."

"All it does is stink up the place," Varana mumbled. "Uglies it out, too."

Sighing, Ysmay set her crimson eyes on her brother, who was still panting excitedly. "You've come here for a reason; I imagine this isn't a lovely family reunion, is it?"

Detlaff nodded and clapped his hands as he calmed down a little. "You have to guess; you get *four* tries."

"Isn't it usually three?" Ysmay asked with a frown as she ignored her sister's mumble of mockery.

"No, four," Detlaff said, shaking his head. "Four because there's four of *us*!" he said as he clapped, looking back at Varana and then at Ysmay.

Varana scowled. "There's three of us, you ugly little mouth-breather."

Pouting, Detlaff crossed his arms and looked at Ysmay. "She's so mean to me."

"News from Father?" Ysmay guessed.

"Nope."

Ysmay frowned impatiently. "Then I'm all out of ideas. Tell us."

Detlaff danced around like a moron, gliding over to the window. He leaned outside, inhaled deeply, and sighed happily as he turned to lean against the ledge. "I found big brother," he said with a proud smile. "Shh!" he then snapped as Ysmay stepped forward to speak. "We have to be quiet, shh...shhhh," he said, looking at Varana, who glared at him.

"Shut up," Ysmay snarled, dropping her pet to the ground. "Where is he? Did you capture him?"

"Uh…no," Detlaff mumbled. "But!" he said, raising his hand before Ysmay could yell at him. "But…but, big sisters, Detlaff knows *how* to find him, yes, he does," he said, nodding.

"What are you waiting for, you moron?!" Ysmay yelled. "Tell me!"

"Why tell when I can show?" Detlaff sang, skipping over to the bedroom door. "Follow Detlaff," he invited, turning back to face them.

Varana frowned as she stood up. "Follow you where?"

"To how we find big brother." He clapped, beginning to lead the way down the hallway.

Ysmay didn't falter. Eager to see what Detlaff had to show her, and just as eager to please their father, she followed him down the hall, leaving Varana's room.

| **Varana** |

Varana stayed on her bed, sniffling and stifling her breaths as her heart ached in her chest. But when Ysmay called her name, she got up with an irritated huff and followed, but dread began to choke her. Was Detlaff going to take them to where Alucard was right now? If he did that, they'd find him with Zalith, and she'd be forced to choose between him and her family. Not only that, but Zalith would disown her—that was for sure. She felt as if she should do something to stop such a scenario from happening, but…*should* she?

She followed her siblings down the stairs, through the castle corridors, and into the hall where Ysmay's naked guests were all still sleeping soundlessly. Detlaff led them past the door and into a lounge lit by the small fireplace in the back wall.

Standing in the middle of the room below the unlit chandelier was a vampire Varana recognized immediately and another man who she assumed to be one of Detlaff's suck-ups. The vampire was Ben, and he looked half-dead if that could be said for a vampire; bloodied, beaten, and barely standing without help from the man beside him. She walked with her siblings over to them both, waiting to hear what Detlaff was about to say—he just had to finish his annoying little song first.

"This delicious creature before you is called Benny-boo," Detlaff sang as he pounced over to Ben and held his hand out to him. As his sisters stopped a few feet away, he sighed longingly and dragged his hand over the vacant, bloodied face of the vampire.

"Vampires possess the ability to locate their master—their master just so happens to be our big brother!" He clapped again, giggling excitedly as Ysmay glanced at Varana with a confused look on her face.

Ysmay then shook her head and looked back at Detlaff. "So, how exactly is he going to help us find him?"

"Shh!" Detlaff insisted. "I'm not done talking about science yet! God, where do you get your manners from?"

"We don't have time—"

"There is always time!" Detlaff insisted as he gripped Ben's jaw and shook his head like it was a toy. "So, big brother created these wonderful creatures this world calls vampires," he continued. "It seems that, unlike us, he possesses the ability to create his own people with his blood. I guess that's because he's not like us, really…well, he's still Daddy's son, but he was made when Daddy—"

Ysmay scowled. "We really don't need the details."

Detlaff giggled and let go of Ben's jaw. He stood behind the vampire, placed his hands on his shoulders, and leaned around Ben's arm so that he could see his sisters. "This beautiful man was made into a vampire through big brother's blood, which means big brother's blood is inside him, which means I can use that to find big brother the same way vampires use it to find him." He smiled glancing up at Ben, who had a struggled but revolted look on his face.

"Then do it!" Ysmay scoffed. "Why the hell are you just standing around here telling us when you could be doing it!"

"Because!" Detlaff screeched, stomping his foot on the ground. "Because…Yayay, if we do it wrong, we could kill him, and I don't want to kill Benny-boo…." He sighed longingly and danced around to Ben's front. He leaned back on him and rested the back of his head on his shoulder, staring up at him. "I've fallen in love, dear sisters."

"Oh, my fucking God," Ysmay grumbled, smacking her hand over her face. "Whatever. Do it without killing him, I don't care. Just take us to him!" she insisted, stepping towards Ben.

Startled, Detlaff sprung back, clinging onto Ben like a child would its mother, wrapping his arms around the vampire's shoulders. "Don't touch him!" he screamed as the guard he had brought with him defensively moved forward.

Ysmay, clearly uninterested in waiting any longer, waved her hand aside, sending the guard crashing into the wall with little to no effort at all. As his lifeless body hit the floor, she stepped forward, ripped Detlaff off Ben, and glared into his panicked eyes. "Take us to him, or I'll work out how to do it myself and kill you *and* your little boyfriend in the process!"

Ignoring most of the commotion as Ysmay began strangling Detlaff, Varana kept her eyes on Ben. She knew who he was, and more importantly, who he was important to. She knew that once upon a time, Zalith had a thing for him, and she also knew that this vampire worked for Alucard. If she could take him to Zalith, perhaps he'd forgive her and let her go home. But…how would she do it? If she wanted to get Ben away from her siblings, she had to do so without implicating herself, and that wasn't exactly going to be easy. She'd figure something out, though. She had to.

"Stop!" Detlaff screeched, ripping Ysmay's hands from around his throat. "You'll kill Detlaff!"

"Good!" Ysmay yelled, shaking her fist as he leapt back and pulled Ben away from his sisters. "I don't know why Father thinks you're so special! You're a fucking idiot! Shit for fucking brains! And a little faggot, too!" she screamed furiously, trying to grab Detlaff, who darted around like a rat, pulling Ben with him.

"Daddy loves Detlaff!" he screamed back, avoiding Ysmay's claws. "Daddy loves Detlaff and all the things he does!"

Varana then scowled impatiently. "How do you use him to find him?" she asked.

Calming down once Ysmay stopped trying to grab him, Detlaff set his eyes on his sister and pouted. "I have to eat him."

Both sisters waited.

"I sip-sip some of his bloody blood, and then I use it to find big brother—but…he's not ready yet."

"Not ready?!" Ysmay yelled. "The fuck does that mean?!"

"He's not READY!!!" Detlaff screamed so loud that the plates on the wall shook.

"Then make him ready!" Ysmay yelled back.

"He needs to SLEEP!!!"

"I'll send you to sleep in…wait." Ysmay frowned, calming down. "If you know how to find him, why are you here sharing the information with us? Father's not exactly going to applaud us all the same way he would one of us for bringing him back home."

Detlaff pouted sadly and shrugged. "Detlaff tried to get big brother himself, but big brother has a boyfriend. Big mean angry boyfriend."

"Literal, or just some guy—"

"Detlaff doesn't know!" he screeched, cutting Ysmay off. "But Detlaff can't fight them both, so Detlaff needs sisters' help," he said sadly, cradling Ben's arm in both of his.

Ysmay sighed and looked at her sister. "Half of me wants to kill him and extract the information on how to use this vampire from his cold dead corpse, but then half of me wants to allow the three of us to work together—since *he* insists we should," she said, looking back over at Detlaff.

Varana snarled in revolt. "Whatever," she mumbled. "How long does he need to sleep for?"

Detlaff, who was dragging his tongue over Ben's bicep, stopped and glanced at his sisters. "Um…." He frowned, standing up straight. "Little…while."

"You don't sound so—"

"I'm sure!" he snapped, cutting Ysmay off once again.

"Are you!?" she yelled, raising her voice.

"I am!"

Varana sighed and dragged her hand over her face. "I'm leaving before I get a headache," she said, turning her back on them both as they continued bickering.

Then, without another word, she left the room. She had already decided that saving Ben was a good idea to gain Zalith's forgiveness, she just had to work out how to do it. She had time, but how long until Detlaff was ready to use him to take the three of them to where Alucard was? She didn't know, and she'd make sure not to take too long. She was smart, after all—smarter than her siblings.

She'd figure out how to get Ben away from Detlaff and how to get herself back home. She just had to wait a little longer.

Chapter Fifty-Eight

— ⋖ ✝ ⋗ —

A Discussion of Technology

| **Zalith** |

As the sun set, Alucard and Zalith arrived back at the house. Zalith pulled the front door open, inviting Alucard inside, and once the vampire entered, he lightly grabbed his collar before he could finish taking off his shoes and pushed him back against the wall. With a smirk, he leaned closer to Alucard's face and kissed his lips.

He'd never felt so happy before. Earlier, he feared Alucard wasn't enjoying their time at the lake; he was terrified that the things Varana had said were going to drive Alucard away forever. And that might have actually happened if he hadn't told the vampire how he felt about him.

But he'd said it. He'd told Alucard that he loved him. For a long time, he'd known that Alucard was more than a game to him—the vampire was more than a conquest, more than a means of entertainment, and more than someone he just wanted to fuck and be done with. No…he loved Alucard in a way that was different to how he'd felt about anyone else. He wanted someone to share a life with, and although he might not know where the future would take them, he knew that Alucard was that someone.

For a few moments, they stood by the closed door, kissing slowly. Zalith's worry and fear had faded—he had no doubts. Usually, 'I love you' was something he said to manipulate and control the people in his life, but it was different with Alucard. He felt no hesitation saying it. The words hadn't filled him with dread or guilt. No, they gave him happiness and relief. And hearing Alucard say the same thing…it warmed his heart so much that it was like it had been woken from a long, lonely slumber. Alucard was all he needed—he knew that now more than ever.

He rested his forehead against Alucard's. "I had a nice time today," he said quietly. "Did you?"

Staring at him, Alucard smiled. "Yes."

"Good," Zalith said, dragging his thumb over the vampire's cheek. "Dinner will be ready soon—unless you don't want to eat."

"We can eat."

Still smiling, Zalith took his hand and began leading the way down the hallway, heading for the dining room.

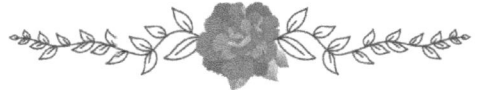

| **Alucard** |

When they stepped into the dining room lounge, instead of immediately sitting at the table, Zalith led Alucard over to the couch under the window and slumped down onto it, pulling the vampire with him.

With a nervous frown, Alucard sat beside the demon, resting his head on his shoulder. He then lay there, staring at the empty fireplace and the painting that hung above it. It hadn't been long since he entered this room and set his eyes on its décor for the first time. The painting was the first thing he'd seen, and the more time he spent looking at it, the more he learned to love it. It was, after all, the first thing he'd seen in the demon's house and the first thing he'd asked about. He wasn't sure why, but something about it was—for the lack of a better word—special.

Taking his eyes off it, he stared into the empty fireplace, his sense of calm increasing as Zalith began to fiddle with his hair. The day's nearing end felt strange; this morning, he'd been so distraught and dismayed by the things he'd come to learn about Zalith, but now, none of that seemed to matter. Zalith explained himself; he'd even told Alucard things about himself that the vampire was convinced he hadn't told anyone else. He trusted Zalith, and despite the sadness that had gripped him recently, he wouldn't dwell on it. Zalith had told him he loved him, and that was all he needed to hear.

He moved his hand and placed it on the demon's free shoulder, holding him tightly as he moved his head closer to Zalith's neck. When he felt Zalith rest his chin on his head, he exhaled quietly and closed his eyes, allowing himself a moment's rest. Love— it was new to him, and he didn't know how to express just how much of it he felt for Zalith, but he'd do his best. Zalith meant more than the world to him, and he'd do whatever he could to hold onto him for as long as he could.

"What are you thinking about?" Zalith then asked.

"What?" Alucard mumbled, opening his eyes.

"What are you thinking about?" he laughed. "When you're quiet, I know you're thinking. I can't read your mind—not that I would without your permission—but sometimes, I do wonder why you're so still and silent."

With a slightly uncomfortable shuffle, Alucard moved his head back to Zalith's shoulder and shrugged lightly. "Nothing, really."

Zalith tightened his embrace around the vampire and rested the side of his head on Alucard's. "*I'm* thinking about how much I'd love to hear you play for me."

Alucard frowned slightly and lifted his head so he could stare at Zalith's face; a smirk clung to it—of course. "Where did you put the violin?" he asked, looking around to see that the instrument Zalith had gifted him wasn't on the table where he'd left it.

"I had one of the butlers move it. Is that a yes?"

Looking down at his lap, Alucard pouted. "Maybe," he said. "Later, though."

Smiling, Zalith rested the side of his head on Alucard's once more. "I look forward to it."

Just then, a quiet knock came at the door to the left of the table. The tall, dark-haired butler, Edwin, stepped into the room and set his eyes on Zalith. "Dinner is ready, sir," he announced.

With a nod of dismissal, Zalith smiled down at Alucard. "Are you ready?" he asked quietly as the butler left.

Alucard sat up and nodded. Zalith then stood up and the vampire followed as he led the way over to the table, where a bottle of wine and two glasses were already waiting. Zalith filled both glasses, and he and Alucard sat in their usual places, waiting for the staff to bring their food to them.

"If you would like—" Zalith started as he handed Alucard his glass— "we can go somewhere for dinner sometime this week."

Taking his glass, Alucard frowned curiously. "To…a restaurant?"

"Yes," Zalith said contently and sipped from his glass.

Alucard tasted his wine and nodded in agreement. "Do you have anywhere in particular in mind?"

"A few places have caught my eye in the time I've spent here. So long as you're comfortable. And I thought I'd let you know that the city law enforcement and I have plans to either chase out or destroy both the Meshuga and the Imperito," he said with a smirk, resting his arms on the table.

Before he could answer, Alucard watched as two of the kitchen staff made their way in with a plate each in their hands. "The Meshuga and Imperito have both been here a long time. They were used to being the government, I guess. They didn't take well to you and your intervention, I can imagine. But they are mostly just humans, so not hard to control," he said as the staff placed a plate in front of them both and swiftly left the room.

Making himself comfortable, Zalith smirked. "Tell me, Alucard, how much do you know of this land and its technology?"

The abrupt subject change bewildered Alucard. He frowned and glanced down at his food—he had no idea what he was looking at.

"It's lasagne," Zalith said, smiling as he picked up his knife and fork.

Nodding, Alucard glanced at him. "It depends what you mean by technology," he said, picking up his fork. "There are… different types, different inventors," he explained, but with caution. Zalith might be his boyfriend, but there were some things he felt he had to protect, no matter who it was he was protecting it from. He trusted Zalith, and perhaps his questions were simply out of curiosity—maybe Alucard's years and years of secrecy had forced him to feel as though he'd have to forever keep secrets—but he didn't exactly want to keep things hidden from Zalith. He'd just have to answer his questions carefully. After all, anyone could be listening.

Zalith smiled. "For example, the lights in every part I've seen of this country, the lights in *my* house. They're not candles, they're not ethos, they run off… technology, connected by wires and posts," he said, taking a bite of his food. "I've tried to look into it myself, and I'm very good at finding sources and answers, but with this, I seem to have hit a dead end. So, perhaps *you* can enlighten me; after all, the only other place I've seen this technology is in your house and castle—I have even seen you creating marvellous things possessing technology like this."

"The people here are not big on ethos; you won't find any ethos in the things you see here. The lights and things like fridges and such, the energy is sourced from either steam power or electricity, which is created in coal-fired power stations; some of the power travels through conduits underground, and some travels through the power lines you see along the roads. Why do you want to know?"

"General curiosity," he said, smirking.

Alucard was certain that was a lie; he'd come to notice when Zalith was fishing for information that he'd later use. He was planning something. But… the vampire felt no need to deny him the information he was asking for. He was, after all, taking control of the country, and the country was powered in ways he knew best to explain. If Zalith's little empire was to be successful, he'd need to know how the place worked.

He looked down at his food and slowly tried some, and to his surprise, it was delicious. He then looked at Zalith. "Well…." He sighed deeply. "There is a lot to it. I can skip the less interesting parts if you wish."

"Indulge me," Zalith invited.

Alucard shrugged. "Fine. Most of the city is powered using steam. There are these factories on the outskirts of the city; inside them, the people heat water into steam. The pressurized steam will move the turbines that produce electricity. The thermal energy of the steam is converted into mechanical energy, which is, in turn, converted into electricity. This electricity can be used for a lot of things—like the lights, and most of what you see working in the Citadel. There are different types, though. The type that creates the electricity and the type you see moving the airships, but that is a whole other conversation."

Staring at him, Zalith nodded slowly, clearly taking in what he'd been told.

"I don't keep up with everything, but I know that they are looking into creating these...communication devices that will let people talk from long distances. Sort of like...how some demons can speak telekinetically. It'll be much easier than sending telegraph things that humans send. I hate those, so I stick to owls and letters."

"How interesting. And I imagine there are inventors...people who discovered these methods of power? You had to have learnt from somewhere."

With a conflicted frown, Alucard rested his arms on the table and asked, "Do you assume I stole this information to build the things I have in my castle?"

Zalith smirked "Did you?"

"No." Alucard snatched his glass and took a sip of his wine. He then placed his glass down and leaned back in his seat. "The Numen don't like this form of power. They want everything to be ethos and ethos only. If that were not the case, I would have spread this knowledge across the world a long time ago—it would have been a much easier way to conquer it than the way I did. To control everything the humans rely on is to control them, no?"

"Quite," Zalith agreed.

"There are people who know this information, yes. Smart people, old people—very old. Close to death now, I imagine. Once they are gone, I'll have to find new people to take their place. Luther suggested I turn them into vampires rather than putting their predecessor's mind inside their own, but the bloodlust of a vampire often distracts one from their work. People think that there are multiple creators—inventors. And there are, but there is only *one* mind behind it all."

"And who might that be, Alucard?" he asked, a smile on his face.

"I just told you," he replied with a smirk before sipping from his glass.

Zalith smiled, impressed, but devious—

"Then there is the matter of medicinal practices. I'm sure such a thing concerns you," he said, looking down at his food before taking another bite. "No ethos, no healers. You want Erwin for that; they are...an elf. I've known them for a long time. Interesting, strange, but knows what they are doing. You won't be able to find them, no matter how many people you send out looking."

"I imagine *you* know where to find this elf?"

"Perhaps," Alucard said, looking at him. "When you tell me what you really want with all of this information, maybe I will tell you more."

Smirking, Zalith continued eating his food, and silence fell over them.

Alucard knew that it couldn't be as simple as Zalith wanting to know how the world around him worked. There was something more to it and he wanted to know what that was. He wasn't going to give out any more information unless he knew what exactly was going to be done with it. Would Zalith be honest with him? He wasn't sure, but what he *was* sure about was the fact that Zalith's need for the information was more of a matter of business rather than casual conversation.

He'd find out eventually.

After a little while passed, Zalith finished his food and picked up his glass. He sipped from it as he set his eyes back on Alucard, who was just finishing up his own dinner.

"Tomorrow," the demon said firmly, "we'll have dinner together in the Citadel. After, we can spend the evening in the city. How does that sound?"

Finishing his food, Alucard pushed his plate forward and rested his arms on the table. "We can do that," he agreed, picking up his glass of wine.

Smiling contently, Zalith finished his wine and sighed quietly, keeping his eyes on the vampire. "Did you enjoy dinner?" he asked, slowly moving his hand over Alucard's.

"Yes, thank you," Alucard said quietly.

"Good. Come," he then said as he stood up, taking hold of Alucard's hand. "We can head to the lounge; it isn't time for bed yet." He smirked as he looked back at Alucard, who followed him. Then, he led the vampire out of the dining room, heading for the lounge.

Chapter Fifty-Nine

Sonata

| **Alucard** |

Zalith led Alucard into the elegant lounge, where the walls adorned in white displayed intricately carved patterns and panelling. A touch of sophistication was added by sage green curtains that veiled the expansive windows along the back wall, and another set that discreetly covered the right-side windows. Suspended from above, a grand crystal chandelier cast a soft glow, complemented by lanterns clinging to the walls throughout the room.

The dark wood flooring provided a rich foundation, enhanced by a central beige and grey patterned rug. Positioned on the rug were three sage-green couches of varying sizes, each boasting a dark wood frame with subtle gold accents. The foremost couch, grand and inviting, could comfortably seat three or four individuals. To its left, a slightly smaller companion, and opposite it, an almost regal armchair. Neatly arranged cushions adorned all the seating, and a stylish coffee table stood gracefully in their midst.

Along the left wall, a fireplace exuded warmth, crowned by a large, gold-framed mirror. The remaining wall space, though largely untouched, featured paintings reminiscent of those in the dining lounge, strategically placed in an artful arrangement. Alucard's gaze was drawn to an intriguing cluster of cushions in the far-left corner, an assortment of beautifully coloured and patterned pillows, some large enough for a person to comfortably rest on, interspersed with smaller ones resembling those on the couches.

With a smirk on his face, Zalith took Alucard's hand and escorted him over to the pile of pillows. He slumped down on them, pulling Alucard with him, and then, they both made themselves comfortable.

The demon looked down at Alucard and smiled slightly. "Are you busy much for the rest of this week?"

Alucard looked up at him. "Well, I'm waiting to hear back from my Paladins, and from Luther. Other than that, no."

Zalith smirked. "Then it looks like you're all mine for a while longer."

"That's fine," Alucard replied quietly with a smile on his face as he tightened his arms around Zalith.

The demon kissed Alucard's head and leaned his back against the pillows. "I think I should get one of the staff to play the piano; a little music could be nice," he suggested but then smirked. "Unless *you* would like to play me a song, Alucard."

Alucard knew that Zalith wanted to hear him play, but he still felt nervous about it. What if he messed up? What if the song he chose to play didn't please the demon? He frowned in confliction and looked down at his lap. He *did* want to try out the new violin Zalith bought him, and he *did* want to let Zalith hear him play; he just had to dismiss his unnecessary worries. He was confident in his skill, and he'd not let his anxiety make him look like an idiot.

He looked back up at Zalith. "Okay," he agreed.

Zalith smiled and looked over at the lounge door. "Edwin," he called. He waited, and as the dark-haired butler walked into the room, the demon requested, "Can you fetch the violin I had you put away, please?"

"Of course, sir," Edwin said with a humble bow. He then left the room, pulling the door shut behind him.

"I'll have to tune it first," Alucard said.

"That's okay," Zalith said, fiddling with his crimson hair.

With a discreet, content smile, Alucard rested his head on Zalith's shoulder and waited. It wasn't too long after that Edwin returned with the dark purple box in both his hands. As he made his way over, Alucard sat up; the butler handed the box to him as he offered to take it, and once the man left the lounge, Alucard opened the box and took out the violin and its bow.

"Thank you again for this," he mumbled shyly as he stared down at the violin.

"You're most welcome," Zalith said with a smirk, keeping his eyes on him.

Alucard didn't falter in tuning the violin. He shuffled away from Zalith so that there were a few feet between them and then rested his chin on the violin's chinrest.

"Is there anything else you can play?" Zalith asked curiously, watching the vampire with a smile on his face.

The vampire glanced at him as he slowly dragged his bow over the violin's strings. "If I tell you, will you ask me to play them, too?" he asked with a smirk, fiddling with the violin's pegs as he tuned it.

Zalith smiled. "Would you?"

"Maybe," Alucard replied, carefully turning one of the fine tuners. "There was a time I also liked to play the cello, but I preferred this," he said, still carefully tuning his new violin. "I also want to one day learn to play the piano, but I'm not sure when I'll have the time. Not that it'll ever get me anywhere, but I put a lot of time into learning the violin. If I didn't have a world to look after, perhaps I'd pursue a career," he said, smiling.

"I'm sure you can do both," Zalith said contently.

"Maybe," Alucard said, lowering the violin and its bow into his lap. "What do you want to hear?"

"Anything."

Alucard nodded, acknowledging Zalith's silent request for a musical interlude. Preparing to play, he stole a quick glance at Zalith, who reclined comfortably, hands behind his head. Determined to maintain his composure, Alucard took a deep breath before guiding the bow along the violin's strings, initiating the melodic journey.

As the first notes filled the room, Alucard closed his eyes, surrendering to the familiar embrace of his music. It had been a considerable amount of time since he last caressed the strings, yet the motions were etched into his muscle memory. The resonating strains carried emotions he'd kept hidden for too long; playing was not merely a skill but a release—a channel for the emotions that lingered beneath his stoic exterior.

In the soothing melody, he found solace, and a subtle smile graced his lips. The rhythmic dance of his fingers on the strings became an expression of emotions long confined. It was a moment of connection with the deepest recesses of his being. Alucard's senses heightened, attuned to the delicate interplay of sound and silence.

And then, in the midst of his musical reverie, he felt a warmth—Zalith's silent appreciation. It added a layer of fulfilment to the experience, the realization that his music resonated not just within the confines of his own soul, but also in the space shared with another. The happiness that welled up inside him was twofold, both a rediscovery of his own artistry and the joy of sharing it with someone who appreciated its essence.

Dragging his bow over the strings, he opened his eyes for a moment to glance at Zalith, and when he saw the demon gazing at him, he smiled and brought his song to a slow, calming end.

As he then lowered his violin, the demon smirked at him, and there was a hint of excitement on his face.

"Put that down and get your ass over here," Zalith demanded.

Alucard stared at the seductive smile on Zalith's face; it told him all he needed to know without even asking questions. He was sure that the demon enjoyed his song, and as much as he'd like to be assured about that, he felt more compelled to abide by Zalith's command.

He carefully placed his violin back into its case, his senses still resonating with the echoes of the music. Returning to the cushions as instructed, he found himself drawn closer by Zalith's commanding presence. The demon pulled him onto his lap, making him straddle it, and in that heated embrace, Zalith's lips sought Alucard's with a hunger that mirrored the passion of a crescendo. A deep, possessive kiss ensued, and the world outside seemed to fade, leaving only the intoxicating blend of their intertwined desires. Zalith's hand found its way to the back of Alucard's head, fingers entwining in the silken strands of his hair, while his other hand claimed the vampire's left arm, a possessive grip that communicated both dominance and desire.

The air thickened with anticipation as each frantic kiss ignited a spark that fuelled the flames between them. Zalith's movements became a silent symphony, orchestrating the intimate ballet of their entangled bodies. As the rhythm intensified, Zalith skilfully rolled over, reversing their positions and pinning Alucard beneath him, and their kisses, once passionate, became a fevered exchange of longing and surrender.

But when he felt the demon's hand wander down from his arm and to his waist, Alucard lightly grabbed his wrist and frowned up at him, halting their kisses. "Did you... like the music?" he asked unsurely; he felt so irritated with himself, but he wasn't sure whether Zalith had enjoyed it or not.

Zalith smiled as he tucked some of the vampire's hair behind his ear. "I loved it," he said and kissed his lips. "You're very talented," he added before kissing him again.

With a nervous frown, Alucard looked away from Zalith. "Thank you."

Zalith didn't give him a chance to hide his flustered face. Gripping his chin, the demon turned Alucard's head to face him and resumed their slow, fervent kiss. Yielding to the unspoken desire, Alucard reciprocated, his hand finding the back of Zalith's head. The demon's touch shifted from his chin to his neck, leaving a lingering anticipation. As the tension rose, Zalith's hand embarked on a tantalizing exploration. Tracing a path down Alucard's body, the demon's touch stirred a mixture of uncertainty and arousal, and when his hand reached the vampire's thigh, he gripped it lightly. His touch aggravated the healing bite which sat upon Alucard's skin, but he didn't care. The anticipation was intensifying, and it was the only thing he could focus on.

The vampire turned his head to the side when Zalith's kisses drifted from his lips to his neck. But after kissing his skin a few times, the demon halted, dragging his hand back up Alucard's body until it reached his throat. The vampire felt Zalith move his fingers over the scars on his neck—those left by the demon's fangs, scars that should have healed by now, but he was sure they'd be gone soon. The demon gently pressed his lips against the marks, and Alucard let out a quiet, yearning sigh, his excitement beginning to increase.

Zalith kissed his way up to Alucard's ear; he leaned into it, moving his hand back down his body to grip his waist. "Can I fuck you?" he asked quietly, his voice almost a whisper. "For real this time."

His words aroused both Alucard's excitement and his anxiety. He tensed up, tightening his grip on the fistful of the demon's hair he had in his hand—and even more so as he felt the demon lightly bite the lobe of his ear. Zalith smirked in response to his reaction, lifting his head so that he could stare down at his nervous face.

With a nervous nod, the vampire gazed into Zalith's seductive eyes and said, "Yes."

Zalith smiled and kissed him a few more times before looking back over his shoulder. "Edwin," he called once more.

The butler made his way into the room and stood in the doorway as he waited for instructions.

"Go and get the black tincture bottle from my bedside table," the demon instructed. Then, as the butler nodded and left, he returned to kissing the vampire.

Tincture bottle? Alucard frowned, and before Zalith could kiss him again, he pulled on his hair slightly so that he'd stop. "What is he going to get?" he asked unsurely.

Zalith smirked. "Lube."

"What?" Alucard frowned in confusion.

"Lubrication to make it easier to put my dick in your ass," he said, still smirking.

With an embarrassed scowl, Alucard turned his head away from Zalith, but there wasn't really much use in trying to hide his face when the demon was on top of him.

Zalith smiled and leaned into Alucard's ear. "And my fingers," he said quietly, followed by an amused laugh as the vampire's embarrassed scowl grew. He descended upon Alucard's neck with fervour, lips tracing a path down the vampire's sensitive skin. The demon's hand navigated down Alucard's torso until it reached the hem of his shirt. With a tantalizing exploration, Zalith slipped his hand beneath the fabric, fingers dancing over each defined abdominal muscle, and firmly grasped a pec as if staking a claim.

Resting his forehead against the side of Alucard's turned head, Zalith exhaled deeply, a breath laden with anticipation. A sly smirk played on his lips as he guided his face back to meet Alucard's, initiating a slow, lingering kiss. Their lips melded together in a dance of passion, synchronized with the movement of Zalith's hand, once more tracing the contours of Alucard's abs.

In response, Alucard abandoned his nervous reservations, reciprocating Zalith's kisses. With a boldness fuelled by desire, he moved his spare hand from his side to Zalith's waist.

Before their intimate exchange could deepen further, though, an unwelcome interruption manifested in the form of another knock at the door.

Zalith stopped kissing him and looked back over his shoulder, setting his eyes on Edwin as he made his way over and handed the demon what he'd asked him to retrieve.

As the butler then left, Zalith set aside the small bottle, swiftly returning his attention to Alucard. In a swift motion, he unbuttoned Alucard's shirt, pulling it off while the vampire stared nervously. Zalith mirrored the move, shedding his own shirt with a smirk, watching as Alucard tentatively placed his left hand on the demon's abs.

Zalith leaned back into the embrace, capturing Alucard's lips once more as his hand traced the contours of the vampire's defined muscles. Pausing the kiss, Zalith gazed down at Alucard, who frowned shyly. Foreheads resting against each other, the demon sighed deeply, his intense gaze meeting Alucard's. The vampire's hand embarked on a journey from Zalith's chest down to his waist, a path that elicited a smile from the demon.

Alucard tensed up when Zalith moved his hand down his body and reached his crotch. He started unbuckling Alucard's belt, and once he removed it, he guided his hand into his trousers. As the demon gripped his arousal, Alucard tensed up a little more, an excited sigh escaping his breath as he turned his head to the side, inviting Zalith to kiss his neck.

The vampire sighed in aspiration as the demon kissed down his neck and to his chest, but then Zalith abruptly and playfully bit his nipple, making him flinch and frown in confusion. The demon didn't stop to look up at him and laugh this time, though; he continued lightly biting it, carefully pulling on it with his teeth, and Alucard couldn't deny that he enjoyed it. He kept his hand on the back of Zalith's head, pulling tighter on his hair as he continued to bite, still caressing his quickly hardening shaft with his hand.

Zalith then kissed his way back up to the vampire's neck as he unbuttoned his trousers. He took Alucard's dick out, and for a few moments, he pleasured him with his hand, kissing him, clasping a fistful of his hair in his spare palm, which he had rested above the vampire's head. Alucard fidgeted beneath the demon as he felt something satisfying tickling its way through his body; he dragged his right leg up, stroking the side of Zalith's body with his knee, and then he pressed it around the demon's waist, urging him closer as he nuzzled Alucard's neck.

The demon, gripping a fistful of Alucard's hair, sighed in aspiration, moving the vampire's face closer to his exposed neck. Alucard knew what Zalith wanted, and he'd not hesitate to comply. His desire for Zalith's blood abruptly intensified when he caught the sound of the demon's racing heart, and the moment he was close enough, he sunk his four fangs into Zalith's neck. The taste of the demon's blood and the sound of his quiet, pleased sigh escalated Alucard's arousal, forcing him to bite harder as he gulped Zalith down. At the same time, he tried to muffle a delighted moaning as the demon continued caressing his dick with his hand.

But then Zalith let go of his shaft and unbuckled his own belt. The demon took Alucard's right hand from his head, and as the vampire pulled his fangs from his neck and frowned curiously, Zalith dragged his palm down over his body and into his trousers.

"Touch me," he whispered into the vampire's ear as he placed Alucard's hand on his dick.

Excitement shivered through Alucard's tense body as his palm wrapped around the demon's hard, thick dick. He began stroking its length, making Zalith sigh in anticipation, and when they started kissing again, the demon returned his hand to the vampire's shaft. Alucard's anticipation grew as he felt the demon's shaft hardening; the longing to feel it inside him again intensified, but he was too nervous to ask for it.

Zalith started kissing his way down the vampire's body; Alucard lost his grip on the demon's shaft, so he gripped a fistful of Zalith's hair. When the demon's kisses reached Alucard's crotch, he slowly dragged his tongue over the vampire's dick and eased it into his mouth. Alucard exhaled quietly in pleasure, tightening his grip on Zalith's hair, and for a short while, he was able to enjoy the warmth of the demon's tongue against his shaft.

But just as the increasing pleasure caused Alucard to fidget, Zalith stopped and gradually kissed his way back up his body, playfully biting his neck once he reached it. As he smirked at Alucard, he pulled the vampire's trousers and underwear off with haste. Alucard thought he might turn away in response to his shyness, but he didn't. He lay there, staring up at Zalith as he removed his own trousers and underwear. Once they were both utterly naked, Zalith returned to kissing Alucard's neck.

Alucard wasn't sure what to expect next; last time, Zalith made him lean over the side of his bed, but there was no bed here. Would he have him lean over the couch? He lay there, waiting for instructions, and once Zalith stopped kissing his neck, the demon grabbed the small bottle he'd earlier set aside. With a nervous frown, the vampire watched him pour the liquid from within onto his hand; he slowly smothered his own shaft with it, and when he caught Alucard staring, he smirked seductively.

The vampire didn't look away; he *did* scowl shyly, but he observed as Zalith put more of the viscous liquid onto his fingers. The demon then leaned his face closer to Alucard's and kissed his lips, and then he slowly eased two of his fingers into the vampire's ass. Alucard frowned as he returned each of Zalith's kisses; the sensation of his viscous-smothered fingers gliding in and out of his body was curiously pleasing, and as the demon massaged the lube into his walls, Alucard tightly gripped Zalith's hair in his hand, his excitement and anticipation beginning to shroud his nervous feelings.

His nervousness returned, however, when Zalith stopped kissing him and rested his forehead against his, slowly pulling his fingers from his ass as a smirk crept across his face.

"Are you ready?" he asked quietly.

Alucard nodded shyly and turned his head to the side. He held his eyes shut, waiting as his heart raced in his chest, enthralled with angst and desperation.

Zalith didn't take long at all to begin; he ever so slowly moved the tip of his shaft into the vampire's ass, and a quiet, satisfied sigh escaped his breath as he nuzzled the side of Alucard's face.

A conflicted frown caught somewhere between uncomfortable and pleased contorted Alucard's expression. Despite this being the second time, feeling Zalith's girth ease inside him still caused him discomfort. But he lay there as delight entwined with the ache; each inch felt more pleasing than the last, sending small but tantalizing waves of pleasure through Alucard's trembling body. The pain was still there, but when the demon's last inch buried itself inside him, Alucard let out a quiet wince of contentment.

Zalith sighed pleasurably and gripped Alucard's leg; he moved it over his back, giving himself a little more room to push his dick deeper, and when he did, they both moaned contently, but a hint of struggle sat upon Alucard's breath. The demon's thick shaft made him feel full, overwhelmed, and at the mercy of Zalith's desires. He flinched when Zalith gripped his shaft, sending another wave of delight through him, and then the demon placed a kiss on his cheek.

The demon hummed quietly, and a satisfied, anticipation-laden moan escaped his breath, "Fuck, Alucard." He nuzzled Alucard's neck and murmured against his skin, "You're so fucking tight." He then kissed his neck and lifted his head as he grasped Alucard's chin and made him look up at him.

As the vampire stared at him with a nervous frown, his body quivering while the demon's hard girth buried deep inside teased him, Zalith smiled and kissed his lips. When their tongues met and entwined, the demon gripped Alucard's shaft in his hand, and as he slowly pulled his dick back out of the vampire's ass, leaving only its tip within, he started stroking the vampire's arousal.

Alucard tightened his grip on Zalith's hair, a struggled groan upon his voice as he dragged his right knee along the side of Zalith's body, trying to relax as best he could, but his nervousness was getting the better of him. He tensed up as Zalith eased his dick deeper into his body, but he tried his best not to whine.

Zalith stopped when his shaft was only halfway buried. "Are you okay?" he breathed.

With a nod, Alucard slowly turned his head to look away again as Zalith smirked down at him. He closed his eyes, exhaling in struggle as Zalith started thrusting into and out of his ass, sending waves of pleasure spiralling through his trembling body. He felt Zalith's breath upon his skin as the demon leaned closer; he kissed Alucard's cheek, his jaw, and then his neck. And while he continued pleasing Alucard with his hand and thrusting into him, he abruptly sunk his two fangs into Alucard's neck.

A wave of pleasure surged through Alucard's body, intensifying into something beyond overwhelming when he sensed the demon's venom seeping into his bloodstream. His fingers tangled in Zalith's hair, gripping as tightly as possible, while the claws of his free hand dug into the demon's bicep. A loud moan escaped him, involuntary and unabashed.

Yet, amidst the pleasure, a conflicting scowl etched itself across Alucard's face. He groaned quietly, the internal struggle evident. Part of him considered telling Zalith to stop, but the desire coursing through him outweighed any rational thought. The intensity of Zalith's attention, as overpowering as it was, became an irresistible indulgence. Every second, though overwhelming, was savoured with a fervour that left Alucard both hesitant and captivated.

But once Zalith pulled his fangs from his neck and began kissing his way back up to his face, the demon started stroking his hand over the vampire's dick faster. His thrusts became more aggressive, enthralling Alucard's body in an overwhelming rapture. The vampire scowled desperately, returning each of the demon's frantic kisses. He was approaching his peak, his body trembling, his heart racing. He fidgeted and frowned, trying to hold on just a little longer; when he was on the very edge, it felt so *fucking* good. But he was powerless against Zalith. With a satisfied, euphoric whine, he climaxed beneath the demon's assertive prowess, and he swiftly sunk his fangs back into Zalith's neck to muffle his pleasured cries.

Zalith wasn't yet done, though. He let go of the vampire's shaft and guided his hand up Alucard's body; he softly grasped the vampire's throat and made him pull his fangs from his neck. The demon then stared down at Alucard's struggled face, quickening his hard, assertive thrusts. Alucard grimaced once again, digging his claws deeper into Zalith's arm. The demon grunted and groaned, the pleasured expression on his face intensifying as he moved faster and faster, and after one final deep, hard thrust, he let out a loud, satisfied moan and nuzzled the vampire's neck.

"Fuck," he groaned as his dick throbbed inside Alucard.

Alucard pulled him closer, tensing up as he felt the demon's hot cum filling his ass, and as he exhaled pleasurably, he stroked his fingertips up Zalith's back.

Zalith then fell still, panting against Alucard's neck as he calmed down and rested his body on Alucard's.

The vampire's racing heart began to slow as he stared up at the ceiling, his trembling body gradually relaxing. The euphoria of Zalith's bite hadn't yet faded, and he felt strangely disorientated, but not enough to take his mind from the moment he was in. He felt tired, satisfied, and content.

He turned his head so that the side of his face was pressed against Zalith's cheek.

"I love you," Zalith whispered, breathing lightly into his ear.

Alucard smiled in both happiness and relief as he exhaled deeply. He dragged down the demon's arm, lightly caressing his skin as he lowered his legs to the cushion he lay upon. "I love *you*."

Zalith lifted his face from the vampire's neck and smiled down at him. He dragged his thumb over his cheek and then started to kiss him. As they kissed, Zalith grabbed the closest piece of clothing—which turned out to be Alucard's shirt—and used it to clean both himself and the vampire once he pulled his dick from his ass. Then, he moved from over Alucard and laid down beside him, sighing contently as Alucard shuffled closer and rested his head on his shoulder.

"I don't want to be without you," Alucard said quietly, moving his arm over Zalith to hold him tightly. "I want... I just want to be with you. You make everything okay," he mumbled.

Holding him just as tightly, Zalith kissed the top of his head. "I don't want to be without you either. I'll do whatever I can to make you happy."

As a dismayed frown appeared on his face, Alucard nuzzled the demon's neck in an attempt to hide it. "Just... don't leave me," he pleaded quietly. "I don't want to be alone again."

"You won't be alone, Alucard," Zalith said sternly.

Alucard nodded, closing his eyes as his fatigue started to increase. But he didn't want to go to bed yet; he wanted to spend more time with Zalith.

But the demon shuffled around and said, "As much as I'd love to lay here and admire you in all your naked glory, I think we should head up and get ready for bed."

Embarrassed, Alucard attempted to hide his crotch by moving one leg over the other. "Whatever," he grumbled.

Laughing quietly, Zalith sat up and handed Alucard his trousers. He then pulled on his own and handed Alucard the grey shirt he'd been wearing. He chucked Alucard's shirt into a nearby laundry basket, stood up with him, and took the vampire's hand. The demon led the way out of the lounge, through his house, and up the stairs. He took them to his bedroom and into the bathroom before letting go of Alucard's hand.

They both undressed and climbed into the shower; as the water ran over their bodies, Zalith smiled and pinned Alucard back against the wall, kissing him.

When they stopped kissing, Alucard gazed at him and placed his hand on the side of Zalith's face. Today, his drowning worries had been silenced, and he felt a whole lot more confident in what he felt for Zalith. The fact that he had imprinted on him no longer caused him distress, but he couldn't help but wonder... had Zalith imprinted on *him*? If Zalith truly meant what he said, then surely he must have already imprinted or done so recently without him realizing. He wanted to ask, but he felt that if the answer was no, it might ruin their contentedness.

So, he remained silent, his eyes wandering from Zalith's face and to the water-covered floor. As Zalith kissed his forehead and pulled him into a tight embrace, he frowned in worriedly, unable to dismiss his thoughts. *Had* Zalith imprinted? He didn't want to think about it. Zalith loved him, and that was enough.

Once their shower came to its end, Alucard followed Zalith out, and they both wrapped towels around their waists as they made their way over to the mirror.

"Tomorrow," Zalith said as he handed Alucard one of the two toothbrushes, "we'll go back to your castle and bring some of your clothes here. Then, we can go somewhere for either lunch or dinner if you like," he said as Alucard took the toothbrush from him.

With a content smile, Alucard nodded. "Okay," he agreed, gazing at Zalith as he began brushing his teeth. He then started to brush his own teeth, staring down at the basin as he did.

Once they were done, Zalith led the way back into his bedroom. Alucard couldn't help but watch Zalith take his towel off as he made his way over to the bed. The demon looked over his shoulder at Alucard, smirking as he watched the embarrassed expression form on his face. But Alucard scowled his embarrassment away and pouted, making his way over to the bed.

As Zalith climbed into bed, Alucard sat on the edge. He pulled off his towel and moved under the covers, shuffling closer to Zalith as they made themselves comfortable.

Alucard then lay there with his head on Zalith's shoulder, holding him tightly as he moved his left arm around him. The day was at its end, and tomorrow was another day he'd get to spend with Zalith—another day of what he hoped to be an endless amount of days.

He smiled slightly as he closed his eyes. "Goodnight," he said quietly.

Zalith kissed his forehead and rested his head on Alucard's. "Goodnight," he replied, hugging him.

Then, in the comfort and safety of Zalith's embrace, Alucard allowed himself to drift off to sleep. For once, his conflicting thoughts were silent. He focused on all the good that had come of today—he focused on the moment he heard Zalith tell him he loved him, and that was a moment he wished to hold onto forever. It saved him from his sadness, from his solitude, and hopefully, it would save him from his constant fear.

DEMON'S FATE
Numen Chronicles | Volume Two

ARCFOUR
†
LILITH

DEMON'S FATE
Numen Chronicles | Volume Two

Chapter Sixty

Memories

| **Alucard** |

The long, winding hallways of Damien's castle haunted Alucard's sleep. He stared ahead, nothing but black walls and a red carpeted floor stretching into the distance and far behind him. Above was the same black, rib-vaulted ceiling, and the silence was plagued by the harrowing screams of someone Damien's cronies were probably torturing. But where exactly was Alucard standing?

He looked to his right, setting his eyes on the barred window. Outside, nothing but deserts of red rock and dead trees. The only wing of Damien's castle that had windows was the Daegelus' private wing, and Alucard remembered... he'd come to ask Damien if it was time for him to go back to Aegisguard.

Three months ago, he'd killed Ada; Damien had come for him, and he'd been in the walls of his castle ever since. And just a month ago, he'd heard Damien speaking to someone about the most curious of things. But the only thing that mattered to him was the fact that Zalith wasn't going to be killed.

Silently, he made his way towards the Daegelus' chamber, the same place he hadn't long heard him talking to someone Alucard had never met before—someone Alucard was undeniably curious to meet. After all, no one spoke to Damien the way this man had without punishment... so who had it been? Who had been able to talk to Damien as if he was inferior? He knew from Detlaff that there was another Numen searching for Damien and his siblings—could that be who he was talking to?

Damien's voice echoed from ahead, becoming louder and louder after each step Alucard took. As he suspected, the Daegelus wasn't alone—that voice, the same voice he heard last month—came after Damien's. Whoever Damien's friend was, he was in that room with him—the room Alucard was moments from reaching. But dare he enter?

He stopped walking—not too far, not too close, just enough so he could hear. But the conversation died before he could understand any of it. Their voices were silenced—

the entire castle was silenced. Then, the movement from within the room told Alucard that it was time to go, but he didn't get a chance to attempt to disappear.

The door to Damien's chamber swung open, but it wasn't Damien who stood in the doorway. With a twisted, mangled smile on his seven-eyed face... was Lucifer. Just as Alucard remembered—hair as red as his own, a look so crazed on his face that it was clear he thought he was more than one person at once.

Alucard's fear kept him standing as if he were frozen, unable to speak, unable to move; all he could do was stare as Lucifer reached out a scaly, clawed hand to grab him.

But that was when everything faded to black, and to his relief, his eyes opened to the familiar gloom of Zalith's bedroom. To his heartache, though, Zalith wasn't beside him. After such an awful dream, the only thing he wanted to see was Zalith's face. But the demon was nowhere.

The door to the bathroom abruptly opened. As Alucard sat up, Zalith walked out, fully clothed, buttoning the cufflinks of his suit. The look on his face was a vacant one, and he didn't smile like he usually would when he set his eyes on Alucard. Slowly, he made his way over to the bedroom door, sighed, and turned to face the vampire.

"Zalith?" Alucard asked, unsure of where he might be going... and why he looked so hesitant. Had something happened?

Zalith sighed again and stopped fiddling with his cufflinks. "Alucard," he said, a tone to his voice that made the vampire tense in worry—he knew something was wrong.

"What?" he asked quietly, staring at him.

"I'm sorry," he said, a regrettable tone in his voice.

Alucard frowned in utter confusion. "For... what?"

"This," Zalith said, glancing around the room before setting his eyes back on Alucard, who stared at him anxiously. "For what I said yesterday."

What had he said that would need an apology?

"I really thought... I wanted to think that what we had was what I wanted."

"What?" Alucard breathed. What they had? He felt an awful pain grip his heart.

"I said... I said what I said because I thought it was what I wanted to say. I didn't want you to leave, so I said what I knew would get you to stay. But... I wasn't thinking straight. I know that I've caused you so much pain, and I don't want to cause you more, but I won't lie to you. You deserve to know the truth, and that truth is that I moved too fast. I made us both think that what I wanted was to be with you forever, but... I don't want that. I'm sorry."

Alucard stared at him, the rest of his words becoming silent, unheard. Zalith... he'd changed his mind. He didn't love him, did he? He'd just said it—Alucard's instincts had screamed at him the moment Zalith said those words by the river yesterday, telling him *that it was a lie, a ploy to get him to stay. And he'd fallen for it. He should have listened to his head and not his heart. All his heart ever caused him was pain.*

He didn't even remember getting outside, walking aimlessly through the forest, his heart broken, his body numb. Unloved, unwanted, alone, and pathetic—everything Damien said he was. He should have listened to the Daegelus—he shouldn't have trusted Zalith.

But... despite Zalith's words, despite the fact that his desire for Alucard had faded, the vampire didn't hate him. He wanted to hate him—he wanted to scowl and yell and hurt him, but he couldn't. Alucard still loved him, and he felt he may love him forever. Zalith might not feel the same, but... Alucard didn't care.

"And that's what makes you pathetic, Aleksei," Damien said.

Alucard sharply turned his head, setting his eyes on the Daegelus as he made his way through the darkness towards him. The vampire stopped walking, watching, waiting for Damien to reach him.

"Was it not I who told you that he was using you?" he asked, a condescending tone in his voice as he stopped in front of Alucard and looked down at him. "But you didn't listen to me, did you? You went crawling back to him; you even crawled into his bed. And where are you now? He's probably already moving on to his next little victim, and you're out here, thrown away, used, useless," he snarled, snatching Alucard's jaw in his hand, making him stare up at him. "I'm looking for you, Aleksei," he said, grinning.

Looking? Alucard frowned in confusion.

"Where are you?" he growled—but he gave Alucard no time to answer. He lifted him up off his feet and pinned him back against a tree. "Where are you?!"

Alucard opened his eyes and sat up, panting, panicking, looking around in horror as he tried to work out where he was. The light grey walls, the dark oak panelling lined along them, the smell of oak and bergamot, and the warm feel of a hand being placed against his back.

"Alucard?" Zalith asked sleepily. "Are you okay?"

The vampire looked down at him, staring at him as he lay there on his left side, his eyes closed, but a frown on his face. He didn't want to concern Zalith with something as stupid as a nightmare, so he looked down at his lap and exhaled quietly. "I'm fine," he answered. "Just... a bad dream."

Zalith lightly gripped his arm and pulled him back down; he wrapped his arms around Alucard as he lay on his back, rested his head on the vampire's shoulder, and sighed quietly. "It's okay, baby. I'll keep you safe."

Laying there, Alucard's anxious frown faded, replaced by a small smile. The fear his nightmare induced withered, and it quickly felt as if it had never happened. Zalith made him feel happy and safe; that was all he needed to think about. So he closed his eyes, and as Zalith fell back asleep, so did he.

| Zalith |

Zalith lay awake for a while. He held Alucard in his arms, breathing in his calming scent. Although he was starting to feel more and more upset about banishing Varana, he tried his best not to succumb to his emotions.

Emotions: they'd been fairly easy for him to ignore, but ever since meeting Alucard, he'd felt a lot of things he *didn't* want to disregard. And earlier tonight was a prime example. When they'd had sex, he'd felt a whole different kind of satisfaction. He was sure that it was because he loved Alucard; that, along with just how pleasing having sex with someone he'd craved for a *long* time felt, had enthralled him in a new kind of delight, and it only confirmed his feelings for the vampire even more. Sex had always been a need, but tonight, it felt like a gratifying reward. It felt a lot more fulfilling... and thinking about it was making him crave more.

He sighed quietly; he wouldn't wake Alucard up for sex, though. He'd let him sleep.

As he dragged his fingertips over Alucard's arm, he tried to fall back asleep. He knew that Alucard would probably have to go home soon and thinking about it made him miss him already. All he wanted to do was be with Alucard every minute of every day. Today, he'd managed to tell Alucard how he felt—he'd told him he loved him... and he meant it for the first time in what felt like forever. He *did* love Alucard and he was going to do whatever he had to to make sure Alucard always knew that.

He hugged the vampire tightly, burying his face into his hair. And then, with one last quiet exhale, he could finally feel himself drifting off. Alucard was all he needed.

| Alucard |

Alucard woke in the warmth of Zalith's embrace. He opened his eyes to stare up at the ceiling, the late morning sunlight shining in through the few cracks in the curtains.

Now, he was so used to Zalith already being awake once he woke up that it was strange to see that he was still asleep.

He lay there, looking down at Zalith, who'd moved around in the middle of the night to rest his head on Alucard's chest. The vampire started gently dragging his fingers through the demon's tousled, unkempt hair, admiring what he could see of him. He wasn't sure how long he waited, but eventually, Zalith stirred and began to guide his hand up from Alucard's arm and to the side of his neck.

"Good morning," the demon mumbled tiredly as he opened his eyes to look up at the vampire.

Alucard smiled as he set his gaze back on the ceiling. "Good morning."

Zalith smiled contently, moving as close to Alucard as he could get, nuzzling his neck as he hugged him tightly. Then, he started to slowly kiss his neck, moving his hand from his shoulder to the side of his head.

Alucard tensed up as the demon kissed his skin; he enjoyed it when Zalith did that. When he kissed him again, Alucard turned his head aside, giving the demon more room to explore, closing his eyes as a small but content smile clung to his face. It didn't take long for the demon to choose a particular part of his neck to suck on. Alucard lightly gripped Zalith's hair and sighed quietly, but after a few moments, Zalith playfully nipped his neck, making him flinch in startlement.

Zalith laughed quietly as Alucard pouted.

"That's not funny," he grumbled.

Still laughing, Zalith hugged him tightly. "Sorry," he said with a smirk on his face and then kissed the love bite he'd left on the vampire's neck. "Are you hungry?" he asked, dragging his hand down from Alucard's head to his shoulder.

With a pout still on his face, Alucard glared at the ceiling. "Maybe."

The demon smirked and rested his forehead against Alucard's neck, guiding his hand down over his shoulder and to his chest beneath the blanket. "Have you ever had waffles before?" he asked, slowly and lightly stroking the tips of his fingers over the vampire's abs.

Alucard frowned in confliction, trying to ignore the relaxing, pleasing sensation he got from Zalith's caressing fingers. "No," he answered, his pout fading as Zalith's hand moved down to his waist.

"You can have chocolate with them," he said quietly as he stroked his hand over the vampire's left leg. "And perhaps…raspberries, too," he added, dragging his hand up Alucard's inner thigh.

The vampire scowled up at the ceiling, tightly gripping the sheets below him with his left hand as the demon moved his hand to his crotch.

"Do you like the sound of that?" Zalith asked with a smirk as he started to caress the vampire's arousal.

Alucard *did* like the sound of that, but he knew that he wouldn't be able to utter his answer without struggle, and that was clearly what Zalith wanted. If he didn't say something, though, would Zalith think he *didn't* want waffles? "Yes," he answered as best he could.

"Would you like that for breakfast?" he asked, slowly tending to the vampire's growing arousal.

With a stubborn pout on his face, Alucard scowled and nodded.

Zalith then stopped stroking his shaft. "I know what *I* want for breakfast," he mumbled into Alucard's ear. Then, he slowly kissed his way down the vampire's body, disappearing beneath the blanket.

The moment Alucard felt the warm touch of the demon's tongue against his dick, he lost his stubborn pout and closed his eyes, sighing quietly in satisfaction as he turned his head, resting the side of his face against the pillow. He lay there, enjoying each moment of Zalith's pleasing attention. He sighed, he groaned, and fidgeted as he gripped the blanket beside him. The minutes passed, the pleasure intensified, and as he sunk deeper into the delight, he let a content moan break free of his lips. He climaxed moments later, and as he grimaced and whined quietly, he heard Zalith hum in gratification from beneath the blanket.

But Zalith wasn't yet finished. He slowly pulled the vampire's shaft from his mouth and kissed his way back up his body, out from beneath the blanket and to Alucard's neck, which he then abruptly sunk his fangs into.

Alucard winced pleasurably and tensed up, gripping a fistful of Zalith's hair as he felt the demon's fangs pierce his skin. The euphoria of his venom swiftly consumed him, and as he lay there, he let it ensnare him.

Zalith carefully pulled his fangs from Alucard's neck and rested his head on his chest, moving his arm around him with a content sigh. Alucard glanced down at him, smiling; he'd really rather not be anywhere else. He could lay where he was for as long as whatever forever was; with Zalith, he felt happier than he had ever been, safer than he might ever be, and above all, he felt loved—he'd let nothing take it from him.

He stared up at the ceiling, placing his hand over Zalith's as the demon rested it on his left pec.

"What are you thinking about?" Zalith then asked quietly.

Alucard glanced down at him again and shrugged. "Nothing, really. Just that... well, you make me really happy. More than I've ever been."

"You make me really happy too, Alucard," he said. Then, he lifted his head to look at him. "Do you want breakfast now?"

The vampire nodded. "Well, I think I want to shave first," he said, dragging his hand over the stubble on his face. "If that's okay."

Smirking, Zalith lightly stroked the vampire's face with his fingers. "Your adorable *red* facial hair?"

Alucard pouted and looked away.

With a slight laugh, Zalith kissed Alucard's cheek. "I'll show you where everything is," he said, moving back over to his side of the bed. He pulled off the blanket, dressed into his trousers from the previous night, and stood up, waiting for Alucard to do the same. He watched as the vampire pulled his trousers on, and as he stood up, Zalith smirked and began to lead the way over to the bathroom door.

Once inside the bathroom, Zalith took a straight razor from one of the cupboards, along with a leather strap to strop it with. From another cupboard, he took out some shaving cream, a small bowl, and a shaving brush; he placed it all on the counter and then handed the vampire the toothbrush he'd given him last night.

"Thank you," Alucard said as Zalith started brushing his own teeth.

The vampire then poured some of the shaving cream into the bowl and used the brush to create a lather, which he then spread evenly on his face.

Zalith finished brushing his teeth and put his toothbrush down. "I'll find you some clothes in a moment," he said as Alucard started slowly and gently shaving his face. "Will you be relieved to be able to wear your own clothes here once we go and collect some?" he asked with a smirk, starting to comb his hair. "Or have you come to enjoy wearing mine?"

Glancing in the mirror at the trousers he was wearing, Alucard pouted. "They are comfortable," he muttered and carefully dragged the blade over his cheek.

The demon smiled and moved nearer to Alucard. "I really enjoyed your music last night," he said quietly, staring at the vampire's nervous face in the mirror. "And I'd love to hear more of it."

Alucard concentrated on shaving but smiled shyly. "Okay," he agreed. It made him happy to know that Zalith enjoyed his music *and* wanted to hear more.

Zalith smiled and placed his comb beside Alucard's toothbrush. "I'll leave you to finish up in here, and I'll also leave some clothes on the bed for you. I'll be downstairs in the breakfast nook," he said, making his way over to the door.

Then, as Zalith left, Alucard focused on shaving off the last of his stubble. It took a short while as shaving always did, but once he was done, he washed his face, brushed his teeth, and tidied his hair. He then cleaned everything and put it back where he'd seen Zalith take it from.

Keen to get back to the demon, he left the bathroom and went back into the bedroom. On the bed was a pair of black trousers alongside a light grey shirt. Alucard slipped both on and then headed downstairs, following Zalith's aura until he found the breakfast nook—a small room in a tower-shaped part of the house with tall rectangular windows on each section of the white hexagonal wall.

The demon was sitting to the right of the small, rounded table in a light grey shirt and black trousers with a cup of coffee in his hands. As Alucard entered the room, Zalith greeted him with a smile. Alucard headed over, sat opposite him, and made himself comfortable.

"Do you want something to drink?" Zalith asked.

Alucard thought to himself for a few moments. He still felt rather sluggish and strangely disorientated—but that was because of the many times Zalith had chosen to bite him. Coffee might help wake him up a little, so he'd ask for that. "Maybe... coffee, please."

"I'll tell them when they bring our food," he said with a smile.

Nodding, Alucard turned his attention to what he could see of the grounds outside. A gardener was watering plants, and a groundskeeper was tending to what looked to be moss on one of the walls. Nothing interesting. He turned his head and set his eyes back on Zalith, who smiled across the table at him as he sipped from his coffee.

Zalith then placed his cup down and rested his arms on the table. "Have you thought about where you want to go tonight?"

"What?" Alucard frowned at him.

The demon looked confused for a moment. "For dinner. Did you forget?"

Alucard's frown thickened but he then remembered that Zalith said they'd go out somewhere for dinner. "No, I'm just a little tired," he said. He then looked down at his hands as he rested them on the table. "I don't know. I've never actually been out to have dinner anywhere—I had no reason to."

"Well, in that case, I'll choose a place for us."

Just then, the door opened, and Edwin, along with one of the kitchen staff, walked in with a plate in each of their hands. Edwin headed over and placed a plate of waffles in front of Alucard—and they looked just as Zalith had said they would. The other man placed an omelette in front of Zalith, and then, they both bowed humbly.

"Could you bring us some more coffee, please," Zalith requested.

Edwin nodded and then left, following the other man.

Alucard hadn't ever tried waffles before, but they were smothered in two of his favourite things: chocolate and raspberries, so he was sure that he was going to enjoy them. He waited until Zalith started eating to try his food—he didn't want to appear eager. But, when he *did* try it, he was surprised, once again. It tasted amazing, and he began to wonder why he'd waited so long to start trying new foods.

"Do you like them?" Zalith asked and sipped from his coffee.

"Yes," Alucard said, a slight smile on his face. Then, as Edwin came back in and handed him his coffee, he took it from the butler with a quiet, "*Multumesc*," and took a sip. He placed his cup down and continued to eat, as did Zalith. His curiosity, however, shifted to what Zalith was eating. He knew what an omelette was, but he'd never tried it.

He felt like he wanted to, but he didn't want to take Zalith's food. So, he continued to eat his own.

"Would you like to try some?" Zalith asked with a smirk on his face, almost as if he knew what Alucard had been thinking—but then again, Zalith seemed to make easy work of reading Alucard's face.

The demon didn't wait for him to respond because he clearly knew what the answer would be. He offered a piece on his fork out to Alucard, waiting for him to try it. And, of course, he smirked suggestively as Alucard leaned forward and ate the food off his fork.

"Do you like it?" he asked as he watched Alucard make himself comfortable in his seat once again.

Alucard nodded. "It's okay," he said with a shrug, returning to his waffles.

Before Zalith could say whatever he was about to say, though, a knock at the front door forced a frown on both their faces. Alucard had no idea who it could be, and it looked as though Zalith wasn't entirely sure either. But they both ignored it and continued eating their breakfast.

"We could go for a ride before we head back to your castle if you like," Zalith suggested.

That sounded rather inviting. Alucard looked at him and nodded. "On the same horse again?"

"Perhaps," Zalith said with a smirk and sipped from his coffee.

Just then, a light knock came at the room door. They both looked over at it, watching as Edwin stepped in—and a rather shaken look clung to his face.

"What is it?" Zalith asked.

"Lady... Varana is at the door, sir," he said, a shiver in his voice.

Alucard watched a bitter frown of annoyance warp Zalith's once-happy expression.

The demon rolled his eyes and looked at Alucard. "I'll be right back," he said with a smile, dragging his hand over Alucard's as he stood up and left the table.

Alucard frowned strangely, watching him leave. Hadn't he sent Varana away? What was she doing back here? He looked down at his food and pushed a raspberry around the plate. He wanted to listen... but he felt guilty eavesdropping on Zalith. And surely the demon would tell him what she was doing here, right?

He sighed quietly and leaned back in his seat, waiting for Zalith to get back.

Chapter Sixty-One

— ⊰ ✝ ⊱ —

Apology

| **Zalith** |

*Z*alith made his way through the house to the entrance hall. He set his eyes on the black-haired woman, who was lingering outside the open front door like a salesman ready to deliver his pitch. Zalith's sights, however, shifted to the man accompanying Varana. Ben. He was beaten, looked over-exhausted, and seemed to have no idea where he was. Why the *hell* was he with Varana?

When he reached the door, he stood behind its threshold and waited for her to speak.

Varana frowned miserably. "Hi," she said with a sullen sigh.

Zalith wordlessly shifted his sights to Ben and back to her.

She looked at Ben. "Oh, um, I have Ben," she said, placing her hand on Ben's shoulder before looking back at Zalith. "Detlaff was using him to find your... friend."

Irritated, Zalith rolled his eyes. She knew that Alucard was more than that but was evidently *still* trying to convince herself and him that he wasn't.

"I found an opportunity to get him away from my disgusting brother and I took it. I figured it was the right thing to do; I didn't want anything bad to happen to you or your fr—"

Utterly, *ferociously* aggravated, Zalith did his best to contain his anger and leaned back and glared down the hall. "Edwin," he called. He then looked back at Varana as he leaned on the door's frame, listening to the butler's footsteps become louder as he approached.

"Yes, sir?" Edwin asked as he reached the door.

Zalith nodded at Ben. "Find Ben somewhere comfortable to rest and let my other guest know of his arrival," he instructed.

Edwin took his eyes off Zalith and set them on Ben. A look of shock clung to his face as he eyed the injured vampire, but he nodded in response. "Y-yes, sir."

"You can come in," Zalith said to Ben, "and keep an eye on him," he added, looking back at Edwin.

"Of course, sir," Edwin replied, taking Ben's arm as Varana encouraged the damaged man to walk forward.

Once the butler vanished into the house with Ben, Varana twiddled her fingers nervously. "How have you been?"

Zalith didn't respond; his anger was dormant, but he could feel it becoming more than just frustration.

Varana sighed sadly. "I miss you," she said despondently. "Do you miss *me*?"

Still with nothing to say, Zalith rolled his eyes ever so slightly.

As tears started to build in her eyes, Varana frowned. "Can you just talk to me?! I know that you're mad, okay? I get it. We need to get over this, though, Z; you're the most important person in my life, and I've loved you since the very first moment I set my eyes on you—"

Zalith sighed in annoyance. "Varana—"

She scowled desperately, a tear trickling down her face. "Let me finish, please," she said sternly. She then wiped away her tears, exhaled deeply, and looked at him with what was clearly a forced look of confidence. "You...you're a creature of habit, Z; you find a routine that works for you, and you stick to it. For centuries, I've watched you find men, put on that charming little smile of yours, make them want you, and then you have sex with them a time or two and let them go. Granted, there were some that you went back to or stayed with a little bit longer than usual, but for the most part, you don't really care enough about them to keep them around long term—"

He rolled his eyes irritably and went to speak—

"Shh! I'm not wrong!" she insisted. "This is *what you do,* Z; it's what you've *always* done. Of course, there were a few outliers, and I know that I personally played a part in *some* of their endings, but facts are facts," she continued. "You were known for this, Zalith—even your parents knew about it. God, I wouldn't even be able to count the number of times your mother *begged* me to find a way to get you to settle down; but I knew you wouldn't, Z, because that's just not who you were. You didn't care about them, even the men you liked were expendable to you in one way or another—but that was fine back then! Things were fine because you had me! And I knew that once you were done playing with your new boyfriends, you'd be right there beside me—and that's all I wanted, really. That's all I ever want...."

Zalith glared at the woman. Of course, he felt bad for her; he knew that she loved him in a way he couldn't love her, and he knew that she was convinced that one day, he and she would share something more than the platonic relationship they had. She was *so* convinced—*too* convinced. But it would never happen.

Varana then sniffled and wiped away more of her tears. "So, when you started seeing...*him*...I thought that it would be over soon enough. When you told me that he kept pushing you away and wouldn't even let you kiss him, I could see your...I don't know, the determination, I guess—desire maybe…and perhaps I should have taken the power of that into consideration, but still, I told myself that it wouldn't last. You'd fuck him, you'd get bored, and you'd be back by my side—but it didn't happen. You stayed. Even when he left you for a year to go God-knows-where, you didn't even bat an eyelash. I thought that you'd find someone to screw around with on the side, and *did you*?"

"No," he answered.

"No! Exactly, and it scared me because that's not like you, Z. Nothing about this relationship is like any of the others and it scares the life out of me. That's why I said those awful things to him in the kitchen. I don't want you to be with anybody else…I want you to be with *me*," she said as she looked down at her hands. Then, she took a step forward, moving closer to him.

Zalith grimaced in discomfort, but he remained where he was; the sympathy he felt for her kept him from moving away.

With a despondent look on her face, Varana shook her head. "It doesn't matter— none of it does—I just don't want you to hate me. You're my best friend, and I love you, and I don't want us to be apart anymore. I need you, Z…" she said as she put her hand on his chest. "I need you."

For a moment, he sunk into his thoughts. He loved her—of course he did—but not in the way *she* loved him. He loved her like a beloved sister, nothing more, and not one thing she said to him would change that. Ever.

Despite what she'd done, though, he didn't want her to be upset over him like this, and he wished he could make her happy; she was his best friend, but he wasn't going to compromise his own happiness just so she could live in her little fairy tale world. For a long time, he'd already been providing for her and going out of his way to make sure she was safe, happy, and healthy, and that she had everything she wanted—he couldn't possibly do anything more for her without sacrificing his own needs, and he just wouldn't do that.

Varana then sniffled again. "You need me, too, don't you?"

He didn't want to cave at the sight of her sorrowful look, so he took his eyes off her and glared at the wall beside him. "Don't do this, Varana," he said. But as she gripped his shirt and moved onto her tiptoes, leaning in to kiss him, he pushed her away. "You need to get a hold of yourself," he snarled irritably.

She burst into tears and collapsed to the ground, sitting on her knees. "Why can't I be good enough for you?!" she wailed.

With an irritated scowl, he glared down at her. "How many times do we have to have this fucking conversation? I'm gay, and I have been for the last six hundred years! No amount of your sad little speeches is going to change me," he said as calmly as his anger would let him—but that wasn't very calm at all.

Crying, Varana squeaked something Zalith couldn't understand and didn't really care to decipher.

"I also have yet to hear an apology from you about what happened in the kitchen," he added.

The woman continued to squeak and perhaps seemed to utter what Zalith thought might be a single 'sorry'.

Zalith sighed, watching her as she cried her eyes out for a short while. She looked so pathetic and sad sitting there in a heap, wailing like a child that had lost its mother. Despite just how awful of a woman she was, he wouldn't deny that he missed having her around, but she didn't yet deserve his forgiveness.

Instead of giving in like she wanted, he crouched in front of her. "Look at me," he said.

With her head in her hands, she shook her head in denial.

He frowned irritably. "Look at me, Varana," he said sternly.

Sniffling, she slowly looked up at him with her tearful eyes.

"You are so important to me," he started. "And I truly hate to see you like this, but you have to accept that things are different now. You'll always, *always* have a place in my heart, but I'm gay, Varana, and I'm in love with another man—"

Varana wailed even louder, almost screaming in what seemed to be grief.

He then frowned at her. "I know that it's not easy for you to accept, but I respect you too much to coddle you with lies, V." He watched as she continued crying, shaking her head, sniffling, and wiping away the soggy mess on her face. Part of him felt as though he wanted to hug her, but he knew that he shouldn't. Instead, he sighed and said, "I'm just going to get right down to it, Varana. I understand your reasoning, but what you did in the kitchen was vile, and I'm nowhere near ready to forgive you for your actions. I don't need a long, drawn-out explanation; I *know* why you said what you said to him. What I need is an apology."

She sniffled loudly. "I said I'm sorry," she cried.

"A sincere apology, not one born from your desire for me to change my mind."

Once again, Varana hid her face in her hands and cried.

"I love him, Varana, and I know this is hard on you, but he's not going anywhere, and you need to make your peace with it," he said sternly. As she continued to cry, he sighed and placed his hand on her shoulder, which she then placed her own hand over. "I know you want to come home, V, but you won't be returning until I believe that you've found it within yourself to accept things for how they are."

Gripping his hand tighter, she looked up at him. "Z, I accept it, okay?! I-I even brought back Ben for you—for the both of you!" she insisted.

Shaking his head, he pulled his hand away from her. "Thank you for that, I really appreciate it, Varana, but I'm not ready for you to come back. Sorry," he said, ending their conversation. She tried to grab his hand, but he stood up and backed off into the house. A saddened frown clung to his face as she wailed and pleaded for forgiveness, but he closed the door and locked it behind him, leaving her to cry and scream outside.

He knew that this would be the first of many dramatic apology attempts, and he wasn't yet sure when he might be ready to forgive her. For now, he'd get back to what he was doing and enjoy his time with Alucard without having to worry about that woman cornering and upsetting him; it was bound to happen again, he was certain. But he'd do what he could to prevent it.

Chapter Sixty-Two

— ⋊ † ⋉ —

The Morose Fate of Benjamin Walker

| **Alucard** |

lucard waited in the breakfast nook; he finished his waffles and pushed his plate aside. He'd heard that woman's voice at the door, and as much as he wanted to listen in, he didn't. He respected Zalith far too much to invade his privacy. He sipped from his coffee and stared outside, watching as the gardener finished watering the plants on one side of the garden. The vampire observed while he refilled his watering can and made his way along the grass with a tired look on his face.

The vampire's eyes, however, soon shifted to somebody who very clearly wasn't a gardener *or* a groundskeeper. A man wearing a black cutaway coat, matching trousers, and a bowler hat made his way along the treeline not too far from the garden wall. He was using ethos that would usually render him unseeable to most, but Alucard could see him clear as day. It didn't bother nor alarm him, though; he could tell that the man was a demon and likely Zalith's security patrolling the grounds.

A quiet knock then came at the door. He took his attention off the gardens and watched as Edwin walked in.

"Excuse me, sir. I was told to inform you that Ben has arrived," the butler said. "I put him in the sitting room."

Ben? Had Luther found him? If so, where was Detlaff? He frowned and stood up. "Take me to him," he said immediately.

"Of course, right this way," Edwin said and led Alucard out of the room and through the house.

Edwin took Alucard towards the very back of the house and into a room similar to the lounge, where Ben was sitting on one of the couches. A vacant look clung to the man's face as he stared out of the window, a look that made it seem as though he might not be sure where he was.

When the butler left, pulling the door shut behind him, Alucard made his way over to Ben, whom he expected to look at him, but the man seemed to be caught in a gaze. So, he stopped beside him and scowled. "Vhere is Zetlaff?" he asked him.

Ben didn't utter a word; he just... stared.

Alucard snarled impatiently and tapped the side of Ben's shin with his foot. "*Vorbi,*" he grumbled.

Slowly, Ben turned his head and looked up at him, and as soon as he realized who he was looking at, he snapped out of whatever trance he was in. For a few moments, he gawped at Alucard as if he was trying to work out whether what he was seeing was real or not.

Alucard felt impatient, but he couldn't blame Ben for his slowness. Detlaff had taken him, and there was no telling what that creature might have done to him. So, he waited.

"A... Aleksei?" Ben stammered.

Alucard sighed, dragging his hand over his face. "Yes."

Ben then abruptly leaned forward—Alucard backed off with a snarl of revolt, but Ben fell to his knees and wrapped his arms around Alucard's legs; he didn't utter a word. He just sat there, trembling, trying to hold back what looked to be agonized tears.

Alucard felt as if he wanted to throw the man off, but again, he had no idea what Detlaff had done to him; he was also Ben's sire, and any traumatized vampire in a state like Ben's would look to him for help, much like a child to their parent. That was basically what he was to vampires—a parent. As much as he hated this unwanted contact, he'd not turn a vampire away when they needed him.

He stood there with a conflicted, uncomfortable look on his face while Ben held onto his legs so very desperately. He wasn't sure what he should do to comfort him, so he frowned and grimaced in confusion. "Uh... you can... let go now," he uttered.

But Ben didn't let go, not even when Zalith entered the room and set his eyes on him, glaring in disgust.

Alucard looked over at the demon; a conflicted look clung to his face as he tried to work out what to say, but nothing came to him.

Zalith took his eyes off Ben and frowned at Alucard. "Is everything okay?" he asked slowly, concern in his voice as he slowly set a disgusted gaze back on Ben.

Sighing, Alucard tried to nudge Ben off. "Fine," he replied to Zalith. Tiring of Ben's need to cling to him, he gripped the man's shoulders and shoved him back so harshly that his back hit the couch, and as he sat there, he stared up at Alucard like a lost sheep. "Where did he come from?" he asked Zalith.

"Varana took him away from Detlaff. I assume Detlaff brought him to his sister's place because that's where Varana's most likely been staying."

Alucard looked back down at Ben. "Was Detlaff using you to find me?"

Ben stared for a few moments, but then slowly nodded in confirmation.

"And how did Detlaff escape?"

The beaten vampire gazed up at him, his eyes empty, his voice silent.

Alucard's patience was wearing thin. With an irritated snarl, he edged closer to Ben, who moved to cling to his legs again, but Alucard hissed quietly in warning. Ben backed off and remained where he sat, staring down at the floor as Alucard crouched beside him. He then sighed and placed his fingers on Ben's face as need be to look through his mind; he concentrated, looking for the answers to his questions.

It didn't take him long to find what he was looking for; he saw Ben leave his office the morning Detlaff had escaped and watched as the man made his way down into the dungeon after hearing voices. Dead on the floor were Felix and Remont—Remont was obviously dead because Detlaff had his voice. Felix, though? Alucard had seen him the day he and Zalith got back from their trip to Avalmoor.

It was time to talk to Felix.

He let go of Ben, stood up, and snarled in both disgust and aggravation. He should have known that Felix had something to do with this, and he couldn't begin to try and explain how angry he was—he couldn't sink into it, though. His anger…he had to keep as calm as he could. The last thing anyone needed was for him to lose himself.

"What is it?" Zalith asked as he moved closer and placed his hand on Alucard's shoulder.

"Fucking Felix," he grumbled, glaring down at Ben.

"That tuft of armpit hair?" he asked with an amused smirk.

Alucard snarled irritably and took his eyes off Ben. "He had something to do with Detlaff's escape."

Zalith frowned in concern. "Perhaps…*now* might be a good time to replace him."

Frustrated, Alucard sighed and moved away from both Zalith and Ben. He walked to the window and glared out at the gardens, thinking to himself. What could Felix possibly be getting out of helping Detlaff? As far as Alucard was aware, Felix was among the few vampires in his castle who had an unhealthy obsession with trying to be noticed by him; did Felix think that betraying him would get him noticed in a positive way? He wasn't that stupid, was he? All betraying him would do is end his life once and for all—and that was what Alucard was going to do.

But then again, what if Felix wasn't involved? What if Felix was simply in the wrong place at the wrong time? Alucard scowled, remembering what Felix said the day he and Zalith returned from Avalmoor. He claimed that he'd gone down in the dungeon to feed Detlaff and Remont was already dead; he'd said that Detlaff had knocked him unconscious. But…Alucard was beginning to find that suspicious. Felix had been told *not* to interact with Detlaff, so why would he be down in the dungeon? Would he *really* ignore yet another direct order?

Alucard couldn't be bothered to think about it anymore. Felix was annoying and defiant, and possibly a liability. It was time to get rid of him for good. It would be irritating to find someone to replace him, but Alucard no longer had the patience to deal with someone so... deranged.

Just then, a quiet knock came at the door, and in response to Zalith's slightly irritated, "What?", Edwin opened the door and stepped in with a stack of envelopes in his hand.

"The, uh... mail, sir," the butler said, holding it towards him.

Zalith took his eyes off Alucard and looked at the butler with an aggravated frown accompanied by a condescending smile. "And where does the mail go?"

Edwin stared nervously as he slowly pulled his hand back after offering the mail to Zalith. "Uh... in your office, sir," he answered.

The demon scowled. "So, I suggest that's where you put it," he said but then frowned and looked at Alucard. "Something came for you while you were recovering." He glanced back at the butler before he could leave. "Go and get the message that came a few days ago—the black envelope."

Edwin nodded. "Uh... where is it, sir?"

Zalith deadpanned. "In my office... with the rest of the mail."

Nodding, Edwin left the room.

"What came?" Alucard asked. "No one knows I'm here."

"It was delivered by an owl, and I assume these birds know how to find you."

Alucard frowned and looked back out of the window. "Maybe it's Attila begging for my forgiveness—or something else uninteresting."

"Maybe. What are you going to do about Felix?" he asked, walking past Ben as if he wasn't sitting there on the floor, huddled up like an orphan. The demon then stood beside Alucard, looking at him.

Alucard glanced at him. "I will kill him."

The demon smirked. "Good," he said, if Alucard wasn't mistaken, there was a glimmer of excitement in his voice.

Both of them looked back over their shoulders as Edwin knocked on the door again, entering with a black envelope in his hand. He made his way over, handed it to Alucard, and then swiftly left.

"When did this come?" Alucard asked, glancing at Zalith as he used one of his claws to open the letter.

"While you were unconscious—the second day."

Looking down at it, Alucard pulled the paper from the envelope and unfolded it, but the message was in Deiganish. As frustrated as he already was, he still felt the need to try and read the letter himself. But the moment his eyes skipped over Felix's name, he scowled and snarled irritably. "Can you read it for me, please?" he asked, looking at Zalith.

"Of course," Zalith said with a smile and took it from him. "Aleksei, I wasn't sure how to contact you, so I asked Attila; he left his address with my brother and me before he left. We're friends…sort of…" he stopped reading and looked at the very bottom of the paper to see who it was from, and then frowned strangely. "It's from Jasper."

"Who?" Alucard questioned, totally clueless as to who Jasper was.

"One of the vampires I sent through with Ben the first night we started that mission."

Alucard had no idea why *he* might be writing to him, but he was sure they were both soon to find out.

Zalith kept reading, "You disappeared three days ago, and since then, Felix has been taking care of things. He insists you left him in charge, and none of us questioned him since Ben isn't around either. But today, he made a call that my brother and I suspect you might not have given the order for, and that's why I went to the levels I did to contact you and find out whether or not what he's been telling us is right. Freja came to the castle looking for you, and I overheard a conversation she had with Felix. Some members of her pack have gone missing, and she assumes it has something to do with the slaughter that happened not too long ago; something about a wizard helping Ada's remaining allies. Freja thinks that some of her pack were involved and fled either in fear of you finding out or because those who got away are up to something, and her pack members are involved."

Alucard scowled and angrily gritted his teeth. He'd hoped any and all drama with the werewolves would be over, but that clearly wasn't the case, and that made him feel so very, *very* tired.

"Felix told her that she and all her wolves were the enemy and threatened her with words I'm sure weren't yours," Zalith continued. "He told her that you'd grown tired of her and her kind, and she'd do best to leave before you came back. Freja obviously suspected he was lying and asked to speak to you directly, but Felix insisted you didn't want to see her and that he was in charge. He's ordered us and the rest of the day and night guards to look out for werewolves and attack on sight. He insisted that Freja threatened him and you, and I think I might be the only one who knows the truth. I'm not sure where you are, but I always saw Ben using these owls to message you whenever you were away, so I hope this reaches you before Felix manages to cause a war or something. From Jasper."

Alucard's frustration grew with every word. Felix, werewolves—what else could he possibly have to deal with today? He turned away from Zalith, dragging his hands over his face as he tried to work out what he wanted to do. He'd already decided that it was time to kill Felix, but he'd not do so without teaching him a lesson first. His anger—it clawed at his skin, desperate to escape, but he couldn't let it. He knew what happened when he let go, and he wasn't going to let it happen.

He exhaled quietly, closing his eyes for a moment as he kept himself as calm and collected as he possibly could. Then, he sighed and turned to face Zalith again. "I need to go back to my castle."

Zalith frowned in concern and put his hand on his shoulder. "Do you want me to come with you?"

The demon's company always helped him to feel slightly better about the shit he had to deal with, so he nodded and said, "If you want to."

With a quiet sigh, Zalith pulled Alucard closer and hugged him tightly. "We'll put Ben somewhere more comfortable, and then we can head out."

Alucard nodded.

Zalith looked over at Ben as Alucard moved out of his embrace. "Ben. Let's go."

Ben looked up at them both, and after a few moments of staring, he climbed to his feet and followed them over to the door and out of the room.

| **Zalith** |

As he led the way through the house, Zalith pondered. He was convinced that Alucard wasn't feeling up to heading back to his castle to fix whatever was going on, but he knew just as well as the vampire did that leaving it would probably only allow things to become worse. He felt bad, of course. Alucard had spent a lot of his time with him lately, time away from his castle and the people he had to keep an eye on. But…at least one of the biggest problems Alucard currently had was going to be dealt with.

Felix…that ugly little cockroach of a man. Zalith was sure that he'd only lived as long as he had because Alucard needed his rank of vampire around, but this time, that wouldn't help him wriggle away. Alucard was going to kill him, and Zalith was looking forward to witnessing it—in his opinion, his death was well overdue. If only he could kill him himself; he'd caused Alucard so much trouble, *so much* unnecessary trouble, and Zalith hated knowing that Alucard was beginning to feel as exhausted as he looked to be.

"I'm sorry for keeping you from your work," he said as he looked at Alucard, his guilt starting to increase.

Alucard sighed quietly as they headed upstairs. "You haven't kept me from anything," he said, glancing back at Ben, who silently followed. "I would rather be here with you, anyway. If Attila hadn't been a piece of shit, and if Detlaff didn't have an obsession with Ben, then none of this would be happening. I don't know why all my subordinates are suddenly falling apart. But...I will find someone else to take over for Ben and Attila. I don't think he's in any state to work," he said, looking back at Ben again when they reached the top of the stairs.

"Do you have anyone in mind?" Zalith asked, leading the way across the hall and towards the stairs which led up to the second floor.

"I don't know. The only other person is Luther; either him or Attila. But I don't exactly like to give people second chances, so Luther."

The second Alucard mentioned that name, a sour frown struck Zalith's face, and he stifled a snarl. He *really* didn't like that guy *at all*, his reason being the comment that Alucard made regarding his appearance. He didn't feel threatened, it just irritated him to know that Alucard thought Luther was attractive, and he felt it always might. But he'd not let it get to him. "Perhaps we should spend more time at your castle until things have settled down," he suggested.

"Maybe," Alucard agreed quietly as they reached the top of the stairs and headed over to one of the guestroom doors.

Zalith pushed it open and invited Ben inside.

"We should go," Alucard said eagerly. "There's no doubt Felix has turned my country into a war zone."

With a slight smile, Zalith glanced at Ben, who sat on the bed. "I'll get someone to keep an eye on him while we're gone," he said to Alucard, who nodded. He then made his way over to the stairs. "Edwin," he called.

The swift butler came running, and once he reached the top of the stairs, Zalith set his eyes on him.

"Tell Tyrus I need one of his men to come here and keep an eye on Ben—as soon as possible," he ordered.

Nodding, Edwin scurried away once again.

Zalith then looked over at Alucard. "Are you ready to go?"

Alucard nodded and followed him as he led the way downstairs and through his house, heading for the front door. They didn't waste much time in heading outside and over to one of the walls, where Zalith created a rift, took Alucard's hand, and led the way through.

Chapter Sixty-Three

— ⸜ ✝ ⸝ —

In His Absence

| **Alucard** |

The pair emerged from a rift in the wall surrounding Alucard's castle. Alucard let go of Zalith's hand, and with his eyes, he scoured the grounds. He glanced up at the dark, clouded sky; rain was sure to fall soon. His sights then shifted to the watchmen standing on the castle towers. They all stared at him, most with a look of fear in their eyes. The groundskeeper stopped tending to the horses and also stared over at Alucard, as did the vampires who were patrolling the paths.

But Alucard's focus was on Felix, and the second Zalith sealed the rift behind him, the castle door swung open. Felix, with a look of glee on his face, burst out and rushed towards Alucard like a wife whose husband had been away at war. A look of utter revolt clung to Alucard's face, but he'd not let his disgust distract him from what he'd come to do.

Just as Felix jumped in for a hug, screaming, "I missed you!", Alucard swung his fist forward and smashed it into the man's face. Felix was launched backwards across the courtyard; he hit the ground, tumbled across the grass, and came to a slow halt as he rolled onto the gravel path.

With a smile on his face, Zalith leaned his back against the wall, observing as Alucard slowly made his way towards Felix, who struggled to scramble to his feet.

The moment Alucard reached Felix, he snatched his collar in both his hands and pinned him against the carriage he hadn't landed too far from. Alucard ignored the man's fumbling, insisting words and glared at him, his anger becoming *fury*.

"What did I do?!" Felix yelled, tears starting to form in his eyes.

Ignoring him, Alucard snarled irritably and threw him to the ground. As he hit the path, the man whimpered and tried to scurry away, stumbling to his feet. For a few moments, Alucard watched him try to run, and just as he came a few feet from the castle's gate, Alucard disappeared and reappeared in front of him. Felix screamed in horror, and

Alucard snatched his throat, pinned him against the wall, and dug his claws into the side of his face, peering into his mind.

Within a matter of seconds, Alucard discovered all that he needed to know. Felix had taken Remont to Detlaff—somehow, Felix knew that Detlaff was Alucard's 'brother', and his estranged little brain made him think that helping Detlaff would earn him some sort of recognition. All Felix wanted was to be seen, to be recognized. But Alucard didn't care. He didn't care about Felix, and he'd make sure he understood that he was nothing but an annoying inconvenience.

"W-why do you hurt me?!" Felix cried.

Scowling, Alucard snarled angrily. "This is the *last* time you piss me off," he hissed. As Felix whimpered in panic, Alucard pulled him away from the wall and dragged him into the shade of a tree as the sun began to creep out from behind the clouds. He made sure he had the attention of everyone who'd been observing and turned Felix so that his back was to him. He held the man's arms behind his back and glared at what he could see of his face.

"P-please!" Felix cried, tears streaming down his face. "I-I just wanted to help!"

"All you've done is cause me an unnecessary amount of shit, and I can't be bothered to deal with you anymore," he snapped, tightening his grip on Felix's arms as he tried to pull free, the sunlight starting to seep through the leaves of the tree Alucard held him under.

Alucard glared at the grass ahead as the sunlight began to flood over it. He waited, holding Felix while he cried and begged to be let go, but Alucard had made up his mind, and he wasn't going to give him any more chances. Every other vampire listened to him and did as they were told, so why couldn't this cretin? *Especially* when the sire link was supposed to compel vampires to do as he asked.

He waited a few more seconds, and then he harshly shoved Felix out into the sunlight.

Felix wailed, screamed, and cried painfully as his skin began to burn; he dropped to his knees, the flesh on his body starting to wither and turn to ash in the light of the sun, and in just moments, Felix became nothing but a small pile of dust. He was gone, and this time, he wouldn't be coming back.

But Alucard wasn't yet done. He took his eyes off what was once Felix and eyed each and every fear-stricken vampire who watched the execution. He didn't even have to say anything to warn them; the looks in their eyes were enough for him to know that they understood not to step out of line. But he had to make sure something like this wouldn't happen again. The day and night guard commanders had followed Felix without question—without coming to him for confirmation. The only one who contacted him was Jasper, so at least he knew he could rely on *him*.

Alucard raised his left hand, pointing at the vampire standing on the tallest tower, and the man made his way down to him in the form of a black shadow. Once he stood before his creator, he shuddered in fear, but he didn't have a chance to speak. Alucard snatched his throat, and without a word of explanation, he plunged his hand into his chest and ripped his heart out. He tossed the body to the side, and it landed beside Felix's ashes. Then, Alucard stood where he was for a moment, keeping himself as calm as he possibly could.

Ben wasn't at all fit to get back to working as his second in command, and Alucard wasn't going to give Attila another chance. So, he'd wait for Luther to get back and have him take over Ben's position. As for the position of the day and night guard's leader, he'd give that to Jasper—wherever he was. For now, though, he'd have to stick around and fix the damage Felix had caused. Usually, he'd have something like this done by Ben, but of course, he'd been made useless by Detlaff.

With an irritated sigh, Alucard walked over to the castle door and made his way inside. Now, he had to go and find Freja and hope that Felix hadn't compromised the arrangement he had with her.

| **Zalith** |

A worried frown clung to Zalith's face as he passed the horrified vampires and hurried towards the castle doors. He'd enjoyed the show very much, but now he was concerned as to how Alucard must be feeling.

"Alucard," he called, catching up to him as he headed through the castle hall. "Are you okay?"

Stepping into the corridor which would take them to his study, Alucard glanced at him. "I'm fine," he grumbled, ignoring Sabazios, who had come running up to him, wagging his tail as he panted excitedly.

The vampire made his way into his study and immediately moved over to his desk. He sat down, sighed, and slouched back in his seat, a tired look on his face.

Zalith made his way over and leaned against the desk beside him. For a moment, Alucard stared up at the demon as he stared down at him, but then exhaled quietly and set his eyes on his hands as he rested them in his lap.

The demon placed his hand on Alucard's shoulder. "Are you okay?" he asked again, but with a worried tone in his voice this time. "Once more, you try to elude me with your attitude," he said with a smirk, trying to lighten the sullen atmosphere.

"I don't have an attitude," Alucard grumbled. He then glared at his hands for a few moments, sighed, and looked up at Zalith. "I shouldn't have left so soon," he admitted, losing his irritated tone. "I feel... tired."

Zalith frowned in concern. "Do you want to lie down?"

Alucard sighed again and sat up straight, resting his arms on the table. "No. I have to make sure Felix hasn't ruined what I organized with the werewolves." He then looked over at Sabazios, who was sitting by the door. "Go and find Freja," he called, and as the hound left the room, he glanced up at Zalith, who still had a concerned frown on his face. "I'll be fine," he insisted.

Zalith started feeling guilt growing inside him again. Not only was Alucard evidently exhausted and still not fully recovered from what Detlaff had done to him, but he was also having to deal with things that may not have happened if he hadn't taken the vampire back to his home with him and kept him there for as long as he had. He wasn't sure what he could do, but he wanted to do whatever he could to help Alucard.

Keeping his hand on Alucard's shoulder, he quietly said, "If there's anything I can do to help, tell me."

Taking his eyes off Zalith, Alucard nodded. "I just need to make sure everything with the wolves is fine, and then I'll contact Luther. Then we must decide what to do with Ben. Detlaff will probably come looking for him, and I don't want any more liabilities. You don't have to wait around with me until Luther gets here, though."

Zalith moved his hand from Alucard's shoulder and placed it over his hand. "I want to stay," he said. Alucard looked up at him, and as he did, Zalith leaned in and kissed him. He then smiled and stood up straight as Alucard looked down at his desk in an attempt to hide his face. "What happens if Felix has managed to compromise your arrangement with the werewolves?"

Alucard shrugged as he leaned the side of his head against his hand. "I will just kill them. I can't be bothered with werewolves anymore."

"Understandable. But the letter mentioned that some of Freja's wolves may have been involved with the wizard you and I killed—"

"I will ask Freja about that when she gets here. If I have to go and do something about it, I will. Sabazios is bringing her now, so hopefully it won't be a long conversation."

As Alucard set his eyes on the entrance to his study, Zalith looked back over his shoulder and watched the vampire's hound lead Freja into the room. The woman had a rather irritated look on her face as she set her eyes on Alucard, but she followed the dog wordlessly and made her way towards the desk Alucard was sitting behind.

"What the hell is going on?" she asked.

Alucard glared at the woman with a look of revolt in his eyes. "Did I ask you to say anything?"

She fell silent and waited to be spoken to.

"I gather you are still on the land I gave you?"

"We are."

"So, I assume you worked out that Felix was acting on his own?"

Freja nodded. "Except when he sent a bunch of your guys to chase us away like rats; you know about—"

Alucard sighed and lowered his hand onto the table. "No, I didn't know because I wasn't fucking here, was I?" he snarled. "Felix is gone. My friend Luther will be replacing Ben, and I will soon find someone to replace Felix. Whatever damages Felix and his orders caused, I will fix. That conversation is over. Jasper tells me that some of your wolves have left to join the survivors of the attack I made on the last of Ada's followers; is this true?"

"Yeah," she said with a nod. "Only three, though. One of my Betas followed them right up to a little camp and then came back to tell me. I came to tell you, but Felix was here."

"You think this little gathering of wolves is planning something?"

"If those three were willing to throw away their lives like that, they must be," Freja answered.

The vampire sighed quietly and placed his forehead in his hand, taking a moment to think to himself. He then looked back at Freja. "Do you know how many of them there are out there?"

She shook her head. "At least twenty—that's what my Beta said, anyway. I don't know if there's more."

"Right," he mumbled. "Get out."

With a slight frown of irritancy, Freja turned around and left the study, leaving Alucard with Zalith.

Once she was gone, Alucard looked up at the demon. "Would you like to come and kill these wolves with me?" he asked, sounding very unenthusiastic and exhausted.

Zalith smirked and nodded. "I'd love to," he agreed. He was concerned that, in his current state, killing werewolves might not be the best activity for Alucard, but he knew that Alucard just wanted to get the problem solved before it escalated—and the sooner it was over, the sooner Alucard could get some more rest. So, he'd not argue with him, but once they got to where these wolves were, he'd do what he could to make sure Alucard didn't strain himself.

"Then we will go now," Alucard said, standing up. He took his blazer from the front of the table and pulled it on. "I'll write to Luther when we get back, and then we can go back home. I'll work out what to do about Detlaff once we've dealt with Ben. I'm still yet to hear from my Paladins about Lucious, but they should contact me soon, too."

The moment Alucard referred to his house as home, Zalith was consumed by a happiness that he couldn't explain. He couldn't help but smile as he watched Alucard take his cape and throw it over his shoulders. Alucard already made him feel so content, but to know that he thought of his home as *his* home, too—it brought a warmness to his heart. He found the fact that he had said it adorable, and it also made him feel glad to know that Alucard felt safe and secure enough to say such a thing. He wanted Alucard to feel as though his home was also his, and now knowing that he *did* only made him feel all the more delighted. He'd not say anything, though. The last thing he wanted to do was embarrass Alucard or cause him to overthink what he just said.

While Alucard finished checking that his weapons were concealed safely inside his blazer, Zalith moved closer and took hold of his hand. He then stood in front of him and placed his other hand on the side of his face. Alucard stared at him expectantly, obviously sure that he was going to say something, but instead, he pulled him into a tight embrace. He didn't want to let go, especially when the vampire wrapped his arms around him. But they now had a new task to complete, and he'd not keep Alucard from it a moment longer.

He kissed him once, stepped back, and smiled. "Let's go."

Alucard attempted to hide his own smile as he looked down at the floor and walked past him, beginning to lead the way out of his study.

Zalith followed beside him, gazing at him with a content expression. All they had to do was get rid of the last of the problematic werewolves, and then they could head home and continue to enjoy their time together.

Chapter Sixty-Four

— ≺ ✝ ≻ —

Pest Control

| **Zalith** |

Zalith walked beside Alucard as he led the way through the forest surrounding Dor-Sanguis. He glanced at the vampire's tired, pale face; the longer he remained on his feet, the worse he began to look. The demon almost wanted to insist that they go back, but he knew that Alucard wouldn't agree to it; the vampire just wanted to get his task over and done with, and Zalith would do all he could to help and make sure Alucard didn't have to do too much.

Something he wanted to do was try and alleviate some of Alucard's stress. He wanted to do something that might cheer him up, something to take his mind off everything. But what? He frowned, looking ahead at the endless path of trees. He knew that Alucard's birthday was in two months; the vampire hadn't mentioned anything about his yearly party, nor had Zalith seen anything as far as preparations went. Was Alucard even planning to have a celebration this year?

He looked at the vampire, still thinking to himself. Of course, he already had a few gift ideas, but event-wise, not so much. He had two months to ponder, though, and if Alucard had no plans, *he* wanted to make a plan for him. He wanted the vampire to have a nice time; it was his birthday, after all, and this year, Zalith wanted to make it better than the last. Last year, Alucard had been sent to another world halfway through his party, and they hadn't even gotten to say a proper goodbye to each other. No, this year, Zalith would make sure nothing ruined his day.

"Your birthday is soon," he started, smiling as the vampire looked at him. "Do you have any plans this year?"

Alucard shrugged and stared ahead again. "No," he answered. "I usually have the party, but…well, I guess I just don't feel like it this year. I haven't been back long, so I haven't really had time to think about it."

"Well, if you want to have the party, I can get some people to organize it for you; alternatively, I can organize something just for the two of us—or both," he said. "Of course, we have two months to plan, but I'd like to get a head start."

The vampire glanced at him, clearly thinking to himself for a few moments. But then, as he set his sights on the path they were following through the woods, he shrugged and said, "I think...this year, I would prefer the quieter option."

"Then it's a date," Zalith said, smirking.

A small smile flickered across the vampire's face, and once Zalith took hold of his hand, they continued through the forest in silence.

| Alucard |

When they approached the place where Freja's three wolves had retreated, Alucard lost his content expression and frowned cautiously. He could already detect the life signs of twenty-two people, all of whom were werewolves. As irritated as he felt to still be dealing with them, he hoped that these twenty-two were the last that would cause him problems. Once they were gone, he could get back to what was a whole lot more important.

As he thought about what was important to him, he glanced at Zalith, eyeing him for a short moment while the demon stared ahead—evidently, he'd detected the wolves, too; his cautious look told Alucard that. But the vampire didn't care to think about the wolves. What he felt was most important in his life right now was Zalith. He wanted to give Zalith as much of his time and attention as he could, and he wanted to focus as much time as he could on their relationship. He wasn't too happy at all to be wasting time chasing dogs, but at least Zalith was with him while he did it. Working with this demon was something he thoroughly enjoyed.

He stared ahead again; the place where the wolves were congregating was just a few minutes away. Of course, both he and Zalith were using ethos to mask themselves from detection, so they could get as close as they needed to be before revealing themselves to their enemy. Alucard didn't feel the need to announce himself, though. He just wanted to kill them and be done with it so he could head back to his castle, get what he needed, and head back home with Zalith.

"Don't let any of them get away this time," Alucard said with a sigh. "I want to end this shit with the wolves right here."

Zalith smirked as he glanced at him. "Okay."

Alucard looked at him from the corner of his eye, a slight smile breaking through his frown. "You take the left. I'll take the right."

"Understood," Zalith said, smiling.

They reached and stepped into the small opening where a camp had been set up. Seven men were sitting with two women around a fire, and the other eleven wolves were off to the left bickering; one man was chopping wood, three women were screaming at one another, and the other men were watching them, laughing. But the moment the two demons stepped into the glade, they all stopped what they were doing and looked over at them.

The second they realized who Alucard was, the pack burst into action, and Zalith nor Alucard wasted time, either. Zalith set his eyes on his targets and raced to the left and Alucard to the right towards the fire, where two of the men had already shifted into their wolf forms.

Despite his determination, Alucard couldn't ignore the slowness he felt. His wounds and healing body were still causing him to struggle, but he'd not let it stop him. He could be half-dead and still be up and fighting—what harm were a few small cuts?

He found out the moment he reached forward and snatched the throat of the man who had come at him with a pocketknife—what idiot charged at a vampire with a pocketknife? Clearly, this idiot. Alucard moved his hand forward to snatch the man's wrist but wasn't as fast as he usually was. He realized he'd not grab the man's wrist in time, so he moved aside, letting the man stumble forward. He then swiftly turned to face the wolf that had jumped at him, grabbed hold of its neck, and snapped it before it had a chance to yelp.

The wielder of the pocketknife then came at him again, but Alucard snatched the man's wrist and shoved him towards the other man running his way. The man's knife impaled his friend's side, and as they shrieked in confusion, the vampire kicked them both into the fire, which he increased in size with his own crimson flames, burning the two men into nothing but ash in just a few moments.

Three were dead, and six were left.

He glanced across the glade at Zalith; the demon was already locked in battle with his targets. Half of them had transformed, and he'd taken out the first three wolves with his ashen flames, their burning corpses not too far from the treeline.

One of the women reached out to grab Zalith mid-transformation, but he snatched hold of her throat and tore her head from her body before she could try and fight back. The man who had been cutting firewood then swung his axe, aiming for Zalith's head as he focused on obliterating one of the charging wolves, but when the wolf was executed, the demon swiftly snatched the axe handle, pulled it from the man's grip, and swung it towards *his* head. The blade cut through the man's skull and embedded itself into the tree beside them.

When the man's half-headless body dropped to the floor, Zalith let go of the axe, leaving it in the tree, and then he grabbed the throat of another wolf who jumped at him. He tore off its head, smothered the last of the people in flames, and sighed in relief.

Zalith then looked in Alucard's direction, and when they locked eyes, the demon smirked and winked.

Flustered, Alucard focused on the last of his own targets.

The vampire kicked away the screaming, burning man in front of him and set his eyes on his next target, but before he could reach the woman, Zalith swiftly snatched her throat, pulling her away from him. The demon tore her head from her body, causing the last two men to stop in their tracks and stare at Zalith and Alucard, who exchanged competitive glances.

One of the men chose to jump at them both, and the other man transformed into a black wolf and scurried away. Alucard took his eyes off Zalith as he snarled irritably and began to chase the fleeing wolf, leaving the demon to deal with the last man.

The vampire raced into the woods, keeping his eyes on the wolf as it panted and wailed in fear, trying to get away. It made erratic turns, trying to shake Alucard off its trail, but he'd not give up until it was dead.

Alucard was no longer alone in his chase, though. Twenty or so feet to his right, Zalith caught up. He smirked at Alucard once he set his sights on him, and there was a look on his face that let the vampire know that *he* was going to kill the last wolf. Alucard scowled stubbornly—this was *his* kill, not Zalith's. So, before the demon could reach and grab the panicking wolf, Alucard disappeared into vermillion smoke and reappeared in front of the wolf. He grabbed hold of it before it even realized he was there and mercilessly plunged his hand into the wolf's body, and with a loud, rapid succession of cracks and squelches, he tore its heart out.

The battle was over, the wolves were dead, and Alucard could rest.

Before Alucard could comprehend it, Zalith gently snatched him by his jaw, pulled him to his feet, and pinned his back against the closest tree. Without a word, Zalith smirked seductively and kissed the vampire's lips.

As stubborn as Alucard felt, he didn't push him away or argue. He kissed back, dropping the dead wolf's heart before gripping Zalith's shirt with his left hand and the demon's wrist with his right. The violence made him feel strangely exhilarated, and being enthralled in Zalith's grip made him feel even more excited. While the demon's assertiveness often made him feel nervous, right now, it made him feel eager, and an almost intoxicating feeling of anticipation was beginning to consume him. He tightened his grip on Zalith's wrist, making him move his hand from his jaw to his throat, and as the demon grinned approvingly, they continued their aggressive, assertive kissing.

But Alucard couldn't let this excitement consume him—not right now. The moment Zalith started to kiss down to his neck, he placed his hands on the demon's chest and lightly pushed him away. If he let it continue, he was sure he'd have a third set of fang wounds on his neck—which then reminded him that those he'd received when Zalith removed the silver from his blood still hadn't healed. As Zalith frowned at him in both concern and disappointment, Alucard dragged his hand over the scars on the left side of his neck. Would they ever heal?

"What's wrong?" Zalith asked as he placed his hand over Alucard's.

"These scars haven't healed yet," he mumbled, dragging his hand away from his neck.

Zalith carefully pulled away the collar of Alucard's shirt so that he could see the scars. He stared at the vampire's conflicted face for a few moments but then set his eyes on the scars once more, lightly dragging his thumb over them. Without a mutter or even a smile, he leaned in and softly pressed his lips against them.

Alucard gave in; all it took was one gentle kiss. He tilted his head to the side, relaxing as the demon slowly and attentively kissed his neck, up to his face, and to his lips once more. Each kiss sent a delightful sensation spiralling through Alucard's body and enticed him even more to let Zalith have his way with him again.

But Zalith then sighed quietly and placed his hand on the side of Alucard's face. "Maybe they won't heal. Your body was under a lot of stress when it happened; your healing ethos may have focused on the damage done inside your body, thus... failing to effectively heal this," he said, dragging his fingers over the scars on Alucard's neck.

The vampire was sure that Zalith was right. He'd thought the scars would heal a lot slower than usual, but now it was beginning to look as though they were permanent.

"They're not so bad, are they?" Zalith asked with a smirk, resting his forehead against Alucard's as he gazed into his eyes. "I'm the one who put them there, so in a way, I've marked you as mine," he said suggestively as he moved his body closer to Alucard's.

His nervousness increased with every word and move Zalith made; he looked away from him and pouted, glaring down at the ground.

"Maybe I'll let *you* bite *me* later," Zalith said with a smirk but then leaned into the vampire's ear. "Unless you want to bite me now."

The demon's invitation was tempting, but Alucard felt it was best *not* to get high in the middle of a forest an hour or so from dusk—*and* he needed his mind to be clear of distraction when he wrote to Luther and explained to Jasper that he was taking over the day and night guard. So, he frowned and turned his head to look at Zalith. "Later," he said, a nervous but stern tone to his voice.

Zalith smirked. "I'll hold you to that."

With the flustered look on his face surely growing, Alucard tried to hide his amused smile and lightly shoved Zalith aside. "We should head back now," he said and started leading the way back to his castle. "I'll get what I need to take back with us, and I'll also contact Luther and Jasper before we go."

Following him, Zalith linked arms with him and contently said, "Okay."

Then, with Zalith at his side, Alucard led the way back to his castle, nothing but the delightful thought of spending the next few days with Zalith on his mind.

Chapter Sixty-Five

— ⊰ ✝ ⊱ —

Loss

| **Zalith** |

A s the sun dipped below the horizon, painting the sky with hues of purple and orange, Zalith and Alucard arrived at the gates of the vampire's castle. Crossing the expansive courtyard, their steps echoed in the fading daylight as they moved toward the front door. A sense of anticipation lingered in the air, both eager to conclude their journey and return to Nefastus, seeking respite from the day's burdens that had weighed heavily on Alucard's mind.

As soon as they entered the castle, Zalith lightly pinned Alucard's back against the wall before the vampire had a chance to take off his cape. The demon smiled and leaned in closer, and then he kissed him slowly for a few moments.

But the calm atmosphere withered away like a flame snuffed out by a cold, sharp breeze. A dismaying bitterness polluted the air, and Alucard immediately turned his head to the left, ending their kiss. Then, as a look of horror chased the smile from his face, he stared in dread, and Zalith's once content-ridden heart was struck with worry.

The demon looked in the same direction—

"Oh, do continue, please," Damien invited, his voice dripping with a sinister edge. He extended his hand toward the duo, a mocking gesture, as he casually leaned against the table at the room's centre. A palpable air of disdain distorted his features, a twisted expression of revulsion plastered across his face. His gaze, however, bore an unmistakable malevolence, an intense anger that honed in on Alucard with a chilling focus, as if the very presence of the vampire fuelled the growing storm in Damien's eyes.

Zalith's grin evaporated instantly upon spotting the Daegelus. Anger surged within him, a fiery intensity that manifested in the piercing glare he directed at the loathsome creature nonchalantly leaning against Alucard's table. The sight of Damien, with his grotesque presence, fuelled Zalith's indignation; the last thing he needed right now was an encounter with someone as repugnant as Damien, someone who'd hurt the man he loved—someone who strived to make Alucard's life a misery.

There was an instinctive protectiveness welling up inside Zalith as the tense, empty silence grew longer. The notion of Damien making a scene and potentially causing harm to Alucard ignited a fierce anger within him; he was acutely aware of the Daegelus aversion to their connection, and he sensed impending hostility. Bracing himself for what might come, Zalith was resolute in his determination to shield Alucard from whatever form of twisted punishment Damien deemed appropriate.

Damien crossed his arms as he eyed the pair. Zalith didn't take his hands off Alucard in hopes that the vampire would understand that he'd protect him, but it didn't seem to wipe the look of dread from Alucard's pale face. He stood there, his back against the wall, staring at Damien as though he was lost and waiting for guidance.

But Alucard soon pushed Zalith away and pulled off his cape, placed it on the table beside him, and then began his approach towards Damien, whose look of disgust grew with every step the vampire took.

At first, every instinct within Zalith's body told him to follow, but he knew that would only make Damien react a whole lot worse. So he stayed where he was, watching, waiting, ready to intervene the moment that creature tried to lay a hand on Alucard.

As Alucard approached him, Damien smiled condescendingly and held out his arm, inviting the vampire to walk beside him as he turned around. When Alucard followed at his side, the Daegelus placed his hand on the back of Alucard's neck, ever so slowly digging his claws in deeper with every step they took.

Zalith stepped forward, but he clenched his fist and fought the desire to attack; the smell of Alucard's blood was taunting him, urging him to take action, but he had to hold off.

"So, Aleksei," Damien said with a skeptical tone in his demeaning voice. "Tell me, how has your search for Lucious been?"

Alucard glanced up at Damien. "I have…made progress," he said. "I—"

Before Alucard could speak another word, Damien grabbed hold of his collar and harshly pinned his back on the wall, slamming him against it so hard that the entire room shook.

Zalith gritted his teeth and scowled; he stepped forward, ready to attack, but before he could move another inch, Damien sharply turned his head and pointed at him—

"Stay the fuck where you are!" he yelled.

Zalith stopped in his tracks, unable to do a thing—just as Damien wanted. He may not respect Damien, he may *hate* him, but the Daegelus' word was law. He couldn't deny him. He couldn't move. All he could do now was stand there and watch as his heart raced, and his body trembled.

The Daegelus glared back at Alucard and snarled in both disgust and impatience. "Don't you *DARE* lie to me!" he yelled, his face mere inches from Alucard's. "I know *exactly* what you have and haven't been doing, you dirty, conniving little fuck!"

As Damien raised his hand towards the vampire's face, Alucard shuddered in his grip, but the Daegelus didn't hit him; instead, Damien held out his index finger, pointing his black claw at his face.

"Did you think I wouldn't find out? Did you think you were so smart that you could sneak around behind my back?!"

Alucard stared vacantly at his enraged face, but Zalith could see the fear in his vampire's eyes.

The Daegelus then harshly dug his claw into the side of Alucard's face just below his forehead—yet, the vampire still stared in silence, not uttering a sound in response as Damien began to drag his claw down the side of his face, cutting at his skin.

Zalith trembled in desperation. He wanted to attack, he wanted to race over there and pull that revolting creature off his vampire, but he couldn't move.

Damien snarled in Alucard's face. "You're a foolish, pathetic little rat! In the year I gave you, you failed something as simple as finding Lucious; yet, I give you more time...and what do you do with it?" he growled, his claw reaching the vampire's jawline. "What do you do with it?!" he shouted.

But then the devilish growl of a hound snatched Damien's attention. Sabazios charged at him, making Damien frown in confusion; the dog pounced at him in an attempt to protect his master, but the Daegelus flicked his left wing out—it smashed into Sabazios, sending him flying across the room, and when he hit the wall, his body broke. He fell lifeless to the floor, leaving a look of horror on Alucard's face.

Damien's abrupt head turn brought a malevolent glare aimed at the vampire. Alucard's gaze, fixed on his now lifeless hound, bore a heart-wrenching expression, a visage that stirred profound sadness. Yet, Damien's reaction was quite the opposite; a sinister grin crept across his face, relishing in the pain he perceived. Zalith, however, could only muster a deep scowl at the Daegelus' cruel enjoyment. The realization that Damien found pleasure in hurting Alucard fuelled an escalating anger within Zalith, intensifying with each passing moment as he stood there, compelled to witness the torment unfold.

Alucard turned his head to look at Damien. "I-I sent people to—"

"People? I don't fucking care about people!" Damien screeched, cutting him off.

Zalith shook his head; he wanted to tell Alucard that attempting to explain wouldn't help, but the vampire kept trying.

Alucard took his eyes off Damien and stared over at his lifeless hound again. "I'm sorry," he said shakily. "I will do better—"

"Will you?" Damien snarled condescendingly. He then let go of Alucard, letting him fall to the floor.

As Alucard hit the floor, he kept his eyes on Sabazios.

Damien backed off. For a few moments, he paced back and forth in front of Alucard but then growled irritably and snatched his throat, pinning him against the wall once again. Alucard grunted quietly as blood trickled down his face and the look of fear that claimed his face grew so thick that Zalith could see him trembling from where he stood.

"Fucking around with werewolves, pissing off wizards, screwing with some fucking demon I told you to forget about!" the Daegelus berated, tightening his grip on Alucard's throat as he slammed him back against the wall.

Alucard frowned in desperation. "I had...I thought Ephriel—"

"Ephriel?" Damien laughed. "What? Did you think she'd want someone as disappointing as you?"

An unsure frown flickered across Alucard's terrified face.

"And then this," he hissed, glancing at Zalith. "I thought I told you *not* to crawl back to him," he snarled to Alucard, "but you couldn't help yourself, could you? You couldn't help but disobey me. You poor, lonely, pathetic little creature. I told you, the next time you fail to do what I tell you, I'd make sure you *never* forget what you are again—"

Before Alucard could do anything, Damien crashed his fist into his stomach so hard that no sound came from his mouth. He grimaced, he scowled, and as Damien snarled in anger, the Daegelus threw him to the ground.

Zalith brimmed with a readiness to strike, his instincts urging him to intervene and shield Alucard from further harm at the hands of that despicable creature. Yet, an invisible force held him in place, an infuriating restraint that left him scowling and gritting his teeth in a futile struggle. The burning disdain he harboured for Damien proved useless against the dark influence exerted over him. Despite lacking any shred of respect for the Daegelus, Zalith found himself immobilized, unable to break free from the grip Damien had over his will. Helplessly, he stood there, witnessing Alucard slowly rising to his feet, accepting the second blow from the Daegelus without displaying even a flicker of desire to defend himself.

Damien's fist collided with Alucard's face, propelling the vampire into a harsh collision with the wall. The Daegelus surged forward, seizing Alucard by the throat, a twisted growl of disgust escaping him as he struck the side of the vampire's face, causing him to stagger. The absence of pained sounds from Alucard only seemed to further fuel Damien's rage. In a swift, brutal motion, Damien grabbed Alucard's arm, flinging him forward until the vampire crashed onto the floor, remaining sprawled where he fell.

In the aftermath, uncertainty hung in the air for Zalith; he couldn't discern whether Alucard couldn't muster the strength to rise or chose not to. Regardless, Alucard lay motionless as Damien advanced, delivering a merciless kick to the vampire's stomach. The force was so brutal that, as Alucard tumbled across the floor, a visible grimace of pain contorted his face.

Damien then seized the back of Alucard's blazer, forcefully slamming him against the wall once more. The side of Alucard's face scraped against the jagged, shattered brick, remnants of the earlier collision. A menacing snarl escaped Damien as he ruthlessly dragged Alucard's face along the broken surface, exacerbating the wounds inflicted by his claws, tearing at the already damaged skin. The Daegelus persisted until he reached the end of the broken brick, where he swung the vampire around and delivered a devastating blow to his face. The impact was so intense that it appeared as though Alucard teetered on the brink of losing consciousness at any moment.

Zalith's heart raced, each beat echoing a fragmenting symphony of despair as he helplessly witnessed each brutal hit and new wound inflicted upon Alucard. The torment unfolding before him seemed to shatter his own sense of agency, breaking him piece by piece. The overwhelming desire to intervene clashed with the invisible force that held him in a paralyzing grip. His limbs refused to respond, rendering him immobilized in the face of the unfolding tragedy.

No matter how fervently Zalith struggled against the invisible constraints, the cruel reality persisted—his inability to move, to shield the man he loved from Damien's sadistic onslaught. The despair deepened with each passing moment, a bitter realization that he was forced to endure the agony unfolding before him. It was a torment not only for Alucard but for Zalith himself, a relentless anguish as Damien revelled in the suffering he orchestrated, ensuring Zalith was a captive witness to the cruel spectacle.

The Daegelus harshly snatched Alucard's jaw, making him look up at him as he scowled evilly in his face. "Reveal," he growled, glaring into the vampire's confused, dazed eyes.

As commanded, Alucard's demon form revealed itself to the Daegelus... but only his horns appeared; that was all he had left of it. Two of them, black as night, similar to those of a kudu in both shape and size.

As the horns appeared, a glimmer of cruel excitement flickered through Damien's eyes. "Sometimes, Aleksei, I wonder why I go out of my way to hide you from my brother—to keep my associates from hunting you like the fucking animal you are," he snarled, glaring down into Alucard's eyes as he murmured in struggle. "Why do I bother with you at all when all *you* do is waste my fucking time and fail to do even the simplest of tasks?! *You're* worthless!"

Then, with a revolted, infuriated growl, the Daegelus swung Alucard around and threw him one final time. As the vampire's back hit the side of the table, Damien sprang over to him, gripping his throat in one hand and his left horn in the other. The vampire struggled and stared in horror, a hint of desperate plea upon his voice as he grunted in pain. He grasped Damien's wrist with his hand, trying to pull his grip from his horn, but that only angered him further.

And then Damien started to pull.

Zalith's heart pounded in his chest, his angst and anger constricting his trembling body. He wasn't going to let Damien take Alucard's horns—he couldn't. He'd already taken his wings; he wanted to destroy Alucard in the cruellest way, and Zalith wasn't going to let that happen to the man he loved. He wasn't going to let *any* of this happen. He wasn't going to lose anything else—not Alucard, not the man he loved, and not the happiness he made him feel.

He gritted his teeth, he struggled, growled, and grunted. He had to protect him—he had to *save* him. He wasn't going to lose Alucard—nothing was going to take him away…not even Damien.

Desperation overwrought him; he struggled as if he were trying to pull his limbs from chains. His body ached as if it were being crushed, worse and worse with each heavy, struggled step…but then, as Alucard's desperate whimper struck Zalith's heart, the invisible shackles around him seemed to break.

Damien's influence wasn't stronger than his need to protect; Damien was nothing, no one, and if Zalith had to kill him, he'd kill him.

Zalith won his struggle. He adorned his demon form and burst forward, crashing into the Daegelus so abruptly that he was torn from Alucard before he had a chance to work out what had happened.

The demon lunged, aiming for a fatal strike. As Damien's back collided with the wall, Zalith instinctively reached for the kill, his hand penetrating Damien's chest, seeking out what he believed to be the beating heart. However, to his profound shock, the Daegelus harboured not a solitary heart but a duplicitous pair. The revelation struck Zalith like a thunderbolt, a jolt of disbelief surging through him. In that moment of realization, he grappled with the shock, the information settling in too late to alter the course of his actions.

Undeterred, Zalith seized one of the hearts, yanking it out with a swift, desperate motion. To his astonishment, rather than the anticipated defeat, a perverse amusement twisted Damien's expression. The grin that spread across Damien's face in response to Zalith's revelation only deepened the shock, leaving Zalith to grapple with the unsettling truth that the Daegelus was not what he seemed.

With a furious yell, Damien gripped the startled demon's wings and forced him back to the other side of the room. Zalith grunted when his back hit the wall; he gripped Damien's wrists with his hands, the Daegelus' clasp on his wings tightening. But he didn't show fear. He scowled in anger, glaring into Damien's eyes with just as much hatred.

"Did you think I'd let *you* get away, too, Eladarin?" Damien grinned. "Did you think I'd just let you defile my boy and walk off?" he laughed as he slowly pulled on the demon's right wing. "If you want to be with him so bad, I imagine you won't mind joining him in exile, will you?"

Zalith scowled in rage, gritting his teeth, trying to fight against Damien's strength, but his own power waned the longer the Daegelus kept his claws in him. His right wing began to tear, blood trickling down his back, and the pain was unlike anything he'd felt before—he couldn't keep himself from groaning painfully in response.

But before Damien could tear any further, the Daegelus suddenly stopped, and a look of struggle melted the grin off his face. He seemed to freeze, his hands trembling as he began to grimace and grit his teeth—but he didn't let go of Zalith, who tried to take the chance to break free. The Daegelus' body shivered as he tried to escape whatever was immobilizing him—and he seemed to know what *that* was. He took his eyes off Zalith, trying to turn his head to look back over his shoulder, a look of both fury and confusion on his face.

Alucard stood where he'd fallen, a gloomy, red-black mist beginning to seep from his skin. He held his hand towards Damien as if he were desperately reaching for something; *he* seemed to be the reason Damien couldn't move. With an agonized grunt, the vampire began to slowly drag the Daegelus towards himself.

Zalith watched in both relief and *awe*. He stumbled out of the Daegelus' grip and his back hit the wall; the force of Damien's attack had injured him more than he'd admit. But he was alive, his wings were intact, and he was fine enough to keep a hostile glare on his face as he watched Damien grunt and struggle while Alucard used his ethos to drag him further and further away.

But Alucard's fight didn't look like it was going to last much longer. The dark aura that surrounded him started to thin, and blood began to seep from his eyes in strain. A condescending grin appeared on Damien's face, but it withered into startlement when Alucard forced his left hand forward, throwing Damien across the room. With an infuriated yell, the Daegelus collided with the wall and crashed through it and into whatever room sat on the other side.

And then Alucard stumbled forward, placing his hand on the table to keep himself from dropping.

Zalith ignored his own pain, taking his eyes off the gaping hole in the wall where Damien had been thrown. He stared at Alucard—immediately, he wanted to go to him; he could see the sealing runes from his back spreading across his skin—they were draining his ethos and looked to be constricting him like snakes. *Of course* Damien had cursed him to feel pain when he tried to resist him. Zalith knew how to stop the runes, and he knew how to remove them, but he'd not get a chance to do anything.

Seconds later, Damien re-emerged from the wall with a horrific shriek of anger. He flew forward so fast that not even Zalith could do a thing to stop him. Before he knew it, Zalith was pinned against the wall, but this time, his trapper was Damien's ethos and not the Daegelus himself. Damien had Alucard, gripping his throat in his hand, pinning the vampire against the wall with such force that the room shook once more, the windows cracking, the floor shivering in his quake.

Damien wordlessly glared at Alucard, gritting his teeth as Alucard gripped his wrist with both his hands. The vampire couldn't breathe, he couldn't fight, and Zalith couldn't do *anything*. He tried—of course he tried. He attempted to counter the telekinesis that Damien was using to keep him against the wall, but he couldn't even seem to dent it. All he could do was stare in rage and desperation, gritting his teeth, not giving up in his attempts to free himself. But Alucard's struggle horrified him.

The vampire choked; the look of pain on his face was so intense that Zalith felt as if he could almost feel it himself. Alucard struggled, but Zalith could see that he was weakening as the Daegelus began to drag him up the wall so his feet no longer touched the ground.

"You…" Damien hissed, glaring at Alucard's face. "You're just like your creature of a father. I raised you for *sixteen* miserable, *repentant*, long fucking years, and *this* is how you repay me?!" he yelled, ignoring the vampire's desperate chokes. "Do you have *any* idea what it took for me to give my time to you?! Do you?!" he growled, tightening his grip. "You ungrateful, selfish, disgusting little shit!" he yelled, so furiously that his voice was distorted and like that of what he must sound like outside of this world—but he gripped Alucard's throat tighter, and as a quiet *crack* silenced the vampire's struggle, Alucard's hands slipped from Damien's wrist, falling to his sides as the life left his face.

Engulfed by a tsunami of horror and disbelief, Zalith felt the very core of his being freeze in a moment of unbearable agony—the nightmare he had dreaded unfolding before his eyes. Alucard, the object of his deepest affections, lay motionless, unresponsive to the world around him. The stark reality of Alucard's lifeless form sent shivers down Zalith's spine, each icy tremor resonating with the profound despair that gripped his soul.

In that agonizing instant, hope dwindled to nothingness. Alucard remained inert, devoid of the vitality that once animated him. Zalith's frantic gaze searched desperately for any sign of life, any flicker of the beloved aura that had now vanished. The crushing weight of despair pressed upon him, rendering him breathless in the face of a reality that he had prayed would never materialize. Alucard, the centre of his universe, had succumbed to an inexorable silence, leaving Zalith to confront a nightmarish void that echoed with the absence of the one he held most dear.

Damien snarled in disgust as he pulled Alucard's lifeless body away from the wall and threw him to the floor. The Daegelus grunted painfully, gripping the side of his body that Alucard's ethos had hit, and slowly dragged himself to where Alucard lay. "Get up!" he yelled, kicking the vampire's back, but Alucard remained still.

The despair engulfing Zalith was so agonizing that he felt like he might utter a sound of sorrow. But he didn't. As they always did, his feelings boiled into anger… anger that he focused on the Daegelus, who stood over Alucard's lifeless body and glared down at him.

"I said—" Damien snarled as he crouched and gripped the collar of Alucard's blazer, lifting him so that his face was inches from his own— "get up!"

As Alucard's eyes gradually opened, fixing on Damien with an unspoken defiance that resonated louder than words, a scoff of disappointment escaped the Daegelus. Though Alucard remained silent, Zalith's keen eyes discerned the undeniable truth—he was alive. A surge of relief coursed through him, a respite from the suffocating horror that had gripped him only moments ago. The pain in his heart began to ease, and for an instant, the world felt less bleak.

However, the fleeting relief was shadowed by the lingering threat that loomed over them. The danger hadn't dissipated; it lingered in the air like an ominous spectre. The realization that they were far from safety tempered Zalith's momentary respite, casting a sobering pall over the acknowledgement that Alucard, though alive, still faced an imminent peril.

Damien's snarl of revulsion echoed through the air as he released his grip on Alucard. The vampire's body met the floor, and the Daegelus loomed over him with a malevolent glare. Without hesitation, Damien's fist collided with the side of Alucard's face, coaxing a slow trickle of blood to escape from the vampire's mouth. The other side of Alucard's head made contact with the floor, a silent testament to the profound agony etched across his face as he staunchly withheld any audible expression of pain.

Unrelenting, Damien seized Alucard's jaw, forcefully turning his head to compel the vampire to meet his gaze once more. "Killing you here would be a mercy," he snarled, harshly pulling his hand from Alucard's jaw. "I'd rather not waste the energy."

Zalith stared in dread, Damien's ethos constricting him tighter and tighter as he watched Alucard choke on the blood filling his mouth.

Damien gripped the vampire's throat in his hands. "It looks like you're struggling, Aleksei." He grinned, watching as Alucard stuttered and choked, the blood seeping through his teeth trickling down the sides of his face. "Let me help you...." He smiled, pressing his index finger into the side of Alucard's face. He then pushed harshly, slowly turning Alucard's face to the side.

The vampire coughed and spat the blood from his mouth, a horrified, pained look on his face—but Damien then turned his head so he was looking back up at him again. Without any warning, Damien sunk all five of his claws into the left side of Alucard's waist. The vampire flinched violently, grimacing as he stared up at Damien.

"You won't be needing these anymore, will you?" he snarled. "Once my brother finds you, I'm sure he'll do well to make you understand that you're alone—more than you ever were. I'm not going to protect you anymore—no one is. You're not worth *my* time. You're not worth *anyone's* time," he growled cruelly as a black aura began surrounding the Daegelus' hand.

Zalith glared in horror—he knew what Damien was doing. He was removing the runes from Alucard's body, prying them like teeth from a mouth, each removal forcing Alucard to writhe and wince. And as the last came away, Damien snarled, stood up, and kicked Alucard's side one last time.

"If by some miracle my siblings don't find you, be sure that I'll come for you myself. Use this time to think about just how much you disappoint me, just how much pain you cause me. All I ever do is look after you, Aleksei, and you betray me for some pathetic, lowly demon?" he asked, a hint of loathing in his voice. "Why would you do that?" he questioned, glaring down at him. "Why would you do that?!" he yelled, stomping his foot down over Alucard's right horn. It snapped, breaking away from his head as Alucard yelped in agony, grimacing to muffle his pained cry—Zalith tried to burst forward, but that forced the ethos around him to tighten, making him grunt. Damien then crouched and glared into Alucard's eyes. "I'll tell you one final time, Aleksei. Maybe you can come home when you wake the fuck up and stop wasting your time with him. Until then, I wish you luck in evading my siblings."

Damien then stood up, glowering down at Alucard for a few moments. Then, with one final revolted glance in Zalith's direction, he disappeared as a blindingly bright flash of crimson lightning broke through the ceiling and wrapped itself around him. In the blink of an eye, he was gone, leaving Alucard alone with Zalith.

The moment Damien's ethos withered, freeing Zalith, he raced over and kneeled beside Alucard, afraid to put his hands on him. He desperately asked him if he was okay, what he could do, and if he needed anything, but Alucard didn't answer. The vampire stuttered and grunted, the pool of blood he lay in growing. And then, as tears began forming in them, Alucard closed his eyes and turned his head to the side.

As he watched Alucard's demon form wither, Zalith scowled in dismay. He hated seeing him like this—it hurt his heart. He wanted to tell him that everything would be okay, but he couldn't find the words. Instead, he gently lifted Alucard so that he was sitting and wrapped his arms around him. Alucard struggled, but he managed to lift his arms to hold Zalith in return, tightly gripping the back of his shirt, and then he cried into his shoulder, his body trembling in Zalith's grip.

Zalith clung to Alucard with a desperate grip, as if his embrace alone could shield the vampire from the crushing defeat etched across his face. The sight of compliance on Alucard's face cut deep, a disheartening and agonizing blow to Zalith's core. There had been no attempt at verbal or physical defence from Alucard as Damien ruthlessly denied him the chance to explain. The motives behind this brutal assault seemed senseless and unjust, leaving Zalith bewildered and infuriated.

The unsettling realization loomed—the palpable aura of trauma suggested that this wasn't the first instance of such cruelty. The vampire's reaction, his subdued responses, and the silent endurance of the abuse painted a grim picture. Zalith sensed that Damien had subjected Alucard to this torment for a *long* time, a revelation that fuelled both dismay and simmering anger within him. Yet, amidst the overwhelming emotions, Zalith vowed not to succumb to the darkness at this moment. His immediate focus was on Alucard, a determination to ensure his well-being in the aftermath of the turmoil they faced.

He wanted to hold him, to tell him that it was going to be okay and that he wasn't going to *ever* let Damien or anyone do anything like this to him again. Despite knowing that he wasn't powerful enough to stop someone like Damien, he knew that he'd find a way. He'd do whatever he could to keep Alucard from suffering any more than he already had. He didn't care what it would take. He'd do it. But again, he'd not sink into his anger yet.

Looking down at Alucard with a sullen frown, he held him tightly, resting the side of his head on Alucard's as the vampire buried his face into his shoulder. "Alucard," he said quietly, listening to the vampire's struggled, muffled breathing. "It's okay," he said—it was all he could manage to say right now… because it *would* be okay.

He'd make it okay.

No matter what.

Chapter Sixty-Six

― ⸲ ✝ ⸱ ―

Zalith

| **Zalith** |

Zalith lay silently beside Alucard, who rested with his head on his shoulder. An hour had passed since he helped the vampire up to his room and cleaned his wounds; he'd offered him his blood, but Alucard had refused. Zalith wouldn't pressure him, though. He wanted to let him sleep.

The demon glared up at the ceiling, sinking into his thoughts. After what he witnessed, he'd lost whatever sense of loyalty he had to Damien—that *creature*. He didn't deserve the respect that people gave him, he didn't deserve the people who were loyal to him, or to be a god, and above all, he didn't deserve Alucard. Zalith knew that Damien would come back for Alucard someday, and the vampire would be forced to believe that he *had* to go back and obey him. Zalith wasn't going to let that happen.

With a sullen frown, he glanced down at his vampire. His ice-pale skin was smothered in black and blue bruises and slowly healing cuts and gashes—he didn't deserve any of it. His physical wounds weren't Zalith's main concern, though; yes, Alucard was in pain, and he *hated* that, but what mattered most was what damage Damien had done to Alucard's mind, to his very being. There was no doubt in Zalith's mind that Damien had been doing this to Alucard for years—decades, centuries…maybe forever. He couldn't be sure how long, but it had clearly been going on long enough to cause Alucard to act the way he had—to act as though he had to stand there and take it as though it was deserved.

Zalith looked back up at the ceiling; he didn't want to try to calm his simmering, smouldering anger. In no way could Alucard ever deserve the shit Damien did to him— and the fact that Alucard seemed to believe he did forced Zalith to feel both enraged and despondent, and it made him wonder just how much damage Damien had done all these years. What had he and his abuse done to Alucard? There were so many things that Zalith felt he could connect to it, but he wouldn't. He'd not assume.

Remorse began to weigh on Zalith's mind. He felt as if he should have done something more, that he should have tried harder to help Alucard. He should have tried harder to break free from Damien's influence—he should have done more; he should have known that a creature like Damien wouldn't be so simple as to have one heart. He felt like an idiot for assuming it would be easy to kill him, and Alucard had suffered for that in his place because the vampire had pulled Damien away from him.

Alucard had risked his life to stop Damien from hurting Zalith, and as grateful as he was, he couldn't let go of his guilt. But he'd not sink into it. His focus was on Damien.

Damien....

He was going to *kill* Damien. He didn't care what it took or what he would have to do. He was going to kill him—there was always a way to kill something, even a god. That creature had caused Alucard so much pain—*too* much pain—and Zalith wasn't going to let it happen a single time more. There wasn't a thing he wouldn't do to protect Alucard, to protect the man he loved with every piece of his heart, of his *soul*.

He couldn't keep his thoughts from shifting.

To Alucard was where they wandered. Alucard, the vampire he loved so truly, so intensely; what he felt for Alucard was as real as he thought love might be. For Alucard, he'd do anything—die, even, and to risk his life to find a way to kill Damien was doing just that, wasn't it? He'd die to save Alucard from the misery that Damien caused him. He'd do anything to make sure that he was safe, to make sure he felt loved, appreciated, and all the things he deserved to feel—pain was not one of them, and Zalith would eradicate it from his life as best he could.

His life—Zalith wanted to spend *his* life with Alucard. The thought felt abrupt, strange to come to him in his moment of processing anger. But he couldn't *not* think about it, about how he loved Alucard, how he would do anything for him, how he wanted him to be as happy as he could possibly make him, and how he'd do anything to make sure that he was safe; how he wanted to spend every moment with him, and how Alucard made him feel every kind of happiness there was—how he made him feel every kind of want and need and desire, how everything Zalith could ever want and need was right beside him.

He looked down at Alucard, his anger completely withering. He tightened his embrace around him, his need to protect him at all times becoming intense. And then, he watched in confusion as a thin, black, snake-like rune appeared on the left side of Alucard's face; it started spreading down his neck and over his body. The faint, fire-like glow that shimmered behind it confirmed that it was exactly what Zalith had first thought, and as he watched his imprint slowly fade into Alucard's skin—where it would remain for as long as Zalith existed—a sensation of both possession and determination gripped him. Alucard was *his* in more ways than one, and nothing would take him away.

But before he could start thinking about how happy it made him knowing that he'd finally found his mate, his thoughts shifted *again*, and anger replaced his contentedness.

Damien was going to die, Alucard would be safe, and Zalith would be responsible for both of those facts.

Safe—he had to make sure the other Numen wouldn't find Alucard, too. Damien removed all the runes from Alucard's body, and Zalith was sure that one of them was responsible for keeping him hidden from the Numen. But Zalith knew a mage capable of creating something that would hide Alucard, something that would keep his aura hidden from *everyone*, even the Numen. Finding that mage would be the first thing he did once Alucard was ready to leave. They couldn't stay there too long; he was sure that the Numen would descend soon. After everything Alucard had said, Zalith was certain that it wouldn't take the Numen long to locate his vampire, and he wasn't going to let that happen.

He then felt Alucard stir; the vampire frowned, a pained but quiet murmur upon his voice as he struggled to make himself comfortable. Zalith waited until Alucard fell silent again after moving his face closer to the demon's neck with a quiet, uncomfortable sigh. Zalith thought he wanted to say something, but what? For once, he didn't know what to say; all he wanted to do was lay there and hold his vampire. They could have both died, they could have lost one another, but there they were…together, just as fate had intended.

Fate…. He'd spent years defying its existence, convinced that he'd never find the man he'd spend his life with. But fate had come through, it had proven him wrong, and now that he'd found his mate, now that his love lay in his embrace, he'd do whatever it took to ensure that he never lost him.

| **Alucard** |

Alucard couldn't fall back asleep. He felt sore, exhausted, and empty. He lay there with his arm around Zalith, holding him as tightly as his injuries would let him, listening to the quiet beating of his heart. But the longer he listened, the less relaxed it made him feel; a familiar craving enthralled him, but he didn't let it take him. He didn't want Zalith's blood—well, of course he wanted it, but he couldn't have it. It would heal him faster, and Damien wouldn't want that.

The things he'd done…. He'd defied Damien. He fought back to keep him from hurting Zalith. The thought of Damien hurting the man he loved had awoken something inside him—his instincts had screamed at him, giving him the strength he needed to resist. And he had. Despite the pain it caused him, he'd managed to ignore Damien's rule over him and force him away from Zalith. He shouldn't have been able to—even Zalith shouldn't have been able to defy Damien's rule, but somehow, they both had.

However, he couldn't help but fear the repercussions. Damien had abandoned him. He'd removed all the runes protecting him from the Numen *and* from himself… and he wasn't sure what might become of him now. He felt so vulnerable—more than he ever had… like the gates of Hell had opened around him and no key was in sight for its lock. The terror pooled in his stomach, angst started to consume him, and the longer he lay there, the deeper he sunk into despair.

But he deserved it. All of it. He *always* deserved it. He was weak, stupid, and pathetic. He deserved to be abandoned, he deserved everything Damien said and did to him. And whatever was going to happen now… he deserved that, too.

He opened his eyes, staring at what he could see of Zalith. He wasn't sure how long he'd been sleeping or how long the demon had been lying wide awake; all he was sure about was the fact that, with Zalith, despite what happened, he still felt safe, and that was all he needed right now.

After a few moments of silence, Zalith slowly and carefully placed his hand on Alucard's head, caressing his hair. "How are you feeling?" he asked quietly, a despondent tone in his voice.

Alucard frowned slightly. He didn't know what to say; he didn't know how he was feeling. He just felt… empty. Without thought, without a voice. He just wanted to lay there in the quiet.

Zalith glanced down at him "Is there anything you need?"

Was there anything he needed? He didn't know. He didn't want to think.

His lack of an answer made Zalith hug him a little tighter. "Alucard," he said, a hint of sincerity to his voice. "I *want* you to drink some of my blood."

Alucard tensed up, a frown starting to appear on his face. "No."

"You don't have to lay here in unnecessary pain."

Alucard struggled but rolled over, taking his head off Zalith's shoulder. "You don't understand," he snapped quietly and pulled the blanket up to cover everything but his head.

"What do I not understand?"

The vampire gripped the blanket tightly and scowled. "I can't."

Zalith frowned again and leaned closer to him. "Yes, you can. Why would you not be able to?"

Alucard scowled in confliction as he held his eyes shut. He didn't want to tell Zalith that Damien would punish him more if he found out he'd consumed blood to heal his body faster. He didn't want to talk about Damien—he didn't even want to think about him right now. He deserved the pain he was in, and he wouldn't do anything to make it easier.

"Alucard."

"What?" he snarled.

Zalith placed his hand on the vampire's shoulder. "Why can't you drink my blood?"

His repeated question forced Alucard to think about the answer; he didn't want to, but he couldn't fight it. He couldn't keep himself from thinking about Damien and what he'd done, and it made him angrier than he felt he should be. He just wanted to lay there in silence without having to think about his pain, about the Daegelus. But Zalith wouldn't let it go. And he didn't know what to say. He opened his eyes, staring at the wall across from where he lay. He didn't want to tell him why… but what use was lying?

He frowned despondently and looked down at the pillow he was resting his head on. "Because…" he said quietly, "I have to wait," he mumbled. He was sure that Zalith was going to ask what he had to wait for, so he'd save him the energy. "I have to heal by myself."

"Why?" Zalith asked confusedly.

Anger began to outweigh Alucard's dismay. He scowled again, glaring at the wall again. But he didn't want to yell at Zalith; he didn't want to raise his voice in any way; he didn't want to let his anger break free. So, he closed his eyes, taking a moment to calm down before answering. "Because it's what Damien wants," he said sullenly. "I'm supposed to feel the pain for as long as it will last. If I don't, he'll do worse."

"Alucard, that's insane," Zalith exclaimed. He took a deep breath and caressed Alucard's head as he softly said, "Damien seemed quite done with you before he left, so I'm sure he isn't going to come back any time soon. It'll be fine."

"I don't want to talk about him anymore," Alucard insisted.

Zalith sighed as he took his hand off Alucard's head. "Okay," he said, a reluctant tone in his voice—it was obvious he didn't agree with Alucard's decision to end the conversation.

That only irritated Alucard more. He was sure he'd made it clear that talking about Damien made him feel worse than he already did, and Zalith's hesitance to drop the subject made him feel—for the lack of a better word—uncomfortable. Before, he'd been fine with Zalith's tendency to intrude, but right now, he didn't welcome it, and the fact that Zalith was discontent with his desire to stop talking about it angered him.

With an irritated but sullen glare on his face, he abruptly tried to get up so that he could find somewhere he wouldn't be hounded with questions, but the second he sat up, his entire body writhed in agony, so much that it forced him to remain sitting where he was, gripping his right side as the pain grew worse with each passing moment. He tried not to utter a sound, but his breaths became stifled.

Zalith instantly sat up and moved closer, placing his hand on Alucard's shoulder. "Careful," he said sullenly, worry in his voice.

Alucard then frowned despondently. He wasn't sure why he felt like he wanted to leave. His conflicting feelings were all over the place—his anger, his pain, his sadness—and he didn't know what to do with any of it. All he wanted to do was be with Zalith, the only man in the world he trusted. Despite his irritating need to ask questions Alucard didn't want to answer, it didn't change how safe Zalith made him feel.

He pouted sadly and stubbornly as he turned his body so that he could wrap his arms around the demon.

Zalith wrapped his arms around the vampire, holding him tightly. "I'm so sorry this happened," he said quietly. "If there was anything I could do to have stopped it, I would have. But no matter what that beast says, you're *not* alone. I'm here, and I'm not going anywhere. I love you, and I'll do whatever I can to keep you safe and happy," he said softly, resting the side of his head on Alucard's.

Tightening his grip on the back of Zalith's shirt, Alucard buried his face in the demon's shoulder. "I want to go home," he said quietly, his voice sullen and muffled. "I don't want to be here anymore."

"Okay. We can go home," he mumbled sadly before gently kissing the side of Alucard's head. Then, as Alucard moved back ever so slightly so that he could see his face, Zalith placed his hand on the side of the vampire's face and kissed him again. He climbed out of bed and moved to help Alucard get up. "We can gather what you need to bring with you, and then we can head back," he said as Alucard slowly stood in front of him.

But before either of them could say another word, the stifling air morphed abruptly into an icy foreboding. In an instant, Alucard was wrenched from Zalith's grasp, the abruptness of the act propelling the demon backwards, slamming against the wall. The atmosphere cracked with tension, leaving a trail of unsettling silence in its wake.

Alucard didn't care who grabbed him. He stared over at Zalith, who had both his arms pinned against the wall by two demons. Their eyes were blush-red, pupils sharp and thin like a cat's; upon their backs, wings as black as night and much like those of a dragon, and atop their heads, horns just as black but with a shimmer of red in the light of the room's candles. He knew who they were…and Zalith seemed to know, too. The look of anger on his face told Alucard that.

And then the vampire turned his head to look at the woman who had *him* pinned against the wall. She held his bruised throat, her white hair flowing down to her waist. She grinned excitedly, staring into Alucard's horrified eyes.

Lilith.

Zalith snarled furiously; Alucard looked over at him, watching as he pulled his left arm free to grab the throat of one of the demons as they both growled in response—

Lilith turned her head, setting her blush-red eyes on the commotion, and as a smile appeared upon her devilish, crimson lips, she laughed quietly. "Don't make me have to hurt the baby." She giggled, tightening her grip on Alucard's throat as the vampire struggled to breathe, but even if he had to strength to, he couldn't fight her.

Zalith glared at her as she stood in front of Alucard, another quiet, hostile snarl escaping his voice as he visibly forced himself to calm down. The two demons who hadn't done very well to restrain him pinned him back against the wall, both of them eyeing him in revolt as he kept his eyes on Lilith and Alucard, watching as she slowly turned her head to look at the vampire.

The white-haired Numen folded her small, carmine-red wings against her back and dragged her clawed finger over the slowly healing gash on the side of Alucard's face. She was a little less than half a foot shorter than he was, leaning on her tiptoes to get her face as close to his as possible. The horns on her head were just as red as her wings, curving back sharply at their tips, a small horn breaking away at either base of them. She wasn't wearing much at all—thigh-high boots, leather straps around most of her body, but with skin space in between to create a corset. She also donned a garter, and a white bikini-like bra accompanied by a white thong. Her long, thin, snake-like tail wrapped around Alucard's right leg as she leaned her face nearer to his.

She looked much different to how she appeared when he was a child—he didn't care to know why. All he knew was that right now, he felt just as uncomfortable as he felt when Ada had thrown herself at him. But he couldn't throw Lilith away. As much as he wanted to, Lilith was a Numen, and the last thing he wanted to do was upset her—there was no telling what she might do to him, or worse, to Zalith. As she leaned her face closer, he turned his head, glaring over at the window. He didn't know enough about her to know whether or not she'd react violently if he acted defensively, so the best he could do was try to avoid her strange affection.

Lilith smiled, stroking her fingers over his sore cheek. "I wouldn't believe that you were the same little Caedis I rescued from that hole all those years ago if it wasn't for this delightfully red hair of yours," she murmured and giggled, flicking a lock of his hair with the top fold of her right wing. She then gasped theatrically and pouted sympathetically. "Who did this to my little baby?" she asked with a babyish tone, stroking her hand over one of the bruises on his right shoulder. "Was it Damien?" she questioned, a revolted look on her face. She then leaned most of her body against Alucard's and looked over at Zalith. "Won't you speak for him?" she asked with a frown on her face. "He's an awfully shy little boy."

Alucard took his eyes off the wall to glance at Zalith. The demon was already looking at him, and as he clearly understood the vampire's look of disagreement, Zalith set his eyes on Lilith.

"Why is it any of your business?" he asked, ignoring the irritated growls of the two demons keeping him against the wall.

Amused, Lilith giggled quietly and looked at Alucard. "I'd just like to know who I have to kill for doing so much...damage to this poor baby," she said with a pout as she stroked the side of Alucard's face again. When he scowled in discomfort, she sighed and stood up straight, unwrapping her tail from around his leg. She then tapped her clawed fingers against her chin, glancing at Zalith, whom she kept her eyes on for a few moments. But she soon looked back at Alucard, who kept his eyes on the wall to his right. "Why don't you look at me, Caedis?" she asked. "Look at me."

Slowly, he took his eyes off the wall and looked down at her. As soon as her eyes lit up with satisfaction, he felt his discomfort grow. He still didn't know much about her—he'd only met her *once* when he was a child—but from this short encounter, he was sure that Lilith was going to continue to make him feel as though he'd rather jump out the window and hit the ground face-first just to get away from her.

She smiled and placed her hand on his bare chest, flicking his crucifix with her fingers as she leaned her face into his. "Where have you been all these years? I told you I'd come back for you once I dealt with those horrible people, but you were...just gone." She pouted sadly as she dragged her fingers over several of his bruises. "There was a rumour that nasty Damien took you away to join his little collection of exceptionally blooded babies. Is that where you were?"

He didn't answer—he couldn't. He was cast out from demon society; speaking to her would be disrespectful, and despite the fact that he didn't care that *he* was a demon, he'd not speak out of line. Even if he *could* speak to her, though, he felt he as if wouldn't answer her questions. He didn't trust her. So what if she helped him when he was a child? Just like the other Numen, she was here to use him—he knew that for sure.

Lilith frowned as she looked back over at Zalith and waited with an expectant look on her face. But Alucard wasn't sure why she was looking to him to answer for him. In demon law, an exiled demon's mate could answer for them, but Alucard had only imprinted on Zalith; that didn't make them mates in the eyes of the demon world; Zalith would have had to have imprinted on him, too, and Alucard was convinced that he hadn't.

Zalith glared at her. "I don't know anything about that," he answered.

Scowling, Lilith looked back up at Alucard. "Why did he leave you, Caedis? After all these years, why did he throw you away?"

Alucard took his eyes off Lilith, staring down at the floor in confliction, but as she pressed her body against his once again, he scowled uncomfortably. If it were anyone else, he'd shove them away so harshly that they'd know not to ever lay a hand on him again. But it was Lilith, and not only could he *not* touch her, he just wouldn't.

Zalith scowled as he watched Lilith place her hand on Alucard's arm. "Do you mind?" he snarled.

Lilith slowly took her hand off Alucard and looked over at him. She giggled in amusement and replied, "I don't, no. Do *you*?"

"Yes," he growled with an irritated frown.

Giggling again, she took her eyes off him and looked at Alucard. "I don't think your little friend likes me," she whispered.

Zalith scowled and questioned, "What do you want?"

"What do *I* want?" she asked, looking over at him. "What do *you* want?"

"I want you to back off and stop touching him," he warned.

Lilith lost her scowl and laughed slightly as she looked back up at Alucard, who kept his eyes on the floor. "Why would I want to do that? He doesn't look like he wants that— *do* you?" She smiled, stroking the side of his face with her fingers.

Zalith scowled with hostility. "You have the use of your eyes," he snarled. "I'm sure you can see you're making him uncomfortable."

She sighed irritably and turned her head to look over at Zalith as if he was an inconvenience. Zalith glared right back at her with the same expression but with much more hostility in his eyes.

But then one of the demons holding him looked at her and said, "There isn't much time left, My Queen."

That was right. Alucard knew that Damien could only remain in this world for so long before it started to drain his ethos, and it seemed as though it was the same for Lilith.

Lilith sighed quietly and dragged her hand down his body, and then she snatched his hand. "Come, sweet Caedis, we will return to my home." She pulled him away from the wall. "I'll help you feel better, and I'll also make sure none of my horrible, awful siblings find you—especially Damien. You want that, don't you? I'll keep you safe." She then looked over at Zalith. "Make sure *he* stays."

The moment she said that, Zalith snarled and began to pull free from the two demons as they tried their very best to restrain him.

Alucard didn't want to leave without Zalith. He didn't want to leave at all, but he knew that he had no choice. If he said he wouldn't go with her, she'd be a lot less calm than she currently was, and he'd rather her think he was coming willingly so that later he'd have fewer eyes on him when he tried to work out what to do to get away from her and the rest of the Numen that were surely coming for him. Going with her *would* keep him safe from the other Numen, but there was no telling what she wanted him for. She wasn't here to simply help him heal and hide him from her siblings. Like them, she was after something.

But he didn't care right now. He didn't care about anything other than Zalith, and he didn't want to leave him behind. Not only was it because he knew that the demon would most likely start a war to find him, but because he didn't want to be alone right now— he *never* wanted to be without him, no matter where he was.

Lilith was going to take him to her home—her castle in her own little domain. Once he was healed, he'd work out how to get away from her and how to evade being found again. But how could he tell Lilith he'd not go without Zalith? He wasn't supposed to talk to her, but… what choice did he have?

As she tugged on his hand, pulling him towards the door, he stopped following her. "I want him to co—"

Lilith's hand smacked the side of his face, silencing him as the force of her slap made him turn his head to his left. He then slowly turned his head, setting his sights on her. When his eyes met her disgusted gaze, he frowned in confliction, attempting to silence his quickly growing anger. What was he expecting? He wasn't allowed to talk to her; of course she was going to react in such a way.

But he had to let her know that he wouldn't leave Zalith, who'd stopped fighting Lilith's cronies the moment her hand hit the vampire's face. Zalith glared at her with such evil in his eyes that Alucard was sure he was about to throw himself at her. But he didn't.

Lilith took her eyes off Alucard and looked at Zalith. She then sighed and looked back up at Alucard. "He can come."

The moment Lilith agreed to Alucard's request, Zalith abruptly pulled free from the two demons trying to keep him where he was and snarled irritably at them both as they backed off. He didn't waste much time in joining Alucard, either. On his way over, he snatched one of the vampire's shirts from a nearby cabinet and placed it over Alucard's shoulders as he began to follow him and Lilith out of his room. The two demons followed closely behind, keeping their eyes on them both.

Once he had the majority of his shirt buttons tied, Lilith took hold of Alucard's hand, pulling him along with her as she made her way towards the stairs that would lead them down to the hall. But Zalith quickly snatched his hand from hers, scowling down at her as she looked back at him with a look just as hostile. Alucard didn't want them to start fighting… but he was sure that it was inevitable.

Chapter Sixty-Seven

— ⋞ ✝ ⋟ —

Lilith

| **Alucard** |

Alucard and Zalith followed Lilith as she led them into her domain—a realm that sat between the worlds of the living and the dead. Guiding them through a rift akin to the demonic portals they were familiar with, they found themselves thrust into their demon forms. As their eyes adjusted, they glanced around the empty, dark cavern and beheld the imposing, towering doors of a concealed chamber, seamlessly integrated into the crimson rock ahead of them.

Behind them, the rift vanished, and they made their way towards the doors. While they waited for them to open, the white-haired woman turned to face Alucard and Zalith, eyeing them fondly. She seemed pleased to see Zalith in his demon form, but when her sights fixed on Alucard, her face contorted into a revolted grimace.

But Alucard kept a vacant stare. He'd lived without his wings for long enough to know how demons would look at him, to know what they would see him as, and he just didn't have the strength to care anymore. He didn't have the strength to care about anything. Lilith's disgust and that of the two guards at the doors would be the first of many derogatory stares.

Instead of sinking into despondency within the gaze of Lilith's disgusted demons, he turned his head ever so slightly to glance at Zalith, who was glaring at Lilith with such hostility that Alucard was sure the demon would be attacking her if it were anyone else.

"Don't worry," Lilith said with a smile, patting Alucard's right shoulder and making him flinch painfully. "I'll fix you."

Alucard wasn't sure what 'fix' meant, but he *was* sure that he didn't want whatever Lilith was going to offer him. He didn't want to fall into whatever game she was playing—he didn't want to let her feel as though she was winning, and he didn't want her to make him feel as though he owed her. He didn't want anything to do with any of the Numen, but whatever she had prepared for him, he was certain that he'd not be able to refuse. She may be acting kind right now, but he knew that it was a façade. No Numen would treat him this way, not even Lilith.

He took his eyes off her and stared down at the ground. He wasn't sure where he might end up now—where Zalith would end up—but a part of him had no strength to wonder. Zalith was here with him, and that was all he wanted to focus on. Damien had taken everything else from him; he'd do whatever it took to hold onto the one thing he had left, the one thing that meant more to him than anything else.

Zalith took his anger-filled eyes off Lilith and glanced at Alucard. Alucard didn't know how to react to the worried expression on his face, so he just looked down at the floor again.

"Come," Lilith then said as she turned her back to them and began leading the way through the doors.

When Alucard started following, Zalith mirrored his strides, steadily closing the distance between them. The yawning doors swung wide, unveiling an abyssal arena teeming with a cacophony of demons. Diverse in size and species, the frenzied crowd clamoured for Lilith's notice. She navigated the expansive platform, traversing toward a throne hewn from a towering black crystal positioned at the room's farthest extremity.

The ceiling, walls, and the darkness below were occupied by her followers, all of whom began to mutter, hiss, and snarl in revolt as they laid their eyes on Alucard. The vampire ignored them as best he could, but he heard Zalith snarl *very* quietly. He could practically feel Zalith's anger, but he wasn't able to tell him not to start something that would get them both killed. All he could do was hope that Zalith would refrain from attacking everyone.

But…instead of starting a war, Zalith slowly stretched out his left, unscathed wing, wrapped it around Alucard, and pulled him closer, taking hold of the vampire's hand as he walked beside him. He kept his wing around him, concealing him from most of the eyes of Lilith's spectators, but it didn't lift Alucard's despondent mood. The crowd might not be able to see but trying to hide only made it worse. The crowd *laughed* at Zalith's kindness, and that hurt Alucard's heart.

They soon reached the end of the platform, where Lilith stopped walking and turned to face them. Zalith evidently suspected that she was about to try and take Alucard from him, so he wrapped both his arms around the vampire, ignoring the repulsed looks of the six demons lined up on either side of Lilith's throne; three on the left, three on the right—four once the two that had accompanied Lilith joined them. The room also started to quieten down as everyone watched the Numen confront Zalith.

"Come, little Caedis," Lilith invited, reaching out her hand towards Alucard.

But the vampire ignored her. He kept his arms around Zalith, not at all interested in listening to whatever it was that Lilith had to say. Zalith obviously had no intention of letting go, either.

Lilith's discontent was palpable. With an impatient snarl, she seized Alucard's wrist, attempting to wrench him from Zalith's embrace. The demon responded with a low growl, issuing a warning glare at the determined woman. Undeterred, Lilith scoffed and pulled with such force that not even Zalith could impede her. Alucard was abruptly torn from his grasp, and in the ensuing commotion, as Zalith stumbled, Lilith mercilessly propelled Alucard toward her throne. The vampire, grunting quietly in pain, was cruelly forced onto his knees, and he didn't make any attempts to get up. He knew where he belonged.

The moment Alucard was taken from Zalith's grip, the demon moved to attack, but *four* of Lilith's demons pounced forward and grabbed him before he could move an inch more.

"Don't make me have to hurt him," Lilith warned, glaring at Zalith, who glowered back at her. She then looked down at Alucard. "Stay there," she hissed, pointing at him.

Alucard took his sights off Zalith and stared down at the floor, holding onto his right arm with his left hand as blood started to seep through his white shirt; one of his healing wounds had torn. He sat there, waiting, ignoring the degrading mutters from the room around him as best he could. He felt a hint of desire to argue and fight, but where would that get him? He wasn't nearly strong enough right now to do much at all, let alone take on a Numen and attempt to escape not only by himself but with Zalith, too. As much as he might like to get away from this, he knew he couldn't. Not yet.

"Why did Damien do this?" Lilith asked sadly as she slowly sat on her crystal-carved throne and glowered down at Alucard.

The vampire couldn't answer, and even if he could, he wouldn't tell her what she wanted to know.

"Did you anger him again?" she asked, smirking.

He frowned in confliction, keeping his eyes on the floor.

Lilith giggled and held out her hand towards one of the demons who had been with her when she'd collected Alucard. "Give it to me," she said. Once the demon reached into his pocket and handed her something, she crouched in front of Alucard. "I found this in the entrance to your little castle," she said with a smile, holding out his right horn in both her hands. "Do you want it back?"

His irritancy grew. She knew that he couldn't answer, so why did she continue to ask questions? Was she enjoying toying with him? Of course she was.

Giggling again, she patted his head with one of her hands. "Of course you do," she said, dragging her hand from the top of his head and to the side of his face. "You'll be my pretty little boy again soon enough." Then, she placed the snapped horn on the base, which still protruded from Alucard's head; she wrapped both her hands around it, and a faint, black glow slithered around them. She effortlessly healed the horn back onto his head, and once it was in place, she let go and smiled, placing both her hands on either side of his face, which she then lifted so that he'd look up at her. "You can look at me now."

Alucard felt less hideous now that he had both his horns, but his lack of wings still made him feel disgusting in the midst of Lilith's temple. He could still feel the revolted looks of every demon on him, but he didn't have the strength to care. His appearance didn't bother Zalith, and that was all that mattered to him.

When Lilith stood up and backed off slightly, she took a deep breath and smiled. "There you go. But your wings—you tried so hard to get them back from Damien, didn't you?" she asked with a sympathetic tone. "You worked so hard, yet he didn't give you what you wanted," she said as the demons behind her snickered quietly.

She was clearly trying to hide her amusement, too, and it made Alucard feel worse knowing that she was playing with him. He wasn't sure why he'd thought just for a moment that she was actually trying to help because she cared; it was probably because there was a single time when he was a boy that he trusted her and seeing her after so long still confused him. But she was a Numen, and he couldn't let his guard down because she'd conveniently helped him *once*.

"You can pick…the wings of anyone here, and they will be yours," she said, looking down at him. "But not my beautiful, hand-crafted scions," she said, glancing at the eight nearby demons. "Once you're fixed, you can begin your life with me. I'll treat you *much* better than Damien, I can assure you." She tapped her chin with her clawed fingers, but as Alucard failed to even glance at anyone else in the room, she frowned impatiently. "Don't be shy," she said. "Look."

He didn't want to.

Lilith snarled irritably and moved forward; she snatched his chin in her hand and pulled him up to his feet. She then forcefully turned his head so that he'd look up. "Look at them. Pick one of them," she insisted. "I'll not have you looking like this anymore."

Alucard glanced at Zalith, who was still trying to escape from the four scions who were holding him back. It was very clear that he wanted to hurt Lilith, but it wouldn't get either of them anywhere. Alucard wasn't going to give in and do what she wanted, though. He took his eyes off Zalith and shook his head from her grip. He then glared down at the floor in hopes she'd understand he wasn't interested.

With a look of disgust on her face, Lilith scoffed and shoved him back. As he stumbled, one of Lilith's scions made his way over and forced him back onto his knees. He grimaced painfully, and as much as he wanted to snarl at the man for touching him, any sound he uttered would result in another wound upon his body. He didn't want that.

She then tutted irritably as she slumped back down in her seat. "Would you calm down?" she growled at Zalith, who was still trying to escape the now *five* men attempting to restrain him. "He's fine, look," she said, waving her hand in Alucard's direction. She then rolled her eyes and said, "If he doesn't want the wings now, I won't force him. He'll change his mind, though; they always do." She sighed and rested her left leg over her right. "And you?" she asked Zalith, her eyes shifting to his right, injured wing, which was almost draping at his side. "Would you like me to fix your little broken wing?"

Zalith calmed down a little but continued glaring at her. "Fine," he snarled.

Lilith smiled, held her hand to her lips, and then laughed loudly in amusement. The entire room laughed with her, but when she noticed that all the laughter didn't affect Zalith at all, she frowned and silenced everyone. She then looked down at Alucard, who had taken his eyes off her to look at Zalith. Something of an irritated frown clung to her face, but she soon set a skeptical gaze back on Zalith. "Would you so happen to know what happened to all of my *other* children? The ones you see before you now were created not too long ago because *something* or *someone* killed my previous creations— coincidently, *you* are the only one to have lived. Why is that?"

Zalith glared at her. "I have no idea," he answered.

She scoffed and set her eyes back on Alucard. "Whatever, I have no interest in you," she dismissed. "If he resists again, kill him."

The five scions holding Zalith glared and growled at him in anger as he rolled his eyes in response to Lilith's threat.

"Caedis," she said with a smile, inviting Alucard to look at her, and as he did, she rested the side of her face in her hand. "How long has Damien had his place in Aegisguard?"

Alucard stared at her for a few moments. He wasn't sure why it had only just hit him that Lilith had now secured her place in Aegisguard—how else would she have been able to walk up there? That meant Ephriel was stuck out in the void, though... as was Lucifer, and Alucard was sure they'd all fight world-shattering battles to try and take each other's places.

The vampire knew that Letholdus didn't like Lilith, which meant he was likely to help Ephriel defeat her, thus securing Ephriel's place in Aegisguard. *That* had to be why Lilith had come for Alucard as soon as she had; Lilith *knew* something like that would happen, and she'd need Alucard's help to fight Letholdus. And if Damien also learned that Letholdus was choosing to help another Numen, then the Daegelus would come looking to get Alucard back as a defence for himself. After all, if Letholdus went after one of them, he'd surely come after another.

This was just the very beginning of it all, and the thought of it made Alucard feel a whole lot more exhausted than he already did. He was just a tool to them. A weapon. A way for them to survive.

"Well?" Lilith asked.

He didn't want to answer, nor could he. Why did she keep asking him when she knew that he wouldn't answer?

Lilith rolled her eyes and looked at Zalith. "Hello?" she snarled. "Speak for him."

Zalith then scowled. "Why do you assume I know what's going on in his head?"

Glaring at him, she scoffed. "Isn't that the point of imprinting? Of being his mate? If we can even call it that," she insulted and then giggled, as did those around her. "You *have* bonded, have you not? He should be telling you what to say for him...." She then paused, her eyes shifting back and forth between them. And then, she gasped excitedly. "Aw, how sweet. The little baby didn't know." She sat up straight and sighed loudly. "How... awkward," she mumbled. "How annoyingly inconvenient."

Alucard took his eyes off Lilith and glared down at the floor. Had she just said that Zalith had imprinted on *him*? He wasn't sure why it surprised him so much—it confounded him. Maybe it was because he thought something like that would never happen to him, for someone to imprint on *him*, especially someone he loved as much as he loved Zalith. It was almost too good to be true, and a part of him felt as though Lilith was simply toying with them both in search of entertaining reactions.

But now Zalith knew *he* had imprinted on him, and he wasn't sure what that information must be doing to the demon. Alucard wasn't sure if it made Zalith feel uncomfortable, to be claimed in such a way, especially someone as broken and shamed as Alucard. He was sure Zalith felt uncomfortable, and Lilith most likely thought that too and had revealed it in an attempt to make Zalith react poorly.

The demon didn't react, though—at least not verbally. Alucard kept his eyes on the floor, too afraid to see whatever expression might have appeared on Zalith's face.

Lilith then exhaled deeply as she leaned back in her throne. "This isn't going anywhere," she muttered, glaring at Alucard. "Caedis," she then said, and as he looked at her, she frowned in something that looked to be concern. "I will give you somewhere you can rest, somewhere you can think about the answers to my questions. You've been through so much lately." She pouted sadly. "But... make sure your boyfriend over there knows what to say. I'll be asking again in the morning. And don't get any ideas; you're not to leave my home." She waved her hand, signalling her five scions to let go of Zalith.

As soon as they let go of him, Zalith barged past them and rushed to Alucard; he helped him to stand and held him tightly as he glared at Lilith, wrapping his wing around the vampire once again.

Relieved to be back in Zalith's embrace, Alucard wrapped his arms around him, resting his head on his shoulder. Despite where they were and what was going on, nothing made him feel safer than being in his arms.

Lilith giggled as she looked at them both. "You can go."

"This way," one of her scions called, looking over his shoulder at them as he prepared to lead the way.

Once Zalith took hold of Alucard's hand, he and the vampire followed the man towards a door not too far from Lilith's throne. He took them into a hallway, leaving the

Numen's temple. Alucard was sure that this was far from over, but all he wanted to do now was rest.

Chapter Sixty-Eight

— ⟨ ✝ ⟩ —

What Was Lost

| **Alucard** |

Alucard and Zalith followed Lilith's scion to an obsidian door at the end of the hallway. The man took a metal key from his pocket and unlocked it, and then he pushed it open before turning to face them.

"You'll stay in here. If you need anything, you'll call for one of the guards," he said, watching them as they passed him and stepped into the room. "Not that you deserve anything... foul creature," he snarled, glaring at Alucard.

Before Alucard could say anything in response, Zalith let go of his hand, swung around, and slammed his fist into the scion's face. The man stumbled back with a pained, confused groan, holding his hands to his face as blood seeped from both his mouth and nose. He glared at Zalith as though he was about to fight back, but the look on Zalith's face seemed to scare him off. He scurried away without another word, not even bothering to try and lock them in as Alucard suspected he planned to do.

Zalith slammed the door shut and leaned his hand against it for a few moments as he calmed down. Alucard stared at him, waiting for him to say something, but after a few moments passed, the vampire took his eyes off him and glanced around the room. No windows, black-stone flooring, and a bed against the wall—it looked a lot like a prison cell, like a room he'd spent most of his life in, and as the sight clawed at his memory, he sunk deeper into despair.

But Zalith then sighed and gently took hold of Alucard's hand. He led him over to the bed, where they both sat down, and as Alucard stared at the floor in confliction, Zalith made him lay on his back, making sure that he was comfortable. The demon made himself as comfortable as possible beside him, and as Alucard rested his head on his shoulder, Zalith held him tightly.

"I'm going to get us out of here," the demon promised.

Alucard frowned sadly. "Even if we get out of here," he mumbled, "she will find me now that Damien isn't hiding me anymore."

"She won't find you, Alucard. None of them will. I'll have something created to hide you from them, and once you've recovered, we'll leave this place, and I'll keep you safe," he said, resting the side of his head on Alucard's.

"But Lilith has seen you. If I disappear, she'll know to look for you."

"I'll give her something better to do than look for me. I assume her siblings would love to know where she's been hiding."

Alucard sat up and looked down at him with a perturbed frown. It seemed as though Zalith had come up with a plan already. "You plan to tell them where she is? You know that will start a war between her followers and the followers of whoever you tell, right?"

"Yes, and she'll be too busy focusing on that to look for us."

"A war that will happen in the world I live in," he said, frowning.

"Yes. But I'm open to other ideas," the demon told him.

Alucard laid back down, thinking to himself for a few moments. If he wanted to hide from the Numen, he knew that it wouldn't be possible without a price. But a war? He'd lived through too many to want to see another vanquish the land he lived in—because that's what would happen. Lilith's followers would fight those of whichever Numen Zalith told of her whereabouts; Alucard knew too well just how much the Numen loved to watch their followers argue and fight for them, and a war would devastate whatever it touched. Did he want to let something like that happen just so he could be safe?

But then…what had the world ever done for him? Why should he care what happened to people he didn't know? People he didn't care about; people who had only contributed to his restless life. If they died, so what? It was no fault but their own for following the Numen. Which of them would Zalith tell, though? Any one of them would act similarly to find and draw her out.

He sighed quietly and rested his head on Zalith's shoulder again. He'd not deny that he liked the fact that Zalith would go as far as starting a war to keep him safe, and he'd also not deny that such an idea was a good one. As barbaric as it might seem, it would work, but he couldn't ignore the confliction. "If we do that, innocent people will die. The war will spread, it'll destroy places and people who have no involvement, and it will be because of us. I guess that we don't know any of these people, and they haven't really done anything for us to care, but…do we want to be responsible for that?"

"I don't know," Zalith said with a sigh, starting to fiddle with the vampire's hair. "But if I don't do everything I can, and something happens to you, I won't be able to live with myself. I don't want to live without you, and I *won't*. So I'm going to do whatever it takes to make sure you're safe and that we're together."

Sadness gripped Alucard tightly. He didn't know why, but Zalith's words brought pain to his heart—like what he was hearing, once again, was too good to be real. Why would someone care about him so much to do the things that Zalith was saying he'd do? Why did it hurt? Why did he struggle to lie there and accept it? He sat up, staring down at the floor as he dragged his hand over the aching, recently opened wound on his arm. Maybe he felt like this because Zalith already did so much for him and was willing to do *so* much more, yet Alucard hadn't done anything for him, had he?

"What's wrong?" Zalith asked, placing his hand on Alucard's shoulder as he sat up beside him.

Alucard glanced at him. A part of him wanted to ask why Zalith did so much for him and was willing to do the things he had said to keep him safe, but he was sure that he knew what the answer would be. Zalith loved him, right? And *he* loved Zalith. Would he do the same for him if their situation was reversed? Of course he would. But it wasn't. Zalith was putting himself in danger to help him, and all he could do was sit there and do whatever Zalith needed him to do. He didn't like that, he didn't like not being able to do anything for him.

There *was* something. His eyes shifted to the demon's broken wing; Alucard knew how much pride demons had in their wings—they were a status symbol, just like fangs and horns; the bigger a demon's wings, or the more horns or fangs they had, the more powerful they were, socially and ethos-wise—and Zalith's wing being broken must be making him feel angry and uncomfortable. The least he could do was fix that for him, right?

"Alucard?" Zalith asked, placing his hand on the side of his face. "If that's not what you want to do, I can think of something else."

He shook his head and tugged lightly on the collar of the demon's shirt. "Take this off."

Zalith smirked suggestively. "Why?"

Alucard pouted irritably. "Just take it off," he grumbled.

"Okay," Zalith said with a smile and pulled his shirt off.

Despite the circumstances, Alucard couldn't resist taking a small moment to stare at Zalith, but he swiftly turned his attention to his wing. It was torn at the very back, and so to heal it, he'd have to get Zalith to stand. He stood up, pulling Zalith with him, and once he was standing, he ignored the curious smile on the demon's face and moved behind him.

He stared at the demon's back; he thought he was examining the tear where his wing connected to his body, but in all honesty, he just liked staring at Zalith without the obstruction of clothes. He'd not stand there for too long, though. He moved to place his hand on the demon's back—

"What are you doing?" Zalith asked with an unseemly smirk as he looked over his shoulder at him.

Trying to hide his embarrassed frown, Alucard scowled and gently gripped the wing's joint. He pressed it against the scar that had been left where Damien had torn the demon's wing. "Stop looking at me," he snarled.

With an amused smile, Zalith took his eyes off Alucard and stared ahead, waiting.

Alucard concentrated. He might not be able to heal the wounds on a mortal body, but he did possess the Numen ability to repair the broken, irreplaceable limbs of demons—in this case, he'd be healing Zalith's wing so that he could use it again. With his hands on both Zalith's wing joint and his back, a faint, black aura began to surround his hands. It used a lot more of the ethos he'd been recovering than he might like to admit, but he didn't care. All that mattered right now was healing Zalith.

And it didn't take very long, either. After a few short moments, and when pretty much all the ethos he'd regenerated since Damien's... attack, Zalith's wing was healed as though it had never been broken in the first place.

Alucard stepped back and leaned on the bed's canopy to keep himself from falling. "There," he said quietly.

Zalith turned to face him, but when he stretched out his wing and realized what Alucard had done, a startled but content smile appeared on his face. He then took his eyes off his wing and pulled Alucard into a hug. "Thank you," he said quietly, both relief and happiness in his voice. Then, Zalith kissed his lips.

But Alucard wasn't yet done. He'd fixed his wing, and now he wanted to ask him about something Lilith had said before letting them go. He wanted to know if Zalith really had imprinted on him or if Lilith was just toying with them. Either way, he was afraid to ask. What if Lilith *was* playing games and Zalith hadn't imprinted? But then... what if he *had*? What did that mean? He'd imprinted on Zalith, and if Zalith had imprinted on him, that had to mean something... right?

He wasn't going to stand there and overthink it. He didn't have the strength to do so anymore. So, as Zalith kissed him again, he frowned and looked down at the floor.

"What is it?" Zalith asked in concern.

As nervous as he was, he'd not let it hold him back. He had to know. "Did... well, did you... imprint on me?" he asked quietly, still trying to fight his anxiety.

The second Alucard asked, an almost nervous, hesitant expression made its way onto Zalith's face. But in his moment of obvious confliction, he pulled the vampire closer and made him rest his head on the demon's shoulder.

"I did, yes," Zalith replied as he caressed his crimson hair. And as Alucard smiled, the demon held him a little tighter. "Did *you*?"

Alucard tensed up nervously... but he nodded.

"When did you do it?" he asked curiously.

Alucard's nervousness grew. It had taken a lot for him to ask, and now he was being asked a question that he wasn't quite sure how to answer. But he was happy; despite where they were and what happened, none of it seemed to matter right now. Zalith really had imprinted on him, and he couldn't hear something more uplifting—more relieving. He wanted nothing more than to be with Zalith for as long as he could and knowing that

Zalith had imprinted on him made him more confident that they'd remain together for what he hoped would be forever.

Standing in Zalith's embrace, he frowned shyly. "Well…when…I showed you my back."

"Really?" Zalith asked with a smirk. "I didn't see."

Pouting, Alucard frowned in both embarrassment and irritation. "It was…when we were…well…I was biting you and you were…you know what you were doing," he grumbled.

Amused, Zalith laughed quietly and then guided him out of his embrace so that he was standing in front of him. He kissed the vampire again, moving his hand to the back of his head; Alucard returned his kiss, placing his hands on either side of the demon's waist. He didn't have the words to explain how relieved he was, how distant he felt from his worries and pain. Zalith made him feel so very content, and he didn't want to let go of it.

But Zalith then stopped kissing him when he nearly dragged his hand over the slowly healing wound on the vampire's face. He frowned, resting his forehead against Alucard's as he gazed into his eyes. "Are you going to bite me *now*?" he asked, not with a seductive tone but one of sincerity and worry. He still wanted Alucard to heal faster, that was obvious.

As conflicted and hesitant as Alucard had felt before, he felt no such reluctance right now. Lilith had him, and Damien wasn't going to find him any time soon. Zalith was also planning their escape, and Alucard was sure that the sooner he healed, the sooner the demon could begin that plan. And…the very thought of the taste of Zalith's blood excited him more than he'd admit.

He looked down at the demon's neck, pondering, but he'd already given in. He edged his face nearer to Zalith's neck, placing his hand on the back of his head. Then, he lightly gripped the demon's hair in his hand, pulling his head aside as he moved closer, and without hesitation, he slowly sank his fangs into the demon's neck.

Zalith exhaled quietly in satisfaction when the vampire's fangs pierced his skin. The high struck Alucard as soon as he eagerly gulped down his first mouthful of blood, the euphoria consuming his already content state as he swallowed more and more. What he felt for Zalith hit him *hard*; he found him *so* alluring, *so* attractive—he didn't want to take his eyes off him. He loved him so much; he needed him, wanted him, *had* him. The thought of Zalith's imprint on him, his hands against his skin—it excited him, relieved him, and aroused him knowing that he belonged to Zalith and that Zalith belonged to him. He wouldn't want anything else.

He tightened the grip he had on Zalith's hair and body, pulling him as close as he could while he bit harder in response to a sudden feeling of desperation. He wanted Zalith so badly—*more* than what he was currently getting. But what more was there? Why wasn't his blood enough? It *was* helping his aching body heal, and he could feel his ethos regenerating; but as satisfying as it was for him, he still wanted more—more of Zalith, more of his body, his touch, his attention; he craved him in every way he knew how. He knew what he wanted, and he wasn't afraid to ask for it.

With a sigh of satisfaction, he pulled his fangs from Zalith's neck and rested the side of his face against Zalith's as he leaned into his ear. "I want you to fuck me," he mumbled, exhaling deeply as he tried to contain his quickly growing eagerness.

"Really?" Zalith then asked, both excitement and concern in his voice. "What about your body?"

"I'm fine," he said, his nervousness quickly beginning to outweigh his sudden eagerness. He nuzzled Zalith's neck, trying to hide his face as Zalith held him tightly.

"Are you sure?" the demon asked, and as Alucard nodded, the demon smiled. "I'll go easy on you," he said seductively.

Zalith lightly gripped the vampire's arms, pushed him back against the wall beside the bed, and initiated a deliberate and sensuous kiss. Alucard, attuned to the palpable thrill in each intertwining of their tongues, found himself growing more enthralled by the moment. His hands gravitated to the demon's chest, and he leaned his head against the wall, savouring the sensation as Zalith's lips descended to his neck.

While standing in the demon's intimate embrace, Alucard explored Zalith's form with his hands, tracing the contours of his body, gliding over his back, and navigating the intricate joint of his right wing. He'd not seen Zalith in his demon form before—not so closely, and not for so long. He'd seen a glimpse once or twice, but that was it, and he hadn't really been conscious enough to appreciate it since their arrival in Lilith's domain.

Alucard placed his hand on the side of Zalith's neck, pushing him back slightly so that he'd stop kissing him. For a moment, he gazed into the demon's crimson eyes as he stared back and moved his hand from the vampire's neck to the side of his face. Alucard felt as if he wanted to say something to him, but his nervousness kept him silent. Instead, he stroked his hand along the side of Zalith's face and dragged his fingers up his left horn, taking a moment he'd waited for to admire Zalith's true appearance.

The demon's smirk deepened, a sly glint in his eyes as he guided his hand to the side of Alucard's face. Maintaining intense eye contact, Zalith's fingers trailed down to the base of Alucard's right horn. He began a slow, tantalizing caress around the horn's foundation, and what started as a soothing sensation swiftly escalated into an overwhelmingly pleasurable experience for Alucard. It was as if Zalith's touch had ventured into more intimate territories, although his hand remained away from Alucard's arousal.

Alucard found himself unable to stifle his response. A mixture of pleasure and surprise contorted his expression, and in an uncontrolled reaction, he grasped Zalith's horn. A quiet exhale of delight escaped him, and he closed his eyes, attempting to conceal his face from the demon, who seemed to revel in the heightened intensity of the moment.

"The base of a demon's horn is one of our most sensitive places," Zalith murmured into Alucard's ear, still lightly stroking the base of his horn with his fingers.

Alucard hadn't known that, and it didn't surprise him that Zalith *did*. He was sure that Zalith knew a whole lot more about demons than he did, and right now, it made him feel... vulnerable—but in a way he liked. He moved his hand to the back of Zalith's head, gripped his hair, and pulled his face away from his neck. He then kissed him, and as he kissed back, the demon stopped dragging his fingers around his horn and stroked his hand down his body, and soon enough, he reached his crotch.

The vampire's anticipation heightened with each passing moment, revelling in every second of Zalith's devoted attention. The demon's kisses were intoxicating, and the subtle caresses over Alucard's arousal sent shivers down his spine. Zalith's hand traversed down his back, and a firm yet gentle squeeze on his ass only added to the building intensity.

Despite the potential embarrassment colouring his face, Alucard couldn't deny the pleasure derived from Zalith's touch. It fuelled a desire within him, prompting reciprocation. He acknowledged the times his gaze had involuntarily fixated on the demon's enticing posterior, and the curiosity about why Zalith enjoyed the tactile exploration as much as he did lingered in his thoughts. Now seemed like the perfect moment to explore and unravel those mysteries.

He fought against his nervousness and dragged his hand from the joint of Zalith's right wing, down his back, and to his ass, which he slowly and nervously began to grip. He felt a smile appear on Zalith's lips as they continued to kiss, and as much as that embarrassed him, he didn't let go. He loved to touch what his eyes would stare at, and the demon's ass was no exception.

Their kissing and touching soon ceased when Zalith carefully turned Alucard so that he was facing the wall he once had his back against. He pulled the vampire's body against his own so that Alucard's ass was firmly against his crotch, and when Alucard felt the demon's hard arousal pressing against his leg, he tensed up in anticipation. Zalith started kissing Alucard's neck while he used his left hand to unbutton his shirt, still caressing the vampire's crotch with his right.

Alucard's desire burned fiercely as he frowned impatiently, swiftly discarding his shirt the moment the demon undid the final button. His hand trailed to the back of Zalith's head; the demon kept placing soft, tantalizing kisses on his neck, and after a few more, he seized control and firmly grasped Alucard's wrist, guiding it to his crotch. Their hands intertwined, and Alucard traced the length of the demon's rigid arousal with his fingers. The pulsating heat only intensified Alucard's yearning, each passing moment fuelling an insatiable desperation to experience the undeniable ecstasy of being taken by Zalith.

Zalith dragged his hand up from the vampire's crotch and started unbuckling his belt. Alucard's anticipation grew, as did his nervousness, but he'd learned to control it better. He gripped the demon's hard shaft a little tighter as Zalith pulled his trousers off, and then the demon made him face the bed as he started kissing his neck again.

The demon then leaned into his ear. "Bend over," he instructed.

With a nervous but excited frown, Alucard did as he was told. Once the vampire got down onto his hands and knees, Zalith gripped his waist with both his hands and pulled his bare ass against his crotch, surely to tease him.

Alucard waited with a grimace on his face that was not of excitement but of discomfort. The way he was positioned was beginning to agitate his wounds, but he didn't want to let that ruin what he so eagerly longed for. He closed his eyes, exhaling deeply as he listened to the sound of Zalith unbuckling his own belt, and once the demon pulled off his trousers, he placed his right hand on the vampire's waist. Alucard heard him spit, and then he felt the wet touch of the demon's fingers press against his ass. He grunted and hummed quietly in contentment when Zalith eased them inside, and when he pulled them out, Alucard's heart raced in anticipation.

The vampire frowned in both pleasure and relief when he felt the tip of the demon's dick against his ass. Zalith placed his other hand on Alucard's waist, slowly pulling him closer as he pushed his shaft deeper into him; Zalith's sigh of pleasure aroused Alucard more, and as he gripped the blanket beneath him, he, too, sighed pleasingly. He ignored the ache of his body as Zalith began to gently and slowly move him back and forth, but the discomfort in his arm outweighed the faint pain that he felt in response to the demon's shaft inside him, a pain that eased more and more each time they had sex.

He didn't want to worry Zalith, nor did he want him to stop, but his discomfort was ruining the excitement that had once enthralled him. However, Zalith seemed to notice; the demon stopped moving and pulled his dick from Alucard's ass. He made the vampire lay on his back, and once he crawled over him, Zalith smiled down at him and started kissing him before he could ask him what he was doing.

To Alucard's relief, he wasn't stopping. Zalith carefully helped him position his right leg over his back and rested his arms on either side of Alucard as he continued kissing him for a few more moments. Then, as the demon started to caress Alucard's head around the base of his right horn with one hand, he used his other hand to slowly ease his dick back inside the vampire's ass.

Alucard exhaled quietly in pleasure as the demon moved his face to his neck and started to gently kiss his skin, resuming with the slow, careful thrusts. The vampire relaxed, his body a whole lot less agitated now that he was lying on his back, and as his pain withered, his excitement returned. He gripped a fistful of Zalith's hair in his right hand, nuzzling his neck as the demon started to suck on his. With each of Zalith's light, gentle thrusts, both of them breathed a little faster and gripped a little tighter. The demon's quiet, hushed murmurs of satisfaction and the feel of his breath against Alucard's neck forced a shiver of exhilaration to surge through his body.

He grimaced in struggle, trying his hardest not to dig his claws into Zalith's skin as the pleasure of his movements began to enthral him. He pulled him closer as he almost whimpered in delight; the last thing he wanted to do was utter a sound so loud that he'd embarrass himself, but the longer he tried to remain silent, the more of a struggle it began to become.

With his face against the side of Zalith's neck, he quickly widened his jaws and bit down, sinking all four of his fangs into the demon's skin. He felt Zalith flinch and heard him groan pleasurably; Alucard's bite made him move a little faster, and his change in pace intoxicated the vampire as he bit harder, gripped tighter, and moaned quietly in pleasure as a struggled grimace clung to his face. His body began to ache and tremble, so much that he stopped swallowing Zalith's blood and pulled his fangs from the demon's neck, resting his head on the bed while a euphoric sigh escaped his breath. Enthralled by the delight of Zalith's blood, attention, and touch, Alucard moaned again, giving in to the intensifying rapture.

The demon started thrusting harder, his pleased groans becoming louder and more frequent. He pushed harder, and harder, and *harder*, and after one final thrust, he plunged his dick as deeply into Alucard's ass as he could and whined loudly in delight. Alucard felt his shaft throbbing inside him, filling his body with that hot, pleasing sensation; he tried to relax his trembling body, allowing his leg to fall from over Zalith's back and to the blanket as he turned his head to look up at him. He felt overwhelmed in so many ways that he couldn't even begin to try and work out where to start. What he *did* focus on was how happy he felt—how happy Zalith made him feel and how much he pleased him.

When he stared into the demon's crimson eyes, Zalith looked as though he was about to say something, but Alucard beat him to it. "I…really love you," he said quietly and shyly. He then took his eyes off Zalith, who smiled down at him. "Don't laugh at me," he said, pouting.

Zalith dragged his thumb over Alucard's forehead, moving a strand of his hair from over his eye. "I really love you too, Alucard," he replied before kissing the side of his face.

The demon then pulled his dick from the vampire's ass and started to kiss his way down his body, but Alucard frowned as hesitation began battling his euphoria. He felt satisfied enough for now; knowing he'd pleased and served Zalith was all he needed, and he just wanted to lay there with Zalith. So, before the demon could kiss any lower than his waist, he gently snatched his horn and looked down at him. Zalith stopped and looked up at him with a confused frown, but he seemed to understand what Alucard was trying to tell him.

Zalith smiled and kissed his way back up his body, kissed his neck, his face, and then his lips one final time before laying on his back beside him.

Alucard carefully rolled onto his side so that he could rest his head on the demon's shoulder, and as he felt Zalith wrap his right wing over him, he sighed quietly and closed his eyes. For a few moments, they lay there in the silence, calming down as they relaxed.

The vampire moved his arm around him and held him tightly. "Whatever you want to do to keep us safe, I'll help. I don't want to live without you, either, and if we have to start a war to stay together, then we will," he said, having decided that he, like Zalith, would go as far as war so that he could spend his life with the man he loved.

Zalith smiled slightly as he rested the side of his head on Alucard's. "We'll work it out," he said quietly. "Whatever it takes, I'll keep you safe."

With a content smile, Alucard hugged him tighter. He already felt safe; even though they were in the midst of Lilith's domain, he felt as safe as he did in Zalith's home. No matter where they were, he'd always feel safe with Zalith at his side, and he hoped that at his side was where he would remain forever.

Chapter Sixty-Nine

— ⋞ ✝ ⋟ —

Alter

| **Zalith** |

Zalith lay wide awake beside Alucard. He kept his left wing around the vampire, holding him tightly as he slept soundlessly with his head resting on Zalith's shoulder. The demon waited. Not too long ago, he'd called for an izuret; usually, the small demon messengers would arrive instantly, but not this time. This time, the izuret had to take a much slower, specific route to get to him to avoid Lilith's detection.

Lilith... he didn't know her personally, but his parents had. They'd talk about her all the time, and from what he'd heard and learned over the centuries, he knew that she was just as deplorable as Damien. She'd toyed around with the fact that Alucard couldn't speak to her; she knew he didn't have wings, yet she'd tried to humiliate him even more. Zalith didn't care, though—Alucard was just as much of a demon as he was, wings or not. He didn't care for demon society.

His anger and skepticism were simmering, his desire to make everything okay gnawing at him like a starved animal. Alucard deserved to be safe, to be okay; Zalith would do whatever it took to make sure that was the case—that *his* vampire was safe.

He looked down at Alucard, watching as he slept in what looked to be peace, despite the fact that they were involuntarily in the confines of a glorified chunk of rock, home to a mantis and her irrelevant guests residing within like a colony of disgusting insects, creeping and crawling. He sighed, gently caressing the sleeping vampire's hair. The wounds on his body had healed, allowing Zalith to feel some relief.

For a moment, though, the silence seized him. It was strange, the sense of emptiness he felt knowing that he was in the centre of a rock floating around the nothingness which was the world outside. Black—endless, murky black. He'd not seen it before, and he'd come to believe that it was the place where the Numen slept—the place they retreated to once their time in the real worlds had expired. And that in itself was a fact he hadn't long come to know; the Numens' power was so infinitely dense that they had to retreat from the worlds after so much time had passed, lest the world's ethos crumble and shatter. It was a fact he'd keep very close to the centre of his mind.

But none of that mattered right now. What *did* matter was what he'd learned about Alucard. His vampire had imprinted on him, and when he'd learned of it, he felt... vulnerable. He'd never experienced this before—the kind of love and need and closeness that he felt with Alucard. Imprinting was one of the most exposing things a demon could do to themselves—it was their way of telling someone that they were going to share their life with them, no matter what; it was a promise of unconditional love and protection, and possession, too. Alucard was his, he was Alucard's, and nothing was going to change that now.

Just then, a very small, silent rift opened in the wall not too far from the door, and an izuret floated out. Its wings were spread, its body was smothered in ash, and the look in the creature's deep-purple eyes was one of annoyance. It clearly hadn't liked having to make the journey to where Zalith was. It floated over as the rift behind it closed and landed silently on the small, crooked table next to where the demon lay. It folded its leathery wings against its back, wiggled around as it planted itself where it had landed, and stared at him.

The izuret tilted its head and chirped quietly, asking him why he was where he was.

Zalith suspected the creature might ask what he was doing there. He rolled his eyes and quietly answered, "None of your concern." He didn't want to wake Alucard.

With a huff of irritancy as if to say *'whatever'*, the izuret shuffled its shoulders and crossed its arms. But as it set its huge eyes on the sleeping vampire, its irritancy faded into excitement. It stood up straight, unfolding its arms as it leaned forward to get a closer look, almost like it was making sure that the man beside Zalith really was Alucard.

When Zalith used the wing he had around Alucard to hide him from the izuret's gaze, it wriggled around excitedly and pointed at him, a flurry of enthusiastic chirps and mutters breaking the sullen silence of the cold room; it pointed to its arm, reminding Zalith that not too long ago, Alucard had seen to this izuret's wounds. How could he forget? It was a moment he found most endearing.

"Be quiet," he said with an irritated grimace, sure that the creature's handclapping would alert the guards—if they were even patrolling Lilith's halls.

Pouting, the izuret crossed its arms again and looked at Zalith. But it then frowned in worry, obviously having not failed to notice the healing wounds on what was visible of the vampire's body. With a few quiet, hushed mutters, it asked if Alucard was okay.

"He's fine," Zalith mumbled. "Tell both Orin and Tyrus to join forces and search for Mage Opus; he also goes by Magnus. I need results as soon as possible," he instructed. For his plan to work, he needed a mage capable of hiding him and Alucard from Numen detection.

The izuret nodded, and as Zalith waved his hand in dismissal, the creature took off, floated over to a wall, and disappeared into a rift, leaving Zalith alone with Alucard once again.

He looked down at the vampire, moving his wing from over him so that he could see his face. *Was* he fine? He was sure that he wasn't. Alucard might say he's okay and try to hide the fact that he was hurting, but Zalith always knew when something was wrong. He knew Alucard was suffering, and he wasn't even sure sleep was a time when he was free of pain. He stared at him, watching as the once-vacant look on the vampire's face became a frown. He'd seen that look appearing on his face ever since he'd fallen asleep several hours ago, and he wasn't sure whether it was because he was struggling to settle or because of what he saw while unconscious. All he could do was hold him and be there for him when he woke.

After a short while had passed, however, Alucard's discomfort became more than a frown on his face. He tensed up, tightening the grip he had around Zalith with his arm. The demon stared down at him, convinced that he was just making himself comfortable—despite his healing wounds, Zalith was sure his body must still ache. But Alucard's frown didn't fade, and his grip only became tighter. His once soundless breathing became a little louder, a hint of panic upon each breath as they grew frantic.

Mumbles soon emerged upon the vampire's voice, all of which sounded confused and fearful, and in a language the demon couldn't understand. Alucard was having another of his nightmares, something Zalith had come to see he experienced many of, and right now, he wasn't sure whether he should wake him or wait for him to settle. But as the vampire's entire body suddenly convulsed, Zalith began to feel panicked.

"Alucard," he said, but the vampire didn't calm, nor did he stop; he flinched, turning his head slightly as the frown on his face thickened with distress. Zalith wasn't sure what he might be seeing, so he gripped the vampire's shoulder and lightly shook him. "Alucard," he said again, but a little louder in hopes it might drag him from his nightmare.

However, it was without avail.

He frowned, watching Alucard mutter and grimace. If he couldn't wake him, what was he supposed to do?

| **Alucard** |

The torment of Alucard's past faded to darkness as he abruptly woke. He opened his eyes, the horror of what he'd seen withering as the candlelight hit his eyes. His panic didn't disappear—it only grew when he saw the four barren walls that surrounded him. He sat up, his heart racing and his body aching as he panicked and gasped for breath. Frantically, he searched the room for a sign of natural light, for a window to the world outside, but no such thing existed.

Where was he? *Why* was he? *When* was he? He had no idea. And the arms around him, the wings beside him—the arms that had suddenly embraced him; he pulled away, preparing to attack whoever gripped hold of him, but when he swung around, his eyes met those that were crimson and familiar.

"It's okay," Zalith said, pulling Alucard into his embrace once again.

Was it okay? Where were they? Panic surged through Alucard as he struggled to make sense of his surroundings. Zalith—he recognized the demon, but the room was an enigma. White walls enclosed him, suffocating and devoid of any openings. No windows, no trace of breathable air, and the corners of the room seemed to be converging, mocking him with their oppressive proximity. The walls pressed in, a relentless force closing in on him, mocking laughter echoing through the sterile air. Despair clung to him like a suffocating shroud. He'd been found again, ensnared once more, halted in his desperate attempts to escape. Each futile effort to break free only led him back to the same claustrophobic space, the gnawing walls of captivity closing in, leaving him to grapple with the haunting question: Why?

He breathed faster, and he held tighter; his body trembled in sheer terror, and he was sure that he'd soon hear footsteps creeping towards his door.

"Alucard," Zalith said quietly, placing his hand on the vampire's head. "It's okay," he repeated with an insistent tone. "I'm here."

Here? Where? Alucard watched as the black wing of the man whose chest he had his head rested against crept around both their bodies, hiding him from the creeping walls, from the sight of the prison he was trapped in.

Zalith tightened his embrace, holding him in his arms within the confines of his wings. "Are you okay?"

It took a moment for him to realize that he *wasn't* in Damien's castle or the room he'd spent the majority of his life in. He remembered where he was—Lilith's domain…her home…whatever she called the mass of rock she hid inside. Zalith was with him…he *was* okay. So, he exhaled deeply, calming down as he placed his hand on the demon's shoulder, nuzzling his neck. He felt so stupid waking up suddenly, thinking he was somewhere else, and knowing Zalith had seen made him feel worse. He scowled in embarrassment, unsure of what to say to him.

"Alucard?" Zalith asked quietly.

With his face against the demon's neck, Alucard frowned despondently. "I'm fine," he said, opening his eyes ever so slightly to stare at Zalith's wing.

What he'd seen while asleep left his mind the moment he woke up, the moment he thought he was in his old room. Now that he knew he wasn't, he let himself relax. He knew Zalith would ask why he'd panicked so much, and he wasn't sure what he might say in response. Did he want to tell Zalith? He wasn't sure, but... if he was going to be spending as much of his life as he could with this demon, would it not be better for him to know? For him to understand why he may sometimes wake in the middle of the night, why he may mutter things of little sense in his sleep, and why he felt so discomforted by the things that unsettled him?

No. Alucard feared that those things would make Zalith think of him differently; the fear had always lingered in every part of his mind, the fear that if Zalith discovered the things he kept hidden, then he'd leave him. But to think so little of the love and care Zalith said he had for him—it hurt Alucard; it made him feel as though he was ignoring his own trust for Zalith, but his worry always outweighed his better judgement. How could he not fear that Zalith would abandon him? He loved him so much, so much that he'd rather suffer in silence than expose himself in the way he would if he told him about the things that kept him from feeling peace.

But... Zalith had seen him wingless; Zalith had seen Damien punishing him, and he'd seen the weak way he acted in front of the Numen. If none of that changed the way the demon felt about him, would *this*?

Zalith then rested the side of his head on Alucard's and sighed quietly as he held him in his embrace. "What are your nightmares about, Alucard? You have them so often, and you wake up so afraid. It worries me."

The vampire held him just as tightly. "Different things," he answered. "But... mostly Damien."

He softly replied, "If you ever want some alleviation from what he did, I can help."

"Help how?"

"I can try to take some of your bad memories away. It could help with your dreams, too," he offered, caressing the vampire's hair.

Alucard frowned as he stared at the demon's wing. He knew what Zalith meant—to go into his mind and remove certain memories as if they hadn't happened... change them, even. But change was something he wouldn't be new to. He was convinced that something like that had already been done. His dream just now made him relive something that happened to him before, but this time, it was different—not the way he remembered. It was as though the memory had been changed to suit its alternator. But who would benefit from altering such a memory? A memory in which before now, he'd been running with the other children Damien had gathered; he'd seen them die for trying to escape. This time, though, Lilith had been there. Although a small change, it brought much to question. Why was she there? Why had she been observing with what could only be explained as glee? And why had someone altered his memory of that moment? He saw no need, no reason… so why?

He closed his eyes, remaining in the warmth of Zalith's embrace. It didn't take him long to assume that the removal of the runes he once had on his back and his dream were connected. He wasn't sure what all the runes on him had done, but… could one of them have kept him from discovering his memories had been meddled with? He was good enough with mind ethos to know when his own mind had been messed with; the only thing that *could* stop him would be something external, something Numen—something *Damien*.

But… how could he be sure? Despite what happened and what was still happening, he didn't want to suspect Damien—to blame him. He didn't want to think about how that made him feel. So, he thought back to Zalith's offer—to his possibly altered memories. "I think… someone's already done that."

"Who?" Zalith asked with what seemed like both curiosity *and* concern in his voice. He'd not think about it. "I don't know," he muttered.

The demon fell silent for a moment but then looked down at him. "What do you think they took?"

Alucard sat up straight so that he was at eye level with the demon and then shrugged as he looked down at his lap. "Things. Changed, rather than took altogether," he mumbled as Zalith slowly slipped his hand into his. "I have this dream sometimes—a memory of when I was a boy. There were other children with me when I was living with Damien; I didn't know any of them, all I did know was that they were scions. I don't think any of them were Damien's—as far as I know, he's never had a child of any type of his own."

Zalith stared at him, listening as he spoke.

"Before, I remembered it being just us and Damien, but… now I see Lilith there. She was there every time Damien would have us gather in the hall. She was there every time Damien trained us. That… involved a lot of injury, and it's what killed most of the others. Those of us who didn't die started doing things for him. Find people, killing things—Lilith was there when we came back, and she was there when Damien caught me and four of the other boys trying to run from him one night. I was the only one to survive that, and I see them all a lot. I could have tried to help them, right?" he uttered, looking at Zalith's concerned face, but he quickly looked back down at his lap.

As he spoke, he discovered that he was becoming a whole lot more convinced that someone *had* altered his memories for a reason. But who? It could have been Damien, it could have been Lilith. Or perhaps it was no one. Perhaps he was only just remembering things the way they had actually happened now that he'd seen Lilith after so long. He didn't know what to believe, but he wanted to know.

With a sullen scowl, he shrugged. "I don't know if it was Damien or Lilith, or if maybe I just forgot some things until now. But… if it *was* Lilith, it would be because she knew one day, I'd end up here, and she'd need me to trust her. Why would I trust her if she was there when Damien… when…" he hesitated and rested his forehead on Zalith's shoulder.

"You wouldn't trust her if she and Damien were friends," Zalith said.

"I don't know," Alucard muttered. "What reason would Damien have to remove her from my memory?" he asked in confusion. "Why… what else is missing?"

Still grasping the vampire's hand with his own, Zalith frowned in sympathy. "Do you want me to help you see?" he offered. "I mean… it makes sense. I've seen you struggle to remember things, which isn't normal for a demon. Brain fog is a side effect of the kind of mind ethos you're talking about."

Alucard felt reluctant. Everything would come to him eventually, right? Sooner if he put effort into searching his mind, but so much sooner if he let Zalith help him. Two minds at work were better than one, weren't they? And he had to get over his fear of Zalith learning things about him and deciding to leave. He trusted him, and he had to trust that the demon wouldn't leave him after finding out more and more about his past—about the things that happened to him.

With a hesitant frown, he nodded. "Maybe."

Zalith smiled slightly as he looked down at Alucard. "I need more than a maybe."

Alucard sat up straight and nodded as he gripped Zalith's wrist, pulling his hand from the demon's. He then lifted Zalith's hand and encouraged him to place it on his face to read his mind, and Alucard did the same, placing his thumb against Zalith's jaw, and his middle and index fingers against his temple. And then, he closed his eyes; they both rested their foreheads against each other's, and after a few moments, Alucard relaxed and allowed the demon to enter his mind.

Chapter Seventy

Secrets and Lies

| Zalith and Alucard, *Witnessing Alucard's altered mind* |

I t didn't take long for Zalith to find the damage. The altered memories. The tangled web of lies and manipulation. Alucard let him dig deeper, and when the demon began carefully unravelling everything, they both witnessed what had been hidden.

From the eyes of a child, they stared up at a priestess' pale, emotionless face as she gripped the offspring in her arms like someone would a most valuable possession. It could see before it its mother—she lay upon a stone altar in the darkness of a dungeon lit only with crimson candles, the fire as black as night. Bloodied, weak, but not dead as a human mother who bore a demon should be. She wasn't human, but a Meridian witch—a woman who held ethos equal to that of an Aegis.

The mother, her eyes as blue as the daylit sky, hair grey as a result of her stress. She reached out with tears on her face for the child within the arms of her midwife, but she wasn't granted what she asked for. Instead, she met her end at the hands of a familiar woman—hair white, eyes red, wings upon her back. Lilith—she dragged her claws through the mother's throat, ending her life before her newborn had the chance to feel her embrace.

Within the arms of the observing midwife, the child reached out its hands—hands scaled, adorned with talons much like a monster. It wept as it watched the life fade from the face of its mother. Lilith scorched her corpse until it was nothing but ash, gone as if never there, as if to be forgotten. A smile clung to her face as the white-haired woman made her way over to the midwife and snatched the child. But it refused to look at her as though she was now its mother. It clawed, leaving the demon Numen with such ghastly wounds on her face. But all she did was laugh a shrill, pleased laugh.

"Caedis Luciferson," she spoke as if the name were a sacred rite. "You have such a glorious purpose."

And then she carried the child away.

A room in the very depths of the catacomb in which he was born was where Caedis would end up—where he would spend the majority of his days until he evolved from a creature to a man. No mother, no siblings, no light—all he would know was the dark of the cage in which he was stored and the midwife who would bring him food at exactly midnight every single day. Days became weeks, weeks became months, and months eventually became years until he grew into a small boy of four.

Lilith made countless attempts to masquerade as his mother, but Caedis knew his true mother's sent, his true mother's aura, and neither was found in Lilith. Still, the woman taught him to speak, to fight, and to respect his owners. Of course, all lessons came with a punishment of injury, something such a small child didn't need. And as each day came to its end, he'd be stored back in his cage, locked away like an animal. Not once in those four years had he seen the sun—the light of the world outside. He wasn't even aware that there was anything beyond the walls of the labyrinth he lived in.

When Caedis reached five, it was time for him to do what he was created to do. A minute past midnight, Lilith dragged him from his sleep and into a hall filled with people he'd never seen. Placed in the centre of a blood-painted pentagram, he was to summon his father from the darkness beyond. So many dead bodies lay around him as Lilith instructed him the way she'd taught him: kill the woman brought to him, chant the words spoken to him.

His father came through the rift that he had created. Lilith greeted the crimson-haired man with adoration—with affection. And they soon turned on the boy they'd used to grant him passage into the world.

"Why kill him?" the white-haired woman asked. "Why dispose of a pathetic little creature who can be crafted, moulded, and used as the weapon we need to destroy Letholdus' world and the children he's polluted it with? Keep him, and no other Numen will dare contest us—Letholdus would dare not intrude upon our rule."

But she and the child's father were not the only ones to have thought of such a despairing fate for Caedis.

The Daegelus arrived. The boy's father was not of right mind and a creature that would only bring destruction to all Numen. Damien cast him out and took the boy from Lilith's grasp. She did fight, but the Daegelus' followers fought for him as he fled with the child. Too young to understand then, but now, it was too clear that the Daegelus and Lilith had shared something, but Lilith had chosen the boy's father over him—and the Daegelus would forever resent the child because he looked so much like his father, the man who had stolen the woman he'd loved.

With Damien was where Caedis now lived. At first, it seemed as though the Daegelus did try to love him, but every time he set his eyes on the boy, he saw only the hatred he had for his father. One mistake resulted in one scar. Two mistakes in another, and every mistake Caedis made from that day on only brought him more injury. But it was all he knew, so who was he to question it? From the very day he was born, he knew nothing but dark and misery and pain—why would it be any different with a new guardian?

Time passed, and once Caedis was eight, Lilith came back. She'd tried and tried to free her lover from the endless dark in which Damien had stored him. She begged and begged for the Daegelus' forgiveness, and he surely gave it. Lilith was back in Caedis' life, and he knew no greater misery throughout the years she stayed. If he so much as looked in the wrong direction, the woman scolded him, and back then, he'd thought it was for his mistakes, but now, he knew that it was because of what had happened three years ago.

But why did Caedis have to suffer? He'd done as she'd asked—he'd opened the rift; he'd freed his father and granted him passage into the world. Why was Lilith so angry with him? Should she not be angry at Damien for destroying everything she and Caedis' father had constructed? And why did Damien still scold him so? Lilith was back in his grasp; he had no reason to hate him—but hate seemed to have become something of a habit. Fun. Enjoyment. To injure and watch as he suffered. It wasn't for reason. Caedis hadn't failed the Daegelus at all—not once. All he ever did was what he asked and more, but all he was ever given in return was hatred and suffering.

Caedis continued with his life, though, with serving the Daegelus. After all, he owed him for saving him from death all those years ago.

For centuries he served, suffered, and continued to live in hopes that one day the Daegelus might see his worth—that he wasn't some pathetic little creature who was only good for summoning Numen. Caedis knew he was worth more, and he did all he could to try and prove it—but not once was he seen.

However, on a night darker than any had been, Damien and Lilith shared a discussion. The subject was the boy, Caedis, and what he was really to do. Summoning his father was one of so many things he was born with the ability to achieve. Why had Lilith killed his mother the moment Caedis was born? So that he'd be without love, and without love, he'd be without hope. Without hope, he had nothing. He'd grip onto whatever hint of acceptance came his way, and that was Damien. He chose to serve Damien, and Damien had become responsible for keeping him from understanding what he was.

Some named him the AntiNumen, for he possessed not only the ability to kill children of the Numen but the Numen themselves. He may need the help of artefacts to do so, but the power resided within him, and both Lilith and Damien had to do their best to keep him from discovering the truth.

Let him know that he would kill Letholdus' children and weaken the hold he had on Aegisguard, but let him not know that he possessed the power to overthrow his holders.

Years passed. Caedis continued serving, only to one day lose a demon's most beloved possession for failing to deliver a message on time. But later that day, he had come to find Lilith had abandoned Damien once more. That was why he was punished, and not until now did he know that. Lilith went to the Daegelus that same night and expressed her hatred, her disgust, for he had caused her nothing but pain, suffering, and misery. No longer could she pretend feelings for him in an attempt to see Caedis' father once more. But she wouldn't leave Damien with the power to stop her once she and the boy's father were united once again. She erased herself from Caedis' memory, leaving nothing but the fact that she had rescued him the night his father's followers attacked his home. In his mind, she remained nothing but an ally who one day might show to grant him the peace he deserved.

Lilith was gone as though to have never existed as more than a blur of a child's memory—a memory that had been played with, but now, a memory that had been untangled, and nothing could be clearer.

| Alucard |

Alucard stared vacantly as both he and Zalith left the depths of his mind. So much had been revealed to him in such a short time that he had no idea what to do with any of it. He could feel both anger and pain boiling inside him like the fire in his eyes. He had to decide what to do with it all.

He watched as Zalith opened his eyes; there was a look of dismay on his face as he stared at Alucard, his crimson eyes full of both sorrow and anger, an anger Alucard knew he wished to scorn both Lilith and Damien with. Alucard felt the very same. To know what they had done and what they might do if they still had him. Lilith thought she had him; she thought her little tricks had worked, that her mind games would cause Alucard to fall at her feet like a good little boy ready to serve the woman who had now saved him twice, or so she had him believe. But he knew. He knew the truth. And he wasn't going to sit around on his ass anymore and let the Numen treat him like a lesser creature.

But now wasn't the time. He was angry—*furious*. His anger clawed at his skin like a caged animal, an animal he had once been. It wanted out—to attack, to injure, to kill. But his targets weren't in sight. Lilith might be down the hall, but he'd wait. He'd let his anger burn; he'd let her continue to think that she was smart, that she had won. And when she least expected it, he'd show her just how much of a monster he really was.

Zalith placed his hand on the side of the vampire's face, his look of sorrow growing as each moment passed.

Alucard had buried his anger, and all that remained was his hurt. He trusted those people—all of them; Lilith, Damien, those who raised him. And for what? To find that he really never was anything but a tool to them. An object that they could reflect their hatred and anger upon. They hadn't cared for him. They hadn't loved him. They just wanted him because he was the only one who could save them. But Zalith—the man before him loved him—cared for him and wanted him because he made him happy, because he loved him and needed him for who he was right now. Not because he was some weapon who could kill Numen.

A despondent frown clung to his face, and as Zalith pulled him closer, he sunk into his sadness. He sat within the demon's embrace, holding him tightly, keeping his eyes shut as he tried to ground himself once more. His anger still clawed—it raged. But he wasn't ready to let it loose. Above all else in the worlds, being in Zalith's embrace was the thing he loved most—the thing he craved most. Not even his anger would steal a moment of closeness from him, a moment he needed so sorely right now. The only person who had ever loved him and who he had ever loved was right in front of him, and he wanted to hold onto that for a moment longer.

The demon hugged him tighter. "I'm so sorry this is happening," he said despondently. "That *all* of this has happened. You don't deserve any of it— you *never* deserved any of it."

Alucard leaned back, staring sullenly at his face as he stared back. He'd not even taken a moment to consider his fear—the fear that Zalith might feel differently after seeing everything that had just come to light. Alucard sensed no change in his presence, his feelings, his aura. Zalith was sad for him and furious at the Numen. Alucard felt a little guilty for having peered into the demon's thoughts for the half-second that he did, but…he wanted to know whether or not what the demon had seen had made him change his mind.

He thought he'd tell him, but he was sure Zalith already knew he'd done it. It didn't need to be talked about. All he cared about was being with him. He placed his hand on the demon's face, and without hesitation, he leaned in and kissed him. For a few silent moments, they kissed and embraced one another, sure that soon enough, things would be a whole lot less calm.

"I'll never let anyone hurt you like that ever again," Zalith said as he rested his forehead against Alucard's. "I won't ever let anyone hurt you in any way."

Alucard opened his eyes to gaze into Zalith's. "I know," he replied quietly and sadly. He then looked down at his lap with a sullen sigh as he slowly lowered his head and rested it on the demon's shoulder.

Zalith hugged him tightly. "I didn't see everything," he murmured, rubbing Alucard's back. "I didn't want to in case there were things you weren't ready for me to see. But I left some trace ethos in your mind, and it's going to slowly untangle everything else for you."

Alucard nodded appreciatively. "Thank you."

The door suddenly clicked and unlocked from the outside.

Zalith snarled a hostile, threatening sound as he sharply turned his head and glared in the direction of the scion who had entered. The demon tightened his grip on Alucard, holding him as protectively as he could manage as he and the scion glowered at one another in a moment of tense hostility.

The man didn't enter the room—the same man Zalith had hit last night. Instead, he hissed quietly and looked away from them both. "Her Highness will see you in the hall now," he said sternly and with a tone of disgust.

"Will she?" Zalith snarled.

Zalith was clearly not at all interested in accepting Lilith's invitation, but Alucard was driven by his anger, by his eagerness to show Lilith just how pathetic she was. He pulled himself from Zalith's protective embrace and snatched his trousers from the floor. He hastily pulled them on, his once despondent look fading to something furious. He snatched his shirt, glancing back at Zalith as he got dressed, too.

Once they were ready, Alucard and Zalith followed the scion down the halls of Lilith's temple. Now, it was Alucard's sadness that had been buried. His anger was rising, his desire to make her pay for everything she'd done increasing with it. No more would he be the little lost boy without love or purpose. No longer would he be Damien's pawn, Lilith's pawn, or the property of *any* Numen. It was a long time coming, but now, he was prepared to take control of his life, and not even Damien would convince him otherwise.

Chapter Seventy-One

─ ⋖ ✝ ⋗ ─

The AntiNumen

| **Alucard** |

Alucard trailed behind Lilith's scion, moving through the shadowed halls of her temple with Zalith at his side. Anger and caution etched across Zalith's face, but Alucard maintained a vacant stare, a façade concealing the tempest of fury brewing within him. Since the removal of his runes, his anger had resurged, reaching a volatile point that threatened to overflow. The catastrophic rage he once struggled to control during the dark night of Ada's demise had returned with an intensity that bordered on uncontrollable.

Yet, in this moment, he found a peculiar sense of mastery over it. Whether it was the looming presence of Zalith by his side or a newfound caution stemming from the need for restraint, Alucard couldn't discern. All he knew was that Lilith wouldn't revel in her false victory for much longer. The simmering anger within him whispered promises of impending reckoning, and Alucard was determined that Lilith would soon face the consequences of underestimating the storm she had unleashed.

His attention fixated on the path ahead—navigating the winding hallways, passing by the stark, windowless walls. In any other circumstance, the absence of a view to the outside world might have induced panic, but not this time. Determination coursed through him, overshadowing any potential anxiety. He remained steadfast, meticulously suppressing the burgeoning anger that threatened to surge forth as he shadowed the scion towards the hall where Lilith awaited.

With every step, the clamour of chattering demons grew louder, a dissonant symphony heralding their imminent confrontation. They drew closer, each footfall bringing them nearer to the threshold, closer to addressing Lilith's atrocious, disgusting behaviour. The anticipation heightened, the promise of silencing that loathsome woman resonating in the air. The time until she would be rendered speechless was dwindling, and Alucard embraced the certainty that her reign of audacity would soon come to a decisive end.

The vampire silenced his thoughts as the scion reached the door to Lilith's hall. He watched when the man pushed the door open and led the way inside as the observing crowds began to quieten down. Lilith's eyes hit him, as did the thousands of others, all filled with disgust, watching every move he made.

But he didn't care about them. He set his eyes on Lilith, who sat on her throne with that same twisted, devious smile on her face. She thought she was so smart, so superior. She'd not think that for much longer.

"Caedis...." Lilith smiled, waving her clawed fingers at him as the scion led him forward, forcing him to stand twenty feet from where she sat.

Zalith snarled in hostility when the scion put his hands on Alucard, and the man let go. He knew his place.

"Take him," Lilith said with a sigh, waving her hand in Zalith's direction. The demon fought, of course, as the other seven of Lilith's scions threw themselves at him and dragged him from Alucard's side.

Alucard reached for Zalith's hand, intending to snatch it before the scions could pull him away, but their fingers slipped through one another as the scions dragged Zalith away so aggressively that he barely had a chance to resist. It dismayed Alucard; he wanted Zalith beside him, but Lilith obviously enjoyed seeing him stand alone because alone was what she wanted him to be. She must have been just as horrified as Damien was when she saw that he'd found Zalith, when she'd seen he'd found someone to love and someone to love him.

"Did you sleep well?" Lilith asked curiously as she leaned her chin onto her hand, smiling down at Alucard once the scion who had led him and Zalith from their room forced him onto his knees.

He stared vacantly at her.

"Well?" she quickly asked, setting her gaze on Zalith, who had calmed down but didn't look any less angry than he had the moment he'd been pulled from Alucard's side. "Did you spend the entire night fucking, or did you decide you'd speak to me?" she questioned with an irritated frown on her once smiley face.

Zalith scowled condescending at her. "We're here, aren't we?"

Lilith scoffed, slowly taking her eyes off him to look at Alucard. "How did my baby sleep?" she asked with a babyish tone.

"You'd think that if he were your baby, you would put him in a nicer room," Zalith snarled.

She tutted, sat up straight in her seat, and crossed her left leg over her right. "I don't know where you get your attitude from, child," she sneered, glowering over at Zalith. "One would think you're of Damien."

Zalith glowered back at the woman. "It came from my mother, who I heard got it from you."

Lilith laughed as she shuffled around in her seat and glanced over at Alucard.

The vampire kept his gaze on the floor, listening to their exchange, waiting for the time to come when she would ask her questions.

"Such a beautiful collection of children; they were my first generation of scions. Did you know that I used the DNA of a very obedient demon to create your mother? I can't remember what I used for your father, but he was just as magnificent." She sighed longingly. "It's a shame that they're all dead—a shame *you* didn't die with them. Now, I have to pry you from my Caedis like a tick upon one's skin," she threatened with a quiet, wicked laugh.

Her laugh was *so* irritating. Alucard wanted to silence her already, and her threat only motivated him more—but he had to wait. Behind him, the hall was full of at least ten hundred demons, most of whom he suspected were children of the scions currently restraining Zalith, whom he also had to consider. What he would do to Lilith would have to be sudden, devastating, and startling enough that he'd have the time to stop the room from descending and attacking.

But Zalith smiled in amusement and laughed quietly in response to her threat; that angered the scions holding him, every single one of them snarling quietly as Lilith glowered at him.

"Is this funny?" she asked with a look of curiosity on her face.

"No, it's not," he answered with sincerity in his voice, but still with an amused smile on his face, almost as if he couldn't help it.

Her smile faded into a vacant stare. "Show him what's funny," she instructed, looking at the scion standing behind Alucard.

The moment she looked at her scion, Alucard suspected that she'd ordered the man to attack *him* in order to get Zalith to cooperate, but instead, the man stormed over to where Zalith was being held and smashed his fist into his face as though it was something he'd been so very desperately waiting to do. Of course, it started a battle of eight against one. Zalith pulled his right arm free and snatched the scion's neck, but his brothers stopped Zalith from injuring him any further.

As one scion snatched his arm, another crashed his fist into the side of Zalith's face. Another's fist collided with his chest, and as Zalith hit the face of another of the scions, one of them kicked the back of Zalith's shin. He stumbled but continued to fight as best he could, given the circumstances.

Alucard was barely able to move in his attempt to get up and assist before Lilith pointed down at him and scowled. "Stay where you are," she hissed.

He watched as the eight men eventually overwhelmed Zalith, clawing and punching and kicking as he slowly fell closer to the ground. Alucard knew that if it were any other situation, Zalith would have made easy work of Lilith's most recent generation of scions, but here, Zalith had no ethos, and he, just like Alucard, had to be careful with his actions.

And for a few awful moments, Alucard had to sit there and watch the eight of them beat the hell out of the man he loved.

Once she felt it was enough, Lilith waved her hand, commanding her scions to step away from Zalith. They forced him onto his knees before leaving but remained close enough to grab him if need be.

A satisfied smile crept across Lilith's face as she watched Zalith spit the blood from his mouth and glare at her with a look so hostile on his bloodied face that it was clear he was eager to kill her.

"Was *that* funny?" she asked, giggling.

Zalith rolled his eyes, not uttering a word that might start another exchange.

As her smile remained on her face, she set her eyes back on Alucard. "Now, where were we? We'll start with something simple. Tell me why Damien did this to you," she said. "Why he stripped you of such beautiful wings."

When Alucard thought about it, his mind went foggy. Zalith's explanation of why he struggled to remember things sometimes made him understand what the feeling meant: the memory of why his wings had been taken had been altered. He tried to remember what really happened, but he couldn't. Zalith's untangling ethos evidently hadn't gotten that far yet.

Zalith hesitated to answer Lilith's question, but when the woman glanced at him, he scowled and said, "He failed to deliver a message at the correct time."

Lilith held her hand to her mouth to hide her smile as she tried to force a look of sorrow onto her face. "Oh... you poor baby. Why would he do such an awful thing?"

"I'm sure you know just as well as the rest of us that he throws a tantrum when things don't go his way," Zalith answered. "And I'm also sure you know that *better* than anyone else."

Taking her eyes off Alucard, Lilith scowled at Zalith. "We all get a little angry when our children disappoint us, don't we? For example, your mother wasn't too pleased to know her son was much less of a man than she had hoped. The many times she pleaded in her prayers that I fix you and your little... problem," she said with a cruel smile as she glanced at Alucard. "To feel such disgusting things for other males. How disappointed in you she was, and still would be if she were alive. But she isn't, is she? And who is to blame for that?"

Zalith's glare grew thicker. "You speak about parenthood as though you have experience properly caring for your child, yet she prayed to you to save us, and you just let her die."

"And *you* speak as though you think I *care* what happened. It wasn't I who chose to have your little family reside in Erich's world; if she had stayed here, perhaps I might have answered her prayers. But.. alas, she and your father ran away to live somewhere else in hopes of leading better lives. How foolish they were, and how foolish you *are*.

This conversation is over. I am here for Caedis; I have very little interest in you—in fact, the only interest I have is that of how you came to find my Caedis, and why it is you cling to him like…like a child would its mother," she said with a grin, eyeing them both.

Alucard glared at the floor; he was sure that she was thinking of the moment she'd stolen *his* mother from him—a moment she clearly loved to reminisce. He lifted his head ever so slightly, setting his eyes on her as she smiled at Zalith.

"You can silence him, children. I don't need his lip anymore." Then, as the eight scions began to attack Zalith once again, Lilith set her eyes on the vampire. "Caedis," she said. "Stand up."

He did as he was told, but with a glance back at Zalith; every instinct within him urged him to rush to his aid, but it might only worsen things. He hated standing there and watching while Zalith was kicked, clawed, and beaten as blood splashed to the ground around him. It hurt to see, and it hurt more to know that any attempt to help the man he loved would only cause Lilith to force more pain onto him.

"Look at me," she then said.

Alucard slowly took his eyes off the commotion and looked at her.

"You may speak to me, considering as your speaker may not possess the ability to do so once my sons are done with him," she laughed.

Alucard stifled a scowl. He had to keep his anger at bay for a little longer.

"Where did you find him?" she asked. "He is not of your world."

"He…came here to do something for Damien," Alucard answered.

Lilith giggled. "I see. And I assume that *you* were also working on that same something?"

He nodded.

"And you two just so happened to…what? Fall in love?"

The horde behind the vampire unleashed a cacophony of unsettling sounds—snarls, twisted laughter, and a disconcerting symphony of noises that encapsulated both mockery and profound disgust. The air reverberated with their malicious expressions, creating an eerie ambience that mirrored the malevolent intentions lurking within the throng. Each derisive sound seemed to weave into a chilling tapestry of scorn and repulsion, amplifying the hostile atmosphere that enveloped Alucard and Zalith.

"I can imagine that Damien wasn't very pleased to see you two doing whatever it is that two males do. Is that why he left you in the state you were in yesterday?"

As the scions continued to beat Zalith, Alucard frowned in dismay and looked back over his shoulder, still eager to intervene.

Lilith sighed loudly and waved her hand in dismissal. "You can stop. That's enough," she said to her scions. "Answer," she then ordered, glaring at Alucard.

For a moment, Alucard kept his eyes on Zalith, watching as he wiped the blood from his face, several cuts on it. And as he felt Lilith's impatience turn into anger, he looked back at the woman. "No," he answered.

She scoffed. "Then why is it that I found you as I did?"

Alucard hesitated; he almost allowed himself to tell Lilith that he had turned on Damien, that he had used his ethos against him. He didn't want to let her know that he would and could do such a thing—he wasn't supposed to know he was capable. But what should he tell her? That he'd failed again so that she could laugh and berate him? What choice did he have? He stared vacantly as she waited in silence. "I took too long to find someone," he answered.

"Of course you did." Lilith smiled condescendingly. "Well, you won't need to worry about him anymore; you're here now, and I'll be taking care of you. Does that make you happy, Caedis?"

It didn't. He took his eyes off her and looked back at Zalith—

"Look at me when I'm talking to you!" Lilith then yelled, slamming her hands against the arms of her seat. "You disrespectful creature!" she screamed.

Alucard took his eyes off Zalith and looked at her. "Yes," he answered with as little anger as possible. He struggled to ignore the scent of Zalith's blood and knowing that he was hurt made him desperate to react, but he had to control himself.

Lilith giggled. "Do you want to go to him?"

"Yes," he said, scowling.

"Then go to him," she said, waving her hand at Zalith. "You may as well say your goodbyes. You won't be seeing him after this. You're mine now, and I can't have something as distracting as your boyfriend hanging around, can I?"

Alucard ignored her threat. The moment he was permitted to approach Zalith, he left the place he'd been standing and made his way over to where Zalith sat. He dropped to his knees beside him, pulling him into a tight embrace as the demon, too, leaned in to hold him. Alucard knew that Zalith was thinking the very same thing: no one would separate them; not Lilith, not Damien—nothing and no one. He was sure that Zalith was already plotting a way to escape, but he need not do so this time. Alucard already knew what he was going to do, and he needed no more motivation other than the thought of having *his* demon taken from him.

He'd lost so much—so many people, too many people. But he'd not lose Zalith. Zalith was the only thing he had left in the worlds; the only one he loved, would ever love, and the only one he'd hold onto so tightly. There was nothing he wouldn't do for Zalith—nothing he wouldn't do to be with him. And what he was about to do was something he would have never even *dreamed* of doing.

But he knew what might happen once he unleashed his anger. Last time, he'd drowned in his rage, and now, Damien wasn't there to stop it from happening.

However, *Zalith* was. Alucard trusted him with his life, and he was confident that he'd save him from sinking into the madness—if not with a rune, then something just as effective. He didn't have enough time to sit there and work out what that might be, but he did have enough time to warn Zalith.

He rested his forehead against Zalith's and closed his eyes. "I need you, my love," he said so very quietly, trying to hide as much of his worry as he could as he placed a message within the demon's mind. All he could do was hope that Zalith understood and that he'd work out what to do to save him.

Zalith stared at him, a look of both worry and confusion on his bloodied face as if he wasn't sure of what was about to happen. "I'm here," he replied, placing his hand on the side of the vampire's face. He then kissed him in what might be an attempt to alleviate some of their worry.

"That's enough," Lilith then called with revolt in her voice. "Get away from him."

Instantly, her scions stepped forward. Two of them pulled Alucard to his feet and escorted him away from Zalith, whom the other six stopped from trying to get up.

Alucard didn't resist as they moved him away from the demon; he took his eyes off Zalith and glared ahead at Lilith as he was shoved back to the very spot he'd been standing in before heading over to him.

Then, he focused on his anger—his *determination*.

He watched Lilith stand; the thought of her believing she'd won only increased his anger; the thought that she felt as if she owned him, that she'd gotten away with everything she'd done. She thought that she was going to control him.

He'd not be controlled; he'd not be owned.

And Zalith—he'd not lose Zalith. No one would keep that demon from him—*no one*. Alucard had to escape with him; he had to fight every single demon in this room, Lilith's scions, and Lilith herself. But he wasn't afraid. He wasn't intimidated. He knew what he was, what he was capable of, and he was but moments away from showing Lilith that she'd made so many very, *very* huge mistakes so many years ago.

"Come, my little Caedis," she said with a smile, holding her hand out to him as she stood in front of her seat. "Let me be the mother you lost so long ago."

"No," he replied. "*You* are not my mother…and you never will be," he snarled.

Lilith scoffed as she lowered her hand. "Such an insolent little child, aren't you? I *ought* to be your mother; I saved your life all those years ago. What did that Lucidian whore ever do for you? Die, disappoint—all she did was bear you, nothing more."

Alucard had so much to say in response. He knew she'd killed his mother; he knew that she was responsible for his lack of a childhood. "You didn't save my life," he growled, watching as Lilith's sour look became something of angered revolt. "If it wasn't for you, perhaps I would have had a life. But I don't resent it—I don't resent the fact I ended up where I did because of you and Damien. If things hadn't gone the way they did, if it wasn't for you, I wouldn't have ever met Zalith, and if I hadn't met Zalith, I'd have no reason to want to kill you," he replied, his voice thick with threat, but his face vacant.

For a few seconds, Lilith stared at him almost as if she was trying to work out whether he'd just said the words that had left his mouth. Her scions hissed in revolt, clearly ready to attack on her word, and the crowd fell silent, the atmosphere of the hall quickly becoming something both tense and ominous as Lilith and Alucard glowered at one another.

Lilith then scoffed. "Excuse me—kill me?" she asked with a little laugh of shock. "You? Oh, my dear Caedis, no." She smiled as she began to slowly approach him.

The vampire didn't move. He stood there, watching her every move as she stepped closer. Both her expression and movements made it seem as though she was almost wary of what might happen next.

She then reached out her hand towards him. "Don't be so silly; you could never hurt me—you simply don't have the means, the will, or...well, you don't have anything, do you?" she asked, placing her hand on the side of his face. "But...you have *me*. You'll always ha—"

Alucard abruptly snatched her throat before she could finish. She gagged and stared in astonishment, gripping his wrist with both her hands as she choked and tried to speak words that might match the look of fury on her face, but the vampire held so tightly that her words were nothing but stuttered, struggled grunts. And the moment he'd snatched hold of her, all eight of her sons flew forward, and the entire hall of demons jumped to their feet and burst into action—but Alucard was much faster than anyone else.

In the blink of an eye, before any of Lilith's scions had taken more than half a step, Alucard burst forward, pinning Lilith against the wall with such force that it shook most of the platform upon which they stood. She gagged, he scowled, and as he dug his claws into her neck, her power began to ooze from her body in the form of black, white, and crimson fog. It soaked into Alucard's ice-pale skin, and as he held out his free hand, the approaching scions were frozen where they stood, powerless against his ethos.

The room was still coming at him, but that didn't unsettle him. He stared into Lilith's mortified eyes, a conniving smirk spreading across his face as the Numen's power began to become his own.

"C-Caedis," she choked, agonizingly gasping for air as she stared into his hell-fiery eyes. "W-what are you doing?!" she screeched.

He tilted his head ever so slightly as the horns on his head began to grow; a second and third pair started to appear as he continued absorbing her power so quickly that no one would have time to reach their queen.

"Did you forget who I am?" he asked, his voice demonic and distorted.

She opened her mouth to scream, but in a blinding, deafening burst of dark Numen ethos, the entire room quaked. Upon Alucard's back materialized his long-lost wings, a manifestation of darkness with a glimmer of crimson on their scales, reminiscent of a night sky tinged with the subtle hues of impending dusk. His head bore three pairs of horns—the first retaining their original form but standing taller, an emblem of his ancient strength. The second pair, mirroring the first in curvature, possessed an inky blackness that accentuated their sinister elegance, positioned not far behind the primary set. The third pair, nestled at the rear of his head, stood as the smallest and darkest, a subtle yet potent display of his unearthly essence. Below these horns, a singular line of small, jagged spines traced a menacing silhouette along his spine, completing the otherworldly transformation that marked Alucard's long-coming return from the despair the Numen had cursed him with.

He spread his wings, sending waves of devastatingly loud bursts of power surging towards the incoming crowds of demons. The eight frozen scions were launched back when the first wave of ethos hit them, thrown off the platform and sent plummeting down to whatever lay below. Zalith was the only one left unscathed, sitting where he'd been left, watching in bewilderment *and* enjoyment as Lilith tried to scream within the grip of Alucard's talon-adorned hand.

Lilith's quickly weakening body began to tremble as Alucard stole the power she so sorely loved. She watched as his form became Numen, demonic scales and fragments of armour-like skin appearing on his body. His glare contorted much crueller, his anger lingered within the black aura that began to pour from his skin, and upon his forearms, his smaller wing-like limbs appeared, folded against his arms.

He held the struggling woman in place while the waves of power emanating from his body eradicated every single follower that had been present within her hall. It was then that she realized that Alucard was no longer the foolish child she had tried to make him believe he was.

Alucard abruptly pulled the woman from against the wall, spun around, and chucked her to the floor. He stood there for a moment, basking in the darkness that was now his power. He stared at her, watching as she struggled, whimpered, and cried, starting to drag herself along the floor. Her wings draped at her side like wet cloths, her body writhing as she clawed at the rocky ground.

Lilith gasped in horror, realizing that she was no longer surrounded by her followers or her sons. There was, however, Zalith. She looked over at him, a look of desperation on her visage as she reached out, but the uninterested look on his face told her that he wasn't going to help. He took his eyes off her, looking at Alucard, who folded his wings against his back and began to slowly prowl towards the crawling woman.

She whimpered and cried in torment, trying to scurry away like an injured animal. But Alucard soon reached her, snatched her left horn, and lifted her from the floor. He swung her around, snatched her throat again, and stared into her eyes. But this time, she stared back with fury and hatred.

"You can't kill me," she hissed. "You can't stop me. You can't hide, you can't run—there won't be a place you can go where I won't find you, creature!"

A small, amused smile appeared on his face. "I hid from you for four hundred years; don't you think I can do it again?"

Glaring at him, she tried to escape his grip and snarled in frustration. She then screamed in anger as he lifted her off her feet. "I'll kill you!" she screamed, kicking and flailing in his grip.

"No, you won't," he said with a smile.

Then, he threw her forward—she flew back, her body twisting through the air until she was in the very centre of the room. She hovered there, forcefully held in place by the ethos that had once been hers.

Alucard stood with a vacant stare on his face, looking up at her as she screamed in desperation. He knew what he had to do next to weaken her. He held out both his arms to his side, resting his elbows against his body while he curved his claws as if to grasp something. Upon his command, every drop of blood that had been spilt began to crystalize into small, glass-like shards, and as he kept his eyes on Lilith, the shards quickly darted towards her. They burst through her body, cutting her skin, shredding her hair. As she was cut, whatever little power that remained within her began to bleed from her.

Her limbs began to crumble, her skin, her horns, her flesh, peeling away like ash in a fire, floating away from where she hung. And once the shards were depleted, Alucard held out his hand, focusing on his need to stop her as he summoned the darkness around him. The fog seeping from his wings slithered towards his open hand and swiftly morphed to form a small, beautifully decorated sheathed dagger. He snatched hold of it, pulled the blade from its sheath, and in the blink of an eye, he burst up through the air towards Lilith.

Alucard mercilessly plunged the dagger into Lilith's heart. The look of defeat and horror on her face was one Alucard had longed to see, and there it was… finally.

He glared into her eyes, and as the entire blade was embedded within her body, Alucard muttered, "Sleep."

A shattering burst of energy erupted from the woman's body. Alucard was flung away by the sheer force, and Zalith stood to rush to his aid, but as Alucard's feet hit the ground, he skidded back and stumbled but purposely fell to land rather gracefully on the throne that had once belonged to Lilith. And there Alucard sat, staring up at her, watching as her eyes closed, any and all life leaving her crumbling face.

And then… nothing.

Dead silence, stillness, emptiness… as her body stopped floating and dropped to the ground with a quiet thump.

It was over.

Or was it?

Alucard wanted to look at Zalith… but the Numen ethos raging inside his body began to possess his mind. The world around him started fading, just as it had the night he'd killed Ada.

And before he could even try to fight to remain in control, the dark took him.

| Zalith |

Zalith stared over at Alucard, who breathed calmly as he slouched on Lilith's throne. The vampire kept his vacant stare on the place Lilith had once been floating, almost as if he was frozen… stuck in the moment of the woman's defeat.

But Zalith didn't forget what Alucard had said to him before Lilith tried to separate them. He had said he needed Zalith, and at the same time, he'd transferred a small message into his mind—*don't let it take me*, he'd pleaded. Zalith was sure he knew what that meant, and it was the only thing he would focus on right now.

Alucard had told him what happened the last time he'd let his anger consume him, and he'd evidently known the same thing was going to happen here—that was why he'd told Zalith he needed him, and Zalith was going to do everything he could to help him. But what should he do? What *could* he do? What would stop Alucard from sinking into whatever was taking hold of him?

He quickly stood up, ignoring the ache of his wounds as he hurried over to where the vampire sat. Alucard took his sights off the space before him and set them on Zalith; the sadness that usually lingered within his hell-fiery eyes was gone, replaced by an ominous, *dark* anger that Zalith hadn't seen before. But it didn't unsettle him. It caused a light shiver to run down his spine, but the intimidation he was feeling might just be the influence of the Numen ethos seeping from Alucard's body.

"Alucard?" he asked quietly, slowing his approach as the look of hostility in the vampire's eyes seemed to grow with every step he took. But he didn't stop at all; he reached Alucard and placed his hand on his shoulder in the space between two black, jagged spines.

The vampire stared up at him, a hint of familiarity glimmering within the black of his eyes' once-white sclera.

Zalith slowly dragged his hand down and over the vampire's arm until he reached his hand, which he gripped firmly. He detected no hostility; it had all faded the moment the demon placed his hand on Alucard's shoulder, so he carefully pulled Alucard to his feet and away from Lilith's throne.

The black, Numen power continued to flow from Alucard's body, seeping along the platform floor and pouring over its edges. Zalith wasn't sure what to make of what he was seeing, what he had seen... but he didn't have time to assume. He had to wake Alucard up from whatever trance he was trapped in.

He stared at the vampire for a moment but then pulled him into his embrace. He held him tightly, trying to work out what to do. The Numen power was leaving his body; did he have to wait until it was all gone? What would even happen once it was? Would it return to and wake Lilith up? He wasn't sure. He *was* sure that Alucard knew, but it didn't seem as though the vampire would utter a word in response.

Holding him, Zalith swiftly thought back to what Alucard had said; the vampire told him that when he'd killed Ada, he'd lost himself in his anger. He said that he didn't even remember half of what happened, almost as if he hadn't been the same person—within the same mind. That had to be what was happening now, and Zalith had to remind him that he was *Alucard* and not what this Numen power and his *anger* were making him think he was.

But how? How could he remind Alucard that he was... Alucard?

Slowly, he leaned back so that he could stare into the eyes of his vampire. "Alucard," he said softly. He then smiled, placing his hand on the side of Alucard's face. "I don't know what I should say," he admitted, glancing to his right as he watched the wings on Alucard's back begin to crumble, floating away from his body upon the fog of Numen ethos. "But... if you're lost, I need you to come back to me—I need you... I *really* need you," he breathed, placing his forehead against Alucard's as he closed his eyes, trying to keep himself from sinking into the sadness that came with the thought of losing the man he truly loved. "I love you *so* much, and I can't lose you—I *won't* lose you," he said, tightening his embrace around him. "Don't leave me," he pleaded quietly.

Zalith's heart pounded in his chest, the grip of desperation tightening with every passing moment. The silence hung heavy, each second without Alucard's response intensifying the tendrils of anxiety that coiled around him. What if he failed to save him? The prospect gnawed at him, a relentless worry that threatened to consume him entirely. What if he was going to lose the man he loved so shortly after finding him? The very thought fractured Zalith's heart, sending tremors through his being, and the spectre of helplessness loomed, casting shadows of doubt over his abilities. What if he couldn't save him?

But his words weren't unheard. Alucard gradually moved his arms around the demon, and as Zalith opened his eyes to stare into his, he watched the vacant, empty stare fade. A weak smile made its way onto Alucard's face, and as it did, Zalith felt relief enthral him, banishing his despair and doubt.

"I…won't ever leave you," Alucard said quietly. "We do, however, have to leave *this* place before she wakes up," he said, looking over at where Lilith's crumbled corpse lay. "Don't let go of my hand until I say," he then insisted, taking hold of Zalith's hand.

Zalith smiled in response. He was glad that Alucard hadn't been consumed by the Numen ethos, and he trusted that the vampire knew what he was doing, that was why he didn't question him when he led him over to the edge of the platform.

"We need to get to the void outside; once we are out of here, I'll take us through a few places to hide our trail. It'll give us a week or so until Lilith works out we're not in any of the places we'll pass through," Alucard explained. "She'll wake up soon, but we'll be far away before then. What I'm about to do should also give you enough time to do what you need to do to hide us from the Numen."

The demon nodded in understanding. "Okay. Let's go."

With the Numen ethos still leaving his body, Alucard wrapped his arms around Zalith as if to hug him—but he then pulled them both over the edge.

They fell, falling… and falling, passing the walls of rock, getting closer to the empty black at the very bottom of the chasm. But when they reached the blackness, they left the confines of the rock, descending into the endless, empty dark space that existed outside the floating mass they had been inside.

Zalith caught glimpses of kaleidoscopic crystal shards, both above and below. He saw stars, moons, and floating masses surrounded by dark auras. He had no idea what it was, but it couldn't be important. He shifted his sights to Alucard; he watched as the further away from Lilith Alucard became, the quicker the Numen ethos poured from his body like blood from a gaping wound. His wings were gone, his new horns were gone— everything was swiftly crumbling other than his own original horns.

The demon watched Alucard stare past his head, presumably watching the crimson rock where Lilith's domain existed become smaller and smaller. Then, the vampire set his eyes on Zalith, gripped the demon's hand tightly, and closed his eyes. Black, sizzling power ensnared them, and in a matter of moments, they dematerialized, and everything went bright red.

Chapter Seventy-Two

— ◁ ✝ ▷ —

Through the Worlds

| **Zalith** |

U nwelcome, intense dizziness gripped hold of Zalith as the crimson light around him and Alucard soon became a spinning array of red, white, and black. He felt the jolt of collision as they hit the ground and heard the quiet chime of the closing rift Alucard had created, and as the world formed around him, he stared down at the vampire, who he'd landed on top of. The fact that they were no longer in their demon forms and laying on lime-green grass made it clear that they were no longer in Lilith's domain, and it brought relief to Zalith's heart.

The demon ignored the irritating motion sickness, keeping hold of Alucard's hand while he placed his other palm on the vampire's cheek. "Are you okay?"

Alucard nodded and huffed in displeasure when he tried to sit up; clearly he, too, suffered the same motion sickness. The vampire placed his free hand on his forehead as Zalith moved so that they could both sit up, and then they sat where they'd landed for a few moments, waiting for the resulting after-effects of their journey to wane.

They were in what looked to be a rather large forest of redwood trees, towering hundreds of feet above the ground. The sky was black and full of stars, and the moons that could be seen from Aegisguard shined brightly; however, here, they were positioned differently. Obviously, the world that he and Alucard were in faced the moons from a different angle than Aegisguard did.

"We are…in Mareaeternum," Alucard said, staring at Zalith, who took his eyes off the moons to look at the vampire. "We'll travel that way," he said, pointing to his left. "Through all the other realms until we get back to Aegisguard. That will scatter our trace very far, and it'll take Lilith a while to find us. I need…ten or so minutes before we can move on, though; the jumps take a lot of ethos, and I need to make sure I keep hold of enough of Lilith's ethos to give us as much time as we can possibly get."

The demon nodded in understanding. Of course, he had questions, and he didn't feel a need to wait. He'd wait to discuss what happened back in Lilith's temple, though, as that conversation would require more than ten minutes. "How long will it be until Lilith recovers?" he asked, looking at Alucard as they slowly helped each other climb to their feet.

Once he stood up, Alucard leaned back against one of the trees and looked at Zalith, who leaned beside him. "Usually, it takes days for a Numen to heal those blades out of their bodies, but someone likely felt all of those demon deaths and will come looking. I would give it...twenty minutes, maybe thirty. But she won't risk leaving that place until she has at least half of her ethos back—that will take a short while to return to her."

Zalith nodded again, slowly taking his eyes off Alucard to look at the world around them. What had Alucard done to Lilith? How? Was he capable of *killing* her rather than putting her down for a while? Alucard evidently knew a lot more than Zalith had originally suspected about the Numen and their weaknesses, and he wanted to know just how much that was. He wanted to know exactly what Alucard was capable of because he was sure that what he'd seen was only a fraction of what this vampire could do, and he wanted to not only *know* but to *see* more. There'd be a time and place to ask all of that, though, so for now, he'd focus on what they were currently doing and where they currently were.

"Have you been here before?" he asked, looking at Alucard again.

"No," Alucard answered, tightening his grip on Zalith's hand. "I only know where we are because of the placement of the moons," he said, glancing up at the night sky. "Mareaeternum isn't too far from Aegisguard, so the moons are only the slightest bit differently angled. I have also studied most of these other realms; I knew one day I'd end up in each of them one way or another," he explained. But before Zalith could say anything else, the vampire stood up straight and pulled lightly on his hand. "We have to go; this world is full of werewolves, and I'd rather *not* have to deal with them. The two gods who live here, Thalis and Kardos, who I told you about recently, are at war with one another," he continued, leading the way through the dark forest. "There are two factions of wolves and they are always fighting to honour the god they follow, always on the lookout for one another. If we are seen, they will not recognize us and assume we are the enemy."

"And thus, we'll find ourselves battling werewolves together again," Zalith said with a smile as he followed Alucard forward. When Alucard looked over at him, the demon then frowned in concern. "Where are we going?"

Alucard looked ahead again. "To avoid emerging from a rift and into the ground where we will inevitably suffocate and die, we need to be falling from a specific height before I can create the rift so that we'll land in open space. The momentum of our fall will create open space around us when we arrive if we do come out under the surface."

"Interesting," Zalith said. He was glad that Alucard knew what he was talking about because he'd rather not end up stuck beneath the ground and have dirt filling his lungs as he tried to escape—it would be much like being buried alive, he was sure, and he'd not like to experience it. "We could fly," he suggested. "If we can't find a suitable drop nearby."

"Maybe," Alucard replied. "But we might be seen, and we don't want to unintentionally pull werewolves with us."

Zalith smirked and said, "An occupational hazard."

"It'll upset the balance of ethos in the world we next go to; I'm an exception because I possess Numen blood, and you are unaffected because I'm holding your hand. If I were to let go, you would start to feel much worse than motion sick as the world tries to eject you like a parasite from a body. So, don't let go of my hand, hmm?" he said, smiling at him.

Amused, Zalith smirked but then frowned as he thought back to what Lilith had earlier said. "This is the second time I've been called a parasite today," he said, keeping his eyes on Alucard. "Am I a parasite, Alucard?"

The vampire frowned at him. "No," he answered. "It was…metaphor," he said, almost as if he was worried he may have offended the demon.

Zalith sighed a fake, dramatic sigh. "I'm not sure. Perhaps I do cling to you far too much."

Alucard scowled. "You don't."

He shrugged. "Maybe I ought to consider giving you some space; the last thing I want to do is irritate you with my parasitic personality, latching onto you like a flea," he said, stifling a grin. "Sucking your blood very much like one, too."

Alucard stopped walking and glared at him. "If you were such an annoyance, I would've told you," he insisted with a scowl of both confusion and irritancy on his face.

Looking at him, Zalith sighed again. "Would you?"

The vampire stared at him, his look of confusion intensifying. He clearly had no idea whether he was being sarcastic or truthful, and it made Zalith laugh. As he laughed, he placed his other hand on Alucard's shoulder and smiled.

"A joke, vampire," he said, moving his hand from Alucard's shoulder and to the side of his face. "I'd rather not spend a moment of my time anywhere else than with you. I just don't want that to become something that aggravates you."

Alucard looked down at the grass and sighed quietly. He then moved closer so that he could rest his head on Zalith's shoulder. "I want you with me all the time, too," he said quietly, tightening the grip he had on the demon's hand. "The thought of not being with you is mostly what kept me from sinking into my anger," he admitted, a nervous tone in his hushed voice.

The demon held him tightly, resting the side of his head on Alucard's. "I'll always be here, always with you, no matter where we are."

Zalith felt Alucard smile while he nuzzled his neck. He, too, smiled as he stood there, enjoying their embrace for a few moments. However, the thought of home soon hit him in a strange way. Home wasn't exactly the same place for them both, was it? Alucard had called the demon's house his home, but Zalith was sure that Alucard still considered his castle his home. Zalith wasn't content with that fact—he wanted Alucard to live *with him*, in *his* home, his house. He wanted it to be *their* home. Not only because Alucard would be a whole lot safer there with him and because Zalith would feel so much less worried with Alucard permanently under his roof, but because it just felt right. He enjoyed Alucard's company so much that he wanted him to live with him. It might seem a little early to want such a thing, but with Alucard, everything was different. There was nothing too early; there were only the exact right times, and this was one of them.

He leaned back so that he could see the vampire's face and placed his hand on the side of it. "Being together would be a whole lot easier if we lived together, you know," he said, smirking.

Alucard stared at him, a look of pondering on his face. It almost looked as though he was confused, and when he frowned unsurely, he looked down at the ground. "You want... me to live with you?" he asked quietly. "At your house... in Nefastus? And... it will be *our* house? Together?"

"Yes," Zalith confirmed with a content smile.

As Alucard's smile returned, he leaned closer and rested his forehead on Zalith's shoulder. But before Zalith could ask him what his answer was, the vampire sighed, stepped back, and looked at him. "We have to keep moving," he said, and as Zalith nodded and followed him, he glanced at the demon.

Zalith stared expectantly at him, waiting for his response.

"When... do you want me to come?" the vampire asked nervously.

"Now," Zalith immediately answered. "Well, once we're safely back in Aegisguard."

Alucard looked down at the grass and smiled slightly. "Okay."

Zalith then stopped walking again, and as Alucard halted to look at him, the demon kissed him. Then, he smirked and continued to walk forward, pulling the vampire with him. "These trees are at least three hundred feet tall," he said, glancing at him. "Would falling from the top of one of them give you the momentum you need? I feel like our search for a cliff might take longer than we'd prefer to spend here."

Alucard looked up, staring at the sky through the very tall treetops. Then, he stopped walking and set his eyes on the tallest tree within the small opening they were standing in. "Perhaps," he answered. "The drop I fell from to get back from Tengetso was around three-fifty and I was fine," he said, looking at Zalith. "If we end up in the ground somewhere, we have no one to blame but ourselves," he said with a shrug.

The demon smirked. "Would you like me to fly us to the top?"

He nodded, and as he did, Zalith adorned his wings and horns.

Zalith wrapped his free arm around Alucard and swiftly took off. He landed on the tallest branch, just over three hundred feet off the ground, and as Zalith's demon form disappeared, he tightened his grip on Alucard's hand. "Lead the way."

"The next world is Glaciaqua; there are dragons everywhere. Hopevully, we arrive in a place where we won't have to run or fight."

"Either way, I'm sure we'll be fine," Zalith said, an assuring tone in his voice.

Alucard then sighed and looked down at the ground. "Are you ready?"

"I am," the demon replied.

Then, holding Zalith's hand tightly, Alucard moved his other arm around him. With no hesitation, he fell back, pulling Zalith with him as they plummeted to the ground. Zalith watched Alucard close his eyes to concentrate, and once the vampire created a rift around them, they disappeared into it moments before they would have hit the forest ground.

Chapter Seventy-Three

Further Beyond

| **Zalith** |

To Zalith's relief, he and Alucard emerged on the other side of the rift a few feet *above* the ground, and because they came through the space lying horizontally, they hit the snow-covered ground and landed on their sides. There were no signs of dragons or anything at all in the wide-frozen valley, and as snow began to fall, they climbed to their feet and made their way over to the shelter of a small dent in the side of a mountain.

"Have you been *here* before?" Zalith asked as he stood behind Alucard, moved his arm around him, and pulled the vampire's body against his own to try and keep him comfortable in the bitter cold.

Alucard turned to face him, burying his face in the demon's shoulder once more as the winds outside became something lethal. "A few times," he answered, clinging onto Zalith as tightly as he could while keeping hold of his hand. "It was a pointless journey, though. At the time, I was simply studying dragons, and this was the best place to come."

But the freezing cold made Alucard shiver violently—*so* violently that Zalith was sure the vampire wouldn't survive the temperature much longer without yelling in anger at it.

The vampire leaned out of the small shelter and glared upwards. "We can make our way up there right now. I don't want to stay here any longer."

Zalith smiled, tightening his embrace around the vampire. "It hasn't been long enough for you to move us again," he said with concern in his voice.

Alucard snarled irritably and looked away from Zalith. "I hate this cold." He adorned a pondering frown and said, "Don't let go of my hand." Then, he disappeared into vermillion smoke and re-emerged in his small melanistic fox form, keeping his paw pressed firmly against the palm of Zalith's hand.

Zalith hadn't exactly been prepared for it, but he caught the fox in his arms. He smiled down at Alucard as he shuffled around and made himself comfortable; the demon knew that the vampire hated the cold, and now it was clear that he hated it so much that he'd take on one of his animal forms to escape it. Zalith thought that was adorable.

He leaned back against the wall behind him and stared out as the snowstorm outside grew worse. Zalith's thoughts were still focused on the conversation he and Alucard were having before they left Mareaeternum, and he wished to continue. He wasn't sure if the fox form of his vampire could respond with words, but that wouldn't stop him from talking.

"Once we return to Aegisguard, and once I've done what I need to do to ensure the Numen won't find us, we can focus on your moving into my home. I know that you'll need workspace, so I can have an office set up for you. You'll need to bring anything that you want to have there, too. I'll have people move it for you," he said with a smile, looking down at Alucard as he stared up at him. With a quiet, amused but endearing laugh, the demon pet the fox's head with his free hand and looked back out at the snow. "I hope that living with me won't cause problems with your work," he then said, remembering the recent troubles that Alucard experienced because he'd been away from Dor-Sanguis for so long. But as he looked back down at him, the fox seemed to shake its head. "Good," the demon said.

The snow began to clear, and Zalith was sure that they'd soon be on their way to the next realm along the path that would take them home. "Will it be cold where we next travel?" he asked.

In his arms, the fox grumbled quietly, and Zalith wasn't sure if that was a yes or a no, but he was sure he'd find out soon.

"Are we ready?" he asked, and as the fox nodded, he entered his demon form once more, stepped out into the cold, and hurried up into the sky. He waited a moment, moving a little higher in case it was needed. Then, he looked down at Alucard, who didn't seem to be willing to change back to his normal self, so Zalith assumed that he could travel no matter what form he was in.

So, without further falter, his demon form disappeared, and once again, they were falling. Just as both times before, a blackness began to swallow them, and in a few short moments, the white of the snowy realm around them became bright red.

The red soon became an array of dark, gloomy shades. Zalith's back hit the ground, and he stared up to find that he was gazing at the ceiling of a room. The muttering of people and the sound of falling splinters caught his attention, as did Alucard's uncomfortable shuffling in his tight embrace.

Still holding the fox's paw, Zalith sat up, leaning his free hand into the floor so that he could look around the area they'd landed in. It *was* a room, one that might belong to a large house, and the wall in front of him was utterly destroyed, a large, circular hole having been burned into it. He could see into the village outside, a growing crowd of muttering, startled people staring in at him as he held onto the fox in his other arm.

It took Zalith no time at all to discover that these humans had never seen ethos before—their thoughts and reactions alike made it clear. How strange it must be for them to see a man who had appeared out of thin air with a fox in one arm, a fox that clearly thought it was funny and refused to turn back into the man he really was. Alucard's amused face made the demon sigh in amused irritancy; he'd not sit there and be gawped at a moment longer.

He climbed to his feet, both wooden splinters and snow falling from him as he used his free hand to clean what he could of his clothes. Then, ignoring the different reactions of the crowd, he made his way out through the hole in the wall and began to walk rather quickly through the village and away from prying eyes.

Once he found a small alley, he calmed down, leaned back against the wall, and looked down at Alucard. He had no idea where he was or what he should do in this strange new world, and he wanted Alucard back to lead the way *and* assure him that the fact they'd been seen just now wouldn't come back and bite them in the ass later on.

"Alucard," he said, looking down at the fox in his arms. "There isn't a single sign of snow here, and there are, in fact, *two* suns," he said, glancing up at the sky. "I'm sure it's safe for you to come back to me."

The vampire seemed to agree. Vermillion smoke surrounded him once more, and to Zalith's relief, the vampire reappeared as a man standing at his side.

"What is this place?" he then asked.

Alucard glanced around. "This is, uh…Letholdus."

Zalith nodded slowly; it was an interesting fact that this realm was named after Letholdus, and he was sure there was a reason behind it.

"Letholdus doesn't come here much, but…he might sense the reactions to our arrival. Ethos is not present here at all, and the people have never seen it. We might have caused a scene they won't soon forget, but…someone will come along with a reasonable explanation that doesn't involve a man falling out of the sky with a fox in his arms," he said, smirking.

Zalith laughed in response. "Will the tale become legend?"

"Maybe," Alucard said with a shrug.

"And here?" he then asked. "Is this a place you've been before?"

"No. I've had no reason to come here; nothing but humans. It's like…cattle farm. The Numen make worlds, and they always populate them with humans first. Those humans have to come from somewhere, right?"

"Quite," Zalith agreed. "Where did you learn that you could do this?"

"Do what?"

"Travel from realm to realm. I thought that, like that to Eltaria, portals existed. Is that not the case?"

Alucard looked down at the ground, clearly thinking to himself again. But he then shrugged and looked at him. "There was a time when I was a boy that I accidentally ended up in the place we were just in. One of the priestesses had a book about dragons; I saw her reading it the night prior. Of course, I stole it; I knew nothing of the world outside the walls of that cathedral, so I was curious. I learned of a place called Glaciaqua—another world, apparently. Then, I sort of just... went there. I only remember now because we uncovered the memories Lilith hid from me. It took them a while to find me out there. It was also where I discovered that I could turn into animals. Much like just now, I became a fox, something I saw a time before that on a tapestry."

Listening, Zalith smiled slightly. He did enjoy learning more about his vampire, but knowing that the memories he was sharing came from the dismaying part of his life upset the demon. Alucard didn't seem very distressed, though, and that gave Zalith some relief.

"As for the portal question... well, there are... factors. The short version is easier," he started. "Eltaria is a pocket world—a world within a world; it's directly connected to Aegisguard because it was created *inside* Aegisguard. The other worlds were made outside Aegisguard, and within the void. Therefore, there was no gateway created to get to them because they don't really have anything to do with Aegisguard. They are out there, though, and all the Numen can travel to them because the Numen can navigate through the void. I am Numen-blooded, so I can do that, too. With them, it's almost instant, but I need a little time to recover from the travel. If I use too much of my Numen ethos at once, it might tear me apart, and I don't think either of us want to see that."

Zalith's smile grew a little. Despite what happened, seeing that Alucard was—to an extent—content made Zalith feel the same way. He was convinced that inviting Alucard to live with him had pulled the vampire from his often sullen disposition, and it had also given Zalith some happiness in all of the upset and concern that recently ensnared them. With that in mind, he smiled and pulled Alucard closer, embracing him tightly. "You're very smart, vampire," he said quietly. "Is there anything you might *not* have facts about?"

Alucard shrugged as Zalith looked at him again. "Probably not."

Zalith felt as if he could list a few things, things that might fluster the vampire, but he'd not do it here. There was a time and a place, and where they were was neither. He looked around again, watching as a small group of villagers obliviously passed the alley they were hiding in. "Where will we be going next?"

A sour look appeared on Alucard's face. "Eh... Tengetso."

Tengetso, the place Alucard was sent to on the night of his birthday last year, the night they had to say goodbye again. But a night upon which they both became pretty sure of how they felt about one another, a night they shared a moment Zalith could never forget. His mind wandered back to the time they'd danced together on that balcony, a moment so sad yet so happy, but a moment that creature of a man, Damien, had interrupted, and the thought of him filled Zalith with rage.

He kept Alucard in his embrace, still holding onto his hand. He remembered what the vampire had said about Tengetso—a wasteland where the Numen disposed of their unwanted creations. Zalith was sure that Alucard didn't want to go back there, but it seemed as though they didn't have much of a choice. It did, however, prompt yet another question. "When you last went to Tengetso, did you have to travel through all of these other realms to get there? Or can you travel to whichever one you want with a single jump?"

"I can go to whichever one I want with one jump, but the further it is, the more ethos is used."

"I see. If you don't want to go back there, would avoiding it be a problem?"

"It would give us less time to work out how to hide me from the Numen, and as much as I would like to not go back there, I'd rather us have more time. We will go now," he said, beginning to lead the way out of the alley.

Zalith followed; he was now sure that Alucard really didn't want to go, but he wasn't wrong about having more time being better for them. So, he let Alucard lead the way once more, setting his eyes on a cliff edge not too far ahead. It would appear that the village they'd arrived in sat very close to the sea, and it saved him from having to take them up into the sky and risk being seen by the so very fragile, oblivious humans that lived here.

As they reached the edge of the cliff, they faced one another again.

"I don't know where we might end up there, but…we might be running a lot," Alucard said with a discontent frown.

"That's fine," Zalith said, an assuring smile on his face.

The vampire then wrapped his other arm around him, as did Zalith, and without hindrance, they fell off the cliff and disappeared into another rift.

Chapter Seventy-Four

— ⊰ ✝ ⊱ —

The Last Stop

| **Alucard** |

Tengetso was the last place Alucard wanted to find himself again, especially on the side of the world that had been ravaged by destruction.

He and Zalith emerged from the rift and into the room of an old sky-high building. The atmosphere hung heavy with an ominous tint, the skies resembling the rich, earthy brown of coffee absorbed into porous paper. Above, clouds loomed in a deep, coal-black hue, casting an eerie shadow over the landscape. The air carried a pungent aroma, a disturbing amalgamation of dampness and the unsettling scent of decaying flesh.

The floor they landed on was covered in ash, but not the type that came from fire—this ash came from the bodies of creatures that didn't manage to escape the light of the raging red sun hanging close to the horizon. To Alucard's relief, they hadn't arrived in the world on the ground, and it was even more relieving to know that they wouldn't have to journey across the land outside, either.

Alucard and Zalith stood up, helping one another to brush the ash off their clothes as the dizziness of their journey wore off. But when the loud, piercing shriek of a creature echoed from the world below, they both turned their heads to glare out of the holes in the walls that were once glass windows.

"This…is where he sent you?" Zalith asked in what sounded like concern and disgust as he stepped closer to the edge of the building to peer outside.

Alucard reluctantly followed him, setting his eyes on the world that lay below. Before them stretched a landscape of desolation—every visible entity lay in ruins, succumbing to decay and destruction. It seemed as though a barrage of fiery explosions had swept across the land, leaving a scorched trail in its wake, even scarring the once pristine sky. Not a trace of greenery remained, no sign of plant life or any living presence. The air hung heavy with uncomfortable heat, rendering the surroundings both miserable and devoid of life.

"It hasn't changed at all since I left," the vampire mumbled. "Nothing ever seems to change here."

"What happened?"

"I don't know," he said with a sigh. "This was a world like Aegisguard once upon a time. Despite being a trashcan for the Numen's unwanted creations, this was still a world—a full world. This side of Tengetso has been lost, and the other side sits behind walls that touch the clouds. One of the Numen sent something awful here, something worse than anything else that lived here, and this is what happened. Half of the world fell apart, everything here died, and this is what is left. There are…things out there, though. Creatures. We'll stay here until we can go."

Zalith was looking at him while he spoke but quickly set his eyes back on the world outside. "Damien had you *here* looking for angels?"

"Yes," he answered, glancing at the demon. "They came here in search of salvation for the world. This place is a source of Numen power—of Damien's, mostly. The death, destruction, and misery all somehow gives Damien influence. The more influence and recognition a Numen has, the stronger they are. Here, Damien is God. The creatures that survive pray to him. I'm sure if Damien was to lose his hold on this world, he'd not be so…powerful. That's why Ephriel sent angels here…to try and remove Damien as God and put herself there."

"I see…." Zalith nodded, an interested, almost devious look on his face. "To remove the belief that he is God here would weaken him."

"Yes," Alucard answered, unsure whether what Zalith had said was a statement or a question. "Anyway, if angels couldn't do that, then who else has hope, huh? We can go in a minute or so."

Zalith nodded and fell silent, a look of pondering on his face.

Alucard stared outside. The desolate, death-ridden world looked like what he thought hate would if it were to materialize. Red, black, brown. Misery. Anger. Destruction. And it made him think about the fact that he almost lost himself to Lilith's power the same way he'd lost himself when he'd killed Ada. But this time, he held on, and he was sure that was because of Zalith. Now, he had someone to fight for—he had a reason to live. Zalith was everything to him, and knowing this demon loved him gave him such a powerful sense of belonging, so strong that he could use it to control himself.

He smiled a little. Zalith had asked him to live with him. The idea scared him at first. What if they got tired of each other? But he was confident that wasn't going to happen. He'd spend every minute of his time with Zalith, and living under the same roof would mean exactly that. He looked forward to the conversation he and Zalith were going to need to have about it.

But right now, he needed to focus on getting them out of this godforsaken place. He looked over the edge of the building, staring down into the crimson murk below.

"Why couldn't the angels do it?" Zalith suddenly asked.

Calculating the drop, Alucard frowned and shrugged. "They weren't ready. Ephriel wasn't sure what lived in this world, so she wasn't sure what to tell her angels to look out for," he said, looking at Zalith. "The angels didn't know what to say, what to do, where to go. They were sent in blind. And then they got trapped here because they didn't know how to get out. They all got infected, too. There are creatures here, just like I said. If they touch you, they infect you, and you die. That's why I'm glad we landed here on a building rather than on the ground."

"What kind of creatures?"

"I don't know what they are," Alucard admitted. "Some would think they are the result of early use of my blood by Janus. Others might call them ghouls. All I know is people that get scathed in any way by them either die or become one of them."

The demon nodded slowly, looking back down at what was left of the world.

"We'll be in Celitrianas next," Alucard said, placing his free hand on Zalith's shoulder as he prepared to fall. "This world is…what I imagine Aegisguard will become in a few centuries."

Zalith set his sights on him and smiled. "Okay. I'm ready."

Without any falter, Alucard fell off the building, pulling Zalith with him. He wasted no time in creating the rift around them, and as quickly as they had arrived, they disappeared, leaving the wasteland behind.

| Zalith |

They emerged on a grassy hilltop. The single sun was setting over the horizon, and the glow of a city sat in the far distance. But the glow was different to that of a city in Aegisguard. The lights were brighter and looked not to be of candlelight but of the electric-powered lights like those in Nefastus. A black brick road lay at the foot of the hill; tall lantern-like lights lined it, lighting the entire path for miles. But there was no sign of a steam-generation factory *anywhere*, so where was the power coming from?

Zalith took his eyes off the lights and looked up at Alucard, who had landed on top of him.

"We must run here," Alucard said, hastily pulling Zalith to his feet. "There are people who would have detected our arrival and will come looking for us. I came here a few times before," he said, pulling Zalith along with him as he ran in the direction away from the city. "To speak to one of Damien's contacts. There are mostly humans here, but there are…werewolves, vampires, demons—they hide, though. Ethos-blooded people here are treated like vermin—hunted, even," he continued as they ran side by side towards a forest.

The demon stared at him, listening as he spoke.

"Wars happened, and eventually, the human numbers toppled those of ethos beings. They hide now, and they don't really put up much of a fight. It's like…it's just normal for humans to live in the light and people like us in the shadows. But little do they know that most of the leaders in this world are ethos-blooded," he said, smirking. "There's a cliff this way; it'll be time to jump when we reach it," he said, looking at Zalith, who nodded.

They then ran through the forest, not taking a moment of the ten minutes Alucard needed to stop and rest. They were only one more world away from home.

The edge of the cliff came into view as the forest began to thin, and Alucard didn't waste much time gripping hold of Zalith and jumping off, forming another rift around them, taking them to the last world before Aegisguard.

| **Alucard** |

The last world was Yilmana. They emerged on a ground covered in golden grass and small circles of blue flowers and pale pink mushrooms. There were trees scattered here and there, but the huge, giant mushrooms were of vaster popularity within the forest they found themselves in.

Alucard helped Zalith up, and then they both took a moment to look around and see if they'd landed anywhere near civilization again, but there was no sign of an animal or man anywhere.

"And this is?" Zalith asked, looking at Alucard as the vampire leaned back against one of the few trees.

Alucard sighed deeply, taking a moment to recover from the journey. "This uh…" he looked around but then leaned his head back against the tree. "Yilmana—elves everywhere," he drawled. "I haven't been here, only heard about it from people I know. Elves always talk about how they come from a different world; I never doubted them, but most people do since elves are mostly stubborn and regard themselves as better than all."

Zalith smirked in agreement. "They think very highly of themselves."

"Come." Alucard sighed, preparing to lead the way.

"Wait," Zalith insisted in worry as he made the vampire lean back against the tree. "Are you okay? You look and *sound* exhausted. If you need to rest for a while, we can."

"No," Alucard denied. "I'm fine. We'll be in Aegisguard next, and then we can find somewhere to rest. I'd rather rest in a world I know than somewhere like this—and full of elves," he muttered, starting to lead the way through the mushroom forest. "I want…can I bring Sabazios?" he asked, changing the subject.

"Your dog?"

"Yes."

Zalith thought to himself for a few moments. "Where will you keep it?"

The vampire shrugged. "Where *can* I keep him?" he asked, sure that Zalith probably wasn't one to allow animals in his house—he didn't, after all, have a single pet.

Zalith asked, "Is he well-behaved? I'd not appreciate him making a mess, either."

"He won't make a mess. He does what he's told, and he knows where he shouldn't go if you tell him."

Zalith thought to himself again…and then sighed. "He can stay in the house," he agreed. "But not in our room, my office, or on the furniture," he stated.

"Fine," Alucard said. "And Drac?"

"He's not going to be coming in the house, is he?"

Alucard glanced at him, unsure whether Zalith was asking in jest or sincerity. "No," he said, pouting. "He needs water. If there's a lake or something nearby, like the one we went to the other day," he suggested.

"Would he be okay in a freshwater lake? He's been living in seawater all his life, I imagine."

"Yes," Alucard answered. "They can live in any type of water."

"Will that lake be big enough, too? What will he eat? I'm sure there aren't any sharks in that lake, and he won't be finding any ships to attack, either."

Amused, Alucard smiled and shrugged. "I'm sure it'll be fine. And he can hunt on land. There are deer in the forest, no? He will eat them."

Zalith nodded slowly and looked ahead again. "Your dragon can stay in the lake, as long he isn't going to travel down into the city and start snacking on the aristos," he said with a smile of amusement.

"He won't."

"How will you get him there?" Zalith then asked.

Alucard pondered. How *would* he get Drac to Nefastus and to the lake that was very far inland? He shrugged and looked back at Zalith. "I'll have him swim to Nefastus, and he will simply make his way along the ground the rest of the way."

Keeping his amused smirk, Zalith glanced at the vampire. "We should make sure that no one witnesses this dragon transferral. The last thing we want is people hunting the legendary lake monster."

"No one will see him."

"Well, I'm sure it's a rather long way for a water-based dragon to slither from the shore to where that lake is. We can arrange to have some people transfer him so that he doesn't dehydrate."

Alucard smiled appreciatively. "*Multumesc.*"

"You're welcome." Zalith smirked and kissed his cheek. "Are there any other pets that I don't yet know of?"

"No," Alucard answered. "Just Sabazios and Drac," he said as he set his eyes on a tree up ahead close to the height of the redwoods from the first world they travelled to. "We can use that tree the same way as we first did."

Zalith nodded, and as he had before, he summoned his demon form, embraced Alucard tightly, and took them both to the tallest branch possible. "Do you know where we'll arrive in Aegisguard?" he asked.

"No," Alucard answered, preparing to leave Yilmana. "I've always ended up somewhere random each time, and this time will be no different. Wherever we end up, though, we should find somewhere to rest. I don't think I can make another journey after this, so we'll go home tomorrow if that's okay."

The demon nodded. "Okay," he agreed with a smile.

"Unless we conveniently arrive in Nefastus," he said, shrugging.

"One can hope."

Then, holding the demon tightly, Alucard pulled them both from the tree, plummeting to the ground below. Just as every time before, he created a rift, and bright crimson swiftly consumed them. But this time, they'd arrive home, and their long journey of world-hopping would be over.

Chapter Seventy-Five

— ◁ ✝ ▷ —

Refroidir

| **Alucard** |

The cold constricted Alucard the moment he and Zalith arrived in Aegisguard. Alucard grappled with the uncertainty of their location. The enveloping darkness revealed little, narrowing down their whereabouts to the nocturnal half of the world. Lying on his back amidst the cold expanse of snow, Zalith leaned over him, and together, they absorbed the mysteries of their new surroundings.

Yet, the latest interdimensional leap had exacted a toll. The reservoir of Numen ethos, drained significantly from his absorption of Lilith's essence, coupled with an uncomfortably substantial portion of his own, left Alucard feeling drained. Seeking respite from the strain, he closed his eyes momentarily, yearning for the ebbing of the ethereal tension and the soothing relief that would hopefully dispel the burgeoning headache.

"Are you okay?" Zalith asked, placing his free hand on the side of Alucard's face.

"I'm fine," the vampire replied, opening his eyes to look up at him.

"Are you sure?"

Alucard nodded, and as Zalith helped him to his feet, he looked around slowly.

"What can you tell me about *this* world?" the demon asked with a smirk, still holding the vampire's hand.

With the realm-hopping journey now over, Alucard sighed in relief, moved closer to Zalith, and rested his head on his shoulder as he did his best to relax in the coldness of whatever country they now stood in. "Well," he mumbled, "there are very few nice places, humans everywhere, wars start every fifty years or so, yet this is the only one of all the realms I find I actually enjoy being in."

Zalith smiled as he embraced the vampire. "Where are we exactly?" he asked, looking around.

They were in a small opening surrounded by tall, ice-covered fir trees. The snow beneath them was a few inches deep, the sky was a very dark purple, and all six moons were shining brightly, as always. There was no sign of civilization nearby, no glow of a city, no candlelight, no torchlight. A large mountain range was just visible in the distance, however, just beyond the vast forest.

Alucard might assume they were in Avalmoor, but of course, there was always something he'd recognize to tell him exactly where he was in the world. In this case, it was the trees, a species with particular patterns that only appeared on them in one specific part of Aegisguard. And the smell: pine and lavender.

"We are in Ascela, at the very top of the world," he said, taking his eyes off the trees he'd been staring at while resting his head on Zalith's shoulder.

"Are we close to Nefastus? perhaps I could phase and take us home," Zalith offered, placing his hand on the vampire's head to caress his hair.

"No," Alucard denied sadly. "I still have a fraction of Lilith's ethos, and I need to let that wane away from where we'll be so that when she eventually comes looking here, she won't know where we are. We should find somewhere to rest and stay until we've found a way to hide me from the Numen. Then, when she comes here, she'll either assume I jumped again, or that I'm somewhere in Ascela."

Zalith nodded in understanding. "Okay. I hope to have an answer for you by this time tomorrow at the latest. Is that enough time for the ethos to leave you?"

"More than enough," he confirmed, looking around slowly. "I've not been to this part of Ascela before; I avoided the colder parts when I came with Attila and Luther in search of someone. I'm sure there are settlements up here near the mountains, though. We can walk," he said, stepping back to look at Zalith. "And find somewhere to spend the night."

"Wait," Zalith insisted, stopping Alucard from walking off. He then focused, looking around slowly, and after a few moments, he looked back at Alucard. "There's a large concentration of life force not too far in that direction," he said, nodding towards the trees behind the vampire. "I assume it's a village or town of some sort. I'm sure there'll be somewhere for us to rest there," he said as he took Alucard's hand and started to lead the way towards the trees.

Alucard didn't argue. He held Zalith's hand tightly and followed beside him, hoping that he'd soon be able to get some rest.

| **Zalith** |

As the night grew later, Zalith led the way through the forest. The snow started falling heavier, and as the glow of a large mountainside town broke through the murk of the increasing blizzard, relief struck both their faces.

Now that he could see the town, Zalith wasn't going to make Alucard walk anymore. The vampire was shivering, and Zalith knew how much he hated the cold. So, he disappeared with Alucard and instantly reappeared at the town's entrance, saving them a trek of ten minutes or so. Now all they had to do was find an inn or hotel.

They made their way into the town, passing under an archway with the town name 'Refroidir' painted on the sign; they followed the salted cobblestone path lit with lanterns hanging along lines of rope, all of them gently swaying in the wind. A lot of the buildings were made of stone and white wood, their roofs thatched and neat. The mountainside was adorned with buildings, too, all of which were connected by long, narrow bridges. It was a small but cosy little town, and the people didn't seem at all alarmed or cautious to see two demons walking through the place. They all went about their lives, closing their stores and preparing to head inside for the night.

Sure that no person here would scream and run in fear, Zalith set his sights on a nearby woman who was packing away her store's wares. He approached her with Alucard at his side, and as she turned to face them, she smiled pleasantly.

"Do you know where we can find an inn or a hotel here?" the demon asked.

Looking at him, the woman frowned and muttered something in a language that Zalith didn't know enough of to understand what her answer was. It sounded very much like Boszorkian, and knowing his vampire knew the language, he glanced at him.

"*L'auberge*," Alucard said. "*Y a-t-il un endroit pour rester ici*?"

The woman looked at Alucard as he spoke and nodded with a smile. She muttered her reply, pointing down the street opposite to where they were standing, and then looked back at Alucard, bidding her farewells.

"This way," Alucard said, taking the lead as he made his way towards the street the woman had pointed to.

They made their way through the town; Alucard followed the directions the woman had given him and eventually led the way into a courtyard that belonged to an estate-like building. There was a single entrance, and the sign above it read 'Mountainside Inn'.

The moment they opened the door and stepped inside, they were hit with the warmth of the fire pit burning in the middle of the room. Several men were sitting around it, muttering quietly to one another as they enjoyed their drinks. Just like the town itself, the inn looked and felt cosy; paintings on the log-carved walls, doors to the left and right that led further inside, and wine-red couches lined under the windows on either side of the doors.

At the very back of the reception was the front desk, and a small, casually dressed woman was sitting behind it, knitting a jumper while she hummed quietly. Like the men around the fire, she was wearing a wool jumper, and it looked as though she may have been the one responsible for crafting the jumpers that everyone in the room wore.

Zalith and Alucard made their way over to the desk, and when the woman noticed them, she stopped knitting and stood up, greeting them in Boszorkian. But Alucard swiftly asked if she spoke Deiganish, and she nodded with a smile.

"Would you like a room?" she asked them.

"Your best suite, please," Zalith said as Alucard rested his right arm on the desk, a somewhat tired look on his face. The demon glanced at him as the woman searched through the inn's logs. "Are you okay?" he asked quietly.

The vampire nodded.

"And you'd like *two* beds, right?" she asked, taking her eyes off the book in front of her to look at Zalith.

"Just the one," Zalith said with a smirk as he winked over at the vampire.

Alucard's face instantly reddened with embarrassment as he looked away.

"Of course," the woman replied, looking back down at her book. "Our best is the mountain view, and it will be five coronam a night," she said, looking back up at them.

Both Alucard *and* Zalith reached into their pockets at the same time, pulling out the required amount of money for the room and offering it to the woman. She didn't know which to take, and as Zalith and Alucard looked at one another, she waited.

Zalith smiled. "I'll pay, don't worry," he said, lightly moving Alucard's hand away from the woman so that he'd put his money away.

But Alucard didn't do as Zalith wanted. "I will," he said, holding his money back out to the woman.

"It's really okay," the demon said as he gently took hold of Alucard's wrist, lowered his hand, and moved him away from the desk. "Here," he said, offering his money to the woman.

Before the woman could take Zalith's money, Alucard snatched it from the demon's hand and placed *his* money into the woman's hand. She'd clearly had enough waiting, so swiftly took Alucard's money, placed it in her pocket, and handed him the key to the room.

Zalith tried to hide his smile of amusement but failed and laughed quietly as Alucard handed him his money back with a sneer on his face.

"To your right; just follow the stairs up to the very back room," the woman said.

Alucard led the way, and as they turned into the wide, window-lined corridor, Zalith lightly grabbed the vampire's ass and smirked at him. He then took his hand as Alucard tried to hide his face in embarrassment and continued through the building in search of their room.

| **Alucard** |

When they located their room, Alucard unlocked the door and led the way inside.

"I guess the people out here are like those in Nefastus," Alucard mumbled as he glanced around the large suite. "Anyone else would have probably refused to serve us."

"Well…." Zalith smiled as he used his ethos to light all the lanterns around the suite's entrance hall. "It looks like many men were saved injury tonight, then."

Alucard nodded slightly as he followed Zalith deeper into the room until they located the bedroom. Like the walls in the entire building, they were made of stacked, carved logs; four windows sat on the wall straight ahead of them as they walked in, along with a door to a balcony—a door that would stay shut because Alucard wasn't at all keen on heading outside.

The room's furniture consisted of a large double bed with a black headboard against the left wall and a dark wood canopy around it. It was adorned with several layers of black and white fur blankets and two pillows on either side. Each side of the bed had a nightstand, and Alucard placed the room key on the right table. A few paintings hung around the room, and a fireplace sat on the right wall with a black couch and matching armchair in front of it. The wooden floors were covered mostly with a brown fur carpet which both looked and felt like bear fur.

As he watched Alucard place the room's key on the bedside table, Zalith smiled and made his way over to where he was. He then wrapped his arms around the vampire, embracing him tightly as he turned to face him.

Alucard sighed in relief as he rested the side of his head on Zalith's, wrapping his arms around him. He enjoyed standing there with him for a few moments in his warm embrace, staring out of the windows at the blizzard. With a discreet smile, he nuzzled the demon's neck, holding him a little tighter. He didn't want to think about how just an hour ago, he might have lost Zalith, that he might have been trapped with Lilith for a very long time, living through his life with Damien once again, only with a woman far worse than the Daegelus. But now that he knew the truth, he'd not let anything like that happen again. He'd not let any Numen try and slither into his life—into *their* lives. Now, it was just him and Zalith.

The demon's sudden descent unexpectedly took Alucard along, depositing them both onto the bed. Alucard found himself sprawled on top of Zalith, a surprising turn of events that drew a quiet chuckle from the demon. In response, Alucard frowned in mild surprise, propping himself up on his arms to peer down at the demon's mirthful expression. Zalith, still amused, smirked and gently rested his hand on the side of Alucard's face. Without the need for words, Alucard intuitively understood, allowing himself to relax and nestle his head against the demon's shoulder.

Zalith then placed his hand on the back of Alucard's head and started fiddling with his hair. "I'm excited for you to come and live with me, baby," he said quietly.

The vampire smiled as he relaxed, moving his left hand to the side of Zalith's neck. "Me too," he replied. He hadn't ever imagined that anything like this would happen—to be so close to someone; to love someone and live with them, and not even in his own house or his castle, but *Zalith's* house. He felt no hesitance, no anxiety to move away from Dor-Sanguis to Nefastus because Zalith would be with him. He felt as if he could go anywhere with him.

"We'll wake up every morning beside each other," Zalith started, still fiddling with the vampire's hair. "And have breakfast; we can walk together, head to the lake often, and ride together, too. There won't have to be a moment where I won't get to be with you."

Everything Zalith said made Alucard feel happier. He smiled a little brighter, closing his eyes as he allowed his feeling of calm to enthral him. "Sounds better than any life I could have imagined before," he murmured. "I never thought I'd feel like this, that I would love someone, or that someone would love me. Sometimes, it feels strange to think about now and back then when I was alone. I never thought I'd be so happy. And now I am, and I don't want to ever be without you."

Zalith tightened his embrace around the vampire, kissing his forehead. But he then shuffled around, moving Alucard so that he was lying beside him so he could see the vampire's face. "But you're so handsome, Alucard—and capable; you have such good taste, and your heart is so kind. How could somebody *not* love you?"

Alucard shrugged, taking his eyes off the demon to look down and away from him. He was sure that Zalith's question was rhetorical, but he couldn't *not* think about an answer. There were so many reasons: his past, his absent wings, his volatile personality, which he was very aware of. Perhaps, though, he shouldn't think about it.

"I love you," Zalith said, resting his forehead against Alucard's. "More than anything. And I never want to be without you, either."

The vampire smiled, gazing into Zalith's eyes for a moment—but before he could reply, he had to look away out of nervousness. "I love you," he said quietly.

Zalith hugged him tightly again, kissing his forehead before they both made themselves a little more comfortable. The demon sighed contently when he rested his head on the same pillow as Alucard, staring into his eyes as he gazed back at him. "How are you feeling?" he asked, using his thumb to carefully move a strand of the vampire's hair from over his left eye, and tucked it behind his ear.

Alucard took his eyes off Zalith; he moved closer, resting his forehead on his shoulder as he stared down in thought. How *was* he feeling? He hadn't given it much thought since their arrival back in Aegisguard. He was tired, that was for sure, but not tired enough to want to sleep yet. He wanted to spend more time with Zalith. "I'm okay," he answered. "What about you?"

The demon smiled. "I'm good."

But Alucard wasn't convinced. "Are you sure?" he asked in concern. "Lilith was a cruel bitch to you because of me."

Zalith shook his head. "I'm with you. Of course I'm okay," he answered, placing his hand on the side of the vampire's face. He then kissed him a single time and pulled him closer, sighing quietly as he embraced Alucard.

However, Alucard couldn't shake the guilt that he felt for what Zalith had endured. Not only had Lilith's scions hurt him, but the woman had said a lot of degrading things that he was convinced had upset the demon. Zalith didn't seem to be very upset, though; but then again, he was good at hiding what was going on inside his head.

Next to his guilt, Alucard also couldn't silence his intrigue. Why did Lilith seem to know so much about Zalith and his family? His mother, to be precise. Alucard knew that Zalith was in Lilith's line of creation—perhaps one or both of his parents were scions, especially if his mother did so much as to *pray* to Lilith and for Lilith to have actually listened. He wanted to know, but was now a good time to ask?

He frowned with both worry and curiosity. "Why...did she know so much about your mother?"

Something of an amused smile clung to Zalith's face. "Because she's my grandmother."

Just as he had suspected. "So...your mother was a scion?"

"My mother *and* my father, yes. They were two of the first Lilith ever created. She boasted about how my mother was created using the DNA of a very obedient demon, but while Lilith thought that my mother was very obedient, she was actually doing her own thing on the side a lot of the time, so I almost want to believe that it's bullshit." He adorned a curious frown. "How *are* scions made? How do the Numen create these unrelated, entirely new species?"

Alucard frowned, looking down again. He knew that Lilith had created some exceptionally powerful scions upon her arrival to the worlds hundreds of years ago, all of which she gave utterly new bloodlines to so that they could populate the realm with her species of demons. And he now knew that Zalith wasn't a scion but the son of two. He wasn't sure if there was a title for such a child, and he was also sure that it didn't really matter. He was Zalith; *that* was all that mattered to him.

He shifted his attention to Zalith's question. "Well, they take the DNA of something or someone and mix it with the DNA of something or someone else. It's pretty much like how mortals make children, except Lilith isn't actually the parent, she's just the... artist..." he explained. "Does that make sense?"

Zalith's intrigued frown thickened as he nodded.

Alucard then asked him, "That's why you don't have a last name, then? Lilith never bothered to give her scions surnames, neither did Lucifer. Just species names."

Zalith smiled. "Yes," he confirmed. "Not that we really needed a surname; we all had strange names. How many other Zaliths do you know?"

With an amused smile, Alucard shrugged.

The demon then rested his forehead against Alucard's again. "*Your* mother was a Meridian witch—a witch with ancient blood; did *she* have a last name?"

Alucard lost his smile and looked away from Zalith's gaze. Sadness gripped him. He hadn't known his mother was a witch until this morning; he had always thought she was a human and a member of a cult that worshipped his father. But now, he knew that not to be the whole truth. He'd found out that his mother was a Meridian witch, a witch with ancient blood, but he wasn't sure which bloodline she'd come from. He'd look into it now that he knew the truth, but not yet.

That also made it clear why Esta, the witch from Boszorkány, spoke to him and nobody else at his meeting. Some witches vowed only to speak to their own kind. There was no way Alucard could have pieced it together back then.

He shrugged again, keeping his eyes on the blankets beneath them. "She was Charlotte Vladislav Reiner. But she was called Emeritus a lot because she was a retired preacher. You're the only person who knows that now. Everyone else thinks my last name is Emeritus."

Zalith smiled and started to fiddle with the vampire's hair again. "I'll keep it a secret," he said quietly.

The vampire glanced at him and smiled slightly, but as he did, Zalith moved closer and kissed him, initiating a long moment of slow, passionate kisses while they lay in the silence.

Alucard wasn't sure what tomorrow might bring for them, but he was looking forward to moving into Zalith's house and living with him. The thought of seeing him every day made him feel happier and a whole lot safer, too. He'd spent so many years of his life in his castle that the thought of living somewhere so very far away was something he could have only hoped for. And to be living there with Zalith, too? It was yet another of those things that sounded far too good to be true. But it *was* true, and tomorrow, he'd be starting a new chapter of his life.

Chapter Seventy-Six

— ≺ ✝ ≻ —

A Declaration

| **Zalith** |

Zalith lay on his back, caressing Alucard's hair while the vampire rested his head on his shoulder. He was looking forward to having Alucard move in; he wanted nothing more than to be as close to Alucard as possible and as often as he could be. Not only that, but he wanted to make sure his vampire was safe, and there was no better place to do that than under his own roof. He was more than glad that Alucard accepted his invite, and the moment the vampire was ready to leave and head for Nefastus, he'd begin the necessary procedures of moving him in, such as setting up a workspace and arranging what would be needed to move Drac.

He glanced down at Alucard and smiled contently. Yet another step Zalith thought he might never take with anyone had been taken in his relationship with Alucard, and he was more than confident that he and his vampire would continue to grow together.

Right now, however, Zalith felt like a bath. Both he and Alucard had been through a lot—and many places, too. It was also cold, and he felt a warm bath might help the both of them relax. "I'm going to take a bath," he said quietly. "You can join me if you like."

Alucard slowly looked up at him with a nervous frown on his face. He then nodded and sat up when Zalith did. "We can do that."

He took the vampire's hand and led him through the large suite and into the bathroom, where towels, bathrobes, toothbrushes, combs, and even an assortment of soaps and shampoos were provided for them. He closed the door, and then he let go of Alucard's hand and made his way over to the white marble tub. He turned both taps on and returned to Alucard, who leaned back against the countertop and fiddled with his earring as the exhausted look on his face grew.

"Are you sure you don't want to sleep instead?" Zalith asked, placing his hands on the vampire's waist as he moved closer to him. "I can join you soon."

Alucard lightly gripped both of Zalith's wrists and shook his head. "I'm fine," he muttered, looking at the bathtub as it gradually filled with water and bubbles.

"Okay." Zalith smiled, nuzzling the side of Alucard's face while he started unbuttoning the vampire's shirt.

They both slowly undressed, and once the bathtub was filled, they climbed into the water. Alucard sat with his back leaning against the front of Zalith's body and rested his head on the demon's shoulder.

Zalith's thoughts were as loud as ever but not as discombobulated as they had been recently. The moment he'd sat in the water and started to attentively drag his hands over the vampire's chest, his mind focused on what he'd seen and discovered over the past few days.

Damien—that was who first occupied his mind. Zalith suspected a lot since growing closer to Alucard, and it was now as clear as day that most of his suspicions were true. Damien had abused Alucard all his life, as had Lilith. Alucard had been made to believe that the way Damien treated him was right, that beating him to near death was a necessary punishment. Zalith *hated* that—he hated Damien, the Numen, and everything about them... but mostly the fact that they *all* wanted to use Alucard for something. Zalith was going to make sure that Damien regretted not killing him—Lilith, too.

He'd already decided that he was going to kill Damien, not only for what he'd done but for what he was going to do. That creature of a man would come looking for Alucard soon enough, and Zalith wasn't going to let him find *his* vampire. He didn't yet know how to *kill* a Numen, but he hadn't long come to know that Alucard possessed the power needed to overwhelm them. Zalith was sure that there was a way to kill them once and for all, and he'd not waste time in finding out what he needed to know to live up to such a promise—a promise to himself, to Alucard, and to Damien.

Lilith was where his mind next wandered. She really was *not* the God his parents had made her out to be. She was a lot stupider than he'd been led to believe and a whole lot easier to take down than he might have thought, too. She may have been caught off guard when Alucard attacked her, but all the same, Alucard made easy work of her, and it made him wonder if it were that easy for Alucard to destroy every other Numen.

This particular Numen was a problem, too—a problem he was going to remove from both their lives. Lilith was going to come after Alucard, and there was no way that Zalith was going to let her have him. He'd not let someone take his vampire away and make him live the life he hadn't long escaped from. Lilith was going to be eradicated, too.

He stopped caressing the vampire's chest and instead started to fiddle with his hair as he stared at the log-carved wall. He was sure he had a lot of work ahead of him; he had to find out how to kill a Numen—two Numen, in fact. He'd already set a plan in motion to hide Alucard from them, he just had to wait for the izuret to return and tell him that his people had located the mage who would create something to conceal his vampire's existence. It was the killing of the Numen that was going to consume his time. But he was sure that he'd find out what he needed to know. There *had* to be people somewhere in this world who knew.

And he still had to help the Citadel deal with the Meshuga and Imperito, especially since Alucard was moving in. He'd work that out once the vampire was settled.

He looked down at Alucard; he was almost certain that Alucard knew the things he needed to know about the Numen, but he wasn't sure whether asking him would get him answers or start a disagreement. Either way, though, he wasn't going to *not* tell Alucard that he was planning to slay the Numen who had made his life such a misery.

"I'm going to kill Damien," he said.

He felt Alucard tense up. "What?"

"And Lilith, too."

Alucard looked up at him from where he lay, probably searching his eyes for a hint of jest, but there was no such thing present anywhere on Zalith's face. Evidently realizing that Zalith was serious, Alucard frowned, sat up, and turned to face him. "What are you talking about? You can't kill them."

"Why not?" the demon asked, but he wasn't exactly looking for an answer. "Everything dies; some things are simply harder to kill than others."

The vampire scoffed in what might be panic. "You can't kill them," he insisted. "They aren't like you or me or anything else. They don't exist, and you can't kill something that doesn't exist."

"I'll find a way."

"Why?" Alucard then questioned, a confused, distressed look on his face. "We'll be fine once I'm hidden."

"But for how long? I want to keep you as safe as I possibly can, Alucard, and killing them will ensure your safety. And not only that, but they both deserve worse than death for what they've done to you. Surely, you agree?" he said, placing his hands on Alucard's shoulders, trying to pull him back towards him.

Alucard shrugged the demon's hands off and stared at him for a few moments, obviously considering his thoughts. But he soon shook his head. "We can't kill them, Zalith," he said with sincerity.

"Can't," Zalith said as he pulled Alucard back into his lap, "or won't, Alucard?" he asked quietly, starting to caress his hair again. "They might've convinced you that they can't die, but nothing is truly immortal, not even Damien."

The vampire didn't reply. He sat there in Zalith's embrace in silence, and Zalith wasn't sure whether he was angry, upset, or thinking about what he was telling him.

"I *will* find a way. There isn't a single thing that can stop me when I put my mind to something, and I'm setting it on keeping you safe from them—all of them."

Alucard sighed in what sounded like defeat.

"If we let them live, Alucard, they won't stop searching for you. How long until one of them finds you? Yes, we can hide you using ethos, but that won't stop them from recognizing you if they see you. I'm sure that Lilith will search every single world without rest for you, as will Damien. They want you for their own selfish needs, and they don't give a shit about what it does to you. But *I* do. I care about you above anything else, and I'm not going to risk letting them find you and drag you right back into the life we just got you away from. And if killing them is the only way to stop them, then I'll kill all of them," he explained firmly.

The vampire looked unnerved. "And if there's no way to kill them?"

"If by some chance there really is no way to kill them, then I'll find a way to keep them out of this world the same way Lucifer is trapped out there somewhere," Zalith answered. "But I've made up my mind. Damien is going to die, and so is Lilith and anyone else who might want to try and take you away from me. They don't deserve you, the rule they have, or even their lives. They sit around and watch the world they apparently love so much fall apart; they watch the people who look up to them die, and they use people like you for their own desires. Every single one of them is false—you said that yourself. If you could remove them for good, would you not do it?"

Alucard sighed again and shrugged lightly. "I don't know. If they die, I'm sure there will be consequences. The people here and all over the realms pray to them, and if their gods die, panic will consume the world. Some of the Numen control factors you don't even know about, and if they die, the world as we know it may fall apart. And for all we know, killing them could be like killing me; if I die for good, every single vampire created using my blood will also die—you could die if Lilith dies."

"I'll find a way, Alucard."

The vampire fell silent once again. Zalith wasn't sure if he'd convinced him or if he was no longer sure how to argue. But one thing was for sure: Alucard wasn't going to get him to change his mind. If he couldn't kill Damien and Lilith, he'd lock them out of the world just as Lucifer had been. Of course, he'd have to take the time to find out what he could about Lucifer's banishment, about the Numen, and how their ethos worked. He already knew from their visit to Tengetso that some of the other worlds were involved in the Numen's influence. He'd find out everything he needed to know, no matter how long it might take, and then he'd do as he'd said.

He placed his hand on the vampire's head again, continuing to fiddle with his hair. "I promised to protect you. I'm not going to let those creatures live knowing the harm they wish to do to you. Just…trust me, okay?" he asked softly. "I'll find a way to remove them from your life forever."

Alucard looked up at him with a tired stare on his face. But he didn't fight, nor did he disagree. Instead, he nodded and stared ahead again.

Zalith then smiled. He was sure that he'd have to talk to Alucard a few more times about it, but not now. Alucard now knew of his intentions, and he could further discuss his plans with him later. For now, he simply wanted to continue to relax with him.

"So," he said as he reached over and chose one of the many small bottles of shampoo. "Tell me about your favourite horse breed," he invited as he massaged some of the shampoo into Alucard's crimson hair.

The vampire thought to himself for a few moments. "Well, it depends, I guess," he muttered. "In general, I like the Clydesdale horses, but they are draught horses and often used for work. For racing, Friesian horses are my favourite. They look like a draught horse, but they are really nimble for their size," he explained.

Zalith listened, carefully and slowly washing the shampoo from the vampire's hair.

"Both are used as show horses, too. Sebastian vas a Clydesdale, and I was hoping to get another like him, but the breeder hasn't been able to raise one for me yet. I've just settled with the common Dor-Sanguian horses for now."

"Is black your favourite colour in a horse?" Zalith then asked as he finished washing all the soap from Alucard's hair.

Alucard relaxed, sighing quietly as he turned his head to lean the side of his face against the demon's shoulder. "I guess so. Colour doesn't really matter, but if I could choose, then I would like to have a black one."

"I see." Zalith smiled, continuing to massage the vampire's head.

"Do you have a favourite horse breed?"

"I can't say I do," Zalith replied, gradually moving his hand down from the vampire's head and to his chest. He then hugged him tightly, resting the side of his head on Alucard's as he stared down at the water.

They sat in silence for a little while, and when the bubbles started to disappear, the vampire shuffled around and sighed quietly.

"What is it?" Zalith asked.

He lifted his head ever so slightly so that he could see Zalith. "I think I want to sleep now. We'll have a lot to do tomorrow."

Zalith smiled down at him. "That we will."

They climbed out of the bath and grabbed the towels; they dried themselves and their hair before pulling on the bathrobes that were hanging on the door. Then, they left the bathroom and returned to the bedroom; the pair climbed into bed, where they made themselves comfortable beside one another.

As he rested his head on Zalith's shoulder, Alucard closed his eyes and sighed quietly. "What will we do first?"

The demon kissed his forehead and relaxed, staring up at the ceiling. "Well, I'll have people work on sorting out one of the rooms and turning it into an office for you. I can also have people move all the things you'd like to take from your castle; you'll just have to tell me or them what those things are. I'll also have people prepare everything needed to move Drac."

"I'll contact my people; they'll guide Drac here, and they can leave my ship in the Citadel docks. There are things on board that I'd rather keep close than leave back in Dor-Sanguis."

Zalith nodded as he embraced Alucard tightly. "All right. It may take a few days to have everything ready, but… I hope you will be comfortable."

The vampire smiled slightly as he wrapped his arm around Zalith. "I will be."

"I should warn you, though, that I haven't finished dealing with the Meshuga and Imperito gangs. I met with the head of the law enforcement division, Margo, just the other day, and we came up with a plan to deal with the Meshuga. I'll likely be working on that over the next week or so," Zalith explained. "But we don't plan to make our move until Decem; that's when Margo's men will be ready."

"That's okay." He paused for a moment. "Do you… want help?"

As much as he enjoyed working with Alucard, he didn't want to risk his safety. "It's okay but thank you. I'd rather you stay at home where I know you're safe. It shouldn't take long to deal with; my demons are very capable, and Margo's officers aren't half bad, either."

The vampire nodded and said, "Okay, well… if you change your mind, I'm here."

Zalith smiled. "Thank you."

He then closed his eyes and held the vampire tightly. The next few days were going to be busy, but he was looking forward to it.

Chapter Seventy-Seven

— ⊰ ✝ ⊱ —

Opus

| **Zalith** |

Zalith was awoken by several taps to his right cheek. He scowled irritably, and when he opened his eyes, he carefully rolled over onto his back, trying not to wake Alucard, whom he'd been cuddling, and glowered at the purple-eyed izuret sitting on his bedside cabinet. He recognized it as Pip, the same izuret Alucard had befriended by removing a thorn from its hand.

"What?" the demon snarled quietly.

With a hushed chirp, Pip reached into a purse attached to his left leg and pulled out a piece of paper, offering it towards him.

Irritated and tired, Zalith snatched the paper from the izuret and opened it with his fingers. There was an address written on it, and as the creature chirped and told him that Orin and Tyrus had found Magnus and that this address was where he would be found, relief outweighed his fatigue and anger. He wanted to leave immediately; the sooner he had something to hide Alucard from the Numen, the better.

"Go to my house," he said to Pip. "In my room on my dresser is a dark wooden box; inside it, you'll find a gold ring with inlaid onyx and black diamonds. I want you to grab it for me and meet me at the Citadel in Nefastus. And don't even *think* about running off with it because I *will* find you," he ordered.

Pip nodded and spread his wings, but before taking off, he leaned to the side so that he could see Alucard and asked Zalith with a series of mutters and chirps how the vampire was doing.

"Go," he snapped irritably.

The izuret pouted and started to slowly float up into the air. He waited for a belayed answer, but he soon understood that he wasn't going to get one and disappeared in a puff of purple smoke, leaving Zalith alone with the vampire.

Zalith looked down at the paper again; it seemed that the mage, Magnus, was living a lot closer than he'd thought, but it meant that he didn't have to go far. He'd already been to the Citadel, so he could phase there, get what he needed for Alucard, and phase back to this very bedroom. But he ought to tell Alucard that he was leaving and might be gone for a while in case the vampire woke to find he wasn't beside him. First, he thought he'd leave Alucard a message telling him where he'd gone and that he'd be back soon, but how could he forget that the vampire's understanding of Deiganish writing wasn't so good?

As much as he didn't want to wake Alucard, he had to. He carefully sat up, using his hands to guide Alucard's head from his shoulder to the pillows. The vampire murmured quietly in question as Zalith climbed out of bed; he swiftly pulled his clothes on and then leaned over the side of the bed to kiss the side of Alucard's face. "Alucard," he said quietly, and as the vampire mumbled in response, he gently caressed his hair. "I have to go and take care of something."

The vampire frowned and lightly snatched Zalith's hand before he could pull it away from him. "What?" he asked in confusion, opening his eyes just enough so that he could look up at him. "Why?"

"I have to go and pick something up," he explained.

He then felt Alucard tighten his grip on his hand as he stared up at him in what looked like worry. "Will you come back?" he asked sleepily, and there was concern in his voice.

Zalith smiled as he leaned onto the bed and rested his forehead against Alucard's. "Of course I will," he answered. He then took his hand from Alucard's and pulled the blankets over him, making sure that he was comfortable. "Go back to sleep, baby." He smiled, kissing his forehead before standing up.

Once Alucard closed his eyes and fell back asleep, Zalith made his way over to the suite door and slipped his shoes on. He silently created a rift in the wall, and before leaving, he took one last look back at Alucard. He'd miss him, but he shouldn't be gone too long. All he had to do was get the mage to enchant the ring he'd sent the izuret to get so that it would hide Alucard from the Numen, and then he'd be back in bed with him.

Keen to waste not a moment more, he stepped into the rift and sealed it behind him.

Zalith emerged from the rift into a gloomy Citadel alley; despite it being the very early hours of the morning, the lights were still as bright as ever, and the city was still beaming with the voices of partygoers. Of course, it wasn't a surprise; he'd lived in Nefastus long enough to know what the city was like all hours of both the day and night.

Where he'd emerged wasn't too far from the address he'd been given, so he left the alley and made his way along a well-lit street, ignoring the bumbling idiots around him as they stumbled, enjoying their night out a little too much—drunk humans were a different species.

He made his way to the centre of the city, where he then stood close to one of the signposts, waiting for the izuret to arrive with the ring.

After a minute or so of keeping a dissatisfied eye on a group of drunk pirates close by, Zalith was greeted by Pip. The izuret appeared from a puff of purple smoke above him and gracefully floated down to hover in front of where he stood. He held out his hand, and the little messenger placed the golden ring in his palm.

"Thank you," he said, slipping the ring into his pocket as the purple-eyed izuret chirped quietly. "You can go now. Edwin will pay you if you head to my house," he told it, turning his back to the creature as he started making his way towards his destination.

The demon headed through the gleaming streets of the restless city, eyeing each sign as he came close to them, searching for the road that had been written on the paper Pip had brought him. Mourning Lane was where his journey met its end, a vastly stretched street lined with homes that resembled miniature mansions.

He made his way down the street, searching for the home numbered thirteen; he came to its front door, which was painted black, and the house itself was white but almost gold in the light of the Citadel. A small set of stairs led him up to the porch; wide, tall glass windows sat on either side, and the inside of the house was concealed by the black curtains.

Zalith knocked loudly and waited, unsure of who or what might come to answer the door, but the sounds of distorted chattering and laughter within told him that perhaps the mage he had come in search of might not be the only one at the residence.

Several clicks came from the door—the sound of at least four locks and two bolts being released—and when the door opened, a butler dressed not in the usual black attire but white stood in front of him. His black hair was jaw length and wasn't neatly combed as most staff would usually have it. The man's shirt was untucked, his tie was loose, and it looked as though he may have been dragged backwards through a hedge a couple of times. He appeared exhausted, and he didn't look very pleased to be where he currently was.

"Yes?" he asked as though he was in a daze. "What do you want? Who are you?" he questioned, glaring at Zalith as he slowly woke from whatever trance he'd been in before looking at the demon.

Zalith, who realized that he hadn't come dressed formally and probably looked like he'd just got out of bed, eyed the man with disinterest. "I'm here to see Opus."

A glare of hostility flickered across the butler's face as he looked up and down the street as though to see if Zalith was alone. He then scowled at the demon, pulling the door shut as much as he could beside him. "Who are you?" he asked again, but this time with skepticism in his voice.

"I'm here as a matter of urgent business," Zalith answered.

The butler frowned again. "Is Opus expecting you?"

Zalith smiled condescendingly. "What do you think?"

With a sigh of exhaustion, the butler pushed the door open beside him and invited Zalith in. Then, after closing the door, he escorted him through the lit hallway and into a lounge to the left. "Wait here," he said, leaving Zalith in the room—a room where four other men were sitting; they didn't bother to cease their loud conversation despite the entry of a stranger into their space.

Zalith couldn't understand what they were saying because they were speaking in a language he hadn't heard before, but he didn't care. They were nobodies to him, and he just wanted to get what he'd come for and leave as soon as possible.

He stood by the door where the butler had left him, staring at the wall ahead of him while he waited. He *really* didn't want to be there; he wanted to be back in bed with Alucard, whom he didn't want to leave alone, but the vampire needed what he'd come to get or the Numen would find him.

His minute of waiting became *five minutes… ten minutes…* and the displeasing sound of the laughter of the men on the other side of the room was beginning to make Zalith wish he could mute the world around him. He kept his eyes on the wall, the wait and constant chatter increasing his frustration. How long did it take to tell someone that they had a visitor?

"*Ohe,*" one of the four men then called. "*Daemonium.*"

Sure that the man had said demon, Zalith glanced over at them. They had stopped their loud conversation and were now eyeing him with demeaning smirks on their faces, holding their glasses of white wine as if they were precious chalices. But Zalith didn't care about what they might be thinking. Each of them possessed the same shade of silver hair, purple eyes, and pale skin, and just like their butler, they were dressed in white, but their attire was much more expensive than their staff's.

They all looked extremely similar and might very well be siblings. The only way to tell them apart was by their different hairstyles. The first had his hair tied up in a bun; the second's was long, loose, and past his waist; the third's hair was just past his jaw and tucked behind his ears, and the fourth's hair was plaited behind his head but rested over his shoulder. It took a single moment of sensing their auras to tell that they were in fact scions, but they weren't demons.

They were angels.

When the man who spoke to Zalith called something that he didn't understand, the demon took his eyes off them and glared ahead. He knew well from his visit to Osiris that angels didn't much like demons, and he could only hope that they didn't try to start a fight with him.

All four of them then muttered to one another for a few moments until the man whose hair was long and loose asked Zalith, "Why do you stand there like cockroach?"

Zalith slowly turned his head to look at them and laughed quietly in amusement. "If *I* am a cockroach, then *you* must be some sort of—" he stopped for a moment and eyed them in disgust— "maggot," he responded.

The four angels looked at one another and laughed, but their laughter wasn't cruel nor was it degrading. Instead, it was as though they were laughing in enjoyment.

"You're going to be waiting there for long time," the brother who had just spoken to him said with a smirk. "Opus is as slow as trade ship. Sit," he invited, holding his arm out to one of the empty armchairs in their circle of white seats.

Why not? If he was going to be waiting a while, he might as well do so comfortably. It confounded him a little, though, that these angels were inviting him to sit with them. He knew how devious their kind were, and he'd not let his guard down. He made his way over and sat where he'd been invited; they offered him a glass to join them in their drinking, but he kindly refused.

The four of them then started talking to one other again in whatever language it was they were speaking, but after a few moments, the Deiganish speaker looked at Zalith. "Why have you come to see Opus?"

"Business," he answered.

The guy appeared to tell his brothers Zalith's answer, and they all muttered to one another again. They then started snickering, laughing, and shaking their heads as they glanced at Zalith a few times, sipping from their glasses.

"You come for…take baby out of human?" one of the other brothers asked as the others laughed amusedly. "Or to put baby in human?"

"No," Zalith said, smiling.

"Opus has weird liking for things baby-related," the brother with the loose, long hair said, shaking his head. "If not here for anything of that sort, are you here for…problems…of male area?" he asked, grinning. As he kept his eyes on Zalith, one of his brothers called something not in Deiganish, something that caused one of the others to scowl in embarrassment and throw himself at him.

Zalith laughed in response to his question. "No. Do people often come here with such problems?" he asked, wondering what sort of mage Opus was if he was seeing people with the kind of problems this man had suggested.

He shrugged as his two bickering brothers were pulled apart by the fourth. "Opus is not just mage—also doctor. Fixes all kind of problem, popular with man problems."

The demon glanced at the others and smirked in amusement. "Is that why *you* are here?"

Laughing, he shook his head. "No, no." He smiled, finishing his drink. "We are older brothers of Opus. Live off wealth he makes fixing problems."

"I see," Zalith replied. He might have guessed they were moochers because they really didn't seem to look as though they were of any use.

The man then held out his hand. "I am Ulric."

Zalith didn't want to take his hand, but he did so to be polite. He smiled in response, shaking Ulric's hand.

"These are Mikel," he said, pointing to his brother with the plaited hair. "Gracien," he said, nodding over at the angel refilling his glass, the brother with his hair tucked back behind his ears. "And Tomás," he muttered, waving his hand over at one of his brothers who had started bickering not too long ago.

"Xurian," Zalith said; he'd often use his brother's name as an alias, and now was a suitable time to do so; it was obvious that Ulric was fishing for his name.

"Unusual name," Ulric said, leaning back in his seat.

Just then—to Zalith's relief—the lounge door opened, and the butler leaned inside, setting his eyes on the demon. "Sir Opus will see you now," he called.

"If he touches you somewhere you don't want to be touched, just scream—I will come to rescue," Ulric said with a smirk, looking at Zalith as he stood up.

Losing all interest in the brothers, Zalith walked away and followed the butler into the hall. He then led the demon up a set of stairs, past several locked doors, and to one rather large door at the end of the landing. He knocked on the door, and as a muffled voice called for him to enter, the butler pushed the door open, invited Zalith inside, and then walked off without a word.

When Zalith stepped into the room, the door closed on its own behind him. The room looked much like a common practitioner's office; a desk ten or so feet ahead of him, doors on either side of it, shelves of herbs, books, and apparatuses, and the floors were lino wood, obviously so that it was easier to clean.

"I was told you were stowed away with my brothers, yes," the silver, silky-haired man sitting behind the desk said, something of a croak to his voice as if he had a cold.

This man could only be Opus. He, too, was an angel dressed in expensive white attire but an angel much different to those who were downstairs. His aura was something Zalith hadn't felt before, and he didn't appear to be a scion—but he was definitely an angel. If he had been a scion, Zalith would have to find someone else for the job; he'd not risk there being any sort of link between this ring's enchantment and a Numen.

"I have no record of any patients today at all, least of this time of the morning, yes." He frowned as he eyed Zalith thoroughly. "Clyde told me of a demon waiting at my doorstep, and of course, this intrigued me, for what demon would come to a household of angels for help? I often have to go to them, yes," he said, kicking out the chair in front of his desk, inviting Zalith to sit.

Zalith eyed Opus. Apart from the fact that his strange aura perturbed him, he felt indifferent. "I'm often an exception," he said, remaining where he was. "For example, I'm not a patient."

Opus placed his pen down on his desk, took off his reading glasses, and frowned curiously. "Then what is it you are here for, yes?"

"I need something enchanted, and I've heard that you're the man to come to."

"Where might you have heard such a curious rumour, yes?"

The demon smiled. "Around town. How does anyone hear rumours?"

Opus deadpanned. "Quite," he answered. "Well, I am not sure where you have heard these rumours, but such an ability requires ethos, and I have no such thing. Ethos was outlawed in these lands many years ago unless you are an elf; surely you know that, yes. Please, do leave and close the doors on your way out," he said, nodding at the door to his office.

With a smirk on his face, Zalith made his way over and sat down. "Your *brothers* are angels, and you're going to try and tell me that *you* do not possess ethos?" he asked, keeping his eyes on Opus.

But no flicker of emotion spread across the man's face. He simply stared at Zalith as if emotion wasn't something he possessed. "If you are smart enough to deduce that we are angels, you should be smart enough to know that not all of us can use ethos in this world, yes."

"I could practically feel your aura the moment I stepped foot in this house. I think it would be much easier for us both if you were to stop with the lies," Zalith suggested, smiling as he leaned back in his seat.

Eyeing him closely, Opus also smiled. For a long, tense moment, they stared at one another, waiting as the atmosphere grew thicker. Zalith wasn't sure what Opus might do, and it was clear that he wasn't sure what Zalith might be intending to do. But after a short while, Opus rested his arms on the table and lost his glare.

"What is it that you need enchanting, yes?" the mage asked.

Zalith reached into his pocket and pulled out the gold ring. "This."

Opus examined the ring with his eyes and then looked at Zalith. "What is it you want done to it, yes?"

"I need to hide someone from a few individuals."

"A masking rune would—"

"I'm not interested in branding a rune onto this person's skin," he said in detest.

The man nodded slowly. "I see.... Come with me, yes," he invited as he stood up.

Zalith also stood up and cautiously followed Opus to the door on the left of his desk. The angel pushed it open to reveal the room inside, which possessed a very different appearance than his office. It was dimly lit, the floor was carpeted black, and the walls were dark gold. The room wasn't much larger than his office, and most of the walls were lined with shelves upon shelves of books, jars, apparatuses, and curious items. A single window sat at the end of the room with a workbench beneath it.

Once Zalith entered, the door shut behind him; he stopped ten or so feet from where Opus had halted and waited, watching as the man pulled a rather large book from a table, placed it on his workbench, and flipped a few hundred pages in.

Grabbing a quill, Opus glanced back at Zalith. "You should understand, yes, that I will not perform any ethos arts without insurance. I will want to know your name, your place of residence, who this enchanted ring is for, and then I will need to know how you would prefer to be contacted. It is for both our benefit, yes. If authorities come looking, I can warn you of such an occurrence, for, as we know, ethos here is unlawful if performed by anyone other than an elf. It is also so I know where to find you if you so happen to cause me... trouble, yes."

There was no way he was going to give this man Alucard's name. He wasn't going to put his vampire at risk any more than he already had. Leaving him back at the inn alone was already a huge risk, and being here was even more so. He understood Opus' reasoning—as ridiculously annoying as it was—but he wasn't going to involve Alucard in any way whatsoever.

"I am Zalith," he answered and watched as the mage wrote it down. "I reside in Cypress Estate, not too far from the Citadel, deep within the forest, and I would prefer to be contacted by either a written letter, a messenger, or telegraph. And it is for my significant other."

Opus wrote down his answers. "I need to know the details of your sig—"

"Are my name and address not insurance enough?" Zalith interrupted irritably. "Why do you need to know so much? Do you ask your patients who gave them a UTI?" he snarled, his irritancy quickly becoming aggression. "No, so I think we'll be fine."

Unshaken by Zalith's sudden outburst, Opus placed his quill down and turned to face him. "Do *you* have a UTI?" he asked unsurely, but with something of amusement in his voice.

Utterly unamused, Zalith scowled at him. "No."

"Yes...." Opus nodded slowly. He then donned a look of sincerity. "Who is it you wish to hide your significant other from, yes?"

Obviously, Zalith had to be honest, and he felt no reason to hold back his answer. "The Numen," he replied, and the moment the word left his mouth, Opus frowned suspiciously.

"Curious," the mage drawled, looking Zalith up and down. "Might I ask why you—"

"No."

The mage deadpanned and leaned back against his workbench. "If you will not tell me why you wish to hide someone from such creatures like the Numen, then I simply cannot and will not help you, yes. And I might as well tell you now that you will nowhere find someone else capable of performing such a spell, nor would you find someone who would not have made an attempt on your life by now, yes. So, tell me, Zalith, why do you wish to hide this person from the Numen?"

Zalith kept his aggravated scowl. "Obviously because they're after him."

"If such people *were* after him, they would have found him by now, yes," Opus said with a doubtful frown.

"Do you think I'd waste my time coming here if I didn't have to?" Zalith snarled.

For a few moments, the mage eyed him... but then nodded. "Yes. Give me the ring," he said, holding out his hand.

Still with an irritated glare on his face, Zalith reached into his pocket, pulled out the gold ring, and handed it to Opus. "You best know what you're doing," Zalith warned. When Opus took the ring from him and sat at his workbench, the demon kept a close, watchful eye on him. "How much do you want?" he asked.

Opus picked up a very small, very fine needle-like blade and started to carve something on the inside of the ring. "I make more than enough income dealing with the rather common genital problems of all the rich men in this city and tending to the needs of their wives and all the women they sleep with. I do not need your money, yes," he said as he smiled back at Zalith in what looked like an attempt to make him laugh. "You will simply, as they say, owe me one, yes," he said, turning his attention back to the ring.

Zalith frowned reluctantly but couldn't help but feel amusement in response to Opus' comment about his work. "I'd rather pay you," he replied with less anger in his voice.

The mage smiled as he worked. "You can pay me either by telling me the name of the man this is for or by owing me a favour, yes."

He rolled his eyes. "What kind of favour?"

Opus finished carving into the ring, placed it in his own palm, and clamped his hand shut around it. He then stood up and turned to face Zalith, his hand beginning to glow a dim gold. "A favour with just as much risk as this, yes. I have become an enemy of the Numen," he said, opening his hand to reveal the ring. "I will come to you when I need you, yes."

Zalith took the ring from him. "Fine."

"As I do not know who it is for, I could not bond blood to it, so the ring will bind to whoever wears it first, yes," Opus explained, leaning back on his workbench again. "It was much of a pleasure doing business with you, yes."

Holding out his hand, Zalith nodded. "Thank you," he said as Opus shook his hand. Then, he turned around, left the mage's office, and didn't waste time creating a rift within the stone wall.

And then, he disappeared, eager to get back to Alucard.

Chapter Seventy-Eight

— ⟨ ✝ ⟩ —

Heirloom

| **Alucard** |

Alucard waited. He lay in bed, staring over at the wall Zalith disappeared into. It had been a little over an hour, and his worry was increasing with each passing moment. He had no idea where Zalith went, only that he'd gone to pick something up. Despite his tiredness, Alucard kept himself from falling asleep, keeping his eyes on the wall, hoping that Zalith would come back any moment now.

He was too tired to sink into his thoughts; all he could think about was what he'd do if Zalith didn't come back. What if something happened to him? What if the Numen found him? Alucard wouldn't even know, and he felt like an idiot for not going with him.

With a sullen frown, he shifted his stare to the ceiling. It had been a *long* day; so much happened and so much had been said. As much as he liked the idea of being safe from the Numen, he didn't feel comfortable with Zalith putting *his* life on the line to protect him. But he knew that Zalith was going to do it anyway, no matter what he said. And...*he* would do the same for Zalith.

Where was Zalith going to find the information he'd need to work out how to banish the Numen, though? Surely, only a Numen would know such things, and not one of them would share those secrets with someone like Zalith, not even to hurt each other.

He tried to remember if there was anything he knew or may have heard long ago that might help, but there was nothing—unless he had to wait for Zalith's ethos to finish untangling his mind; if he *did* know anything, Lilith and Damien would have definitely made him forget. But as of right now, he didn't know if killing them was possible; he didn't know how to banish them, all he knew was how to hurt them the same way he'd hurt Lilith. But he trusted Zalith, and Zalith seemed confident that he'd find the answers that he needed. And if the Numen somehow caught word that Zalith was looking for ways to work against them, then Alucard would do everything in his power to protect him. After all, he knew that he was capable of *fighting* the Numen, so at least he'd be able to get himself and Zalith out of trouble if it came calling.

The Numen and Zalith's plans weren't the only things occupying his thoughts; since mentioning his mother, he also wanted to find out which bloodline she belonged to— he'd do that once he was settled in with Zalith in Nefastus. He'd also have to update Luther, who was going to be working as his second in command; he'd be controlling things back in Dor-Sanguis for him and would have to report to him pretty much every day. Alucard was sure that wasn't going to be a problem, though. He would also have to inform Jasper, who had taken over for both Ben and Felix; he'd get Luther to do that once he returned from his hunt for Detlaff, wherever that had taken him.

Then, there was Ben. That man was clearly broken after what Detlaff had done to him, and Alucard couldn't let him continue to work for him—he couldn't exactly expect him to be able to do so, either. But he was a liability, and he couldn't let him go free and wander the world just to be caught and used to find him again. He wasn't sure what to do with him, but it was beginning to look like killing him was the best option. Killing him wasn't what Alucard wanted to do, but if he had to do it to keep himself and Zalith safe, then he would.

Suddenly, a rift opened within the wall Zalith had left through, and to Alucard's relief, the demon returned. An irritated look clung to his tired face, but other than that, he looked fine.

Zalith smiled when he caught Alucard's gaze and made his way over to the bed. He pulled off his clothes, took something from his pocket, and then climbed into bed. "Hey," he said once he made himself comfortable beside Alucard. He placed his hand on the side of the vampire's face and stared into his eyes. "Have you been awake this whole time?"

Staring at him, Alucard shrugged slightly. "No," he lied. "Where did you go?"

Zalith moved closer, resting his forehead against Alucard's. He then sighed deeply and took a moment before looking back into his eyes. "I went to see a mage—Opus is what he called himself," he explained. But he then lightly grabbed hold of Alucard's left wrist from beneath the cover and pulled it out so that they could both see his hand. The demon revealed what he'd taken from his pocket—a gold ring with inlaid onyx and black diamonds on either side of the onyx. "This used to belong to my father," he said quietly, taking his eyes off Alucard's curious face for a moment as he stared down at the ring.

Alucard also looked down at it, watching as Zalith slowly slipped it onto his left middle finger.

"It's one of the only things of his that I have left, and I want to give it to you because I love you...more than anything," he continued, making sure that the ring was sitting comfortably around the vampire's finger. He looked back at Alucard's tired, curious face and smiled. "If my father knew about the circumstances, he would have wanted me to give it to you; I think both he and my mother would have liked you very much," he said, resting his forehead against Alucard's again.

The vampire stared into Zalith's eyes but then glanced down at the ring on his finger as Zalith took hold of his hand. He'd given him yet another gift, and one that had so much meaning to it. Alucard didn't know what to do or what to say; all he could do was think about how much Zalith had done for him and how little he felt he'd done for Zalith. Should he be getting Zalith gifts, too? Was giving a partner something *this* important a part of being in the kind of relationship they were in? It all confounded him, but he felt that maybe this wasn't what he was supposed to be thinking about right now, so he silenced his confliction.

He looked back at Zalith, and a content smile stole his tired face.

"It will also keep you safe," Zalith continued before Alucard could say anything. "I had the mage enchant it so that it'll keep you hidden from the Numen, so don't ever take it off," he said with a smirk.

"I won't," Alucard said. "Thank you."

Zalith smiled and wrapped his arms around Alucard, pulling him into his warm embrace. Alucard moved his arms around the demon to hold him in return, but Zalith soon leaned back to stare at his face once again. He leaned closer and kissed his lips, and then he seemed to look at him and wait for Alucard to let him know whether or not he wanted more.

Alucard guided his hand to the back of Zalith's head and pulled his face closer to his own, and then they started kissing. They started off slow and passionate, but after every few strokes of their entwined tongues, they got a little faster. Eventually, Zalith moved so that he was leaning over the vampire, who he made lay on his back, kissing him softly as he started lightly dragging his fingers over and down Alucard's naked body.

It didn't take long for Alucard's tiredness to be muted by his anticipation— anticipation that had abruptly arisen the moment Zalith's hand moved down his arm and to his waist. He exhaled quietly but deeply as the demon's attentive kisses wandered from his lips and to his neck; his growing excitement felt so abrupt, but he was sure that it was because not only did he find everything about Zalith so enthralling and enticing, but because he loved him, and that had a way of making his desire for him harder to contain. And the desire he felt right now was for the demon's bite—for the pleasing, drowning euphoria that his venom would give him.

Alucard's hand slid to the back of Zalith's head, closing his eyes in anticipation of the demon's seductive bite. Zalith, however, had different plans; he trailed teasing kisses along Alucard's neck, his fingertips dancing over the vampire's taut muscles. Alucard frowned and eagerly pulled Zalith's face closer to his neck, so close that he could no longer kiss him; as he felt the demon smile and widen his jaw, he lost his impatient pout and stopped holding his face so tightly against his skin.

To his surprise, Zalith deviated from his expectations; instead of sinking his fangs into Alucard's body, he traced his tongue provocatively along the vampire's neck. A sly chuckle resonated in his voice as he detected the pout forming on Alucard's lips; the demon then playfully blew air over the vampire's wet skin, sending an electrifying shiver down Alucard's spine, and although it irritated him, it left him yearning for more.

The demon smirked, kissing the side of Alucard's face and back down to his neck as he continued dragging his hand over his body. Every time his fingers came close to the vampire's crotch, he moved his hand away, denying Alucard the touch he was desperately waiting for. He tried his best not to smile and struggled even more so when the demon glanced at his face in search of a reaction. Zalith lightly stroked his fingers down and over the vampire's abs, past his waist, and to his inner thigh, all while watching the anticipation on Alucard's face increase.

Alucard fidgeted with impatience, desperately awaiting the feel of Zalith's fingers against his crotch. And finally, the demon moved his hand close enough to lightly caress Alucard's arousal, breathing against his neck as Alucard slowly tensed up in response to his long-awaited touch. But Zalith then stopped and moved his hand back down to the vampire's inner thigh.

Irritated, Alucard sharply turned his head and glared up at Zalith, stopping him from kissing his neck. But Zalith smirked deviously, dragged his hand back up Alucard's leg, and lightly gripped his shaft. Alucard's irritancy withered into anticipation, and when he tried to look away to hide his face, Zalith carefully snatched his jaw, keeping him from looking away from him.

With his right hand, Zalith started to slowly tend to the vampire's arousal, staring into his nervous eyes with a smirk on his face. Alucard tried to keep himself from sinking into his angst, but when he felt the demon's hard, thick arousal digging into his leg, he huffed vehemently, fidgeting a little while trying to encourage himself to tell Zalith how badly he wanted him.

But Zalith then leaned closer and kissed his lips. Alucard gripped a fistful of the demon's hair, his heart beginning to beat faster as each moment passed. His eagerness grew so much that he let go of his nervousness for just a moment to allow his free hand to wander down Zalith's body and to his crotch. He didn't hesitate and lightly gripped the demon's shaft, and a pleased groan sat upon Zalith's breath as the demon lightly bit the vampire's bottom lip.

The vampire turned his head to the side in hopes that Zalith might now bite his neck, but he clearly knew what Alucard wanted and wasn't going to give it to him just yet. Alucard was growing used to how Zalith thought in these moments, and he was sure that he'd have to wait a little longer to feel the demon's fangs pierce his skin.

But to Alucard's bewilderment, Zalith released his arousal, seizing his waist instead and orchestrating a sultry relocation; the demon reclined against the headboard, coaxing Alucard into his lap, urging him to straddle it. Caught off guard by the sudden move,

Alucard placed his hands on Zalith's chest as he gazed down, a haze of confusion clouding his eyes.

The demon, undeterred, guided his hand to the back of Alucard's head, compelling their faces to draw near. Leaning in, Alucard met the hunger in Zalith's eyes with his own, succumbing to another passionate kiss.

Alucard could sense the palpable excitement pulsating between them. Zalith's hands traced a searing path down the vampire's body, claiming his waist with a possessive grip that lingered in the intoxicating embrace. The demon, however, momentarily withdrew, turning his head to the side; Alucard watched as he reached into a small rift and pulled out a bottle of lube from what looked like a vault, and when the rift closed, their lips met once more, and the fusion of desire and arousal intensified, leaving Alucard breathless in the aftermath. Zalith then rested his forehead against the vampire's shoulder, the lingering heat between them igniting a slow burn that promised an evening of unbridled passion.

The vampire exhaled in anticipation when he heard Zalith open the bottle, and when he felt the demon moving his fingers down his back and to his ass, his heart raced a little faster. But it was then that the demon abruptly sank his fangs into his neck, making him flinch and whimper in startlement, a grimace appearing on his face—but it soon withered into a relieved frown, the brief moment of pain that came with every bite disappearing as pleasure and euphoria enthralled him. At the same time, Zalith slowly guided his lube-smothered fingers into his ass. Alucard frowned, resting the side of his face on Zalith's as the demon kept his fangs latched onto his neck for a little longer than he usually would, slowly swallowing his blood as it poured into his mouth. But when he did eventually stop, he tightly gripped the right side of the vampire's ass and exhaled deeply in satisfaction.

Zalith then let go of his ass, gripping his own shaft as he firmly held Alucard's waist with his free hand. Alucard felt him guide the tip of his shaft so that it was against his hole and then moved his hand to his waist. Zalith started to gently kiss his neck, encouraging Alucard to slowly sit, thus gradually taking the demon's dick deeper into himself. At first, of course, the familiar discomfort greeted his body, but he didn't care. Ignoring it, he tightened his grip on Zalith's hair as he felt each thick inch easing deeper and deeper until he was sitting in the demon's lap.

The demon exhaled pleasurably against Alucard's neck, a satisfied sigh upon his voice as his grip on the vampire's waist tightened. Alucard's excitement intensified, the euphoria of Zalith's bite silencing any nervous thoughts he might have. A shiver of pleasure travelled through him when Zalith made him move his body up so that he was no longer straddling his lap but then back down again until he was sat firmly. He kept hold of Zalith's hair in one hand, placing his other on the side of the demon's neck as he continued to slowly move in the way Zalith had shown him, sliding the demon's dick into and out of his ass, and he quickly found that being in control excited him even more.

He breathed deeply and pleasurably, holding onto Zalith as tightly as he could without hurting him. Zalith kept his hands on Alucard's waist, his own deep, satisfied breaths enticing Alucard to sink further into his enjoyment. He might be moving slower than Zalith usually did, but the demon didn't seem to dislike that. He groaned quietly, as usual, pulling Alucard closer, burying his face into his neck to muffle his pleased moans.

Alucard didn't hold back his own sighs of enjoyment. But the enthralling pleasure soon forced him to glance at Zalith's neck. He caught himself craving the demon's blood so often that he'd not wait a moment longer to take it—and he was sure that Zalith was waiting for his bite, too; the demon dragged his right hand from the vampire's waist and to the back of his head, slowly pulling his face closer to his neck each time he moved his body.

When Alucard reached where he'd chosen to bite, though, he didn't instantly sink his fangs into the demon's skin. This time, he gently pressed his lips against Zalith's neck, kissing him a single time, a quiet, pleasured groan upon his voice as he sighed, still moving his body back and forth over the demon's shaft. He thought he might do as Zalith did and tease the demon into annoyance, but he couldn't keep himself from biting long enough. He slowly sunk his four fangs into Zalith's neck, listening to the demon as he sighed in delight, tightening the grip he had on Alucard's body.

The moment he felt Zalith's blood seep onto his tongue, Alucard hummed quietly in satisfaction, allowing the euphoria to pull him deeper from his senses; the pleasure of the demon's dick moving in and out of his body, Zalith's venom, and his blood quickly ensnared him, making him whine quietly, but the moment he'd bitten Zalith, the demon— as he moaned quietly—gripped each side of Alucard's waist with his hands and started moving the vampire's body faster. Alucard complied, allowing Zalith to take control as he sunk into the intense, drowning pleasure.

He grimaced in struggle, pulling his fangs from Zalith's neck as he continued moving his body for him, and as he rested the side of his face on Zalith's, he couldn't contain a quiet, pleasured mumble of his name. "Zalith," he breathed, digging his claws against the demon's back as he tried to contain his enjoyment. The utter of his name only seemed to enthral Zalith more as he moaned quietly in response, both of them breathing frantically as he pushed and pulled on the vampire's body.

Just as Alucard was approaching his peak, Zalith stopped moving his body for him after a final assertive thrust, burying his throbbing dick as deeply into the vampire's ass as he could. The demon grimaced, nuzzled the vampire's neck, and quietly groaned, "Fuck," against his skin, holding Alucard's trembling body against his own.

The vampire moaned in startle but then exhaled in delight when he felt the demon's hot cum ooze and pool inside him, and with a content hum, he nuzzled the demon's hair.

But it wasn't over. Zalith took a moment to catch his breath but swiftly pinned Alucard on his back. The demon kept his dick inside the vampire's ass and made Alucard move one of his legs over his back. Alucard's once-settling excitement started to return, and as he exhaled deeply in struggle, the demon started thrusting into him.

Alucard turned his head to the side, clasping his fists shut as Zalith held his wrists above his head. He frowned and scowled in pleasure, moving his other leg over the demon's back so that they were both firmly clamped around him. He pulled Zalith closer with his legs, struggled cries upon each frantic breath as Zalith thrusted harder and harder, resting his forehead on the side of his head as he breathed just as desperately into the vampire's ear. And after just a few short moments, Alucard's body tensed up, his excitement peaked, and as he grimaced and moaned quietly in satisfaction, he climaxed, a sheer delight enthralled every inch of him.

The vampire lay there, calming down as Zalith exhaled deeply and rested atop him. The vampire's tired, trembling body began to relax, and the euphoria started relenting. He turned his head to stare up at Zalith, who rested his forehead against his and smiled. The demon then kissed him a few times, letting go of Alucard's wrists to use his hand and move a few strands of hair out of the vampire's eyes.

"I love you so much," Zalith breathed with a content smile on his face.

Alucard smiled shyly, taking his eyes off Zalith for a moment. "I love you, too."

Zalith dragged his thumb over the side of Alucard's face and sighed quietly. "Wait here," he said, and as Alucard nodded, the demon snatched one of the bathrobes from the floor. He pulled it on as he stood up and wandered off down the hall.

Alucard took his moment of solitude to admire the ring on his middle finger; he held his hand above his face, staring at the small black diamonds. He loved it. But when Zalith returned with a small towel, he lowered his hand and stared curiously at him as he sat beside him. Zalith used the towel to clean the cum off his dick and body and then smirked as he took off his bathrobe and climbed back into bed with him.

The demon pulled Alucard closer as the vampire rolled onto his side, making himself comfortable. He smiled slightly, waiting as Zalith wrapped his arms around him and rested his head on the side of his. It was strange but exciting to think that things would always be like this from now on. He'd be moving into Zalith's house, and it would be where he'd spend all of his time—at least he hoped so. He'd still have work to do, but he didn't want to think about that. It didn't matter right now. All that mattered was Zalith and what might come next for them in their lives together.

He relaxed as much as he could, closing his eyes as he focused on the content thought of spending every night with Zalith like this. He couldn't want anything more. Zalith was who he wanted to spend his life with—he was sure about that already. And tomorrow, another step in their life together would begin.

DEMON'S FATE
Numen Chronicles | Volume Two

DEMON'S FATE
Numen Chronicles | Volume Two

Chapter Seventy-Nine

─ ≺ † ≻ ─

A Month Later

| **Alucard** |

A month and twelve days had passed since Alucard and Zalith escaped Lilith's domain.

Alucard stirred to the comforting symphony of birdsong, a melody that gracefully rode the gentle currents of the morning breeze in Nefastus. Even as the cold season began to settle in, the warmth of Zalith's bed enveloped him, a familiar embrace that felt like home—their shared sanctuary. The reality of it all still carried a touch of surrealism, a departure from the life he'd once known.

Lying there, with the soft glow of dawn casting a subtle glow on the room, Alucard couldn't help but marvel at the unexpected turns that had led him to this moment. Sharing his life with Zalith had been an unforeseen journey, one that had taken him to a place he never imagined. As he lay beside the demon he'd come to love, the realization of living with Zalith settled within him, a notion that brought both warmth and a sense of contentment.

In the quiet intimacy of that morning, Alucard found solace in the simple truth that he hoped would endure—the hope of waking up beside Zalith for as long as fate allowed.

He opened his eyes, and as they met the sunlight shining in through the gaps in the curtains, they faded from hellfire to ice blue, and the familiar discomfort electrified through his head. A faint smile of contentedness clung to his face as he sunk into the warmth of Zalith's arms, but it soon faded. He'd often wake from his nightmares and wonder if he was still trapped within them, but lately, he woke to find that he didn't remember what he'd seen in his sleep only to recall it moments or hours later, and in this instance, he remembered *moments* later.

With a look of unrest on his face, he shuffled around uncomfortably, trying to dismiss the haunting thoughts of what his life had been like before he met Zalith and what his life might have become if he'd never allowed himself to understand just how much the demon beside him meant to him—if Zalith had never fallen in love with him, and if *he* had never gained a reason to live an actual life.

He then felt Zalith hug him a little tighter, resting his head on the side of Alucard's, embracing him from behind. "Good morning, baby," the demon said quietly, lifting his head just enough to kiss the side of Alucard's face.

Alucard turned his head and his body so that he was lying on his back; Zalith leaned on his left arm, smiling down at the vampire as he stared up at him, and Alucard smiled in response. He was relieved to see Zalith, as always, but his discontent didn't wither much.

Zalith never failed to notice when something was wrong. The demon frowned and placed his hand on the side of his face as he frowned in concern. "Are you okay?" he asked tiredly.

The vampire sighed deeply, sure that his habit of waking up like this every morning was beginning to tire Zalith. Near enough every morning, he'd either wake up suddenly or depressed. He wasn't quite sure why it always happened—why *would* he feel sad? He had everything that he thought he'd never have; someone who loved him, someone he loved, and a home that was safe. There wasn't anything to be sad about...yet, he still felt despondent, often empty, and he wasn't sure why.

But Zalith made him feel better—better enough so that he wouldn't sink into the sadness the way he used to; the sadness only really seemed to be there when he woke, and once their day started, he was confident he'd be fine.

He smiled a little brighter, placing his hand on the side of Zalith's face. "I'm fine," he said but this time with truth and not a wish to dismiss his feelings. Because he *was* fine. Nothing awful was going to happen again; he was safe, he was with Zalith, and he didn't have to worry about any of the Numen anymore.

Zalith kept his look of worry, a look that seemed almost upset. "You look sad," he said, staring into his eyes.

He took his gaze off Zalith, looking over at the windows as he contemplated whether or not he wanted to talk about what had saddened him this time. He was sure that if he didn't tell Zalith, the demon wouldn't let up until he knew why he felt so despondent. So, he shrugged and sighed quietly. "Just a stupid nightmare or something," he muttered.

The demon stroked Alucard's face with one of his fingers. "What happened?"

"Just the same thing," he mumbled. "Lilith had us, but we didn't get away like we did," he paused and grimaced almost painfully. "And she took you from me."

Zalith sighed sadly as he rested his forehead against Alucard's. "I wish there was something I could do to stop all of these bad dreams."

He stared at the wall, a sullen frown possessing his face. "Maybe they will go away eventually."

Still staring at him, Zalith lifted his head from Alucard's and tucked a strand of his tousled crimson hair behind his ear. "Is there anything I can do to make you feel better?"

"No," he answered. Zalith already did enough, and he was sure that he would be feeling a whole lot worse if the demon wasn't with him—*that* was enough.

Zalith seemed to think to himself for a few moments. But he then leaned closer and gently kissed Alucard's neck before leaning into his ear. "Do you want me to suck your dick?" he asked seductively. "*That* might help."

As embarrassment smothered Alucard's face, he pouted and scowled over at the wall. He didn't even have to look at Zalith's face to know that he was smirking. "No," he mumbled, refusing to look at the demon as he leaned around a little more to try and get him to look at him.

"Are you sure?"

For a moment, Alucard thought about it; he'd not deny that he enjoyed Zalith's attention, and he was certain that it would take his mind off his sadness for a while, but his moment of contemplation faded before it even became anything close to desire. He didn't feel as if he had the energy, not even enough to become aroused. So, he nodded stubbornly.

"Okay," Zalith said with a smirk. "But if there are any sexual favours you might need, I'm ready and willing," he said, grinning.

He knew that his face had become red; he thought he'd shove Zalith away to get him to stop flustering him, but he knew that the demon would only find enjoyment in the struggle.

"What about a kiss? Would that help?" Zalith then asked, starting to fiddle with his hair.

Alucard sighed quietly and turned his head to look up at him. He *did* love to kiss Zalith and loved it even more when Zalith kissed him—he enjoyed feeling the demon's lips against his own; it gave him a feeling of contentment that nothing else did. So, he kept a nervous, stubborn pout as he glanced away from his face and nodded slowly.

With a smile, Zalith leaned in and kissed Alucard a soft, single time before resting his forehead against his. "My grumpy little vampire," he said quietly, admiring Alucard's face while the vampire tried to hide his fluster again. The demon then laughed slightly in response to his stubborn face and leaned closer, kissing him again.

Each slow, gentle kiss pushed Alucard's feeling of discontent further and further away until he felt calm. Zalith always knew how to pull him from his despair, no matter how far he may have fallen into it, and that was only one thing of many that he loved about this demon.

He placed his hand on the back of Zalith's head and dragged his fingers through his hair. It didn't take very long for Alucard's desire for more to make itself known, his longing for every ounce of affection he might get. There was nothing he enjoyed more than Zalith's touch, especially at times when he felt sad.

Zalith's hand shifted from the side of Alucard's face to his neck; his kisses soon moved from his lips to his jaw and the opposite side of his neck. Alucard exhaled quietly, starting to tense up as he felt the sharpness of Zalith's fangs press against his skin. The demon began lightly sucking on his neck as though he were biting and draining him of his blood, but Alucard knew what Zalith was actually doing. There'd be a mark on his neck by the time the demon was done, a mark that would remain in place for a few days, but he welcomed it. He *wanted* it.

He then frowned as he felt Zalith's right hand move from his neck, under the blanket, and down his body, caressing his abs. His own hands found their way to Zalith's body, specifically his arms; his biceps were one of Alucard's favourite physical things about Zalith. He gripped the demon's left one in his hand, resting the side of his face on Zalith's head while the demon continued sucking his neck.

After a short while, Zalith's hand wandered back up to Alucard's shoulder, and he returned to kissing his lips. Alucard kept hold of the demon's arm, slowly dragging his hand down it until he reached his wrist. He lay there, consumed in their moment, his need for affection intensifying. He might have turned down Zalith's offer before, but now he wished that he hadn't. He wanted more, he wanted to be overwhelmed; he wanted *Zalith*, but more than what he was currently getting.

His left hand started to wander down the demon's body, and over his pecs and his abs, places he loved to see and touch. But they weren't where his hand wished to end up. He slowed as he passed Zalith's waist, and when he dragged his hand over his hip, he felt Zalith stutter in his current kiss as though he was surprised. Of course he'd be; Alucard was sure there hadn't been a time before now when he'd touched him without Zalith having first put his hands on him, but his eagerness encouraged him.

With a nervous frown beginning to appear on his face while Zalith continued kissing him, he lightly stroked his fingers over the demon's crotch. He felt Zalith's body tense up against his as he breathed a sharp breath onto his lips. The demon's hand moved from the side of Alucard's neck and to his hair, a handful of which Zalith gripped as he kissed him one final time, softly biting his bottom lip as he lifted his head enough to look down at his nervous face.

A smirk then crept across Zalith's face. "Do you want me to fuck you, vampire?" he asked quietly.

Alucard's nervous, stubborn pout returned as he took his ice-blue eyes off Zalith's seductive face and turned his head in an attempt to hide his look of embarrassment. He didn't hesitate and nodded, and Zalith didn't waste a moment in complying. The demon kissed the side of his face and slowly made his way down his neck and to his chest. But that was where he stopped. He didn't move any lower, and Alucard wasn't sure why until he felt Zalith kissing closer to his left pec.

Zalith reached it and started playfully and gently biting his nipple, making him flinch in startlement. He heard the demon's amused snicker, and it made him pout harder. He relaxed, though, as Zalith placed his lips over his nipple and started to lightly drag the tip of his tongue around it. It was a strangely sensitive area, and Zalith seemed to know that too—of course he did; it wasn't the first time he'd surprised Alucard with his sexual knowledge.

The vampire fidgeted in agitation, even more so when Zalith's left hand made its way down to his right pec. He frowned in delight as the demon pinched, licked, and sucked his nipples, flinching in confusing pleasure and surprise when Zalith occasionally bit his left one.

Zalith soon stopped and kissed his way back up to the vampire's face. He pressed his lips against Alucard's while his hand wandered beneath the covers. Alucard was once again able to reach the demon's crotch and did so when Zalith started to caress his. The feel of the demon's arousal excited him more; he gripped Zalith's shaft lightly in his hand, their kisses intensifying as they both started to breathe a little heavier.

But that was when a puff of purple smoke appeared beside them; out came Pip, the purple-eyed izuret, with a cheery chirp, but he stared bug-eyed when he set his sights on Zalith and Alucard.

Alucard hesitated, immediately let go of Zalith, and sharply turned his head away from the creature as a look of horror smothered his face.

Zalith, on the other hand, snarled irritably, refusing to look over at Pip. "What?" he grumbled, gritting his teeth in impatience.

Pip, who had two white envelopes in his small hands, held them out to his boss and informed him that they were from Eltaria...and that they were urgent.

"Put them on the dresser," Zalith ordered, glancing at the creature.

The izuret pouted but did as he was told and floated over to the closest dresser. He placed the envelopes on top of it; obviously aware that he wasn't welcome to stay, he disappeared in another puff of smoke, leaving Alucard and Zalith alone.

With his irritated expression fading, Zalith looked down at the vampire and made him turn his head so he'd look up at him. "I'm sorry about that," he said. As Alucard stared up at him with a look of irritancy, Zalith smiled and stroked the side of his face with his fingers. "Where were we?"

He started kissing the vampire again, but Alucard could tell he was distracted. His kisses felt snappy, and after just two more kisses, the demon stopped and sighed.

"Give me a moment," he said. He held out his hand and telekinetically pulled the letters over to him, and then he sat beside Alucard.

Alucard stared at Zalith, his anticipation slowly withering as each moment of silence passed. He watched while the demon read the first message, and a look of concern appeared on his once-content face. Alucard was sure that what he was reading wasn't good news and that any moment now, he was about to tell Alucard that he had to leave.

As expected, with a quiet sigh, Zalith lowered the letters and looked down at Alucard. "I'm sorry. I have to work."

Every ounce of happiness and lust that Alucard had felt disintegrated as Zalith spoke, and his feeling of discontent returned. But he'd not get angry or upset with him; he had work to do, and now that he was living with Zalith, he knew to expect things like this to happen. He nodded, sure that if he spoke words, he might unintentionally make Zalith aware of how he felt about the fact that he'd probably not see him for most of the day—and he wouldn't see him tonight either because he'd be in the city dealing with the Meshuga. He didn't want to seem selfish or like he didn't understand, so he sat up and shuffled to the end of the bed. "I should go and work anyway," he muttered.

Zalith leaned over as Alucard started to pull his clothes on. "We could have lunch together if you like," he offered with a smile, placing his hand on the vampire's shoulder.

Alucard looked back over his shoulder at him and smiled, trying to ignore his returning sadness. "Okay."

The demon kissed Alucard's forehead before getting out of bed to get dressed. As he did, Alucard pulled on his shirt and made his way over to the bathroom. For a moment, he stared sullenly down at his hands, but when he heard Zalith coming to join him, he snatched his toothbrush, spread some toothpaste on it, and started to brush his teeth. Zalith joined him, standing at his side as he did the same.

Once he was done with his teeth, Alucard took one of his combs brought from his castle and began tidying his hair.

Zalith then pecked his cheek with a kiss. "I'll see you a little later," he said, and as Alucard nodded, the demon left the bathroom through the door that led into the hallway and headed for his office.

Watching him leave, Alucard frowned and looked back at his hands. A few moments later, the familiar clipping of Sabazios' claws echoed down the hall, and surely enough, the dog poked his head around the bathroom door and stared up at him—except he was no longer a *dog*, but a puppy. No more was he a hound reaching the vampire's waist in height, but a much smaller, fluffier form of Sabazios just reaching the vampire's shin.

When hellhounds like Sabazios died, they would later burst into flames and re-emerge from the ashes, much like a phoenix, except every time a hellhound died, they looked a little more dead each time they came back to life. Now, the once husky-looking dog had an awful tear in his right ear, which stretched down over his face to form a scar, one which crept over his right eye. It was the wound that had killed him and a scar that would forever remain upon his body.

Sabazios strolled into the bathroom and sat at Alucard's feet as the vampire took his eyes off the dog and continued tidying his hair.

"I'm not feeding you," he muttered. "That's what the kitchen staff are for."

The dog whined quietly, gawping up at him with a pleading look in his eyes.

"Go," he mumbled, waving his hand over at the door.

But Sabazios didn't leave. He shuffled closer to Alucard's leg, whining.

Once he finished tidying his hair, Alucard sighed deeply, looking down at his dog. Sabazios rubbed his face on the side of Alucard's shin, so the vampire rolled his eyes, leaned down, and picked him up. "Fine," he muttered, carrying his puppy like an infant as he left the bathroom and pulled the door shut behind him.

It looked like he'd be feeding the dog after all, and once he was done, it would be time to get to work. He knew better than to sit around in silence doing nothing. That would only encourage his tendency to overthink, and that was the last thing anyone needed.

Chapter Eighty

— ⸲ ✝ ⸱ —

Updates From Dor-Sanguis

| **Alucard** |

Alucard made his way downstairs; he glanced at Sabazios, who looked a little *too* content to be in his arms, and he couldn't help but smile a little. When he reached the bottom of the stairs, emerging into the wide-open space which was the hall, he turned left and walked into the hallway that would take him to the kitchen. However, once he came to the open floor space between the kitchen and a set of stairs, he set his eyes on Sabazios' bowls to see that they had been filled, but the dog hadn't eaten much of what he'd been given.

"Why are you being fussy?" Alucard muttered, looking down at him.

The puppy wagged its tail, staring up at him and panting happily.

Alucard rolled his eyes and put the dog on the floor. "Finish your food," he grumbled, turning away to head back towards the hall.

But Sabazios yapped quietly and followed, sticking close to him while he made his way back down the hallway.

Alucard stopped walking to look down at the dog, and as it stared up at him wide-eyed, he crouched and sighed quietly. "What do you want?" he asked, patting the puppy's head.

Sabazios sat in front of the vampire and held out his paw, waiting for Alucard to take it. The vampire eventually did so, waiting to be told what it was the hound wanted, but Sabazios just stared at him.

Perhaps he wasn't hungry, or maybe he'd sensed the vampire's despondency and simply wanted to be there for him. Either way, Alucard had work to do. As much as he'd rather be back in bed with Zalith, he knew that he'd not get such a thing any time soon. Zalith was working, too, and Alucard wasn't sure how long he might be doing so.

"Okay," he said with a sigh, scooping the puppy up in his arms again.

Alucard headed through the house until he reached the main hall again. Straight ahead as he came out of the hall was the door to *his* office, sitting between the entrance to Zalith's office and the door to the casual lounge where he played his new violin not too long ago for the demon.

He headed into his workspace with Sabazios in his arms. Unlike most of the house, *his* office was fully carpeted with black, fluffy carpet, just as his office had been back home in both his old house and his castle. One of his favourite white dragon fur rugs sat in the centre of the room, too.

His desk sat ahead in front of the large windows with two armchairs in front of it. The black, red-trimmed curtains were already open, the sunlight shining in; nearly all the wall space was lined with book-packed shelves, and to his right was a large corner table upon which he'd work on his inventions. Beside it were two leather couches, one against the shelved wall, and one against the wall with a staircase leading up to his study behind it.

Alucard closed the door behind him and placed the puppy on the floor. Sabazios scurried over to his bed, which sat under the window behind Alucard's desk chair, where the vampire sat and rested his arms on the table. For a moment, he sat there and stared, trying to forget about both his sadness and frustration. He felt selfish for feeling the way he did, for being a little irritated that his time with Zalith had just been cut short. But it wasn't like it happened all the time or would be happening all the time, and he felt as if he just needed to calm down and get on with his day.

He exhaled quietly, reaching for the small stack of envelopes that had been left on his desk. Most of them were from Dirk, and two were from Attila—he could tell by their handwriting. The last didn't look familiar, but it couldn't be urgent; otherwise, it would have come directly to him rather than to his office. So, he placed it back down on top of the pile and rested the side of his face in his hand, sighing quietly.

Sabazios raised his head, staring in the direction of the door. He burst out of his bed as footsteps approached, and when the door opened, the puppy glared at the butler, Edwin, as he stood in the doorway.

"What?" Alucard grumbled.

"Luther has arrived, sir. Should I send him through?"

"*Da*," he grumbled, waving his hand in dismissal.

Edwin nodded and pulled the door shut.

Alucard then set his eyes on Sabazios, who was staring intensely at the door. "What are you waiting for?"

The dog looked back at him and whined quietly.

Not too long later, Edwin opened the door again, this time with Luther behind him. As Luther stepped in, Sabazios wandered away from the door with a look of disinterest on his face. He curled back up in his bed and lay in a slump as he watched Luther make his way over and sit in one of the chairs in front of Alucard's desk.

"I see Dirk still sends daily letters," Luther said, making himself comfortable as he glanced at the envelopes.

"What is that ugly little man doing?" Alucard grumbled.

Luther shrugged. "He hangs out in Dargamoore most of the time. He got himself a little condo not far from the centre. Close to Ben's old place, actually." He paused and frowned. "Where *is* Ben? He still here?" he asked, shuffling around in his seat.

"You ask a lot of questions when you're nervous," Alucard said with an irritated scowl. "Did somebody die? Lose an eye, maybe?"

With a forced laugh, Luther shook his head. "Nah, just uh...I've not done so well finding someone to replace Felix. We have Jasper in charge of his old jobs; it's just the looking after fledglings that we haven't covered yet. The creepy little guy deserved what he got, I just wish he wasn't the one thing that's close to impossible to find, you know?"

Alucard stared at him with little interest. "Close to impossible, not impossible. If no one at the castle fits the criteria, then you can tell Attila to contact these people I have in DeiganLupus," he said, pulling out a piece of paper which he then began to write on. "Lawrence's coven lives in the capital city, and he possesses a rather talented teacher— one I would have chosen if Felix wasn't around. Send this to him; I gather he's back from his trip?" he asked, handing the paper to Luther.

Glancing down at the woman's name written on the paper, Luther sighed quietly.

"Problem?" Alucard questioned. He knew that Luther had a history with the woman he'd selected, but he didn't care. The work was more important.

"No," he mumbled, tucking the paper into his pocket.

"There better not be one if and when she comes to work with you. Perhaps this will encourage you to look harder for a replacement, hmm?"

Luther sighed again. "What about Ben? If I knew where *he* was, then the problem would be solved. He's old enough, experienced enough, and—"

"Dead," Alucard interjected.

A disgruntled look appeared on Luther's face. "Detlaff really got him that bad, huh?"

"How is that cockroach doing?" Alucard muttered, leaning back in his seat.

"Locked up in the dungeon, same place I put him when I got him last week. Six guards at a time, all the time. He isn't getting out again."

Alucard stared at him, waiting.

"I'll keep searching for someone to look after the baby vamps. If I don't find someone by next week, I'll get Attila to contact...*her*," he uttered.

"Good," Alucard said.

"Regarding your other interest," Luther then said, reaching into his suit.

Alucard watched as he pulled a small file of papers from inside his suit and placed them on his desk. The vampire immediately took them and opened the file to stare at the first page, adorned with very fine print, strange symbols, and scribbles.

"I went as far back as I could find; a lot of it's covered in blood—or maybe it's wine, who knows? It's older than I am," Luther explained.

Uninterested in Luther's attempt to amuse him, Alucard looked through the papers.

"There's uh...drawings, too. I guess even cultists get portraits done."

Alucard continued ignoring Luther as if he wasn't there. He looked through the papers, reading every single name within the records, glancing at every picture until he came to one page among them all, a page that banished his vacant look and replaced it with something discontent.

On the page in front of him, there wasn't much written other than a name, a date of birth, a few small pieces of background information, and a hand-drawn portrait. Her face was just as he remembered. He might have only seen his mother once, but it was enough for her face to forever remain in his memory. It was all he had of her, and ever since discovering the truth of her death, he couldn't settle.

He took the paper from the folder, which he then shut and placed into one of his desk drawers. "I want you to find out whatever you can about this woman. I need to know of her heritage," he said, sliding the paper across the table.

Luther leaned forward and took the paper. "Charlotte...Vladislav Reiner?" He frowned, slowly looking back at Alucard. "She died over four hundred years ago."

Alucard glared at him, his impatience beginning to stir.

With a nervous nod, Luther folded and tucked the paper into his pocket. "All right, I'll get right on that."

Then, with an irritated glower on his face, Alucard looked away from Luther and down at the mail on his desk. "I still haven't heard from my Paladins about Lucious. I sent to have them come back two weeks ago."

"I'm confident they'll be back any day now. They went pretty far out looking for this guy. Oh, that reminds me, actually—the Diabolus. There's nothing there yet, either. I suspect they're either all dead or maybe they just gave up, huh?" he said, smirking. "Got tired of chasing you around for four hundred years."

"One can only hope. Don't let your guard down; ever since Damien disappeared, they would have been free to find me. I'm surprised not one of them has turned up in Dor-Sanguis yet, especially considering I killed one of their operatives a while ago."

"Well, the first sign of any Diabolus we see, we'll be on it," Luther said firmly.

With a slight nod, Alucard looked at him again. "Did the lady in Avalmoor take well to your 'death'?"

"Honestly, she seemed more than happy to be rid of me; my 'brother' tells me she's a hell of a lot more happier with a guy that's actually into her," he admitted.

"Right," Alucard muttered.

Silence then fell over them. Alucard stared down at his desk, not thinking about anything in particular, but rather more just staring in hopes that something other than irritancy and sadness would come into his day. He was sure that everything that needed to be covered had been, and all he really needed to do now was send Luther on his way.

"Might I ask...how you're doing?" Luther then asked with a cautious look on his face. "We haven't really spoken lately other than about business. Sometimes, I feel like you forget you and I were friends once upon a time."

"I don't forget," Alucard denied. "And I'm fine."

Luther then looked around his office for a moment. "I guess you and this demon are really serious, then? You've set up in his place pretty fast; feels weird knowing you're not holed up in that castle somewhere working on your latest contraption that makes absolutely no sense to me or Attila whatsoever," he said, smirking.

Alucard shrugged. "This is my home now. Living with a castle full of vampires who see me as their father wasn't exactly comfortable—for a while, maybe, but once I learned that I'd be back here in Aegisguard for longer than any time before, I began to feel as though I wanted my house back. We all know what happened to that," he grumbled.

"Could have built a new one. Being all the way out here in Nefastus, a place where ethos is pretty much as illegal as the Book of Lore says it is to love and sleep with another man. What happens if you get caught? I haven't seen any other vampires out here, only scummy little humans and stuck-up elves. Are you prepared for torches and pitchforks, Alucard?"

"I'm always prepared for torches and pitchforks," he said with a smirk.

"Well, I guess you best make sure your demon is."

"We're fine. Elves are much loved out here, and that's what Zalith and I say we are," he mumbled. "We sure have the ears."

Looking at him with a smile, Luther shrugged. "I suppose you do."

Just then, Alucard's attention shifted to his office door. He heard Edwin approaching, but he didn't knock on *his* door, he knocked on Zalith's. The vampire didn't listen to their conversation—he'd never do such a thing, but he *did* hear Zalith leave his office moments later and head through the hall. It was most likely that someone was at the front door for him.

Alucard sighed quietly and looked at Luther again. "If there's nothing else, you can go," he said dismissively.

"Nothing else," Luther said, shrugging. "Unless there will ever be a time when you're not too busy to hang out with us again."

The vampire's vacant stare didn't wither. "Eh, maybe one day."

"Soon," Luther said with a grin. He then stood up and straightened his white suit. "I'll see you in two days."

Alucard nodded with a dismissive wave of his hand. Luther then swiftly left his office, leaving the vampire alone with his puppy and his thoughts.

Chapter Eighty-One

— ⋞ ✞ ⋟ —

A New State of Affairs

| **Zalith** |

Zalith made his way to the front door. Although he'd been told that Varana was waiting for him, he couldn't stop thinking about the messages he'd read from Eltaria. It looked like things were taking a turn for the worse over there, and he might have to go back to fix it sooner than he'd like. But he'd deal with that later.

Once he pulled the door open and set his eyes on the crimson-eyed woman dressed in a navy blue dress that seemed to reflect both her sadness and desperation, he leaned on the door frame and donned a vacant stare. "Yes?" he asked.

Varana frowned up at him. "Well, hello to you, too."

He didn't have anything to say to her. He stood there, waiting, watching as her frown intensified with each moment of silence.

"You're not even going to ask me how I've been?"

Zalith sighed and lazily asked, "How have you been, Varana?"

"Horrible!" she exclaimed.

He didn't care, nor did he feel bad for her. "I'm sorry to hear that," he lied tonelessly.

Another moment of silence fell over them. It was clear that the woman wasn't *at all* happy with his tone; the displeased look on her face became something revolted as she waited in desperation for him to show some sort of emotion.

She pouted slightly and sighed. "Can I at least come in so we can sit and talk?" she asked calmly.

It was then that Zalith's expressionless face adorned an unsure frown. "Varana, I..." he paused, leaning back into the house to see if Alucard was anywhere within either eye or earshot, but his vampire was still in his office talking to Luther. He then looked at Varana. "I don't think it's a good idea."

Her calm faded into a scowl. "What? Why can't we talk?!"

Zalith stepped out of the house and pulled the door shut behind him, sure that the volume of Varana's voice was only going to increase. "We can," he said, ushering her to a nearby bench as she lightly protested. "But let's just sit out here."

They both sat down.

Varana kept a skeptical, irritated glare on Zalith as he sat beside her. "What are you hiding?"

"Nothing," he answered.

She scoffed in disbelief. "Nothing? You expect me to believe that?" she asked, glaring at him. "Why can't I go in? Has another one of my siblings found their way into your bed? I wouldn't be surprised," she muttered, taking her glare out at the grounds.

Not at all bothered by her need to be repulsive, Zalith questioned, "Is this what you came here to talk about?"

She sharply turned her head and glared at him. "No!" she insisted angrily. "I came here to talk about—" she paused, hesitation on her face. It seemed as though she was reluctant to wander into an argument and took a deep breath before looking at him again. "I came to say I'm sorry," she said, but still with irritation in her voice.

"For?"

Varana sighed sadly and looked down at her lap, resting her hands in it. Then, after a few seconds of silence, she started, "I crossed a line when I said those things to...*him*. I was just acting out for my own selfish reasons and didn't stop to consider what it might do to either of you. Our time apart made me realize that, at the end of the day, all I want is for you to be happy...and if *he* makes you happy, then who am I to get in the way of that?" She sounded upset, but surprisingly, she wasn't crying yet. "I don't want to be the cause of your unhappiness, Z, and I'm sorry if what I did made things difficult between the two of you. You've lost so much, and you work so hard.... You deserve to have somebody to come home to."

Zalith's doubt didn't fade. He wasn't entirely convinced that she had somehow managed to turn over a new leaf in her time of exile. She'd been after him for centuries, after all, and he knew that she wasn't going to give up *at all* despite Alucard's significance in his life. But he acknowledged her remorse for what happened in the kitchen two months ago; she appeared to be taking a step in the right direction and felt that maybe now she was deserving of some forgiveness.

He sighed quietly and slouched back, making himself comfortable. "Thank you."

Staring at him, Varana nodded. "I'm just glad that you're not done with me," she said confidently.

Then, Zalith glanced at her with a look of incredulity on his face, but it didn't hide his slight smile. She seemed so sure that he wasn't done with her and her petulant, selfish behaviour, and her altogether. It was somewhat amusing, but he'd not let her know that he found her assumption so. "A bold conclusion for you to jump to," he said.

Varana scowled in irritancy. "Shut up!" she snapped, shoving his arm ever so slightly with her hands. "We both know that we wouldn't be sitting on this bench if that were the case."

His amusement didn't fade; his smile grew a little, but he sighed it off his face and looked out at the grounds. "So, what now, Varana?"

"I want to come back," she said sternly.

"Is that so?"

"Yes," she said with a single nod. "I can't *bear* to be at my sister's for a moment longer."

Zalith smiled amusedly. "How bad is it?"

She scoffed and adorned a look of disgust. "Well, here with you, it's nice and clean and quiet, and everybody is always fully clothed—"

"Not always," Zalith said with a shrug.

The woman grimaced. "You know what I mean."

"Not to mention that sheer robe you're *constantly* wearing—"

"All I'm saying—" she interjected— "is that I just want to be able to eat breakfast without having to see *and* hear an orgy. I'd like to look out of my window and see a nice garden like this, not a nasty heap of bones and some postman getting eaten alive only for his body to join said piles of bones," she grumbled. But then, she cringed in utter revolt. "Ysmay has this...pet, too, and it's just..." she shuddered.

Zalith smiled, humoured by her discomfort.

"It's *such* an *ugly* little thing! She calls it Pickles," she mocked. "Funnily enough, considering it smells like cheese."

Staring out at the grounds, Zalith shrugged as a smirk crept across his face. "I don't know, V, her place doesn't sound *that* bad."

"Whatever," she said, frowning. "I just...I'm lonely there. You and I have been together for so long; it's strange being apart. I don't care for it much."

Another sigh broke his smirk. He nodded in agreement, for he had missed his best friend, too. He felt that, if things hadn't played out the way they did, if Varana hadn't caused the tension she did and just left of her own accord, then he might be the one asking her to come back home. However, Alucard was now a whole lot more involved in everything, and he thought it was best to tell her that he had his vampire move in with him.

He glanced at her, certain that she was about to explode like some kind of hellish chasm made up of several raging volcanos. "I have something to tell you," he started.

"What?" she asked, setting her gaze on him.

Although he'd just braced himself, he felt as if he had to do so just a little more. He kept a calm look on his face, preparing for her inevitable breakdown. "Alucard moved in with me a month ago."

Varana seemed to freeze beside him, a look of both shock and horror on her face, almost as if she'd seen someone she loved so very dearly die before her eyes. But she soon snapped out of it enough to scowl unsurely. "I can't tell if you're joking," she said, searching his face for a sign of sarcasm.

But there was no such thing on his face or in his voice. "I'm not," he answered, watching as her horror grew. "I converted the library into an office for him, and he also has the big guest room as his own private area to do with what he wishes," he explained.

Glaring at him, she gritted her teeth, clearly trying her best not to burst into flames. Her left eye twitched as a result of her attempts to do her very best to remain calm. "Wow..." she said, unable to dispose of her struggling grin. "That's...fantastic news...I'm so...happy...for you," she said with strained enthusiasm.

"So," Zalith continued, "I'll have to speak to him about whether or not he feels comfortable with you living with us."

Varana clenched one of her fists. "I lived here *first*."

Zalith rolled his eyes. "If you're not going to be civil with him, Varana, then I'm afraid you're going to end up living with Ysmay and Pickles for much longer than anticipated."

Yet another grimace clung to her face. "I can be civil."

"And if you pull another stunt like last time, you're going to wish that you and I never sat on this bench," he warned her.

She nodded, keeping her eyes on him. "I'm done with all of that nonsense, Z. I swear that I'll never do it again."

He scowled a little, still doubtful that she was totally over it. "Don't make me regret this, Varana."

Varana nodded in agreement, but the sadness on her face gleamed like sunlight on water. She sighed once more, looking out at the grounds. For a moment, she was silent, but it was clear that she was working out how to approach *something*.

After a few moments of quiet, she looked at him again. "Can I ask you something?"
He nodded.

"Why *him*? Honestly, what makes him *so* different from all the millions of other men you've been with?"

A content smile found its way to his face; he truly didn't know where to begin. He loved Alucard so much, everything about him was beautiful and wonderful, and Zalith never wanted to lose him. "It may be cliché," he started, staring out at the grounds as he smiled at the thought of Alucard, "but when I'm with him, I feel like I'm home. There's a comfort there; it's like everything that has ever caused me pain ceases to exist when he's with me. He's just different. My heart has been so fickle in the past, but with him, it's like everything inside of me has been rewritten," he beamed.

The woman pouted angrily. "Is that it?" she asked sarcastically.

Zalith glanced at her to see a sour look on her face. He knew that she was being sarcastic, but her comment was rude, so he wasn't going to stop talking—he didn't *want* to stop talking. "Of course not. I love his smile, his voice, his ass," he said with a smirk. "Well, his body in general. You know that V area near a man's hips?" he asked as he made the shape of a V with his hands and held them against the centre of his pelvic area. "This thing?" he asked, watching a look of revolt appear on her face.

She nodded but then looked away in disgust.

"Drives me crazy," he continued, sure that he was agitating her even more.

"Ugh," she uttered.

He smiled. "I just love everything about him, and I'm not afraid to show it."

Varana rolled her eyes and glared at him, almost turning her nose up as she eyed him up and down. "I mean, you reek of his imprint, so you must be laying on the affectations."

Just then, the front door to the house opened, and Luther walked out. Zalith watched him with a slight glare as he made his way away from the porch and towards the stairs that would take him into the grounds.

Varana obviously noticed his look of annoyance and giggled quietly. "Uh oh," she muttered as she also watched Luther pass, but with a look of curiosity. "Trouble in paradise?" she asked slyly. "Does your boyfriend have another boyfriend?"

"No," he grumbled.

"Who is he?" she asked curiously.

"Alucard's subordinate. Luger or Lumbar or something; I can't quite recall."

"He's kind of cute," she said with a smile as Luther made his way down the steps and into the grounds, following the path towards the estate's exit.

"Please," Zalith scoffed quietly. "He looks like something one might string up to keep pigeons away from the house."

Amused, Varana laughed and leaned her head on Zalith's shoulder. She sighed happily, obviously content to have been told that she may be coming home and escaping her sister's lair. "He seems nice," she continued.

He shook his head in disagreement, taking his eyes off Luther once he reached the gates.

The demon's thoughts then wandered back to Alucard. He was going to have to talk to the vampire about Varana returning home, and he knew that it wasn't going to be an easy conversation. But it was one they had to have. He also had a lot to think about regarding his work; Eltaria wasn't in good form as of now, and the thought of having to return to help with that lingered like a potent miasma in the back of his mind. He had a lot to do and a lot to think about, and none of it was going to be simple.

"I better get back," he said. "I'll talk to Alucard about your return; he's not going to be happy, though, so it might take a while to convince him."

She didn't look too happy, but she nodded in acceptance and squeezed his hand. "Thanks, Z."

He sighed and stood up. "I'll send an izuret."

She also stood up and smiled in what might be excitement. "Okay. I'll see you soon," she said, remaining where she was as he started to walk off.

"Goodbye," he replied, glancing back at her. Then, he made his way back into the house, now preparing himself for a conversation with Alucard. He was certain that it would be a long one.

Chapter Eighty-Two

— ⊰ ✝ ⊱ —

Settling In

| **Alucard** |

In his office, Alucard was still sitting behind his desk, staring vacantly at the bookshelves. Despite the fact that he had work to do and letters to read, all he could think about was what he'd seen this morning.

He'd had yet another dream—nightmare, memory, whatever it was—on top of his vision of losing Zalith to Lilith. He hadn't told Zalith about the prior because he felt as if he didn't yet understand it himself. Of course, he knew that a lot of his memories had been either altered or permuted by Damien and Lilith; he'd learnt many truths, both harsh and enlightening, but even though that was over a month ago, he was still uncovering new truths.

Last night, he remembered Damien; the Daegelus possessed his thoughts and memories near enough all the time, and no good ever came of it. What he remembered was the first night Damien had come to him, the night he'd said he'd keep Alucard safe and that he'd take care of him. Damien may have hidden him from the other Numen, but Alucard never felt safe, nor did he feel like anyone cared for him. Even now thinking about it hurt; he tried to outweigh his pain with the fact that he had Zalith, though. Zalith loved him, cared for him, and made him feel safer than he ever had...so why didn't that stop the sadness or memories?

Before, being with Zalith and sleeping beside him had kept the nightmares away, but the pain of his past seemed to be growing more potent as each night passed, as each memory slowly came back to him, and as he remembered just how little of a creature he was. Damien had told him so. Lilith had told him so. Everyone he had ever stood before told him so. Everyone had only ever used him, stolen from him, done things he'd never forget and probably never be able to speak of. What was he supposed to do with all of it? Four hundred years' worth of...that.

He took his eyes off the wall and glanced down at his puppy as it whined quietly, staring up at him. What he had here with Zalith...he wished it would last forever, but everything inside him told him that eventually, something would take it away from him, no matter what he tried to tell himself, no matter what Zalith convinced him with. He never got to keep the things he wanted. He'd lost all his friends, all the people who mattered to him, and he'd nearly lost Zalith too many times already.

But then he felt bad for underestimating the demon. Zalith had already done so many things that no one else could do—he loved *him*, after all, something everyone in Alucard's life had always told him would never happen. He'd even imprinted—they both had. He smiled a little and looked down at the black and gold ring sitting on his left middle finger, the same ring that would keep him hidden from *all* the Numen. Somehow, the demon had done that for him, too. So why did he still feel afraid? Why did he still fear that one day he might lose everything? Was it part of loving someone? To fear losing them?

He sighed and swivelled around in his seat, staring ahead at the door. He knew too well that it wasn't safe for him to sink into his thoughts, and he always tried his best not to. But the dismay he felt this morning hadn't helped. He just wanted to be with Zalith, to spend as much of his time as he possibly could with him, to lay beside him, and to rest his head on his chest or his shoulder and forget about everything bad that had ever happened. But he'd have to wait for that—and that was okay. Zalith had to work, and Alucard understood that.

With another quiet sigh, Alucard reached into his drawer and pulled out the file that Luther had brought for him. His primary interest had been his mother, Charlotte, but the file also contained the names and information of the people who had been a part of the cult he was born into. Not that it mattered anymore, since it happened over four hundred years ago, but a part of him felt that he'd still like to know everything he could about that part of his life.

Before he could read much into the file, however, someone knocked on his office door, snapping hold of Alucards attention. He lifted his head and watched as Zalith stepped into the room with a smile on his face.

"Hey, darling," the demon said, leaning back against the door once he closed it behind him.

Alucard felt content to see him and smiled in response. As the demon made his way over, he placed the file down on his desk and looked up at him.

"What are you reading?" Zalith asked as he walked around the desk and leaned against it beside the vampire.

"Just some information regarding the people who were around me when I was born and raised."

"Did you find anything of interest?"

He shrugged as he leaned his arms onto his desk and looked down and them. "No. I haven't really looked through yet. I sent Luther to gather information on my mother, though. I want to know which Numen she was descended from."

Zalith stared curiously at him. "Do you have a hunch?"

"No, but it doesn't really matter, I guess. Being related to them doesn't really do anything for me other than give me the ability to become them when I kill them. I don't want to be any of them, so," he said, looking ahead as he slouched back in his seat. "But I might prefer it to be one of them who doesn't look for me, like Erich or Letholdus. They just mind their own shit. I guess there was a time Letholdus wanted to find me for some things I did, but he got bored."

"Well, I hope your little friend Looper helps you get the answers you're looking for," Zalith said with a smile.

Alucard looked up at him. He knew that Zalith didn't particularly like Luther and evidently found it amusing to act as though he didn't know or care who he was or what his name was. But the vampire didn't exactly want to talk about that right now. "Who was at the door?" he asked, trying to change the subject.

Looking down at him, Zalith smirked and laughed slightly. "Why the sudden change in topic, vampire?"

Still looking at him, Alucard frowned slightly. Zalith obviously didn't want to change the subject, and he felt as though maybe he should let Zalith say whatever it was that he wanted to say about Luther. But first, he'd try one last time *not* to get into such a conversation. "I know that you don't like Luther, so we're not going to talk about him, demon," he sneered.

Amused, Zalith kept his smirk and laughed quietly once again. "I see. A convenient excuse."

"There is no excuse."

"Am I irritating you?" Zalith asked amusedly.

"No," he answered, keeping his eyes on Zalith. "Why would you be irritating me?"

"You seem irritated."

Alucard then scowled. "Do you have problem with him?"

"Should I?"

"No," Alucard grumbled, taking his eyes off him. "You seem to have one."

Zalith's amused smirk didn't fade. "You didn't want me to catch you blushing at the thought of him, so you changed the subject. That sounds like an excuse to me."

The vampire then rolled his eyes. "The thought of that man makes me wish I vas human so I could die."

"That's not what your eyes say when you look at him."

Alucard was convinced that Zalith was trying to make him mad, and he was sure as hell doing a pretty good job of it. He scowled irritably. "Why do you find such amusement in pissing me off?"

"I didn't know Luther was such a sensitive subject," Zalith teased.

"What are you trying to say?" Alucard snarled, glaring at him. "What do you want?"

The demon laughed and stood up straight. "I'm only joking. Come here," he said, moving in to hug him.

Alucard didn't deny his hug but pouted as he stood up into Zalith's embrace and moved his arms around the demon.

"I just like to look at your cute little grouchy face," Zalith mumbled, hugging him tightly. But then he leaned back a little and kissed the side of the vampire's face with *so* much exaggeration that the loud sound of the smooch made Alucard's aggravated expression grow. The demon gazed at his irritated face and laughed in response before using his fingers to move a strand of Alucard's hair out of the way of his left eye. "I'm sorry," he said. His eyes then wandered down to the vampire's neck, the same place he hadn't long left a love bite. He smirked and looked at Alucard's face. "I can be serious if you'd like me to."

With a quiet sigh, Alucard looked down at Zalith's collar. "It's fine," he mumbled.

The demon smiled and rested his forehead against Alucard's. "Okay," he said, staring into his eyes as Alucard shyly stared back. "How's your new office?" he then asked, placing his hands on either side of Alucard's waist to pull his body against his own and hold him in place.

Alucard took his eyes off Zalith, sure that the demon had noticed his shy expression. "It's comfy."

Zalith moved one hand from Alucard's waist, lightly grabbed hold of his jaw, and turned his head to face him. "Good," he said before kissing him a slow, soft, single time. "It makes me happy to know that you're comfortable here in your new house." Then, he kissed the vampire again, but this time, not just once, and for a few moments longer.

The vampire smiled slightly as he looked down, attempting to hide his expression. "I really like being here."

"Good," Zalith said, stroking the side of the vampire's face with his hand. "Are you hungry?"

It was almost lunchtime, and Zalith had said that they'd have lunch together. But he didn't yet feel like eating. So, he frowned unsurely and said, "Not really."

"Then would you like to continue from where we left off earlier?" the demon asked with a curious smirk.

A nervous look instantly plastered itself to Alucard's face. He looked away again, frowning as he tried to hide his expression. Alucard knew that Zalith enjoyed flustering him just as much as he enjoyed making him mad. But the question still remained: did he want to continue from where they had been before the izuret turned up? He craved every ounce of Zalith's touch and attention despite what just happened, and he didn't want to say no out of irritancy.

He rested his head on Zalith's shoulder and nodded slightly. "Yes," he muttered.

Zalith's smile took on a tantalizing, almost devious edge. He lightly gripped Alucard's jaw again, coaxing the vampire to meet his gaze for a kiss that bore the promise of an impending intensity. As their lips converged, Zalith orchestrated a slow, deliberate manoeuvre, guiding Alucard until he found support against the sturdy surface of the desk.

Breaking the kiss, Zalith's hand transitioned from Alucard's jaw to the side of his neck; simultaneously, the demon's other hand ventured from the vampire's waist, embarking on a journey upward. A gentle, teasing glide traversed Alucard's body until Zalith's fingers reached the collar of his shirt, a subtle invitation to unravel the layers that stood between them.

The demon's fingers skilfully worked through the buttons of Alucard's shirt, each one yielding to Zalith's deliberate touch. As the final button succumbed, the kiss that bound them momentarily halted, and Zalith's gaze wandered over the revealed expanse of Alucard's torso. Despite the vulnerability of the moment, Alucard resisted the urge to retreat, meeting Zalith's intense stare with a steady gaze.

Zalith's fingertips embarked on a sensual descent, tracing a path down and over Alucard's defined abs. A thrill of anticipation coursed through the vampire, his composed exterior belying the electric sensations surging beneath his skin. A quiet sigh escaped him, surrendering to the touch that promised an intoxicating journey. As Zalith's lips found their way to Alucard's neck, the vampire tilted his head, offering a silent invitation for more.

When Zalith's fingers reached the precipice of Alucard's waist, the demon boldly followed the lines that traced down from his waist to his crotch. An eager smirk played on Zalith's lips as he lifted his head to lock eyes with Alucard. Faced with the intensity of that gaze, Alucard averted his eyes, attempting to mask a nervous frown that betrayed the thrill of anticipation brewing beneath the surface.

Zalith's touch was a teasing caress, his hand delicately tracing the contours of Alucard's arousal through the fabric of his trousers. A trail of kisses, fervent and hungry, painted a heated path from lips to cheek and then down to the vampire's neck. The lingering mark of their earlier intimacy beckoned Zalith's lips, and as he pressed against the love bite, he unbuckled Alucard's belt, causing a soft exhale to escape the vampire, a quiet testament to the mounting anticipation. Alucard's belt dropped to the floor, discarded, as the demon skilfully unbuttoned the vampire's trousers, and with a confident yet desperate hand, Zalith ventured inside.

But then Sabazios whined and snapped Alucard out of his moment of enjoyment. Zalith stopped what he was doing to look at Alucard as he looked down at the puppy, who was curled up in his bed behind where Zalith was standing.

"Go," Alucard mumbled, a look of embarrassment on his face.

As he was told, Sabazios got up out of his bed and wandered off up the stairs, leaving them alone.

Zalith took his hand off Alucard's face and moved a strand of hair away from his eye again. Then, he kissed his lips as he started caressing the arousal in his trousers. He returned to kissing Alucard's neck, which Alucard enjoyed enough to let himself hum contently. After a few moments. Zalith took his hand from the vampire's trousers and pulled them down. Alucard tried to keep his nervousness from getting the better of him; he returned Zalith's kisses, moving his hand down the demon's chest. But once his trousers fell to his ankles, Zalith stopped kissing him and smirked before he kneeled in front of him.

Alucard sighed quietly in satisfaction as Zalith placed his lips over the tip of his dick; he gripped the bottom of it with one hand and pressed his other against the vampire's abdomen. Alucard closed his eyes, holding the desk's edge behind him with both his hands as he leaned against it. Something pleasing electrified through his body as Zalith slowly moved his mouth over his shaft; he sighed quietly, moving his left hand from the desk and to the back of the demon's head.

As each moment passed, Zalith sucked a little faster, forcing a louder moan of enjoyment to escape Alucard's quickly increasing breaths. He tilted his head back ever so slightly, a grimace of struggle on his face as he gradually approached the end that would come.

The demon didn't relent; he sucked harder, and when he took Alucard's dick deeper into his throat, the vampire tightened his grip on the demon's hair and let out a pleasured groan. And as his climax quickly came, he moaned quietly in delight, and his shaft throbbed in Zalith's throat. He could feel the demon swallowing his cum, and it brought a satisfied smile to his face, a smile which grew when Zalith hummed quietly in content.

But Alucard then flinched in startlement as the demon abruptly took his shaft from his mouth and sunk his fangs into his right inner thigh. Alucard grimaced, a confusion of pain and pleasure conflicting with one another when Zalith bit harder. As the demon's venom took hold of him, however, he lost his grimace and frowned in relief, a familiar euphoria enthralling him as Zalith then kissed his way back up his body.

Alucard thought that Zalith was leaning in to kiss him, but Zalith smirked and instead rested his forehead against Alucard's. For a moment, the demon stared into his eyes, both of them calming their frantic breaths, and once Alucard frowned in confusion, Zalith's smirk returned.

"Turn around," the demon demanded seductively.

The vampire did as he was told; with a nervous frown, he turned around, and then the demon pressed his hand against his back, making him bend and lean over his desk. He then felt Zalith gently moving his lube-covered fingers into his ass; he hummed contently but grunted in startlement when the demon immediately eased his dick inside him. His euphoria from Zalith's bite continued increasing, and as the demon started slowly thrusting into and out of his body, his grimace of struggle became a frown of delight.

Zalith held Alucard's waist, thrusting a little harder as Alucard rested his forehead on his arm, breathing frantically in response to his growing excitement, which only intensified once Zalith started to move faster than usual. A struggled grimace found its way to his face as he tried to keep quiet, but hushed mumbles of pleasure sat on each breath while he felt the demon dragging his hand down his back.

The demon moaned pleasurably as he tightened his grip on the vampire's waist. His thrusts grew more aggressive, enthralling Alucard in utter delight as his heart raced and his body trembled. But the demon then leaned forward, pressing his left hand into the desk beside Alucard. The fact that Zalith moved faster and then slowed a little, only to move faster again, convinced Alucard that the demon was struggling to control himself, and as much as he wanted to tell Zalith he didn't have to refrain how aggressive he *really* wanted to be, he wasn't brave enough to say anything.

Zalith moved his hand from the desk, gripping Alucard's wrist as he groaned in contentment. Alucard felt him tense up, and he moved faster and faster as his moans became louder, laced with desperation and desire. He thrusted *hard*, burying his dick as deeply inside Alucard as he could, and then he moaned loudly. His shaft convulsed, and as Alucard felt the warmth of his cum oozing into him, he exhaled deeply and hummed in delight.

The demon then leaned forward and rested his body against Alucard's as he breathed frantically, his tense body gradually relaxing. Alucard also let himself relax, and after a few moments, the demon stood up and pulled Alucard to stand with him. He made Alucard turn around, and then he crouched down and pulled the vampire's trousers back up to his waist for him. Once Alucard had buttoned his trousers, Zalith rested his forehead against his, smiled, and stared down at what he could see of his body.

With a quiet but deep exhale, he placed his hand on Alucard's chest and stared into his eyes. "Are you okay?"

Alucard nodded, placing his hand on the demon's shoulder as he looked down at Zalith's hand.

"Good," Zalith said with a smirk, moving his hand to the side of Alucard's face. Then, he kissed him a few times before leaning back to stare at his face. "I'm going to go and take a shower before lunch. Do you want to join me?"

The vampire thought to himself for a short moment but shook his head. He just wanted to sit and relax. "I'm fine."

"Okay. Then I'll meet you out on the patio in about fifteen minutes."

Alucard nodded. Zalith then kissed him a few more times, and as Alucard sat back in his seat, he watched the demon leave his office, smirking back at him when he pulled the door shut behind him.

With a quiet sigh, Alucard leaned back in his seat and relaxed. He really *did* love being here.

Chapter Eighty-Three

Pessimistic News

| **Alucard** |

After a short while, Sabazios slinked back into Alucard's office.

The vampire looked down at him as he curled up in his bed. "Did you eat the rest of your food?"

Sabazios licked his muzzle in response, which obviously meant yes.

Taking his eyes off the puppy, Alucard buttoned his shirt up and tidied his hair, and once he was done, he snatched his belt from the floor and re-buckled it around his waist.

He was sure that Zalith was going to be a short while longer, so he began tidying his desk. After he'd had lunch, he'd resume looking into the information Luther had brought him and read his mail, too.

Once his desk was tidy, he stood up and made his way over to his door. Leaving his office, he walked through the hall and towards one of the back doors that would take him out onto the patio. Zalith was still upstairs, but he didn't mind waiting for him.

When he emerged outside, he made his way over to the table and sat down. He then stared out into the distance, waiting, and not too long later, Zalith came out onto the patio. The demon smiled as Alucard looked back over his shoulder at him and kissed the side of his face before sitting across the table from him.

"Hey," Zalith said, resting his arm across the table to take Alucard's hand, which he then pulled from beneath his crossed arms. "You haven't been waiting long, have you?"

Alucard smiled slightly. "No, I just got here."

The demon smiled again and let go of Alucard's hand, sitting up straight as one of the kitchen staff made his way over to the table with two dishes in his hands. He placed them on the table and left as silently as he had arrived. Another staff member came shortly after and put a few differently sized glasses and a selection of beverages on the table. He then left, leaving Alucard and Zalith alone.

Alucard looked down at what had been placed in front of him; it was different to anything he'd eaten with Zalith before; it looked to be some kind of pasta...maybe ravioli smothered in sauce and topped with pecans.

"This is butternut squash ravioli," Zalith said.

Glancing at him, Alucard nodded and tried a piece. It tasted particularly sweet, and he had nothing negative to think or say about it. So, he continued to eat.

But his curiosity soon urged him to look at the demon. He wanted to know what Zalith had to deal with this morning. "So...how was your morning? What did the izuret bring you?"

Zalith finished what he was eating and glanced at him. He sighed and leaned back in his seat. "Things back home aren't looking so great," he started, a hint of worry in his voice. "I fear my work with Eltaria is going to become more demanding, and I may have to make trips back and forth over the next month or so. But I might not have to; it just depends how bad things are."

The vampire frowned in concern as he also stopped eating. "What's happening?"

"The humans," he grumbled. "Making their moves—*big* moves. My people are dying, and I need to keep them safe. We can't really fight much anymore, as our numbers have dwindled—especially recently."

It was obvious that the war in Zalith's world was only worsening; the demon had done so much to help Alucard that he felt no hesitation in offering to help him. "Do you want me to come and help over there? Things here are calmer for me now that Damien is gone...and Felix...and the werewolves. I want to help," he said sternly.

Zalith smiled appreciatively. "If things become worse, I may take you up on your offer. As for now, I'm trying to move people to safer locations. I believe I can manage."

"Okay. Well, if you want my help at any point, just tell me. And I still don't mind helping you tonight, either."

"Thank you. I'll be having my subordinates over later," he then said, continuing to eat his food. "To talk about the problems back home. I'm not sure how long they'll be here for, but we should be done in time for dinner."

Alucard nodded, looking back down at his own bowl. "And you're leaving after dinner, right? Do you know when you'll be home?"

"A few hours at least. But not too late," he answered. He took a bite of his food and then asked him, "What are you going to do with the rest of your day?"

With a slight shrug, Alucard took his eyes off his food and looked out at the forest in the distance. "I will...see to Ben."

"Do you know what you're going to do with him?" he asked curiously.

"Well...." He sighed, thinking as he spoke. "I don't exactly want to kill him; what happened wasn't really his fault, but...I don't want to leave any liabilities around. I'll offer him two choices: I'll either kill him, or I'll make it so he is no longer a vampire and erase all the memories he has of working for you and me. That way, he can live a life and be no danger to us or himself."

"It's unfortunate that all of this happened to him. Ben's a good man, and he doesn't deserve any of this. But sometimes, these things happen."

Alucard exhaled deeply and nodded in agreement. "I hope he picks the latter. I'd rather not kill him. But he did lose his wife in all of that, so I can't really be sure whether or not he'd rather die and go to wherever it is she went."

Zalith nodded slightly. "I'm not sure what *I* would do if I were him."

With a perturbed frown on his face, Alucard questioned, "What?"

"Well, if I were Ben, I'd be torn between wanting to die rather than live without the love of my life and experiencing something almost entirely new. Of course, Ben was born a human, but he's been a vampire for much longer. The change might be difficult." He ate a little more of his food. "What would *you* do, Alucard?"

Alucard already knew the answer to that. Of course, the question was if he were Ben, but his mind instantly jumped to what he would do if it were him and Zalith. He'd rather die than live without him, something he had discovered a long time ago. "You know the answer to that," he replied. "I don't want to live without you."

Keeping his eyes on Alucard, Zalith frowned in adoration, but a hint of concern flickered across his face. "I wouldn't want to live without you either, Alucard. But...if someone were to be responsible for your death, I'd be on the warpath; my anger and hatred would be so potent that I simply would not stay dead if I were to choose to die," he said, almost as if it was a promise.

The look on Zalith's face became a lot sterner and Alucard didn't want to make him feel any angrier than he looked. "Well..." he started. "It's a good thing no one can kill me, then, no?"

"Either way, I'd never let it happen," Zalith said and then finished his food.

"Neither would I."

With a smile on his face, Zalith leaned over to a small, covered bowl on the tray that the drinks had been delivered on. He placed it in the middle of the table and pulled off the lid to reveal a small selection of diced fruit. "How is Drac settling into his new home?" he asked, stabbing a piece of strawberry with a fork and then offering it out to the vampire.

The demon's question made him feel a little guilty. He hadn't been to visit Drac much since his transferral from Dor-Sanguis, the last time being two weeks ago. He was sure that the dragon was fine living and hunting on his own, but Alucard always made sure to check in on him often enough. He did, however, know that the dragon was content living in the lake. "He's fine," he answered and ate the strawberry off the fork as Zalith smirked. "He likes to sit on the shore and watch the deer. Thank you again for letting me bring him; I didn't want to leave him."

"You're welcome," he said with a smile and ate a single grape. "Is he getting enough to eat?"

"I think so," Alucard said with a nod, looking out at the forest again. "He seemed fine every time I went to see him. If he was hungry, he would have slithered out here to complain to me."

"Well, we'll have to make sure he's kept well-fed," Zalith said with a hint of concern in his amused voice. "The last thing we want is him over here tearing up the gardens."

Alucard nodded in agreement. "He's fine, I'm sure."

"And your puppy?" he asked, offering a piece of what looked like grapefruit out to him.

First, he ate the fruit, and then he shrugged and said, "He's okay, too. He's just being fussy with the kitchen staff. He's fine, though. He eats all his food eventually."

Zalith ate a piece of pineapple before offering Alucard some, too. "There's something I need to talk to you about," he drawled cautiously.

Alucard frowned as he swallowed the pineapple. "What?"

The demon sighed deeply. "To answer the question you asked me earlier in your office, it was Varana who was at the door."

Upon the mention of that woman's name, Alucard grimaced and tried his best not to let his hatred for her consume him.

"I know that the two of you didn't get off on the right foot, but I miss her very much, and I'm just wondering how you might feel if she were to come back."

Alucard didn't want that *at all*. But he had to keep himself from blurting it out. He didn't want to sound rude or controlling; however, the thought of having to see that woman waltzing around the place put him off his food.

Zalith continued, "Obviously, you live here now, too, and I don't want to make any decisions without you. But I was also thinking that I could get a guest house built on the property so that she's not in the main house and won't be a bother."

Guest house or main house, Alucard was certain that Varana would still be as much of a pain in his ass. But...this was Zalith's house, she was Zalith's friend, and Alucard didn't want to give Zalith the impression that his choice was the only one that mattered. However, he *did* want more time to think about it. Zalith had put him on the spot, and he suspected that the pressure was making it harder for him to come to a decision that *he* would be comfortable with.

The vampire looked at Zalith. "I want to think about it."

"That's okay," Zalith said, smiling. "You can take as long as you need."

His irritancy didn't fade, though, and the last thing he wanted to do was upset Zalith with his attitude. The sooner he thought about it, the better. So, he stood up. "I need to go and deal with Ben," he mumbled.

Zalith stood up and placed his hand on the side of Alucard's face. "Okay. I'll see you later, then."

Alucard nodded.

The demon then kissed him and rested his forehead against his. "Let me know if you need me."

"I will," he mumbled. Then, as Zalith let go of him, he wandered off back into the house. He had a long afternoon of thinking ahead of him, but first, he'd deal with Ben.

| Zalith |

Zalith frowned sadly as he sat back at the table. He hadn't wanted his and Alucard's lunch to end on a negative note, but it couldn't have been avoided. He needed to tell Alucard about his conversation with Varana, and he had been confident that it would upset him.

Of course, Alucard's feelings about the matter were just as important as his own, and he'd not do anything until he knew how the vampire felt about it. He'd give him as much time as he needed, and he'd not press him for an answer, either. Varana could wait.

With a quiet sigh, he got up and left the patio. He still had a long day of work ahead of him.

Chapter Eighty-Four

— ⊰ † ⊱ —

Choices

| **Alucard** |

A lucard silently made his way through the house and up to the first floor. He crossed the landing, headed to a spiral staircase, and climbed it to the second floor, where there were five guest bedrooms much smaller than the one he'd been given when he first stayed at the house.

He turned left on the landing, heading towards one of the bedroom doors close to the front of the house. As he walked, his thoughts remained with the conversation he and Zalith had not long ago. That woman wanted to move back in, and Alucard felt irritated about it—so irritated that he didn't want to keep thinking about it. Right now, he had to focus on what he'd come to do, and *that* was to give Ben his options.

When he reached the bedroom door, Alucard knocked a single time. He heard an utter of Ben's voice telling him to come in, so he did so. He pushed the door open, made his way into the room, and set his eyes on the man, who was huddled up on the cushion-lined ledge of the window. His wounds and scars had healed, and he looked a little less pale than he had done before, but he still looked miserable and broken.

"How do you feel?" Alucard asked.

Ben shrugged lightly but didn't say a word.

Obviously, he wasn't *feeling* any better, but at least he wasn't crawling on the floor, hugging Alucard's legs, and begging for safety.

But Alucard felt as though it was time to decide what to do with him once. He'd been staying in this room for over a month and that was more than enough time for him to have recovered to a point where he'd be able to decide what he wanted to do with his life. After all, Alucard didn't exactly want him to be lingering around his and Zalith's house; he was a subordinate, and he was lucky to have received this much kindness.

Alucard remained where he was but closed the door behind him. "Look," he said.

With a sullen frown on his face, Ben looked over at Alucard.

"You've been here for over a month now. That's more than enough time for you to get your head straight and for you to be ready to choose what you want to do with your life."

Ben frowned unsurely. "What do you mean?"

"You cannot stay here. You cannot go back to my castle, for you are a liability. It's not your fault that these things have happened, and that's why I'll be lenient. I have some options for you, and you will think about them very carefully and tell me which of them you'd like."

"What...are my options?"

"One, I kill you, and you go to wherever it is vampires go when they die. Two, I return you to a human form, and you'll live a normal human life. If you choose this option, I'll erase all memories you have of me, Zalith, and working for both of us. You'll have a new life, a new identity, and be free to do whatever you want—within reason."

Ben just stared at him. It was clear that he was overwhelmed, conflicted even. Of course, Alucard didn't expect him to answer right away; he'd need time to think.

"I'll come back either later tonight or tomorrow and see if you have an answer," he said, turning to open the door.

"Did...you catch him?" Ben asked shakily.

Alucard stopped and looked over his shoulder at him. "Detlaff is in the most secure dungeon in my castle. If you choose to live, you don't have to worry about him finding you again—neither of us do."

Ben nodded, looking down at his lap.

"Take your time to think about it," Alucard repeated.

"How...how did you catch him? He took me to some...place. I don't remember it that clearly," Ben said hauntedly.

Alucard frowned as he turned to face him and leaned his back against the door. "You don't have to talk about it."

But Ben didn't seem to hear his words. "It looked like...maybe a castle or...something—he took me to a lot of places."

He waited.

"The last place I remember before here...there was snow—a lot of it."

"I've been made aware that Detlaff visited Avalmoor a few times, and that's where he took you."

"There were two women there, too; they looked exactly the same."

"I know of them."

"And then...how did you catch him?"

"I have people all over the world, and there is no one who can hide from me for too long. This also means that I am very good at hiding people. If you want to live, I will do my best to hide you away from this life."

Ben nodded slowly, staring out of the window again. "But then...what do I have if not my job? I lost Lillian. I feel. .empty."

Alucard took his eyes off Ben and sighed quietly. He didn't really know what to say about him losing his wife; he could only try to imagine how he was feeling.

"Will you not let me stay?" he asked, looking at him. "Some other job someplace? Maybe I can help somewhere."

"No," Alucard denied. "You're too much of a liability now. Given that it's not your fault, I'm willing to help you start a new life somewhere. But working for me or Zalith is no longer an option."

With a nod of understanding, Ben looked down at his lap again. "I guess I'll be made to forget you both, huh?"

"Yes, that's what I said."

"And everything I ever did here, in Eltaria...everything linked to you two."

"Yes."

"Or...I can die."

"That is also an option," he repeated.

Ben sighed and looked back out of his window. "Can I ask how things are back in Dor-Sanguis?"

"Everyone thinks you're dead, and that is for the best."

"Right," Ben said with a single nod.

"The idea of a new life might scare you, but...if it's any consolation, I don't want to kill you or think you deserve to die. But if you want to be with your wife, then I'll respect your choice."

He looked over at him. "How long do I have to think about it?"

"I would prefer you to take no longer than a few days. I have other things to start prioritizing."

"Right. I'll try and make a decision soon."

"You can either ask one of the staff here to fetch me, you can come to my office yourself, or...just find some way of telling me," he muttered.

Once again, Ben looked out of the window. "All right. Thanks...for giving me options."

Alucard nodded. Then, without another word from either of them, he left the room.

He made his way back through the house until he reached the ground floor. As much as he might like to get the situation with Ben sorted, he now had other things to think about. He was quite sure that he didn't want to see the face of Zalith's rude little friend again, but it seemed as though the demon was confident to have her move back one way or another.

For a moment, he thought that he might go and talk to Zalith about it right now, but when he reached the bottom of the stairs, multiple voices came from the demon's office, which had to mean he was currently meeting with the subordinates. Alucard would have to wait.

Sabazios came to greet him, having hurried out of his bed by the front door the moment he saw the vampire coming downstairs.

The puppy panted happily as he stared up at Alucard, frantically wagging his tail.

Alucard sighed, sinking down to sit on the second step. Despite the fact that it had only been half an hour or so since he left Zalith, he missed him as though it had been half a week. But he was busy, so he'd have to wait until he was done with his subordinates.

Looking down at his dog as he patted his head, Alucard frowned. "Do you want to go for a walk?"

The puppy bounced up and down like a confused rabbit, panting loudly as he watched Alucard stand up. He then clung to the vampire's side as he made his way over to the door, took his cape off the coat rack, pulled it on, and slipped into his shoes. Then, he headed outside.

Sabazios pounced up and down impatiently while he waited for Alucard to shut the door behind them, and once it *was* shut, Alucard looked down at the enthusiastic hound. Staring up at him, Sabazios sat down and waited. He didn't need to be put on a leash, though; Alucard trusted Sabazios not to wander off, and so, without any further falter, he made his way through the grounds, glancing down at Sabazios as he followed at his side.

When he left the gates and followed the country road, he sunk into his thoughts. He wasn't pleased to know that Zalith's friend wanted to move back and that the demon seemed very confident to have her return. Although she hadn't really done anything *that* awful, Alucard just didn't like her. Not only had she tried convincing him that he should leave Zalith, but she also seemed to have a strange obsession with the demon, one that he didn't like *at all*. Zalith may be gay, but his woman didn't seem to understand that.

Alucard rolled his eyes and turned left, entering the forest to follow the path to the lake. He was sure that if that woman moved back in, she'd be nought but a bother. Lingering around, flirting with Zalith, muttering rude, snarky things. Most of all, though, she was one of Lucifer's scions, and Alucard would never trust her. So what if she brought Ben back? That could have been a part of some plan to work her way in and give him up to Lucifer once his and Zalith's guard was down.

With another sigh, he looked down at his dog. Alucard had only recently become completely settled in his new home, and he wasn't exactly comfortable sharing it with someone he not only didn't know but someone who clearly despised him and would most likely be keeping a close eye on him. He didn't like that—to be watched, studied. She was going to do just that, and despite having been punished for the things she'd said back then, he was sure that was only the beginning.

Glaring ahead again, he slipped his hands into his trouser pockets and continued forward. As much as he might like to say no for the sake of his privacy and self-security, he almost felt like it didn't matter. That woman, *Varana*...she was Zalith's friend—best friend, even—and Alucard suspected that someway, somehow, she'd end up back home.

And he really didn't feel significant enough to be the deciding factor. Zalith may say it was his choice, but he didn't feel like it was. He might say no, and he was sure that Zalith would try to convince him otherwise. He'd already done so by suggesting a guest house to be built for her—a guest house that Alucard was certain she wouldn't stay in.

Maybe it was best if he accepted it. He knew Zalith missed his friend, and he didn't want him to be sad about it anymore. Alucard didn't trust her or want anything to do with her; from their brief interactions, he'd already decided he didn't like her and probably never would—not only because she seemed infatuated with *his* demon, but because she seemed to have made it her personal mission to sabotage what he and Zalith had. She'd not win, though; she might be coming back, but that didn't in any way mean she was victorious.

He felt as if he should stop thinking about it for a little while or he might become mad. So, he silenced his thoughts surrounding that woman and continued his walk with Sabazios.

Eventually, they reached the river he and Zalith sat by last month, the same river he first ever heard Zalith tell him he loved him. He'd never forget that and how happy it made him.

A small smile found its way to his face as he walked out into the opening, setting his eyes on the tree they'd sat under. Sabazios raced off the moment they left the trees and headed straight for the water, yapping madly at it as he reached the bed.

Alucard made his way to the tree and slumped down against it. A flicker of sadness travelled across his face as he looked down at the grass; he'd much rather Zalith be with him right now. Why was he missing him so much? They lived together, so they saw each other pretty much every day. Why did he feel so...needy? If that was even the word for it. He just wanted to be with him, see him, talk to him...he only ever felt okay when he was with Zalith.

Why did he always feel so sad? So empty and alone, even in the company of others. His dreams only played a small part in his despondency, and as much as he tried to work out what else might be making him feel this way, he had no answers, no solution other than being with the man who made him forget the sadness just enough that it didn't drag him into the drowning loneliness.

With an irritated yet saddened huff, he shuffled around uncomfortably and stared out at the lake. Maybe it was because all of this was new to him. Before Zalith had come along, he'd paid no attention to his own needs, emotions, or feelings, but now that he loved someone, he couldn't *not* focus on the things he felt.

Before, he'd just focused on his work, dealt with the people who needed dealing with, and kept the humans at bay and the people they fought with safe. Was he missing the wars? The battles, the danger. Was his current excessive free time making him feel this way?

He snarled irritably, a manifestation of his smouldering frustration as he attempted to decipher his predicament. But that was when Drac's silhouette gracefully glided beneath the water, growing nearer with each sinuous movement. An internal tempest brewed within Alucard, a maelstrom of annoyance that threatened to consume him. Yet, as the dark figure approached, Alucard released a resigned sigh, banishing the tumult of his thoughts to the recesses of his mind. The dragon, a formidable presence beneath the surface, demanded his attention, and he was more than happy to give it.

Sabazios stopped his frenzied barking and scurried to Alucard's side beneath the tree; the puppy, sensing the impending majesty of the approaching dragon, sought refuge beside the vampire, trembling in fear. The waters stirred, and with a graceful emergence, Drac ascended from the lake's depths; he positioned himself just at the water's edge, partially submerged, with his head poised before Alucard.

"I'm sorry I didn't come to see you sooner," Alucard said as he placed his hand on Drac's snout. "You know I was busy."

The dragon grumbled quietly, staring at him with sorrow in all four of his eyes.

"I know. I would've come before, but I had to sort things out at the house. I'll come and visit you more often now, though. I don't really have much to do right now; there are no wars, the werewolves have accepted defeat, Detlaff is caged up, and Damien is gone. All I really have to do is keep an eye on things, but I have people doing that for me," he explained as Drac gawped at him.

But then, the dragon murmured quietly and rested his head in Alucard's lap, shifting his sights to Sabazios, who watched the dragon very carefully.

Alucard sighed, placing his hand on Drac's head. "I gather you miss the times of war too, no?" he asked with a smirk, looking down at him. "All those people you got to eat."

Drac looked up at him and grumbled in agreement.

"Well...." He sighed. "This is Aegisguard, and war always happens here. I know Zalith is trying to deal with the gangs here in Nefastus; that's likely to cause tension with people. I want to help him; that would give me something to do. But he doesn't want my help."

With a mumble, Drac shook his head in disagreement and pouted.

"What?" Alucard frowned, looking down at him. "I don't know why you worry. I trust him."

Drac, however, wasn't so convinced. He seemed to currently only tolerate Zalith and blamed the demon for taking Alucard away from him. But the vampire felt that they just needed to get to know one another a little better. Hopefully, Zalith would come with him next time he came to see Drac. The demon said he might be busy for a little while, and Alucard wasn't sure when he might have time to bond with an animal. Either way, though, he'd make sure it happened. He loved his dragon, and he loved Zalith; he wanted them to get along.

He sighed again and leaned back against the tree; Sabazios curled up beside him, and Drac also made himself comfortable in the afternoon sunlight. He didn't have anything else to do, so he thought he might as well just relax for a small while and hope that once he headed home, Zalith would be finished with his meeting.

Chapter Eighty-Five

— ⊰ ✝ ⊱ —

The Demon's Subordinates

| **Alucard** |

A   cold breeze woke Alucard, sending an awful shiver down his spine. When he realized that he'd fallen asleep under the tree, he frowned and sat up straight in an attempt to shake the fatigue. But that was when he noticed that the sky had greyed, and ashy clouds were beginning to form overhead. It was clear that at any moment, rain would fall, and he didn't want to get caught out in it.

He nudged Drac's head, waking the dragon from its slumber. Drac grumbled irritably but moved as Alucard climbed to his feet.

"Come on," he said, glancing down at Sabazios. He then looked down at his pouting dragon. "I'll come back tomorrow."

Drac rolled all his eyes and slithered back into the water, disappearing once again.

Alucard quickly left the opening and headed back into the woods as his dog trotted along at his side. He wasn't sure what time it was, but the sun was setting, and Zalith's meeting had to be over by now. A relief warmed him as he thought about seeing the demon despite seeing him just hours ago.

He felt irritated that he kept thinking about how he missed Zalith so much and how they hadn't even been apart that long; it didn't matter how long they'd been apart, did it? He missed him for the five minutes he'd take in the bathroom every morning and the small moments when he simply had to leave the room to get something. He missed Zalith whenever they weren't together, and he wasn't going to deny it.

Rain splashed onto his face, and he snarled irritably. Now, his hair was going to get wet, and it would be the first thing Zalith would point out when he got home. He didn't care about the impending fluster, though. He was looking forward to getting back to him, seeing his face, and hearing his voice. If Sabazios wasn't here, he could simply vanish and be home in moments, but the dog couldn't transform with him, so he'd have to keep at his fast-paced walk.

When he finally reached the tree line and emerged onto the country road, Alucard set his fiery eyes on his home, where he knew he'd find Zalith. The rain was pouring, Sabazios was whining, and rumbles of thunder were drawing nearer. He picked up his pace and ran as the puppy followed him down the path and into the estate's grounds, through the gardens, and up onto the porch. He pushed the door open and stepped into the entrance hall, but swung around before Sabazios could come in.

"No," he warned, pointing at him. "Shake first."

As he was told, the puppy relentlessly shook his body on the porch, spraying water everywhere. Then, Alucard stepped aside and let the dog wander into the hall. The vampire took off his cape and shoes and proceeded into the main hall, where Edwin had come to greet him.

"I need a towel," Alucard said.

Edwin nodded and swiftly disappeared as Sabazios scurried over to his nearby bed and curled up in it. The butler then returned with *two* towels; he handed one to Alucard— which the vampire immediately used to dry his hair—and wandered over to the damp dog with the other one.

"Make sure you get his ears." Alucard said, watching the butler struggle to dry the uncooperative dog. "He doesn't like wet ears."

Just then, Zalith's office door opened, and of course, Alucard couldn't help but immediately look over there. He watched as a group of three demons made their way out, talking quietly to one another as Zalith exited behind them, pulling the door to his office ajar. He caught up with them, but his eyes instantly met with Alucard's the moment he turned to face his direction.

The demon smiled and moved ahead of his subordinates, who followed slowly behind, still chatting with one another.

"Hey," he said, his voice a little hushed but excited as he approached and moved in for a hug.

Alucard welcomed his embrace and rested his head on Zalith's shoulder as they hugged tightly.

"I missed you," Zalith said quietly. But when he stepped back, a smirk found its way to his face as he tucked a few damp strands of hair behind Alucard's ear. "You're wet."

"I got caught in the rain," he mumbled, glancing at Sabazios as Edwin continued to dry his paws. "How did your meeting go?"

Zalith moved to stand beside him as his subordinates stopped chatting and halted in front of them both. "These are my Alphas: Orin, Tyrus, and Idina," he said, gesturing to the three demons who had come out of his office.

Alucard eyed them all closely; he hadn't forgotten that Zalith was an Apex demon, an Alpha of Alphas, and he knew that it was only a matter of time until he met some of his subordinates.

Orin, the tall, pale man with silvery-blonde hair and silver eyes, smiled and bowed his head a little in greeting.

Tyrus, the dark-skinned man with golden-orange eyes and hair so short that it looked like he might not even have any, smiled slightly and greeted Alucard with a casual, "Hey."

The last, Idina, was an olive-skinned woman with long brunette hair and light green eyes, and as she set her sights on Alucard, she smiled pleasantly. "It's nice to finally meet you," she said. "We've heard *so* much about you."

Alucard frowned. Zalith...spoke about him to his subordinates? He wasn't sure how that made him feel. But it wasn't anything bad. In fact, it made him feel content to know that Zalith spoke about him.

"Not *too* much, I hope," he then replied, offering his hand out to the woman.

She shook his hand and laughed a little. "Never *too* much."

Her voice suddenly faded away from Alucard's attention. In a short moment, flashes of the woman's face stole his vision, and along with it came some sort of intuition that she was going to be around for a while...*and* that her presence would become more significant. Why?

Once she was done talking, she slowly let go of his hand with a conflicted smile and then looked at Zalith. "We'll inform Danford and the others about what we discussed here and will see you again soon."

Zalith nodded, placing his hand on Alucard's arm as his subordinates made their way over to the front door. "Are you okay?" he asked the vampire.

"I'm fine," he said, frowning.

"You just...froze for a moment."

Alucard shrugged. "I'm just tired," he mumbled; he didn't want to make a big deal out of whatever just happened. He felt like it was nothing. "I went for a walk with Sabazios, went to see Drac, and then it started raining, so I came back."

With a smile on his face, Zalith kissed his forehead and then left his side. "I just have to see them out, and then we can dry you off," he said, smirking.

The vampire nodded and began to make his way through to the lounge beside his office. When he entered, he lit the fireplace with his ethos and slumped down on one of the couches with a quiet, deep sigh. He felt relieved to be home, relieved to see Zalith, and relieved to get to spend more time with him before he had to leave to take care of the Meshuga.

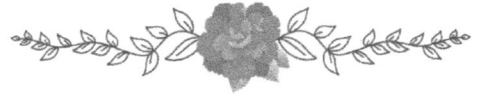

| Zalith |

Once he was done seeing his subordinates out, Zalith made his way into the lounge. He set his eyes on his vampire, whom he'd longed to see the entire time he was away. Being in Alucard's company brought him so much comfort and joy, and he'd not waste a moment of the time he now had to spend with him. After all, the next week or so was most likely going to be busy; things in Eltaria required his intervention, and he'd have to leave rather early each morning and probably wouldn't return until dusk. He'd have to explain that to Alucard, but he was sure that the vampire would understand.

He made his way over to where Alucard was and sat beside him. He wanted to rest his head on the vampire's shoulder, but his shirt was damp, and he was sure it wouldn't be very comfortable for either of them. "You should take this off," he said, pinching the collar of Alucard's shirt.

The vampire frowned nervously, obviously having taken his comment as something flirtatious. Of course, Zalith always loved to see what lay beneath Alucard's clothes, but this time, his suggestion was purely of concern. He wasn't sure if Alucard's species of demon got sick, and the last thing he wanted was for the vampire to catch a cold.

"Edwin," Zalith then called.

The butler came and stood in the doorway. "Yes, sir?"

"Could you fetch a blanket, please?" he asked.

Edwin nodded and disappeared.

"Blanket?" Alucard asked.

"So you don't get cold," Zalith said, smirking.

Alucard frowned shyly, but he seemed to understand Zalith's concern and started to unbutton his shirt.

The butler returned with a black wool blanket and handed it to Zalith, who wrapped it around himself and Alucard once the vampire removed his shirt.

With a content sigh, Zalith cuddled up with him and rested his head on his shoulder. "So, how was your walk?" he asked quietly.

The vampire leaned the side of his head on Zalith's and stared into the fireplace. "Vas okay," he answered. "I didn't really have anything else to do today, so I thought I'd take Sabazios out and check on Drac at the same time."

"How *is* Drac? Is he okay in that lake?"

"Well...he's sort of mad at me for not visiting him in a while. I told him I'll go and see him tomorrow. Do you want to come with me?"

Regret consumed him. How he'd love to go down to the lake again with Alucard, but he had to head to Eltaria and start dealing with things before they became worse. "Sadly, it will have to be another time. I have to head to Eltaria tomorrow morning and start trying to make the problems less dangerous to the people I left there. I feel as though I'll be busy with that for the next week or so. I'm sorry," he said quietly.

Alucard was silent for a moment, and Zalith felt him shuffle a little in what might be discontent. "That's fine," he then said. "What about what you're doing here? Are you still dealing with the gangs?"

"Yes, but after dealing with the Meshuga tonight, I'm going to have to put it aside while I deal with this," he answered. He'd made a lot of progress establishing grounds and relationships in Nefastus. But right now, he had to prioritise Eltaria. The thought had occurred to him to use what he was building here to help with what was going on back home, but it wasn't yet time to consider it.

"Are you sure you don't want my help?" Alucard asked.

Zalith smiled. "It's okay. I'll keep your offer in mind still, though."

"Okay."

"What will you do tomorrow while I'm gone?"

"Well, I'll still go and see Drac. I don't really know what else. I don't have much to do now that things are calm all over the world. Maybe I'll practice or...I don't know," he mumbled.

"You can always take my horse out if you like," Zalith offered, well aware of Alucard's love for the animals.

"Maybe," the vampire mumbled. "I guess I could look into my dreams or something. I want to see if there's a way to stop them."

Alucard's awful, terrible nightmares. Zalith was familiar with them and with the way the vampire woke from them. He always seemed so afraid, so confused, but Zalith always made sure to be there for him. His nightmares had only seemed to worsen as each day passed, and he didn't blame Alucard for wanting to find a way to stop them. Of course, he'd offered to help, but just like with most things, Alucard preferred to deal with it alone. He respected that, though, for these nightmares were Alucard's, not his, not *theirs*. He wouldn't force his help on him.

"Do you have any ideas?" the demon asked.

"There are many things I've heard over the years regarding dreams and dream ethos. I'll just research them, try some, and see if anything helps me."

"If you need my help, I'm here," he said, moving his hand up to stroke the side of Alucard's face with the back of his hand.

The vampire smiled slightly. "I know."

For a short while, they lay there in front of the fire, wrapped in their blanket, enjoying the silence. But Zalith soon remembered that Alucard had been to talk to Ben this morning and was curious to know how that had gone.

"What happened with Ben?"

Alucard sighed again. "Well, I told him what his options are, and then I said he can have a little while to think about. He'll either choose to become human again, or I'll have to kill him."

Zalith frowned curiously. "What does the process involve? Making a vampire a human again."

"I just remove my blood from them, untangle my ethos from theirs...that's all, really. It's my blood that made them vampires and taking it away will make them human again."

"Will it have any negative effects on his body?"

"No," Alucard answered. "Ben will not be the first I've done this to. There was a time when I was younger that I wasn't at all happy with the people around me; I was used to working alone, and after a while, I grew tired of the vampires I made. I turned them all back into humans and sent them on their way. That was...hundreds of years ago, though, when I was only just deciding that I would take Aegisguard for myself."

Zalith smirked in amusement. "How I love to hear about the times you were younger, Alucard. Mr Warlord, Mr God Slayer...King Slayer, creator of explosions and city-wide destruction because of boredom; you travel between worlds, possess the power to beat the shit out of a Numen. What else have you not told me, vampire?"

"Maybe you'll find out more someday," Alucard answered with a smirk. "Where's the fun in telling you all at once, hmm?"

"Quite," Zalith said in agreement. Then, he sat up just enough to lean into Alucard's face. "Whatever I learn, I know I'll love." He smiled, placing his hand on the side of the vampire's face. "I love *you*," he then said quietly, closing his eyes as he rested his forehead against Alucard's. He'd missed him so much today, and he felt so relieved just to be able to spend some time with him, and all he could think about was how much he really did love and appreciate him.

And how glad he was that this vampire was *his* vampire.

Chapter Eighty-Six

— ⋖ † ⋗ —

Of Pirates and Berserkers

| **Zalith** |

The Royland Shipyard was quiet, shrouded in thin, silvery fog and lit by the nearby streetlights and six full moons hanging in the pitch-black sky. Salt and gunpowder sat upon the light, warm breeze, and the accompanying stench of human and lycan made Zalith discreetly grimace in revolt as he and his allies covered their clothes in the rosemary-like concelo herb.

They stood outside the shipyard, covering behind the tall brick walls. Margo, Sheriff Reed, and the posse of police officers checked their weapons, and Zalith's men, all demons in Tyrus' pack, waited for the operation to begin.

While he waited for Tyrus to get back with the necessary intel, Zalith worried about Alucard back home by himself. He felt bad for leaving him alone for so much of the day, and he felt even worse knowing that he was going to be busy over the next few weeks trying to deal with things in Eltaria, but he was certain that Alucard understood; after all, they *both* had their business, and there were likely to be times when the vampire had to spend weeks at a time dealing with huge problems or operations.

He missed him, though. What he wouldn't give to be in bed with him right now rather than in some putrid shipyard dealing with pirates. But he had to focus on the bigger picture; if he was going to be successful in becoming a part of the Citadel Government, he needed to prove his valour, his resourcefulness, and his dedication.

Tyrus returned, emerging from the shadows. He stealthily crept past the shipyard gates and re-joined the group. "Twenty-seven guards, boss," he said to Zalith. "Thirteen with dogs. There are two men in each spotlight tower, one each with long-range rifles. Grimclaw is in the cabin stuffing his face."

"Doesn't surprise me," James, one of Margo's men, said with a scoff. "Scoffing down stolen food is a Meshuga common practice."

"Well, it ends here," Sheriff Reed stated.

"Too right," Margo agreed.

"I've selected a route," Tyrus said to Zalith. "We'll take out the shipyard guards, and you'll be clear to head up onto the boat."

Zalith nodded and looked at Margo and Reed. "Are you ready?"

Everyone nodded.

The demon then looked at Tyrus again. "Go."

With a nod, Tyrus left the group, leading his men to a narrow hole in the brick wall poorly covered with pieces of rotting, wet wood. One by one, they headed into the shipyard, and once they were all in, Zalith peeked through the small hole in the bricks beside him and watched his subordinate disappear into the fog.

"Not your first rodeo, huh?" Margo asked him quietly.

He could hear the nervousness in her voice and suspected she was the kind of person to talk when they were anxious. Although he didn't feel like indulging her, he needed to ensure that both she and her co-workers trusted and liked him. "No," he answered. "Elves faced a lot of problems where I come from; we had to deal with more than disrespectful pirates and petty bandits."

"Where *did* you come from?" James asked skeptically.

Zalith shot him a condescending smile. "You know I can't tell you that."

"Elves are very private," Sheriff Reed said. "If everyone knew where they lived, their way of life would be destroyed." He looked at Zalith. "Right?"

"Exactly," the demon confirmed. "Our lands are sacred."

James rolled his eyes. "Spiritual nonsense."

"Don't be fucking rude," another of the officers said just as Margo was clearly about to snap. "The elves here have done nothing but help us."

"Quiet," Margo then muttered. "Focus on the operation."

The posse nodded and rechecked their weapons.

"Sorry about that," Margo said to Zalith quietly. "Some people take much longer than others to accept new species into their fold."

Zalith smiled at her in response and then peered through the gap in the bricks again. He caught a whiff of human blood, but it was quickly covered up by the concelo herb that Tyrus and his men had been instructed to place on every pirate that they killed. He waited a moment, focusing on Grimclaw's aura, hoping that the berserker didn't catch the scent, too, but Zalith didn't detect a shift in his ethos; it appeared that he was far too busy gorging to notice that his men were dying in the fog.

"How's it looking?" Margo asked.

"I can't see too well through the fog," he told her.

"That's the thing about fog," Reed said with a sigh. "Gives us great fucking cover but makes it just us hard for us to see as it does for our enemies."

Zalith focused on the human auras on the other side of the wall. He felt each of them change one by one; some faded when Tyrus and his men knocked the pirates out, and others disappeared entirely, evidently assassinated because they were either too difficult to subdue or weren't any of the targets Margo wanted alive.

Minutes passed by, and the night grew later; Zalith focused on Tyrus' aura, tracking him through the fog, and *finally*, twenty minutes later, Tyrus let him know that the guards were down, the only thought inside his head being: *it's done*.

"Let's go," Zalith said to his allies.

As the demon led the way, Margo, Sheriff Reed, and the posse of officers followed him. He crouched and went through the gap in the wall, and as he traversed the muddy terrain towards the galleon, he focused his senses on the men on and inside the ship.

"I count thirty-seven men inside," he said, keeping his voice hushed. "And nine on deck."

"Be ready," Margo whispered to her men.

Zalith concentrated, ensuring that he hadn't missed any auras as he approached the boarding ramp. He stopped by the gangway fence and looked back at his allies. Margo and Reed both gave him a nod, letting him know that they were ready, and then he began leading them up towards the deck.

He prepared himself for the battle that was about to break out, discreetly extending his claws; when he reached the top of the ramp, he set his eyes on the silhouette of a man with a rifle patrolling mere feet away. He held his hand back towards Margo, letting her know to wait, and once she and her men halted, he continued forward on his own.

Swiftly and silently, he grabbed the patrolling guard and held his hand over his mouth to keep him from screaming. He glanced at his face, and when he saw that the man wasn't one of the men Margo wanted alive, he mercilessly dug his claws into the pirate's neck and tore his throat out. The demon then carefully lowered the man's body to the floor and looked back over his shoulder at Margo. He nodded at her, and as she and her men filed onto the ship to begin their part of the operation, *he* made his way towards the cabin.

He could smell Grimclaw from halfway across the ship. That wretched stench of wet fur, old blood, and sweat. The smell of a whole bouquet of food hung in the air, mixed with tobacco, salt, and gunpowder; the men up on the quarterdeck were smoking, and two others sitting by the stairs that led up there were cleaning their rifles. Zalith didn't need to worry about them, though. He kept himself hidden, edging closer to the cabin doors.

To his relief, Margo and her men hadn't yet blown their cover, so he might be able to sneak up on Grimclaw and knock him out without a fight. He wouldn't count on it, though; any second now, one of those officers—likely James—would fuck up. But they were all ready for it.

Zalith reached the doors. He very slowly and very carefully twisted the handle, and as he pushed the door open, he peered inside.

Grimclaw, the stout, overly hairy man was sitting with his back to the doors in front of a table overflowing with food. Expensive and likely stolen meats, luxury cheeses, pastries, fruits, and sweets—it was enough to feed at least a hundred people. The man greedily and rather disgustingly stuffed his face, grunting and groaning and slurping. Even in his human form, he looked like a dire bear ready for hibernation.

Zalith stepped into the room and silently closed the door behind him. "Are you expecting visitors, Trent?" he asked with an amused smile.

The man flinched violently, dropping his greasy turkey leg as he turned his body to look at Zalith. His eyes grew wide, and a confused expression slapped his disgusting, food-smothered face. "Who the fuck are you?!" he roared.

"That doesn't matter," the demon replied. "This can go either of two ways. One: the easy way, where you give yourself up to the entire police regiment currently taking out all your friends. Or two: the hard way, where I send you off to sleep and you wake up in a cell," he explained slowly.

But Grimclaw laughed as if he'd been told an absolutely hilarious joke and stood up out of his seat. "You think you can scare me? My men can handle a few puny pigs," he spat.

Zalith grimaced in revolt. "I was rather hoping you'd choose option one so I could avoid getting covered in all that grease," he muttered, glancing at the table.

The man scowled angrily, but before he could speak, gunfire broke the silence, and the deck outside lit up with the firing of rifles.

Grimclaw immediately attempted to shift into his bear form, but Zalith burst forward, got behind him, and wrapped his arm around his neck, pulling him into a headlock.

"Get off me!" the man yelled, trying to hit Zalith with his elbows.

The demon dodged each of his jabs, tightening his grip, waiting for the man to succumb to being deprived of air. Yelling voices of both the Meshuga and Margo's men came from every direction, and the gunfire grew more aggressive. Zalith telepathically signalled Tyrus and his pack to assist, and then he tightened his grasp just a little more but not so much that he broke Grimclaw's neck.

He kept struggling, putting in a little more strength; Zalith started stumbling back, trying to keep the man where he was, and when his back hit the table, the demon grunted irritably.

"Get... off!" Grimclaw growled, gripping Zalith's arm. He then yanked, managing to loosen the demon's grip, and the man pulled out of Zalith's lock and lurched backwards.

Zalith snarled irritably and went to grab him again, but Grimclaw took his chance and shifted into his bear form. The beast let out a savage roar, and then he charged at the demon. Zalith dodged by mere inches, and when the bear skidded to a halt and turned to face him, he backed off and scowled challengingly at the monster. He had to be *very* careful now, but this wasn't his first time dealing with powerful lycans. Usually, he'd send it up in flames or tear its throat out, but Margo wanted Grimclaw alive, so he couldn't do something that would kill him.

A maniacal grin stretched across the huge bear's face. "Come on!" he urged.

The demon scoffed at him and quickly glanced around the room for anything he could use to his advantage, and he saw exactly what he needed behind Grimclaw. He just had to get over there. "What are you waiting for, Trent?" he taunted with a smirk.

With a furious growl, the bear burst forward, teeth and claws bared.

Zalith waited, his heart starting to beat a little faster; he wasn't going to lie, he *was* a little nervous because berserkers were very unpredictable, and the last thing he wanted was to get home to Alucard looking like he'd been mauled by a pack of dogs. He had to time his moves just right.

The bear got faster, reaching him in just seconds, but Zalith skilfully dodged its charge, and as he backed off towards the back wall where a giant steel beam stood, he watched the bear smack into the wall he'd been standing in front of as it attempted to halt itself.

Unfazed, however, the bear turned around, shook its head, and charged at Zalith once more. Zalith waited, watching its every move, and just as the bear was about to collide with him, he lunged to the side, and as planned, Grimclaw crashed face-first into the steel beam. The bear groaned and shook his head, stumbling around, but it wasn't enough, so Zalith cautiously edged a little closer and slammed his fist into the side of the beast's face with just enough force to knock it out... but Grimclaw still didn't go down.

Zalith tried to back off, but the massive bear roared confusedly and threw its huge body at him. Its sheer weight made Zalith collapse as it landed on him, but before it could clamp its jaws around any part of him, he grabbed hold of its muzzle and held it back. The bear growled and roared, and Zalith snarled and grunted; they struggled, and every time the bear attempted to slam its paws down on Zalith, the demon dodged, and the wooden floor beneath them cracked and splintered.

With a struggled grunt, Zalith took one hand off the bear's muzzle and slammed his fist into the side of its head once, twice, and a third time, hoping each hit would be the one that knocked it out. The bear kept fighting, but the disorientated look in its eyes was increasing. So Zalith kept hitting it, over and over and over, and after one final harsh punch to its head, the beast let out a defeated groan, its eyes rolled to the back of its head, and it fell still.

Zalith snarled irritably when the huge bear collapsed on him, but once he was unconscious, just like all lycans did, Grimclaw reverted to his human form, and Zalith harshly pushed him off with a disgusted grunt. It was then that he noticed the gunfire had died down, and the only voices he could hear outside were those of Margo's men.

The demon stood up and wiped his coat with his hands; he then reached down and grabbed Grimclaw's leg and dragged him towards the doors. He dragged the man out of the cabin and onto the foggy deck, where he was met with Margo and Reed's surprised but impressed stares.

"I was about to come in there and see if you needed help, but you clearly have it all handled," Margo said with a smirk.

Zalith left the unconscious man by his handcuffed minions. "Did you arrest everyone you were after?" he asked.

"More than half of them," she said with a nod.

"A few of them were... difficult," Reed said.

"It's only thanks to your men here that we managed to get as many as we did," Margo said, glancing at Tyrus and his pack, who were waiting by the ramp. "Thank you for your help, Zalith. We honestly never thought we'd see the day where all of these assholes were brought to justice."

"It's no problem," Zalith said with a nod.

"I reckon we owe you a drink," Reed suggested with a smirk.

Zalith laughed a little but shook his head. "I appreciate it, but it's late, and I should get home. I trust you and your men will manage getting them back to the station; I'll leave Tyrus to help with him," he said, gesturing to Grimclaw, who James was putting a pair of silver shackles on.

Margo looked disappointed, but she smiled and said, "Okay. Thank you again. We really couldn't have done any of this without you."

He smiled one last time and then made his way down the ramp to the dock. All he wanted to do now was get home to Alucard, and the moment he was deep enough in the fog, he created a rift in a stone wall and stepped inside.

The demon emerged through the wall surrounding his estate. He made his way through the gardens and to the front door, and once he stepped inside, he let out a deep, tired sigh and pulled his coat and shoes off. As he headed upstairs, he unbuttoned his blazer and shirt, and when he got into his bedroom, where Alucard was already asleep, he undressed and carefully climbed into bed beside his vampire.

Alucard stirred a little when Zalith moved his arms around him, but he didn't wake up, so the demon nuzzled the back of his head and held him tightly. He kissed him, closed his eyes, and let himself relax. It had been a long night, but now that he was home with Alucard, the weight of its events withered. He could always count on Alucard's presence to relieve him of his stress.

Chapter Eighty-Seven

— ⚔ ✝ ⚔ —

The Chicken

| Zalith |

Zalith woke as the sun started creeping over the horizon, lighting the bedroom a dim orange. Beside him, sleeping soundlessly with his head on the demon's shoulder, was Alucard, and a smile instantly made its way to Zalith's tired face. But he wouldn't get to lay in bed for an extra hour or so with him *this* morning. He had to get up, get ready, and head to Eltaria.

Sadness quickly consumed him as he carefully moved a strand of hair from over Alucard's face. He had a strong feeling that what he had to do back home would only become more demanding, and he didn't want to leave Alucard alone while he dealt with it. But he wouldn't ask him to come; he didn't want Alucard to get hurt, and that was likely to happen in the midst of the depravity that had swept across his homeland.

With a quiet, sad sigh, he carefully moved Alucard's head off his shoulder and onto one of the pillows. But his attempts to not wake him were futile. The vampire murmured quietly in disagreement and stretched out his arm to pull Zalith back to where he was before trying to get out of bed.

Zalith sighed and smiled slightly. "I have to get ready to go," he said quietly as he caressed the vampire's hair once Alucard rested his head back on the demon's shoulder.

A stubborn pout appeared on the vampire's tired face, but he relented and let go, resting his head on one of the pillows.

"I'll see you later today, okay?"

Alucard muttered something in agreement and made himself comfortable once again.

Zalith placed his hand on the side of the vampire's face and kissed his cheek, sure that he was going to spend all day missing and thinking about him. The day was going to be a long one, but the thought of coming home to see the man he loved kept him focused.

He climbed out of bed, made sure that Alucard was comfortable, and headed into the dressing room. He selected one of his black suits, got dressed, tidied his hair, and then made his way over to the bedroom door and looked back at Alucard. Leaving him had become so hard; even though he'd be back later, he felt so despondent when he thought about spending almost the entire day without him. But he had to help his people back home.

With a frown of hesitation, he pulled the door open and left, preparing to head back to the place where he'd lived for six hundred years of his life.

| **Alucard** |

Alucard woke from his slumber hours after Zalith's departure. He slowly opened his eyes, a painful feeling of sadness consuming him as he stared at the empty space where Zalith slept. He'd become so used to waking up beside him that it felt strange *not* to see him there. Of course, he knew that Zalith had to return to Eltaria to deal with the problems there, but Alucard still wished he could have gone with him—to help and to just be with him. But he couldn't be with him *all* the time, could he?

He rolled onto his back, staring up at the dark ceiling as he tried to will himself to get out of bed. If he fell back asleep, not only would he sleep the day away, but he'd sink back into whatever despondent dream had haunted him this time round. He didn't remember it much now, but he was certain that it would all come to him once he started to progress through his day.

With a frown of discontent, he slowly sat up and stared down at his lap, still trying to find the motivation he needed to get up. He wasn't sure what to do with his day; he said he'd go and see Drac, so he could do that. He'd also decided that he was going to look into his dreams and a possible way to stop them, so he could do that, too. He also had to read Dirk and Attila's letters—he was confident that they weren't too important, for all the annoyances and problems he had to deal with before were now settled.

He wished he knew how last night went for Zalith, though. He didn't get the chance to ask, but the fact that the demon wasn't panicking or covered in wounds assured him that things went fine. He'd ask for details later.

The vampire sighed quietly but dragged himself out of bed, tidied the bed covers, and then made his way into the bathroom. He stepped into the shower, staring at the floor as the water poured over him. He tried to focus on what he'd do when he headed downstairs in an attempt to silence his incoming dismaying thoughts. He might go and see his dragon first.

Once he finished showering, he wrapped a towel around his waist, headed over to the countertop, and as he did every morning, he brushed his teeth, tidied his hair, and made himself look presentable. Then, he left the bathroom and walked through the bedroom and into the dressing room. He pulled on a long-sleeved white shirt and black trousers, a combination he had come to wear a lot more often, and then he started to make his way downstairs.

He might as well take Sabazios with him to see Drac again, and Zalith had said he could use his horse, so he might do that, too.

When he reached the bottom of the stairs, he searched for his puppy, but he wasn't curled up in his bed by the door, nor was he wandering the hall looking for food. Maybe he was still eating.

Just then, Edwin came down the hallway that led to the kitchen and set his eyes on Alucard. "Sir," he said, approaching him. "As instructed, your breakfast has been prepared and will be brought to you out on the patio when you are ready."

Alucard frowned. Instructed? That must mean Zalith had made sure he'd eat in his absence. It made him feel a little better knowing that Zalith did his best to make sure he was okay even when he wasn't around.

"Fine," he said. "You can bring it now."

The butler nodded and turned around, heading back towards the kitchen.

As the butler left, Alucard made his way through the house and to the patio. He sat down at the table, staring out into the distance as he waited. Once again, all he could think about was Zalith, how he should be sitting across the table from him right now, and how he wasn't. A saddened frown clung to his face again; it irritated him to think about how much he missed the demon despite the fact that he would be back in five or so hours, maybe less, maybe a little more. But it just didn't feel right without Zalith around.

One of the kitchen staff came out onto the patio with a plate in one hand and a tray in the other. He first placed the tray, which had an empty glass and a small glass jug of orange juice. The man then placed the plate in front of him, on which sat waffles, but they were topped with cuttings of strawberries lain out in the shape of a heart.

The vampire waited for the butler to leave before smiling down at his plate. Although Zalith wasn't currently with him, he felt a lot less despondent knowing that he thought about him enough to do this to his breakfast just to remind him that he loved him. The sight of it made him so happy that he felt as if he didn't want to eat it, but Zalith had asked for it to be prepared especially for him, and he'd not be ungrateful. He did, after all, like both waffles and strawberries, and perhaps eating something would help him to feel less miserable.

He picked up the knife and fork that lay on the tray beside him and started to eat, enjoying his food along with the content thought of seeing Zalith tonight.

When he was done, he leaned back in his seat for a short while and stared out at the forest. He watched as another of the grounds' guards patrolled past just behind the treeline, watching the property with the several other people Alucard had seen over the past weeks of living with Zalith.

He then sighed and looked over his shoulder, glancing into the lounge behind him. He was sure that Sabazios must have finished his food by now, so he got up and made his way into the house in search of him. Surely enough, the pitter-patter sound of the dog's claws against the flooring echoed through the hall, and as Alucard stepped into it, the puppy trotted over to him with a smile on its face.

"Did you eat *all* your food?" Alucard asked skeptically.

Sabazios sat down and licked his muzzle, slowly wagging his tail as he waited to be told that it was time for a walk.

"Good," Alucard said. He then made his way over to the front door as the puppy followed him.

Sabazios watched as Alucard slipped his shoes on along with one of his calf-length overcoats. The vampire then unlocked the door and stepped out onto the porch, and the brightness of the sun forced his eyes to fade to blue as pain shot through his head.

He waited for the pain to pass, and then he set his sights on the stables. As he walked over there, though, he caught sight of a small bird pecking at the ground as it slowly lurched forward. Alucard stopped walking, staring at the cat-size, brown-feathered bird as it clucked quietly, rapidly turning its head from side to side when it stopped pecking at the ground to look at him. A chicken?

Alucard frowned curiously and looked around for whoever might own the bird, but there was no one else in sight. Why was there a chicken by the stables? Where had it come from? Who did it belong to? And why was it slowly making its way over, pecking at the gravel as if it were seeds?

Sabazios also watched the bird, but he didn't attack or chase it. Instead, he sat at Alucard's side, waiting to be told what to do about the approaching animal.

The vampire looked around again, hoping that someone would come to collect it before he claimed it as his own, but no one was coming, so when the bird reached him, he crouched and eyed it closely. "Why are you here?"

It gawped at him with its gold, beady eyes, turning its head from side to side. It clucked, cooed, and waited in front of him.

Alucard frowned. He couldn't detect anyone other than the staff inside the house and the guards patrolling the grounds, and there was no sign of a tag or badge on the creature that might indicate someone owned it. Maybe it was a wild chicken; perhaps it wandered afar and found its way there. Whatever the case, Alucard felt as if the bird wouldn't be safe out here on its own for long.

He scooped the chicken up and held it in his left arm. It clucked again and looked up at him, and with a hesitant frown, Alucard moved his free hand closer to the bird and patted its small head with a single finger. "I will call you...Hana."

Hana clucked quietly and continued looking around as though she was afraid something might find her.

Alucard smiled slightly and continued towards the stables.

Suddenly, a woman's voice called, "You with the chicken!"

Alucard frowned and looked over his shoulder at a blonde-haired woman dressed in an orange and white trimmed dress, who was waving her hand at him as she approached. She waved a handkerchief in her left hand, an impatient look on her face as she glared at him. He'd never seen her before, and he was fairly certain that she wasn't there for him or Zalith. So, why *was* she there?

"I'm sure you must be very busy with your chicken job," she started as she stopped in front of him. "But I'm just wondering if you know if Varana is here."

An irritated scowl struck his face. Of *course* she was there for that woman. But his irritancy then shifted. Chicken job? "I don't have chicken job," he uttered.

The woman stared at him; her dark blue eyes flickered to the chicken, back to him, and to the chicken again, and as she frowned, her sights settled on him. "Why are you holding a chicken, then? Ew."

As she took a step back, glowering down at the chicken, Alucard's scowl became a vacant look. He wasn't going to conversate about his new friend. Instead, he rolled his eyes. "I have no idea where that repugnant woman is," he answered.

An astonished look spread across the woman's face as she gasped. "You can't talk about your employer like that!" she snapped.

"She is *not* my employer," he snarled.

She scoffed doubtfully. "Then why are you standing here holding a chicken if you don't work here as a chicken boy? Some sort of...chicken...keeper..." she said, waving her hand towards the chicken with a look of disgust on her face.

"I live here," he grumbled.

The woman frowned, looking down at the chicken again as it stared at her. She then leaned aside to look at the barn behind him. "In...the chicken coop?"

"In the house," he growled, trying not to lose his patience with her just in case she was also a friend of Zalith's.

She frowned again. "Do Varana and Zalith know you let chickens run loose in their house?"

"This is *my* and Zalith's house," he corrected.

Yet again, the woman scoffed and frowned. "Uh...Varana lives here, too, does she not?" she laughed slightly. "I know she's been away on vacation to see her sister in Avalmoor, but she still lives here...she's Zalith's wife, after all," she said with a matter-of-fact tone.

Alucard then scowled in aggravation. Obviously, Varana had chosen to tell whoever this woman was that she and Zalith were married, and he was sure that there was a lot more she'd lied about—such as her reason for not being home right now. She wasn't on vacation; she had been kicked out for being a bitch.

He deadpanned. "Is that what she told you?"

"Of course she told me! She writes to me all the time," she said smugly. But then a skeptical, curious look appeared on her face. "Wait...is that not the case? What happened?"

This woman wanted to know...and who was he to turn away yet another person who Varana had lied to for her own benefit? "She and Zalith are *not* married."

With a perturbed frown, the woman laughed a little. "Uh...I'm sorry, who are you again?" she asked, an almost demeaning tone in her voice.

Alucard felt no need to lie. "I'm Zalith's boyfriend," he answered, and as he watched a bewildered look appear on her face, he became convinced that he'd just caused Varana the drama she deserved to have to deal with.

The woman gasped in shock as she stared at him. "You're..." she paused for a short while, clearly trying to find her words. "I..." she stuttered. But then she shook her head. "I have to go; it was very nice meeting you!" she called as she turned around and scurried off like a schoolgirl with a look of both excitement and astonishment on her face. Obviously, she was about to go and cause exactly what Alucard suspected would come of their conversation, and it made him feel no sympathy or worry for the rude, intolerable woman who had clearly spread a mountain of lies.

He watched the orange-dressed woman hurry through the gardens and to the carriage that waited outside the gates. He had no idea where she might be going, but he didn't really care. All that mattered was that Varana was going to get what she deserved.

With Hana the chicken in his arms, he turned around and wandered into the stables, setting his eyes on Zalith's horse. It lifted its head to look at him, watching as he approached, and once he reached it, the horse moved forward to greet him.

But...he couldn't take the chicken to the lake with him, could he? He looked down at Hana, who was still in his arms, gawping up at him. He sighed quietly and put Hana on the ground as he said, "You can stay here. I'll come and find you when I get back."

She stared up at him, clucked, turned her head, and then waddled away back outside.

Alucard then mounted Zalith's horse and looked down at Sabazios. "Let's go," he said as the dog wagged its tail excitedly.

Without any further hindrance, he steered the horse out of the stables, through the grounds, and began his journey to the lake.

Chapter Eighty-Eight

— ᰔ ✝ ᰔ —

Gossip Among Friends

In the Citadel, two elegantly attired women were sitting in a small, cosy coffee shop, seated in front of a large window. The décor boasted ornate, handcrafted wooden panels and delicate lace curtains, casting a warm, inviting glow courtesy of crystal chandeliers overhead.

The air was filled with the inviting scent of freshly ground coffee beans, served in dainty cups with intricate designs. The subdued murmur of conversations and occasional clinking of cutlery provided a gentle backdrop to the women's exchange of hearsay. Attendants, dressed in refined uniforms with tasteful bows, moved gracefully among the tables, offering trays of exquisite pastries and an assortment of fine teas.

Beyond the window, the cobblestone streets of the city echoed with the sounds of horse-drawn carriages and the distant hum of daily life. The coffee establishment, a refined sanctuary within the lively city, allowed the women to indulge in the art of gossip, their laughter blending seamlessly with the sophisticated atmosphere of their retreat.

The first of the women was a slender redhead, her shoulder-length hair a dull, almost-brown-orange. Her eyes were chocolate-brown, and the dress she wore was a light blue with patterns of white around its sleeves. She sipped from her small teacup, a content smile on her face as she glanced at her hazel-haired friend, dressed in a rosy-red dress similar to that of her companion.

"Do you think she got lost?" the redhead asked with a hint of concern in her voice, placing her teacup back on the table. "Cadence and V are usually the first ones here."

The other woman frowned slightly and glanced out of the window. "We all know what V is like," she said with a sigh. "She probably had the carriage turned around halfway through the trip because she wanted to change into something more revealing."

Both girls giggled. However, as a carriage pulled up across the road, they watched with expectant looks on their make-up-plastered faces. It wasn't Cadence *and* Varana who stepped out onto the street, though; it was Cadence on her lonesome. The honey-blonde, orange dress-wearing woman hurried across the road after her carriage left, a look of excitement on her face as she spotted her two friends inside the small building.

Neither of them asked the question they were both thinking—where was Varana? They did, however, wish to know why she looked so enthusiastic today, for Cadence was usually rather snooty.

"What do you think she knows?" the redhead giggled quietly.

Cadence rushed into the shop and joined her friends at their table. They stood up to greet her, all of them kissing each other's cheeks before asking how she was. Then, they returned to their seats, and as Cadence made herself comfortable, her two friends waited eagerly to know what she was surely about to tell them.

"Guess what!" she exclaimed, her voice hushed and eager.

The girls looked at each other excitedly. "What?" they both asked just as quietly.

But then Cadence frowned hesitantly for a moment. She picked up the teacup that had been waiting for her and took a sip. "Maybe I shouldn't say it," she said, batting her eyelashes.

Her friends frowned eagerly.

"Tell us!" the redhead insisted.

"Okay!" Cadence giggled quietly, needing no persuasion at all. She leaned closer, as did her friends; she looked at them both and frowned slightly. "A certain someone's husband is having an affair!"

Again, her two friends looked at each other with intrigued looks on their faces. Then, they gazed back at her. "Who?" they both asked at the same time.

Cadence hesitated again.

The redhead then huffed in disbelief. "Well," she said, sipping from her tea. "It's not my Roland. He is absolutely *horrible* at keeping secrets from me," she said with a boastful expression.

"Your Roland is quite stupid, Selena," the hazel-haired woman said.

"Agreed," Selena said, nodding.

Cadence shook her head. "No, no, it's none of *our* husbands...but someone *very* close to us," she said, nodding over at the only vacant seat at their table.

The two girls gasped.

"No!" the hazel-haired woman exclaimed.

Cadence nodded. "Yes!"

Selena leaned closer. "Tell us *everything*!"

With an excited shuffle in her seat, Cadence smirked. "So, as usual, I went to Varana's house so that we could share the carriage into town, and—"

Just then, the waiter arrived with a plate of sandwiches. The girls all deadpanned and eyed him in silence as he placed the plate down.

"Thank you..." Cadence mumbled.

The waiter bowed respectfully and walked off with a roll of his eyes as the women leaned back in to whisper to one another.

"So, as I was saying, I went to Varana's house to share the carriage with her like usual, and I came across this...individual out front holding a *chicken*!" she said quietly, looking back and forth at them both.

"Ew," Selena uttered, "gross."

"I know, chickens are awful. Anyway, I asked them if they could tell me where Varana was, and we kinda just got to chatting, and—"

"Why all the 'them' and 'they'?" the hazel-haired woman asked. "Just say her!"

Cadence bit her lip as she held back a giggle. "That's the thing, Mary-Beth," she said, a matter-of-fact tone in her voice. "It wasn't a woman...it was a *man*!"

Mary-Beth and Selena gasped. "Not Zalith!" they both exclaimed in astonishment.

"And-and the worst part is that he thinks Zalith and Varana aren't even married!" she added.

Selena held her hand to her mouth in shock. "Zalith's so horrible for doing that—"

"Shh—shh, it's her!" Cadence then whispered.

"Shh!" Mary-Beth insisted as Selena did her best to hold back her giggles.

"Shh!" Selena added as they all stared out of the window, watching as the black ebony carriage pulled up outside.

"Don't say anything!" Cadence whispered.

Then, the three of them waited for Varana to join them.

| **Varana** |

Varana climbed out of her carriage with a quiet sigh. She made sure that her black hair was perfect and then made her way into the café. As she stepped inside, all three of her friends stood up; they hugged her, kissed her cheek, and said their hellos and how are yous.

"You smell like paint," Varana said, turning her nose up at Selena as they sat at the table.

Selena giggled and waved her hand as she sipped from her tea. "Oh, Roland is having the porch painted—again!"

Varana wasn't interested and sat there with a glum look on her face.

"So...how was your time away?" Mary-Beth asked with a smile.

"Awful," Varana answered, snatching a sandwich. "My sister has this ugly little pet named Pickles, and I can still smell its ugly, revolting stench in my nose!" she exclaimed.

"Ew," Selena uttered.

"Was it...as gross as a chicken?" Cadence asked with a giggle.

As Selena giggled, too, Varana frowned. "Even worse than a chicken!"

"Who calls their pet Pickles, anyway?" Mary-Beth questioned.

"My annoying sister," Varana mumbled, taking a bite of her sandwich.

"What's Avalmoor like?" Selena asked. "I hear it's so, *so* cold out there—I could never go somewhere like that unless I had at least *two* of my thousand-gold fur coats."

"That's so true," Cadence agreed with a shiver.

Varana sighed as she sipped from her tea. "The cold isn't all that bad," she answered as they stared at her. "But I suppose that's because I'm just built differently," she said with a condescending smile. "However, the people—and the scenery, ugh!"

"Sounds awful," Mary-Beth said with a sympathetic frown. "Are you back home now for good?"

With something of a smirk, she nodded. "And I won't be leaving again."

"Yes, I'm sure Zalith missed you *very* much," Cadence said with a smile. "He must have been very lonely in that *huge* house all by *himself.*"

As Varana—who wasn't paying much attention—stared at her nails, her three friends hid their smiles behind their hands and giggled quietly.

"Hmm? Oh, yes," Varana mumbled in agreement, fiddling with her nails.

The girls looked at one another before looking back at Varana.

"So, Varana." Cadence smiled as she sipped from her tea. "We were all *so* surprised to hear that you headed off to your sister's place so abruptly; you're such a free spirit. Was she surprised to see you, too?"

"I'm always a welcome guest at my sister's house," Varana replied, taking her eyes off her fingers to eye each of the women.

Cadence pulled a frown of concern—but it wasn't very convincing. "You left so out of the blue. We were all worried that something might have happened at home."

Varana then scowled, sure that they all knew something that they weren't supposed to. "What?" she growled.

"O-oh," Cadence stuttered with a small giggle. "We were just worried."

Selena then leaned in. "It must be nice to get away from your husband from time to time. I'm sure he missed you."

Varana kept her scowl, drinking from her teacup.

Then, they all went silent, sipping from their tea. It was unusual for her friends to be as silent as they were, and Varana wasn't sure why. She scowled, looking around at them all as they slurped their tea for a strangely long time. "What?!" she exclaimed. "What is it?"

All three of them glanced at one another in suspense, clearly unsure of what to say.

Varana had never really had much patience. "Tell me!"

Cadence shook her head in denial. "N-nothing, we just—"

"Cadence, you should just tell her," Mary-Beth interjected, concern in her voice.

"Tell me what?!"

Scowling at Mary-Beth, Cadence rolled her eyes as Selena giggled behind her hand. "Well?!"

"Just tell her!" Mary-Beth urged sadly, staring at Cadence.

With a deep exhale, Cadence looked at Varana and frowned sympathetically. "Your...husband is having an affair," she revealed.

Varana scowled irritably. "What?"

All three of them seemed to brace themselves for Varana's inevitable outburst.

Cadence frowned a little. "Well...I went to your house so that we could share the carriage, and no one answered the door. However, I saw this chicken boy over by the stables, so I went to ask him. He had...red hair—"

Varana cringed at the thought of Alucard.

"And blue eyes. I asked him where you were, and he said he was Zalith's boyfriend!"

Selena giggled behind her hand again, and Mary-Beth stared with a look of sympathy.

Varana calmly sipped from her teacup. Her first thought was Zalith and how he didn't need or want the people here to know that he was gay. It may have been said countless times that in Nefastus, people didn't care if you were straight, bi, gay, or anything different, but in reality, they *did* care. If people were to find out that Zalith was gay, they'd not respect him nor treat him the way they would if he were straight—as they currently thought. Zalith had been working so very hard to gain a place of control in this country, and his plans were working. Varana wouldn't let that be taken away from him.

She was also sure that if she lied about Zalith's sexuality, Alucard...as much as she hated him...might become involved, and it would cause drama that would only aggravate Zalith. She didn't want that, either, so she was going to have to be smart about what she next said.

Once she was done sipping from her drink, she lowered her cup from her face and rolled her eyes irritably. "He is," she answered in response to Cadence's revelation. As much as she hated to know and admit it, Alucard *was* Zalith's boyfriend.

All three of her friends gasped in astonishment.

Varana glared irritably. "Calm down!"

They did as she said, falling silent as they stared expectantly at her.

"Really?" Mary-Beth asked. "But...you two *are* married, right?"

Varana scowled again. "No," she grumbled.

Her friends all gasped in shock once again.

"But we're practically married," she then said confidently. "We've been best friends for as long as I can remember."

Selena shook her head in startlement.

"Well, the chicken boy said that he lives there!" Cadence said. "How long have you been hiding this from us?"

Varana rolled her eyes again and glowered irritably. "I wasn't hiding him. Z just moved him in while I was away without asking me first!"

Cadence pouted. "So you really *did* just decide to visit your sister out of the blue?"

"Yes."

"Well, chicken boy seemed to imply that that wasn't the case."

In response to Cadence's intrusive tone, Varana frowned bitterly. "Okay, and *your* husband implied to me that you aren't sufficient enough at your wifely duties and asked me to sleep with him. But do you know what I did? I walked away and minded my own business. Maybe there's a lesson we can all learn from that," she sneered.

As Cadence backed down with a sad little pout, Selena frowned slightly in astonishment. "There's no need to get hostile, Varana, my goodness."

"We're your friends," Mary-Beth concurred. "We just want to know what's going on with you, that's all."

Varana scowled but took a sip from her drink and deadpanned. "Fine," she muttered. Then, she sighed deeply. "Yes, Z *is* seeing a man, and *yes*, I am not his wife, but I still love him dearly, and if any of you tell your disgusting little husbands or *anybody else* about Z being gay, I will ruin your life without a *shred* of remorse," she warned, something of a hostile growl in her voice as her friends all looked at one another in shock.

But Selena frowned in sadness. "My Laurence isn't disgusting."

"Oh, please!" Varana exclaimed. "He looks like a bleached raisin, and his teeth are made out of wood!"

Selena pouted sullenly and stared down at her lap.

"What did he look like exactly?" Mary-Beth then asked. "This blue-eyed boyfriend?"

Cadence giggled quietly. "If I'm being honest, he was *very* attractive," she answered.

Varana grunted in revolt. "No, he's not—he's ugly!" she snapped.

"You really think so?" Cadence frowned doubtfully. "I thought he was quite handsome."

Keeping her scowl, Varana tutted. "Ugh, gross. It would be weird if I was attracted to him," she said but then realized that she shouldn't have just said that.

"Why?" Mary-Beth asked. "Because he's gay?"

"No...." She frowned, unsure of how to escape.

"Why would it be weird?" Cadence asked.

Varana hesitated but then sighed and shrugged. "Because...he's my brother—"

Cadence, Mary-Beth, and Selena all looked at each other and gasped in utter disbelief.

"Be quiet!" Varana snarled.

"No wonder you left!" Cadence giggled.

Rolling her eyes, Varana finished her tea and prepared to get up. "Whatever. You best remember what I said. It doesn't leave this room."

All three of her friends glanced at each other warily.

"Let's go," she then said.

They didn't falter in getting up to follow her.

"We didn't finish our lunch!" Selena protested.

Varana didn't care. She was leaving with or without them—and as they always did, they followed her anyway. "I don't care," she muttered. "I just want to get this day over and done with already."

And then, all four of them left the small café, disappearing into the city.

Chapter Eighty-Nine

— ⊰ ✝ ⊱ —

Chicken Parmesan and Linguini

As the evening drew nearer, Alucard arrived back home on Zalith's horse and escorted the animal back into the stables. Sabazios left his side and ran towards the door, waiting to be let into the house. Alucard, however—once he left the stables—looked around for the small, feathered friend he'd made before leaving. But there was no sign of Hana.

He frowned, stopping outside the stables as he looked around for the chicken, hoping to see her pecking at the ground again in search of food. But she was nowhere. Maybe someone had come to reclaim her. He wasn't sure, but it made him feel a little sad to have not been able to say goodbye.

With a quiet sigh, he made his way over to the porch, opened the front door, and stepped into the house. After taking off his shoes and blazer, he walked through the hall and retreated into his office.

Zalith wasn't yet home, so he'd try to preoccupy himself while he waited for him to come back; if he didn't do *something*, he'd sink into his thoughts about how much he really missed the demon.

He slumped down on one of the couches and huffed deeply, tired from his day of doing practically nothing—how had *that* made him feel so exhausted? It didn't matter. Now, he could spend his time researching dream ethos just as he planned.

The vampire got up, wandered over to one of the book-lined shelves, and picked out a black leather-cased book. He returned to his seat, opened the book to its first page, and started reading. But coincidently, *that* was when the front door to the house opened once again.

Alucard knew that it was Zalith and didn't waste a moment getting up to go and greet him. He left his office and set his eyes on the very tired-looking demon who'd just stepped into the hall. Zalith smiled through his frown of fatigue when he spotted Alucard approaching, but before the demon could say anything, Alucard wrapped his arms around him, embracing him tightly.

The demon hugged him back, and after a few moments, Alucard moved back ever so slightly so that he could see his face. The demon placed his hand on Alucard's cheek and kissed him.

"How was your day?" he asked quietly.

The vampire shrugged. "Slow. What about you?"

"Pragmatic," Zalith answered with a slight sigh. "But I managed to get a fair amount done."

The vampire nodded slightly as he donned a shy frown. "I missed you," he said quietly, looking down at the floor in an attempt to hide his face.

Zalith's content smile widened. "I missed you, too," he replied, pulling him closer for another tight hug. "Let me just tidy myself up a little and then we can have dinner," he said, glancing at the few patches of dirt on his sleeve. "Meet me in the dining room?"

"Okay," Alucard replied.

As Zalith left and disappeared upstairs, Alucard turned around and headed to the private dining room. He sat in his usual seat, two glasses and a bottle of wine already laid out for them; he poured himself and Zalith a glass and then waited.

Zalith didn't take too long at all. He came into the room now dressed in a white shirt and a new pair of trousers and kissed the side of the vampire's face as he walked past. He sat at the head of the table, as usual, and smiled at the vampire.

"Will you have to go back to Eltaria tomorrow?" Alucard asked.

"I'll be going back and forth a lot for the next few weeks, but you'll have me all to yourself in three weeks."

"Three weeks?" he asked with a frown.

"Yeah...for your birthday. I'm not going to leave you to spend it alone."

How could he have forgotten? So much had happened lately that he'd managed to completely forget that his four hundredth and twenty-sixth birthday was this month. Four hundred and thirty, almost—how old, such an age...to have lived for almost five hundred years. It was unprecedented.

"I forgot," he admitted.

Zalith placed his hand over Alucard's. "*I* didn't," he said. "We'll spend the entire day together."

That excited him. Zalith had told him that he'd organize something for the two of them a while ago, and he was eager to know what he might have planned. "What will we do?"

"You'll find out when it's time," he said, smirking.

Alucard knew that asking questions wouldn't get him anywhere, so he wouldn't try to get answers out of him. Instead, he shifted his focus to something more important. "How did things go with the Meshuga last night?"

"Good," the demon said. "We didn't lose any of Margo's men, and they were able to arrest more than half of the Meshuga as well as their leader. We also rescued some guard dogs; I'm going to have someone train them up to guard the grounds here," he explained.

"Are you still going to deal with the Imperito, too?"

"Yeah, eventually. But not now. Like I said, I'm going to have to put a hold on that until I've sorted things in Eltaria. If they start causing too much trouble, though, I'll work something out."

Alucard nodded and said, "I still really don't mind helping."

"I know, and thank you," the demon said with a smile. "But it's okay. I just want you to be safe here at home."

Two kitchen staff then came in to deliver their food. They placed the plates in front of them and then left as silently as they entered.

Alucard glanced down at his plate, unsure of what it was he was looking at. Something smothered in a red sauce sitting on a bed of pasta. He wasn't going to sit there and try to work out what it was, so he stared at Zalith, who had already started eating.

"What is this?" he asked.

Zalith smiled. "It's chicken parmesan and linguini."

Chicken?

Dread and realization struck Alucard like a fist to his heart. He wordlessly stared at the demon, unable to find his voice.

"Is everything okay?" Zalith asked, a hint of amusement in his voice.

Alucard then looked down at his plate, staring at the food.

"Do you not like it?"

"The...chicken?" he asked in dismay, looking at Zalith again.

Zalith frowned. "*A* chicken.... What do you mean *the* chicken?"

He stared down at his plate again. Now it made sense. That chicken he'd met earlier wasn't someone's lost pet or some runaway bird; it was livestock. It had obviously been delivered for tonight's dinner, and now what was once his friend was a meal. He frowned despondently, an almost pained glare in his eyes. If he'd known then, he would have rescued it.

"What's wrong?" Zalith asked, placing down his knife and fork and placing his hand over Alucard's.

"They...cooked Hana?"

"Hana? Who's Hana? Cooked?" But the demon then glanced at his own plate, and a look of realization appeared on his face.

Alucard felt utterly devastated. His little, feathered friend was no longer carelessly pecking around outside but dead and sitting on a plate. A dismayed pout found its way to his face as he hung his head in sorrow, unable to accept that the bird he'd earlier met was meant for nothing but food.

Zalith frowned sadly and gripped Alucard's hand. "Come here, baby," he said sympathetically, evidently trying his best to hide the laughter in his voice.

Alucard was hesitant, but he stood up and moved closer. Zalith pulled the vampire into his lap and then hugged him tightly.

"I'm sorry about your friend," he said quietly. As the vampire hid his face in his shoulder, Zalith glanced back at the door. "Edwin," he called, and when the butler came in, he nodded at the plates, telling him to take them away. Once the butler had taken off with them, he started to gently caress Alucard's hair. "Would you like me to get you a baby chicken?"

"No," Alucard mumbled sadly.

Zalith kissed the top of his head as he held him tightly. "Do you want to go and cuddle in bed?"

Alucard nodded, trying to fight his sadness.

Then, with a smile on his face, Zalith took hold of Alucard's hand and led the way out of the dining room.

The vampire followed him, trying to keep himself from sinking into guilt and instead attempted to focus on the excitement that he felt for his upcoming birthday. It might be three weeks away, and he was sure that he'd struggle to find ways to keep himself busy while Zalith was away in Eltaria, but he was looking forward to it.

For now, though, he just wanted to cuddle with Zalith and forget the day's dismaying turn of events.

Chapter Ninety

— ⋖ ✝ ⋗ —

Alucard's Birthday

| **Alucard** |

Alucard woke when he felt Zalith gently caressing his hair. He was sure that the demon had been awake for a while now, and it always made him feel content to know that Zalith waited for him to wake up, too.

He opened his eyes, glancing up at what he could see of Zalith's face from where he had his head rested on the demon's chest.

"Hey," Zalith said with a smirk, looking down at him. "Happy birthday."

The vampire smiled shyly and looked down at the covers, ever so slightly tightening the grip he had around Zalith. "Thank you."

"Did you sleep okay?" the demon asked.

He couldn't remember nor feel a belated reaction to what he might have seen while asleep, so he nodded. As he did, Zalith rolled onto his side so that he could wrap his arms around him and embrace him.

"Good," the demon said, smiling.

Alucard felt both content and nervous. He wasn't sure what Zalith might have planned for him today, but he was sure that he was going to enjoy every moment of it. Of course, he wanted to ask for details, but he knew that Zalith would keep them from him.

Zalith leaned the side of his head onto his hand so that he could look down at Alucard. "Are you ready to get up for breakfast?"

Although he didn't feel particularly hungry, Alucard knew that it was probably time to get out of bed, anyway. Like always, he'd slept in, and he didn't want to stay in bed so long that it spoiled what the demon had planned. So, he nodded as he looked up at Zalith.

Zalith kissed Alucard's lips and then shuffled to his side of the bed. The vampire sat up and pulled on his trousers, and when Zalith got out of bed, he got up, too, and followed the demon into the bathroom. Despite the fact that he felt nervous about doing so, Alucard undressed again and followed Zalith into the shower.

Once he stepped in, Zalith took Alucard's hand and slowly guided him until his back was against the cold wall. The hot water poured over them as the demon placed his hands on either side of Alucard's waist, and with a smirk, he leaned in and kissed him. Alucard smiled, placing his hands on Zalith's waist to pull him closer as their lips met. Of course, Zalith's hands didn't stay in the same place for long and began to wander up the vampire's wet body and over his defined muscles.

Alucard leaned his head back against the wall, allowing the demon to kiss his way down to his neck. But Alucard then frowned in hesitation when he felt Zalith stop; the demon lifted his hand to his shoulder, dragging his thumb over the place where the scars that his fangs had left remained. They'd been there so long that Alucard had accepted that they were permanent, and Zalith seemed to enjoy seeing them there.

They stopped kissing to wash their hair and bodies, and when they were done, the demon lightly dragged his tongue over the scars on Alucard's neck as the vampire frowned in confliction. Then, the demon resumed kissing him. Alucard enjoyed every moment of Zalith's affection, and the longer he stood there with the demon's tongue entwined with his own, the more a familiar desire began to consume him. But when Zalith kissed his lips one more time, the demon smiled and rested his forehead against Alucard's.

"Let's go and get breakfast," he said with a smile.

Alucard frowned for a moment; he'd felt sure that their kissing was leading to sex, but it clearly wasn't, and he did his best not to become frustrated. He nodded in response, and once Zalith switched the water off, Alucard followed him out of the shower.

The demon handed him a towel as he wrapped one around his own waist, and then they made their way back into their bedroom.

They headed into the dressing room and started getting dressed. Zalith pulled on a white shirt and a black turtleneck sweater, as well as a pair of black trousers. Alucard didn't possess casual attire, so he just pulled on a pair of black trousers, his only red shirt, and a black waistcoat.

As they then made their way downstairs, Alucard couldn't keep his eyes off Zalith, not only because of the excitement he had to silence once their shower ended but also because enjoyed seeing Zalith in what he had chosen to wear. He wasn't sure why, and his confusion irritated him, but he didn't take his eyes off the demon. Perhaps the way the black sweater tightly hugged the demon's body caught Alucard's attention; he did, after all, love to see Zalith's defined physique, and the sweater he wore complimented every aspect of it.

He frowned slightly, trying to ignore the strange attraction as he followed Zalith through the lounge and out onto the porch.

When they sat at the table, Zalith curiously asked, "Are you excited for today?"

Alucard took his focus off Zalith's appearance and thought about how today made him feel. He'd never had a surprise planned for him, and he wasn't sure what it could be. But it was Zalith who'd set everything up, so he was certain that he was going to love everything that was to come.

He nodded, resting his arms on the table as he did his best to hide just how shy he felt. "No one has ever planned anything for me."

The demon smirked as he leaned forward and kissed him a single time. "You best get used to it."

Just then, two kitchen staff came out onto the porch with their breakfast. Alucard stared in surprise as a stack of chocolate chip, icing-sugar-covered pancakes were placed in front of him, adorned with slices of banana and an enticing chocolate drizzle. Zalith's plate had only two of the same pancakes and a side of egg.

Eager to eat his breakfast, Alucard picked up his knife and fork and started, a content smile on his face.

"After we've eaten, I have a surprise for you out front," Zalith said as he started to eat his own food.

Alucard glanced at him, his nervousness returning. What surprise? He smiled shyly in response and continued eating his pancakes.

While he ate, Alucard started to think about the past three weeks. Zalith hadn't spoken much about his work in Eltaria, and he wanted to know. "You never really told me how work has been going. I know that the last thing you wanted to do was talk about that after all those long days...but I'm curious."

Zalith smiled slightly. "Today's your birthday. We can talk about that another time."

He was right. Today was meant to be a day free of business, the only one Zalith might have for the foreseeable future. But then *that* reminded him: he hadn't told Luther *not* to come today. He wasn't sure when his associate would turn up, but he didn't really care. He'd just send him away again.

"Okay," he said with a smile, continuing to eat.

Once breakfast was over, Zalith smiled and took hold of Alucard's hand. "Come on," he said excitedly, standing up to lead Alucard back into the house.

The vampire followed with a curious but nervous stare on his face as the demon led him to the entrance hall and out the front. He had no idea what might be waiting, so he didn't exactly look anywhere specific; he realized that Zalith was leading him over to the stables, though. Were they going for a ride? He looked to see if the horses were being prepared, but when he set his eyes on what was waiting, his nervous frown became an excited, surprised smile.

Standing in front of the stables was a black Friesian stallion. His eyes were light brown, his mane and coat as black as night, and around his neck was a bright red ribbon tied into a bow.

Zalith moved his arm around Alucard and pulled him closer, squeezing him tightly. "Happy birthday, baby," he said with a smirk and kissed the side of his face.

Alucard glanced at the demon, a little lost for words. Zalith's horse questions evidently weren't just casual conversation and seeing that the demon had gone out of his way to get a horse that looked so much like Sebastian made him smile brightly, filling him with happiness and banishing his shyness. He wrapped his arms around the demon and murmured, "Thank you," his voice muffled as he pressed his face against the demon's shoulder.

Zalith smiled, hugging Alucard tightly. "There's also a brand-new saddle and tack inside for him."

"Really?"

"Mm-hmm," he confirmed.

The vampire's smile grew brighter as he pulled away from Zalith and headed over to the horse. All he wanted to do was get his new steed ready for a ride, so he made his way inside the stables and found all the new tack wrapped in red ribbons, and beside it sat a heart-shaped box of chocolates.

Today was already turning out to be the greatest birthday in all his four hundred years.

| **Zalith** |

Zalith stayed outside and waited for Alucard to return. He wanted to make sure that today was the best birthday Alucard had ever had; he *knew* that his vampire hadn't experienced a fun, exciting birthday as someone deserved, and he was going to take it upon himself to ensure that Alucard had no less than a *perfect* day.

He watched as Alucard wandered out of the stables with the new saddle and headed over to his horse. First, he placed and secured the saddle on the beast's back, and then he started to inspect the animal, his look of excitement increasing as he did.

Seeing Alucard as happy as he was right now made Zalith feel content—seeing him happy *always* made him feel delighted, especially since he'd learned of the vampire's tragic, dismaying past. He deserved to be happy, and birthday or any other day, Zalith would do his best to make sure he was.

However, his happiness subsided enough to make him frown when a familiar, repulsive aura caught his attention. He turned his head, watching as Luther made his way through the gardens. Of course, he'd come to update Alucard, but in his right hand, he carried a small white gift box. It would be selfish of Zalith to think that he'd be the only one giving Alucard gifts today, but he felt like Luther's intentions were more than simply giving Alucard a present for his birthday.

The demon eyed the man as he approached, smiling and unbothered by Zalith's presence—a mistake, for Zalith would make sure that Luther *was* bothered and uncomfortable because of him.

"Alucard," Luther called pleasantly, ignoring Zalith's glare.

Zalith looked over at Alucard as he took his attention off his new horse to look at Luther. The vampire didn't seem all that content to see Luther, either, but made his way over and stood beside Zalith.

"What?" Alucard asked.

"Happy birthday," Luther said with a smile, holding out the small white box. "It's been a while since I've been around for such an event. No party this year?"

"I didn't feel like a party."

The fact that Alucard hadn't yet taken the box amused Zalith; he could see the concern building in Luther's eyes as each moment passed.

"Do you like your horse, darling?" Zalith then asked, looking at him.

Alucard took his eyes off Luther and stared at him—

"A Friesian?" Luther asked before Alucard could answer.

Zalith gained a look of displeasure, becoming aggravated. He glanced at Luther, eyeing him closely as he stared at Alucard's new stallion. As much as he might like to tell the ugly man to scurry back to whatever hole he lived in, he didn't want to cause any drama that might ruin Alucard's day. So, he waited.

"What do you want?" Alucard then asked, taking the box from him.

"Nothing. I just came to give you this," he said, nodding at the box.

Alucard looked down at it, frowned, and set his blue eyes back on Luther. "Fine. Thank you."

Luther smiled in satisfaction. "You're welcome. Do you want to do anything today?"

"No," Zalith immediately answered.

"I wasn't asking you," Luther said, scowling at the demon.

He smiled condescendingly. "My answer is the one you will be receiving, regardless of who you ask."

"No," Alucard then answered before Zalith or Luther could say another word to each other. "I have things planned with Zalith. Thank you for the gift, though. You can go now."

Luther took his look of irritancy off Zalith and looked at his boss. "Another time, perhaps."

Without a farewell, Alucard then turned around and returned to his horse, but Luther, on the other hand, didn't leave. Instead, he set his eyes on Zalith, who'd been waiting for him to do just that.

"You look at me as though I'm a pest," Luther said, a hint of hostility in his voice.

Zalith simply smiled in response. "And?"

Luther's smile swiftly turned into a challenging frown. "Do I intimidate you?"

The demon laughed amusedly as he looked over at his vampire, watching as he set aside the small white box and started to fit the horse's reins. "No."

"Then why do you feel the need to try and belittle me in front of people? Do you think I didn't hear what you said a few weeks back to that woman?"

Once again, Zalith laughed in response. Then, his condescending smile returned. "That wasn't born from intimidation; I was simply making an observation."

Luther scowled irritably.

"If you want to stop being mistaken for a scarecrow, perhaps you should try wearing something different," Zalith suggested, looking him up and down.

"Perhaps *you* should keep your suggestions to yourself. I don't come here to be observed by you; I come here for Alucard. I'd advise you to keep your opinions to yourself in the future unless you wish to end up somewhere very far away, cold, and dirty. I've been in Alucard's life a lot longer than you have, and I'm sure he wouldn't be happy to know how rudely you treat me."

Zalith then laughed again. "Well, Alucard is within earshot, isn't he? It's rather strange that he has yet to react," he said, slowly turning his head to glance at Alucard again, who was still dressing his horse. "Alucard," he called quietly. "Am I to end up somewhere cold, dirty, and far away?" he asked, sure that the vampire had been listening.

Alucard set his sights on them both for a moment but then frowned and returned to his horse.

"It would appear as though you're wrong," Zalith said to Luther.

Luther scoffed. "Think what you like. I—"

"Alucard and I have plans. Therefore, I think it's time you left," Zalith uttered as he turned around and walked away from Luther.

The man scowled. "We're not—"

"If you cannot find your way to the gate, I'll have someone escort you," he said with a smile, still walking away.

Luther seemed to give up and walked off in a huff as the demon reached his vampire.

Alucard took his eyes off his horse and set his sights on Zalith. "Do you enjoy aggravating him?"

"I enjoy making everyone mad," he replied, smirking.

The vampire frowned. "And here I was thinking you only liked to make *me* mad."

Zalith took hold of Alucard's hand. "You're my favourite person to make mad; it's so cute," he said, leaning closer.

With a pout, Alucard looked at his horse.

"Have you named him yet?" the demon asked curiously.

"No." Alucard sighed quietly. "It often takes me a day or so to name something."

Zalith smiled and squeezed the vampire's hand. "Well, I'm sure you'll think of something by the day's end. Come on, there's a lot to do today. The stablehand will take care of your new horse," he said as he took Luther's gift from him and placed it on the fence.

With a curious frown, Alucard followed Zalith as he led the way forward. But when Zalith created a rift in the closest stone wall, the vampire hesitated. "Where are we going?" he asked.

"That's the surprise," Zalith said, smirking. Then, he led the way inside, taking Alucard to what he liked to think was the day's main event.

Chapter Ninety-One

— ≾ ✟ ≿ —

Solitudinem Animal Sanctuary

| **Alucard** |

When Alucard and Zalith emerged from the rift, the warm Nefastian air transformed, becoming bitter and dry. As the demon closed the rift behind them, Alucard looked around slowly; the sky was grey, the ground was paved with stone, and the birdsong was strangely peculiar, possessing the voices of birds from all over Aegisguard.

Zalith took Alucard's hand again and smiled at him as he led the way along a path. They seemed to be inside some sort of building complex; he could see the stone walls through the thick flora lined along either side of the trail—flora found in several different parts of Aegisguard; trees that could only be found in Samayō-Akuma hung very close to those found in DeiganLupus. Where the hell were they?

"Welcome," came an enthusiastic voice.

Alucard took his eyes off the strange scenery and stared ahead as Zalith stopped leading the way forward. In front of them stood a uniformed man; his hair was tied back, glasses clung to his tired face, and in his hands, he held a clipboard. What stood behind him, however, was more interesting. A tall, vast archway that read 'Solitudinem Zoo and Animal Sanctuary' in many different languages, some of which Alucard could understand.

An animal sanctuary? He looked at Zalith, who smiled in response.

"As requested, we've organized for you to be able to get a lot closer than usual to some of our residents," the man said, looking at them both. "If you would like to follow me," he said as he turned around and started to lead the way towards the archway.

The vampire couldn't hide his excitement. An entire place full of animals? He'd have never expected Zalith to take him somewhere like this, and his surprise only grew when they entered the sanctuary and he saw that there wasn't a single person in sight. Zalith had clearly paid for them to have the place to themselves.

As soon as they entered, the man started ranting about how good of a place the sanctuary was, but Alucard didn't care to hear about profits or business. His eyes located a vivarium, and he felt no hesitation in wandering over to it to see what might be inside, pulling Zalith with him.

The glass tank was full of leaf litter, fallen logs, and a small pond with lily pads floating atop its surface. It took him a moment, but he soon located a lump of a creature sitting on a rock. It possessed two large, goat-like eyes, its body looked much like a stone, and as it basked in the light of its artificial lamp, it croaked loudly. A toad.

"I want to touch this," Alucard said, glancing at the guide, who'd been ranting the whole time about the breed of toad.

The man laughed nervously. "Uh...did you miss the part where I said its skin is poisonous to humans?"

Both Zalith and Alucard stared vacantly at the man, waiting.

Intimidated, he looked to his left and pointed to a woman who was standing by with a large set of keys tied to her belt. She made her way over, unlocked a small door on the side of the cage, and pulled on a pair of leather gloves before reaching in to grab the toad. It just sat there and let her pick it up, a deadpan stare on its face as it was lifted from its home and placed on Alucard's palms.

Alucard stared at the toad while it slowly turned its heavy body to look up at him. He glanced at Zalith, who had taken a few steps aside, obviously not at all interested in getting the toad's slime on his clothes. Alucard didn't care. The slime that oozed from its body kept it cool when need be—the little guy couldn't help it. He lifted his hands closer to his face, staring at the toad as it croaked quietly and gawped at him.

"Y-you probably don't want to get *that* close to it," the guide warned.

"Does he have name?" Alucard asked, ignoring his warning.

The man frowned. "Uh...no. We don't really—"

"They don't name their animals," Alucard said condescendingly, looking at Zalith.

The demon pulled a look of offence. "You don't name your animals?" he asked, looking at both the guide and the woman, who glanced at each other unsurely.

Alucard handed the toad back to the woman and cleaned his hands with a wet towel and some soap that another man had come to give him. He and Zalith then walked hand-in-hand again as they followed the chattering guide through the sanctuary.

The second exhibit they came across was one of three Drydenan dogs. They looked a lot like hyenas, but they possessed six legs instead of four and were four times the size. In their habitat of grassland and forest, the beige, striped female was sleeping under a tree, and the two slightly smaller, non-striped males were chasing each other around in the open.

"We saved these three from hunters," the man said as Alucard and Zalith watched the dogs play around on the other side of the glass. "Drydenan dogs are often hunted for their teeth—mainly their larger fangs. They contain—"

"I know what people use their teeth for," Alucard grumbled despondently. "It doesn't work," he said, glaring at the man as he nodded slowly. People misused a lot of animals in practices such as low-level alchemy and fake for-profit witchcraft, all of which animals were made to suffer greatly for. Drydenan dog teeth were used to create a pain reliever, one that was well known for not working, yet people still made it anyway, charging an extortionate amount to desperate people with no other options left.

Zalith placed his hand on Alucard's shoulder. "Would you like to pet one?" he asked quietly with a smile on his face.

"No," Alucard said with a sigh. "They pee everywhere when they get excited."

"I see," Zalith said.

They followed the guide forward, passing exhibits containing snakes, spiders, and even a family of foxes. It wasn't until they approached the home of a group of chickens that Alucard felt the need to stop for longer than ten minutes. He watched the group of twenty birds as they pecked at the ground, waddling around carelessly.

"Where did you find them?" Alucard asked, looking at the guide.

The man laughed slightly. "Uh...these are what we feed the carnivores we have here—"

"What?" Alucard frowned, looking back in at the chickens. Why was it always chickens? They were so small and stupid and funny and harmless.... Why were *they* always the food? He then scowled sullenly, remembering his late friend, Hana, who had suffered at the hands of Zalith's chefs. He pouted sadly, thinking about her small face, her beady little eyes, and the way she pecked around at the ground without a care in the world—

"What's that over there?" Zalith suddenly asked, placing his hands on Alucard's shoulders to escort him away from the chicken pen.

The demon steered him to the front of a habitat containing a large blue, green, and red-feathered bird. It was the only other animal exhibit close by, and as Alucard glanced at Zalith, he could see a hint of discomfort on the demon's face. Why?

"It's...uh, keunsae," Alucard answered, taking his eyes off Zalith to look into the snowy habitat and at the herd of large, seven-foot-tall birds. "They are what a lot of people use to get around in Avalmoor. We might have ended up using them if the place we had to get to was further away."

Zalith shook his head slowly. "They are unnecessarily big...for a bird."

"They can get bigger. Do they scare you?" he asked, smirking at Zalith.

The demon scoffed slightly in amusement. "No," he answered, but Alucard suspected that was a lie.

"We rescued this herd from the feather trade," the guide said. "These birds are meant to be strictly used as mounts, but apparently, their feathers made wonderful pillow filling, rumoured to aid in the best night's sleep. Disgraceful."

Alucard asked the guide, "Where did you get them? Where do all of these animals come from?"

The man sighed as he leaned against a nearby lamppost. "Some of them were donated by people who could no longer look after them, and others we went out and rescued ourselves. However, we haven't been able to do much lately. The tickets you paid for are probably the most we've made in years," he said with a saddened laugh. "Our investors have sort of just...lost interest."

"Why?"

"It's Aegisguard. War makes more money than sick, hurt animals, I guess. And who wants to risk their lives to come out here to see them, anyway?"

Alucard frowned sadly and looked back at the keunsae. "What will happen to all of the animals if you run out of money?"

The man shrugged. "We'll have no choice but to let them go. It would be cruel to keep them here if we can't give them what they need." He sighed and smiled as best as he could. "Anyway, if you'd like to follow me this way, I'll show you to our most impressive resident."

As the guide wandered off, Alucard took his eyes off the birds inside the habitat and looked at Zalith. The demon looked somewhat concerned, and Alucard felt even more so. All the animals obviously needed to be there to be safe; he didn't want to see them all sent back out into a world they were mistreated in.

"Come," Zalith said with a smile, taking Alucard's hand as he used his free one to tuck a loose strand of the vampire's hair behind his ear.

Alucard followed him, taking one last glance back at the grazing keunsae as he did.

They came to the entrance to a tunnel that seemed to lead quite far underground. Alucard didn't exactly like the idea of being in such a dark, enclosed space, but the suspense of what lay below encouraged him to follow Zalith and the guide down the stairs.

As they went deeper, small lanterns attached to the walls lit their way. The reflection of water danced across the cave-like walls, a blue glow emanating from the now visible bottom of the stairs.

When they reached the bottom of the stairs, a long, wide corridor stretched ahead for at least a mile. The ceiling was made of thick glass, and it was soon clear that they were underwater. The surface of the water could barely be seen, and around them was a large, colourful reef. Oceanic fish of all sorts of different shapes, sizes, and colours swam around, the corals and sea flora floating in the light current—Alucard even spotted a shark lurking in the distance. But he felt as though *that* wasn't what this huge tank was home to.

He walked at Zalith's side as they followed the man through the submerged tunnel, staring into the water above and beside through the glass. The suspense only grew as Alucard searched for what might live here; a glacier floated atop the water close to the end of the corridor, and as the man stopped leading the way, the vampire tried to piece together what might live there.

"Huh...." The man frowned "She's usually here this time of day."

Alucard stared into the water, searching it with Zalith, but all either of them could see were fish and sharks.

However, just as he was about to look at the man and ask what lived there, something that sounded like a whale song echoed from behind them. Both he and Zalith turned around, wandering over to the other side of the tunnel as a dark shadow approached. It swam closer, its body appearing to be long and sleek like that of a snake, spines lined along its back. And it took Alucard just a few moments to work out exactly what he was staring at.

Four aqua-green eyes, two on either side of the creature's dragon-like face. Frill-like ears, shimmering blue-green scales with hints of gold and red—Alucard knew what this creature was.

"We found her stuck in a rockpool," the man said, standing beside Alucard as the serpent stopped in front of the glass to stare in at her observers. "Female kori serpents are one in every thousand; we were all quite surprised to find her."

The first thought that came to Alucard's mind was that he wanted to take this dragon for himself; Drac needed a friend, after all. But he was sure that Zalith wouldn't be too happy to have *two* dragons living in the lake back home, so Alucard kept his thoughts to himself. He did, however, look over at the guide again. "There is...a lot of space here, no?"

"Yeah. We've been looking for some friends for her; kori serpents often live in schools."

"I know," Alucard muttered.

"Huh, well...she used to be our main attraction. A lot of people would come to see her, but as I said earlier, people don't come here much anymore. Anyway, if you'd like to spend some time here, I can meet you back on the surface when you're ready to continue," he said, and when both Alucard and Zalith nodded, the man then left and made his way back upstairs.

The demon smirked as he gently pushed Alucard's back against the glass wall and kissed his lips. He then rested his forehead on the vampire's as the dragon behind him slithered away into the dark water.

"Are you having fun?" Zalith asked.

Alucard smiled in response and nodded. "I never knew there was a place like this," he admitted. "How did you find it?"

"I have my ways," he said, smirking.

With a nervous smile, Alucard looked away and stared into what he could see of the water behind him. However, he then frowned as something came to his realization, and looked back at Zalith. "Did you know there was a dragon like Drac here?"

"No," Zalith replied, lightly stroking his thumb over the side of Alucard's face. "I heard that it was an animal sanctuary, and I knew I had to bring you here."

The vampire stared at the carpeted floor beneath them. "Thank you," he said quietly.

Zalith smiled and pulled him into a tight embrace. "I just want you to have fun and enjoy your day."

"I am having fun," Alucard said, his voice muffled as he buried his face into the neck of Zalith's sweater. "I've never done anything like this before, and...I don't really know what else to say."

"You don't have to say anything." Zalith smiled, resting the side of his head on Alucard's as he continued to hold him. "Come on," he then said, stepping back as he took hold of Alucard's hand. "There are probably still a few more things to see."

Alucard nodded, following Zalith as he then led the way up the stairs so that they could continue their walk through the sanctuary.

As the day grew later, Alucard and Zalith's tour of the animal sanctuary came to an end, and the pair made their way out. Alucard made a point of holding the toad once more, which he had come to name Grog; he simply looked like a Grog, particularly because of how groggy and angry he looked.

Their guide waved goodbye once Zalith and Alucard made their way along the stone path, heading back towards the wall they'd come out of upon arriving. When they reached it, the demon created a rift to an entirely different place, and that place *wasn't* Nefastus as Alucard had been expecting.

Alucard stared ahead when he stepped out of the rift into a dark forest edge. The rift they emerged from had appeared within the side of a cobblestone wall, one that seemed to outline an area of land. Sitting in the distance in front of a large lake was a log cabin with light in every window; a small pier stretched out onto the water not too far from it, and a small rowing boat floated nearby. A well sat a small distance from the cabin, too, and so did a stack of chopped firewood.

The moonlit opening was surrounded by tall fir trees and a range of towering, snow-tipped mountains which seemed to stretch for miles upon miles. Alucard felt he was right in suspecting that they were in Ascela—it was surely dark and cold enough.

Once he was done closing the rift, Zalith took Alucard's hand, but instead of leading him forward as Alucard had thought, the demon lightly pushed him back against the wall and leaned in to kiss him.

They stood in the light of the rising moons for a few moments, slowly kissing one another until Zalith sighed contently and rested his forehead against Alucard's.

"Are you okay?" the demon asked.

It might feel a little unprompted, but Alucard was used to Zalith's need to check in with him often. He nodded, relaxing as he stared into Zalith's eyes. "Yes," he answered.

"Good."

Alucard rested his head on Zalith's shoulder, closing his eyes for a moment as he allowed the silence of their new location to calm him. He always felt so content in Zalith's company—it felt so right to him...so much like home, more than any four walls could ever provide.

Each time he was with him like this, he always thought about just how much he loved him, how much he needed him, and how he'd not rather be anywhere else. He was Zalith's, and Zalith was his. He'd never let anything take that from them.

He opened his eyes, expecting to set them on the soft skin of Zalith's neck, but he'd forgotten that the demon was wearing a turtleneck sweater, one that hid from him something he enjoyed staring at. For some reason, his inability to see Zalith's neck made him feel increasingly enticed. He thought about his blood a lot—he'd not lie about that, but right now, he found himself wanting it more simply because Zalith had unknowingly inconvenienced him.

But the demon smirked before Alucard could stare a moment longer. "Let's head inside," he said, taking Alucard's hand again.

He led Alucard towards the cabin and up onto the porch. The demon pulled a key from his pocket, unlocked the door, and stepped inside—of course, Alucard couldn't yet follow and let go of Zalith's hand as the demon moved over the cabin's threshold.

Zalith turned to face him with a smirk on his face and leaned on the doorframe. "Would you like to come in?"

Alucard pouted in annoyance. "Why do you find this funny?" he asked, the amusement in Zalith's voice as clear as the smile of enjoyment on his face. He knew that Alucard couldn't enter a place without having been given permission first.

The demon's smirk didn't fade. "On the contrary, I find it curious...to have to invite you to enter my house so that you may do whatever you wish inside, to have to give you permission to potentially...suck the life out of my body within the safety of my own home." He grinned, watching Alucard's pout worsen. "If I let you in, are you going to make a meal of me, vampire?"

Glaring at him, Alucard wasn't sure whether this was some kind of game or if Zalith was flirting with him—maybe it was both. If he wasn't so nervous, perhaps he would play along.

Should he?

His enticing thoughts quickly outweighed his nervous ones, perhaps enough so that he could see where Zalith was headed. He crossed his arms and scowled impatiently. "Do you not trust me?"

A flicker of surprise glimmered in Zalith's dark eyes as his smile became something devious. "I'm not sure," he said with a sigh of sadness. "You've been staring at me all day as if I'm some kind of hot, delicious snack. For all I know, the second you enter the safety of my home, I could become your dinner."

Alucard slowly raised his left eyebrow in concern. "I don't make a habit of playing with my food; if I wanted to eat you, I would have done so this morning."

Zalith smirked and stood up straight. "If you insist. Who am I to question you? You can come in," he invited as he took a few steps back.

The vampire stepped into the cabin, letting his arms fall to his sides as he closed the door behind him, but Zalith failed to move and lead the way in and stared at him expectantly.

"What?" Alucard asked, frowning at him.

Obviously, Zalith had been expecting him to do something, but as he realized that perhaps Alucard hadn't been playing along, he smiled slightly and turned around. "I have already had our—"

Before he could finish, Alucard swiftly grabbed Zalith's shoulder, turned him to face him, and pinned him against the closest wall. He ignored the demon's confused grunt and leaned his face closer to his neck. The vampire didn't speak a word while he moved his left hand around Zalith's neck and up over the back of his head to grip a fistful of his hair. For that brief moment, he let his sudden desires lead him, and now that he had Zalith against the wall, he wasn't quite sure what he wanted to do with him.

The enticement that had gotten him to where he now was had come so suddenly; it hadn't happened before. But he felt that it was because the suppression runes he'd had placed on him had been lifted—he'd felt it with his anger, he'd felt it with his need for affection, and now he assumed he was feeling it with his desire, too.

It was more than simply wanting to touch, see, and feel Zalith—more than wanting something intimate. It was like he wanted and needed Zalith in any and every way he could possibly have him. And right now, the way he wanted him was against the wall and helpless as he drained the blood from his body.

He gave into his need and edged his face nearer to what little was exposed of Zalith's neck. The vampire parted his jaws as if to bite but instead gently pressed the tips of his fangs against what he could of the demon's skin. As much as he wanted to bite, he enjoyed his moment of being so close to the demon.

Zalith didn't fight him, nor did he move at all; Alucard had pinned the demon's left wrist against the wall, keeping him where he was. He could feel Zalith's angst increasing the longer he made him wait, the longer he held him in place without sinking his fangs into his body.

For a moment, Alucard let his senses consume him. He listened to the sound of Zalith's once calm beating heart—as the demon's angst grew, so did the rate of his heartbeat, and although he might like to make it look like he was calm and collected, Alucard could tell that he was eager and anxiously waiting. The demon's natural scent of sandalwood, bergamot, and white sage *always* enticed Alucard, and so did the smell of the demon's blood.

He moved closer, pressing his body against Zalith's as he exhaled quietly on the demon's neck. Zalith shuddered in anticipation, something Alucard may not have been able to notice if he weren't focusing on all his senses—something he had never taken the time to do before, and something he felt he might only do when it came to Zalith—after all, he was the only person he could ever enjoy with all *five* of his senses.

However, as he felt Zalith's eagerness increase, a devious thought came to mind. Zalith seemed to find it so very funny to tease him with bites, and he thought that he'd let him know exactly how it felt.

Alucard stopped and moved his face away from Zalith's neck as he let go of him and stepped back. He might have sorely wanted to sink his fangs into him, and Zalith had clearly been expecting it, but this time, Alucard managed to resist and would leave the demon to suffer as he often let him.

"We have dinner?" he asked, catching the scent of cooked food coming from the dining room. Then, he took his eyes off Zalith's astonished face, turned around, and headed through to the dining room, leaving the demon with his thoughts. It was about time he knew how that felt.

| **Zalith** |

Zalith watched Alucard leave the room, surprised and a little gobsmacked. He felt confused and maybe even embarrassed; he wasn't even sure what just happened. He'd somehow become lost in whatever it was Alucard had done—he had no words to explain it, all he could think was: *what the fuck?* but in a way that made him smile. He'd never felt so bewildered before, and of course, it could only be Alucard who could do that to him.

He'd become so discombobulated in that moment; so many different things warped his thoughts that had once been devious. The moment Alucard pinned him against the wall, he'd felt some kind of angst...something like uncertainty. He had no idea what Alucard was going to do, and that excited him in a strange, conflicting way. He hadn't even tried to move at all. It was so sudden, so new, and so unexpected; he'd become enthralled in a haze forced on him by the vampire's attack-like approach, and he wasn't sure what to make of it. All he could think of now was how he liked it and how he wanted to feel it again.

But Alucard seemed to be interested in the dinner he'd had his people make sure was set out at the right time. Trying to disguise his unsettlement with a smirk, he headed into the dining room in search of his vampire. Their night was far from over, and once they had dinner, he'd continue with what he'd planned for the evening.

Chapter Ninety-Two

— ⋖ ✝ ⋗ —

The Lake

| **Zalith** |

Zalith and Alucard sat at the table in the cabin's cosy dining room. As usual, the demon made himself comfortable at the head of the table, and Alucard was in the seat to his right. They both enjoyed the salmon with feta, tomatoes, and risotto that had been prepared for them, sitting in the light of the fireplace burning not too far from the table.

The demon smiled in adoration while he watched his curious vampire try each of the things on his plate. He had discovered long ago that he enjoyed simply watching Alucard, no matter what it was he might be doing—even when he was doing nothing at all, Zalith would find such serenity in staring at him.

As he ate his own food, his mind wandered back to what happened when they entered the cabin. He still hadn't let go of what he felt when Alucard attacked him; he was still perplexed as to why he'd felt so startled and unsettled but in a way that he enjoyed. Perhaps it was because it was the first time anything like that had happened to him—the first time anyone had managed to make him feel both afraid and aroused at the same time. What a strange feeling.

He smiled, resting his arm on the table as he looked at Alucard. "Tell me," he said with a look of intrigue on his face, "why is it that you and all vampires have to be invited into someone's home before entering? It's often been said that it's something vampirism causes, but you're not a vampire, are you...vampire?"

Alucard finished what he was eating and set his sights on him. "It's hereditary curse," he answered. "The other Numen put a curse on Lucifer that would keep him from entering this world without being invited in by one of its inhabitants. That curse was passed onto me when I was born, and so it was in my blood. My blood is what makes vampires, so they inherit it, too."

"I see," Zalith said, his curiosity increasing. "And are there rules to this curse?"

"Only the homeowner can invite a vampire in; say...your butler was here and he invited me in, I wouldn't have been able to enter."

"And for Lucifer? Could anyone who lives here in Aegisguard invite him into the world?"

"I don't know," Alucard admitted, looking down at his plate. "If that were the case, I'm sure the Diabolus would have invited him in by now. Maybe...Letholdus, since he's the one who constructed the world." But then he frowned. "There's also the fact that Lucifer is in some kind of prison, so...maybe that's why."

"Prison?"

Alucard frowned harder, almost as if he was trying to recall, but he didn't look successful. "I don't know."

Zalith knew that the memory recovery ethos was likely still untangling Alucard's mind, so he wasn't going to pressure him. He took a sip of his drink and asked him, "What if I were to ask you to leave? Would you have to?"

"No," Alucard said with a shrug. "I only need permission once to enter, so once I have that permission, I can come and go as I please."

The demon smirked. An opportunity to make an inappropriate joke lay before him, but he was sure that Alucard wouldn't understand it, and as much as he loved to see Alucard become flustered, he felt like it was best not to discomfort him right now.

His smirk faded into a smile as he asked, "If the owner of a house you'd been invited to changed—say, someone else signed the lease—would you have to be invited into that house again?"

Alucard nodded. "The new owner of that place would have to welcome me."

"What about stores and restaurants?"

"They are public places, and anyone is always welcome, so the inviting rule doesn't apply," he explained.

"What if the store was inside someone's house?"

The vampire went to answer confidently but then frowned before the words left his mouth. He shrugged, an unsure look appearing on his face. "I don't know...."

Zalith smiled again as he stared at the vampire's conflicted face. "Well, you didn't actually need an invite to come in earlier," he revealed, watching Alucard frown in confusion. "This cabin belongs to the both of us."

Looking back down at his plate, Alucard pouted and continued to eat.

"Did you enjoy your day?" Zalith then asked; he was sure that Alucard was irritated.

Finishing the last of his food, Alucard glanced at him. "I did, thank you," he said quietly, a nervous smile on his face.

The demon finished his dinner. "I'm glad. I'm sure that...Grog misses you," he added, remembering the frog his vampire had made friends with the moment they entered the animal sanctuary.

As he pushed his finished plate away and near the centre of the table, Alucard rested his arms in front of him and looked at the demon. "I would have never thought anyone in this world cared enough to build something like a sanctuary for the creatures that need safety. All the humans I've met only really care about themselves and their ideals."

Zalith smirked slightly as he sipped from his glass. "There are a lot of people who care more for animals than humans; I've come to learn that a lot of humans can't even tolerate each other."

Alucard nodded slightly. "They will still only prioritize themselves in the end, though."

The demon smiled in agreement, but as he watched Alucard stand and take both of their plates, he frowned. Obviously, the vampire was taking it upon himself to take their dishes out into the kitchen, considering that there was no butler to do it for them. However, he needn't do such a thing; not only was it his birthday, but there was also another surprise in the kitchen that Zalith didn't yet want Alucard to see.

So, he stood up and took the plates from Alucard before he could take a step closer to the kitchen. "You don't need to do that," he said, smiling. "You can go and sit back down, and I'll be back shortly," he said.

Alucard frowned but nodded, and as the vampire returned to his seat at the table, Zalith turned around and headed into the kitchen.

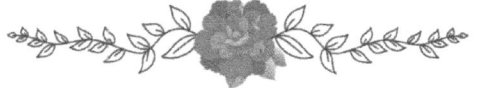

| **Alucard** |

Alucard returned to his seat and waited. He felt tired but content. His day had been more than he could have ever hoped for; Zalith always had a way of exceeding his expectations, and he had been confident that today would have been no different. Zalith had taken his love for animals into account and took him to a place where he'd seen so many of them. He'd got him a new horse—his favourite breed, too—and proceeded to end their day in a quiet, cosy little cabin next to a lake.

The demon always seemed to know how to make him happy, and today, he'd gone out of his way to make sure he was content *all* day long—and he had been, and still was. For the first time in a long time, all Alucard felt were feelings of contentedness. His birthdays before today had always been the time of year when every boring person gathered to try and get closer to him; desperate people would turn up at his castle in hopes of forging a deal or relationship so that they would feel relevant. But not tonight. Tonight, it was just him and Zalith, and he couldn't ask for better.

But it was obvious that Zalith had more planned. Alucard looked over at him as he walked back into the dining room, but in his hands, he had a three-tier chocolate cake. It was adorned with chocolate-covered strawberries, blackberries, and purple grapes. There were also a few rose flowers here and there.

"Happy birthday," Zalith said with a smile as he placed the cake down on the table. Then, he sat in his seat, leaned over, and kissed Alucard's lips.

The vampire smiled, watching as Zalith cut them both a piece of the cake and handed him his on a small plate. "*Multumesc*," he said quietly.

"So...." Zalith smirked. "Four hundred and twenty-six."

"So? Six hundred and something," he sneered.

"Six hundred and twenty-five," Zalith corrected with a matter-of-fact tone.

"Old man," Alucard mumbled.

"And yet, young, prosperous, and undauntedly handsome."

With a stubborn pout on his face, Alucard took a bite of his cake. "Whatever."

Zalith leaned closer and lightly gripped Alucard's jaw with his hand, making him look at him. "*And* wholeheartedly in love with a stubborn, adorable little vampire," he added, smiling.

Alucard was sure that his pout faded as he felt embarrassment consume him. He couldn't keep a smile off his face but pulled his jaw from Zalith's grip and looked away in an attempt to hide it. He knew how Zalith loved to fluster him, and he hated the demon seeing the face he made when he was embarrassed.

"Do you like it?" Zalith then asked.

"What?" He frowned at him. "Like what?"

"The cake," he said, smirking. "Do you like it?"

He did—in fact, he loved it. Chocolate was one of his favourite things, and so were strawberries. "Yes," he answered, looking at the three-tiered cake in front of them, having finished the slice that Zalith had cut for him.

The demon smirked as he took one of the strawberries off the cake and offered it towards him.

Alucard didn't hesitate and leaned forward to take the strawberry from him. As he ate it, he leaned back in his seat and continued to think about how much he enjoyed his day.

However, he found that he couldn't stop thinking about the animal sanctuary and how their guide had hinted at the fact that it might soon shut down. No one was visiting enough to help them keep up with the costs of running the place, and Alucard didn't want to see the injured and vulnerable animals sent back out into the wild. He thought that...perhaps he could do something. He had more money than he would ever need; maybe he could help—the animals more than the people.

A matter to think about later. Tonight wasn't supposed to be about business.

He dismissed his concerning thoughts and looked at Zalith, who was already staring at him.

Embarrassed to have met his gaze, Alucard looked away. "What?"

"The sky is beautiful tonight," Zalith said, turning his head to stare out of the window. "Perhaps we could head outside and enjoy it," he suggested, looking back at Alucard.

The vampire gazed at him and then looked over his shoulder to glance out the window. From where he was sitting, he could see that the very dark blue sky was clear and full of stars, and he'd not deny that it was a rather wonderful sight. The only thing that made him feel conflicted about heading outside was the fact that it was currently winter; he hated the cold, and Ascela, winter or not, was the coldest place in Aegisguard.

He looked back at Zalith, who was waiting for his approval. "But...I don't want to be cold."

With an amused laugh, Zalith stood up. "You won't be cold." He smiled before pulling off his sweater. He then made the vampire stand up and handed it to him. "You can borrow this."

Alucard looked down at the demon's sweater. "Won't *you* get cold?"

"I'll be fine," he said with a smirk, pinching his white shirt.

He didn't need much convincing. Zalith always seemed to be fine in the cold weather, and that—as well as his naturally hot body temperature—told Alucard that perhaps the cold didn't affect Zalith as much as it might others. So, he pulled the sweater on over his head and then took hold of Zalith's hand as the demon offered it out to him.

They made their way over to the cabin door and stepped out onto the porch. The moment they did, the cold of the night smacked Alucard in the face; he shivered and scowled, but the biting cold began to wane a few moments later. Both the sweater *and* the demon at his side helped him feel warm.

He followed Zalith down from the porch and along the gravel path to the small pier, where a single rowing boat was docked. As Zalith climbed in, so did Alucard; the boat swayed gently on the water, and as Alucard sat down, he took a moment to glance up at the sky. The six moons were full and bright as ever, yet their colours didn't taint the blackness of night. Hundreds of thousands of stars were scattered all over the place, and it was by far one of the calmest nights Alucard had experienced in a long while.

As the demon started to slowly row the boat away from the pier, Alucard took his eyes off the stars and looked at him. Zalith smiled at him, and as he always did, the vampire looked away nervously. It was rather late, and soon, his birthday would be over; he'd had such a nice day that he didn't want it to end, but Zalith always made him feel happy no matter what day it was.

He had no idea how to thank the demon for doing everything he'd done for him. He still wished that he could do more for Zalith—and he would. The demon's birthday was in a few months, so he'd do what he could to make sure that Zalith had just as much of a nice time as he had today.

Zalith stopped rowing, and they stopped near the centre of the lake. He made himself comfortable, shuffling closer to Alucard, who also moved closer to him, the bitter cold slowly managing to creep past his layers of defence.

"Do you do anything on *your* birthday?" Alucard asked as the demon wrapped his arms around him and leaned his head onto his shoulder.

The demon sighed quietly. "I used to have a party. But I haven't really done anything for the past five years."

"Why did you stop?"

He sighed again, ever so slightly tightening his grip around the vampire. "Well, the war, to start with; all my friends died, and it didn't feel right to stop and celebrate myself when I had a million other things to do and when there were people who needed my help, things that needed to be done. It was all more important than me having a birthday celebration. As for the more recent years, again, I haven't had big parties because either all my friends are gone or I've been dealing with the war, and it didn't feel right. And to plan something for myself, too...it just...doesn't feel the same," he answered, despondency in his voice.

Of course, Alucard understood. He'd never done anything for his birthday because he had no one to do anything with. His birthday had always been the day of a party used to benefit his growing empire and not to celebrate an occasion with friends or family. How very alone he felt, and how very alone Zalith must have felt, too. But he didn't want to focus on the negative; now, they had each other.

He denied his nervousness to take hold and looked down at what he could see of the demon. He frowned sullenly and rested the side of his head on Zalith's. "Well...you have me now. We can do something together when your birthday comes."

"I'd love that," Zalith said quietly and then sat up and kissed his lips.

Alucard smiled as the demon relaxed again, resting his head on his shoulder. "What about...those three people who were with you a few weeks ago? Your Alphas. Are they your friends?"

Zalith went to immediately answer but then fell silent for a few moments. Eventually, Alucard felt him shrug a little. "I suppose...in a way, they are."

"There is...also Varana," he uttered, an unpleasant taste lingering in his mouth as he spoke the name of that woman.

"Sometimes she's more of a nuisance than anything else, but...you're right," he said, a smile clearly on his face.

The vampire set aside his dislike for that woman and focused on his attempt to make Zalith feel better. "So, you won't be alone or without friends when we do something for you this time."

Zalith smiled up at him. "All I need is you, Alucard," he said, placing his hand on the side of the vampire's face.

Alucard smiled but then pouted and looked away as he watched a smirk creep onto Zalith's face. "Well," he mumbled through his embarrassment, "you'll always have me."

"You'll always have me, too," Zalith said. He then leaned up to kiss him again—however, this time, he didn't stop with just one or two.

They kissed for a while, a while that resulted in Alucard being pushed onto his back so that Zalith could rest his body over his. And then they kissed more—slowly, passionately, and in a way that made Alucard feel so much closer to the demon than he might have before.

Zalith stopped briefly so that he could stare into Alucard's eyes. "I love you," he said quietly.

Alucard's face went red as he looked to the side and smiled shyly. "I love you," he replied.

The demon leaned in to kiss him again. But as he pressed his lips against Alucard's, he moved his hand to the vampire's side and pinched his waist—

Alucard flinched violently in startlement and uttered a sound of both shock and annoyance as Zalith laughed amusedly. "Don't do that," he snarled, trying to push Zalith away, but the demon kept his smirk and struggled with him.

The vampire tried to get up, but Zalith kept him on his back; Alucard even tried to use his legs to push Zalith from over him, but he wouldn't yield. So, for a few moments, Alucard scowled and snarled irritably as he tried to sit up and push Zalith away, and Zalith laughed in amusement as he resisted each of Alucard's attempts and kept him where he was.

Throughout their battle, though, the boat began to sway. Alucard put a little more effort in and managed to push Zalith back enough so that he could sit up, but that was when Zalith started to pinch *both* his sides, laughing as Alucard uttered in complaint.

"Stop," Alucard snarled, snatching one of Zalith's wrists, but the demon didn't do what he asked and laughed more. So, the vampire pouted and put more effort into shoving him away—maybe a little too much. He pushed Zalith back, and as he did, the swaying boat jolted violently.

Looks of startlement clung to both their faces as the boat tipped to the side; Zalith snatched Alucard's wrist, Alucard grasped the other side of the boat, and before either of them could do anything to stop it, the boat twisted on its side and they both crashed into the bitter, freezing water.

The cold clawed at Alucard, an icy grip that constricted him on all sides, enthralling and strangling him, pulling him into its bitter depths. Panic surged through him every movement became a struggle, and a haunting memory seized him, anchoring him in place. The darkness, the biting cold, and the eerily familiar sensations of this moment—

all felt just as they had in the past. The only differences this time were the fact that he wasn't a child and the warm hands gripping his arms were trying to save him.

Alucard gasped for air as he was pulled from the water's depths and to its surface; his panic didn't wane as he searched around frantically, and as he set his eyes on Zalith, he frowned in confusion. The demon helped him to the bank of the lake, and as he reached dry land, he clung onto Zalith as though for dear life. He shivered and trembled—he *hated* the cold as much as a feline hated the wet. But it wasn't just his hatred keeping him in his state of panic; his memories taunted him, they taunted him so much that Zalith's calls of concern were nothing but mumbled sounds that seemed as though they were miles away.

For what seemed like a long while, he sat there, his knees digging into the mud while the demon sat with him, holding him tightly as the vampire refused to let go. But soon, the cold managed to outweigh the fear, and Alucard began to feel his senses returning to him.

"Alucard?" Zalith asked for what might be the hundredth time.

Snapping out of it, he slowly leaned back so that he could look up at Zalith's face.

"Are you okay?" the demon asked, sincere concern in his voice.

Was he? Of course he was. He had Zalith. He didn't need anything else—except...maybe someplace a lot warmer than the bank of a lake. He nodded, slowly releasing the grip he had on Zalith's soaking wet shirt.

"Come on, let's get inside," the demon insisted, helping Alucard to his feet.

Alucard was more than happy to hear that. He hastily followed Zalith back towards the cabin, longing to sit in front of the burning fire, and he hoped that his memories wouldn't ruin the rest of the night.

Chapter Ninety-Three

By The Fire

| **Alucard** |

When Alucard and Zalith returned to the cabin, they pulled off their wet clothes, swiftly wrapped themselves in a black, fluffy wool blanket, and sat in front of the lit fireplace.

Alucard shivered frantically as he glared into the fire, waiting for the warmth to caress him. Beside him, Zalith seemed absolutely fine, resting his head on the vampire's shoulder as he held him tightly. It took a while, but eventually, the vampire stopped shivering so much, his glare faded to a tired stare, and they both relaxed.

The vampire felt as though he might soon suggest they headed to bed. He was now warm, dry, and comfortable—he might even fall asleep right where he was. But he'd not allow that to happen. He wanted to spend as much more time as he could with Zalith, so he'd wait until the demon decided that it was bedtime.

Zalith might have other plans, though; Alucard frowned slightly as he felt the demon's hand wandering from around him and up his body beneath the blanket. But Zalith's hand only found its way to the side of the vampire's face, and as he looked down at him, the demon leaned up to kiss him.

"I'm sorry for launching us into the water," Zalith said with a quiet laugh.

Alucard sighed. "It's fine."

Zalith smiled and stroked his cheek. "I hope today was as fun for you as it was for me."

"It was," he agreed. "No one has ever done so much for me."

The demon sat up straight, making sure that the blanket stayed wrapped around as much of their bodies as he could. "There *is* one more thing I'd like to do," he said with curiosity in his voice.

Alucard wasn't sure what to expect, but he'd not deny that he felt as curious as Zalith sounded. "What?"

Zalith guided his hand to the back of Alucard's head as he rested his forehead against his. "Have you ever heard of binding?"

"W-what?" Alucard stuttered, unsure whether Zalith was referring to something sexual.

He laughed slightly. "Demons can bind their beings together—a sort of...soul to soul connection. In that instance, the demons would be able to feel everything they both feel at the same time. It's similar to the ability our imprints give us to see how one another is feeling, but it's more intimate. It's only possible because we've both imprinted on each other, and we have to consent to one another, too."

Listening to his explanation, Alucard frowned and looked back into the fireplace. He'd never heard of binding before, nor had he ever heard of anything quite like what Zalith had just explained. But he *was* curious to know more, to feel what Zalith was feeling; that seemed to attract him. He was just concerned that Zalith wouldn't be content feeling what *he* felt. He didn't want to say no, though.

He looked at Zalith. "What...do we do?"

An excited smile appeared on the demon's face. He took hold of his right hand. "Just...give yourself to me. That's the best way I can think to explain it," he said with a quiet laugh. "And you must also accept me giving myself to you."

Staring into his dark eyes, Alucard nodded slowly. "Okay," he said.

Alucard shut his eyes, mirroring Zalith. With an intense focus, the vampire directed his concentration to welcoming the demon into the depths of his mind, soul, and every fibre of his being. Simultaneously, he delved into the essence of Zalith, embracing the demon's entirety. Initially, doubt lingered as if the connection might elude them, but after a brief span of silence, a peculiar sensation enveloped Alucard—an odd yet gratifying experience. Zalith's presence crystallized, gaining clarity beyond the boundaries of mere physical touch. Their auras merged seamlessly as if their very souls were engaged in an intricate dance of intertwining energies.

A unique euphoria swept through Alucard, accompanied by a profound sense of understanding and an indescribable pleasure. It was as if an unseen veil had lifted, revealing layers of comprehension that transcended the limitations of words. In essence, the connection surpassed the depth he felt when they held each other in their arms, amplifying Zalith's presence to an intensity that defied explanation.

He slowly opened his eyes to meet the demon's gaze. They both stared for a few moments, the intertwining of both their existences intensifying into an intoxicating caress. Alucard watched Zalith's pupils dilate, and he felt a soothing warmth burn inside him. Zalith smiled...and Alucard could feel his delight, his happiness. He smiled back at the demon, placing his hand on the side of Zalith's face as they leaned closer, and when their lips met, a pleasing sensation spiralled through him.

The demon clearly knew what he wanted next, and Alucard hesitated a little when Zalith's desire for intimacy echoed in his own mind. He always felt so nervous about it, and Zalith could now feel his confliction as if it were his own.

The demon stopped kissing him, opening his eyes to stare into Alucard's as he shyly stared back. "Is something wrong?"

Alucard shook his head.

Zalith surely heard his thoughts of annoyance towards his own nervousness and smiled slightly in amusement. "It's okay," he said, dragging his fingers down the side of Alucard's body beneath the blanket.

In breathless anticipation, they exhaled into each other's mouths, lips melding in a fervent kiss. Zalith, with a gentle yet insistent touch, guided Alucard to recline on his back. Alucard's hand traced a seductive path up the demon's arm, entwining in the tousled strands at the back of his head. Their mouths fused with an intensity as Zalith's right hand ventured beneath the veil of the blanket; the clandestine exploration kindled an immediate response, the intimate touch stirring a hunger that coursed through both of them.

When Zalith gripped Alucard's arousal, the vampire exhaled both nervously and eagerly, turning his head to the side and pulling Zalith's face closer to his neck as he began to fidget in struggle. He could feel the demon's desire for him, and he knew that Zalith could feel the desire *he* had, too. There was nothing he craved more than Zalith's affection.

He frowned in angst, a sigh of enjoyment escaping his breath as the demon kissed his neck and caressed his hardening dick. But then he felt Zalith's yearning for *his* touch...so he complied. He still kept hold of Zalith's hair but allowed his free hand to wander below the blanket so that he could grip the demon's arousal.

They both smiled and exhaled excitedly, breathing frantically as they allowed themselves to become lost in one another for a short while.

But Zalith stopped after placing one final kiss upon the vampire's lips. He smiled down at him, resting his forehead against his again. "Do you want to try something?" he asked, a curious smile on his face as he fiddled with the vampire's crimson hair.

Alucard stared up at him; it took a moment, but what Zalith wanted projected from the demon's mind and into his. Zalith craved him in a different way tonight; he was curious, eager, and excited to reverse the roles they had taken. Alucard felt hesitant, for he had no idea what to do and feared that he might do something wrong. However, he was undeniably intrigued to experience what Zalith felt each time they had sex.

He nodded anxiously, watching as Zalith's smile became a smirk.

"I'll be right back," the demon said, letting go of Alucard to leave the blanket—utterly naked. Zalith grinned down at him as Alucard couldn't take his eyes off him, but the vampire pouted and looked away once the demon snatched a spare blanket from the couch and wrapped it around himself.

As Zalith left the room, Alucard looked over at the fire and waited. His anticipation didn't fade; being made to wait only caused him to feel more eager. He could still feel Zalith's excitement, which grew as the demon made his way back into the lounge. Zalith crawled into the blanket with him, smiling as he leaned over the vampire and made himself comfortable. And then they started to slowly and passionately kiss one another again.

Alucard traced his hands over the demon's warm, defined body, his heart racing as he eagerly awaited what would come next. The demon continued tending to Alucard's arousal, lightly gripping a fistful of his hair in his other hand. But Zalith then took his hand off the vampire's shaft; he continued kissing him, their tongues eagerly entwining, and then he kissed Alucard's cheek and his neck. He once again gripped the vampire's shaft, but this time, his hand was cold and smothered in viscous lube. The cold made Alucard frown, but before he could utter a sound of complaint, Zalith sunk his fangs into his neck, making him grimace and grunt in startlement.

He shuddered in response, but as the demon's venom entered his bloodstream and enthralled him in pleasure, he relaxed and gripped hold of Zalith's dick, letting out a quiet, pleased hum. Zalith exhaled deeply in satisfaction, biting harder as he swallowed Alucard's blood; the vampire could feel Zalith's euphoria increasing, and it was unlike anything he'd felt before—to feel both his own pleasure and that of Zalith.... It was overwhelming.

Zalith straddled the vampire's lap and leaned his body forward. Holding the vampire's hard dick, he pressed the tip of it against his ass and began to slowly move back, easing Alucard inside himself with a hushed, content moan. Alucard moaned, too, tensing up as Zalith took his dick deeper into his warm, tight ass; he could feel his walls ensnaring his shaft, each inch deeper urging him further into sheer delight. Zalith then pulled his fangs from the vampire's neck, sat up, and groaned in satisfaction as he sat firmly in Alucard's lap, taking the entirety of his shaft into himself.

"Fuck," the demon breathed as he gripped Alucard's wrists and made him place his hands on either side of his waist. "You feel so fucking good inside me."

Alucard let out another pleased groan as he turned his head to the side in an attempt to hide his grimace of struggled pleasure. Zalith then leaned forward, resting his arms on either side of Alucard as he kissed his bleeding neck, and then he sat up again, pressing his hand into the vampire's abs as he took a moment to stare down at his body.

The demon began gently gyrating his hips, angling his body so he could kiss Alucard, who exhaled and moaned contently. Zalith started slow, watching the struggled looks of pleasure appear on Alucard's face. Alucard grew more nervous by the second, and when

Zalith smirked and started moving his body over his shaft a little faster, he frowned in delight and turned his head to try and hide his face.

Alucard moaned pleasurably, tightening his grip on Zalith's waist, his heart starting to race, his body beginning to tremble as he fidgeted beneath the demon. Zalith's pleased moans excited him, sending spiralling waves of pleasure through him every time he made so much as a grunt.

Zalith then gripped one of Alucard's wrists and guided the vampire's hand to his own dick; Alucard complied and gripped hold of it, making the demon moan in satisfaction as he began stroking it. Zalith moved his body faster, leaning forward and nuzzling Alucard's neck as they moaned pleasurably together.

When Zalith got aggressive with his movements, Alucard felt himself approaching his peak, and he was sure that Zalith could feel it, too.

Zalith groaned in delight as he rode the vampire harder. "I want to feel you cum in me," he said with a long, pleased groan.

Alucard could feel Zalith approaching his peak, too, and it was all starting to overwhelm him. The both of them breathed frantically, moaning, their bodies trembling against one another. Zalith moved a little faster, pressing his hand down into Alucard's abs a little more. Alucard whined and fidgeted, his body writhing as he edged nearer and nearer. And then, as his body became utterly enthralled in pleasure and euphoria, he reached his peak and moaned feverishly; his dick convulsed inside Zalith's ass, the sensation of the demon's walls engulfing his shaft forcing Alucard to whine contently.

Zalith tensed up as a look of sheer delight appeared on his face. He moaned and hummed, moving his body a little faster, encouraging Alucard to caress his shaft harder, and then, with a content, relieved groan, the demon climaxed, his shaft throbbing in Alucard's grip and his hot cum oozing onto the vampire's abs.

"Fuck," he cried, tilting his head back and exhaling in relief as he dragged his fingertips down Alucard's trembling body. And then he leaned forward, resting his body against Alucard's as he laid his head on the vampire's shoulder. He laughed a little, kissed the vampire's neck, and said, "Happy birthday."

Alucard smiled, moving his hand to the back of Zalith's head. "Thank you," he murmured through his slowly calming breaths.

"The first of many we'll get to spend together, I hope," Zalith said with a smile.

"I want to spend *all* of my birthdays with you."

His smile grew. "Me too, baby. We'll spend every day together—every holiday, too," he said, stroking the vampire's neck.

"I'd like that," Alucard mumbled contently.

Alucard wanted to spend forever with Zalith. He loved him more than he'd ever loved anything, and he'd do whatever was necessary to ensure that he was always at this demon's side. *Nothing* would take them from each other. He'd make sure of it.

DEMON'S FATE
Numen Chronicles | Volume Two

THE NUMEN CHRONICLES
SERIES ONE

Nosferatu
The Numen Chronicles | Volume 1

Demon's Fate
The Numen Chronicles | Volume 2

Light
The Numen Chronicles | Volume 3

Demon's Bane
The Numen Chronicles | Volume 4

Ascendant
The Numen Chronicles | Volume 5

Icarus
The Numen Chronicles | Volume 6

Demon's Curse
The Numen Chronicles | Volume 7

Renascence
The Numen Chronicles | Volume 8

Demon's Reclamation
The Numen Chronicles | Volume 9

[And more…]

THE NUMENVERSE
OTHER SERIES/STORIES

Aldergrove Chronicles

Set in the year 1176 after Aegisguard's second world war. After being told he has only six months left to live, Clementine decides to track down his sister's murderers, leading him to Aldergrove Academy, a place where a hundred students must fight to the death to earn their right to travel to the New World. But he soon learns that the students aren't the only ones prowling the corridors at night in search of blood.

Where The Wild Wolves Have Gone

Set in the year 1330. Following Luan, a young transman werewolf who belongs to a pack owned by Lyca Corp., a military-focused organization. The pack have served them for generations, but after a mission goes sideways, Luan begins to learn the horrifying truth about the people they serve.

Greykin Chronicles

Set in the year 1332, following Jackson, a journalist who heads to the snowy mountains of Ascela in search of his missing best friend, Wilson. But he discovers that not only is there a whole different world hidden out there, but death isn't necessarily the end for some creatures.

The Numen Chronicles Series Two

Set in the year 1335. While hunting for his missing friend, Elijah stumbles upon a fiery journalist, who so happens to be looking for the same people as him: the doctors who experimented on him when he was a child. But when the two are forced to go on the run together, Elijah's healing wounds are opened, and he realises that Lyca Corp. took more than his childhood.

To stay up to date with future releases, follow the author through their website!

www.numenverse.com/

DEMON'S FATE
Numen Chronicles | Volume Two

Milton Keynes UK
Ingram Content Group UK Ltd.
UKHW040309130224
437741UK00002B/17

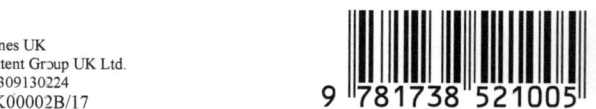

9 781738 521005